The Memory of Lost Senses

Also by Judith Kinghorn and available
from Headline Review

The Last Summer

JUDITH KINGHORN

The Memory of Lost Senses

headline
review

First published in Great Britain in 2013
by HEADLINE REVIEW
An imprint of HEADLINE PUBLISHING GROUP

1

Cataloguing in Publication Data is available from the British Library

ISBN 978 0 7553 8601 7 (Hardback)
ISBN 978 0 7553 8602 4 (Trade paperback)

Typeset in Perpetua by Palimpsest Book Production Limited, Falkirk, Stirlingshire
Printed and bound by
CPI Group (UK) Ltd, Croydon, CR0 4YY

Headline's policy is to use papers that are natural, renewable and recyclable products and made from wood grown in sustainable forests. The logging and manufacturing processes are expected to conform to the environmental regulations of the country of origin.

HEADLINE PUBLISHING GROUP
An Hachette UK Company
338 Euston Road
London NW1 3BH

www.headline.co.uk
www.hachette.co.uk

For Max and Bella.

In Memoriam

JME Shepherd 1895–1917

'Rome, before 1870, was seductive beyond resistance . . . shadows breathed and glowed, full of soft forms felt by lost senses.'

Henry James

'If any one faculty of our nature may be called more wonderful than the rest, I do think it is memory. There seems something more speakingly incomprehensible in the powers, the failures, the inequalities of memory, than in any other of our intelligences. The memory is sometimes so retentive, so serviceable, so obedient; at others, so bewildered and so weak; and at others again, so tyrannic, so beyond control! We are, to be sure, a miracle every way; but our powers of recollecting and of forgetting do seem peculiarly past finding out.'

Jane Austen, *Mansfield Park*

Sometimes it's easy to be blind, to run into the blackness and know you are heading in the right direction. Know that beyond the dark is light, and that behind you all is dark. Know that your destination — wherever it may be — will be infinitely better than your point of departure. This is how it was that night.

And though the girl already knew about the need to take flight, she had not anticipated her own escape, had never been out in the dead of night, the witching hour, grazing dripping brick and corrugated iron, the backsides of tenements and factories and warehouses; clamouring over ramshackle fences, sidestepping rat-infested ditches and sewers.

But fear of the night — its other-worldliness — was nothing compared to what had just taken place at home.

At the end of the alleyway the woman finally stopped, released the girl's hand and dropped the bag to the ground. The girl was still whimpering, and shaking; shaking so violently she thought her legs might give way, thought she might fall to the sodden ground and be swallowed up by Hell and Damnation. Her feet were numb, her shoes and the hem of her dress caked in wet mud from cutting through the market gardens. She could smell the river, its stench permeating the fog, and knew they

1

were close. But she must not make a sound. No, no sound. She had been told that, and slapped.

And so she tried to hold in her sobs, her breath, and kept her hand — its congealing stickiness — clasped over her mouth, her eyes fixed on the blurred shape of the woman beside her, now pulling a shawl back over her head. Ahead of them, a solitary hansom cab creaked westwards, wheels spraying, lamp swaying.

'Was he . . . is he . . . dead?' the girl whispered.

The woman made no reply. She watched the yellow light fade, picked up the bag, and led the girl on across the highway, into the blackness, into the night.

Prologue

England 1923

The photograph had been torn in two and later repaired. Now, a crinkled line of severance ran through the background pine trees, the top of the tented gazebo and the statue by the gate to the sunken garden, decapitating the marble lady. But the image continued to exude the effulgence of that day, and Sylvia squinted as she brought it closer, glancing along the line-up and then at herself: eyes closed, hand raised, as though about to sneeze, or laugh, or speak; the only one to have moved. I was nervous, she thought, remembering, not used to having my photograph taken . . . not used to posing.

She lifted the magnifying glass, levelling it over the figure seated at the centre: a broad hat shading the eyes, the memory of a smile about the mouth, the dated costume, out of time – even then. Accustomed to scrutiny, impervious to the occasion, she thought. But she could hardly bear to think the name. She was still in shock.

She sat back in her chair, closing her eyes, already moving

through shadows towards brightness and warmth, and the sound of a band and the hullabaloo of children drifting up from a village green, and that day, that day, that day.

But something else tugged at the edge of her senses. Another memory, faded almost to white and worn thin as gossamer with time. And emerging from it, into it, a familiar dark-haired young man, standing by a fountain in the sun-drenched piazza of a foreign city. As he moves towards her she feels the incandescence of the stone surrounding her, the weight of it upon her, and one name, on their lips, about to be spoken, about to be broken.

'My dear,' he says, reaching out to take her hand, 'your note has me quite bamboozled . . .'

He holds her gloved hand in his. His dark eyes are serious, searching; his brow is furrowed. He is indeed perplexed. But there is no turning back, she must tell him, she must tell him everything. And so she releases the appalling words in whispers, and as he leans towards her she can smell turpentine and stale sweat. When he steps away from her he raises a paint-smudged hand to his forehead, and she can feel his pain. But it had to be done. She had no choice.

'I had no choice,' she said, opening her eyes, coming back to now. 'He needed to know . . . needed to know the . . .'

She had been going to say *truth*. But it would have been a lie.

Book One

England 1911

Chapter One

Within weeks letters would be burned, pages torn, photographs ripped in two. Names would be banished, memories abandoned and history rewritten, again. Within weeks promises would be broken and hearts made fit to bleed.

But for now there was little movement or sound.

The countryside languished, golden and fading and imbued with the lassitude of weeks of unwavering heat. High above, the cerulean sky remained unmoved. It had been there early. Stretching itself from treetop to treetop, resolute, unbroken, never touching parched earth. Only the ratter-tat-tat of a woodpecker interrupted the wood pigeon's lullaby coo.

It was shortly before noon.

Sylvia would remember this – the time of her arrival – ever after, because she would later write it down, along with the words and events of that day, and the rest. She would for years to come ponder upon whether she could have, should have, done things differently. But when she stepped down from the vehicle her heart knew only love.

As the wagonette disappeared back down the curving

driveway she gazed up at the house, smiling. It was typical of Cora to have played it down. Now, I shall be able to imagine her *here*, she thought, lingering beyond the shadow of the building. Ahead of her, the front door and glazed inner door stood open. It was fine weather and they were expecting her. But still, it seemed a tad foolhardy, reckless even, to her. Anyone at all could walk in.

The hallway was dark and cool, the place silent, and as she put down her bag she called out, 'Hello-o! It is I, Sylvia . . . anyone home?' She immediately recognised the long ornately carved table next to her and, placing her fingertips upon it, reassured by familiarity, she moved along its length. A red leather frame – next to a large earthenware bowl containing an assortment of calling cards – read, 'OUT'. A folded newspaper and yet to be opened letters lay on a silver tray beneath an oversized and, to her mind, rather haphazard arrangement of flora. She glanced through the letters – brown envelopes, all bills – then lifted her hand and tugged at a large open bloom, pulling it free from the tangle of waterlogged bark and stems, plunging it back into the centre of the vase. Raising her eyes to the wall, she gasped. It was not a painting she recollected having seen before, and was surely inappropriate to have hanging in an entrance hall, or anywhere else, she thought, turning away.

Opposite her, a settee of gilt and pink velvet she remembered from Rome made her smile. And above it, the zebra's head, mounted high upon the wall. But hadn't Cora said she loathed the thing? Would never have it in any of her homes?

She walked on, glancing through open doorways into tall sunlit rooms, revealing more familiar polished mahogany – magnificent antiques, glinting crystal and objets d'art. She smiled at Gio and Louis – Cora's two beloved pugs, stuffed by a renowned Parisian taxidermist and now sitting either side of an ottoman, staring glassy-eyed at the empty hearth – half expecting the little things to scramble to their feet and clip-clap across the ebonised floorboards to greet her once more. Oh, but it was marvellous to be in a place where one could immediately connect with so much of it. Almost like coming home, she thought. And yet it was queer to see it all again, together, here, in this place. Cora's world could never have fitted into any cottage. 'A cottage indeed!' she said, shaking her head. Cora was a collector, a traveller, and her new home was testament to this. Each of her homes — her apartments in Paris and Rome, her chateau in the Loire — had surely been testament to this. And though Cora had never planned to return, had vowed she would die in Rome, circumstances — tragic as they were — had dictated otherwise, and Sylvia had secretly been pleased. For Cora was finally back in England, and back for good.

A young male voice broke through the silence and she turned.

'You must be Sylvia,' he said. 'I'm Jack.'

Jack. So this was he. Ah yes, she could see the resemblance.

He smiled, stretched out his hand to her, and as she took hold of it she said, 'What a pleasure to meet you at last.'

He told her that they had been expecting her a little earlier. And she explained that she had taken the later train in order to avoid the day trippers. She did not tell him that this plan had failed, that the train had been chock-a-block with families bound for the coast.

Unused to children, their eyes and their noise, she had sat in a tight huddle on board the train, her notebook and pencil in her lap. She had pretended to be busy, keeping her mouth shut, restricting her breathing to her nose. In her notebook she wrote the word *miasma*, then doodled around it in small squares and boxes, interlinking and overlapping. Until the word itself was covered. When the child dropped the ice cream at her feet, splattering her shoes and the hem of her skirt, she simply smiled.

And when a nursing mother unbuttoned her blouse and exposed her breast to feed a screaming infant, she smiled again, and then looked away.

'All tickety-boo? Cotton was still there, I presume.'

'Yes, Mr Cotton was there, waiting on the platform as arranged.'

When she stepped off the train, with her small leather satchel and portmanteau, she had stood for a while with her eyes closed. She had seen the man at the end of the platform, knew from Cora's description that it was Cotton, but she needed a moment – just a moment – to herself. She had allowed him to take her bag but not the satchel. She had hung on to that.

'And the train? Not too busy, I hope.'

'No, not too busy at all,' she replied.

'I imagine Linford was quite deathly . . . by comparison to London,' he added.

The market town had been quiet, very quiet. Sylvia had noticed this. Sun-bleached awnings sagged over the darkened shop windows and empty teashops, and the wilting flags and bunting and banners proclaiming 'God Save the King' still draping buildings and criss-crossing the street looked sad and incongruous; like Christmas in summer, she thought. But the coronation and its celebrations had been quickly forgotten in the stifling heat, the effort of remembrance too much.

Sylvia shook her head. 'It's the same up in town. *Everything's* shut down, ground to a halt . . . the streets are quite deserted.'

This was something of an exaggeration. Though many city businesses had been closing early, the main thoroughfares quieter, the pulse of the capital continued to throb. People had adapted, altering their habits. The city's parks were busier than ever and any pond, stream or canal, not yet dried up, filled with bathers. And though Mrs Pankhurst and her suffragettes had called a truce to their window smashing for the coronation, and for summer, they were still out and about with their banners and placards: 'Votes For Women'.

'Ah well, perhaps you won't find it quite so quiet here after all,' he said and smiled.

Yes, she could see the resemblance, in the line of the jaw, the nose and, most particularly, the eyes. She said, 'You remind me very much of your grandfather.'

He looked back at her, quizzical for a moment, then said, 'Of course, I forgot . . . forgot that you knew him, that you lived in Rome as well.'

'A long, long time ago,' she replied, glancing away, removing her gloves.

'My namesake,' he said, wistfully.

She kept her eyes fixed on the ivory lace in her hands. They were talking at cross-purposes. He knows nothing, she thought.

'Come,' he said suddenly, and with an assurance that surprised her. He walked on ahead of her down the passageway, saying, 'I was outside . . . it's not too hot for you, is it? We can sit in the shade . . . I'll organise some coffee, if you'd like . . . wait here.' He turned, walked back along the passageway, put his head round a door, and Sylvia heard him laugh and say, 'Yes, please, if you don't mind . . . on the lawn, please.'

She followed him out through a broad sunlit veranda, across a south-facing terrace to stone steps leading down to an expanse of yellowing grass. He pointed out a gate to a sunken garden and spoke of a woodland path. It was perfect, she said, all quite perfect. And she wouldn't have expected anything less of his grandmother. They sat on cushioned wicker chairs and made polite conversation. A young maid appeared and covered the table between them in a white linen cloth. When he said he was enjoying 'getting to know' his grandmother, Sylvia was reminded how little the two had seen of each other, of Cora's absence.

She was careful not to mention his mother, or his father; careful not to mention too much at all.

He said, 'I'm afraid you'll be back on the train next week,' and she immediately wondered if something else untoward had occurred, if she was to be despatched back to London, a superfluous guest.

'She's agreed to be a judge at some flower show or other on the coast.'

'Ah, I see,' she replied, relieved.

He was casually dressed in the way young people were now, his shirt collar unbuttoned and open, his sleeves rolled back. And his manner, too, was relaxed and informal, in that modern way. He stretched out his legs, placed his hands upon his head and looked into the distance, smiling. It was hard to imagine what he had been through. But there appeared to be no trace of any lasting trauma.

'Mm, such a perfect day,' he said, closing his eyes.

She looked away. At the edge of the lawn, under the shade of beeches, a hammock – grubby and fly-covered – hung between two trees. An overturned glass and a book lay on the ground beneath, and she supposed this was where he had been before her arrival.

'I hope you weren't busy . . . hope that I haven't disturbed you.'

'Busy doing nothing,' he said, and slid further down his chair.

It was strange the way young people lolled about. Particularly young men – always sprawled. It struck her in the same way a loose thread hanging from a frayed cuff would: unravelling, untidy. She had noticed it more and more of late. In the park near to her flat, on any fine spring or summer's day, they would be there, lying about, clothing askew, sometimes without even a rug beneath them. The things she had seen in that park . . .

When the maid returned with the tray, he sat up, and Sylvia

saw them exchange smiles. He was a handsome boy, of course, but the maid perhaps a little too forward in her demeanour, and her uniform much too tight.

Eventually, she said, 'And so, where is she, where is Cora?'

'She took a stroll, to the temple I suspect. I'm sure she won't be long.'

'The temple?'

He raised a hand and gestured behind him. 'In the woods . . . a tiny replica of ancient Rome. She likes to sit there.'

'I see.'

Gestures to ancient Rome were scattered all about the place: the sculptures and bronzes within the house, the urns and more sculptures outside in the garden. Sylvia had seen some but not all of them before, and at that moment she noticed and recognised the marble figure next to the gateway in her line of vision.

'She was always a connoisseur, you know? Not just of painting and sculpture, but so very well-informed and knowledgeable about architecture as well. Far, far more than I,' she added and laughed.

At one time in her life it had seemed unfair. Cora's blessings – her beauty, aptitude and style, her ability with people – had inspired resentment, left Sylvia feeling impoverished, lesser. But fate had intervened, the way it did with the appearance of good fortune. Cora, she had come to realise, many years ago, was not to be envied. She was to be loved, cherished and, above all, protected.

He moved forward in his chair. 'I understand you're penning my grandmother's memoirs,' he said, without looking at her, lifting his cup and saucer.

'Yes, that's right, I am.'

'Well, I shall be the first, the very first to read it. But I rather think it'll be an interesting exercise for you. She seems somewhat reticent to talk about the past . . . to me, at any rate.'

Sylvia did not say anything, not immediately. She was a little irked to be classified as the memoirist. It made her feel like a hired amanuensis. After all, she and Cora *were* dear friends, close friends; they had known each other for over half a century, been through so much, confided in each other. Added to which, she was doing this as a favour. Memoirs were not her expertise. She was a novelist. Some would say *romantic* novelist. She preferred the term *literary*.

She said, 'Sometimes it's not easy to revisit the past. It involves confronting everything we've done and said, all our actions, mistakes, and regrets.'

The memoirs had always been Sylvia's idea, always. Though it had, admittedly, been many years since it was first mooted, and then later begun. At that time Cora had been angry about the innuendo and gossip surrounding her marriage to her late husband and Sylvia had suggested to her that if she were prepared to write about her life, the truth, it would at the very least silence her critics. 'After all,' Sylvia had said, 'in the absence of fact people do rather like to invent things.' Cora had agreed, then, and they had made some headway, mainly via their letters to each other. But later Cora appeared to change her mind, writing cryptically to Sylvia that she felt the enterprise to be *somewhat foolhardy* and *possibly dangerous*. Over the intervening years it had become something of an issue between the two women, with Sylvia often writing to Cora, *when we finish your memoirs* . . .

However, when Cora stayed for a few nights with Sylvia prior to coming down to the country, she had been surprisingly enthusiastic, appeared newly committed to the plan. Yes, she wanted to put the record straight, she said, not least for Jack's sake, and added, 'The truth needs to be told. Indeed, the truth *must* be told.' To that end, Sylvia had been invited to stay for an indeterminate time at Temple Hill. When Sylvia mentioned that she would have to return to London – once a week, perhaps – to check on the flat, collect post and so on, Cora had clapped her hands: 'Barely an hour by train!'

'Of course,' Sylvia began again, 'your grandmother and I have known each other for a very long time. We have few secrets from each other . . . and writing one's memoirs is a . . . an intimate process. I don't suppose she would wish just *anyone* to record her memories.'

'Of course,' he replied, smiling. 'I understand you met when you were both quite young.'

'Yes, at Rome, when Cora first arrived there. Though my parents and I had lived there for a good few years by then . . . My father managed the English bank there.'

He nodded, and they moved on. She asked him if he had met any other young people in the village, and he mentioned some names, including two girls: a Sonia and a Cecily. She smiled. 'Nice girls?' she asked.

'Perhaps,' he replied, shrugging his shoulders, glancing away.

A few minutes later, Cora appeared. She emerged from what Sylvia already knew to be the gateway to the sunken garden. She raised a hand and then moved towards them, slowly, looking downwards and pausing to tap at the dried lawn with her cane. Sylvia and Jack rose to their feet. 'Dandelions!' she called out. 'Coming up everywhere.' She did not smile, did not ask Sylvia about her journey or how long she had been there. But later, when Sylvia finally said, 'I do like your *little cottage*, my dear, but think it rather cramped by comparison to Bayswater,' Cora had laughed. And the joy Sylvia felt at hearing her laugh was incomparable.

Weeks earlier, when Cora had arrived at Temple Hill, the yellow gorse was still in bloom and tiny pink flowers covered the branches of crab apple trees. Trees she could not recall having seen before. But it had been over twenty years since she had visited the place, it was quite different to how she remembered. The house itself was smaller, its interior – the layout and dimensions of rooms – not at all as she pictured, and the landscape surrounding the place more wild and rugged.

She had acclimatised quickly to the unseasonable warmth and to her new surroundings. After all, it was home. She had come home. And though she was privately anxious – and by this thought more than anything else – she considered the place an oasis of calm in a troubled and turbulent world; a world she no longer fully understood.

Before Jack arrived, before Sylvia came, she had spent a great deal of her time in the garden, wandering the overgrown pathways with Mr Cordery, her gardener, explaining her vision, how it had looked in her mind's eye: remembering, or trying to. And as the heat grew increasingly intolerable, building up day by day, and the house, despite every sash being pulled open, so claustrophobic, she sought refuge in the temple.

The temple – a small, circular structure, comprising seven ivy-clad Doric columns and a cupola atop – had been erected some years after the house was built, the limestone shipped from Tivoli. But inclement weather, damp and spores from the trees had aged it prematurely, bestowing it with the look Cora intended: a well-preserved ruin. Open to the elements, it had once been open to the views also, north, south, east and west: across the valley to uninterrupted pastures and meadows; across the village with its clusters of smoking chimneys, picture-postcard green and church steeple; and westwards, to glorious sunsets. These vistas were now obscured by woodland but light continued to filter down through beeches and birches, bouncing off stone encrusted with tiny particles of glass and silver and sand. It was a quiet, private place, a place of meditation and remembrance.

And yet it appeared to commemorate nothing. There were no carved initials or dates, no inscriptions in Latin or lichen-covered busts, no statues here. But for Cora it was a small piece of Italy, a reminder of a time and a man. Here, there was still-ness and peace; here, she liked to ponder what had been . . . and what might have been, had her life been different.

But facts were inescapable now she had come to a halt. And reflection, the inevitable backward glance, the search for a perfect moment in which to luxuriate and wallow and take comfort, offered up other moments too. Reminding her of how and where her journey had started. Reminding her of who she had been, and what she had done. An involuntary remembrance that caught in her throat and sucked out her breath. A memory she had spent a lifetime trying to forget.

And yet, and yet, surely the only fact that mattered was her love: her love and devotion to a man, one man. And it was at this place, the temple – her temple – that she often saw him, spoke with him. That he had been dead almost two decades mattered not. When he came to her there he was young and beautiful, exactly as he had been when they first met, and exactly as he had been at Lucca . . .

She stands before him, aware only of his gaze, his concentration upon each curve, each undulation, each and every part of her being. And in the silence, in the dusty ether that lies between them, the possibilities are endless and eternal, beyond a here and now. And when he finally meets her eyes, when he looks at her and says her name – as though it's the very first word he has ever spoken, the first word to ever escape his lips – there is a frisson, a frisson that will sustain her and fire the years to come.

Sylvia made it her business to find her bearings, to learn her way about the place and be at mealtimes promptly. She wished to be an inconspicuous houseguest: a pleasure to have. Thus, each morning, whilst Cora – never an early riser – remained upstairs in her suite of rooms, Sylvia quietly worked on her new novel. She had been instructed on the morning room. The light was better there, Cora told her, and there was a desk in front of the window. Perfect, said Sylvia.

Jack, too, it seemed, was not a morning person, which perhaps explained why that particular room, with its lack of curtains, crates and boxes, had had so little use. When eventually he rose – an hour or so before his grandmother, who made her entrance on the day at around eleven – he appeared to Sylvia to float about the place aimlessly. She sat listening to the sound of him moving through rooms, opening and closing doors, as though unsure of what to do, where to be, or perhaps looking for something: a clue. She watched him through the window, wandering, lost in thought. Understandable, she supposed, that he'd need time to himself. Time to take in the events of the preceding months, his circumstances and new situation. Time to ponder the woman who had broken her vow and quietly slipped back into England, his only living relation. Understandable.

And it was understandable, too, that Cora had a lot on her mind. Understandable she appeared so distracted. How could she not be? Sylvia thought, trying to imagine, trying to imagine what it must be like to be Cora.

During those first few days Sylvia watched Cora closely. She tried to access that troubled mind, watching and waiting for signs. She noted and logged each nuance in manner, each and every hesitation or tremor. She smiled a great deal, asked few questions, and sometimes hummed through a silence.

It was plain to see that Jack knew nothing and it was certainly not her place to tell him. If truth were told, he made her nervous, though she would, she thought, be the first to admit that all men, young and old, remained an enigma. There were, had always been to her, things off-putting – in their countenance, shape and smell. And it was the way they breathed. It must have started, she presumed, with her father who, banker or not, had always been a heavy breather . . . and with some decidedly queer habits, too. And it was, she imagined – whenever she looked up and saw Jack at the table – in no small part due to the way they chewed and swallowed their food, as though they had not eaten for weeks, as though no one was watching, as though they were not human, but animal. But Cora seemed not to notice, and who was she to cast aspersions?

Seven days after her arrival, Sylvia did indeed find herself 'back on the train'. It was in fact her fourth train journey that week. The day-return to London had been arduous enough, the tube like a furnace, and now, less than twenty-four hours later, she was on board another, this time heading south. Of course it was an altogether different experience travelling with Cora. There were no filthy children or bare-bosomed women in first class. And the upholstered velvet seats, gilt-framed mirrors, oil paintings, polished brass, and mahogany panelling made it an altogether more enjoyable and aesthetically pleasing experience. But still, so much toing and froing had left her feeling quite lacklustre.

And she had had to tread carefully with Cora, for there seemed to be issues, new issues. Whether to do with Jack or something else Sylvia was not yet sure. But today her friend appeared more distracted than ever, and Sylvia could not help but wonder if it was related to a letter she had received in the morning post.

In anticipation of their day Cora had risen early, been at the breakfast table – in navy blue silk and smelling sweet with the fragrance of violets – by nine. She had pronounced it a 'glorious' day, telling Sylvia that she was in fact an early riser at heart, and that the lack of a siesta was the root cause of many of the problems in England. 'Tiredness! Fatigue!' she declared, raising her hands in that way she did. 'It so interferes with one's judgement . . . one's ability to enjoy life . . . its simple pleasures.'

Sylvia watched her pick up the envelope, slice the pale yellow paper with a silver knife, pull out and open a single sheet – typewritten, it appeared from the reverse. She saw her wince, heard her gasp. And as Cora put the page back inside the envelope and the envelope inside her pocket, Sylvia tentatively enquired, 'Is everything quite all right?'

At first Cora offered no reply. She stared straight ahead at the open window, and with such intensity that Sylvia, too, turned and looked in that direction. Then Cora rose up from the table and said, 'We must make haste, Sylvia. Cotton will be here in a few minutes.'

Perhaps because of these matters, matters yet to be disclosed to Sylvia, they had made no progress on the memoirs. None whatsoever. Each time Sylvia mentioned it Cora shook her head. 'Not now,' she'd say, 'now is not the right time.' But when, Sylvia wondered, would it be the right time?

On board the train, Cora sat for some time with her eyes closed. She was not sleeping, Sylvia could tell. She watched Cora's breathing, watched her lips part and move, saw the flicker of a smile. And Sylvia knew she was remembering, knew she was back there with *him*. She was always back there with him: *George Lawson . . . Lord George Lawson.*

Sylvia had been there when they very first met, when they were introduced to each other at Mrs Hillier's palazzo apartment on the Pincio hill in Rome, so many years ago. They exchanged few words that night, Sylvia remembered, though it had been enough for Cora; enough for Cora to change who she was or had been, enough for her to forget what came before and look forward. She had been beautiful, then, young and beautiful, Sylvia thought, studying the lined face opposite her. And he? Yes, he was handsome, and exceptionally talented, that was undeniable, but he was also conceited, and selfish. He did not deserve her love. Had never deserved her love. That had been proven by his actions. He had been put to the test – and failed. And yet, when Cora finally took her revenge, and it *was* revenge, Sylvia was in no doubt about that, she had actually felt sorry for him. 'Him!' she said out loud, and then quickly raised a finger to her lips. But Cora did not look to her, did not hear her.

And to think she had allowed Cora to take him back – after everything, after everything he had done to her; to think she had allowed Cora to nurse him through his final days . . . *and to think what he knew about Cora* . . . But she tried to push that thought away. After all, he had spoken to Sylvia in Paris about *that* matter. And he had been the one to bring it up, not she. She would never have done that. Would never have mentioned it. And it was not the right occasion, a wedding: Cora's wedding. Oh yes, he had quizzed her, and just as though *she* were guilty, as though she had committed the crime! None of it was how it should have been, not in her mind; not the way she had envisioned or written it.

When Sylvia lifted her satchel, slamming it down upon the table between them, Cora opened her eyes. Sylvia smiled at her. Then, pulling out her notebook and pen, she said, 'You know, I've been thinking . . . we could change certain names if you wish . . .'

'Hmm. It's an idea. But then it's not the truth, is it?' Cora replied. She opened a small mother-of-pearl case with two intertwined silver 'Cs' upon its lid, slipped a cigarette into an ebonised holder. Sylvia looked on as a liveried guard swiftly appeared with a match. She watched Cora tilt her head, release a plume of smoke towards the lacquered ceiling of the drawing-room carriage. '*Grazie*.' She looked back at Sylvia. 'Well, we can think on it, can't we? It's not as though we're in any rush.'

'No, but I rather thought now might be a good time to make some notes.'

Cora frowned, raised her hand to her brow. 'But I'm still not altogether sure where to begin,' she said.

'At the beginning, of course. We must begin at the beginning. It's what I came down here to do . . . the beginning.'

'But I'm not sure, not sure it's relevant.'

'Not relevant?' Sylvia repeated, attempting a smile.

'Yes. I think we should simply begin at Rome.'

Sylvia tried to laugh. 'But if we are to write the truth—'

'Sylvia!' she snapped. 'If you had any real notion of how life can be . . . if you had had children, for instance, a husband, or husbands,' she went on, in a terse, hushed voice, and leaning forward now, 'homes to run, others to think of, you would understand how exhausting it can also be. *Exhausting*.' She turned her head away, and Sylvia watched her as she gazed at her reflection in the carriage window, puckering and pursing her lips.

Morning coffee was served.

The sight of starched linen and polished silver appeared to assuage Cora's nerves, and she smiled benignly to the young waiter as he bowed and disappeared off down the carriage. Earlier, the stationmaster himself had helped her to board the train, and Sylvia had seen him whispering to the guard as though he knew a secret. Oh, it was plain enough to see that Cora was someone, or had been, once. And though men had always been dazzled, as much by the enigma as by any reality, there had only ever been one who had dazzled Cora.

Sylvia knew that in Cora's mind it had been a Great Love Affair. She knew that in Cora's mind it still was, for she had not been able to let him go. But what niggled Sylvia more than anything else was, why? Why did she hold on to him? And, more importantly, why did she hold on to her secrets? After all, *the beginning*, that part of her story she would not speak of, happened long, long ago. Everyone involved would surely be gone by now. And she owed *him* nothing. Nothing. He had broken promises: promises of marriage, children and that bohemian gypsy life Cora had described to her all those years ago: '*We will move around, he says; live like gypsies. Spend winters here in Rome, spring in Paris, and summers . . . oh, I'm not sure now where he said we would spend the summer . . . but I'll be back each year, so I'll still see you.*' Then he abandoned her. Left her high and dry in Rome. And all because of *circumstances*, circumstances so appalling and shocking as to be unbelievable, circumstances Sylvia had waited over fifty years for Cora to confirm. But patience seemed to count for nothing, and now Sylvia was determined.

Before coming down to the country, in anticipation of the weeks ahead, Sylvia had gone through some of their early correspondence, archived, and filed in chronological order in various numbered shoeboxes at her flat. It had been a time-consuming process due to the sheer volume. And confusing, because of the crossings out: corrections made at earlier dates in Sylvia's own hand. She had half-wondered whether to bring the letters with her to the country. But no, there were too many of them, and Cora would have reacted badly, for she had long ago asked Sylvia to burn them. Why? Because Cora's tales from overseas (commentaries spanning half a century) had been illuminated by observations others would have had neither the courage nor inclination to put down on paper, and because of the names involved.

Sylvia wanted Cora to elucidate, she wanted to hear her final version, and from her own lips, face to face and in person. *Not* the stories around the Story. That was what Cora was good at, had always been good at, deflecting, detracting. Even now, so many of her sentences began, 'You know, I had a dear friend in Paris who once told me . . .' or, 'My friend, so and so, in Rome used to say . . .' and continued by way of a circuitous route of name-dropping and digressions to a startling revelation. From a peccadillo to a double life, her tales of scandal had always been littered with abandoned wives, illegitimate children, lunatic asylums, mistresses, lovers, murders and duels. Sylvia had heard them all before and, even when they were fresh, even when they were new(s), nothing, no matter how scintillating, had ever been able to compare to Cora's own and yet to be concluded story.

'I do hope Jack enjoys his cricket,' Sylvia said at last.

Cora said nothing. She appeared to be deep in thought, and continued to stare at the pane of glass, transfixed by her own image.

'It's so nice that he's able to join in with the other young people,' Sylvia persevered. 'Lovely that he's made a few friends . . .'

Silence.

Sylvia lifted her cup, looked down into it. 'I believe he's rather taken by a certain girl in the village.'

Cora turned to her.

Sylvia took a sip. 'I must say, this coffee's really very good.' She placed the white china carefully back upon the saucer, lifted the napkin to her mouth. 'Yes, awfully good,' she said again. She looked up at her friend, smiling. 'You haven't tasted yours.'

Cora sighed. 'Well . . .'

'Well?'

'Are you going to tell me? And don't, for heaven's sake, ask *what*. You know perfectly well *what*.'

'He mentioned two names . . . but the hesitation before the second gave him away.'

'And the name?' Cora asked.

Chapter Two

Cecily remained indoors. Spread out on the long, blue-cushioned window seat in the square bay of the parlour, she was immersed in her new novel, *Zuleika Dobson*, which had arrived in the post the previous day. The summer curtains were drawn halfway across the open window, shading the room, Cecily and the book from the glare of the afternoon sun. And but for the distant sound of Rosetta's singing, all was quiet.

When the doorbell rang Cecily jumped, dropping the book to the floor. It seemed unnecessarily loud and whoever it was, they were of determined character, she thought, pushing the book beneath the cushioned seat.

'I'll get it, Rosetta,' she said to the maid in the hallway.

She turned the brass handle, pulled opened the door. 'Annie—'

'There's a cricket match on the green this afternoon and *he's* in it, he's bowling, Walter just told me,' Annie said rapidly, clutching the handlebar of her bicycle. 'I thought I should come . . . come and tell you.'

'I'll get my hat.'

The girls cycled slowly down the track, through the shallow ford and up the hill on the other side, moving in and out of the shadows of overhanging hedgerow and trees. At the newly gated entrance to Mount View, where the road widened and the sky suddenly seemed bigger than ever, they passed the rector, Mr Fox, wobbling back towards the village on his bicycle, and Stephen Burrows, emerging from a field with a reap hook in his hand. They parked their bicycles under the trees by the steps down to the village hall and walked up the pathway towards the green. The match was already underway. Languorous half-hearted shouts and desultory clapping drifted through the air. Barefooted children zigzagged about with hoops and people stood in huddles. A group of young men raised their boaters, smiled and nodded to the girls as they passed. 'Too hot for cricket, eh?' one of them said, wiping his brow with his hand-kerchief. 'Hottest day so far, I reckon.'

In the middle of the green the yellowing grass turned to molten silver, the players blurring into the pool of liquefied metal: like a mirage, Cecily thought. Only a few wore white flannels, the majority were in their usual working clothes, with shirtsleeves rolled back and braces exposed. And beyond them, at the other side of the field, clear and solid, and dazzlingly white, stood Bramley's new pavilion.

'Oh cripes,' said Annie, 'look who's here . . .'

Sonia Brownlow stood out that day, but for none of the reasons she would perhaps have wished to. In a broad-brimmed, top-heavy hat, tight-fitting frilled blouse, and skirt, tightened further by a broad belt, she resembled a great white galleon about to set sail. Sonia lived with her parents, brothers and sister at Mount View, the biggest and newest house in the village, situated opposite the village green. Mr Brownlow had made his money in shipping, enough for his family to live in deep-piled comfort, with every modern convenience and luxury and a dazzling array of new, gilt-edged furnishings. Sonia had been born in Rangoon and, as she liked to remind people, had travelled the world. And to Cecily and Annie she had made some bold claims: she had swum with giant turtles in the Pacific, shot wild boar in Africa, and learned to ski at St Moritz. And she could, she had told them, if she wanted – though not to them – speak half a dozen languages.

When Sonia saw the girls, she flapped a hand about under her fringed parasol, beckoning them over to where she and a few others stood. Cecily glanced at the figures in the centre of the field. She could see Walter, Annie's brother, standing in front of the wickets, bat in hand, and she recognised a number of other familiar figures, but she could not see *him*. And the possibility of his absence, of his not being there, gave her a sudden pang, a quick and sharp sensation of loss.

Sonia was laughing, wobbling her head about in that affected way Cecily loathed. As the girls drew nearer she turned to them, wide-eyed, and asked, 'Here to watch the match, are we?' And then quietly added; 'Don't worry, none of us gives a monkey's about cricket, but perhaps we rather like certain *cricketers* . . . hmm?'

Cecily whispered, 'I think I'm going home.'

'Now? But we've only just arrived.'

Cecily turned, about to walk away.

'But Cecily . . . Cecily,' Annie hissed.

She glanced over her shoulder, saw Annie's nodding gesture and, beyond, a white-clad figure striding out across the pitch, rubbing a ball against his thigh. For a while all conversation stopped as the girls focused their collective attention on cricket, without any commentary. Then, with her eyes fixed ahead, Sonia said, 'I don't suppose you know Jack.'

'Jack?'

'Jack Staunton.'

27

'Yes, I've met him,' Cecily said. 'I met him last week, very briefly, though I didn't catch his name.'

It was true. She had crossed paths with him, literally crossed paths with him. He had been heading up the track when she stepped out through the garden gate and almost collided with him. And she had known, known immediately, who *he* was, even before he mentioned the word 'neighbour'. But so unprepared had she been that she missed the name and then stumbled over her own, reducing it to *Silly* Chadwick. 'Cecily,' she had said again, shaking his hand and looking downwards, too embarrassed to ask him to repeat his own, too embarrassed to say anything else at all. She had swiftly turned and walked on, cringing at the clumsy introduction. But at the bottom of the track, on the bend before the ford, she had glanced back, and caught him doing the same.

Sonia moved closer. 'I was introduced to him the day he arrived. *She* invited us over . . . wanted him to meet some young people he'd have things in common with, I suppose.'

Annie said, 'Is he her grandson then?'

'Well, yes,' Sonia replied, sounding vaguely amused. 'But he's only just finished at school. Because of all of his travels he's a year or two behind – which must be rather odd,' she added, crinkling her nose. 'He's going up to *univarsity* in October. Better late than never, I suppose.'

'And is he really an orphan?' Annie whispered.

'Indeed he is,' she replied. 'His father died *yars* and *yars* ago, when he was no more than a baby, and his mother . . .' she paused, looked around her, 'committed *sewicide* . . . only earlier this year,' she whispered.

'Suicide?'

'Sshh! Yes. Awful business, one imagines.'

'But how do you know all of this?' Annie asked, moving closer, narrowing her eyes. 'Did *he* tell you?'

'No! My mother told me. She read about it in the newspaper. There was an inquest and it mentioned the name, said the old lady had returned to this country after a lifetime abroad. His father's death was in the newspapers too, apparently. He died in a hunting accident, you know. He had just returned from South America.'

'South America,' Cecily repeated.

'Mm, thrown from his horse. Tragic really. Mama says the poor woman must be cursed for everyone around her to die in such tragic circumstances.'

Cecily was about to ask the name, the full name, for no one ever seemed inclined to refer to it, but Sonia continued, 'To lose all of her children, and five husbands . . .'

'Five!' Annie repeated.

'I believe so.'

'And is she English?' Annie asked.

'Oh, I should say so. Old aristocracy . . . titled family scattered the length and breadth of Europe. You know how they all intermarry. She has a palazzo in Rome, and a chateau somewhere in France, I believe. And of course one can see from her manner and style that she's from a very old family. Temple Hill is quite something, I can tell you. Wall-to-wall antiques and art . . . Though Papa says old families like hers always like to have their heirlooms on display, no matter how chipped or tatty, just to remind them of who they once were.' She laughed.

'And Jack, Jack Staunton, he has no brothers or sisters?' Cecily broke in.

'No, he's the only one left.'

'So what happened? To the others, I mean,' Annie asked, leaning in once again, her eyes fixed on Sonia.

Sonia shrugged her shoulders. 'I have no idea but I believe they all died in quite tragic circumstances.'

29

'Golly, a curse . . .' said Annie, sounding excited.

'And what of the companion?' Cecily asked.

'The novelist?'

'She's a novelist?'

'Oh yes. And one imagines she could tell you the whole story.' She threw back her head, and affected another, this time silent, laugh, then continued, 'They've known each other forever, since they were girls in Rome.'

'Rome?'

'Yes, she grew up there with—'

'But I heard it was Paris,' Cecily interrupted.

'Paris and Rome.'

'Paris and Rome,' Cecily repeated quietly, trying to take it all in.

'Crikey, she gets about,' Annie said, not entirely untruthfully, Cecily conceded.

'She's a peculiar sort though, awfully timid . . . scribbles away all the time.'

'Which one?' Annie asked.

'The novelist! Miss Dorland.'

'Dorland?' Cecily repeated. The name was vaguely familiar. Wasn't there a Dorland in the village? Hadn't she seen or heard that name somewhere recently?

'And is he Italian?' Annie went on.

'Jack? No! He's more English than you or I, dear. Oh, but yes, I see . . . he does rather look *Latino*,' she added dreamily, staring across the field.

Then Annie said, 'And so, what's he like, Sonia? Do tell.' And Cecily wished she hadn't; wished she hadn't sounded quite so eager.

'Well,' Sonia began, without looking at either one of the girls, 'he's really rather charming, and quite different to anyone here, of course. You see, he's travelled a great deal, like me . . . like us.' She glanced at Cecily and smiled. 'And I told him Bramley's really rather dull . . . perfectly suitable for a summer, perhaps, but not to spend one's *entire* life.'

Cecily looked away. She longed to know more, wanted to ask questions, but it seemed to her that both she and Annie, particularly Annie, had indulged Sonia Brownlow long enough. And she resented the remark about Bramley. Despite her desire for new horizons, a desire growing ever stronger, Cecily felt inherently loyal and protective of this small world. She gazed out across the field, watched Jack Staunton run forward, describe an arc and release the ball.

Due to Mr Cotton's wagonette having over-heated and breaking down en route from the rectory with scones, cakes, sandwiches, as well as the tea urn on board, there was only a very brief interval at 3.30p.m., when the players filed into the pavilion for cold refreshments. Tea would be served after the match, Mrs Moody informed everyone, circumnavigating the field with a megaphone as Miss Combe tried to keep pace holding a parasol aloft. And every so often, forgetting to remove the mouthpiece from her lips, and entirely forgetting her public-speaking voice, Mrs Moody's offside remarks reverberated through the sultry air: 'This ruddy heat'll have me yet . . . it'll make us all go mad . . . as though I haven't enough to do . . . well, I'm not carrying anything from that blessed motor . . .'

Minutes later, Mr Fox, Mrs Fox, Miss Combe and a few others could be seen weaving their way through the long grass of the rectory field in a crocodile formation, carrying trays and platters, with Mrs Moody a few yards behind, bringing up the rear. And later still, inside the sweltering pavilion, laid out upon a long trestle table, were the plates of curling sandwiches, scones with dollops of melting cream on top and fat slices of cake that had been rescued and carried through the fields. Mrs

31

Moody stood poised with a knife behind her lemon meringue pie; Mr Fox, his whiskers smeared with jam and cream, was already seated and tucking in.

The girls sat in a row on a bench outside the pavilion with their tea. Beyond them, on the far side of a densely wooded valley, the tall chimneys of Temple Hill rose up into the blue. And it was this vista Cecily was contemplating when Jack Staunton emerged from the pavilion holding a cup and saucer in his hand. Sonia quickly rose to her feet and invited him to join them.

He smiled. 'Miss Chadwick.'

'Oh yes, you two have already met . . . and this is Miss Annie Gamben,' said Sonia, wafting a hand, 'from the post office.'

He reached out and took hold of Annie's hand. 'Jack Staunton, a pleasure to meet you,' he said, and then sat down on the grass in front of her.

Annie said, 'You played very well. I'm not sure we'd have won without—'

'*Remarkably* well,' interrupted Sonia, seated once more. 'One rather thinks you were the man of the match, Mr Staunton.' And as she arched her back and lifted her head up to the sun, he glanced at Cecily, smiling, and said, 'It's Jack, please, and I have to say it was a team effort . . . the whole team played well.'

'My, but it's hot!' Sonia went on, tugging for a moment at the lace of her blouse, and then fanning her face with her hand. 'Makes one think of the South Seas . . .'

'Or Southsea,' said Annie, 'on a hot day. No different.'

'Southsea? Ha! Oh Annie, you do make one laugh. The South Seas are, I think, a tad different to Southsea. Wouldn't you agree, Mr . . . Jack?'

'I'm afraid I really can't say. I've never been – to either.'

Sonia laughed, as though Jack Staunton's reply was the funniest thing she had ever heard, as though there was some private joke hidden in his response to her, Cecily thought.

'But I'd like to,' he added, quietly.

'Southsea or the South Seas?' Cecily asked.

'Both,' he replied. 'But perhaps one is nearer, more accessible than the other.'

'And duller.'

'Hmm. Not necessarily, not if it's where one wishes to be, not if the sun shines.'

'*If* the sun shines . . . that's a condition.'

'A secondary condition. Happiness can't be dependent on fine weather.'

'No. But it can be defined by a sense of *place* . . . and . . .'

'People?'

'Yes, people,' Cecily agreed.

'Then we're in agreement. Nowhere is dull, only people are dull.'

Cecily smiled, and Sonia, whose head had been turning from Jack to Cecily and back again, said, 'One hasn't the foggiest notion . . . what *are* you two on about?'

'Only the weather,' Jack replied. 'So queer you should mention fog . . .'

Sonia laughed again, and for a few minutes they sat in silence before she started, 'I must say, your grandmother's a remarkable lady, Jack. It was such an honour to be invited to meet her . . . to hear about Rome and Paris and all. One could listen to her for *ars* and *ars* . . . and one simply can't wait to read the book, the memoirs. But,' she paused and frowned, 'it must be unspeakably dull for her here.'

Jack looked at Cecily and smiled. And Annie, leaning forward, staring along the bench at Sonia, said, 'Oh dear, one appears to have spilled some tea on one's blouse, Sonia.'

Sonia glanced down at her frilled bosom, 'No . . . really? Where?'

'Perhaps not,' Annie replied, sitting back, turning her face away. 'It must've been a shadow.'

For what seemed to Cecily excruciating *ars* and *ars*, Sonia monopolised the conversation, determined Jack Staunton should understand the nuances of being Sonia Brownlow, determined to make the distinction between herself and the two sitting next to her. When, eventually, she rose to her feet, she said, 'Well, my dears, I'm afraid it's toodle-pip time *pour moi*. One has one's pianoforte lesson at six.' She opened her parasol. Jack Staunton stood up. She extended a gloved hand to him. He took it in his. 'So lovely to see you again,' she said, blinking. 'I believe you and your grandmother and Miss Dorland are to dine with us tomorrow.'

'I look forward to it,' he replied.

Cecily watched him as he watched Sonia stroll off across the grass. She wondered what he made of her. She was handsome, yes; and she could certainly speak of things that neither she nor Annie – nor most in Bramley – had any experience of. Sonia wanted to impress, and she was impressive. How could she not be? How could anyone not be impressed by her knowledge, accomplishments, even her wardrobe? And Jack's grandmother was obviously impressed too. After all, she had invited Sonia up to Temple Hill to meet him, her beloved grandson. Hand-picked, Cecily thought. But then Sonia had a proper family, a mother *and* a father, and the requisite full complement of siblings. And the family had money, more money than anyone else in the parish. Mr Brownlow's seemingly endless pounds had funded the modernisation and extension of the village hall, an extra classroom at the school, and the new cricket pavilion. Oh yes, the Brownlow's weren't short of a bob or two, or ten.

When Walter, Annie's brother, appeared, he squeezed himself

on to the seat and turned to Cecily. 'My, my, you're looking very fetching today, Cecily.' He placed his arm along the bench behind her, moved his head under her hat. 'And we don't usually see you here . . . do we?' he whispered, his mouth to her ear.

Cecily stared ahead, smiling, and said nothing. Walter liked to tease her. He was two years older than Annie and had recently celebrated his twenty-first birthday with a rumbustious dance at the village hall, which Cecily, her mother and sister had attended, and left long before its end. Cecily considered Walter solid and dependable, a brick: Annie's big brother. And he was. He was easily over six foot tall, with broad shoulders and huge hands. Like Annie, he was fair-skinned, with mousy coloured hair and pale far-seeing grey eyes. His disposition, too, was like Annie's, with a natural inclination towards happiness. Walter, Cecily thought, was innately kind; comfortable with himself and his lot in life, without pretension, malice, or ambition.

Jack Staunton sat tugging at the grass, his head bent, listening to Annie. She was going on and on about a fair at Linford, saying what a ripping idea it would be for them all to go. It had been at the Whitsun fair, right there on the green, that Annie had been told she would be married before she reached twenty. She had been euphoric, over the moon, had spent all of the following week cogitating upon her future, that forthcoming marriage, and with whom it was likely to be.

'So where's Ethne today?' Walter asked.

'Oh, probably at church,' Cecily replied.

He threw his head back and laughed.

'It's not *that* funny Walter.' She turned to him: 'She may well be.'

He leaned closer. 'Really?' he replied, looking into her eyes, 'But you always make me laugh.'

Walter had been like this a lot recently: staring and intense. And it made her feel awkward, uncomfortable. Weeks before, at his twenty-first birthday, a little befuddled and bleary-eyed, he had pulled her close as he danced with her and said, 'You know I have plans, Cecily Chadwick . . . plans for the future. I'm going to make something of my life. You wait and see.' She had said, of course, she wouldn't expect otherwise. Because Walter had a brain, a very good brain, and it would be wasted at a post-office counter, she thought. 'So don't you go running off with anyone whilst I'm not looking,' he had added, smiling, half-joking. She had laughed. 'I'm not planning on running off with anyone,' she replied, turning away from him, towards her mother's watchful gaze.

Now, she could hear Annie telling Jack Staunton everything the fortune-teller had told her at the Whitson fair. '. . . she said she saw the letters R and W, and a large stone-built house and lots of animals.'

'A farmer?' Jack suggested.

'Yes! You know, that's exactly what I thought. It has to be, doesn't it? But I can't think of any farmers, not round here, with those initials . . .'

'Could be middle names.'

'Yes, or someone who's going to take up a tenancy, because I've got almost another year yet, you see. He might not have arrived yet.'

'There's that old buffer, Richard Wakeford,' Walter broke in. 'He's got a big stone-built butcher's shop, no wife, and plenty of *dead* animals.'

'Ha-ha,' Annie replied, flicking a hand in her brother's direction. 'I seem to recall that you, Walter Gamben, weren't quite so glib at the time, were you?'

'It's bunkum, Annie. All of it.'

'Oh really? And I suppose that's why you were so keen to know if your name had been mentioned in connection with a particular young lady – whose name I shan't mention . . .'

Walter's face reddened, and for a short while no one spoke.

When Cecily stood up, saying, 'I should go now,' Walter and Jack simultaneously rose to their feet.

Walter said, 'I can walk you home . . . if you want.'

'There's no need. And anyway, I have my bicycle.'

Jack Staunton stood kicking a toe at the grass, his hands in his pockets. 'I'll walk with you,' he said. And then, looking at Walter, as though he might say something, object, he added, 'After all, I'm going that way too.'

At first, without Annie and Walter there to chivvy things along, the atmosphere was awkward, and they walked in silence down the road. He had insisted on taking her bicycle, pushing it along between them.

He said, 'Annie's a jolly sort.'

Cecily smiled, nodded her head.

'And Walter,' he said, turning to look at her: 'He seems like a nice chap.'

'Yes, he is, although . . .' she paused.

'Although?'

'He's become a little . . . solemn of late. But he's a very nice person. One of my favourite people.'

'I could see,' he said, looking away.

'Sonia says you're going to university, to Cambridge.'

'Yes. I've been offered a place at Trinity.'

'How exciting.'

'I suppose it is. Yes . . . I suppose it is,' he said.

'So you're here for the summer then?'

'Mm,' he said, pushing the bike along, lost in his thoughts.

'Well, you know a few folk here now,' she went on, wanting him to feel . . . What was it she wanted him to feel? At home, welcomed, part of the village? Yes, all of those things and more.

She wanted him to feel happy. She wanted him to look forward, not back.

'You know Sonia,' she said, 'And now you know Annie and Walter, and me.'

'Yes, it's good to make new friends.'

When they reached the hill that led down to the huddle of the village, he stopped, stepped over the bike, turned to her and patted the seat behind him. 'Come on, hop on.'

He stood upright on the pedals and she sat on the saddle, her hands behind her, clutching it, as they glided down the hill. As they swerved to the right, towards the ford, she felt the tilting of the bike and grabbed hold of his waist. 'Not through the water!' she shouted, but their approach was too fast, and then they were in it, and through it.

He stopped the bike on the dirt track on the other side of the stream. 'Sorry about that, I forgot about the ford,' he said, laughing.

'And I'd forgotten it's almost dried up,' she replied, climbing from the bike, glancing along the path of the stream to the pool where watercress and forget-me-nots grew. The yellow water lilies were in full bloom, the air above thick with tiny white butterflies.

They continued up the track. He said, 'I'm getting a motor-cycle next week. I'll take you out on it, if you'd like.'

'A motor bicycle? I don't suppose my mother would allow me to go out on one of those.'

'Don't ask her . . . don't tell her. I shan't go too fast, you know. I promise. Just a spin through the lanes, but only if you'd like to, of course,' he added, without turning to look at her.

When they reached the privet hedge they stopped. She took the bicycle from him. The rubber grips of the handlebar were warm and wet where his hands had been. He pushed his palm up over his forehead into his hair and said, 'My God, it's hot. Hard to believe we're in England, eh?'

'Yes,' she said, though it wasn't for her, because she had never been anywhere else.

He stepped away from her, to the other side of the track, staring out over the scattered rooftops, the straggling line of the village beneath them. Across the valley a hot-air balloon rose up above the trees and he raised his hand to his brow, watching it. 'Wouldn't it be wonderful to do that? To go up into the sky, just float above the world,' he said, and she smiled. Because every summer, every time she had seen one of those huge, coloured balloons rise up over the hill, intermittently roaring, breathing fire, she had thought the very same thing.

'One day I'm going to fly,' he said, his eyes still fixed on the balloon.

'You mean go up in a flying machine?'

He turned to her. 'Yes, why not? Geoffrey de Havilland's already building himself another flying machine, as you call it, at the balloon factory at Farnborough. He'll be taking it up sometime next year, I imagine. And you know, one day, one day soon enough, people will be flying all over the place in them, across mountains, land and seas, travelling the world through the air.' He smiled. 'It's a stunning thought, isn't it?'

'I'm not sure. I think a balloon's far safer, and more sedate.' She moved the bicycle towards the open gate.

'If we only ever did what was safe we'd never learn anything, never have new experiences . . . never move forward. We have to take risks in order to progress. Science has, at the very least, taught us that much.'

'I'm afraid I'm not very scientific, and I simply can't believe science has *all* the answers.'

He stood with his hands pushed deep into his pockets, looking downwards and kicking at the ground once more. He said, 'No, well, you might be right . . . I don't know anything really. I thought I did. In fact, up until quite recently I rather thought I knew it all. But things happen, inexplicable things that one never saw coming . . . that one couldn't possibly have foreseen or anticipated, and then everything . . . everything goes back to the beginning. Right now, I'm probably as clueless as the day I was born.'

'Sometimes all of us, no matter what our circumstances, feel like that,' she offered, searching for something better. 'I lost my father when I was very young, rather like you . . . but of course I still have my mother.' No, that wasn't what she meant, not what she meant to say at all. 'What I mean is . . .' she faltered, and he smiled.

'It's all right, I know what you mean.'

Seconds later, when she turned her head, saw his white figure disappearing into a tunnel of shadows, it was all she could do to stop herself from dropping the bicycle to the ground and running after him.

Chapter Three

He says he thought it was her in the bed, and she simply stares at him, her breathing loud and fast – as though she has been running, running very fast, her chest rising and falling, her jaw clenched. She shakes her head and speaks quietly when she says, 'It can't happen . . . can't happen again.' He laughs, turns to walk away and she reaches out, grabs hold of the back of his shirt, pulling on it and saying, 'Do you hear me? I'm telling you now.' His fist glides through the air so smoothly, so swiftly, swivelling his body, almost lifting him off his feet, meeting the side of her face in a loud crack. Then he looks across the room at the girl sitting on the chair by the fire. And he raises his finger to her as a warning.

Cora sat alone, staring out towards the tops of pine trees. Had she needed a prompt, a visual reminder, they would have served her well, for she had stared at that very same image – a blur of darkest green against brilliant blue – many times before. But at that moment she saw no wooded hillside and no English sky; she saw only the blush of ancient stone, the sunlit ruins of a

41

distant place. She saw the velvet contours of seven hills, a hundred steeples and domes and, beyond them, the windswept meadows where the land met the sky in an azure haze. And with this image came the remembrance of the weightlessness of youth, when her world had been a small empire of infinite possibility.

'Such plans, such dreams,' she whispered, 'such promises.' Had it really only been a season? Yes, between autumn and spring. He had swept into her life without warning, turning winter into summer and her world upside down. But hadn't she known, even before she met him, even before she set eyes on him? Wasn't there something in the name, she thought, trying to remember that very first time she had heard it, which sounded . . . familiar, anticipated? She could hear her aunt say it, picture her standing in the hallway of their apartment in Rome. That was the beginning, she thought; that was when I came alive, truly came alive, when I heard that name for the first time.

Knowing he was in Rome for only the season made every minute of every hour of every day count. 'It's why and how I began to live . . .' She smiled as she recalled her boldness on that first solo visit to his studio, and she could see the place once more: the violets she took him, standing in the dirty jam jar; the canvases stacked up against the walls; the kettle on the open fire; the paper-strewn floor; and him, standing in his chalk-smeared, crumpled velvet jacket, holding up a teapot. 'China or Darjeeling?'

'China or Darjeeling,' she said to herself, half laughing.

But her memory, as it was wont to do now, moved on at random to a later date, and with an intake of breath she closed her eyes . . .

'We'll come back each year,' he said, lying back, folding his arms behind his head. 'Yes, we'll return here each winter.' He glanced at her. 'What do you say?'

'I say, *yes*!'

She threw herself down next to him. The remnants of their lunch – grapes and peaches, cheese and bread – lay scattered about them, the bottle of wine and two almost empty glasses on the table next to him.

'Of course, once we're married I'm going to have to sell heaps of bloody pictures to support you and our horde of badly behaved children.'

'And how do you know they'll be badly behaved?' she asked.

'Because I do . . . because they'll be just like you,' he said, turning to face her.

She lifted her hand to his brow. 'We'll be happy,' she said, tracing a dark curl with her finger, 'so happy.'

'We will, and we'll live in total squalor.'

'Squalor?'

'Chaos . . . Total and blissful chaos.'

'But where will we live, George?'

'I've already told you, everywhere. We shall live *everywhere*! All over the place and wherever we like. We'll live like gypsies . . . but we may need more than one caravan. We'll come here each winter, divide our time between Rome and Florence, head to Paris in the spring, and the south of France perhaps in autumn.'

'But not England?'

He stared at her and smiled. 'No, not England. Who needs England?' he asked, pulling her to him . . .

She opened her eyes, glanced down at her hands, her wedding band – immovable now. 'I was the gypsy,' she said out loud.

There was a muted rhythm to the evening. The air was soft and still. But it had been a long and arduous day: too long, and much too hot. And it had been a relief to get back to the solitude and peacefulness of her garden, the place that was now her home. Stiffly upholstered in navy, faded with age and wear, she felt heavy and weary. Not simply from that day's journey, but from a lifetime's journeys, and the journey of a lifetime.

A seasoned traveller, undaunted by timetables, foreign languages and customs, she had spent decades criss-crossing Europe by land, by river and by sea. But there would be no return to Rome, not even for the winter, and there could be no more trips to Paris. She would never again stroll through the gardens of what had once been the Tuileries Palace, or catch a steamer and sail from Rhône to Avignon, or from Marseilles to Civitavecchia and, later, stand on the deck of another, heading upriver to the Ripetta. Her wings had finally been clipped.

But there were other things sapping her once renowned energy. Things she could not speak of, which thrashed on the periphery of her thoughts and lay heavy on her conscience. If she could only exhale, fully exhale, she thought, she might be able to release the burden, feel lighter. *Breathe*, her aunt had told her, breathe, as though it was the easiest thing in the world to do. But it had never been easy. And now, this holding-in was almost too much.

She moved her hand, feeling for the paper in her pocket: yes, it was there, still there. She had not dreamt it. She would look at it again later, in private; decide then what to do. She must not panic, must not imagine the worst. After all, it had happened before. Been dealt with before. This time would be no different . . . though there was, of course, Jack to think of now.

She had thought of telling Sylvia, and had come close to it on the train earlier that day. Sylvia's instincts had always been so very acute. She knew when something was amiss. But it would be wrong, selfish, to burden poor Sylvia, who would undoubtedly panic and imagine the very worst scenario. And yet, when Sylvia had taken hold of her hand and said, 'Something is troubling you, Cora, I can tell,' she had longed to tell her: to tell her everything, all of it, from beginning to end.

But the train's movement, a gentle rock and forward motion, that familiar sensation of transit, and a landscape, albeit foreign to her, gliding swiftly past had soothed her. The upper windows of the drawing-room carriage had been pulled open, and she had closed her eyes, savouring the caress of warm air upon her skin, searching for that familiar bouquet of cedar, cypress and pine. And fleetingly, for a second or two, she caught it, the memory of it, heady, intoxicating, life affirming; then it had gone. Gone forever, perhaps. And the tightness about her chest – the restriction, lack of breath, the weight – returned, and with it a sense of sorrow.

When she caught her reflection in the carriage window she had been surprised once more by the aged face staring back at her; the inclination of what had once been upturned to now be downturned; the eyes, once sparkling and wide, now small; unreadable, even to her. Oh, that she could turn back time, that she wasn't in England, surrounded by English people and their need to know; their voracious hunger for information. And for what reason? To know where and how she fitted in? People had stared, people had smiled; yes, they always did. They bowed their heads as she passed by, and then bowed them again each time she caught their eye.

Early on in life she had become aware of this dichotomy: how easily the succour of attention turned to the discomfort of scrutiny. Now she thought, how queerly people stare. Was it age? she wondered. Or was it that they perceived something different, not English, something foreign to their sensibilities and tastes perhaps? Or was it something in her expression? Impossible surely. No one knew: no one *living*.

She was pondering all of this when Jack appeared, looking hot and exhausted in his cricket whites. And the shape of him, his gait, and those familiar dark features pulled her back and made her smile. He bent down, kissed her cheek, and then fell into the chair next to her with a sigh. He told her about the match, inquired after her day.

She said, 'And did you see your friends?'

He stared out over the manicured lawn in front of them. Yes, he told her, he had seen his friends.

He was distracted, she could tell. And she knew it was not the cricket.

'If there's someone you'd like to invite here . . . to tea, or to dine with us . . .' she ventured.

He turned to her. 'Someone?'

'Someone in particular . . . a girl, perhaps.'

'There's no girl.'

'I was thinking of Sonia Brownlow, or perhaps Cecily.'

He tried to laugh. Repeated Sonia's name and rolled his eyes.

'Or Cecily?' she said again.

He stood up, pushed his hands into his pockets and swivelled round on his feet.

'This is your home now. It's *our* home. I want you to know you can invite your friends here,' she said, reaching out to him, placing her hand on his bare forearm.

He looked down at the ground. 'Her name's Cecily Chadwick . . . she's our neighbour. But I don't suppose we've much in common, not really.'

'I'd rather like to meet her.'

He shrugged his shoulders. 'I'm not sure when I'll see her again.'

Cora laughed. 'She's our neighbour, you said. I'm quite sure it's not beyond you to walk a few hundred yards and invite her here. You can tell her that I'd like to meet her.'

He pulled away. 'I can't say that! It sounds perfectly dreadful, as though we've discussed her, which we have now, but . . .'

'Jack, you simply say that your grandmother is keen to meet

46

her new neighbours. That's all. I'm sure she's not a mind-reader, not yet.'

He looked down at her. 'What do you mean by that?'

She smiled. 'I simply mean that I'm quite certain she isn't able to read your thoughts.'

'Can you?' he asked.

'Perhaps . . . but that's because you, your heart, are so very precious to me. You're all I have.'

'I should go inside, clean myself up,' he said, moving away from her.

She smiled as she listened to his footsteps fade, lifted her glass to her lips. The liquid, like the air, was syrupy and warm. She thought about Jack and the girl from next door, tried to picture them together, and wondered what they had spoken of. She wondered how her grandson appeared to a young, innocent village girl. Handsome surely. Burdened? Damaged? She closed her eyes. No. He was neither burdened nor damaged, she told herself, firmly, silently. Poised on the brink of magnificent manhood, Jack was her legacy to the world, the embodiment of everything good in her life, its sum total, distilled to one. And she lifted her face to the sun once more.

But it was in such moments she was catapulted back. For there was no forward, her life lay behind her. Anamnesis: when the journey ended, this was all one was left with, memories. Of foolishness, pride, rapture, pain, sorrow, and regret. Sweet and bitter and bittersweet, they floated about the ether like thistledown in the wind, difficult to catch hold of and, once caught, never quite as lovely.

It was impossible for her to remember what she had said to whom and when. Had she ever told Sylvia the truth? She could not recall what, exactly, she had told her all those years ago in Rome, though she knew she had told her something – something of the truth. That's what had whetted Sylvia's appetite, surely, that glimpse, the glimpse of a story. Oh yes.

The problem, she realised, one of the problems, stemmed from the fact that history had been overwritten, and not just once, and not just by herself. Now, it seemed increasingly hard to unravel the facts, the truth of events and circumstances. Could history change its shape with time? Had her subconscious mind intervened and run rampant, editing and rewriting her own story? Memories did indeed change shape with time, she knew and understood this. The conscious mind followed instruction, could be controlled. By reason and logic, and survival? Yes, survival. It could even override the heart, sometimes, for a while. But the heart was infinitely powerful. It could be ignored – to an extent; it could be restrained, repressed, but it could never be controlled. One could never control one's heart.

But now there were gaps and missing links, for seasons and, sometimes, entire years had been erased, people discarded, abandoned along the way, left standing at a dusty crossroads without so much as an adieu. Distant recollections were worn-out flimsy things that only occasionally had resonance, the ring of truth about them. And that once sharp mind, the very foundation on which her life had been built, had slowly come to let her down.

Old age. It was frustrating and yet queerly liberating at the same time. Made frustrating by the obvious and anticipated limitations, both physical and mental, and made liberating by those very same things as well: not being able to remember, not being expected to know or get things right. What does it matter, she thought, if I make a mistake? No one will know. Everyone is gone.

She heard a door close behind her.

'Good gracious,' Sylvia began, sitting down with her notebook and pencil. 'I do believe the air is hotter now than it was this afternoon.'

Cora said nothing. She smiled as she watched Sylvia open her notebook, flick a few pages, scanning the pencilled scrawl: *so childlike*.

And why would she not be? Nothing had occurred to induce her to leave that state, to make her grow up. Sylvia's entire life had been an uninterrupted, solitary affair, without claim to either requited or unrequited love. No lovers, no children, no husbands, Cora thought, continuing to watch her. Had her lips ever once been kissed? No. She would die a virgin. And yet, she had known passion, of a sort, for had she not spent a lifetime imagining it, picturing it, writing it? But dear Sylvia's novels were so very naive, so clichéd, and they were all the same. Sylvia had admitted as much herself. 'It's my formula,' she had said only the previous day, looking quite put out.

In truth, Sylvia had assumed Cora too busy to notice the coincidences, the synchronicity. But Cora had always known, always been aware that she had been the source of inspiration; that it was her experience, her unique perspective, that had expanded Sylvia's understanding of the universe, and of men. And Sylvia was not the only artist whose vision had been inspired, for the soft contours of Cora's once youthful shape were frozen in tinted marble, the symmetry of her young face captured in oils.

'You know, it astounds me how you find so much to write about,' Cora said now.

'Words, dear, just words.'

'Words,' Cora repeated, fiddling with the locket about her neck. 'And how many of those, I wonder, have been spoken and written only to be rued. We have too many words now, too many words for too many things. And new ones being invented all the time.'

'But that's the beauty of language, dear. Man's need for expression is, I think, the most powerful urge of all, the need to say who we are, how we feel, what we think, hmm?'

'And perhaps also to shock, to inspire reaction,' she shrugged, 'instil fear?'

Sylvia appeared pensive for a moment. 'Yes, they can be powerful tools.'

'Indeed. And illuminating. One can, if one is so inclined, identify one's friends and one's enemies simply by examining their choice of words. Even one word, a name . . .' Cora said, staring at her.

Sylvia nodded but made no reply. And Cora watched her as she peered through her spectacles at a particular page, then lifted her pencil to her mouth.

'You really oughtn't do that, you know. I read somewhere recently that lead is not good for one to ingest.'

Sylvia glanced up at her. 'Oh?'

'Poisonous, I presume.'

'Really?'

'Yes, but don't look so worried. I hardly think one can take one's own life in the lick of a pencil.'

'Unlike arsenic,' Sylvia said.

'Or carbolic acid . . .'

They stared each other.

'I meant to ask you, does he know? Have you ever told him *how*?'

'Of course he knows,' Cora replied sharply. 'It was in the wretched newspapers, though I did my best to stop it. I imagine everyone knows, or knew at the time. But I've never discussed it with him, and neither do I intend to.' She paused for a moment, exhaled loudly, and then added, 'Hopefully he does not allow himself to dwell on it. Any of it.'

'Well, yes, and he seems so . . .'

'Fine?' Cora suggested.

Sylvia tapped her pencil on her lip, then nodded. 'Yes, fine.'

'Well, I rather think he is. He's not like her, you know? Good gracious no, nothing like her. He's like his father, and like . . .'

'George?'

Cora turned to her. 'Like his grandfather,' she said.

'You know, the timing of it has always struck me as a queer thing,' Sylvia began again.

'The timing of it?'

'Yes. The fact that it happened immediately after the government's census . . . that she recorded herself and then, almost the very next day, was no more.'

'They're abominable things,' Cora said, raising a hand dismissively.

Sylvia smiled. 'But you've never had to do one, dear.'

'No, and nor would I!'

Sylvia shook her head. 'It's the law, I'm afraid. Everyone has to.'

'The law is an ass.'

'You know, you'd have had to give them your *full* name' Sylvia went on. 'Yes, and oh my, that *would* confound them!' she said, clapping her hands, and then intentionally mispronouncing Cora's full name. 'And 'ow you spellin' that, ma'am?' she added, in a mock cockney accent, Cora presumed, and giggling.

'I do not use Lawson, Sylvia, as you very well know. My name is quite long enough without it. And anyway, the name proved . . . problematic. I have no desire to raise my head above the parapet again.'

'No . . . no, of course not,' Sylvia replied, gathering herself. 'And you're right, censuses are awful things and ask all manner of questions: what one's occupation is, how many children one has given birth to. Oh, it goes on and on. And for the life of me I do wonder why. Wonder who all this information is for.'

'Statistics,' Cora said, with great emphasis. 'Statistics and pigeonholing, placing us all into tidy identifiable groups. The modern world is becoming obsessed by statistics . . . utterly intrusive and condemnable, I think.'

'Well, I can't help but wonder if all those questions were simply too much for her. For Cassandra, I mean.'

'I don't think it was the census, Sylvia. Cassandra had always been fragile, always of a melancholic nature. No, I think she'd teetered on a brink for years, and but for Jack, who knows? Perhaps she'd have taken her own life many years ago. But she waited, she waited until . . . until he was an adult.'

'Unfathomable . . . and I don't imagine she ever thought you'd come back,' Sylvia mused aloud. 'I suppose that's why she waited until he was grown up, had finished his studies. But,' she gasped, shaking her head, 'such a dreadful thing to do to him, poor dear.'

'Best not spoken of, I think, Sylvia. 'Twas a wicked and selfish act and I have nothing more to say on the matter.'

'Well, we have had rather a lovely day to ourselves, have we not?' said Sylvia, after a moment or two. 'And certainly, everyone considered it a great honour to have *you* there to judge and present the prizes today. Oh yes, it's quite clear that they hold you in very high esteem. In fact, you appear to be something of a celebrity, my dear.'

'I don't think so. A foreigner, perhaps, an outsider.'

'But you're not. And you really mustn't say such things. People will take you at your word, especially country folk.'

'Perhaps not but I feel like one, and I'm never entirely sure where my allegiance lies . . . Though dear Bertie used to laugh at me whenever I said such things.' She paused, smiling, remembering. '"My dear," he would say, "you are as English as I." Of course he was being ironic because he was a Saxe-Coburg-Gotha, and his mother a Hanoverian.'

'The King was fond of you, wasn't he?'

'Oh yes, he was a dear friend, and of course a very dear friend to . . .'

'George?'

'Mm, yes, George,' Cora replied vaguely.

George. His face had haunted her dreams and waking hours for half a century. And yet it was hard to fathom the passing of time and nearness of him, the years between then and now. George. Each and every day of her life she remembered him. His face stared back at her through open doorways and panes of glass, through seasons and years, across a continent and a sea. All of her imaginings led her back to him: the what ifs, the whys, the silent conversations stretching through time. And sometimes, alone, she spoke his name out loud, lengthening that one adored syllable. But what would he think of her situation now? she wondered. *He never knew, never knew any of it, I never told him . . .*

'And would he have loved me any the less?' she murmured.

'What's that, dear?'

Cora started. 'Oh, nothing . . . nothing at all.'

'You know, you quite put me to shame today,' Sylvia began again. 'I'd never realised that you had such an understanding and knowledge of flowers and plants.'

'Not really, my dear, I just know a little about many things – and don't they say a little knowledge is a dangerous thing?'

'But it always seems to me that you know a great deal about *everything*,' Sylvia replied. 'And I insist, you must tell me where this knowledge came from.'

Cora turned to her friend. 'You know, I'm rather beginning to think you'd be better employing your investigative talents in writing crime thrillers instead of silly romances that . . . that have no bearing on real life!'

For some minutes the two women sat in silence.

'I'm sorry', Cora said, 'I've a great deal on my mind.'

'Is it about Jack?' Sylvia asked, leaning forward.

'No, not entirely . . .' She paused, looking at her friend with newly anxious eyes.

'Then what is it, dear? Please tell me what it is that's troubling you so.'

Cora reached over, placed her hand upon Sylvia's. 'I'm not sure I've ever told you how much your friendship means to me,' she said, her eyes on their hands. 'You've been the best, the very best.'

'We've been good friends to each other, dear. And you've been more than a friend to me, you have been family to me. But I can't bear to see you like this, not now. We're both much too old for any more drama.'

Cora tried to smile, shook her head. 'Oh, it's nothing . . . nothing sinister. Complications to do with the trust estates, that's all.'

'Ah, I thought as much. But you know, you really mustn't worry so. All will be well. Edward was a good man, a good husband. I'm quite certain he'll have made sure that you're looked after, provided for.'

'Well, I'm not destitute, not yet.'

'Nor will you ever be, not whilst I'm alive. But it's a scandal,' Sylvia shook her head, 'for you to be so fretful at this stage in your life. Dear Edward would turn in his grave!'

'It is what it is, we all have our crosses to bear . . . and I have spent too much of my life creating heroes and villains out of mere mortals.'

She saw Sylvia open her notebook once more and scribble something down. And Cora smiled. '*Dolce far niente*,' she said, closing her eyes.

'Ah yes, *dolce far niente*,' Sylvia repeated, without looking up.

'You know, I close my eyes and I'm back there.'

'It's this blessed heat. Easily as hot as Rome in August, and to think . . .'

Cora could hear Sylvia's voice, but she could no longer make out the words, and she had no wish to. She wanted to go back there, to that time, always that time, always that place.

Weeks away from England, isolated and undisturbed, Rome had been a small city then, shrivelled within its walls. A place of lopsided crucifixes and littered shrines, and scattered ruins tangled up in weeds and undergrowth, and centuries of rubble and dust, where cows and sheep grazed about the tumbled pillars of ancient palaces and ragged clothes lay out to dry upon their scorching stones. Where animal carcases, flasks of oil and balls of cheese dangled against the crumbling plaster of windowless shops; where tailors, milliners, shoemakers and carpenters huddled in doorways, a shrine to the Madonna and a candle flickering in the dimness behind them. And in the summer months, when the Tiber exposed her yellow banks and a fetid air hung over the city's ruins, the place languished in that sweet idleness the Romans called '*dolce far niente*'.

'Never look back,' her aunt had told her. 'Your life . . . *our* life began here in Rome.' And for so long, so very long, she had not looked back. She had only ever looked ahead, always ahead. But that *other* time, that time before Rome – for so long pushed away, denied, so much so that it had almost been forgotten – seemed determined to be acknowledged. And names for so long unuttered, buried in the past, had been written down for her to see: *John Abel*.

She opened her eyes. Sylvia was watching her, and she smiled. Now, a new secret hung between them, an invisible pendulum swinging between each and every glance. And Sylvia's constant surveillance, that seemingly relentless albeit well-meaning scrutiny was awaiting answers, waiting for her to elucidate upon then and now, and everything in between.

But no, she couldn't. How could she? She would have to introduce Sylvia to new words – words even she found hard to say. And it would mean going back to the beginning, the beginning of everything. It would mean unravelling seven decades of careful arrangement. She thought of her aunt, of all the times she had warned her about any permanent return to England. But she had had no choice in the matter. After all, the boy had no one, and she had nowhere else to go.

Such a tawdry business, blackmail.

Chapter Four

'A French cook, I ask you!'

Rosetta was rolling out pastry once more, sprinkling flour across the pine table, wiping her brow between every roll. The kitchen was airless and hot. Cecily sat watching her, only half engaged in their desultory conversation which had meandered from shortcrust pastry to the shortcomings of the soon-to-be-appointed cook at Temple Hill.

'How's she going to find a French cook round here? And what do the French know about English food? It'll all be foreign, oh yes, you mark my words, and then she'll have to eat humble pie, advertise again,' Rosetta went on, oblivious of any pun. 'Never trusted the Frenchies, never would – look at what they did to their own King . . . wouldn't want one in the house, rob you as soon as look at you. And she's half-French – at least.'

'Actually, I think she's English,' Cecily said without looking up. 'Her grandson's certainly English.'

'Hmm. He might be,' Rosetta said, sceptically. 'But there's been stuff said, hasn't there? And there's no smoke without fire.'

She glanced over at Cecily. 'But that's not to say he's got her ways.'

'Her ways?'

'All them marriages, that life abroad. It's not normal, is it?'

Cecily didn't answer. What was normal? Was Rosetta's life normal? Was her mother's? Normal was surely whatever was normal; normal was subjective. Normal meant nothing, she concluded swiftly. There was little point in debating semantics with Rosetta.

'I'm not altogether sure what you mean,' she said.

'Well, seems to me she's had a *pecular* sort of a life. Moving about all the time, marrying willy-nilly. It smacks of one thing . . .'

'Mm, what's that?'

Rosetta put down the rolling pin and leaned towards Cecily, her broad hands flat on the table. 'Lustfulness.'

'Lustfulness!' Cecily repeated.

'You may well smirk, my girl, but it's what robs men of what little sense they're born with and sends women to the county asylum.'

Lustfulness. It was not a word Cecily had heard spoken out loud before, or not that she could recall. Lustfulness: is that what had driven their new neighbour from one country to another, one man to another?

'And it all comes from the French . . .' Rosetta was saying, stuck on her theme now. 'I don't want to know what they get up to over there, and I don't want them bringing it over here neither.'

Diminutive, dark, and comfortingly round, Rosetta, Cecily thought, would have made a brilliant actress. She understood drama, knew how to deliver lines. But her talent had been wasted – in service, and in a kitchen, someone else's kitchen.

For that was where she had spent her life. She had never been married and Cecily couldn't be sure how old she was. Like so many others, she appeared to be ageing and old at the same time. She was suspicious of any written word apart from those in the Bible, which she read most evenings, and she took enormous comfort in prayer. 'I'll make sure I include him/her/them/it in my prayers,' was one of her stock replies, and to almost anything. And though she liked to complain about the rector – his choice of hymns, his sermons, and his fondness for the New Testament – she was an ardent churchgoer, attending all three services on a Sunday in her waist-length cape and tiny bonnet tied tightly under her fat chin.

The only thing Cecily knew for sure, the only thing she could relate to, was that Rosetta had loved and lost. She had only mentioned him once: someone named Wilf. He had been killed in the Boer War.

'But if she has known great love over and over, is it so very wrong for her to have accepted it? How many hearts could have been broken? How many tears shed? And which is nobler, to take love and cherish it, or to throw it back because one has already known it?'

But Rosetta appeared not to hear her. She continued with her rolling pin, eyes cast downwards, and said, 'And who knows where she's come from . . . could be anyone at all . . . anyone at all . . . I've read about folk who go overseas and come back all la-di-da, oh yes . . . could be anyone at all. Makes you wonder what happened to all them husbands,' she added, glancing up at Cecily with wide eyes.

Cecily laughed. She said, 'Oh Rosetta, only *you* would suspect the poor old lady of murder!'

Rosetta made no reply. She pursed her lips and stretched her short neck as though trying to swallow words. Then she said,

'You should go and tidy yourself up, missy. The Foxes are due here at seven.'

Cecily Chadwick had been born towards the end of a century, and towards the end of a life. Her first proper word, whispered – as she'd been taught – was 'Daddy'; her first sentence, with a finger to her lips, 'Daddy not well.' She had taken her first steps the day of a great earthquake in Japan, but there had been no tremor of excitement in her small hushed world. And then, at the end, it had gone quieter still and all black and white as her ashen-faced mother, already in mourning, with the nurse and the rector by her side, explained, 'Daddy has gone.'

Since that time there had been little physical alteration in Cecily's life. She had stayed on at the village school teaching the infants, and continued to live with her mother and sister in the house her father had built. But lately she had begun to feel a suffocating tightness about the village, like a gown she had outgrown but was still forced to wear. The sameness of each and every day was inescapable, the prospect of change remote. A yearning for excitement, she had been told, was the ambition of a shallow and idle mind, the ambition of *pleasure-seekers*.

Then, early in the spring of that year, the Countess From Abroad had moved into the house on the hill, the place known as Temple Hill. For days before her arrival all manner of vehicles had come and gone, struggling up the steep track, knocking branches from trees, churning up rocks and sand and dried mud. One wagon had failed to make it up at all, had stopped right there in front of Cecily's garden gate. The men had had to carry each piece of furniture up the track, resting halfway, upon tables and in chairs, for a smoke. She had watched them disappear over the brow of the hill, stepped out through the gate and peered inside the wagon at the ornate antiques, rolls of carpets, tapestries, paintings, cabinets, settees and chairs. Stacked high at the back were crates and tea chests, a marble sculpture of a naked woman and, immediately in front of her, uncovered and gazing out into the sunshine, the bronze head of a Roman-nosed bearded man.

In the weeks that followed, as news of the countess's arrival gathered pace, Cecily heard many things: the lady had lived in exile for almost all of her life, the lady was of foreign blood; her manner was unusually forthright, her manner was curiously reticent; she was Catholic, she was Protestant; she was penniless, she was rich. There was, however, consensus on one thing: the countess's style was universally acknowledged as *cosmopolitan*.

It was the rector, Mr Fox, who first alluded to royal connections, and there was talk of lineage and ancestry, albeit unspecific and somewhat vague, linking her to Louis Philippe, the last King of France. To Cecily, Mr Fox appeared to know more than anyone, and certainly more than he was prepared to divulge. But once, over tea and cake, he slipped up and offered Cecily another tantalising scrap, a chink into that rare knowledge. Oh yes, she had indeed been *someone* in her day, he said. 'But the dear lady has come here in search of privacy and peace . . . and we must grant her that.'

As time went on, a selected few had been invited to the house for tea, always at a quarter past four. These, the chosen ones, had seen for themselves the fine French and Italian antique furnishings, paintings, sculptures and souvenirs; the paraphernalia of a life spent in a far more sophisticated milieu than their village. They spoke of the countess's knowledge of Italian and French art and architecture, her apparent fluency in both languages. And when they learned that she had grown up in Paris, well, it came as no surprise.

But there was also talk of lost children, and husbands long since deceased, and though some appeared to consider this careless, almost wanton behaviour, Cecily began to sense something of unutterable tragedy lying at the heart of the story. She pictured marble tombstones scattered across the desolate hillsides of foreign countries, and she could not help but view the countess as the sole survivor of an epic adventure. That the lady's Grand Tour – gone horribly wrong perhaps – had finally, albeit inexplicably, led her to Bramley seemed a curious fluke of fate. And meaningful? Perhaps.

That the countess had had a remarkable life Cecily was in no doubt, for already she knew that her neighbour had lived in a way others had not. But Cecily's mother remained unconvinced. She appeared, to Cecily at least, somewhat piqued by the rector's unquestioning predisposition towards their new neighbour; said he appeared 'a little star struck'. But yes, she had conceded, smiling, the lady had undoubtedly led a colourful life. 'But then, what goes on abroad, what's acceptable on the continent, is different. Quite different.'

'You mean the husbands, the marriages?' Cecily had asked.

'I mean everything.'

For weeks Cecily had been desperate for a glimpse of the Countess From Abroad. And once, driven by that desperation, that need to know, to see for herself, she had ventured up the track, and then further still into the tangled hollow of rhododendrons bordering the driveway to Temple Hill. Like a spy on a mission, gathering intelligence, she had crouched there, waiting. But nothing happened. No one emerged from the house and no one arrived. And to Cecily there appeared to be no signs of life within it.

'But does she never go anywhere?' she had later asked her mother.

'I believe she's quite old, dear. So no, I imagine she doesn't go far. Not now.'

'It must be strange,' Cecily continued, 'to have travelled so much, so far, and then come to a stop. A stop *here*.'

Madeline Chadwick looked at her daughter: 'But she might not be stopping, dear. I heard talk that she's only here for the summer, is returning to the continent for the winter.'

'Only here for the summer?' Cecily repeated. 'But all that . . . stuff – surely she can't be thinking of moving again?'

And then her sister, Ethne, said, 'I don't know why you're so fascinated. Is it the title, dear? Because you know they're two a penny on the continent.'

Encouraged by Cecily, Annie Gamben had made it her business to try and learn more. As village postmaster, Annie's father was privy to almost everything that took place within the scattered parish: births, deaths, engagements, marriages, and scandals (though there were few); who was writing to whom, who despatched and who was the recipient of a telegram; and, crucially, what those telegrams spoke of.

It had been Annie's mother who had first mentioned the *young man*: a relation, she presumed, and from what she had heard – judging by his looks – foreign, possibly Italian. Then Mrs Gamben mentioned the *companion*: a lady only recently arrived by train from London. The companion had been into the post office twice, once to buy a packet of birdseed and some buttons, and once to despatch a large brown paper package to a gentleman in north London.

On the first occasion Mrs Gamben had not taken much notice of the bespectacled lady. It had been a Wednesday and the post office had been busy, as it always was on half-day closing. Realising the lady to be a visitor to the village, and assuming her to be staying with one or other of her customers, Mrs Gamben had been courteous but not overly so. But after the lady had thanked Mrs Gamben and left the shop, Mrs Moody, standing to one side beside the brooms and trugs and baskets, emerged from the shadows and told Mrs G exactly whose guest her previous customer had been. On the second occasion, when the lady arrived with the brown paper parcel, Mrs Gamben had been prepared. She had noted the absence of a wedding band on the lady's left hand, a distinct lack of eye contact, and what she described as a 'rather shifty manner'. Mrs Gamben had politely inquired after the countess, been reassured to hear she was in very good health, and that Miss Appleby – who came to the post office each Tuesday to cut and dress hair – was expected up at the house that very afternoon. The countess, Mrs Gamben surmised, was still very particular about her hair.

Rosetta had been the first to use the word 'orphan'. She had bumped into the gardener, Mr Cordery, 'had it from the horse's mouth', she said, that the boy was quite without parents *and* that there were 'suspicious circumstances.'

Everyone was curious. Everyone wanted to know more.

It was Cecily's mother, Madeline, who raised the subject later that evening at dinner, saying, 'Do tell me, Mr Fox, how is our new neighbour, the countess, settling in?' And Cecily looked up and sat forward.

True to form, Mr Fox appeared delighted to be offered the opportunity to speak about *the dear lady*. Oh yes, he began, she was settling in well, and delighted with the modernisations made to her new home. 'Of course, she's used to continental ways, and finds English sanitation a trifle primitive, to say the least,' he added. And Cecily saw Rosetta – standing behind Mrs Fox, waiting to remove plates – roll her eyes.

That evening, Rosetta had changed into the dark gown, long white apron and cap Madeline had made for her and liked her to wear on the rare occasions they had visitors to dine with them. But the dress had become a tad too tight around her waist, causing her to tug and pull at it, and the cap, secured with elastic about her head, too loose. It slipped this way and that, and at one point, as she leaned forward to serve the rector, it slowly slid down her forehead until it entirely covered one eye before she managed to free a hand and push it back in place. Cecily knew these evenings to be enough of an ordeal for her, standing about, waiting at table and managing the kitchen on her own, without the added encumbrance of a faulty cap. Also, despite every window in the house standing open, the place was uncomfortably hot. And permeating the smell of meat and pastry and stewed vegetables, like the top note of a cheap perfume that catches the back of one's throat, was the malodorous reek of Mr Fox.

'And do remind me of her full name,' Madeline continued. 'I've been told, of course, but it's somewhat unusual. French, I think, isn't it?'

Cecily turned to the rector.

He smiled, nodded. 'You are correct, Mrs Chadwick. It is the name of one of the most ancient and noble families in all of France, de Chevalier de Saint Léger. Thus the dear lady is la Comtesse de Chevalier de Saint Léger.'

'The Countess de Chevalier . . . de Saint Léger . . .' Madeline repeated hesitantly, as Cecily said it silently.

'And there were how many husbands?' Madeline asked.

'Someone told me there had been five,' Cecily broke in, without thinking, and she heard her mother and Mrs Fox both gasp.

The rector cleared his throat. He picked up his glass of wine, studied the liquid for a moment. 'It is unfortunate but perhaps understandable,' he said, glancing at Madeline, 'for there to be conjecture of that nature. I can tell you only the *facts*. Facts I am certain the countess would be happy enough for me to share with the assembled company.' He paused again, took a sip of wine. 'The first marriage was to a gentleman by the name of Staunton, in Rome, many years ago . . . perhaps as many as fifty years ago.'

'Fifty,' Cecily repeated.

'I would estimate so . . . yes, I would estimate so. But that union, that *first* marriage, was cut tragically short when Mr Staunton was killed.'

There was a loud clank from the sideboard. Madeline jumped. 'Killed?' she repeated.

'An accident, I believe,' said Mr Fox, without elaborating further. Cecily caught Rosetta's eye and quickly looked away as he continued. 'And thus, the countess – little more than a girl at that time – was left to raise her sons alone.'

'Ah, so she *does* have children,' Madeline said, smiling, sounding relieved.

'Sadly, no longer. I'm afraid her children, like her husbands, are all deceased. Her grandson is the only one left . . . all she has left,' he replied, newly baritone.

'What about the count?' Cecily asked. 'What happened to him?'

He shook his head. 'It was another short-lived union. They were married but a brief time before he was killed.'

'*Killed?*' Cecily said, at that moment conscious only of the repetition of this word, its connotations, and Rosetta's steady gaze.

'Killed in battle during the Franco-Prussian war, and buried there in the battlefield, at Servigny, near Metz.'

'The Franco-Prussian war. That was forty years ago.'

'Bravo, Cecily, it was indeed. Forty-one years ago, to be precise. And so our dear lady was tragically widowed once more, cruelly robbed of another husband, her children robbed of another father. At that time la comtesse,' continued the rector, warming to his theme, 'divided her time between France and Italy, between her fine chateau nestling in the glorious Loire Valley and her home in Rome, where her aunt, the dear lady into whose care she'd been placed as a very young girl, continued to reside. And of course she also kept an apartment in Paris, off the rue du Faubourg Saint-Honoré,' he added gutturally. 'Paris, like Rome, is I think very dear to her heart. For thither she was sent as a child, to live with her aunt . . .' He paused, glancing about the table, his eyes twinkling, smiling, 'who was none other than the Contessa Francesca Cansacchi di Amelia!'

Cecily looked at the others; was this a name she was meant to know?

'Gracious!' said Madeline.

'Indeed, indeed,' said the rector, lifting a napkin to his whiskers.

'Golly,' said Ethne, who'd remained silent until now. 'So she's true aristocracy.'

The rector looked at Ethne, narrowing his eyes. 'Almost more than that,' he said, enigmatically.

Cecily felt her heart shiver. More than that? What did he mean? And she wanted to say, 'Do tell us, please tell us more,' but for some reason, right at that moment it seemed inappropriate. The rector had stopped his story at a very specific point, and quite obviously for a reason. There was more, she realised, much more. She glanced to her mother and Madeline smiled back at her; but now with tightly sealed lips, as if to say, no more questions. Did her mother know something? she wondered. Was her mother familiar with the aunt, the Italian contessa? Did everyone know something she did not? She looked over to Ethne, who appeared more engrossed by the summer pudding in front of her. No, Ethne would not know. She turned to Mrs Fox, seated on her left, but she too appeared more interested in fruit and cream than the unfolding roll call of European nobility. And then she couldn't help herself.

'Is she descended from royalty, Mr Fox?'

He smiled at Cecily, raised a finger to his face and tapped his nose.

'Well,' said Madeline, lifting her glass of watered wine, 'what a life . . . what a life she has had. But it must be hard for an expatriate to settle,' she added. 'She must find Bramley awfully quiet after Rome and Paris and . . . all that,' she petered out.

The rector shuffled in his chair, clearing his throat, and Cecily knew another instalment was on its way.

'I believe the dear lady was ready for a change,' he began. 'The daughter-in-law's tragic demise served to propel that need for change, and here we are, with her and her beloved grandson in our midst. I think we're honoured, Mrs Chadwick, truly honoured, don't you?'

'She must find everyone here pretty dull,' Ethne broke in, sucking raspberry seeds from her teeth. 'I don't mean that in a derogatory way, of course. I don't think Bramley's dull at all, I'd far rather live here than in some horrid smelly city like Rome. But why on earth did she come here?'

Hallelujah! Cecily thought, at last she's managed to spit out one pertinent question.

'Because Temple Hill is her home,' Mrs Fox piped up, soft and sweet, like the pudding in front of her. 'It belongs to her, was built for her, I believe,' she added, glancing along the table to her husband.

'But surely it's much too old,' Cecily said. 'And it's been standing empty for years, hasn't it?'

'That is correct,' Mr Fox quickly replied, silencing his wife, who was about to continue. 'The place has never been lived in, certainly not in my time. Though I've heard tell that it was for a while rented out to a succession of tenants, and then no one. Of course, when I first arrived here, almost twenty years ago—'

'Good gracious, Mr Fox, is it really that long?' Madeline interrupted.

Cecily sighed and Mr Fox smiled. 'Yes, indeed it is, Mrs Chadwick. And oh, what changes I have seen in that time . . .'

Diverted, the rector began to speak about the village and surrounding area as it had once been. Cecily pushed the congealing ruby-coloured mess about her plate. Had her mother changed the subject on purpose? Who in their right mind, apart from her mother, would want to hear about Bramley as it once was rather than Rome and Paris? It was beyond frustrating. All Cecily could do was wait. He'd get back to it, eventually. She knew he'd only just begun.

Bramley had always struck Cecily as an untidy, straggling sort of place. The roads passing through it rose and dipped and rose once more before heading out through tunnel-like lanes to the outlying farms, scattered cottages and huts of the parish. The village had no railway station or market, but it had carpenters, builders, blacksmiths and wheelwrights; saddlers, farriers and millers; broom makers, shoemakers, coal merchants and drapers; grocers, bakers and butchers. The surrounding heathland provided for the broom-squires and thatchers, the bees for honey, hop fields for beer, and the meadows for milk and butter and cheese. It had three public houses, a school, an undertaker and a post office. And there were regular 'entertainments': evenings of poetry, music and amateur dramatics in the village hall. The lending library was administered by the rector's wife, Mrs Fox, who checked and monitored exactly who was reading what each Thursday afternoon.

For hundreds of years those who had been baptised at St Luke's – and then, against the odds, survived infancy – had been wedded there, and later buried there. No one left, no one moved. Bramley had always been self-sufficient, able to supply and occupy its inhabitants' hands and heads and hearts and stomachs.

In her final year at school Cecily had written about 'The History and Times of Bramley'. Most of what she had learned had come from Old Meg, who may have been Young Meg, once. Meg had been the village midwife and had, she reckoned, delivered over one hundred babies and laid out almost as many corpses. But by that time Old Meg confined her activities to the reading of tea leaves – and knitting. She told Cecily that in times not so long gone by *runagates* had skulked about the mist-shrouded wilderness surrounding the village. Yes, it had been a place for fugitives then, she said; a place to hide away, a no-man's-land people travelled through at their peril due to the vagabonds and highwaymen who preyed upon those journeying between London and the coast. She told Cecily that the unplanned ragged lines of the village probably owed something to those lawless folk and squatters, who had erected cottages by night, depositing children in them by dawn so the bailiffs could not remove the heather-thatched roofs above their heads. Then, the railway came to Linford, bringing rich city folk and consumptives from London. Yes, Cecily thought: Daddy.

Daddy – Cecil Chadwick – lay next to the ancient yew tree on the western side of the churchyard. Cecily had grown up knowing him only as a name chiselled on a tombstone. When she was young, she had been taken to his grave twice each week. Then it fell back to once a week, on Sunday afternoons. Now it was as and when – high days and holidays and special occasions, and Madeline alone each wedding anniversary. But sometimes Cecily took a walk through the churchyard on her own. She thought of the dead beneath her feet and pondered on all those long unspoken, long forgotten names: someone's daughter, someone's son, someone's father: hers. In Loving Memory . . . Sacred to . . . Beloveds one and all.

In the churchyard, history – his story and her story – was condensed to names and dates. Nothing more. Lifetimes, no matter how extraordinary, had no narrative, no triumphs or

70

defeats. There were no clues, no achievements listed. And yet there, just below Cecily's feet, lay hundreds of untold stories, stories spanning centuries, bridging generations, linking then and now. Tales of derring-do and recklessness, wisdom and folly, passion and pride and honour, stories Cecily could only wonder at and imagine. The names themselves often conjured an image, the date adding context and detail. So much so that she could often see them, not as bones beneath the sandy earth but in the flesh, alive and animated once more.

Cecily's allegiance with the dead had started at an early age, reinforced by all those visits to the cemetery and bound up in a fascination with Loss. And most particularly, Love and Loss.

Finally, and after some confusion about the point of his lengthy monologue (of which Cecily had heard not a word), the rector found his thread again. Yes, his wife was correct, Temple Hill, as far as he understood, had always belonged to the countess. The rector leaned towards Madeline. 'But you must know,' he whispered loudly, 'the land this very house sits upon was once part of the gardens of Temple Hill.'

Madeline shook her head and, glancing at Rosetta who stood by the sideboard, a dish in her hands, mouth open and cap askew, she said, 'You can clear away now, thank you.' And the maid bustled out of the room.

Madeline then quietly explained to the rector that she had not been involved in her late husband's business affairs. She had no recollection of him ever having mentioned from whom he had purchased their plot of land. But then, after some thought, she admitted she couldn't be sure he had not; he had been ill, her attention focused entirely upon him, his comfort and well-being. And then, as though still taking in what the rector had told her, she said, 'So, our house, the land this house is built upon, actually belonged to *her*, the countess?'

He nodded.

'Well I never,' she said.

Cecily listened as the rector explained that Temple Hill had originally had some one hundred acres of gardens and paddocks and woodland. But slowly, he said, over the past twenty years or so, parcels of land had been sold off for development, mainly on the other side of the hill. Now, he estimated the house would have only a fraction of those original acres; certainly less than ten, he thought.

The evening, Cecily realised, was producing answers to questions even she had not thought of. And as the conversation altered its course, touching briefly on the strikes and unrest spreading through the country, before turning to the recent and not so recent changes to the village, and Mr Fox to his favourite subject – the loss of the old country ways – Cecily sat in quiet contemplation.

So, she was right, she thought, the countess was indeed the survivor of an epic adventure, one that had cost her dearly, robbing her of husbands, children and, it seemed, money. But how had it started? she wondered. She knew the end of the story – or almost, because the countess had arrived there, possibly penniless, and with no family to speak of apart from Jack – but where, exactly, had it begun? And why had she not returned to this country before? After all, she mused, having done the calculation earlier, she was a great age, and had had a house standing empty, waiting for her. If her only family had been in England, why had she chosen to stay overseas? It was incomprehensible. Something didn't make sense. Was she so very selfish that she had allowed Jack's poor widowed mother to sink further and further into her loneliness, her melancholia, while she continued her gallivanting across Europe? No, surely not.

She had come here eventually, yes, but that, it seemed from what Cecily had heard, had been after Jack's mother's suicide. Then it dawned on her: the countess had had no plans to come back, ever.

Later, in the room Madeline Chadwick referred to as the parlour to her daughters and the drawing room to her guests, Cecily sat down next to the elderly rector. She wanted to ask him more about the countess. She had obviously led a fascinating life, she said, smiling brightly, eagerly, knowing he'd be flattered by her continued interest. 'And what stories she must have . . .'

'Indeed! What stories,' he repeated. 'But like any noble lady – all old nobility – she is in possession of discretion, Cecily. She is a very private person, without inclination to divulge her credentials or esteemed connections to all and sundry. Oh no, *la comtesse* chooses whom to confide in with great discernment, great care. After all, she has no need to impress the likes of we humble country folk.'

'She has confided in you then?'

The rector smiled, closing his eyes momentarily. 'To an extent,' he replied, nodding his head slowly. 'And thus it falls upon me to be prudent in my judgement of any disclosure. You see, Cecily, the dear lady has no desire to court fame or publicity, in fact quite the opposite. She has come to this parish in search of solitude, perhaps one could even say anonymity.'

'Anonymity? But why? Why would she wish for anonymity?'

'I imagine that if one has lived one's entire life under the glare of public scrutiny, even adulation, one eventually craves the luxury of invisibility.'

A tiny moth fluttered above the oil lamp on the table next to the rector, dipping down towards the yellow light, then back up, round and round, up and down.

'Of course, many of those she was once on intimate terms

with have passed away,' he continued, raising a hand to wave the moth from his face, stretching out his breeched legs. 'At one time she knew everyone, in Rome, Paris, and in London: royalty, dignitaries, aristocracy; writers, sculptors, poets . . . and some very famous painters as well,' he added, turning to Cecily with a smile.

'Such as?'

'George Lawson, for one.'

'George Lawson? *The* George Lawson? Lord George Lawson?'

The rector shuffled along the settee towards Cecily. She noticed the silver hairs sprouting from the tips of his lobes, could smell his body odour, and his rancid breath – alcohol, rotting gums, and that evening's dinner. 'I believe they met in Rome, many years ago,' he said, turning to her, breathing full into her face. 'He was there as a young man, before he became famous. It's where he painted his "Madonna", which of course the Queen herself later bought.'

'So they knew each other?'

He nodded. 'I believe so. He was a regular visitor to Paris and often travelled to Vichy to take the cure. Yes, Vichy . . .' he said, drifting. 'It's a place Mrs Fox and I have often contemplated visiting ourselves, but I fear we've left it too late.' He looked down at his empty glass, and Cecily quickly took it and rose to her feet.

Seconds later, handing the rector his replenished wine, Cecily sat down and said, 'But you know I do wonder, Mr Fox, why she didn't return to this country before now. Particularly in view of the fact that she was on her own, and her family, her only family – Jack and his poor mother – here in England.'

The rector pondered, stroking his whiskers. 'Let me say this: I believe the dear lady had good reason to stay away and, unprotected as she was, and is, no wish to rouse her enemies.' He turned to Cecily. 'Jealousy and envy can poison the heart and inspire untruths and wickedness. It is down to all of us here in Bramley to protect her now. I'm afraid I am not at liberty to say any more, but I know you to be an intelligent young woman, Cecily, and I hope I can rely on your discretion.'

Bewildered, Cecily nodded. 'Of course.'

Chapter Five

He slaps her face and says, 'You little bitch, you told her . . . you told her, didn't you?' She shakes her head. 'No . . . no, I didn't, I promise.' She places her palm to her cheek and she can feel the heat, the burning stain he has left on her.

It was another sultry evening, with no movement, no breath of wind. The hillside lay quiet in the warmth of the setting sun, and in its reflected glory appeared brighter than ever, the tops of the pine trees ablaze, illuminated by a light that spoke of the perfection of that day.

Inside the house, Cora had finally given in to exhaustion. Her head rested to one side, slowly rising and falling in time with her breathing, a stray curl across her brow. Her still brilliant blue eyes were shut, and her lips, the crinkled curve of a Cupid's bow, occasionally twitched and moved without sound. Her hands lay upturned and open in her lap, in a simple pleading gesture, as if to say, here I am.

She sat in a modern English wingback armchair, a token to

English taste in a room boasting European style. In front of her, an ottoman, upholstered in deep red velvet, piled with books and magazines; adjacent to her, a Louis XV settee and matching chairs; and against the wall opposite, an Italian black walnut bookcase, bowing under the weight of volumes of English, French and Italian literature. Scattered about the long room were various chairs and side tables, another settee, a desk in front of a tall window overlooking the garden, and, hanging from picture rails, framed oil paintings, watercolours and drawings of all sizes. Within the recess of an arched alcove to one side of the fireplace stood an almost life-size marble sculpture of a naked woman, and at the other side, in another alcove and standing upon a plinth, the bronze head of a bearded man.

That evening, she, Sylvia and Jack had dined early once again. Though she preferred to take a light supper later in the evening, this was not the custom in England and had proved something of a problem with Mrs Davey, her housekeeper, who was standing in as cook until a permanent one was appointed. Nine o'clock was much too late to be busying on in the kitchen, Mrs Davey had told the countess; her day was long enough.

After dinner, Jack had disappeared upstairs to his room, to read, he said. She and Sylvia had remained seated at the dining table, lingering over their coffee. But Sylvia had annoyed Cora with her persistent questions. The memoirs, which Cora was quietly beginning to have second thoughts about, seemed to be coming between Sylvia and her wits. To Cora's mind, Sylvia was becoming possessed with an unhealthy obsession about her life. And she had told her so.

Sylvia had abruptly risen to her feet, saying she wished to take a stroll about the garden, and Cora had retired to the drawing room. She sat by the window on the western side of the house, flicking through the dog-eared pages of one of Sylvia's *Lady's Pictorial* magazines, peering through her old lorgnette at murky images and out-of-date advertisements, keeping thoughts at bay. But as daylight dwindled her eyes had grown heavy, and as the sun slipped down behind the trees she put the magazine to one side, allowed herself to sit back in her chair and closed her eyes.

Now she was lost in her dreams. But her dreams, like her memories, had fused, muddling people and chronology, muddling everything. Nameless yet familiar faces spoke the wrong words, borrowing sentences; people were not what they seemed, not who they appeared to be, and places were unreliable, altering their shape and form to a different city, a different country, taking her back to where she had started . . .

She feels sick, the ship is listing, but she does as she is told, placing her hand upon soft leather and promising, 'No one.' She repeats words over and over: this is what she must say. Yes, yes, she knows, she says, she will not forget.

When she walks down the plank and steps ashore, she stands amidst rubble and ruins and dust, and stone columns stretching all the way up to the heavens. The sky is brighter here . . . but she must not forget, she must remember the words . . . and the name.

Cora asked for dreams. She asked for them to refresh her memory. But chaos was her recurring nightmare. And in this chaos her overriding desire was to find George, to get back to him. And sometimes she did, and sometimes she did not. But when she did, in those rare dreams when she finally found him – waiting for her, beside the steps – he held out his arms to her, wrapped them around her so tightly she could feel the warmth of his breath upon her forehead, the softness of his velvet jacket against her cheek. And when she awoke, fresh from his embrace, she remembered, remembered it all: the heady sensation, the hunger for another's touch, the rise and fall of each wave, and that feeling of complete abandonment, where only the senses were alive, and yet lost at the same time.

Lately, she had begun to enjoy that blurred landscape which often bridges slumber and wakefulness, that place of semi-consciousness. She liked to linger there, in that glow, aware it would come to her with more substance if she remained within it. Hoping *they* would come to her if she remained within it. For it was then, in that place, she could hear them: cherished voices, whispering and murmuring from another century. Occasionally she heard music – a piano, someone singing – beyond the open window, drifting across the garden, in the next room or upstairs, faint and impossible to place. And once or twice of late she had known with absolute certainty that he was there, standing so close to her she could sense his presence with all of her being. Close enough for her to feel that frisson once more.

When Sylvia, Jack or one of the maids entered the room, she kept her eyes firmly shut, as though in defiance of her own physical decrepitude as much as her circumstances. And perhaps because when she finally opened them nothing ever looked quite as it should. Things were all wrong, she was all wrong, like a sole survivor washed up on a foreign land with the material contents of her life tipped out around her, sad mementos, conspicuous and out of place.

In conscious moments, she revisited her most favourite times, working through them slowly and in detail, backwards and forwards, forwards and backwards, savouring each second of a moment again and again. And there was Lucca. No longer a place, but a memory, a time. Sacrosanct. Fortified.

She was careful never to near unhappy memories, or venture back too far. Once, it had been easy, or easier, to steer clear of those dark places and difficult times. But now, like coming to the end of a road, a place where there is no further way forward, she had no choice, she had to turn and look back upon her path. She saw herself at different stages as different people: the young woman of almost twenty in Rome; the woman of thirty, mistress of a castle in France; the woman of forty, part of the beau monde of Paris; mother of two sons, wife of three men, lover of one: all different people with different lives. And that time before Rome, the place her journey started, obscured from view by those people she had become, had once been.

Numbness had come with old age, but to her bones, not to her heart. And though in public she was careful to keep her emotions in check, to maintain – or try to maintain – a ready smile, a relaxed countenance, in quiet, solitary moments, moments of reflection, and often when least expecting it, she was sometimes plunged under, submerged, left gasping for breath; drowning in a great swell of sorrow and joy and pain and rapture. And it was this, the memory of senses and sensations, that made her weep. She wept for lost children, she wept for lost love; she wept for a life slowly ebbing, and for things still inexplicable to her.

And now, at this great age, she wept for her mother too. Not simply in sorrow at her distant passing, or the loss of her, but in need of her. The child within the aged body and creaking bones, the little girl who had not been allowed to say goodbye, finally wanted to be heard. Mother. The word itself had piercing resonance. For she, too, had been robbed of that particular title.

'. . . mother, . . . mother? Grandmother?'

She opened her eyes.

'You're in darkness,' he said, lighting the lamp on the table beside her.

'I must have drifted off.'

'You were talking about your mother.'

She blinked, staring at the shape of him, allowing her eyes to adjust to the new light. 'I was dreaming,' she said.

He sat down on the chair opposite her. 'And what were you dreaming of? Your mother, obviously.'

'I'm not sure. This and that. It was all a muddle, it always is.' She glanced about the room. 'Is Sylvia back indoors?'

'Yes, and retired for the night. She said she didn't wish to disturb you. Actually, she was rather upset.'

'She gets upset too easily, far too easily. Always has. It's part and parcel of having had so little in her life.'

He smiled. 'Perhaps we need to remember that,' he suggested. 'That she has had so little.'

'You're right, of course you're right. I was sharp with her. I shall apologise in the morning.'

'I know we've had very little time together,' he began, staring down at the floor. 'Growing up . . . well, you were overseas, I couldn't see you, but now we have the opportunity . . . I'd like to know more about everyone: Father, Grandfather, Fanny, and you, your family, your parents. You see, it strikes me I know nothing about my own family. Mother,' and he paused after he said the word, 'Mother was unable, or perhaps not inclined, to tell me anything about the Staunton side of my family. She always claimed she knew little about you.'

Cora smiled, looked at the clock on the mantelshelf. 'Good gracious, half past ten. I've been asleep for two whole hours. I rather think it's time that I, too, went to my bed.' She struggled forward in her chair. He rose up, took hold of her hand and helped her to her feet. He looks so like him, she thought, observing his features in the lamplight; so like him.

'Will you tell me sometime? Will you tell me about the family, *your* family? I'd like to hear about them all,' he said, holding her hand in his.

'Yes, yes, of course I shall, but not tonight, my darling,' she said, trying to smile, placing her hand upon his cheek.

As she moved away from him, towards the door, he said, 'Oh, and I was thinking of inviting Cecily Chadwick to tea on Tuesday . . . You said you'd like to meet her.'

She turned to him. 'Yes, I would, and that's a splendid idea. Goodnight, dear.'

As she closed the door and moved across the hallway, she felt a constriction about her chest. She grasped the handrail, began to climb the stairs, and the rustle of her petticoats momentarily distracted her: that swish-swish-swishing sound that had accompanied her every movement, all of her life. A fleeting image of her younger self dashing up steps two at a time flashed through her mind's eye, and she caught that sensation once more: the weightlessness of youth. Whalebone, she thought, can't really be good for one's breathing. But lodged deep in her breast was an ever-tightening dilemma, and one name playing on a loop inside her head: John Abel . . . John Abel . . . John Abel.

After Cora retired to her bed, Jack sat alone for a while, cogitating. He reflected on the conversation he had had with Sylvia, earlier, in the garden, and it concerned and perplexed him in equal measure.

'Of course, it could be the heat,' Sylvia had said. And he knew she was being polite, as any good friend would be.

'I'm sorry,' he said. 'I can only apologise.'

She had recounted Cora's harsh words, had been tearful, and understandably so.

'That she thinks I'm *possessed* . . . with an obsession about her . . . her life, and after she invited me here, asked me to record her memories . . .' She shook her head, removed her spectacles and dabbed at her eyes. 'I don't know what I've done, Jack, to make her turn on me like that.' She raised her head, staring straight ahead. 'I fear for her,' she continued, 'that she can turn on *me*, her oldest, most devoted friend, and with such . . . such venom, such passion. Hatred, that's what it was. Pure hatred.'

'No, no, she doesn't hate you. You mustn't for one moment think that. She's very fond of you, I know.'

But he was at a loss. Why had Cora turned on Sylvia? Sylvia, who wouldn't say boo to a goose. Sylvia, whom Cora herself had claimed was such a dear friend. After a while he said, 'You may be right. It may be the heat. I know she was used to it once, but we must bear in mind she's a good deal older now.'

Sylvia sniffed, tucked her handkerchief inside her sleeve, and for a while they sat in silence, side by side, looking out over the garden.

'I only hope she comes back to us soon,' she said. 'That we haven't lost her.'

'Lost her?'

'It happened in Rome . . . in the summer. July and August. The heat brought it on, the delusions, the fever . . . paranoia . . . madness,' she said, so quietly that he had had to lean forward to catch the last two words.

Now, he thought Sylvia had overreacted. His grandmother was right: she had had so little in her life, was as unsused to drama as Cora was used to it. Poor Sylvia. But as he rose to his feet and moved towards the lamp, something surfaced. At first, a mere sensation, a glimpse and flash of yellow. Then, slowly, more: his mother, another lady, unrecognisable, faceless; a yellow-walled room, long forgotten, unidentifiable; and a small dog – sweet little thing, grey – rolling about on the rug in front of him. His mother and the other lady are behind him, talking. They don't say the name but he knows that the 'she' they speak of refers to his grandmother.

His mother says, 'She'll never come back here to live, not permanently. She's too afraid.'

'But afraid of what?' the faceless woman asks.

'Being discovered . . . being found out. Oh, she'll come back for a drawing room at the palace . . . spend a week or so gadding about. But she's terrified of any of *them* finding her. She thinks I don't know, but I do.'

The faceless woman says, 'Did *he* know?'

'No,' his mother replies, and she almost laughs as she says, 'My husband adored her.'

Upstairs, Sylvia lay awake in her bed. Too hot to sleep, too distressed to write.

It had all started with the blessed letter, another letter. It had arrived in the afternoon post, and it had been she, Sylvia, who had taken it in to Cora. Sylvia had noted the pale yellow paper, the name and address typed in red ink . . . but perhaps only because of the somewhat clashing colours. Never could she have foreseen that she would later be attacked as the messenger.

Cora took the envelope from her, and as Sylvia spoke of something else – she couldn't now recall what – Cora glanced at it and then simply placed it to one side, upon her desk. She was dealing with bills, settling accounts. There was no reason for Sylvia to suppose the yellow envelope contained anything more than another invoice. But even then, Cora had been dismissive, sharp with her.

'Is there anything else?' she had asked, interrupting Sylvia, and just as though she was a wittering servant.

'No, nothing else,' Sylvia had replied, and far too meekly she thought now.

Cora had stayed in that room, at her desk, for the remainder of the afternoon, which was odd, because she had told Sylvia at luncheon that she would take no more than an hour over her correspondence and accounts, and then, she said, they would take a walk. So Sylvia had sat on the veranda, waiting. She had used the time productively enough, making a new list of questions to ask Cora, and pondering an idea for a short story. But by four o'clock, and with no sight or sound of Cora, Sylvia had crept along the terrace and peered in through the south window. She could clearly see Cora, in profile, doing absolutely nothing at all but gazing out through another window – the one immediately in front of her desk. She could also see that there were no papers, invoices or even pens out upon the desk.

She had been pressed up against the climbing hydrangea for some minutes, watching her friend daydream, for that was how it appeared, when she noticed Cora's lips moving and realised that she was in fact speaking. And so she tiptoed quietly along the wall of the house to the open window, on the other side of which sat Cora. At first, it was impossible to make out what, exactly, Cora was saying. She spoke in a strange, low, monotone voice but, after a little while, Sylvia recognised the words, and listened to her as she continued: 'The dew of the morning, sunk chill on my brow . . . it felt like the warning, of what I feel now. Thy vows are all broken, and light is thy fame: I hear thy name spoken, and share . . . in its shame.'

Byron. Sylvia almost said the name out loud. She had been there the very first time Cora recited it – 'When We Two Parted' – at her aunt's soiree, in Rome. And he had been there, too: George. Had he known the lines were for him? Had she ever told him? But yes, he must have known. For it had all been for him; even then, everything was for him. The two of them had crossed paths a number of times by then, and Cora had already visited his studio – in secret and alone – once, or was it twice? Sylvia could not recall.

But Cora had told her, certainly, of that first visit. He had been nervous, fumbling and awkward. They had spent time looking at the sketches and studies from which he was working, and he had talked her through his vision, his 'Madonna'. He had explained to her how he would use only one or two models for the multitude of minor characters, but would add detail to their dress so that they would appear different. The painting would tell a story, he said, but each section of the vast canvas was as important as the whole, with a separate story to it. Cora said he talked with such conviction and passion, such intensity in his eyes that it made her feel as feeble as a child and yet more alive than ever before. And then he had said to her, 'And I want you, Cora, to be my Madonna.'

Sylvia closed her eyes. Cora continued to murmur.

Even then, after that first visit to George's studio, Cora claimed they had confided in each other. She said she had told him things she had never told anyone, which Sylvia found hard to believe. And yet, wasn't that when Cora had begun to drift away from *her*? Wasn't that when Cora had begun to change, altering her story, telling Sylvia she had made mistakes in her recollection of events? But Sylvia had already written things down. And he knew nothing. How could he love her if he knew nothing about her?

Silence. Sylvia stood perfectly still, hardly daring to breathe. Then Cora began again. She seemed to be in some sort of trance-like state, reciting the poem over and over. What on earth was she doing? Trying to summon him from the grave?

It was after Sylvia returned to the veranda and had pondered on this bizarre occurrence that she began to think the worst, began to wonder if Cora was in fact losing her senses.

Later, at dinner, Cora had been unusually quiet. And afterwards, as the two women sat alone together, Sylvia had tentatively mentioned the memoirs; had suggested that perhaps they could make a fresh start on it the next day. Cora appeared to be in agreement. She had smiled and nodded, with a degree of magnanimity. But then, when Sylvia very gently said, 'I heard you reciting your poem earlier today, dear,' she had flown off the handle, accused Sylvia of spying on her. That was when she had also said Sylvia was obsessed, obsessed with her life. And it was a ridiculous accusation in view of the circumstances.

'Ridiculous,' she said out loud, wiping her nose. I have simply loved her, loved her and been a loyal and true friend . . . for all of these years, all of these years . . . and she's never appreciated me, all I have done for her . . . never appreciated.

Sylvia had made no mention of the letter to Jack, or the queer poetry recital. She had no wish to burden the poor boy further. He had already been through enough. Quite enough. But, if Cora would not tell him the truth, it would, in time, surely fall upon her to do so.

Chapter Six

The door slams shut. Neither one of them moves. The woman lies crumpled, motionless on the floor, the girl sits in petrified silence, waiting, listening, hardly daring to breathe. Only after his footsteps have faded, only when there is complete quiet does the girl slide down from the chair and run across the room. The woman reaches out, tries to speak, but her mouth is filled with blood, her teeth coated red, and the girl can't distinguish the words in the gurgling, swelled sound. And so she says, 'It's all right . . . he's gone now.'

At one time in her life Cora had been a brilliant listener. She had asked a great many questions, keen to hear about the minutiae of others' lives. Long anecdotes, digressions tedious to anyone else, had been met with an unerring patience and attentiveness. And this skill alone had won her many friends. But now Cora liked to talk. Not necessarily about herself, but of those she had once known, the places she had once lived or visited.

She had made Tuesdays her 'at home' day but other days, too, had seen a steady stream of callers. Once or twice, as many as ten had sat down to take tea with her, glancing about her drawing room with eager eyes and a seemingly endless list of questions, some surprisingly intelligent, others less so. What had Rome been like before the reunification? Had she met Garibaldi? (Of course, she had.) And the Pope? (Yes, many times.) Had she been in Paris during the Commune of '71? (No, thankfully not. She had been residing in Rome at that time.) Did they still speak Latin in Rome? Was it true that they made the Jews race in bare feet through the streets and locked them up at night?

The fact that she was able to answer these questions, that she could enlighten, educate and inform her new neighbours had given her a sense of satisfaction, and pride, even a raison d'être for the short time they were in her midst. She was flattered by their interest in her, in her life and her possessions. She pointed to paintings – a watercolour of her former home, the Chateau de Chazelles in France, a portrait of her at twenty-one years of age, and another of the count in uniform. She spoke of her early days in Rome, pronouncing the unpronounceable, rolling her Rs and slipping into Italian here and there. She explained to them that the English expatriate community, then, had been strong, with an English quarter situated around the Piazza di Spagna – yes, where the famous steps are – and with English shops selling English produce, English tea rooms serving English tea, English hotels, English banks, even English employment bureaus offering English servants. 'Well,' someone said, 'that is a relief!'

Rome, she told them, had had no fewer than thirty-five thousand foreigners living within its walls when she first arrived. 'Of course, many of them were visitors, there for only the season. And it is without doubt the perfect place to spend the winter months. The light is altogether different then,' she went on, staring out of the window. 'I'm not sure how I shall cope

with winter in England. I haven't spent a winter here since—'
She stopped. 'Since I was a girl.'

'And, if I may ask, where was that, ma'am? Whereabouts did
you grow up?'

'Gracious, now you are testing me!' she said, affecting a laugh.
A few followed suit, and she added, 'I rather think I grew up
in some distant county that no longer exists, for the world has
changed and the place of my childhood is no more.' Heads
turned and nodded. 'Like many of us here,' she continued,
gauging a consensus, 'I grew up in a different world.' She turned
to the gentleman. 'I'm afraid my early life is very dim and distant
to me now. And, I fear, decidedly dull by comparison to my life
overseas,' she said, smiling.

She was long used to navigating difficult conversations. It was
easy enough, or had been, to chart a course. Deflection was a
useful tool, to turn the tables, ask the same question back, and
then another, and another, so that that the original question,
addressed to her, was abandoned, forgotten. She imagined it
similar to driving a motorcar and avoiding the potholes on the
road ahead. The driver sees them coming and swiftly takes action.
The passengers remain oblivious, distracted by a newly pointed
out vista. But it would, she thought, be nice not to *have* to drive
the blessed motor every time, to be able to be a passenger, be
able to sit back and simply take in the view.

Thus, motoring on, across the Channel and back to Rome,
she spoke of glittering entertainments and tableaux vivants, of
the torch-lit parties and moonlit charades within the walls
of the Coliseum, and casually sprinkled a few famous names.
She spoke of a vibrant hubbub of noise and colour, and they
could almost hear the carriages, carts and wagons, the thunderous clatter of hoofs and wheels. They sat in spellbound silence
as she led them down dark and narrow streets, across sunlit
piazzas to fountains and churches; they followed her up ancient

steps, through vast doorways into cool, candlelit basilicas where saints lay at their feet beneath a marble floor. And they could see it, see it all; hear the fountains gently flowing, smell the incense within the church.

She chose not to tell them of the eight o'clock curfew, which locked up the poor Jews *Pio Nono* called 'dogs'; she chose not to mention the dead cart, which crossed the piazza beneath her bedroom late at night, swaying this way and that, heavy with lifelessness, and bound for a pit in the Sacred Field beyond the city walls. She chose not to tell them about the city's lepers and beggars, who slept in filth on the streets and sat outside the bakers each morning, waiting for crumbs to be thrown. These poor souls, and others, she kept to herself.

And what about that first journey, someone asked, that must have taken some time? Indeed it had. It had taken over twenty-five days to reach Rome. She tried to recall the route: 'From Le Havre by public coach to Nevers, across the mountains to . . . Chalon-sur-Saône . . . down the Saône to Lyon . . . then another steamer, to Avignon . . . from there, overland to Marseilles, and thence onwards to Civitavecchia.'

Yes, that was the route, she thought, staring through a shaft of light at a memory . . . *a place so far away no one will ever find us.*

She watched the light break through the small porthole, splintering into a myriad of dust-filled rays. She stepped down from her bed and moved over to the window. 'We are here,' she said, turning to her aunt. 'We're in Italy.'

They had originally expected to sail upriver to Rome, but the captain advised them to continue their journey overland. The French government steamers, which commuted between Rome and the coastal port, transporting the French army and supplies to its protectorate, did so only on appointed days, and this day was not one of them, he explained. He mentioned Palo, some Etruscan tombs at Cerveteri, and though Cora was keen, Fanny said she had no desire to see Palo or to visit any ancient tombs. They needed to get to Rome before nightfall.

Sidestepping horse dung and beggars, amidst the cacophony of street vendors, soldiers, sailors, horses, dogs, carts and barrows, the two women moved along the quayside towards the carriage office. Italian men, women and children of all ages vied for their attention, desperate to sell their wares, and filthy barefoot children with eyes as black as coal stretched out grubby hands and tugged at their skirts. 'Don't worry, dear, Rome will be quite different,' Fanny said, taking hold of Cora's arm and guiding her through the quagmire.

A group of young Italian men attached themselves to the women, walking alongside them. 'Inglese? Inglese? *Benvenuta!*' One pushed forward. 'Good day, fine ladies, I speak the English . . . and I will be your guide, yes?'

'No, thank you, you will not,' Fanny replied, grasping Cora's hand.

'But signora, please, we are your friends . . .'

Cora knew their lack of chaperone made Fanny more nervous than ever, and it had been the same in Marseilles. There, a Monsieur Saint Léger had kindly offered to act as their guide and chaperone, and for a while Fanny appeared quite taken by the attentive Frenchman. Her attempts at his country's language, as well as her knowledge of Paris, seemed to have impressed him too. However, when he became what Fanny described as 'uncommonly interested' in them, asking too many questions, she had had no alternative but to abruptly end their arrangement. 'We can't afford to make any mistakes now,' she had told Cora.

Two more young Italian men were now walking alongside

them, gesticulating and speaking effusively to Cora in Italian, and then English. 'I love you!'

When Cora's broad smile began to erupt, Fanny halted. 'Please!' she hissed. 'You're encouraging them, and I have already warned you about Italian men – they need no encouragement.'

Before arriving at the carriage office the women found the apothecary the captain had recommended, and there, with the help of Cora's book, its section 'Useful Phrases and Words for the Traveller in Italy', they purchased a foul-smelling concoction which Fanny was assured would settle her stomach. Cora had wanted to browse the shops and stalls – the drapers, with its bundles of exotic coloured silks propped up outside, the milliners, housed in no more than a cupboard, but Fanny said not. They must make haste. 'And we must remain on our guard, Cora,' she said, sitting down inside the carriage and pulling the blanket over her lap.

'Of course.'

The palette of the landscape glowed in the late morning sun. The air was fresh and cool, and the light very different to the thin midwinter veil of England. As the carriage creaked and swayed, Cora tried not to think back but forwards. Italy was her home now. And for a while she kept her eyes closed, knowing that if she opened them tears would escape. For her aunt's sake, she had for the most part been animated on their journey, pretending to be excited about their new life in Rome, and she was, in a way. But then and there all she could think of was her mother, weeks away and lost to her. For how would she ever find her again?

Through the lonely meadows and pastures of the campagna the carriage stumbled on, occasionally passing another heading back to the port, or a cart, piled high and swaying perilously from side to side. Abandoned houses languished at deserted crossroads, and scattered about the desolate wilderness were the ruins of a temple, the fallen arches of an aqueduct or the shell of a dilapidated church.

Late in the afternoon, as the air grew cooler and colours faded, the hazy outline of the city's rooftops finally came into view. And as the carriage passed by the lopsided tombstones and broken pedestals of the Protestant Cemetery, and entered the gate of Saint Paul, Fanny turned to her niece and smiled. 'Now we *are* here.'

But the city the women had anticipated had shrivelled and shrunken with age. For within its crumbling walls lay only more scattered ruins, tangled up in stunted trees and grass, and wide-open fields, woodland and empty space, with no signs of life. Then, slowly, the inhabited city began to emerge: dilapidated buildings, half built and unfinished, weathered by time and neglect, with tattered shutters of flaking paint, festooned in ragged garments hanging out to dry in the winter sun. The noxious aroma of sewers and festering rubbish permeated the bouquet of cedar, cypress and pine, and the two women sat in silence, each one afraid to speak. Rome was not as they had expected.

Twisting and turning, the carriage continued, in and out of shadows, shaving doorways, grazing peasants and statues and littered shrines, scraping off plaster and paint. Cora took in her new home. Was it really any different to where they had come from? And those suspicious dark eyes staring back at her, what did they say, what did they ask? *Who are you? Why are you here?*

Then, turning on to a wide avenue, Cora gasped. The splendour of the city spread out before her in ruins she recognised from pictures, white marble fountains, sculptures and pillars, columns stretching up to the sky, pink in the twilight. Rome became Rome, ancient and grand, rising up from the muddle of her unruly young buildings and capturing one heart, one imagination.

It had been upon her arrival in Rome that Cora had made decisions about her life: how it could be, how it would be, and how it would end. She had decided then that she would never suffer the ignominy of being passed over by life and discarded in death. She had decided then that she would have a rich and full life. It lay ahead of her, a blank canvas simply waiting to have colour and texture added. She would live, love and die in Rome, and be buried amongst England's lost poets in the Protestant Cemetery, where a white marble angel would stand guard and a carpet of violets would cover her grave. This was what she decided when she became intoxicated by possibilities, and fell in love for the first and last time.

'The photographer from Linford is coming today and I rather think we should be outside, on the lawn,' said Cora, standing by the window, her back to Mrs Davey. 'Yes, the light will be better for him . . . perhaps by the horse chestnut,' she added, turning to the housekeeper. 'It's a little cooler and more shaded there. If you and Sally can erect the gazebo, and perhaps induce Mr Cordery to help you, that would be perfect. We shall take tea there.'

'I'll see what can be arranged, ma'am,' Mrs Davey said, sounding less than enamoured by the idea.

'Tea in the garden, how delightful,' said Sylvia as the door closed. 'I've always loved taking tea in an English garden at the height of summer. Tea and scones, and white linen . . . and green, green grass and buttercups, and daisies and butterflies and sunshine,' she went on, quietly, whimsically. 'It all fits together so beautifully, don't you agree?'

Cora glanced towards her and sat down.

'Like tea and crumpets toasted over a roaring fire in winter, when it's dark and stormy and snowing outside, hmm?'

Cora nodded. 'But the grass is hardly green, and I fear we, too, may wither and perish in this heat.'

'Oh, but we'll be fine in the shade. You have your fan, and you're more used than any of us to a torrid climate.'

The two women had made up their differences the previous day, after Cora had apologised. Sylvia had assured her that she had not been spying, would never dream of doing such a thing. Cora had shaken her head. 'Please,' she said, 'let's not speak of it. I was out of sorts. You know me well enough by now, I think, to know it meant nothing.'

Too hot to be outside, they had spent the day together indoors, comparing notes on specific times; lost for the entire afternoon in their shared recollections, almost laughing at their younger selves. But Sylvia could see that her friend was still troubled, deeply troubled. She knew it would only irritate Cora if she asked again what the matter was so instead she attempted to distract her friend with prompts beginning, do you remember when . . .

Whilst Cora spoke, Sylvia took copious notes, and then later, in the evening, read them back to Cora, who nodded her head all through, and seemed perfectly happy with what was recorded. Before retiring to bed, Cora had thanked Sylvia for her patience, told her that she had enjoyed their day together. And Sylvia had gone to bed satisfied, happy. At last they had made a start. They had begun at Rome but Cora had assured her that they would 'deal with' the beginning – Paris, and even Suffolk – all in good time. And Sylvia, keen to cement their new understanding, had said, 'There's no rush. We have plenty of time, dear.'

Shortly after they had first met in Rome, Cora had mentioned her family – her parents and siblings – to Sylvia. 'All gone,' was all she could say as a tear rolled down her cheek. Later, she had elaborated on this, telling Sylvia the story of her poor family's demise. Her mother, a renowned beauty, feted by society and despised by other women, had died in childbirth, leaving her heartbroken father to bring up their four children alone. At that time, she, her father and siblings had lived with their grandparents on their vast estate in Suffolk. But in the aftermath of this tragedy her father had taken to drink and gambling, and within twelve months of her mother's death he had shot himself. It was then that Cora had been placed in the care of her mama's sister, Fanny, who was living in Paris at the time with a distant French relation. Her younger brothers and sister had continued to live with their grandparents, but in the course of the following two years all three of her siblings died: one of pneumonia and two in the cholera epidemic.

But the very next day Cora appeared to regret telling Sylvia this version of events, for she had called on her and said, 'What I told you yesterday . . . about my family, you haven't repeated it to anyone, have you? You see, it's not necessarily the truth . . . not the whole truth. I am not allowed to tell anyone . . . but I'll tell you one day, I promise.'

The mystery had been compelling enough for Sylvia thereafter to be vigilant. But as she listened to Cora, and to others, rather than be able to piece together what might have happened, she had only become more confused. Locations changed, names altered, and siblings were unborn. Then, not long before George left Rome, and in an angry and highly strung state after an argument with her aunt, Cora blurted out another version of events, one that Sylvia, to her everlasting and eternal regret, *would* repeat.

Now, Cora said, 'By the way, Jack has invited a girl to tea.'

'Well, how lovely, how marvellous.'

'Cecily . . . Cecily Chadwick.'

'Cecily Chadwick,' Sylvia repeated, whispering the name, as though it were a secret in itself. Then she opened her eyes wide: 'Aha! Quelle surprise! Le Double Cs.'

'Yes, a queer coincidence.'

'He's quite taken with her, don't you think?' Sylvia said, tilting her head, peering over her spectacles at Cora.

'He barely knows her,' Cora replied. 'But it would seem he likes her enough to invite her here to tea, to meet me,' she added.

'How exciting!'

Never having been married, never having had children, never having known pain and heartache or love and loss other than the deaths of her parents at ripe ages, and after calm and orderly lives, Cora believed that Sylvia viewed the world through a child's eyes, with a child's propensity for emotion. Life to Sylvia was exciting, splendid and marvellous, or perplexing and unfathomably queer, or sad. No two states, no two emotions, co-existed, for there had been no dichotomy, no duality in Sylvia's world. She remained, Cora thought, oblivious to the complexities of the human heart, the nearness and sometimes overlap of love and hate. She had had no reference to, no real understanding of the characteristics of a passionate nature: that a woman could both laugh and cry with grief, or hate the man she loved, or be driven to madness, and even murder, by a thing as sweet and tender as love.

Sylvia had written about love, of course, and continued to do so. But her stories were about a particular type of love, a certain sort of character: the requited type, the fathomable sort, leading to a happy ending. Cora knew that as far as Sylvia was concerned, her life had been rich and filled with love: the love of her husbands, the love of her children and friends. Each seemingly unhappy ending had reshaped itself, altering to a happy one. And, even now, Sylvia determined a glorious sunset on Cora's life. Oh yes, she kept saying, it would all turn out fine in the end. But would it?

The memoirs remained an issue, and in truth Cora regretted

ever having agreed to it. There were ways round it, she had decided, though she was not yet entirely sure how to navigate them. In the meantime, the focus of their attention would be Rome: her first years there, meeting George, his early work. She could not let Sylvia down. The book seemed to be her raison d'être. And Cora had promised her, promised her years ago, that she would be the one, the only one, to tell her story.

Earlier that morning, alone in the temple, she had stared at the name once more. Typewritten in capitals and red ink, it was designed to shock her, warn her, she knew. But what was she to do? There was no demand for money, not yet. That would come later, perhaps. No, this was simply to let her know that the past – her past, her secret – was not forgotten.

She would just have to bide her time. After all, what was the worst that could happen? The man in question was long dead. No one would remember; no one would be interested. Any self-respecting newspaper editor would throw the story out. But as she rose to her feet her resolve sank. She had come too far to allow anyone to besmirch her name, the Lawson name, or jeopardise Jack's future.

Chapter Seven

By noon, the thermometer outside read eighty-seven degrees Fahrenheit. By three o'clock it had risen to eighty-nine. Rosetta predicted another of her turns if the heat did not abate, and sat holding a damp towel to her head at the kitchen table, from time to time muttering expletives. Madeline was in her workroom, as usual, wrestling with swathes of green velvet: the Brownlows' new winter curtains. And Ethne was noisily, laboriously, practising – what sounded to Cecily like one long, thumping dirge – on the pianoforte.

In a white cotton dress with broad blue sash, Cecily descended the stairs. The dress, once her mother's, had never appealed to Ethne and thus had come direct to her. Originally, in Madeline's day, it had had a profusion of lace ruffles running from its high neckline down over the bodice, but Madeline had altered it to fit Cecily's specifications: a narrower skirt, a flat sailor-style neckline and collar, no lace and a shortened hemline.

'You look very pretty, dear,' said Madeline, raising her head. She stood at the cutting table, scissors in hand. The room smelled of lavender and camphor and newly cut fabric. 'Enjoy your tea party.'

Cecily walked across the hallway and picked up her straw hat. Earlier, after lunch, she had managed to find a few roses in the garden, a few the drought had not yet killed off, and had pinned them to the ribbon round the hat's crown. She placed her hat on her head, checked her appearance in the mirror, and walked on, to the kitchen.

Rosetta removed the towel from her forehead and looked up as she entered. 'My, you do look a picture . . . you look like a bride . . . on her wedding day!' she said, tearfully, red-faced.

Poor Rosetta. Her face, her hands – even her body – appeared to have swollen in the heat. She had dispensed with her stockings and her strangely misshapen shoes, which lay on the floor next to where she sat, and her feet were resting in a large pail of water.

'Poor Rosetta,' said Cecily, bending down and kissing Rosetta's thick warm hair.

'My little angel, that's what you are. My little angel, sent from him above . . . the only one who cares about poor old Rosetta.'

Cecily moved swiftly through the darkened scullery, where flies buzzed at the mesh-covered window and crawled about the leftover ham lying out on the slate bench. She stepped out into an incandescent day. Nothing moved, nothing stirred. The air was still and silent, heavy with the weight of an oppressive heat. Even in the last hour the temperature seemed to have risen. And as she walked down the pathway and turned on to the track, she felt that weight, a pressure upon her head and in her chest, and with it, a strange sense of foreboding. Not nervousness, exactly, but the queerest sense of some future sadness, like the fluttering of an ill-conceived notion, or the fleeting scent of misfortune. For a moment, even the track ahead appeared portentous, darker. As though the arching branches had eyes, fixed on her, watching her. As though they knew a secret not from the past but from the future.

Breathing in deeply, dispelling doubt and moving on, she wondered who else might be at the house, and she hoped that Sonia Brownlow would not be there. 'Sycophant,' she said out loud. Oh, how she wished Annie had been invited too. But the invitation had been for her alone.

It had been Jack who had invited her. He had called at the house himself. But he had been rather offhand, she thought, flippant. 'You're very welcome to drop by for tea on Tuesday, if you fancy,' he had said, staring towards the gate to the orchard.

'That would be nice. At what time?'

'Quarter past four.'

Then he turned and marched off down the path.

As she walked down the driveway towards the house, Cecily could hear voices drifting over the bank of rhododendrons on her right. She could hear Mr Fox quite distinctly, too loudly, speaking about the falling attendance at church. Then another voice, unrecognisable and vaguely apologetic, saying something about faith being carried in the heat . . . or was it in the heart?

She wasn't sure how, exactly, to announce her arrival: should she go towards the voices, take a pathway and wander through bushes, then emerge, unannounced, in front of them all; or should she go to the front door?

She walked on, towards the shadowed north-facing front of the house, where the gritted driveway merged with a large circular space big enough for carriages to turn. At its centre was a bed of tall grasses and a small oriental-looking tree. Immediately in front of the house, defining its lines, emphasising its symmetry, was a neatly trimmed box hedge. She slowed her pace as she passed two shaded windows, noting her reflection in each, and trying to see beyond the glass; but the blind within one was drawn down and the shapes within the other too indistinct to make anything out.

The front door stood open and, next to a substantial boot-scraper firmly fixed to the ground, a coconut mat said 'Welcome'. Ahead of Cecily was a small anteroom with a highly polished black and white marble tiled floor, another boot-scraper with brushes, a mirrored coat stand to the wall on the right, draped in a variety of cloaks and coats, and a pair of discarded galoshes beneath; directly opposite her another half glass-panelled door remained closed. Cecily stared into the glass, straightening her hat, checking and smoothing her dress, then pulled on the bell.

It took a while for the young maid to emerge from the shadows and open the door, but as soon as she did, and before Cecily could speak, she said, 'Good day, do come in, please follow me, miss,' and beckoned her into the darkened hallway. She led Cecily past a long ancient-looking table, where a red leather frame announced 'IN' and where an arrangement of wilting flowers had shed petals and pollen on to letters and papers scattered beneath. Above the table hung a large oil painting: a Pre-Raphaelite-looking woman with golden flowing hair, standing by a pillar and staring back at Cecily over a bare shoulder. They passed a settee of chipped gilt, faded pink velvet and tattered brocade, a stairway of threadbare carpet leading up to a half-landing where light flooded in through a tall arched window, illuminating dust motes and cobwebs. She followed the maid down a passageway, past a marble sculpture of a naked man, to another glass-panelled door, and then out on to a can-opied veranda. Here stood two more sculptures, some aged wickerwork chairs and a table, and a passion flower, thick and rampant and twisted around posts. They stepped out on to a wide stone-flagged terrace, which looked out over flowerbeds and lawns, beyond the formal terraced gardens to a wilderness of trees. The maid lifted her arm, pointing to a green and white striped gazebo set out on the grass. 'Her ladyship's yonder. Tea's to be served outside today,' she said, bobbing her head and turning away.

As Cecily descended the steps leading down to the lawn, she heard the rector say, 'Aha, and here she is!' Ahead, under the canvas and seated in a variety of chairs, were the rector, Sonia Brownlow and her sister, Marjorie, Miss Combe, and a bespectacled lady with thinning grey hair and a book in her lap, whom Cecily immediately and instinctively knew to be the lady novelist.

In the centre of the huddle, majestically upright and watching Cecily as she crossed the lawn, was an elderly lady in an old-fashioned rigid ensemble of navy blue and white striped silk with lace cuffs, and a broad-brimmed navy blue hat atop a cloud of white hair. She wore an inscrutable expression, her eyes almost closed, her mouth unsmiling. Even if Cecily had not known who she was – and she knew exactly who she was – her eyes would have been drawn to this one person. Wherever she had seen her, whether in some busy city street, on a train, in a painting or photograph, she would have noticed her, been drawn to her. For her presence was compelling, without need of name or identity. Cecily felt a new sense of trepidation.

The rector rose to his feet: 'Allow me to introduce you to Miss Cecily Chadwick, ma'am,' he said, with a nod to Cecily and a half-bow towards the lady. And without thinking, completely spontaneously, for she had not planned it, and had never in her life made such a gesture before, Cecily placed one foot forward and lowered her body in a deep curtsy. As soon as she raised her head she caught Sonia's pinkish smirk, and felt her own face tingle. But the countess's demeanour shifted; she opened up her bright blue eyes and smiled.

'Cecily. How lovely to meet you. Do sit down, my dear,' she said, gesturing to the empty chair at her side. 'I imagine you know everyone here.'

Cecily glanced about and nodded as the others said hello.

'And this is my dear friend, Miss Dorland,' she went on. 'Miss Dorland and I grew up together in Rome. Miss Dorland writes novellas,' she added, with a sudden and definite emphasis on the last word.

'Novels,' the bespectacled lady said quietly. 'I write novels.' And she smiled at Cecily.

'I thought we'd take tea outside today, Cecily. I do hope it's not too much for you, dear, this heat.'

'No, no, it's—'

'One so loathes abandoning summer, peering out at it like a sick child from beyond a window, never being able to step out into this glorious light,' she said, gesturing bejewelled hands upwards. And then she tilted her head back, closed her eyes and breathed in deeply.

Cecily watched her. She saw that her skin was tanned, more tanned than any one else's she knew, though she had seen people – even women of a similar age – at the fair with that same sort of colouring and had always thought it attractive. But the countess was nothing like any woman at any fair. In fact, the countess was nothing like any other woman. The combination and contrast between the colour of her skin, her eyes, and the whiteness of her hair was striking and, despite her age, quite beautiful. In repose, the corners of her mouth slipped downward, lending age and an air of sadness to a face that still had something of the glow of youth about it, in spite of its lines. And that mouth . . . the mouth was – or certainly had been – a very pretty mouth, Cecily thought. But it was impossible to put an age – a definite age – on the lady. To Cecily, the countess appeared settled in that ill-defined place women reach, eventually, sometime after forty. A place her mother had happily, voluntarily – and prematurely – entered; a place where white hair alone did not necessarily denote years. She glanced at the novelist:

girlish in demeanour, ancient in looks, she surmised. Confusing. She looked back at the countess: ancient in demeanour, but something still girlish around that mouth, puckering, pursing, smiling and pouting in turn. Then, as though sensing the scrutiny, the countess opened her eyes and turned to Cecily with a curious smile.

'Sunlight!' she said, dramatically. 'It's what feeble bodies crave, what troubled souls hunger for.'

'I just adore sunshine,' said Sonia, emulating the countess and tilting her head upwards. 'I think it's perhaps something to do with having been born in the tropics.'

'You should be careful, it can make folk feverish. Look at the deaths in the newspaper, and one here in Linford only last week. It's taken its toll, that's for sure,' Miss Combe said, ever the voice of sobriety and caution, and tucking her chin into a froth of lace. 'And it's been proven it can make people go quite mad.'

'It is not the heat which makes one go mad, Miss Combe,' the countess said, 'though it is, I grant you, a contributory factor. No, it's the lack of sleep, the broken nights . . . the nightmares. The lack of peace our consciences need and require in order for us to face each and every new day.'

'Hear, hear!' boomed Mr Fox.

Cecily noticed Miss Dorland open the notebook in her lap, lick her pencil, and then scribble something down. She heard Marjorie whisper loudly to Sonia, 'That doesn't make any sense. Why do babies need so much sleep then? Surely they have clear consciences.'

'It's always so refreshing to have the young amongst us, wouldn't you agree, Mr Fox?' the countess continued, ignoring Marjorie and turning to the rector. 'One always feels invigorated by their . . . sheer zest and joie de vivre.'

'Ah, yes, indeed, ma'am,' he said, nodding, his eyes fluttering shut.

She turned to Cecily. 'So, my dear, do tell me a little more about yourself. I hear that you've lived in Bramley all of your life.'

'Yes, that's right. And in the same house too . . . the place my father built.'

The countess released a short gasp. 'Mr Chadwick, such a talented man!'

'You knew him?'

'No, my dear, sadly I did not. But I'm always impressed by men who build, design or make things. What gifted, talented souls they are, as all artists are. But such a great loss to you and your poor mama . . .' She shuddered. 'Oh, to be robbed of a father, that paternal, guiding force, that fountain of knowledge and wisdom. 'Tis arguably the second greatest loss for our sex to endure.'

The countess did not appear to notice Cecily's blush, or Miss Dorland's nervous glance towards the rector.

'Yes, indeed,' she continued, 'far worse, I think, than the loss of a spouse, a husband, but of course not as great as the loss of a child,' she added quietly. 'No, that is the greatest loss for any woman to endure.'

Minutes later, as two maids came across the lawn towards them, carrying the tea paraphernalia, and whilst the others talked amongst themselves, the countess turned to Cecily. For a moment she did not speak, but simply smiled at Cecily, studying her face. Her blue gaze moved across Cecily's features, her nose, her mouth, then back to her eyes. And it was intoxicating, a scrutiny that made Cecily feel light-headed, quite dizzy. The countess said, 'You know, we have the same intials, you and I. The double Cs.' She leaned closer. 'My name is Cora, Cora de Chevalier,' she said, lifting her arm, stretching out her hand. On her little finger was a heavy gold ring engraved with two intertwined Cs. 'So you see, already, we have a great deal in common.'

As tea was served and sipped, and plates of scones and queen cakes, and shortbread and small triangular sandwiches passed about, the conversation meandered from this to that and back again. There was no sign of Jack, and the countess made no reference to him, offered no apology for his absence. Cecily watched Miss Dorland, noted how quietly she sat. An observer, she concluded. And from time to time she caught the novelist's eye, and they smiled at each other.

Mr Fox spoke at some length about Lady Agatha Withenshaw (she had recently donated substantial monies to the clock tower and war widows funds). And then Miss Combe interjected, stretching her neck from a sea of ruffles and white lace to say that Lady Agatha had a vested interest: she was a war widow herself. Mr Fox smiled, said that was not the point, but then failed to elaborate further, and Miss Combe, glancing away, tucking in an already receding chin, murmured something, and Cecily heard the word 'gold-digger'.

There were debates on the temperature, reckonings – and a tally – on local deaths the heat had caused, and then discussion of the growing unrest across the country. The countess spoke about the trouble in the Balkans, about Germany's egotism, and then, shaking her head and genuflecting, said something in French. At which point, Mr Fox tried to laugh but it came out all wrong, and the countess threw him a withering glance. Cecily made a mental note to read up on foreign news, and to look up the Balkans in the atlas when she returned home. The countess appeared to know about everything: history, art, empires, civil-isation, science and social order; the future of India, the future of Germany, the future of mankind; and wars. Listening to her, it seemed as though the whole world was in turmoil, standing on the edge of the abyss, looking down into the void. She told Mr Fox that he and all of England needed to wake up, and Cecily heard Miss Combe gasp. Then she proclaimed that England itself was on the verge of civil war, to which the rector responded with mirth, and teased her, saying, 'You have spent too long, ma'am, in countries not your own. We are civilised here.'

'Civilised?' she repeated. 'Someone once told me England was filled with civilised philistines and cultured barbarians.' She paused, smiling coquettishly, and perhaps more to herself and a memory than to anyone present. 'London, I was told – and yes, it was a very long time ago – was a capricious city dressed up in finery, pretending to like art without ever knowing what art is. London, I was told, was a place of ignorant snobbery! No, I'm not sure the English are civilised, not yet, Mr Fox.'

'I'm afraid I have to disagree,' he replied. 'We may have lost some dignity . . . certainly since the eighties and nineties, but this country remains the most civilised of the Western world. Our culture, our manners, our society – and our Empire – are envied the world over.'

'Pffsh,' she cried, with a rapid gesture of her hand. 'We *have* lost our dignity, Mr Fox, and we have lost our way: morally, spiritually and culturally. What made us great has made us arrogant and will surely pull us down. Look at Liverpool, and London for that matter. How can we speak of civilisation, what pride can there be in our Empire when people here are starving? Such poverty is the direct result of that insatiable appetite for Empire. Imperialism, profit, expansion – it all comes at a cost. And I have seen the squalid tenements and courts and alleys that are also a part of our Empire, Mr Fox. They are nothing to be proud of.'

For a moment Cecily wondered if the countess had been poor-peopling, like Sonia's mother – visiting those desperate families who lived in only one room. She saw Mr Fox smile, close his eyes, and then heard him say something quietly about history. But the countess interrupted him again, saying that history could never record the truth, or any individual stories. They would be lost, gone forever. It would take an overview, it would generalise, she said, diminishing real stories and identities, personal perspectives, and within them truths, turning triumph, defeat and tragedy into something else: popular entertainment, she suggested.

The rector made no reply, and for a minute or two no one spoke.

Then Miss Combe began: she was considering electricity, canvassing opinion on its safety. Someone had told her that it was not compatible with long hot summers, which seemed prevalent nowadays. (And there was a brief exchange about English summers of the past, whether they had in fact been hotter, longer, better.) Mr Fox advocated that electricity, the sort that travelled through wires, was quite unnecessary. Wires, he said, were the problem. Wires were not compatible with the British way of life and should not be tolerated. It was the countess's turn to laugh. And she did. Then she mentioned someone named Marconi, a friend of hers, Cecily presumed. Yes, the rector conceded, the Italians were good with wires. Or rather, that's what he seemed to be saying.

And thus, like the ebb and flow of waves upon a shore, the tide drifted back to Italy, to Rome. The countess spoke of people whose names Cecily knew she really ought to know, but the countess seemed to know so many. For every name she mentioned was followed swiftly by another, and then another. And Mr Fox in particular – in fact, alone – turned quite giddy and began to rub his thighs, like one of Cecily's infant schoolboys when they were allowed to clean the blackboard. And Cecily, embarrassed for him, for a moment distracted by him, missed the beginning of another story: about a doll in Rome, a doll that performed miracles.

'The Piazza d'Ara Coeli,' the countess was saying, 'lies at the heart of medieval Rome, close to Monte Palatino and the Roman

Forum. Like all piazzas, it has a fountain at its centre, and a church: the church of Santa Maria d'Ara Coeli. Situated on the Capitoline hill, overlooking the piazza, it is built upon the site of the ancient Roman Temple of Jupiter, where Augustus heard the sibyl announce the birth of Christ. It houses the Santissimo Bambino, a wooden doll carved from a tree that grew on the Mount of Olives, and said to have been painted by Saint Luke himself. There are many stories about how the Santissimo Bambino found its way to Rome, and each one includes a miracle. Romans believe the doll has divine powers and is able to heal the sick. And, up until quite recently, it was often carried from Maria d'Ara Coeli and transported through the city's streets in its own carriage – with footmen and priests in attendance – to visit those sick and infirm. In return, grateful Romans continue to bring the Bambino gifts – money, jewels and gold. And each Christmas the children of Rome visit the doll, to sing to it, and offer up prayers and thanks. It is an ugly, macabre thing,' she added, wrinkling her nose. 'Though I've oft enough prayed to it myself.'

'I was always frightened of it,' the novelist said quietly. 'I never liked its face, never liked to look into its eyes.'

'Did it really perform miracles?' Marjorie asked.

But the countess suddenly appeared distracted. She gazed towards some steps at the edge of the lawn, smiling and frowning at the same time, as though she had just noticed an old friend.

Miss Dorland said, 'So the Romans believe.'

There was something childlike about the novelist's voice, something innocent and tremulous and sweet. And just as one could see that the countess had been a great beauty, one could also see that Miss Dorland had not. Her looks accommodated themselves well to age, and Cecily imagined she possibly hadn't altered very much in appearance since her youth. Her face was unexceptional, unremarkable, like so many others – forgettable.

And yet there was an innate softness to her, in her manner, and genuine warmth in her unforced smile. She deferred to the countess in all things, it seemed, and watched her closely, her eyes constantly moving back to her. And the countess for her part appeared to treat Miss Dorland like a younger sister, or perhaps a daughter. She looked down at the grass and up at the sky as she listened to her friend speak, occasionally correcting her on a detail, or on her pronunciation. 'No, dear, it wasn't actually then . . . the D is silent, dear . . . no, Sylvia, she was his aunt, not his mother,' and so on. But it was clear, to Cecily at least, that the two women knew each other very well, and had known each other for many years. Like an old married couple (rather like Mr and Mrs Fox, Cecily thought), they finished each other's sentences and corroborated each other's anecdotes with nods and murmurings; and when one could not remember – a detail, name, time or place – the other swiftly stepped in.

Cecily noted the elderly novelist's hands, fidgeting and busy all the while, playing tunes between fingertips, tapping a beat on an invisible machine. She spoke in short precise sentences, and, every so often, lifted a hand and touched the small gold-framed spectacles perched upon the bridge of her nose.

To look at, the two women were the antithesis of each other: one still voluptuous, with a shape Cecily imagined to have been envied in youth and that extravagant cloud of white-white hair; the other angular and flat, with dull grey hair scraped back into an impoverished bun. Unlikely friends. And yet, Miss Dorland was – and must always have been – a calm presence in the countess's turbulent life, Cecily supposed.

Cecily could have listened to the countess all day, particularly when she became caught up in a reminiscence, for there was something, then, in her style, the mellifluous sound of her voice, her enunciation and consideration of each and every syllable, as though she was reciting poetry. She paused, pursed her mouth, and sometimes pouted; she sighed mid-sentence, looked heavenward, closed her eyes, opened them, leaned forward, raised her hands, breathed in deeply, then stared into the distance, ponderously, as everyone waited for her next word, next sentence, next exhalation.

There was one queer moment though, when Miss Combe mentioned a story that had appeared in the newspaper about a local woman who had been sent to prison for bigamy. A name was mentioned, and Mr Fox nodded solemnly; yes, he knew the woman in question. Had he married her? Cecily wondered. But Miss Combe went on to say that the woman had had no fewer than three bigamous marriages, and that the variety of children from each totalled thirteen. The countess listened to all of this, and to Mr Fox's murmurings, then, with a great intake of breath, she said that bigamy was a very complex issue and, in many cases, an understandable course of action. It had been common enough, she said, in times gone by; indeed, she herself had known bigamists, both male and female, who were quite respectable people as well. She cited a number of hypothetical cases, reasons why it could not, perhaps should not, be viewed as a crime, and she spoke – seemingly with some authority – about the archaic divorce laws. Mr Fox then leaned forward, wide-eyed, and spluttered, 'But you sound as though you're advocating it, ma'am.'

She smiled at him, closed her eyes and shook her head. 'No, not advocating it, Mr Fox. Rather, trying to *understand*. This woman has been locked away, her family broken up, her children farmed out to strangers. The law refuses to look at the reasons for the action, it simply sees the crime and punishes the perpetrator. But, like self-defence, a crime is not a crime if it can be justified, understood . . . and then, perhaps, forgiven.'

Mr Fox sat back in his chair. No one spoke.

When the photographer, Mr Trigg, appeared, Cecily at first thought that he, too, was there as a guest. Then the countess raised her hand to him and said, 'Dear Mr Trigg, do please say if you require anything. I'm afraid my grandson is not yet back from his motor excursion and we can't possibly go ahead until he is here.'

Sonia said, 'Ooh, are we to have our photograph taken, ma'am?'

'Mr Trigg is here to photograph some of my paintings, but I thought it rather a nice idea for him to capture us as well,' she replied, as the photographer quietly busied himself, arranging his equipment on the lawn.

By the time Jack finally appeared – leaping over a small box hedge and striding across the lawn towards them – Miss Combe was on her feet saying she felt rather queer about having her photograph taken; she had not expected it. He wore no jacket, no necktie, and the waistcoat of his suit was unbuttoned. He apologised for his tardiness, explaining to them that his motor-cycle had had a puncture somewhere south of Linford, and his soiled white shirt – as the countess pointed out – seemed to verify this. Miss Combe sat back down; Sonia sat up; and Cecily stared down at the grass. Mr Fox laughed. 'Motorcycles indeed!'

'Well, my darling, I'm afraid you've missed tea but I'm sure Mrs Davey will bring out a fresh pot soon enough.'

'I'm fine,' he said, catching Cecily's eye.

He moved forward, hovering over the plates on the linen-covered table, picked up a handful of sandwiches, and then sat down on the grass. The rector spoke to him about his new motorcycle, and Cecily heard him say, yes, he was running it in, but had taken it up to almost forty on the Linford straight. And she pictured him, flying along that road she knew so well, with the wind in his hair, looking out at the world through goggles. Speed, she thought, he likes speed.

Mr Trigg announced that he was set up and ready, if it was convenient to her ladyship. Chairs were moved about. Sonia put on her gloves, Miss Combe dispensed with her parasol, and Jack and Mr Fox took their places, standing behind the ladies. Then Mr Trigg told them all to remain perfectly still until he gave the word . . .

And it was all over in a flash.

The countess clapped her hands. 'Bravo! Well done, Mr Trigg!'

Shuffling and smiling done, conversation resumed. Sonia asked Miss Dorland about her next novel. It was to be titled *Lord of Nivernais* and set in France, the lady novelist replied. Then the countess explained that Nivernais was a region of France where she had once lived. She laughed. 'I don't believe I'm being too immodest when I say I suspect the book owes something to me.' Miss Dorland replied, 'Well of course, they all owe something to you, dear.' Sonia said she would love someone to write a book about her one day, Miss Combe said she could think of nothing worse, and Marjorie quietly helped herself to another queen cake. Mr Fox and Jack continued to talk about motorbikes, and motorcars, and aeroplanes. And Cecily heard Jack telling him, too, that one day soon enough people would be travelling all over the world by air.

'How about that, Mr Fox?' the countess interrupted. 'You and Mrs Fox could fly to Rome!' she said.

He shook his head. 'Mrs Fox would never entertain such a notion. And I certainly shan't be volunteering. The modern world is unsettled, in a state of flux, I fear, and this need for continual change, invention, reinvention!' he shouted, to make his point, Cecily presumed, 'is too much for me. But I must admit, I do rather like the idea of a motorcar,' he went on, turning his attention back to Jack, seated at his feet. 'Yes, Mrs Fox and I were discussing the possibilities only this morning and—'

'I think you've been rather neglectful of your guest, Jack,' the countess broke in, waving a hand in Cecily's direction. 'Perhaps you'd like to show Cecily around the place . . . the gardens?'

'Of course,' he replied, rising to his feet. 'Would you like to to see around the gardens?'

Sonia stood up. 'I'd love to see the gardens,' she said, oblivious of any faux pas. 'You know, we never did get to see them last time,' she added, turning to the countess.

'Ah, your enthusiasm is to be commended. But I was looking forward to having a little conversation with you, Sonia. I've barely spoken to you, my dear.'

Sonia looked from the countess to Jack and then back at the countess, and then sat down.

The countess turned to Cecily. 'Allow Jack to take you on a little tour. It's hardly Versailles, but I think we're making progress,' she said, smiling beguilingly at Cecily.

They walked across the lawn to steps leading down to another, fringed by wide herbaceous borders and swathes of overgrown wilting rosebushes. A gritted pathway crossed the second at right angles in the centre, where an ancient-looking sundial stood, and, beyond it, a long pergola, festooned in creepers and trailers, and dangling tentacles like cobweb-covered hands. At the end of the pergola, next to an arbour, a tall, black, wrought-iron gate stood open on to the wooded hillside, where centuries of fallen leaves had made a thick carpet of the earth. Here, under towering beeches and pines, the brightness was diffused, the air cooler.

He said, 'I'm sorry I was so late. I hope it wasn't too much of an ordeal for you.'

'No, it wasn't an ordeal,' she replied, walking on.

The sound of a motorcar's engine drifted over from the other side of the valley, its horn honking loudly as it approached the last hairpin bend before the village. And when its noise finally abated the voices on the lawn were no longer audible. But the sound of the fair on the village green – a brass band and children shrieking – drifted up through the wooded dell.

'You know, when the house was first built there were very few trees here, on this part of the hill. Apparently one could see Linford and beyond, almost as far as the coast on a fine day.'

'This place was built for her, for your grandmother?' Cecily asked, glancing towards him.

'I believe so. I suppose she wanted to have somewhere to come back to, eventually. And all these pine trees,' he added, looking upwards, 'are a nod to Rome. She'd have no doubt moved the Roman Forum here if she could've done.'

'But she never lived here, until now.'

'No. She preferred to live in Rome, and Paris. It's where all her friends are . . . or were. And,' he looked at her and smiled, 'she's not overly fond of England.'

'Why is that?'

He shrugged his shoulders, ran a hand through his hair. 'She considers herself European, and having been an expatriate for so long, I think she feels somewhat estranged from English ways and customs. She finds people here . . .' he paused, pondering, searching for the words, 'perhaps a tad judgemental, narrow-minded. She abhors snobbery, says England invented it,' he added, amusement in his voice.

He stepped from the pathway, pulling back overgrown laurel and waist-high ferns to reveal stone steps leading down to another path. And as he held back the branches and Cecily moved down the steps, she caught the pungent musky scent of fox.

'She's had a such an interesting life,' she said, ducking cobwebs, stepping from the hard stone on to a deep brown carpet of pine needles and leaves.

He leapt down the last few steps, landing in front of her.

'Yes,' he said, breathlessly, looking back at her. 'Though bizarrely I don't know a great deal about it. You see, we've not seen an awful lot of each other. She was always overseas and, well, I was here with my mother. I'm only just getting to know her . . . and about her life.'

'Must be queer,' Cecily said, glancing away, 'to only now be getting to know each other.'

'I suppose it is,' he replied, turning and walking on. 'She loves to speak about Rome, as I'm sure you've gathered this afternoon. And she loves to talk about Paris, and the old chateau, but she's not too fond – seems almost reluctant – to speak of her childhood and early life. I imagine it was a sad time for her. She lost both of her parents so young, was left with no one apart from her aunt, who was more like a mother to her. Watch out for the holly,' he added, over his shoulder.

'Did you ever visit her in Rome?'

'No, sadly not. I saw her on the rare occasions she came to London, but she and my mother never saw eye to eye, and there was always . . . always a strained atmosphere. I used to think she blamed my mother for my father's death.' He reached down, picked up a stone and, just as though it were a cricket ball, ran forward, described an arc and hurled it out across the valley.

'But that was an accident, surely?'

'Yes, of course it was. But I'm not sure my mother was my grandmother's ideal choice of wife for my father. Her background was so different. Her father – my maternal grandfather – was South American, Argentinian.'

'I thought you said she hated snobbery?'

He laughed. 'She's contradictory, if nothing else,' he said, shaking his head. 'No, my mother, or perhaps more specifically her father, were not the match my grandmother had in mind. He was an opera singer, or wanted to be. He had no money when he arrived here in this country, sang for pennies, by all accounts. His name was Virdeon Cazabon. Rather a good name for an opera singer, don't you agree?' he said.

'That's where you get your dark looks from.'

'Both of my parents were dark. I'll show you a photograph later, if you'd like.'

She nodded. 'Yes, I'd like to see.'

'I was born there, in Argentina . . . Buenos Aires. My mother for some reason decided that I should be born there and not in England.' He paused. 'It was shortly after we returned here that my father died.'

'He fell from his horse?'

He stopped. 'Yes, and not very far from here, as it happens. He was out hunting . . . it was January, the earth was hard . . . and his horse took a tumble. A rabbit hole, I believe. He was thrown . . . landed on his head . . . died hours later.' He turned to her. 'Fate, eh?'

Cecily shook her head. 'Fate . . .'

They continued on in silence down the steep path, deep into the valley and taller woods, zigzagging briars, thickets of holly, bracken and ferns. When they reached the dried-up mud of a stream, he said, 'This was flowing quite magnificently at Whitsun.' And he kicked at the hard earth with the toe of his shoe. All around them, high above them, the great beeches loomed, cathedral-like, majestic and timeless, effulgent in the sunshine. Magical, Cecily thought.

They followed the path of the stream, spoke of incidental things: the new bridge planned for the ford; the cricket teams' fixtures for the forthcoming weeks; and the entertainments planned in the village hall. Then Cecily told him of her wish to travel, to visit far-flung places, see cities and live in them, perhaps. And he told her of his wish to live in the country, in a place such as Bramley, and be settled and happy. 'It must be marvellous to belong somewhere. To live in a place where everyone knows who you are,' he said.

She spoke of her father, the last time she had seen him, or the last time she could recall. And he told her a little more of his, adding, 'My grandmother speaks very highly of him, of course . . . And now there's only me.' He shrugged. 'I have no relations, no cousins, you see. Quite a responsibility . . .' He spoke of his mother, briefly. She had, he said, suffered from melancholia all of her life, had had that artistic temperament. But with each year her depression had grown worse. He knew, he said, but he was away at school. 'What could I have done?' he asked. 'She longed for someone who had gone. She became more and more reclusive, hardly venturing anywhere towards the end. She wanted to go back in time . . . to sleep, that was all.'

Eventually, they turned and slowly climbed back up the hill. And as he held back the branches on the steps once again, as she passed by him, he said, 'I'm pleased you came today.'

The countess appeared to be dozing. Mr Fox and Miss Combe – who had been on the point of leaving for at least an hour – were discussing a recent drowning in a nearby pond: the perils of bathers. Miss Dorland was quietly reading her notebook, and Sonia and Marjorie were nowhere to be seen. As Jack and Cecily sat down, the countess opened her eyes and smiled. 'I'm afraid the Brownlow girls had to leave,' she said. 'Their father's chauffeur came to collect them.' She turned to Jack and said something to him in French.

He replied in English. 'No, we went the other way, took the path down through the woods.'

The countess turned to Cecily. 'You didn't get to see my temple?'

Cecily shook her head. 'Temple? No, I've not seen it.'

'I shall show it to you next time,' she said. She leaned forward and whispered, 'It's a very special place, a memorial to—' She stopped, turned towards the rector. 'I'm sorry, what was that, the name you just mentioned?'

Mr Fox appeared momentarily confused. He had been speaking about some new tenants at the farm on the edge of the village. 'Ah, John Abel!' he said, remembering. 'Yes, he and his family moved into Meadow Farm two weeks ago. Nice people, from somewhere in Suffolk, I believe. I was there earlier today and—'

'John Abel? Are you quite certain that was the name?'

'Oh yes, absolutely.'

'And you say they're from Suffolk?'

'Yes, that's what he said, that's what he told me,' the rector replied, a little mystified. 'A name you're familiar with, ma'am?'

'I believe my aunt once knew someone of that name. But that was many, many years ago,' she replied, glancing away. And then she reached to the table and picked up her mother-of-pearl cigarette case. 'Would anyone care for a small sherry?' she asked.

Chapter Eight

That night, Cecily dreamt of the Bambino Santissimo. She dreamt it came to Bramley, carried through the lanes and up the track to her house in a sedan chair, waited on by Mr Fox and Jack Staunton, who said, 'We have to get it back to Rome by teatime.' But the chair became stuck in the garden gate, and her mother said, 'Expatriates always require a wide gate.' And when Cecily peered inside the chair, she saw that the doll was not a doll at all, for it was smoking a cigarette, and appeared to be . . . the countess.

When she awoke, she dismissed the dream, and then lay in her bed for some time, remembering the events of the previous day, working through it all once again, trying to recall the exact words and sequence of conversations. Had he said he was pleased that she came? Or had she dreamt that? No. He'd definitely said it: I'm pleased that you came. She could remember exactly where they were, could walk back to the very spot. And hadn't he looked at her in a certain way? Had he not had that rather serious, concentrated look in his eyes? The same expression Walter had worn when he told her that she always made him laugh? She pictured Jack once again, standing in his white shirt, with that black smear across the front, holding back a branch. She could see the shadow of his beard, the line of his mouth, beads of perspiration glistening above his top lip. That beautiful lip . . . had it ever been kissed? she wondered.

She turned on to her side. The room was warm, already bathed in sunlight. A somenolent coo drifted in through the open window. She closed her eyes, took herself back twelve hours.

She had bid the countess goodbye at around six o'clock. Mr Fox and Miss Combe had finally left, together, and the countess wished to go indoors, saying she felt the air becoming cool, though how – at around eighty degrees Fahrenheit – Cecily could not fathom. Jack said he would walk her home, and they had come by way of the eastern side of the house so that he could show her his motorcycle.

Around a gritted yard was a row of little cottages, a coach house and some stables; and connecting the main house to the coach house, another entire wing, less grand but easily as big as her own home, that Cecily had never seen.

'What's in there?' she had asked, pointing.

'There? The game larder and pastry larder, lamp room and scullery, the china closet, and Mrs Davey's bedroom and sitting room. And the servants' hall, of course,' he replied.

The yard led on to a lane, bordered on one side by a paddock, where a few rabbits sat about on the grass, and rotting hen coops and hutches butted up against a fence. On the other side was a pink brick wall, which Cecily already knew to be the wall of the kitchen gardens.

'And where does the lane lead to?' she asked.

'The cinder track? Down to the main road, eventually, at the very bottom of the valley,' he replied, pulling open the coach-house door.

Then he began talking about his motorcycle, mentioning all sorts of numbers and letters, and then more numbers, none of which meant anything to Cecily. Well, yes, she said, it looks marvellous. She had not known what else to say. I'll take you out on it, he said, again. 'But please don't ask your mother, she's bound to say no.'

They walked back by way of the house and the main driveway, and lingered there, at the top of the drive, before turning out on to the track. He said, 'I meant to say to you earlier, I rather like your hat, what you've done with it – the flowers,' he added, gesturing to it in her hand. She had been embarrassed. But why? If anyone else, even Walter, had commented on any hat she'd worn it would not have made her feel anything other than pleased to receive the compliment. She'd have smiled, said, 'Thank you.' But instead, with him, she was momentarily speechless, quite unable to put together any words that made sense. She had stammered, said something disjointed and nonsensical about it being one of her sister's hats, that it was Ethne who had attached the flowers, and that she didn't particularly like it. And, just to prove it, she had pulled one of the roses out and thrown it into the rhododendrons behind her. He had stood back, hands in pockets, smiling, as though he knew, realised; so she had pulled out another and flung it across the driveway.

She shuddered as she recalled it.

They had sauntered down the track, stopping every once in a while, extending minutes . . . or had they? Had she been extending each minute while he had been wondering why she walked quite so slowly?

She turned over on her bed, her head in her hands.

'You know, you've hardly told me anything at all about yourself,' he said. 'I've spoken about me and my family, added to which you've had to listen patiently to my grandmother, and

124

to Mr Fox's ramblings – when he could get a word in edgeways – and to that awful Combe woman.'

She laughed. 'There's nothing much to tell,' she said. 'I was born, I grew up, and here I am. That's it, so far.'

He nodded. 'Hmm. I like that. And it's actually the *from here* I'm interested in.'

Had he said that? Was that what he said?

She turned on to her back, looked up at the sloping ceiling. And she could see them, there on the track, walking down the hill together, beneath that tunnel of branches.

'Where would you like to go from here, Cecily Chadwick? What do you wish for?'

She had pulled the last wilting rose from her hat and thrown it into the hedgerow. 'I wish for happiness, of course. I wish for fulfilment, to do more with my life than simply marry, have children, grow old and then die. I want to see other places . . .' She stopped, looked at him. 'And I want to write.'

She turned on to her stomach, buried her face in the pillow, moaning. 'I want to write! Ugh! I can't believe I told him that . . . I've never told anyone . . . no one knows.'

But what had he said? She turned on to her side once more.

'You want to write? You write?'

'Yes, I try to. It's what I want to do, all I've ever wanted to do.'

It *was* what she wanted to do. It was what she wished for. She wanted to be remembered for being more than just someone's wife, someone's mother, or someone's daughter. She didn't want to have to marry simply in order to validate her existence upon this planet. What good had that done her mother, or anyone else? Husbands made decisions, yes; they offered respectability, safety and, usually, a home, a lifestyle. But they also went away, they also died, leaving pale-faced widows and confused children, bereft and adrift; leaving a gap far bigger than if they had never been there. Marriage brought status, she knew that, but it also brought a sort of invisibility, anonymity.

'Do you allow anyone to read what you write?' he asked.

She shook her head, already rueful.

'Well, you must allow Sylvia to. It'd be good for you to get her opinion, wouldn't it? She's had perhaps as many as a dozen books published, I think.'

They reached the gate, and she hadn't wanted to look at him, hadn't wanted to in case he was quietly laughing at her. But she had – and he hadn't been. He'd stood quite close to her, his eyes cast downwards, flicking the peeling paint from the gatepost. Then he'd looked up at her and said, 'You know, you could call by tomorrow, bring some of your writing for Sylvia to read . . .'

'I'm not sure.'

'No, perhaps not . . . But you could call by anyway, if you'd like to.'

'Or you could call here,' she said, feeling bold.

'I could,' he replied, smiling back at her. 'Should I?'

She nodded.

'Then I shall.'

They had stood there in silence, staring at each other, smiling. Neither of them had spoken for some time. And the queerest thing was she couldn't now be sure whether that silence had lasted only a few seconds or some minutes. In her mind it was interminable. In her mind, it went on and on. And yes, she had been bold, forward in that look, which said, quite simply, she thought now, 'I like you.' For surely that particular smile couldn't have said anything more, could it?

She rose quickly from her bed, reached to the window and drew back the curtains.

'He started it . . .'

Yes, he started it. He had looked into her eyes, smiled, glanced away, glanced back, smiled some more; and then, finally, as she'd pushed on the gate, as the latch had dropped – clickety-click – he had slowly backed away.

It had been later that evening, as she sat with her mother and sister, that she said, 'I've invited Jack Staunton to call on us tomorrow.'

And Ethne had smirked but said nothing.

'For tea?' Madeline asked, a note of mild alarm in her voice.

'Yes, I suppose so. I think I said around four . . .'

'I see.' Madeline put down her sewing, cast her eyes about the room, as if reckoning it from another's perspective. Then she said, 'I think perhaps it impolite not to also invite the countess. You said she's very nice . . .'

Nice: it was not the best-chosen or most accurate word to describe the countess, Cecily realised. Nice meant . . . unthreatening, well-intentioned, amiable. The countess was amiable, but as for well-intentioned, Cecily wasn't altogether sure, and unthreatening? The lady was formidable. She smoked cigarettes, took sherry in the garden, possessed ardent opinions on almost everything, and used words like *sex* without even noticing. What on earth would her mother make of it all, of her? But it was decided that Rosetta would deliver a note to Temple Hill the following morning, formally inviting all three – the countess, Miss Dorland and Jack – to tea, but not that day. It would appear a little hasty and ill-conceived to send an invitation for the very same day, Madeline said.

'But I've already asked him, told him to call by tomorrow.'

'That's fine, dear. I shall explain in my note.'

'You must admit, it would be rather strange if he came to call here alone,' Ethne began. 'People would assume you were courting,' she added, glancing at Madeline.

By mid-afternoon a date had been set, but not for tea at the Chadwicks'.

Rosetta had begrudgingly taken the note, and returned with

another – a counter-offer. 'I can't be doing with going back up that track, not again, not in this heat. It's a hundred degrees out there, and there's about to be an almightly storm,' she said, handing over the sealed envelope and falling into a chair. She fanned herself with her hat. 'Just look at my feet,' she added, lifting her skirts.

Madeline opened the cream envelope, unfolded the paper. Cecily could see two elaborate gold letter Cs at the top of the page. Madeline read the note in silence, reflected, and then reread it, aloud: 'My dear Mrs Chadwick, thank you so very much for your kind invitation to tea. I was however on the very point of extending an invitation to you and your daughters to dine with me here on Saturday evening. I know from dear Cecily how busy you are, and I am quite sure dinner is perhaps less of an interruption to your day, and it will be such a treat for me to have you all here and to meet you at last.' Madeline paused, reflective once more. 'Shall we say seven p.m.? I do hope this isn't too early but I know people here prefer to dine earlier in the evening.'

She turned to Cecily, a furrow of wariness about her brow. 'Well, would you like to go to dinner? Ethne, you won't be able to come of course, you agreed to go with the Foxes to the concert at the Jubilee Hall,' she reminded her elder daughter. 'So it would only be you and me,' she said, smiling at Cecily.

And thus Cecily found herself under an ominous sky, clutching another note from her mother to the countess. As she walked up the hill she recalled the time, years before, when she and Annie had ventured there together. 'You do know that we're trespassing,' Annie had said, making it all the more thrilling, all the more frightening.

Perched high on the hill and surrounded by woodland, the only way to see the place was to trespass. With their hands pressed up against dusty panes, they had peered in at empty rooms, and then wandered about the gardens, traipsing across overgrown lawns and down mossy pathways, through tangled woods and bracken, ducking branches. When they stumbled upon the temple – almost lost in holly, its pillars covered in ivy – they quickly concluded that it pre-dated the house, had been built centuries before, an ancient relic. And the word 'sacrifice' had been enough for them to run back up the hillside, out of the shadows and on to the track.

The house had struck Cecily then as the perfect place to hide away from the world, to be invisible. Mothballed and forgotten, it had felt to her like a sleeping place; a place waiting for someone to come and rescue it and bring it back to life.

Cecily's own home, the brick house her father had built, though considerably smaller and less secluded, was – she had thought then – much prettier. It had a low-pitched roof with exposed rafters, a number of unusual stained-glass windows, and, inside, panelled walls, a parquet floor and built-in shelves, cabinets and window seats, all in the same honey-hued oak. It had been his idea of home, his and her mother's vision, where they would grow old together. And Cecily knew this because her mother had told her, and told her when she was still in mourning. It was one of Cecily's monochrome memories, a flashback to that other time, before her mother finally discarded her widow's weeds and brought colour back into their lives. And though that colour had always been muted, for Madeline was not overly fond of brights, there was, Cecily knew, something intrinsically safe in those indefinite shades.

Like all bright things, money had never been a topic of discussion with Madeline. Its vice or virtue, surplus or lack were never addressed. It was a blessing, she had said, to have a roof over one's head, food on the table, a bed to sleep in; and they must count themselves lucky. Growing up, Cecily had come to realise that their own situation veered more towards lack than surplus; that her mother's frugality was not born of idiosyncrasy of character but of necessity. Gowns, blouses, skirts and coats were patched and mended, Ethne's old dresses adapted and taken in to fit Cecily. Nothing was discarded or thrown away, every remnant – every hem from every shortened gown, every frayed cuff and sleeve and collar – was kept and stored, and used again, ingeniously. Then Madeline bought her Singer sewing machine and began to take in work: altering waistlines and hems, removing collars and stitching new ones, adapting fashions and tastes. She made quilts, cushions and curtains, loose covers and bedspreads. And spent each evening darning linen, embroidering table napkins and antimacassars. She worked hard, built a repu-tation, and became known as the best seamstress in the area, receiving commissions from local gentry, including the Brownlows, whose bespoke curtains and blinds she had labori-ously finished by hand.

But to Cecily, there was something else, something born of loneliness – and perhaps denial – driving her mother's industry. Why else would each and every single moment be spent cutting, stitching and sewing, as though her whole being depended upon it? As though to stop would allow her time to think, to remember. Rosetta had said, 'When you've loved, truly loved, and then lost, you can never again give yourself to another.' And Cecily had immediately thought of her mother, and not of Rosetta. She thought of the love between her parents, the woman she lived with, who had given birth to her, and the man she had never known. How had their love been? She tried to imagine them together, the couple in the silver-framed wedding photograph. She imagined her mother bright and young in her father's arms, imagined them looking into each other's eyes, dancing towards the future, laughing. And she began to feel that sense of loss, that feeling of the world being not quite complete, not whole; that feeling of something – someone – missing, a future taken. No, there could be no brightness in Madeline's world, not now, not ever. But would there be brightness in hers?

By the time Cecily arrived at Temple Hill, the sky had darkened further. The maid glanced upwards at the heavens, then ushered Cecily inside, slamming the front door behind her, shutting out all dwindling light. She asked Cecily to 'please wait there a moment' and disappeared into the shadows, then re-emerged and led Cecily to a room. The countess was alone and sat by a window, rather formally attired, Cecily thought, in a stiff costume of pale lemon and white lace. Perhaps she was going out, or perhaps she had just returned. She did not rise from her chair but reached out and took hold of Cecily's hand, saying, 'I think you're just in time . . . we're hoping for a deluge,' and then asked her to take a seat. Cecily handed over the note, at the same time informing her that although Ethne had a prior engagement, she and her mother would be delighted to come to dinner on Saturday evening.

'*Perfetto!*' said the countess. She glanced down at the small brown envelope in her hand, and Cecily saw her momentarily frown. Then, without opening it, she placed the envelope on the table next to her, beside a small red leatherbound book, and went on to explain that *darling* Jack and Miss Dorland had gone to Linford with Mr Cotton. They were both catching the train to London, she said, Jack to visit a school friend, where he would be staying for a night or two, and Miss Dorland to meet with her publisher and sort out various matters at her flat. And Cecily felt the sting of disappointment, for she had hoped to see Jack, if only to explain the altered arrangements. The countess said, 'Of course, he'll be back by Saturday, when you come to dine,' and offered Cecily a smile.

Outside, daylight shrivelled. The room shrank into dimness. And as the first crack of thunder took hold of the house, shaking chimneys and timber and glass, the countess gazed out through the window and said, 'So desperate . . . desperate for relief.'

But the storm rumbled on without any relief. There was no deluge.

They spoke about the village, the school in particular. And the countess told Cecily that she herself had once, when young, taught at a Sunday school in Rome, a place called the Granary Chapel which had for a while improvised as a church for the English expatriates there. And Cecily immediately wondered if she had lost her faith; if something had happened in her life which had caused her to question and then denounce God. The countess had not been to any service at Saint Luke's, the village church.

'Children,' the countess said, dreamily, as though thinking aloud, 'are not simply the future, they're the light in all our lives.'

She looked away, shook her head and raised a hand dismissively. At first, it was as though a new thought — contradictory or conflicting — had come to her at that very same moment. But as she continued to stare across the room, seemingly at something fixed, Cecily turned, half-expecting to see someone, a figure, even a ghost. But there was no one there. Seconds after this, the countess glanced at the clock on the mantelshelf and pulled on the bell by her side. 'I find a small glass of wine at this time of day reinvigorates the senses, opens one's heart, prepares one for . . . for evening.'

So Cecily took a glass of sherry with the countess. And when the countess opened the small mother-of-pearl cigarette case and held it out to her, Cecily took a cigarette. It burned her throat and she coughed. The countess told her they were 'Best Venetians'. A count — with a strange-sounding unpronounceable name — sent them to her, she said; she'd never smoke English cigarettes, 'but these are actually very good for one'.

When the clock chimed six, Cecily said she really should be

going soon. But she didn't want to. And the countess, turning her head away, glancing out through the window, said, 'Had we but world enough, and time . . .' She looked at Cecily. 'Time's winged chariot . . . to his coy mistress? Andrew Marvell?'

'The metaphysical poets.'

The countess smiled, nodded. 'You remind me a great deal of myself when I was young. Seems but a moment ago.' She lifted her glass to her lips, and Cecily noticed her hands: bejewelled fingers, still slender. She watched her sip from the glass, place it down upon the table next to her, and then glance about the room, her hooded eyes moving swiftly from one object to another, as though checking it was all there, in place. Each surface, every table and shelf, was littered with memorabilia: china and glass and photographs and, Cecily noticed, on the table immediately next to her, two framed black silhouette cameos of cherubic infants with tousled hair.

The countess said, 'Freddie and Georgie. My babies, my boys . . . gone now.'

'Freddie?'

'My firstborn, my eldest, taken from me when he was barely six years old. He is in Rome . . . left there now.'

Sadness slipped down her face. She reached to the locket about her neck, mouthing silent, inexpressible words, struggling perhaps with the need to remember, something, someone, all of them. Wishing perhaps to say their names again, Cecily thought, watching her. Then sunlight broke into the room, under the sash, under the blind, bouncing off china and glass and mirror, and Cecily heard a thin mournful sigh, like the tail-end vibration of a sad song. The clock on the mantelpiece chimed the quarter hour and the countess dissolved into the light, spectral with her white hair and pale gown.

'They're all there,' she said. 'Freddie, my aunt, Jack and—'

'Jack?'

'My first husband. He passed away when . . . before Georgie was born.' She raised a hand to her eyes. 'Do draw down the blind a little, will you, my dear.'

Cecily rose to her feet, moved over to the window and lowered the blind. She wanted to ask questions: were there only two children, two sons, or had others, too, been lost along the way? What about the daughter Mr Fox had mentioned? And how many husbands had there actually been? And which children were born to which husbands? And how had the first husband died?

'My family is rather a muddle,' she said, as if able to hear Cecily's thoughts. 'Perhaps all families are . . . my first husband was also my aunt's stepson.' She paused as Cecily sat back down, and then continued. 'My aunt married a man named James Staunton. He lived in Rome with his son, Jack, whom I later married.'

James Staunton had been contracted by the papal government to set up the Anglo Romano Gas Company and begin the long process of installing gas in the city, she told Cecily. 'When I first arrived, the new gas works were still in the process of being built – on the banks of the Tiber. They were ugly, something of a deformity, particularly there, surrounded by such antiquated beauty. But Mr Staunton was an *industrialist*,' she said with emphasis. 'He and my aunt fell in love so very quickly. It was rather a whirlwind courtship. She was an intelligent woman, calm and measured, a remarkable woman . . .' she petered out, and remained silent for a moment or two. 'She and I had been living in Paris,' she began again, remembering, 'and it was there, in the room of Roman Antiquities at the Louvre, that I first became acquainted with Rome, fascinated by its relics . . . And then, lo and behold, my aunt married Mr Staunton, and there I was *living* in Rome!' she said, smiling at Cecily.

But the story was too fast; there were gaps. How had they

come to be in Paris? Why had they gone there? And how, exactly, had her aunt met Mr Staunton? And what about Jack? What happened to him?

Her early days in Rome were spent just as any other tourist, the countess said, moving on again swiftly, 'visiting and revisting the ancient sites, piazzas, picture galleries and churches, so that within a very short time, I needed no map or guidebook. And I did not care what anyone said, to me it was heaven, *heaven*!'

'What anyone said?'

'Oh well, in comparison to other European cities, Rome was still considered by many to be backward and shabby, third rate; a place to visit, to stay for a while, but not to live, not permanently,' she replied. 'And it had something of a reputation . . .' She glanced at Cecily, 'for fugitives, all sorts of shady characters.'

'Not unlike here then.'

She laughed. 'No, possibly not,' she replied. 'And yet, for those of us who chose to live there, it offered a kind of freedom, and the chance to be whoever one wished to be,' she added wistfully.

'Yes,' said Cecily, imagining.

'And behind every doorway, no matter how humble, were masterpieces, friezes depicting ancient stories, magnificent frescoes, statues, intricate mosaics and richly marbled floors. Every window and balcony overlooked the antiquities, like one's own museum, one's very own art gallery. It felt to me like the centre of the world. And of course it had been, once. Everywhere one looked were relics, history and art, stupendous art. How could one fail to be inspired in such a place? All of it shaped me, who I am, and like those I have loved, it remains here,' she said, placing her palm flat upon her chest. 'It lives within me . . . that place.'

And how could it not? Cecily thought. To have spent one's

formative years in such a place was indeed an extraordinary privilege.

The countess gazed out of the window. 'I would like to go back there,' she said, 'just once more.' And she began to describe a vista in such extraordinary detail that Cecily too could see it: a view across jumbled terracotta rooftops, across a sea of steeples and domes, across scattered ruins and pillars to crumbling walls, and beyond those walls to wide empty pastures and distant hills.

This was what had awakened the countess to beauty, Cecily thought, what fed her senses and continued to nourish her soul.

'And your first husband, Jack . . . he died there?' Cecily ventured at last.

'Yes, that is where he rests, where they all rest.'

'But not George?'

She flinched. 'George? Why, George is in Rome . . .'

'Oh, I'm sorry. I was sure Jack said his father had fallen from his horse somewhere near here.'

'Ah yes,' the countess said, closing her eyes, nodding. 'Forgive me. I sometimes get a little confused with names. You are correct. Georgie,' she said, with emphasis on the 'ie' sound, 'did fall from his horse, and not far from this place. He was so dashingly handsome,' she said, smiling, remembering, 'invincible to his fellow officers and to everyone else . . . and much too brave to suffer the ignominy of an accidental death. He always thought he'd die a heroic death on the battlefield – if any at all. And he made me think that too. But . . .' she paused, shook her head, 'he was mortal. Mortal like his father.'

'So sad.'

'Yes, it was a difficult, painful time, for me – for all of us. He left a young wife, Cassandra, and of course little Jack, only weeks old. I was in Rome . . . I returned here, of course. As soon as I received the telegram I left Rome and returned here as fast as I could. But I was too late.' She lowered her head. 'We buried him in the snow . . .' she said quietly, 'we buried him in the snow as his father passed away.'

'His father?'

She looked up at Cecily. 'Godfather,' she said. And then she glanced once more across the room, towards the bronze head in the alcove. 'They stay with us, of course. Departure from this life, death of the physical body, is not an end. We merely cast off the trappings of this realm for another. The soul is immortal. I know this now.'

Cecily nodded.

'And yet, 'tis the queerest thing,' she began again, quietly, 'to find myself here, at this age, in this place. Peculiar to find oneself anywhere, to still be here, when those one has known are all gone.' She turned to Cecily. 'But of course I have Jack to think of,' she said, in a louder, firmer voice, and picked up her glass. 'He is the future and all that matters to me now. And he's a darling, darling boy, so very like his grandfather in looks and thought and deed. And that is my comfort. It's what we leave behind us that defines who we have been, not our birth date, or death date, nor whom we married or where we were born. Those are the facts, of course, the details, but they're minor details, they mean nothing on their own, tell nothing of the story of a person's life. What made one's heart quicken, what one saw, how one felt; the decisions made, the regrets: all of this is lost, forgotten. And when one reaches my age, 'tis hard to recall one's early life and first impressions.'

Without thinking, Cecily said, 'And what *are* your earliest memories?'

The countess tilted her head to one side. 'My earliest memories . . .' she said, turning away with eyes half-closed, 'my earliest memories are of a place called Standen Hall, a place in Suffolk. It is where I lived before I went to Paris, before my mother . . .' she paused, 'before my mother departed.'

'What was it like?' Cecily asked, leaning forward in her chair.

'It lies a few miles to the west of Woodbridge, off the old London road. And you know, I can picture it now, the view from a carriage window. One passed through an immense gated entrance with a towered gatehouse to the right and headed down a long, long winding driveway, through breathtaking woodland and gardens, and then the vast red-brick Tudor sprawl came into view – the tallest chimneys you ever saw. There was an enormous front door, easily as large as any of the grand doorways in Rome, which opened directly into the oak-panelled medieval great hall. I recall suits of armour, stag's heads mounted high up upon the walls, and a vast wooden staircase rising up to galleried landings lined with portraits. It was truly a splendid place.'

Cecily smiled. 'Home.'

The countess nodded and smiled.

'And you never went back?'

'No. Never. Once my parents were gone . . . well, there was nothing left for me there, no one left. And my life had moved on. I was in Paris, and then Rome, and then married with children. It was impossible to go back, and there was no reason to go back. Life moves on and we must move with it,' she added, smiling, weary.

'Sad. Sad for you, ma'am, to have had to leave everything behind.'

'Please, no more "ma'am". Cora. My name is Cora.'

Later, as Cecily strolled back down the track, she felt quite different to the person who had marched up the hill only hours earlier. The fortified wine had undoubtedly mellowed her senses, but it was more than this: there was something new and altered in everything around her, and within her. As though the world – and herself with it – had passed through a spectrum. She knew that nothing would ever be the same; nothing could ever be or seem as it had earlier that day, or before that day. And though the ground felt softer, like a cushion beneath her feet, and the sun, now exposed and still high in the sky, spilled out upon that dark umber carpet in soft slanting rays, something inexplicably sad had attached itself to her, and she felt its burden.

The atmosphere within the room she had just left had been peculiarly insulated, and not just from the heat and light of the day, but from everything, almost from time itself. Three whole hours had passed by in a flash, and in those three hours she had had a glimpse of a life, a different life. A door had opened – an inch, no more – and she had been allowed to step forward and look through it – for a moment, no more. But in that moment, in that glimpse, how much she had seen. Time had slipped away, and she and the countess had been equals, had spoken as friends.

And before Cecily left they had made a pact.

'I'm a very private person, Cecily. I would prefer you to keep these things we've discussed to yourself. I'd like to think I could trust you.'

'Of course, I wouldn't dream of betraying your trust, Cora.'

'I knew . . . knew we were going to be good friends, you and I. And there's something else, something I'd like you to do for me, Cecily, a small favour.'

Cecily nodded.

'You must mention this to no one, no one at all,' she said, 'not even to Jack. In fact, most especially not to Jack. It's to do with the man at Meadow Farm,' she began.

Chapter Nine

*I*t was late Saturday morning. The village was busier than usual, and noisy. And temperatures were running high. The horse-drawn van of the baker, the butcher's bang-tailed cob and the omnibus to Linford – already running ten minutes late – were locked in dispute and remained stationary, surrounded by bleating sheep being moved from one parched field to another by way of the main street. As the bus driver – coerced, Sylvia presumed, by his hot and impatient passengers – honked on his horn and shouted, she and others had spilled out from the post office to watch tempers fly.

Sylvia had already been to the Sale of Work at the village hall, but when she spotted Cecily emerge from the festooned doorway of the hall into the maelstrom she had waved her hand. But Cecily appeared to see nothing, least of all Sylvia. She marched off at some speed, weaving her way through the livestock which was running this way and that and up the wrong lane. As Cecily disappeared, Sylvia too had moved on, through the stupid animals, holding her bag aloft. Once clear, on the decline to the ford and with Cecily in sight once more, Sylvia quickened her pace. She called out, twice, and both times Cecily stopped, just as though she had heard her name. But she failed to turn and simply marched on. And when, eventually, Sylvia caught up with her, Cecily had been unusually abrupt.

'Oh, hello, Miss Dorland,' she said flatly, and sounding quite put out, Sylvia thought.

They had stood for a while in one spot, while Sylvia caught her breath.

'I hear . . . I hear you're to dine with us . . . later,' Sylvia said, fanning her face with her hand.

'We're supposed to be, yes,' Cecily replied, in the same cold voice.

She had not reckoned on Cecily Chadwick being a moody sort, not at all. Something must have happened, Sylvia thought, for her to be so . . . so rude.

'Is anything the matter, dear? You seem a little out of sorts, if I may say.'

Cecily shook her head. 'It's nothing,' she said, without meeting Sylvia's eyes.

As they began to walk, Sylvia told her that she, too, had been to the sale earlier, and they stopped again as Sylvia produced the woven bookmark and bag of pot-pourri she had bought for her friend.

'Oh yes, I'm sure Cora will like them,' Cecily said, barely looking at the things.

At first, Sylvia thought she had imagined Cecily saying the name.

'Cora?' she repeated.

'Mm. I'm sure she'll like them.'

Cecily moved on, but Sylvia remained fixed, the bookmark and muslin bag in her outstretched hands, and a strange giddy feeling, which tilted the pathway ahead. For a moment she thought she might faint. And when Cecily turned, looking back down the hill at her with a queer smile, she appeared to Sylvia rather smug, even triumphant.

She put away her gifts and continued up the hill towards Cecily. 'So, you've been up to the house . . . been to call on her?' she asked.

But Cecily appeared not to hear her. She stared straight ahead, a look of concentration furrowing her brow. And so Sylvia rephrased the question: 'I take it you've seen the countess recently?'

'Oh yes,' Cecily said, and then added – a little defensively, Sylvia thought – '*You* were in London.'

'Ah, when Mr Fox was also there?'

'No. There was only me,' Cecily replied.

But Cora had made no mention to Sylvia of Cecily's visit. She had mentioned only that the rector had called on her. And Sylvia had become increasingly suspicious of that man. To Sylvia's mind, he seemd uncommonly interested in Cora's life. She was worried that her friend, troubled as she was and, perhaps, in need of succour, might feel inclined to unburden herself to him. He had taken to calling at the house almost daily, and had arrived, quite out of the blue, earlier that very morning, before Sylvia set off for the village. It was most irregular. People did not make calls in the morning, and Cora usually refused any callers at all before 3p.m. But then, when Cora informed her that she wished to speak to the rector alone, in private, Sylvia suspected that they had had a prearranged appointment, that Cora had in fact been expecting him. Sylvia loitered in the hallway, tidying papers and adjusting an arrangement of flowers, but not a sound had permeated the closed door.

Now she heard Cecily say, 'I spent quite a while with her. She told me about her boys . . . Jack's father, George, or Georgie as I think she calls him. And also about her childhood, where she grew up.'

'Her childhood, where she grew up?' Sylvia repeated.

'Don't worry,' Cecily said, turning to her, 'I promised I'd not breathe a word to anyone, and I shan't.'

'I see.'

They walked on in silence and when they reached the privet hedge bordering Cecily's garden, Sylvia said, 'I must tell you something, Cecily.'

She then explained how worried she was about Cora, about her friend's recent outburst, the sitting alone in the temple. 'I know that Jack, too, is concerned . . . very concerned,' she added, grimly. 'Recently, she seems . . . she seems to be more confused than ever, almost delusional.'

'It's the heat,' Cecily said, with a shrug of her shoulders, and quite dismissive to Sylvia's mind.

'No, it is not the heat. She's long used to that. No, there's something else. I know it. And my worry is . . .' she turned her head away and sighed. 'She's become so muddled about everything, her past, the details of her birth, her childhood. I'm not sure what, exactly, she told you, Cecily . . .'

Cecily stared back at her but said not a word.

'But the chances are it was fantasy. Fantasy,' she repeated.

'I see, and yet she didn't appear muddled to me, not about *that*, anyway. She remembered it all in great detail. But don't worry. I shan't break my promise. You have my word on that.'

At that moment Madeline appeared at the garden gate. Sylvia said hello, Cecily said goodbye, and Madeline said how much they were looking forward to dinner later.

Sylvia moved away, newly troubled.

It was not that she did not trust Cecily, not exactly. It was perfectly clear Cecily Chadwick could keep a secret. But her manner had been strange. She had been abrupt and decidedly reticent when Sylvia first caught up with her, almost as though she had been trying to get away from her. Is that why she had rushed from the hall? Had she in fact seen Sylvia before Sylvia had seen her? And why had Cora made no mention of Cecily's visit?

As she continued up the track, a sensation of estrangement enveloped her, and she paused at the top of the hill and caught her breath in a loud gasp. She was being sidelined, excluded, left out and cut out of Cora's story. And that Cora had spoken to Cecily – Cecily Chadwick, a nobody, a young slip of a thing she barely knew – about her life, her childhood, was incomprehensible. But the facts of the matter were simple enough: Cora had elected to confide in another the one thing she herself had been waiting a lifetime to hear, to have confirmed. 'And after everything I've done for her, everything she's promised me,' she whispered, walking on, her heart pounding. 'Does my loyalty and love count for nothing?'

She stopped. Questions sprang up in profusion, like the nettles on the side of the path, stinging her mind. *What* had Cora told Cecily? *Why* had she told Cecily? Was it possible that Cecily Chadwick knew more about Cora than she? What on earth was Cora playing at? After all, Cora had invited her down here for that very reason, to tell *her*! To once and for all explain the truth of events before she arrived in Rome.

She walked on. One thing was clear, an alliance had been formed, memories annexed, and Cora was now a protectorate of Cecily's.

'Cecily Chadwick!'

She stopped again. She needed to compose herself, needed to think things through. But the sense of betrayal was agony, *like a dagger plunged into her heart she thought*. Oh, but it was not her who was adrift, she reasoned, it was Cora who was adrift; drifting away from reason and sanity, away from a lifelong and tested friendship. Had I known, she thought, I should never have come . . . never have come.

She moved off the track, through the long grass towards the rotting timber of an old gate, placed her arms along its length and allowed her head to fall forward. The world was spinning and she with it. 'It's not jealousy . . . not jealousy,' she whispered, eyeing a spider weaving a silvery web around a wasp twice its size. Then she raised her head, wiped her mildew-covered hands on the skirt of her gown, and as she crouched down to reach through the gate for her hat, she heard a voice. 'Miss Dorland, is everything quite all right there?'

It was Mrs Moody, walking her goat.

'Yes, fine. I was just admiring the foliage and lost my hat,' she replied, pulling the boater through a gap in the gate and rising to her feet.

'Beautiful day for it,' Mrs Moody said, staring at the skirt of Sylvia's dark gown.

'Indeed . . . yet another.'

'Bernard and I always have a little stop here. You're standing on his grass,' she said, and laughed.

'And I must away. Cor— my friend will be waiting for me.'

'Oh, and how is her lay-ay-dyship?' Mrs Moody asked, jerked forward, towards the grass, by Bernard. 'The rector mentioned that she's not been herself of late. Troubled by the heat, he said. Well, I said, that doesn't make sense, not being that she lived abroad for so many years, but he said it takes a while to *climatise* and I suppose it's true enough. It happened to me when I went to Brighton, you know, and it was enough to—'

'I really must get on,' Sylvia interrupted, and as she turned away, Mrs Moody called after her.

'Do give her my regards . . . And tell her I know what it's like.'

Sylvia closed her eyes: *Mrs Moody sends you her best, and wishes you to know that she, too, has suffered climatisation.*

No, of course it wasn't the heat that was troubling Cora; it was laughable that anyone would think so. It was the situation she found herself in: having to come back to England and confront her past.

By the time Sylvia reached the laurel-lined driveway, she had made one decision. There was nothing else for it, she would have to speak to Jack.

Cora was in the garden. She sat upon a bench by an herbaceous border clutching the red, leatherbound volume of Byron's poems: the one George had given her, still with the dust of a pressed violet marking the page. She watched butterflies: tortoiseshells, peacocks, chalk-blues, and a single red admiral. It was safer to love these ephemeral things, she thought, than humans. Their lives were brief and fleeting but when they died there was no pain, no need for grief. They always came back, came back each year . . .

If only he could come back . . . if only I could go back.

She glanced about the garden. To think it had all been excavated and planted for her. And yet, how queer it was to be sitting in it in England. That had never been her plan. Her plan had been to die in Rome, to be buried there, alongside George. But she had had to leave him, had had no choice, just as he had had no choice all those years before.

So many parallels . . .

'So many parallels,' she said out loud and sighed. She liked to think of the path of their lives — criss-crossing and overlapping — as synchronistic, and the events within them mirroring. But the only parallel had been each of their liaisons with people old enough to be their parents, although Cora had trumped his sixteen years with her thirty, and then trumped him again in her choice of third husband. If it had been a contest, Cora had certainly won, and by much more than a mile.

She thought his name, heard his voice: 'I have to go. It's a tremendous opportunity for me.'

Yes, it *had* been a tremendous opportunity, history had proved it so. And yet . . . and yet . . . George's opportunity had been the undoing of *them*, and the undoing of her. But fate had also conspired in the form of that wretched woman, Mrs Hillier. Without her, who knows what might have happened.

She glanced up to the heavens, wondering briefly, fleetingly, if dear George and Mrs H were reconciled there. *No, it was a . . . a business arrangement, a commercial partnership. There was nothing more to it. He told me so, told me so himself.*

And John Clifford had also told her, or had tried to, once, all those years ago. A pupil of Canova, Clifford had been considered Rome's finest sculptor, and his studio the liveliest in the city, a Mecca for all visiting English artists. It was the place Cora had first been exposed to long philosophical discussions and passionate political debate, which had in turn educated and informed her thinking. The gentle and paternalistic Clifford had taught her how to draw and, in quieter months when the city's many visitors returned home and only those who had no desire to be anywhere else remained within its walls, Cora had spent hours listening to his anecdotes and reminiscences of how Rome 'used to be'.

Cora's aunt had, initially, been concerned at the amount of time Cora spent in the company of artists. She had been agitated about the morality of a *mal entourée* whose sole occupation seemed to be the pursuit of pleasure. But Clifford had reassured her, told her not to worry, that he would keep an eye on young Cora.

In his self-deprecating way Clifford liked to allude to a vague and unrequited love in his life but it was commonly accepted that he had no great desire for requited love; he appeared ambivalent in matters of the heart, indifferent to the opposite sex. But for Cora, his position as unattached observer gave him an advantage others could not possibly have.

'My dear, George is not the man for you,' he said. 'He is

simply not a man for marrying, or for belonging to anyone. He is married to his art.'

'And what of Mrs Hillier?' she asked.

'Mrs Hillier? Mrs Hillier is a married woman, and almost old enough to be his mother.'

'But George spends so much of his time with her.'

Even then, she was aware that she sounded like a lovestruck jealous child, but she did not care. Clifford was a dear and trusted friend, and she knew he would not repeat their conversation. She also knew that what he so enjoyed was the knowledge that he was trusted with such tender secrets.

'Yes, but she is his advocate and patron now. Thanks to Mrs Hillier, dear George has made some fine connections, and will have some worthwhile commissions, of that I'm sure.' He looked from Cora to his easel. 'He knows it's perfectly safe to spend time with her. She is married, unavailable, but more importantly, perhaps, he knows there is no danger of falling in love with her.'

Cora stepped down from the upturned crate and, wrapping a sheet around her body, moved towards Clifford, looking over his shoulder at the sketches for his 'Tinted Venus'.

He went on; 'Mrs Hillier's a delightful lady, a sophisticate, and undoubtedly accomplished, but the relationship she and George share is platonic, I'm quite certain of that. They share passions but not for each other, and their . . . their friendship is mutually advantageous. George needs Mrs Hillier to be his champion, and she needs him for . . . reflected glory. She has the contacts and the influence, not only in London but here in Rome and in Paris, too. Think about it. George is a very clever fellow. By Jupiter, he is!'

'But you're inferring that George is using Mrs Hillier to promote himself, to further his career.'

'He's ambitious, Cora, very ambitious, and determined to prove himself, particularly to his father. And that means being successful and selling pictures! Dear George, perhaps more than any of us, feels a need – nay, a pressure – to be accepted and successful, to make money. And, sadly for you, my dear, his compass directs him to Mrs Hillier.'

George had already spoken to her about his father, and at some length. Mr Lawson Senior had wanted George to follow in his footsteps and study architecture. He had told his son that only a very tiny proportion of painters, only the most God-given talented ones, ever made any money at it. 'All he cares about, or seems to care about, it is that I have a profession, a noble profession – oh, and that I marry well,' George told her.

'Marry well?'

'Yes, marry someone of standing, someone *known*, someone he approves of.' He glanced to Cora and added, 'But if I really cared what *he* thought, would I be here in Rome, would I be painting?'

'He does not care what his father thinks,' Cora said to Clifford. 'I know, he's told me.'

Clifford smiled at her. 'But what he says and what he does may differ. Particularly where you're concerned.'

Despite her misgivings, despite Clifford's words – was it a warning? – Cora held on to her fantasy. John Clifford was an old man and love had passed him by. She and George shared something – something different, something private, something no one else would understand. They were going to travel together, live like gypsies, and while he produced art, she would produce his sons and daughters. They might never be rich, but they would have enough, he said, and that *enough* was more than enough for Cora.

Cora winced. She did not wish to recall that time, nor what came immediately after. She preferred to remember those last few months together. How perfect it had been, despite the ticking of the clock. 'How it could have been, how it should have been.'

He had said, 'Tell me you love me, and kiss me . . . kiss me goodbye.'

Yes, that was what he said.

'I love you but I shall never ever say goodbye to you, George.'

'Not even after I am gone?'

'No, not even then . . . not ever.'

She had held on to his hand, listening to his breathing, watching his eyes flicker and close, and open and close.

'I shall bring you violets,' she had said, 'every day. I shall sit with you, talk to you . . . tell you all the things I never told you. And then, at the end, I'll be there. I shall be there with you for all eternity.'

'For all eternity,' she heard him say now, and repeated it with him.

But in the distance she could hear another voice, and through a pathway in the rhododendrons she spotted Sylvia on the driveway, talking – it seemed – to herself. She smiled. Always busy on a new plot, she thought. She called out and Sylvia stopped, and then looked about her with an expression of panic. She appeared rather flushed, quite wrung out, Cora thought. But when Sylvia finally located Cora, her expression altered, and she smiled as though in relief and waved back. She then made her way through the bushes, lowering her head as she passed under a tangled archway. And as she stepped down on to the grass, Cora thought she heard her mutter something about a ditch.

'There is no ditch, dear, not there.'

In her room, Cecily was still seething.

She lay upon her bed staring up at the sloping ceiling, unable to stop the sequence of images of *them*, together, larking about in boats, motoring down wide city streets, posing for the camera. Like picture postcards, they laughed and smiled back at her from each one, with Sonia in the foreground, smiling broadly and calling out to her, 'Hell-o-o, Cecily, look who I am with!'

Oh God, the agony! How could he? How could he have been with *her*?

It had been at the Sale of Work in the village hall that Sonia had told her about London. She had only just returned, she said, had been there for a few days, helping her mother select furnishings for their new Knightsbridge apartment.

'And so we came back on the train with him,' she said, glancing at Cecily. 'Well, we bumped into him travelling up there, you see, so I saw quite a bit of him, and his friend, Noel . . . so charming. And the coincidence is, Noel's parents keep an apartment in the same building as mine! Can you imagine? I'm sure you'll meet him at some stage. I rather think he said he might drive down here sometime. He has his own motorcar . . . Oh, it was a hoot! We motored all over London, up the Mall, through Trafalgar Square, with Noel and Jack pretending we were tourists and calling out to people in French . . .'

She went on and on. Then she said, 'And yesterday evening, Millie Compton – my oldest, bestest friend from school – Noel, Jack and I took a boat out on the Serpentine. Oh, it was heavenly! We had a picnic, and naughty Noel brought along two bottles of champagne! Can you imagine? I was almost blotto!'

'Real champagne?' Annie asked, and Cecily could have kicked her.

'Oh my dear, the best, the very best *real* champagne. And rather potent stuff too, I can tell you.' She threw her head back and affected a laugh. Then she leaned over the table in front of them and whispered, 'Poor Jack was quite fuddled by the end of the evening, he had something of a sore head this morning.' And then she did another of her silent laughs.

Cecily had picked up her basket, turned to Annie and said she hadn't realised the time, and before either girl could speak, she marched off out of the hall.

She could barely remember the walk home, so angry had she been. Then Sylvia Dorland had appeared out of nowhere, wittering on about the sale and some silly bookmark she had bought for Cora. At first, she had not listened to a word Sylvia said. She had been picturing the London foursome, lounging on rugs and sipping champagne, and Sonia tossing her head about in that way she did. She had been wondering who was paired with whom: Jack and Sonia, or Jack and Miss Millie Compton? Wondering if Jack Staunton had wrapped his fuddled arms around Sonia, for she had freely admitted that she had been blotto.

But then Sylvia said something about Cora being muddled, and had given her such a queer look; and she realised almost immediately Sylvia's concern. So she had quietly reassured Sylvia, and given her word. Now she wondered if Sylvia had actually come looking for her on Cora's instruction. For it seemed odd to her that Sylvia would say such things about her friend, almost disloyal. More likely, she mused, that Cora regretted their conversation of earlier that week, and had asked Sylvia, devoted as she undoubtedly was, to ensure that she, Cecily, kept to her promise. But what about the people at Meadow Farm? Was she still to pursue her line of enquiry and find out who they were and where they hailed from? Why on earth does she want to know about them anyway?

'What does it matter?' she said out loud. 'We're simply the poor neighbours, briefly dazzled – like everyone else.'

She sat up on her bed. She would not let Jack Staunton know. No, she must not give away so much as an inkling that she knew or cared about his sojourn in London. It would be so obvious, so cheap. And jealousy was a low emotion, possibly the lowest, along with envy and greed. And pride? Hmm. She was not sure about pride. But now was not the time to ponder upon pride, she decided. The facts of the matter were simple enough: if Sonia Brownlow was his cup of tea, she had misjudged him, overestimated him.

No, she would not give away anything to anyone from now on.

She rose to her feet feeling resolute and strong. Tonight was definitely the night to wear the turquoise silk chiffon.

Chapter Ten

 ecily stood with her mother and Sylvia in Cora's drawing room.

'Oh yes, a remarkable life,' Sylvia was saying, addressing Madeline Chadwick but with her gaze fixed on Cecily, 'and we've known each other *almost* our entire lives.'

She had been explaining to Madeline that she was to write the final part of the countess's memoirs, and, in case Madeline was in any doubt, that this was indeed a great honour.

Minutes earlier, the maid had led Cecily and her mother through the hallway, past the painting, which Cecily saw Madeline raise her eyebrows at, telling them that the countess would be 'down shortly'. She had shown them into the room, moved to a table and, without asking, poured each of them a small glass of sherry from a decanter. Madeline, who rarely drank alcohol, took the glass and said thank you. Cecily could tell that her mother was nervous, apprehensive. For Madeline glanced about the room like a hungry animal, keen to take it all in before the countess or anyone else appeared, and sipping perhaps too frequently from her glass. Cecily had watched her mother's eyes move from the polished curves of one sculpture to another, and across the walls from one naked breast to another.

'And these are the countess's sons,' Cecily said, pointing out the cameos to her mother. 'And that is the Comte de Chevalier de Saint Léger,' she added, gesturing to a portrait. 'And that one is Cora when she was young.'

'Cora?' Madeline blinked, taking another sip.

'Oh yes, she asked me to call her by her given name.'

Sylvia appeared, wearing the same dark grey dress they had seen her in earlier, and just as though she had heard Cecily's last words, she requested that they dispense with formalities, abandon the Miss Dorland, and simply address her as Sylvia.

Looking at Cecily, who had pinned up her hair and wore a gown of pale turquoise silk chiffon, Sylvia went on, 'We have no secrets, of course, dearest Cora and I. When two people have known each other as long as we have, well . . .' she shrugged.

Seconds later, Jack entered the room. He wore a tuxedo, with a wing-collared shirt and white bow tie, and was more dashing than any man Cecily could recall ever having seen. Still busy fastening a cufflink at his wrist, he smiled at Cecily. 'Good evening, ladies,' he said, moving into the room. His hair was damp and slicked back, and his face more tanned than it had been earlier that week when Cecily had last seen him, when they had loitered at the garden gate in silence, exchanging smiles.

Cecily introduced her mother. He shook her hand, said he was honoured to meet her, and Madeline flushed. 'Please, do sit down,' he said.

'I'm sure Sylvia's already explained, my grandmother sometimes takes quite a while to dress for dinner. It's a ritual, a lifelong ritual,' he said, looking from Cecily to her mother and then back to Cecily. Madeline drained her glass, and he sprang to his feet, took the glass and refilled it.

'I heard you weren't feeling awfully well earlier,' Cecily said, looking towards a sculpture upon a plinth in an alcove.

He frowned, shook his head. 'No, I'm feeling tip-top, actually.'

She turned to him. 'Not too much champagne then?'

'Cecily!' Madeline gasped.

'Sonia seems to think you were quite fuddled by it.'

'Cecily!'

'You and naughty Noel and silly Millie . . .'

'Really, dear, whatever's come over you?'

'I'm just ragging Jack, Mother. Aren't I, Jack?'

He smiled. 'It would seem so.'

Cecily turned to her mother: 'Jack and a few others, including dear Sonia, were partying up in London yesterday. I saw Sonia earlier and she was telling me *all* about it,' she added, forcing a smile and glancing at Jack. Then she put down her glass and stood up. 'Do please excuse me a moment.'

She walked out into the hallway, her head spinning, angry with herself, and then down the passage to the veranda. The sherry made her feel hotter than ever and she stood in the open doorway fanning herself with her hand. Nothing ever went as she planned; she had certainly not planned that. The plan had simply been to look as lovely as possible whilst appearing as indifferent as possible. 'Stupid, stupid girl,' she whispered. She moved out on to the veranda and glanced about in the vain hope that Cora might have been there earlier and left her packet of Best Venetians lying out. Then, like a miracle from above, she saw a plume of smoke rise up from behind a hedge.

'Yoo-hoo! Hello, excuse me,' she said, moving across the terrace.

A man's head appeared.

'You're Mr Cordery, aren't you?'

'That I am, miss.'

'You don't happen to have a spare cigarette, do you?'

'Yer not really a smoker, are you?' he said, holding the match to her, watching her.

'No, I'm a beginner,' she said flatly, finally getting the thing alight.

She walked back to the veranda and stood on the steps, picking bits of tobacco from her lips. The cigarette made her head spin more, made her feel more out of control.

'Bloody stupid!'

'What's that?'

It was Jack.

'I hadn't realised you smoked,' he said, moving alongside her.

'I don't.'

'I see.'

She caught his smile.

'It's gone out,' he said. 'Would you like me to fetch you another?'

'No. No, thank you,' she replied, tossing the thing into a nearby shrub. And as she turned to him, she saw him quickly look away. 'Is it funny?' she asked.

'Are you angry about something?'

'You don't answer a question with a question, Jack. Anyhow, we'd better go back inside, we've left my mother on her own with Sylvia.'

'My grandmother's with them, and they'll be fine. Probably best for them to have a moment without us.'

She looked away, across the terrace, across the tops of the trees.

He said, 'You're looking very nice tonight.'

'Thank you.'

'But you seem different . . . different to how you were on Tuesday.'

'Hmm, well, a lot can happen in four days.'

She felt his hand on her arm, her bare arm, his skin touching hers. 'What's happened? Tell me?'

She pulled her arm away, moved along the step.

'It's not . . . it's not about me and Sonia . . . or silly Noel or whatever it was you were referring to just now, is it?'

There was nothing for it; she had crossed a point, a point of no return, and she would have to ask. She turned to face him, took a deep breath . . .

'Please, tell me what it is?' he said, now frowning, looking into her eyes.

Oh dear, it was tempting, so tempting. *He* was tempting. And right at that moment she wished she could tell him everything – all of it, everything about her – from beginning to end; for him to know and understand her . . .

'And this is the veranda . . . ah, hello, children.'

It was Cora, leading Madeline, obviously giving her a guided tour of the place.

Cecily exhaled, loudly; and Jack swiftly stepped down from the step, on to the terrace.

'Dear Cecily!' said Cora, reaching out to her, taking hold of her hands, and then kissing her upon each cheek. 'And my word, what a vision!' she gasped, stepping back. She turned to Cecily's mother. 'Madeline, you must be very proud to have a daughter like Cecily . . .'

Madeline, Cecily thought: that hadn't taken long. No one called her mother by her first name. How had that happened so fast? She glanced towards her mother, who looked a little pink in the face and was shrugging her shoulders like a bashful schoolgirl. And then she turned to Jack, who smiled back at her knowingly.

'I'm giving your mama a little tour, Cecily dear, and then we shall dine,' Cora said, turning away. And as she disappeared back through the doorway and into the house, she said in a loud whisper, 'No wonder poor darling Jack's so distracted.' And Cecily saw him close his eyes and bite his lip.

For a moment he didn't speak, and neither did she. They could hear the two women's voices echoing down the long passageway. And as they slowly faded, he sighed.

'Madeline!' Cecily said.

'Mm. I knew it was best to let them get on with it. My grandmother has a way with people.'

She caught his gaze stray from her face to her body. But as he turned away, his awkwardness struck her, and she felt guilty. For hadn't she pushed him? And wasn't he lovely? Wasn't he perfect?

She stepped down from the veranda, sat on the step and looked up at him. 'Did you get drunk in London then?'

He ran a hand over his hair. 'A little,' he replied. 'Was that why you were angry?'

She tried to laugh. 'No. Of course not!'

He sat down next to her. 'So, are you going to tell me? I think you were about to – a moment ago.'

She shuffled, fiddling with the soft fabric of her gown, and as she leaned forward, flicking at the dust on the toes of her satin shoes, she said, 'I . . . well, I . . .'

'Yes?'

'Yes,' she repeated, absently.

Then she heard the smile in his voice as he said, 'Come on, you've got to tell me now.'

'Now, I'm not sure.'

'Not sure of what?'

She turned her head towards him, his knees. 'Did you . . . did you . . .'

He leaned forward, tilting his head, levelling his gaze with hers. 'Did I get drunk? Yes, a little. Did I flirt with Sonia

Brownlow? No. Did I flirt with Millie Compton? No. Would I ever want to? No.'

She stared back at him and didn't speak.

'Does that answer everything?' he asked.

She nodded.

'Is that what it was all about – in there, out here, is that it?'

For a moment she wished she wasn't there, wished she were invisible. She shut her eyes, opened them again, and he was still smiling at her, a different sort of smile, one she hadn't seen before.

'How could you possibly think I'd be remotely attracted to someone like Sonia Brownlow? Do I appear desperate?'

She laughed. 'No, no. But she, Sonia, has,' she shrugged, 'her ways.'

'*Her ways*? Short of wearing a placard, I'm not sure what else she could do to advertise her ways.' He paused and Cecily laughed again. 'And let me tell you, her friend Millie is rather a knockout too. But perhaps slightly thicker built – in brain *and* body.'

And at last she unfolded herself and sat up, smiling now at the spectacle of the London foursome. 'But why did you go about with them, you and your friend, if they were so ghastly?'

'It was all set up by the delightful Mrs Brownlow and Noel's mother – you know how they do. Let's get the young people together, sort of thing. Anyway, as it turned out, it was quite a laugh. I don't suppose Sonia told you that she fell into the Serpentine.'

'No!' Cecily shrieked.

'Yes, truly,' he said, beginning to laugh. 'She was trying to step out of the boat – and I don't think Noel did it on purpose, he swears he didn't – but the boat suddenly moved away from the pier and Sonia . . .' he was laughing, struggling to get the words out, 'Sonia almost did the splits before going in!' He wiped away tears. 'It was so funny . . . you'd have died. She managed to keep her hair dry, but she wasn't at all happy when we finally dragged her out . . .'

They sat giggling for some minutes, and every so often he added to the story, offering Cecily another comic detail. Then he said, 'I so wished you'd been there. Noel and I were fit to explode by the time we dropped her home. Every time she moved about the leather seat in Noel's motor, there was a squelching sound, and she apologised!'

She felt his hand graze the middle of her back, his palm rest flat there. He said, 'So you see, you have nothing to be angry about. There's only one girl I'm interested in.'

And though she said nothing, did not look at him and made no reply, she wanted to. She wanted to hear him say her name. She wanted confirmation. But the moment passed. He moved his hand away and moved on. He asked her if she had been writing, and she told him that she had. She told him of her idea for a novel, inspired, she said, by Cora's life overseas. Then the gong sounded. And as he rose to his feet, he offered her his hand. 'Cecily.'

In years to come, Cecily would return to that evening, his words, his smile – and even the sound of the gong. She would relive it again and again, because it was a beginning, *the beginning*. Everything that had happened in her life up until that point had been a prelude to that moment, moving her forward, leading her to that touch, that smile, those words. Her life had arrived. She could see the future, the possibilities, and she could see Jack Staunton walking towards her from each and every horizon.

Dinner was a success, Cora charm itself, if a little distracted from time to time. It was, Cecily thought, as though the past was still with her; as though those she spoke of were there, in that room. Once or twice Cecily followed her gaze, turning her head towards the baize door, the wall, the salamander, as though she, too, would be able to see something, someone standing there. At one point she was sure she had seen Cora nod and then raise her hand, just as if she was dismissing someone from the room. But no one was there.

Cora spoke of Rome and Paris, relishing a few well-worn anecdotes that Cecily had heard once and Jack and Sylvia perhaps tenfold but that Madeline had not yet heard. They all laughed at her reminiscences of the mischievous antics of her young sons, specifically Jack's father, Georgie. And she spoke once more of her aunt, a woman of impossible glamour and style, it seemed, who had been such an influence over her life – a mother to her, she said. But when Madeline enquired about her mother, her real mother, Cecily saw that veil of melancholy descend once more. She had simply been too beautiful for this life, Cora replied.

All through dinner Cecily and Jack exchanged smiles as though they had a secret, which they did. For hadn't he said there was only one girl for him? And so, although Cecily heard the conversation and joined in from time to time, and although she ate some of the hors d'oeuvres and a little of the clear velouté, the roast pigeon and then the meringues with fruit and whipped cream were barely tasted. All she could think of were those words, that *one girl*.

But when Sylvia leaned towards her and said, 'It's awfully nice that you and Jack have become friends,' and then added, 'But it's such a shame that he won't be here for very much longer,' she felt her heart sink, and knew Sylvia was reminding her. And at the end of dinner, as they all filed out of the dining room, when Cora stood in the doorway, saying, 'Oh Cecily, do please wait here with me a moment,' Cecily was sure it was going to be about Jack; that Cora, too, perhaps wished to remind her of the opportunity he had ahead of him; that nothing should stand in his way; that attachments were superfluous at this stage in his life. And as the others disappeared from the room, she was already practising one line: *I understand everything*.

So when Cora whispered to her, barely audible, and beginning, 'I don't wish to put you under any pressure, dear, but I need to warn you about *him*,' Cecily was already nodding, already saying, 'I understand everything.' She failed to hear the last two words of Cora's sentence: *John Abel*. And, intoxicated by the evening, the wine, the words, the possibilities, and the giddy feeling that others – in their concern and warnings – had her best interests at heart, she went on, adding, 'Sylvia has already spoken to me about him and I understand.'

'Sylvia?' Cora sounded surprised.

'Yes. She didn't need to say a lot, and neither do you.'

'I see,' said Cora. 'Well, it seems dear Sylvia is ahead of me – in all things.'

'And don't worry, I shan't say anything to him.'

Cora appeared aghast. 'I should hope *not*. He must know nothing. Nothing at all!'

It was then, at that moment, Cecily noticed her eyes – intense and glistening, bright with tears. And so she reached out and took hold of Cora's hands. She said, 'I was not expecting . . .' then she paused, searching for the right words. 'You must remember that up until quite recently I had no idea of his or your existence . . .' she shrugged. 'Neither of you were here, in Bramley. And yet, you and he and all of this has changed me, and changed the way I see the world. But I know, I understand, the timing. I *do* understand.'

Cora closed her eyes. 'Well then, we should perhaps leave it be.'

'But there's one thing, one thing I must tell you,' Cecily said. 'He'd quite like to know more about you, simply in order to understand who he is.'

'Who *he* is?' Cora repeated. 'No,' she said emphatically. She

163

shook her head. 'I'm afraid it cannot be.' Then she released Cecily's hands and walked away, into the hallway and then on into the drawing room. Cecily followed her. As she entered the room, Jack stood up. He helped himself to two of Cora's Venetian cigarettes and asked Cecily if she'd care to join him. And so they returned to the veranda and sat down side by side in wicker chairs, looking out over the pale evening sky.

He smiled as he asked her, 'So, are you going to tell me what it was my grandmother wished to speak to you about?'

She turned and smiled at him when she said, 'No.'

He sighed. 'Secrets, eh? Do all women keep secrets?'

'Hmm, possibly . . . probably, but I imagine men do too.'

He laughed. 'Well, I don't but I suppose there's till time for me to accumulate a few.'

'Plenty of time.'

'And no doubt at Cambridge . . .'

'No doubt.'

'I'll be going off there in a matter of weeks.'

'Yes, I know.'

'I have to go up before term starts to sort out lodgings, that sort of thing.'

She nodded.

'Will you go back to the school? Continue teaching?' he asked.

She shrugged. 'I suppose so.' Then she said, 'Oh well, it'll be Christmas before we know it.'

He looked down at the ground. 'I'm not sure I'll be here at Christmas. I've been invited to Neufchatel. Noel's parents have a place there . . . and I've sort of said yes.'

'How wonderful.'

He turned to her. 'But I'll definitely be back here next Easter.'

She stared ahead. 'I may be travelling then.'

'Really? You're going away?'

164

'Oh yes. Did I not tell you? I'm going away with my aunt.'

'No,' he shook his head. 'You never said.'

'Yes. France, Germany, Austria, Switzerland . . . and Italy, too, I think.'

'So you'll be away for some time?'

'Mm.'

After a while he said, 'Will you come out for a spin with me? You really must, you know. Not tonight, of course, but perhaps tomorrow, or . . . Monday?'

'Monday . . . I'm not sure.'

'Well, think about it. I'll take you out from here, we can go down the cinder track.'

When they returned to the drawing room, Madeline was already on her feet. The light was fading, she said, and they must get home before darkness fell. Then they all shook hands, and a maid appeared to show them to the door.

Cecily did not hear a word her mother said as they walked home. In the space of a few hours she had been raised up into that pink and orange sky – then dropped. Or that's how it felt. For now she saw only the long winter ahead. She saw time stretching out – the months, seasons and years to come – and herself slowly shrivelling, shrinking, drying up; withering in Bramley. And she saw Jack Staunton in a place called Cambridge, surrounded by impossibly glamorous and erudite young people, and beautiful young women. She felt such a fool. What on earth had made her think that he could ever be interested in someone who had been nowhere and done nothing?

As her mother closed the front door, she said, 'Oh, Ethne must be back,' but already Cecily was halfway up the stairs pulling the pins from her hair; already she saw herself as the *one girl* who had gone overdressed to dinner.

Chapter Eleven

When Sylvia found the small brown envelope on the table in the drawing room, the first thing that struck her was that it was in the wrong place. Unopened post belonged on the silver salver on the hallway table. Cora only moved letters from there when she was ready to open them, and then always at her desk. This letter, Sylvia could see, remained sealed, unopened. Picking it up, she noted the hand, small and somewhat malnourished, and the strange spelling. But people had forever been confounded by the name, and Cora was used to being addressed in a variety of fashions (once, Sylvia could recall Cora telling her, even 'Her Royal Highness' had prefixed the misspelt name). But this was a brown envelope which, upon feeling it, contained nothing more than a flimsy, insubstantial sheet. A bill? Perhaps. Turning the envelope, Sylvia could see that it was not properly sealed, easy enough to open. But as she lifted it up to the lamp, leaning forward to examine it further, the door opened.

To Sylvia's mind Cora overreacted. She was not snooping, not at all. She was simply concerned that this was yet another of those wretched letters. And she wished nothing more than to protect her friend. But oh, how Cora had gone on, saying that Sylvia had no right to be 'prowling' about the place, rifling through her papers and letters. What was it, exactly, that she was looking for? she asked, sounding angrier than Sylvia had ever heard her. But she gave Sylvia no opportunity to reply, for she went on, saying, 'Had I known you wished to play detective whilst here I should never have invited you.'

Sylvia tried a number of times to speak, to explain, but Cora would not stop. 'You were about to open that envelope, Sylvia, I saw you. No, don't even try to deny it. I was here, standing right here in the doorway, watching you. Do you wish me to read it to you? Do you wish me to read every one of my letters to you? Is that what you want? Must I show you every single part of me, my life? Am I to be allowed no privacy at all? And all of you . . . all of you crowding in on me, demanding answers . . . wanting to know everything, every tiny detail!'

Her breathing, always a problem, had become quite rapid and she raised a hand to her chest as the words tumbled forth. Her face was flushed, shining, and strands of her white hair stuck flat to her brow, wet and dark. When she finally sat down, breathless and still clearly agitated, she grimaced as though in pain, and Sylvia rushed to her side and laid her hand upon her forehead. 'You have a temperature, dear. A fever,' she said, reaching for the bell on the wall. 'We must get you to your bed.'

Cora remained silent as Sylvia led her upstairs to her room, cooing words of contrition. 'You should know by now I'd never do any thing to hurt you . . . only your best interests at heart . . . always have . . . always have.'

When Cora's maid appeared, Sylvia moved aside and stepped out of the room into the lobby. She could hear Cora saying something about it all being too much for her, and the maid softly hushing and fussing. When the maid finally emerged through the doorway, Sylvia stepped back into the lamplit room to say goodnight.

'Don't think I don't know . . . I know everything,' Cora said, without looking at Sylvia. She was not lying flat and not quite upright, but propped by a multitude of white linen pillows, against which her hair, now plaited in two thick ropes, all but disappeared. In the great galleon of a bed she suddenly appeared very small, Sylvia thought, small and frightened. And it was the same fearful look Sylvia recalled having seen before, a very long time ago.

'You've been talking about me to Cecily . . . talking about *him*.'

'Him?' Sylvia repeated. She presumed Cora meant George. 'I most certainly have not,' she replied. 'But that girl is determined, oh yes, you mark my words.'

'You're all determined . . . won't be satisfied until I've lost my senses and been committed . . . like her, and like John Abel.'

Sylvia stood at the end of the bed. She ran her hands over the sheet. 'Hush now, you must rest, dear. I shall tell Jack that—'

'You shall tell Jack nothing,' Cora said, fixing her eyes on Sylvia.

'All I meant was—'

'You shall tell Jack nothing,' she said again.

Sylvia hovered, watching Cora's hands plucking at the bedcover.

'You were always there for me, weren't you, Sylvia?'

'Yes, indeed I was, and I still am.'

'Yes, always there for me . . . always able to tell me about George's new lover, the very latest rumour.'

'Aha, so that's what this is all about. You've been remembering Evie Dip—'

'No! Don't say it! I don't want that name uttered in this room! I don't want to hear that name now or ever again.'

Sylvia had been the one to tell Cora, the one who had written to her in Paris of the Dipple Affair. She wrote to Cora that she had heard from various 'reliable' sources that George had become *quite obsessed* with his latest sitter. She had mentioned the girl's age, telling Cora that it was *the talk of all London*.

'But I had no intention of . . .' Sylvia began and then stopped. There was no point. Cora was, Sylvia thought, delirious, quite delirious. So she simply bid her friend goodnight. But as she turned to close the bedroom door she heard Cora mutter something about *revenge*.

'I'm sorry, I didn't quite catch that,' she said.

'It wasn't revenge . . . my marriage, it was never about revenge . . .'

'Of course,' she replied. 'Goodnight, dear.'

Minutes later, when Sylvia eventually located Jack, sitting on the candlelit veranda, doing nothing but staring out into the dusk, she stopped in her tracks and stood perfectly still for a moment, struck once again by the likeness. The profile could be him, she thought: George, before he grew his beard. And she could not help but wonder if it was in fact Jack's presence that was tipping Cora. For how must it feel to have him there? The only one left, all she had left: a constant reminder.

She sat down beside him, explained to him that Cora had retired for the evening and that she was not at all well. She was concerned, she said, for her well-being and for her state of mind. But like all young people, it seemed to her, he was distracted, and spoke only in short sentences containing those ubiquitous words – *age* and *heat*.

'She has a fever, Jack. She was quite delirious. I wasn't going to mention it to you, I don't want to worry you, but . . . she accused me of spying, snooping on her.'

He turned to her. 'Do you think we should send for the doctor first thing in the morning?'

'I'm not sure. She hates doctors, has never had any time for them. I told her that she should remain in her bed tomorrow. Her room is cool . . . I think she needs to rest.'

'You're a very good friend to her, Sylvia,' he said.

She could have told him things then, could have told him how betrayed and hurt she felt, how very odd Cecily Chadwick had been with her the other day, her suspicions about that girl, and about Mr Fox. And she could have told him about the letters, and about George Lawson, and Edward. But when he yawned, stretched out his legs, then turned to her and said, 'You know, Cecily writes. She's working on a novel,' Sylvia simply smiled.

He sat up in his chair. 'She wants to write a book based on Cora's life.'

She stared ahead. 'Oh, really? I rather thought that was my role.'

'Ah, no, nothing like a memoir. A sort of mix of fact and fiction, I suppose, something *loosely* based on her life. I think she's made quite a few notes, has begun working on it.'

'Well, well.'

'I thought you might take a look. I told her I'd ask you . . .'

Sylvia rose to her feet.

She was not a violent person, had never struck or been struck by anyone, but right at that moment, had Cecily Chadwick been there, she thought she might very well have slapped her. She said, 'Oh, I shall have to see, Jack. I'm rather busy, as you know, with your grandmother's memoirs, and finishing off my own novel.'

Jack nodded.

He was not to know, she thought. He was innocent in all of this. But as she moved towards the doorway back into the house, another thought came to her, and she stopped and turned to him. 'As a special favour to you, I shall take a look at Cecily's book, the one she's writing about Cora's life. It makes sense for me to see it. After all, I *was* there.'

'Thank you, Sylvia,' he said, smiling.

Upstairs, Cora had returned to Italy.

She dreamt of that time so long ago, when George announced, 'I have to go. It's a tremendous opportunity for me.' And she was young and she was desperate, and she was begging him to stay in Rome with her. He said, 'I'll be back, I promise. I'll be back in the autumn.'

It was shortly after George's departure that Cora married Jack Staunton, her aunt's stepson. She gave birth to Freddie five months later. George did not return to Rome; already, by then, he was famous and much in demand. The Queen had bought his 'Madonna', Cora read in the English newspapers. And it was via those newspapers she caught up on the events in his life, often weeks after they had happened. From time to time she received first-hand reports: he had attended some party, been present at someone's wedding, been in Paris, or Florence, or Munich, but not Rome, never Rome. She heard that he moved within the highest echelons of English society, was a regular dinner guest at Buckingham Palace, counted dukes and duchesses amongst his closest friends, was courted and feted, and hailed as 'England's greatest living painter'. Royal patronage, it seemed, had catapulted him into a different stratosphere.

And she had heard the gossip, the rumours about the women in his life. But those whom he chose to escort and appear in public with, and those he allegedly entertained in private were quite different.

She pictured him, then, in glittering company, and wondered if he ever thought of her, ever wished her by his side. And sometimes, lost in a daydream, she allowed herself to indulge in fantasy once more. She imagined herself with him, standing under a bright chandelier. 'Your Grace,' he would say, holding on to her hand, 'I don't believe you've met my wife . . .'

She had not been angry, could never be angry with him. He had not known. And he could not know, not then, not ever, that she had given birth to his son. Aunt Fanny had said so, and had dealt with the crisis swiftly. She had spoken to her husband, and the marriage had been arranged within weeks. Freddie came early, Fanny told everyone, though Cora knew there was gossip.

And the gossip continued about George, also.

His relationship with his patron, Mrs Hillier, the woman who had introduced him to society in Rome and was his most devoted advocate and champion, had come under scrutiny. It was reported that the two were inseparable, that the married lady, some years George's senior, was always at his side, and that her husband turned a blind eye. It was reported that the two travelled together frequently to Paris, and that Mrs Hillier, a former opera singer, acted as hostess at the many dinners and musical soirees at George's home in London. Some suggested that George Lawson was using the well-connected older lady, that his ambition knew no bounds, and that his success was in no small way due to Mrs H's introductions.

But Amy Hillier had long dazzled everyone in Rome, particularly Cora's aunt. An invitation to one of her musical soirees had become a highly sought-after ticket of entry to the exclusive expatriate set. It had been at Mrs Hillier's sumptuous home on the Pincio Hill, with its long windows and sunset-coloured walls, that Cora had first met George, though she had heard his name before that day, heard that George Lawson, the most promising English painter in a lifetime, had come to Rome.

She and George had spoken together only briefly that night, although they had exchanged many glances. Mrs Hillier barely left his side. It was just as Cora's aunt had predicted when she said, 'Mrs Hillier has a new raison d'être: his name is George Lawson.' That evening Cora had been introduced to any number of people: various English aristocrats wintering in Rome, politicians, Austrian and Italian counts and countesses, and a coterie of English and American artists and writers. And she was introduced to George's father as well, who had been passing through Rome on his way to Greece. It was also the first time Cora had heard the famous diva, Mrs Hillier, sing, though she had heard tell of the exquisiteness of her voice, and would later say that it was Mrs Hillier's *bel canto* that finally stirred her from an adolescent slumber.

Some years later, when Mrs Hillier returned to Rome with her husband, Cora found herself once more on the Pincio Hill, when she and her aunt were invited to tea. She learnt that George was working in Florence. Mrs Hillier had visited him en route to Rome and spoke of him at some length, saying that she was worried about his health; that he worked much too hard and had had such problems with his eyes. Cora's aunt nodded sympathetically throughout, then asked, 'And will we see him here in Rome?' But Mrs Hillier said not. He would be returning to London from Florence, she said, glancing at Cora.

It was in fact Cora's aunt who insisted she take up Mrs Hillier's invitation to join her house party at Lucca. And the doctor had already suggested that a change of environment would be good for her. He told Cora that her melancholia was due to nothing more than a sensitive disposition. And he suggested to her that another baby would set things right.

But how could there be another baby? Jack never touched her, had no desire to touch her. He was sometimes kind and affectionate, and he undoubtedly loved little Freddie, but he was not and never had been her lover. Their marriage had been arranged, hastily arranged. It was not what a marriage should be. And she told him so, in their increasingly frequent whispered arguments. He said, 'But what more do you want? I've given you my name.'

She was – she had known from the start – simply the wrong sex for Jack's tastes. And yet she was grateful to him, for though the marriage was a sham, a respectable sham, he had married her and given her son his name. Whilst Jack's father remained in denial, oblivious to his daughter-in-law's predicament, Cora's aunt knew. 'One can't have everything,' she told Cora, alluding vaguely to her niece's circumstances. 'And you should consider yourself fortunate, very fortunate. You have a husband *and* a child you love.' A passionless life was, it seemed, the price to be paid for a youthful intoxication, the penalty for having loved outside convention.

When Cora spoke of the excursion to Lucca to her husband, he had been his usual distracted and dismissive self. 'Yes, why not? You should go,' he said, without looking up from the *Giornale di Roma*.

There had been no mention of George when Mrs Hillier first suggested the trip, though Cora had privately wondered if he would be there, if he would join the party. Two days before she was due to leave Rome, she discovered that George was to meet up with them at Florence and come on with them to Lucca.

It would be their first meeting in almost four years.

Chapter Twelve

She wishes he were dead, hopes he'll catch the consumption or the cholera, or step out in front of a carriage and be trampled to death by horses. He calls her 'my pretty' and she turns away. He says, 'Don't be like that now . . . come here.' And because she's alone with him, she has to go to him and sit on his lap. 'My pretty,' he says, stroking her hair . . .

The sun rose early over Temple Hill, breaking through a narrow gap of pale chintz, throwing a searchlight over Cora's bed, her pillow, her face. She had had another difficult night of interrupted sleep and broken dreams and was exhausted. Now, the effort of another day – and within it another lifetime – seemed almost too much. For what would she remember this day? How many times would she be confronted and challenged by her own memory?

She lay still for some time, cogitating, deliberating, pushing away, reordering people and events, sequences and words. She was used to the heat, used to the light, but she was not, and never would be, used to the weight of years, or that unyielding inflexibility that had become so much a part of her body. Resistance, she thought, had made her like this, for she knew that the mind and body were inextricably linked, and that much – perhaps all – of the weight of her burden was due to her fight against it. And hadn't it started when she was still young? Hadn't it started with George? With that need to be someone unstained, without blemish, or past or future? But no, it was not right to blame him. Too easy, too easy, she thought.

The situation she found herself in was her fault and no one else's. She had returned there knowing that she would perhaps be found. 'A place where no one will find me . . .' she said out loud, and then closed her eyes. She had wanted to speak to Cecily about the letters, had wanted to tell her – and she had had the opportunity, after dinner, when Cecily freely admitted she had been *changed* by what she knew. But what did Cecily know? And how could she, Cora, tell her anything without knowing what, exactly, she knew? It had been a perplexing conversation. He was desperate, Cecily had said. Yes, of course he would be. But was it him? Was it really the farmer, John Abel, sending the letters, reminding her?

'It could be any one of them . . .'

She turned her face to the window. The light was quite different, not of the same quality as Italy. She could hear someone outside beneath her window, the sound of sweeping, whistling, and then song. And the light and the song, and the sudden and fleeting sensation of another time momentarily lifted her spirits. If she closed her eyes she could be back there in a split second. One of the benefits, the very few benefits, of old age was having that menu of moments: moments to return to and relive, over and over. This was control. And one had to control one's memories, otherwise . . . otherwise they could run rampant, leading one to places and times best forgotten. But oh how they seemed to be running amok on her now. The way to do it, she thought, the way to stop all of this is to train the mind, restore one's history. *I must take control and focus my mind . . . I must remember, I must forget.*

She had never been an early riser and there seemed little to rise for now. Ten o'clock was quite early enough to greet the day, take breakfast – always coffee and rolls – and plan, yes, plan what was to happen. But what was there to plan? What was there to happen? Lunch, and tea, and dinner, a walk about the garden, perhaps. Nothing more arduous. Accounts to be settled, bills to be paid, correspondence to be dealt with – and what would the post bring today?

She wondered what time it was, but the numbers on the clock were blurred. Was that one o'clock? No, Sylvia would have come in by now, come to check on her. Someone would, surely. They would not leave her there, sleeping, dozing, drifting. Perhaps she had been asleep for days, sailing through time. But it was rather nice, to be left alone, to not know the time, not know the day . . . not know.

Sylvia had said not to get up, said that she would see to things. She could remember that. Yes, she could remember that. Sylvia had helped her upstairs to her bedroom . . . But they had had words, harsh words, and it pained her now to think of them. Had she overreacted? Sylvia *had* been snooping, there was no doubt at all about that. She had seen her, holding the little envelope from Mrs Chadwick up to the lamp. And later, when Sylvia had loitered at the end of her bed, guiltily, awkwardly, what was it she had said? Something about Edward?

'Edward,' she said, and sighed.

For a moment she could hear music, a distant serenade, swept over countries and rooftops and into her room. And she closed her eyes once more, drifting back to a wedding in Paris . . .

She can see George standing in a huddle at the other side of the room. He has not spoken to her and he does not look at her. As she moves about the palatial room holding on to the arm of her new husband. She smiles, says hello, kisses people and takes hold of their hands. She turns to her husband and listens to him as he speaks. From time to time he places his hand over hers resting on his arm, and he says her name. But it's not the same. Can never be the same. And yet, what was she expected to do?

'You've been dreaming,' Sylvia said, smiling at her.

The windows in Cora's room were open wide, but the air was thick and hot, and when she tried to speak her words were syrupy and stuck in her mouth. She tried to move, tried to sit up. Sylvia quickly rose to her feet, leaned over her, adjusting the pillows behind her head. She said, 'I've told Jack you're not feeling quite yourself. He's gone off out, said to give you his love, and tell you that he'll see you later.'

She nodded, tried to smile and closed her eyes. She saw Jack and Cecily, and herself and George; he was there, he was not there; and Jack and he were one and the same. She felt a touch, a hand upon her forehead, and in her dream it was him pushing back her hair, stroking her brow. She heard herself say his name and then a female voice, 'No, it's me, dear.' But when she opened her eyes and glanced down, she fleetingly but clearly saw his hand resting upon her own. She saw the lines of his knuckles, his fingernails – the smudges of paint beneath; his gold rings glinting yellow and white, bright white, in the sunshine.

The female voice said, 'But you do look a little better . . . more like yourself. And I've asked Mrs Davey to bring up a tray. Just a scone and some tea, I said.'

She turned to Sylvia. 'What time is it?'

'Half past three . . . and I know you abhor tea being served

178

before four, but you must have something. You've missed break-fast and luncheon.'

She raised herself up, and as Sylvia pushed and pulled at the pillows behind her she wanted to say, 'Please don't . . . please let me be . . . I'd like to be on my own.' She watched Sylvia sit back down, saw her pick up her notebook, then make that kissing noise with her mouth and tap her pencil on the page. Here they come, she thought, more questions. She can't leave it alone, can't let me be.

Questions, once eagerly anticipated and enjoyed, now seemed relentless, intrusive. And she was certainly in no mood for them today. It felt too close, too raw. As though the intervening years had been peeled back and the past was there, in that room with her. As though everyone was in that room with her, standing about the bed, waiting . . . but what were they waiting for? She was not about to die. Not yet.

Then, Sylvia spoke again. She asked if she could go over the details of a landscape, said it would help her describe the setting for a particular chapter in her novel, *Lord of Nivernais*.

'I've gone back to it,' Sylvia said. 'Seeing as we're not making much headway on *your* book.'

'Aren't they *all* my books?' Cora asked. 'And anyway, you visited France enough times yourself.'

'No, no, not France, Lucca.'

Cora narrowed her eyes. 'Lucca? You've gone to Lucca?'

'Yes,' Sylvia replied. 'I hope you don't mind. It's where Harriett, my protagonist, and Armand—

'I can't believe you've gone to Lucca. Why Lucca? You could have gone anywhere, taken them anywhere. Why there?'

'Oh Cora, really,' Sylvia stammered, 'it's just a place . . . the place I've put them for their reconciliation. You see, Harriett is returning to Rome, and Armand is now back from the war. I wanted to—'

179

'But why Lucca? It's not on the way anywhere, and which war? You never mentioned any war to me. And you know how I feel about Lucca.'

'Well, I suppose I could move them, place them in Siena, perhaps, but really, I wanted somewhere quiet. And it has to be Italy, you see, because . . .'

Cora did not hear any more. In a split second she had been thrown back half a century, to Lucca.

They had lain entwined as dawn broke through the shuttered window, casting golden stripes across their bodies. He said, 'I never want to leave you.'

'But you will, you will . . . you have to.'

He had to . . .

Cora travelled by train to Florence. The party headed out on foot from the hotel for luncheon with George. But when the moment came, 'Hello, George,' was all she could summon. He asked after her aunt, and Jack, and then he said, 'And your boy? How is Freddie?'

She smiled. 'He is well.'

He sat with Mrs Hillier at lunch and, though as attentive as ever to *her* needs, Cora was aware from his gaze, his frequent glances, that something of the chemistry remained. Towards the end of lunch, when everyone decided to return to the hotel for a siesta, he leaned forward and invited her to take a walk with him, to Santa Croce. As they strolled through the streets arm in arm, he told her about the Italian sculptor with whom he was working, and Cora listened, slowly coming alive for the first time in four years.

Within the Gothic splendour of Santa Croce, and with her arm linked through his, they walked along the monumental walls, surveying the marble tombs of Dante, Galileo, Vasari and

Michelangelo. They lit candles and sat down, side by side, in contemplative silence in a shaft of warm light.

'Not homesick for your beloved Rome, I hope?' he whispered.

'No, I needed to get away – you have no idea how much.'

'Oh, but I do. It's why I asked Amy to invite you.'

She turned to him. '*You*? You asked Mrs Hillier to invite me?'

He looked back at her, frowning. 'I heard . . . that you've been unhappy.'

She glanced away. 'A little,' she said.

'I don't like to think of you unhappy. I always imagine you smiling, always smiling. And I wanted to see you . . . It's been a long time.'

Even then, she had wanted to wrap her arms around him, to tell him about Freddie and explain her marriage to Jack. She wanted to tell him everything. But she simply smiled at him and said, 'Yes, too long.'

Early the following morning the party set off in two carriages, travelling from Florence to Prato, then on via Montecatini to the house, three miles east of Lucca, arriving as night fell. But that evening, on a terrace ablaze with torches, candles and brightly coloured paper lanterns, Cora felt awkward, in awe of the assembled company and, in particular, of their hostess, Mrs Hillier. Dinner was served late in the large but simply furnished dining room, where four ostentatious silver candelabras lined the long table. Cora sat between George and an American, named Grant Duvall.

'Alicia and I just adore Florence, but Rome . . . Rome was a disappointment. I'm not sure what we expected but it's a mess of a place. It needs tidying up; and it needs a different government! And you know, there's no mention in any guidebook about the smell, the aroma di Roma! Anyway, we won't be going back, not unless all those pretentious English expatriates and fugitives move out!'

When the conversation moved on to politics, Garibaldi and the supposed imminent reunification of the Italian states, Mrs Hillier held everyone's attention. She knew Giuseppe Garibaldi, knew everyone, and spoke with authority on the very latest political developments. And George, Cora noted, sat in spellbound silence as he listened to her speak. He respects her, she thought; he loves and respects her.

The following morning, afraid she had overslept, Cora hurriedly dressed and went downstairs, but the place was quiet, no one stirred. She walked out on to the terrace, where the hum of cicadas and sound of a nearby stream soothed her haste. Here and there, the mist of night lingered, clinging to the curves and sloping vineyards beneath her. A valley of pale umber and myrtle, the shapes of cypress and pine, and high up in the distance the walls of an ancient fortification glinted in the morning sun.

Somewhere beyond it all is Rome, she thought. And she imagined her son asleep in his bed, and wished she were there, at home in Rome.

Those first few days had been spent idly. There were walks and picnics. Mrs Hillier was carried across the bumpy terrain in her *chaise à porteur*, while Cora and the others walked on ahead in search of the perfect location for lunch. Each evening there were *tableaux vivants*, readings, poetry recitals and charades on the terrace. Cora adopted the role of observer, and learnt much from watching the dynamics at play. She was able to see how Amy Hillier orchestrated proceedings, commanding the attention of her guests with an obvious need to be centre stage, and yet at no time appearing overbearing or insensitive to her friends. But Mrs Hillier was a seasoned hostess, and a performer, Cora concluded.

She was able to see for herself the intimate bond between George and his patron. But she was no longer jealous. She realised that her friend John Clifford had been right all those years ago when he had told her that George's relationship with the older woman was based upon mutual need. And it was obvious, obvious to her, that George respected and admired Mrs Hillier. And he was undoubtedly grateful for her support. After all, it was she who had launched him on his path to success. His talent, good manners, his educated background and love of music had enthralled Mrs Hillier from the start, even before he officially became her protégé. But now Cora realised that George and Amy Hillier had a great deal in common: they were both perfectionists, and egotists, absorbed in a private, mutual admiration.

It had been towards the end of that first week at Lucca that George asked Cora if she would sit for him. He wanted her to pose outside, on the loggia, and at first she was not sure. She had sat for him before, years before. But her shape had altered, become fuller, more curvaceous, and that confidence of youth and lack of inhibition had been replaced by the modesty of a mother, and a respectable married woman. She knew Jack would be furious, knew she should refuse.

'No. I don't think so.'

'Please?'

'But I'm too old to sit for any painter now, especially you, George.'

'No. You're perfect. Please?'

He wished to paint her in a Grecian-style robe, and it had been Lottie Davenport, the retired American actress, who had insisted that she should be the one to style Cora, taking her upstairs to see what they could find. And so, in a white muslin sheet with an ornate brooch pinned to her shoulder, and a belt of twisted silk tied around her still slender waist, Cora had returned to the loggia, where George, with Clifford's help, had arranged the scene already set in his mind's eye. Lottie then suggested to George that Cora's hair be loose and flowing, something which embarrassed Cora more than the frayed sheet she had been bullied by Lottie into wearing.

'Really? Why does my hair need to be down?' Cora asked.

'Because no one in ancient Greece wore their hair in a modern up-do!' Lottie replied.

'That's not strictly true, Lottie. I've seen paintings of Grecian women – goddesses – with their hair taken up,' Amy Hillier interjected, before looking at Cora and adding, 'But it would certainly be a more romantic vision if you were to have your hair down, Cora.'

George said nothing but smiled at Cora, appealingly. And so, with Lottie's help once again, she disappeared upstairs to unpin her hair.

'I'm not sure my husband would be pleased,' she said, as Lottie unpinned her hair.

'Does he not like you to be admired?' Lottie asked, but Cora made no reply.

'You're a beautiful woman,' Lottie went on, 'and your husband need never know. Secrets are quite often beautiful in themselves, you know,' she said as she brushed Cora's hair. 'We should all keep a part of ourselves for only us to own. We must never share the essence of who we truly are, for then we are lost, well and truly lost.'

'But that means one can never give oneself completely . . . never truly love.'

'I suppose it does. But true love is a curse as much as a blessing, you must know that.'

'I'm not sure I've ever truly loved anyone, apart from my son.'

'Oh, I think you have; I think you know how to love deeply,

profoundly, passionately, but you have not been loved back like that, yet.'

She felt Lottie's hand upon her bare shoulder. 'I think that's George calling. We'd better go back down,' she said, moving away.

Downstairs, the tension evaporated when Lottie blew an imaginary trumpet and then called out, 'My lords, ladies and gentlemen, her Serene Highness Queen Cora of Lucca!'

George smiled. Clifford, pipe in mouth, broke into riotous applause. And Amy Hillier looked from Cora to George but remained silent.

Over the next three hours George made what appeared to Cora to be dozens of sketches, some discarded in crumpled balls upon the floor, others placed on a marble table next to his easel. Eventually, and despite Cora's complaints that her bare feet were cold and that her back ached, George at last began to put paint upon the canvas. Unlike Clifford, he worked silently, lost in the execution of his work, studying each fold of material, each shadow; perfecting the lines and shape of his model's features; scraping off paint with a palette knife, adjusting his composition, perfecting the balance and harmony of his vision.

The others had long since left the makeshift studio and moved inside, and Cora could hear them, arguing and laughing over card games. Part of her longed to go inside so she could sit in a chair, be comfortable and warm. And yet she savoured each moment alone with him, knowing his attention on her was so intense, so complete, his dark eyes moving from her to the canvas and back to her. From time to time, he spoke, asking her to straighten up, move a finger or raise her head, but there was no conversation, and the silence between them seemed only to heighten the atmosphere of intimacy.

He walked towards her, adjusted the sheet where it was knotted at her shoulder, his warm flesh brushing against her bare skin. He lifted the back of his hand to her jaw, gently raising her face, his eyes upon her mouth, her nose, and then her eyes. He touched her hair, arranging it down her back, the tips of his fingers grazing her spine. He stepped away, casting his eyes over her, her body, and smiled. '*Perfetto*,' he said, then returned to his easel and picked up his palette and brush. She could hear his breathing, each grunt and sigh, his tongue in his mouth as it opened and closed in varying degrees of concentration.

And looking back at him over her shoulder, she watched him as he watched her. She studied his face once more: the hooded eyes, the Roman nose, that so familiar high forehead and tousled hair, now greying at the temples. The lips, a mouth she knew so well, and a beard, from time to time tugged and pulled at. The crumpled collar of his velvet jacket, the ruffled silk of his necktie. The concentration in his eyes: the perfectionist at work.

Finally, as the afternoon light began to fade and the air grew noticeably cooler, he looked up at her and said, 'Shall we continue tomorrow?'

'You said an hour or two, George, not a day or two!' she replied, stretching her arms out in front of her, and then up over her head.

'But you're a vision, my perfect vision . . .'

The following morning, as everyone was about to depart on an expedition to the town, Mrs Hillier asked Cora if she would mind staying there with her to keep her company. She had had a headache the previous evening, retiring to her bed early and requesting supper on a tray, which George had taken up to her. But she still felt 'under the weather', she said.

'George enjoys your company very much, Cora. I'm so pleased that you decided to join us here. As you know, I'm sure, he gets bored so easily, can never be in one place for too long,' she said, as the two of them walked slowly down the hillside. 'It's good for him, I think, to see old friends, people his own age . . .' She stopped. 'Though age itself is no barrier to friendship, of course, and really means nothing at all.' She smiled at Cora. 'One person may take a lifetime, fifty, sixty, seventy years to reach the wisdom another attains in thirty. We are all different in our ability to acquire knowledge, to mature and learn; it is not dependent upon a number. The ability and rate at which one learns from experiences is in itself fascinating. There are those who take a lifetime and learn very little, and others whose hunger to learn the lessons of life enables them to gain wisdom from a tender age. I have met idiotic and immature old men, no more than little boys, devoid of any wisdom or clarity, and I have known exceptionally wise young men, custodians of great knowledge. Dear George falls into the latter category of course.' She paused and smiled. 'And happily, he does not see my age, only my wisdom. We are kindred spirits, you see, and have probably shared many lifetimes together before this one.'

'Do you truly believe that?' Cora asked, remembering her aunt's word for people who held such views: 'pagans' she called them.

'Yes I do. There are people we meet who are so familiar to us, not in their physical appearance perhaps, but in their aura. Instinctively we recognise them and feel an inexplicable but deeply powerful connection. It is the recognition of a kindred soul. You see, Cora, the soul is immortal. Have you never felt that rush of familiarity upon a first meeting?'

'Yes, indeed I have, but I've never been able to understand it, and I'm not sure I'm able to believe in reincarnation. It would be nice to think we are reborn, but where does that put heaven and God?' she asked, looking up at the cloudless sky.

'Does one have to be exclusive of the other?' Mrs Hillier asked.

'No, perhaps not, but if we keep on returning to a physical body, at what stage do we ascend to heaven?'

'When we have acquired wisdom; when we have learnt all there is to know about ourselves. What did Socrates say? "Know thyself"? I think we have to know ourselves, and that is the most difficult thing. The most difficult thing!'

When the women reached the bench by the stream, they simultaneously closed their parasols and sat down. Cora could hear the older woman breathing in deeply, as though savouring each sensation, and she felt mildly irritated by her own inability to clear her mind. It seemed a cluttered untidy mess over which she had no control. And yet she knew that beyond that mess of unanswered questions lay vast pools of wisdom.

'I think you know how very dear and precious George is to me,' Mrs Hillier began again after some minutes. 'It is my mission to nurture his talent, to support him in any way I'm able. His well-being is of the utmost importance to me . . . indeed, to the world.'

'Of course.'

Mrs Hillier sighed. 'His art is God-given, a gift from the Almighty. He is not like ordinary men. He cannot allow himself to be encumbered by attachments that will burden him and stifle his creativity. He must have peace – peace of mind, space, freedom from the ordinary and mundane activities which the rest of us are unfortunately so taken up with. No, he cannot be burdened. And it is why he will never marry, why he prefers celibacy.'

Cora stared ahead and said nothing.

'Passion, lust, romantic notions, he knows these things are fleeting, that they will rob him of what he so desperately needs in order to fulfil his life's purpose. Oh yes, he knows this, he knows this now.'

Later, that evening, after the others retired one by one to

their beds, Cora and George were left alone on the terrace. As the candles around them flickered and burnt out, they sat in silence watching fireflies in the blackness. Then Cora said, 'Do you believe in reincarnation, George?'

He turned to her. 'What a question to spring on me! Why do you ask that?'

'Because Mrs Hillier told me today that she believes we have all lived more than one lifetime.'

'Ah, well, Amy has such notions.' He looked away and smiled, obviously familiar with Mrs Hillier's view of the universe. 'I'm not sure,' he said, hesitantly. 'Based on what I've read recently, no, I do not. Science has taken over our theories and seems to be challenging all of our beliefs. And yet it cannot answer all of our questions. But reincarnation? Well, it's a fanciful and rather egotistical notion, is it not? That we are given another chance? That we go on and on. No, I'm not sure I can subscribe to that. But what do you think? You've obviously been pondering this.'

Cora shrugged. 'Of course I would rather like to think I had at least a few more lifetimes ahead of me – one is definitely not enough. But then I am greedy by nature and wish for too much.' She paused. 'It's just that Mrs Hillier, well, she believes you and she have known each other before . . . in other lifetimes.'

He laughed, shook his head. 'She's testing you, sounding you out.'

'But why? Why do that?'

He shrugged his shoulders: 'Perhaps because she's intrigued,' he said, a smile in his voice.

'Intrigued? By me? How ridiculous!'

He turned to her. 'But why does it astound you?'

'Because I am nothing by comparison.'

'You have youth. You have physical beauty. And you know yourself, I think.'

Cora turned to him, her face clearly visible in the moonlight. 'But I am hardly youthful, and as for knowing myself . . .'

'Does your husband know you?' he asked, staring ahead, into the night.

'Marriage is no guarantee of knowledge, George.'

'I always thought marriage, commitment, meant *truth*, opening up one's heart.'

'Opening up one's heart . . . Is that why you've not married yet? Are you afraid to open up *your* heart?'

'Perhaps. But I tell my dear father it's because I've not yet met the right woman, lest I appear a coward . . . which of course is the truth of the matter. The one unalterable truth.' He turned to her. 'I fear I am destined to be on my own now. And that is my sadness. I have everything I ever wished for and nothing at all; no one to share with; no one waiting for me at home; no sons or daughters to climb up on to my lap and tease me and love me; no wife who knew me before my success, who loves me for me, for who I am. And why? Because I chose for it to be so. I chose, didn't I? So, now tell me, how brave am I?'

She rose to her feet. 'I think we should go inside. It's getting cold,' she said.

He reached out, grabbed hold of her hand. 'Tell me you love me . . . tell me you still love me. Tell me you forgive me.'

'George, please.' She pulled her hand free. 'I can't tell you that. I can't, it's too late.' And then she turned and walked quickly towards the house, and as she moved through the open doors she heard someone call out her name: an unfamiliar, broken voice.

Upstairs, in her room, she slammed the door shut and stood perfectly still for a moment. I must leave here, she thought; I should never have come. I must leave here . . . go home. She moved across the room to the wardrobe, began pulling out her gowns, letting them fall in a heap at her feet then sat down amongst them. 'I must go home,' she repeated through tears.

She did not notice the door swing open, or hear it close. And as he fell on to his knees by her side, she whispered, 'I must go, I must go home.'

'My darling, my own dearest . . .'

He took hold of her hands, lowered his head and kissed her palms. 'Forgive me,' he said, and she felt the wetness of his tears slip between her fingers.

'We cannot do this, I cannot . . .' she began, but then his mouth was over hers, his hands cradling her head. And as he ran his fingers through her hair, pulling it loose between breathless sobs, kissing her lips, her face, her neck, repeating her name over and over, she felt his hands move down her body, his fingers untying the lace of her gown, against her skin, exploring, tracing. And with his tears in her mouth, she pulled him closer.

'Who's sad to see you in England, dear?' Sylvia was saying, leaning over her, over the bed. Daylight had faded. It was late in the afternoon, or perhaps early evening, Cora thought. And then she heard herself say the name, 'Edward.' She had not meant to say it; she had heard Sylvia's question and thought it, merely thought it.

'Edward? I don't think Edward was ever sad to see you back here. Was he?' Sylvia asked.

'No, no, sad about George . . . about George and me,' she replied.

'But did he know? I thought he'd never known . . . hadn't realised.'

She raised her hand. 'Sylvia, you must stop. You don't understand.'

191

'Oh, but I do. You see, I never listened to anyone else, only you. And so I . . . I believe you, and I know it was *not* revenge . . .'

She turned to Sylvia. 'I'm sorry, but I must ask you to leave, Sylvia,' she said, clearly and calmly, with complete clarity. 'I want you to leave now.'

Chapter Thirteen

The lanes were bathed in a soft dappled light, and the air, gliding over Cecily's arms and face and through her hair, blissfully cool. The hedgerows, arching branches and trees and fields flashed by in a blur of colour, and the engine throbbed and roared. And sometimes, as they slowed, as they tilted, rounded a corner and changed gear, the machine made a strange and unnerving put-put sound. From time to time they came to a junction and stopped, briefly, then moved on, accelerating down the straight and into the sunshine. And once or twice, when the engine cut out and he had to restart it, he turned to her, smiling, his face half covered by goggles. 'Hold on! Hold on tight!'

Speed: it was, quite simply, intoxicating. Too thrilling for words. He was right. It made her heart thump and made her feel alive. She closed her eyes, savouring the new sensations: the light and shadow swiftly moving over her, over them, light shadow light shadow light shadow; the feel of the air, warm summer air, brushing her skin, moving her hair, her clothes; the sound of the engine, the thrust of its power; and even the spine-tingling, heart-wrenching, nerve-wracking threat of danger.

Speed. It was modern and daring and brave. It was the Future. Or that's how it felt to Cecily that day.

When they reached the Bracken Pond, he pulled over, on to a gritted pathway under the trees. He turned off the engine and pulled off his goggles as he climbed from the bike. He stared at her, smiling broadly, and then laughed. She said, 'Please, don't laugh, don't say anything. I can well imagine what I look like.'

He stepped forward, took her hand. 'But you look wonderful. You look . . . wild and exciting.'

She had received his first note, in a sealed envelope, on the Sunday morning, the day after dinner at Temple Hill. It had been delivered by hand; her reply and the others were posted.

Cecily,

Did we part as friends yesterday evening? I am not sure and this bothers me more than perhaps it should. I sincerely hope that I have not offended you . . . & that we are still friends.

JS

Dear Jack,

Of course we are friends! I was, I admit, a little tired, and rather hot. Perhaps it was that . . .

In haste,

CMC

Dear Cecily,

I think you are perhaps being disingenuous . . . but that may be your prerogative. Either way, I hope that we ARE still friends, and that you are well.

Jack

PS. What is the M in your name?

Dear Jack,

I am very well, thank you, & assure you that I was most definitely not being 'disingenuous'. This misunderstanding has arisen, I believe, simply from an absence of knowledge of each other & of our respective characters.

As ever,

Cecily

PS. The M is for Madeline, after my mother.

PPS. Do you have a middle name/names?

Dear Cecily,

I think you are right with regard to the not knowing, & so, though I am unable to furnish you with any detailed (objective) observations on my own character (and though I could perhaps provide you with names for 'character references'), I can, in the absence of said knowledge, offer the following:

Middle name: George (after my father, of course)

Birthday: December 2nd

Favourite place: the top of a hill near the Bracken Pond

Hobbies: hate the word. Makes me think of a children's toy horse . . . & suggests solitary model-making et cetera.

Ambitions: to learn to fly, and to have an outrageously long & blissfully happy life.

Likes: ski-ing, cricket, the English countryside (about here); Sherlock Holmes & anything else by Conan Doyle; the theatre, the pictures, Lily Elsie; music, my gramophone, Bach, Beethoven, ragtime; meringues, and very cold beer.

Dislikes: Shakespeare, Chaucer, jelly (a pointless food), pomposity & lies.

Enough for now, I think. But I would be grateful for similar from you . . .

Yours,

Jack

PS. I wonder what you are doing at this very minute. I am in the garden, lying under the horse chestnut — writing to you!

Dear Jack,

Yes, I too was in the garden, reading (Far From the Madding Crowd, if you really wish to know).

So, here goes:

Likes: reading (Austen, Hardy, Dickens, George Eliot and almost every English poet), writing, daydreaming (& quite extraordinarily good at the latter); jelly (definitely NOT a pointless food), blackberries (picked fresh from the hedgerow & popped straight into one's mouth), wild strawberries and CREAM; sunsets, long twilights, & storms, wild skies and moonlit starry nights; music . . . Beethoven and Debussy. Honeysuckle, snowdrops, four-leaf clover and forget-me-nots. My bicycle. The smell of hay, the greenness of the beeches, and breezes. (Yes, breezes!) Breathing in the world. Here & now . . . and everything this very minute. And the future — what is to come!

Dislikes: people who pretend to be something other than what they are; cruelty, inequality, and spitefulness; Mr Fox's long sermons, Rosetta's (our maid) stew and dumplings, Ethne's incessant piano practice, and Sonia B's silent, head-throwing laugh. Gossip, supposition and small-mindedness.

Ambitions: to LEAVE Bramley and travel, to write, live in a city, & to attend the opera at least once in my life. And of course to be 'blissfully' happy (surely that goes without saying?)

Favourite colour: violet.

Favourite place: . . . not yet discovered!

Favourite sound: possibly the wood pigeon that I am listening to now . . .

That's about it. I think.

Cecily

Cecily,

Show off! I had already surmised that you are without doubt cleverer than me. Did you perchance see the sunset yesterday evening? I wondered if you were outside . . . was half tempted to come over.

Jack

Jack,

Ha! I was not showing off . . . I was doing my very best to be honest! Yes, I did see the sunset. Mother says it means a storm . . . & almost 100 degrees today. Hard to believe we're in England.

C

Cecily,

Are you free tomorrow? I thought you might like to come out . . . a picnic? Just a thought . . . if you are we could meet here . . . 11 o'clock?

J

Hitherto, the only letters Cecily had received had been from her cousins or Aunt Kitty. And so Madeline, witnessing the arrival of at least two of Jack's letters, had asked, 'Who are your letters from, dear?' And Cecily said, 'Oh, just Annie. She's testing the service for her father.'

'How very enterprising!' Madeline replied.

The first note had made Cecily tremble, more than was warranted by its sentiments, she thought. And she had spent hours thinking of her reply, then penning it, perhaps ten times over, before finally reducing it to little more than a sentence. But after that, it had been easy: a written rather than spoken conversation. Was he flirting? Possibly. But that possibility was the most exciting thing about it all. Jack Staunton was corres-ponding with her. He was not only writing sentences *to* her, he was thinking about her, and that thought alone altered her world, and her consciousness of it.

The evening she had written about her likes and dislikes – outside in the garden – she had felt as though she was sharing something of herself for the very first time. Because no one had ever asked before, because no one had ever focused her mind in that way. What did she want? What did she like? He wanted to know. He wanted to know about her, her thoughts, how she felt, what she saw, how she saw. He wanted to know.

And everything around her – the garden, its colours, the sounds, lack of sound, even the fly-filled air – suddenly seemed more real than ever, and inexorably linked to him: linking her to him, yards away, minutes away. It was an inevitability; it was fate. All of it. Everything. She saw her life flash before her, and she saw him, Jack Staunton, with her throughout. Yes, it would be; it had to be.

That night she had fallen asleep smiling, blissfully happy in the knowledge that she was worthy of his interest, inebriated by the possibilities ahead.

He organised the picnic, telling her he had put it together himself (this, she could believe): hard-boiled eggs, pork pie, cheese, bread and butter, apples, and ginger beer (non-alcoholic, he'd assured her, but after one mouthful she realised he'd lied).

They had lounged about on the rug on the sand, watching ill-clad bathers, the rigmarole of families and children and dogs. At one point Cecily thought she spotted Mrs Moody paddling at the water's edge and ducked down, lying flat upon the rug on her stomach. But no, it was not the village gossip, just someone who resembled her.

'So, what did you tell your mother? Where did you say you were going?' he asked.

'With Annie, of course – to Linford. She's a brick, won't say a thing,' she replied, turning over, sitting up, wrapping her arms around her knees.

'I don't imagine you lie to her often – your mother, I mean.'

'Oh yes I do. Well, not often, but sometimes.'

He lay with his arms behind his head, staring up at the sky. 'It's a rotten business, isn't it? Having to lie, especially when there's no reason. But sometimes . . . sometimes it's so much easier than telling the truth.'

She glanced at his legs, stretched out next to her, the shape of his bony kneecaps and slender calves through the fawn-coloured fabric. His shoes looked expensive, and new; and she wondered if Cora had bought them for him. Above one navy blue sock was a patch of bare, pale skin covered in a down of dark hair. And she had an impulse to reach out and touch that patch of skin – which shocked her.

'I rather think my grandmother lies,' he said, pensive.

'No, surely not,' she replied. 'She might not wish to divulge things about herself, her life, but that's quite different to lying.'

She remembered Cora's words of the week before: 'I have never been a person to place too much store on truth,' she had said, as if declaring it to the world and not just to Cecily. 'The truth is an enigma. I may say that I've never known truth. I have known great love, great pain and loss, but not necessarily truth.'

'You mean withholding the truth?' Jack asked her.

'Gracious, no. I didn't say that. I really don't know . . .'

He sat up. 'But you see, I think you're right, I think that's exactly what she does. I think she offers people a rather sanitised, edited version of events in her life. The only one left to corroborate her version is Sylvia, and she appears to be sworn to secrecy on all things.' He paused. 'I imagine Sylvia could tell me so much, but of course she daren't; she worships the ground my grandmother walks on.'

Cecily smiled. 'She is awfully fond of her, isn't she?'

'Irritatingly so. I rather think poor Sylvia has spent her entire life hanging on my grandmother's every word. She's like a devoted pet, or some lady-in-waiting,' he added, kicking at the sand. 'I've asked her, of course, about my father . . . and about the others.' He turned to her. 'She knew them all, you see, she's been around forever.'

'What did she tell you, what did she say?'

He looked out across the water. 'Nothing. She answers each question with a question: what has your grandmother told you? Don't you think you should ask her? And so it goes on. Good luck to her with the memoirs, that's all I can say. I don't imagine my grandmother has any intention of collaborating on that particular project, which may explain the tension between them,' he added.

'Tension? What do you mean?'

'I can tell that my grandmother's becoming irritated by Sylvia's presence. She's been avoiding her. Yesterday, I found her in the garden, at the temple, and it seemed to me as though she was hiding. She asked, "Where's Sylvia?"' He mimicked his grandmother's clipped voice, and an exaggerated wide-eyed stare. 'And then, later,' he continued, 'Sylvia came up to me and implied that my grandmother was going potty.'

Cecily laughed. 'What did she say?'

'That she was worried, *deeply worried*,' he said with exaggerated emphasis, 'about my grandmother's state of mind. She talks in riddles, that woman. She told me that *it* had happened before, and I had not a clue what she meant, whether she was referring to some former madness in the family or something else. I suppose I should sit down and have it out with her.'

'With Sylvia?'

He turned to her. 'With my grandmother. I should just ask her outright about everything. You see, I'd rather like to know who I am. Does that make sense?'

'Yes, of course,' she replied. 'And I'm sure she'll tell you everything you want to know, if you explain.'

He looked down, shook his head. 'It's a queer thing not to know about one's family, where one comes from.'

'I'm sure there's no great mystery, nothing scandalous.'

He moved forward, resting his chin on his knees. 'But perhaps there was. Perhaps there was a scandal. Perhaps my grandfather's death was not an accident.' He ran his hands through his hair and sighed again. 'And I know – am very much aware – that the only reason she came back here is because of me, my situation. But I have this feeling . . . this . . .' He paused, staring down at the ground, then turned to her. 'She talks around everything. Haven't you noticed? She talks in anecdotes, the same stories over and over, but none of it's real, not to me at any rate. Don't get me wrong, I'm very fond of her, and I recognise that she's . . . elderly, forgetful perhaps, eccentric most definitely,' he added, smiling. 'But there are too many things she won't discuss with me, so what am I expected to think?'

She nodded. What was he expected to think? It was perfectly reasonable that he should want to know about his family, his father and grandfather. Already, perhaps she, Cecily, knew more than he did. But Cora was wise; she would choose her time, know when it was best.

'I don't suppose it's anything sinister, you know. I imagine she's simply being cautious, protective of you.'

'I'm not a child.'

'No.'

They had been there for an hour, no more, when he rose to his feet and said, 'I'm bored of this place. Let's move on.' His mood had changed. He was quieter, reflective, and Cecily wished she could tell him, tell him something. But she had promised Cora. So they gathered up the rug and half-eaten picnic in silence. As they walked back to the bike, Cecily yearned to reach out, to take hold of his hand, his arm, to offer a touch. She said, 'It doesn't really matter who our families were or are. I like to think we can be whoever we want to be.'

He glanced to her and smiled. 'A romantic notion, I think.'

As he pulled on his goggles, he said, 'I want to show you a place. It's not far from here, only ten or so minutes away.' He climbed on to the bike, averting his gaze as she carefully climbed up behind him. Seconds later, they roared off down the road circling the perimeter of the pond.

They climbed up the sandy track hand in hand, through waist-high heather to the top of the hill. And all around them, as far as the eye could see, was heathland: an undulating purple landscape broken only by the shapes of birch and pine. In the distance was the small looking-glass pond, its bathers now almost invisible to the eye, its sailboats tiny white dots upon its sky-filled surface.

'This is where I wanted to bring you, where I've wanted to bring you for some time. Isn't it glorious?' he added, staring up at the sky.

She watched him, his head thrown back, his pale throat exposed, his hand to his brow, as if searching for something above. 'Glorious,' she said.

And then he lowered his head, and staring into her eyes, he moved closer. 'I like to come here and look up,' he said, 'look up at the sky and imagine I'm up there, looking down. Looking down on the world.'

'And what do you see?'

'Sometimes I see you. In fact quite often I see you, sitting alone, reading in your garden, writing your stories,' he replied. 'I see Cecily, and I wonder what she's thinking.'

She smiled. 'Perhaps she's thinking of someone called Jack Staunton, wondering what he makes of her.'

He lifted his hand to her cheek and moved closer. 'What he makes of her . . .' he repeated, but his sentence petered out as his lips touched hers.

His kiss was achingly tender. So gentle at first that Cecily was the one to move forward, pressing her lips more firmly against his. And as he wrapped his arms around her, drawing her to him, she could feel the world spinning, that vibration, and his heart, her own heart, their lips, that kiss: the moment. He spoke her name as no one had ever before said it, and she knew then and there that no one ever again would express it so.

'I didn't plan that,' he said, looking at her with smiling eyes. 'I didn't bring you here to . . . to kiss you.'

And she couldn't speak. Words deserted her. But she could feel a trembling. A wobbling sensation rising up from the ground through her feet to her legs, and up her legs to her body, her stomach, her chest, her arms and hands and fingers, and neck and head. Even her eyelids seemed to be not completely fixed. And her mouth, lips – still parted, but soundless, wordless – seemed to be caught in that vibration: quivering. For a moment she thought she might cry. She felt tears sting her eyes, as everything around her, already spinning, blurred more.

He reached out, took hold of her hand, lifted it to his mouth and placed his lips there, softly, lingering. And she thought she might fall over. For the earth seemed to be moving quite rapidly now, the sand on which she stood slipping away from under her feet. It must be heatstroke . . . must be the ginger beer, she thought, focusing on a tree, a single tree, trying to steady herself.

'I don't want you to think I'm taking advantage. It's not why I brought you out today . . .'

And she couldn't look at him, couldn't look at his face, his eyes. But she could hear herself breathing, breathing loudly;

or was it him? Everything seemed muddled, blended, too connected . . .

She felt him pull her towards him once more, his arms around her, his hands upon her spine, and she closed her eyes, lifted her face – her lips – to his again. And then her head spun, upside down and all around, and up and down again. And she thought, if he releases me I will surely fall. But he didn't. And even when he moved his mouth away from hers, gently grazing her jaw, he kept his arms around her, and through half-closed eyes she saw his mouth curve upwards at each side.

In time to come Cecily would revisit that moment; that perfect moment. She'd return to that place, that day, reversing the world on its axis, spinning it backwards through sunsets and dawns, and sunsets and dawns and seasons. Sometimes she'd look down from the sky, see two small figures, together, entwined; feel his arms about her once more. And she'd see everything and everyone else, too: the bathers stepping out of the water, shivering and wet; the picnickers on the shore, gathering up rugs and baskets and children and dogs; and the lanes, sleepy and silent and dappled in light, waiting for them to pass through. Waiting for them to pass through once more, young and with hearts fit to burst; young and with lives still ahead; young and with kisses still wet on their lips. And their lips still trembling and damp from kisses; racing through lanes with lips damp from kisses; racing though lanes with skin still warm: his skin still warm.

Chapter Fourteen

he earth is hard. Dampness has permeated the rug beneath them. Jemima is asleep, cocooned within the quilt they share. High above are infinitesimal stars: glistening, eternal. Her father has promised her some shoes when they get to Colchester. There's work there, he says, moneyed folk there, he says. Suffolk's no good, no good now the farmers are all poor. They'll be able to get a room there, have a bed and perhaps a fire, too. And she pictures the room, the bed and that fire . . . and she tries to imagine the warmth. But the soles of her feet are blistered and torn, and her back aches from carrying little Johnny.

Sylvia waited in the garden for Jack. Her bags were packed. She would go, if that were Cora's wish. It had been the mention of *that* marriage, of course, and the word revenge, she knew that. And yet, hadn't she said that she knew it *wasn't* revenge? That she did not care what others had said, that she had only ever listened to Cora? And she had, almost.

Truth was, it had been impossible to ignore the gossip, impossible to ignore the facts. Oh, she could understand it, understand why Cora did it, but there was bound to be talk. George was renowned, famous by then. But he had treated her badly, very badly. That was undeniable. And he had had his chance, and often enough. He had used her. He had slipped in and out of Cora's life as and when it suited him, and never, not once, offered to marry her. In Sylvia's mind he was nothing more than a selfish – albeit talented – bounder. And Cora deserved better, much better.

As soon as Sylvia heard the sound of the motorcycle coming up the hillside she made her way through the bushes on to the driveway, and flagged down Jack. Her words spilled out before he had time to pull off his goggles, and, turning off the motor, he asked her to repeat them. He was shocked, she could see. And she was tearful. He took hold of her hand, told her not to worry; his grandmother quite obviously did not know what she was saying. He would go and speak with her, go and speak with her immediately, he said.

So Sylvia sat in the arbour by the sundial, as agreed; for she would not set foot inside the house until Cora had taken back her words. Her bags were packed, she had told Jack. Cotton could easily be sent for. There was a train at 6.46 p.m.

It took Jack almost half an hour to return to the garden, to Sylvia. But he was full of assurances and told Sylvia that of course Cora did not *really* wish her to leave, particularly not on such bad terms. It was all a misunderstanding, he said, more than once. But he was noticeably perplexed by the escalated quarrel, and, once Sylvia had agreed that she would stay on, at least for another day, he asked how the whole thing started.

'I am in a most difficult situation, Jack,' Sylvia began, 'because your grandmother does not wish me to speak to you . . . about anything at all.'

He shook his head. 'I don't understand.'

'There are matters to be resolved, things I am not at liberty to tell you, things that she herself is unable to speak about, even now after so many years, even to me. Unfortunately, *others* are forcing the situation.'

'Others?' he repeated. None of it made any sense.

She nodded. 'It may surprise you, but I have been quietly noting Mr Fox's, and your friend Cecily Chadwick's, keen interest in your grandmother's life. I believe their questions, their scrutiny, at a time when Cora is struggling, grappling with deeply personal dilemmas, have simply been too much for her. This, I fear, is why she turned on me. There is no other explanation for her . . . her paranoia.'

Jack, who had smiled as Sylvia said Cecily's name, now looked away, frowning.

'Oh, but there is one other matter that I should perhaps mention.'

Jack turned to her and, after a moment's hesitation, Sylvia made him promise with his hand upon his heart that he would never breathe a word to Cora; would never disclose to anyone her suspicions about the nature of Cora's recent correspondence.

A letter had in fact arrived late that very afternoon. Sylvia had found it lying on the silver salver in the hallway shortly after she had packed her bags. It was in a strange childish hand, not typewritten, and bore a London postmark. It was plain to see that the sender did not know Cora, for the name was not quite right. Had she not been quite so upset, she might have been tempted to take it, tear it up or burn it, Sylvia told Jack. For these letters, she believed, were at the root of Cora's agitated state of mind. She did not tell Jack that this particular letter was different to the others. It was not her place, she decided. But when he rose up from the bench, saying he would fetch and open the damned thing himself, she did not stop him. Minutes later, he returned, empty-handed. The letter had gone. It had been taken up to Cora.

The following morning, heeding Jack's advice to carry on as normal, as though nothing had happened, Sylvia simply smiled and said, 'Good morning,' when Cora appeared and sat down to breakfast. She and Jack had agreed, in view of the circumstances, that Cora needed their patience and protection more than anything else. So Sylvia had tried to make conversation. She said, 'You know, you really should have stayed in your bed. After all, there's nothing happening today.'

Cora stared straight ahead. 'I spent yesterday in bed. I've never been a malingerer and I don't intend to become one now,' she replied.

'Can I get cook to do you some eggs?' Sylvia asked.

She shook her head. 'No, thank you, I'm not hungry. I think I might take a walk.'

'A walk?' Sylvia repeated. 'To where?'

'About the garden. I need a change of air . . . fresh air.'

'I'll get my hat.'

'If you don't mind, I'd rather like to take a walk on my own.' She rose awkwardly from the table, and Sylvia quickly disappeared from the room into the hallway and returned with her cane.

'Thank you,' Cora said, taking the cane, without looking at Sylvia.

Cora knew that Sylvia had spoken to Jack, despite her plea. She knew an allegiance had been formed. She knew that Sylvia would say she was going mad, losing her senses. And perhaps she was. Beneath her clothing she could feel the heat of a fever, still there upon her skin. She felt weak, unsteady on her feet, and in her heart. And her sense of loneliness was more acute than ever.

As she stood on the terrace, looking south, directly into the sun, she closed her eyes: I have outlived them all, and outlived any purpose, she thought. Am I to spend the remainder of my days in hiding, in fear? Will I ever know freedom, be able to breathe?

She moved on, carefully descending the steps to the lawn, nodding to one of Mr Cordery's men as he raised his cap to her. The garden was quiet and a cloudless sky promised another languorous hot day. She walked slowly across the grass, pausing every few steps to look about or upwards, preoccupied. If only there was someone she could talk to. If only she could tell someone the truth. But what was the truth? What were the facts?

'Really, what does it matter?' she said out loud.

'Beg your pardon, ma'am?'

'Another glorious day!' she called out, without turning.

She descended more stone steps, standing still for a moment on the last to look out across the garden. Put things in order . . . I must put things in order for him, for Jack. Perhaps write it down . . . yes, that would be sensible. She stepped on to a gritted pathway. I can only be as honest as I recall . . . what more can I do? She walked under the shade of the pergola, already vaguely aware of a presence – a shadow on the periphery of her vision – flickering amidst the tangle of jasmine and clematis. She emerged from beneath the pergola, sat down on the bench inside the arbour, and looked back across the lawn.

She had seen him there before, conspicuous, incongruous, entirely out of place. This morning he was standing by the sundial, with one hand flat upon the lichen-covered stone surface. He looked so very out of date, over-dressed and old-fashioned, she thought, watching him watching her.

They did not speak. Not in audible words. Their conversations – the few they had had – had been conducted almost entirely in silence. He seemed to prefer that.

She took him in: his hair, a single curl hanging down upon his forehead, his beard, greying, his crumpled trousers, well-worn burgundy velvet jacket and usual necktie. He was, she supposed, about forty. Forever forty.

'You should never have left me,' she said, in barely a whisper.

'I never wished to leave you,' he replied, without moving his lips.

'But you did. You always went back to her.'

'No. There was only ever you.'

'You say that now, but it's too late. It's all gone. Over.'

'I'm here, aren't I?'

She looked away for a moment, irritated. 'No, I am here. I'm here without you, and I don't know what to do, how to be. And I'm no good at being old.'

She saw him throw his head back in a noisy silent laugh. Then he fixed his gaze back upon her. 'You'll never be old. Not to me. Look at you now. How old are you? Twenty? Twenty-one?'

'I was when you first met me. But you've been gone these past twenty years . . . and gone from me long before that.'

She saw him look away, shake his head.

'But I have Jack,' she added. 'You never saw him, never knew him.'

He glanced back at her, frowning, perplexed.

'Not that Jack. That Jack passed away years ago, in Rome, remember? I have another Jack . . . our grandson.'

'Our grandson,' he repeated, silently, smiling. He lifted his hand from the sundial and held it out to her.

'No. No, not yet.'

And she watched him dissolve into the sunshine.

She had had numerous conversations with him like this, and could never be sure when or where he would turn up. Once or twice he had appeared at the most inconvenient times, and she had been forced to ignore him, shushing him off in a glance, lest anyone else should see. Later, she had inevitably felt guilty, had had to apologise to him, explain that she couldn't always be at his beck and call. Life goes on, she had told him. I am back in England now, and the English do not like unannounced callers. She could always make him laugh.

It bothered her, somewhat, that he never quite seemed to know who Jack was and always appeared confused. But it was understandable, she supposed. The only Jack he would recall would be her first husband. And neither one of them ever mentioned him, or the others. They had an understanding, and had never needed names, or indeed words. They shared a tele-pathy that went beyond the grave and was integral to the force that bound them to each other; she had never needed to confirm or deny anything to him. He knew, had always known . . . surely?

But now she reminded herself, he had lived in ignorance about so much – and for so long.

After Lucca, and weeks after Jack's death, Cora had given birth to another George: Geor*gie*. Despite letters, one 'in sympathy', the next promising a visit, and another proclaiming delight at being asked to be godfather and stating that he was 'honoured' she had chosen his name, George did not visit Rome after Jack's untimely death, or for the christening of his godson.

As etiquette decreed, Cora spent two years in mourning. Dressed in black parramatta silk and bombazine gowns, she lived her life quietly and rarely ventured out. She was still young, people told her; she would, perhaps one day, have another husband, more children. But she had had her children by the man she loved and the man she loved had gone. Her two boys, she decided, would be her life; she would be a mother first and foremost.

When Freddie became ill, Cora and her aunt took it in turns to nurse the five-year-old. It was a fever, nothing more. For two days and nights they sat by his bed, watching him doze, bathing his body with cold compresses. But on the morning of the third day, as dawn broke across the city, and as her aunt finally gave in to sleep, Cora noticed her boy's breathing become more laboured. She climbed up on to the bed, folding his small body into her arms, holding him close; willing his heart on. She ran her fingers over the curves of his face – his cheeks, his nose, his mouth – memorising the softness, each rise and fall, each undulation; those pale purple-veined eyelids fringed with long lashes; that high brow and dark chestnut hair. And in that final hour, she prayed to every saint whose name she could recall, and to every god of every creed; she bargained with them, made promises to them all.

The sun had set by the time Dr Small convinced her to release the dead boy from her arms – still rocking. 'He cannot hear your lullaby now. He is gone, my dear. You must let him go . . .'

Two days later, Cora watched her son's tiny coffin as it was lowered into the ground outside the city walls. And that night, after she had been found, and after Dr Small had been called once again, she lay on her bed and quietly told her aunt that she knew with certainty that there was no God. 'Look at me, what has he done for me? Everything I love he takes away, everything I beg him for he snatches from me . . .'

From that day onwards Cora rarely, if ever, spoke of Freddie. And thus, over time, people forgot; forgot that she had in fact had two sons, not one. But in the locket round her neck she kept a curl of dark chestnut, five-year-old hair.

Freddie's death swept away the last remnants of girlish fantasies, certainly any girlish fantasy of a romantic hero. No one, it seemed to Cora, was going to rescue *her*. Happy-ever-after endings belonged to novels and, perhaps, to those her aunt referred to as 'people of quality'. For their journey had not started as hers had, they had not had to flee from anything. Sometimes, in quiet moments, she would unravel the thread of her life and work backwards, revisiting that season when she and George had first met. If he had married me, she thought, how different my life would be, how different I would be. And if I had been *someone* . . . he would have married me.

But there was so much George did not know, had never known. How could he love her? He did not know her. And how could she love a man who had turned his back on her in order to pursue ambition, success?

As Cora's life continued quietly in Rome, George's soared noisily in England, and echoed across the continent. His name appeared more often than ever in the newspaper. It was by then a name everyone knew. And though a few continued to speculate on the nature of his relationship with his patron and constant companion, Mrs Hillier, most in Rome and back in England assumed the bachelor artist and married lady – sixteen years his senior – to be dear friends.

It was the year after Freddie's death, at a ball at the Palazzo Ruspoli, that Cora was introduced to an officer in the French army named Antonin de Chevalier. Dashingly handsome, stationed in Rome, he was younger than Cora by five years. And later, that same winter, three years after he had bid adieu to Cora at Lucca, George Lawson returned to Rome – with Amy Hillier.

In the carriage en route to Mrs Hillier's soiree, Cora tried to explain to Antonin the nature of the relationship between George and the older married lady. But he laughed and simply said, 'Darling, I am not a baby. I know about these things.' Minutes later, after Mrs Hillier had greeted them both in the lobby, he whispered, 'No, I think I am a baby. I do not understand.'

'Not all love is bound by physical attraction, Antonin. I used to think it was, and I used to think it was simply Mrs Hillier's patronage that drew him to her, but now I'm not so sure. Yes, George was always ambitious, but their relationship is . . . is

213

more complex than that. She has a hold upon him I've never been able to fathom. She's not beautiful, not in the traditional sense, but perhaps her soul radiates a beauty for him. I think George became bored by physical beauty long ago; there had to be something more enduring than mere physical beauty.'

'Perhaps, but I hear he is, as you English like to say, a *snub*, and she has good connections, no?'

'The word is snob, Antonin. But no, I don't think so. George is not a calculating man. He would not use someone in such a way, and has no need to. He's a creative soul, an artist.'

'Aha! They are the worst. And Rome is full of them, aristocratic creative English souls, rich and idle and sitting in the Greco putting France, Italy and the whole entire world to rights.'

She moved away from him with obvious irritation.

'Why are you so defensive about the painter and the aged singer?' he asked in a whisper, following her through the room.

She stopped. 'I'm not defensive, Antonin. But when you refer to my friend as a snob, I am *slightly* offended. It is no compliment. You're implying that he assumes some sort of superiority, and I happen to know he's not like that. People misunderstand him, that's all.'

'And you, my darling, do you understand him?'

'Yes, I think I do.'

'He is an old love of yours, yes?' he asked, smiling.

'No, he is not an old love in the way that you mean, but he is an old and dear friend of mine.' She looked up at him and smiled in a conciliatory way.

'*Il est bien beau?*' he said after a moment, looking across the room at George.

'He used to be compared to a Greek god – Jupiter Olympus, I think . . .'

That evening, Amy Hillier's apartment looked as grand and

opulent as ever, like the backdrop to a painting or the stage set of an opera. Everything in her home appeared to be an *objet de beauté*; each and every item carefully and thoughtfully placed to afford harmony and symmetry. Panelled walls, painted dark pink and gold, were adorned with the work of her many painter friends. And a portrait by George now hung above the fireplace, though it often took guests a moment or two to realise that the attractive woman in the painting was in fact their hostess.

Finally out of mourning, Cora wore a gown of deepest burgundy silk, made for her by the latest French dressmaker to arrive in Rome. It showed off her figure to perfection and complemented the rubies adorning her throat: a gift from Antonin.

George stood with his back to Cora, talking to other guests, but as she walked towards him, something of her presence must have stirred him, for he turned as she approached. He took her hands in his, stepped back to look at her and for a moment, neither one of them spoke – or seemed sure how to navigate their conversation. But the moment passed, and it was Cora who charted their territory. It had been a long time since she had attended such a party or been dressed as she was that evening; a long time since she had sipped fine champagne, and a long time since she had stood in front of George, his full attention upon her. She felt exhilarated and bold, and something in her wanted to toy with him and his safely guarded emotions.

'You know, George, I'm so pleased that we've caught up with each other at last.'

'As am I.'

She smiled. 'It's been a while.'

'Too long.'

'Yes, too long . . . feels like a lifetime . . .'

'You've been through a great deal. And I want you to know

215

that I'm sorry, so sorry that I've not been able to visit until now. But I've thought of you, often, and I must say you look remarkably well.'

'Older, wiser,' she replied, glancing about the room.

'I'm sure.' He nodded. 'He was a good man, Jack. I . . . I,' he stumbled, 'I wish I'd had the chance to know him better, and little Freddie, too. I never met him.'

She stared at him. 'No, you never met him.'

'I can't imagine—'

'No, you can't,' she said quickly. 'There's so much you don't understand, George. You're like a child, a cosseted little boy, protected from the truth.'

He looked away and made no reply.

'And there's something I've been pondering for quite some time. It's a secret, but one I may need to explain to you at some stage,' she continued, turning her head, looking about her and sipping her champagne. And as she ran the tip of her tongue along her unpainted lip, she felt his eyes upon her.

'You're angry with me, again . . . and as intriguing as ever,' he said. 'But tell me this secret.'

'I did not say that I would tell you, George dear,' she said, turning to him. 'You see, I wonder *if* and how I should tell you. It might capsize you,' she added, wide-eyed. 'God forbid, it might quell your creativity . . .' She gasped. 'Or even tarnish your reputation!'

'You're mocking me, teasing me, Mrs Staunton.'

'Certainly not, Mr Lawson,' she replied, already giddy from the mix of champagne and sensation of power. 'I know how much you cherish secrets. Didn't you once say to me that a secretive nature is the most alluring, most intoxicating thing in a woman?'

'Did I really?' he answered, playing nervously with his beard. 'Perhaps I did.' He shrugged. 'It was a foolish thing to say and

I'm not altogether sure what I meant by it. The foundation of friendship, true friendship, should always be honesty. I'd like to think that I've been a true friend to you and in turn I hope that you can be candid with me.'

For some minutes they stood in silence. She was aware of George's eyes upon her, and she was determined not to look at him.

'You're playing games with me. Why mention your secret if you have no intention of telling me?' he said, moving closer, beginning to enjoy the clandestine nature of their conversation.

'Perhaps because it's about you.'

'About me?' he repeated. 'Well, it could be so many things, and I would be a fool to venture—'

'Then I don't suppose you shall ever know,' she said, altering tempo and turning to him. 'But I want you to know this, when I stood up and spoke those lines from Byron, all those years ago, they were for you, George, only for you . . . it was all for you, everything.'

For a moment he seemed unable to speak. He stared down at the floor, frowning. Then he whispered, 'I don't know what you want from me . . . I don't understand. I can't—'

'I want nothing from you, not now, other than your friendship.'

'But of course, you have that, and more, much more.'

At that moment the piano stopped and they looked away from each other to clap for a performance neither one of them had heard.

As Amy advanced towards them, Cora said, 'Don't worry, I would never do anything to compromise or embarrass you,' and she placed her hand upon his arm.

'You two are always to be found in a corner together. So what are the secrets you share? Please, do tell,' Amy asked, standing in front of them.

217

'No secrets, simply catching up on idle gossip,' Cora replied. 'Do please excuse me, I must find Antonin,' she added. And as she walked away she heard Amy say, 'Are you quite all right, my dear? You look as though you're in pain.'

Amy Hillier had watched Cora closely that night. But what had she seen? Amy advocated beauty, like youth, too transient to admire on its own merit. Real beauty, she said, radiated from the soul and found its expression in music, art, literature and poetry; it did not wither or age. Later, many years later, Cora realised that Amy Hillier had seen what she herself could not possibly have seen then: that she, Cora, had altered and matured; that the blandness of youth and inexperience had given way to something else. And that life – pain and heartache – had not taken away but had added. And perhaps Amy Hillier had realised then, that night, that there was only one woman able to wield power over George's tightly guarded emotions and upset his equilibrium.

'I was cruel . . . I wanted him to suffer . . . I wanted him to feel my pain, my loss. I wanted him to feel regret,' Cora said now. She stared down at the lawn in front of her, parched and dry; thirsty, she thought, like Chazelles. The grass had always been thirsty there, too, would never grow like English grass . . .

No, she had never told him, she thought, returning to that memory. But she supposed he knew, had always supposed he knew. And then, at the end, hadn't she told him? Hadn't she raced to him to tell him that *their son* had died, and hadn't he placed his hands over his head and wept like a baby? 'But how could he not have known? I tried to tell him, tried so many times. And they looked so alike . . .'

It was then, at that time, she thought, that she had finally told George about Freddie, too. Freddie, who had died so long ago; Freddie, whom he had never met. Yes, she had told him on his deathbed that he had fathered not one but two sons. But it was not to hurt him, not then. She told him because she wanted him to know that she had loved him enough to raise his sons alone, without him. Because she wanted him to know how much she had loved him. She wanted him to know and understand.

She looked up, saw her younger self running barefoot across French grass chasing a small boy, and he, standing under the shade of trees, watching them, laughing. He had flitted in and out of their lives, Uncle George, famous Uncle George. She had not been his wife, had not been his mistress, not the acknowledged one, at any rate. She had been the mother of his children, kept in the shadows, overseas.

For years Cora had hoped – indeed, longed – for George to return to her, to declare his love to her. But his life, always a complex, compartmentalised world, became even more so. His talent, his fame and, more importantly it seemed, his reputation had trapped him. He inhabited another world, was part of an establishment foreign to Cora in every way, and the respectable public image of the English aristocratic painter, the image on which his commercial success had been built, served only to force his deeply private nature further into hiding. He carefully nurtured his public persona and vehemently guarded his private life. And as a close friend of the Prince of Wales, he lived at the very epicentre of fashionable London society. But there had always been gossip about him. He had once been rumoured to be having an affair with a notable duchess and, before that, embroiled with a former mistress of the Prince of Wales. He had moved on, and then on again.

There had still been Mrs Hillier, of course, and Cora had had no doubt that there were others, younger and prettier, and hidden away from public view. Once, over dinner in Paris, George had confided to her that he was neither inspired by nor attracted to the respectable eligible women of his class. And she had wondered if the rumours were true about the 'sitters' with whom he was reputed to have affairs.

But Cora made no demands. How could she? Clifford had been right all those years ago when he told her that George could never be owned; that he was owned only by his art, his vocation. So, instead, she had valued their friendship, and took comfort in *it* and her knowledge of him, the years that they had known each other. And she had her son; she had Georgie.

She raised her head to the sky. Hard to believe it was an English sky. Hard to believe it was the twentieth century. 'Nineteen eleven,' she said out loud, and she shook her head. It sounded absurdly futuristic. For she wasn't yet used to the twentieth century, the sound of it, its dates and strange fashions and new-fangled gadgets, and the year nineteen hundred seemed but a moment ago, or still in the future. But it had come and gone, and then, another decade. And I am here, she thought, in nineteen eleven, in England.

He had always said, 'You're too vibrant and colourful for England, too much of a free spirit, they won't be able to let themselves trust you . . .' And hadn't Edward warned her, too, all those years ago, that the dream would end, that it had to? That she would, eventually, leave Rome and return to England?

Edward . . .

But she did not wish to think about him, not now. 'It was a mistake . . . a mistake,' she said, rising up from the bench.

She walked towards the wrought-iron gate. A jackdaw flew up from the trees overhead, squawking as it rose into the blue. She could hear Mr Cordery's voice in the distance, the hum of a mowing machine. She stood by the gate for a moment, then turned and looked back across the garden, tapping at the earth with her cane. Had I done things differently, if I could have done things differently . . .

Then she heard them, the voices, all talking at once, still desperate to be heard.

'He was always so *ambitious*.'

'A snob!'

'A social climber!'

'And so fond of a title.'

'You simply weren't good enough for him – in his eyes.'

'Enough! Enough!' she called out, moving on along the path.

It wasn't like that. He had no choice . . . he had an opportunity, here in England, he had to return. He had no idea, he did not know . . .

'Yes he did. He had a responsibility to you and to—'

And she called out, 'No! I will not have it. Do you hear me? I will not have it . . .'

Then no one spoke. And the only thing she heard was the beating of her heart, the rushing of her blood through her narrowing veins, and his name, always his name.

Chapter Fifteen

Her father has gone. She knows not where. But two whole days and nights have passed since he left. He told her to be good and look after the others. That was all. And it seems queer to her now that he didn't say more, and so she wonders if he has gone to look for her mother. But she has run out of stories, and the penny he gave her is gone. If he has not returned by morning she will take the others and walk back to the big house.

The sun continued to burn down, bleaching colour from the landscape. By the end of July the pastures around Bramley had turned brown; local farmers had been forced to raise the price of milk, and wells were running dry. The dock workers' dispute, which had begun in Southampton in June, had gathered momentum and spread to the north, and the threat of strikes erupted again. But now women were joining the fight for better pay, better working conditions, with jam-makers, pickle-makers, biscuit-makers and tea-packers all threatening to take action. And whilst the countryside lay in deep torpor, the cities in turmoil, an oppressive haze hung over Temple Hill.

Cora wondered if she, and perhaps the whole country with her, was going mad in the heat, and if it would ever abate. Sleep had never been easy and now it seemed impossible, apart from those daytime exhaustion-induced nightmares, and journeys into the past. Each one seemed so real. It was as though in returning to England she was having her life, that journey, forced back on her — to review, to reckon with, to atone. And she could not tell anyone. Could not say, 'I am afraid, afraid to close my eyes, afraid to remember.'

But Sylvia knew.

When Cora said, 'I need to talk to you,' Sylvia's heart leapt with joy. It did not matter to Sylvia what her friend was about to tell her, whether a confession, an anecdote, an apology, or nonsense. The fact was, Cora wished to speak to her again. Cora had barely uttered a word to her, had barely looked at her or spent any time with her since their fracas. Instead, she had chosen to spend an inordinate amount of time sitting about the garden, in her temple, alone, contemplating goodness knows what. And though Sylvia had tried to reach out to her, to offer the proverbial olive branch and words of comfort, Cora's isolation was such that she might as well have been in another country, Sylvia thought.

'You know I'm here for you, always,' Sylvia said, shuffling forward in her chair.

Cora nodded, glanced away momentarily, and then took a deep breath. 'The thing is, I appear to be the victim of some sort of blackmail attempt, again.'

'No!'

'It's a queer affair, and I'm not altogether sure what to do.'

Though the two women spoke at some length about the letters, Cora was careful not to divulge to Sylvia the exact nature of the contents of these missives. She told Sylvia that she suspected she had more than one blackmailer. For she had thought about the letters long and hard, she said, and there were obvious differences and discrepancies: in the hand, the spelling of her name, and the demands. Whilst one demanded money, and a paltry amount at that, the other seemed to want nothing more than confirmation of her identity.

'You must not give in to any of their demands,' said Sylvia.

Cora turned to her. 'But your advice, as I recall, was to cooperate.'

Sylvia looked blank, shook her head. 'No. You've never spoken to me about any of this, dear. I never said that. When did I say that?'

'The other day, in my room. I was sure I heard you tell me to *cooperate* with whoever is sending me the letters. I thought you knew about them.'

Sylvia almost laughed. 'My dear, you were delirious, imagining all sorts of things.'

'Hmm. Well, I'm thinking of dealing with it differently this time. I'm contemplating bringing in the police.'

'Really? I thought you said you'd never do that. And what about the publicity? What about Jack? You have to think of him now. I'm quite sure if you ignore them, they will eventually realise the futility of their actions.'

'You may be right,' Cora replied, nodding, pensive. 'I shall deliberate.'

'I really think you should,' Sylvia said quickly. 'I think any haste on your part – in any sort of response – could be counter-productive and have damaging consequences. You said so your-self, the last time.'

'That was almost thirty years ago and, if you remember, the circumstances were very different. I was not residing here . . . was here only very briefly. This time,' she paused, staring at Sylvia, 'this time, I can't escape to another country.'

Sylvia shook her head. 'Astonishing that they've managed to keep track – of you, I mean, after all these years.'

'It's all because of that wretched business with Cassandra, I suppose, my name being in the newspapers again.'

'But which name?' Sylvia asked.

Cora smiled. 'De Chevalier de Saint Léger, but people have long memories, particularly those with . . . tawdry motivations.'

Sylvia reached out, placed her hand upon Cora's, and said again, 'I'm sure if you ignore them, offer no response at all, they will stop. They have to stop. What else can they do?'

Cora lowered her eyes. 'They can carry out their threats, go to those publications who appear to take such delight in printing cheap gossip. And I can't allow that. I can't take that risk. Not now.'

'You know, and I've told you so before, if we finish your memoirs, tell the truth, the whole story, it will once and for all silence your critics. You need to be open and honest about that time before you went to Rome, you need to record the facts.'

'Yes. I have been thinking this too. We must get to it, Sylvia. After all, it's what you came down here to do,' she added, looking up at her friend and attempting a smile.

And Sylvia suddenly felt quite emotional. It had been a trying few days but now, despite the gravity of the situation, despite that painful exchange, it seemed reason and friendship were restored. At last they could get to work on the book that would, in Sylvia's mind, once and for all quell any festering rumours and innuendo about Cora's past and her marriage to Edward. There was not a moment to lose, Sylvia said, and now was as good a time as any to make a start.

For the next few days the two women worked in harmony. They sat together each afternoon, sometimes in the house, sometimes outside in the garden, and as Cora reminisced, Sylvia took it all down. They were, once again, covering ground already recorded, but Sylvia decided to keep quiet and allow Cora to lead the way. At the end of each session Sylvia read back to Cora what she had written, and Cora would nod, say yes or no, offer amendments and sometimes check Sylvia's spelling. Occasionally, Cora had second thoughts and asked Sylvia to omit a name or event for unspecified reasons. But Sylvia was happy enough to strike a line through a page or a name.

They were sitting on the bench by the pergola when Sylvia said, 'Oh, I must make a note of Antonin's medals and honours.'

Cora shook her head. 'There's no need.'

The war that claimed Antonin de Chevalier's life was a short war, over in a matter of weeks. After his death, Cora and her son left France and returned to Rome, where they remained as those that had been part of the Commune were rounded up and executed in their thousands. Paris was no place to be, France was no place to be, and Cora, not yet forty, was a widow once more.

She had no desire to return to the Chateau de Chazelles, she said. There, weeks passed by without any visitors, and she knew the slow passing of time and sense of isolation would compound her melancholia and sense of loss. With Antonin so often away, she had lived there alone but for the servants and her young son for almost two years. There was little to do other than walk and read, or ride out across the empty fields and rolling hillsides. Her time had been punctuated by regular trips to Paris, to visit her dressmaker and select new gowns, and catch up with friends, including George, once.

He had written to her to tell her he would be passing through Paris, en route to Vichy with Mrs Hillier. But when Cora and her son went to meet them for tea at their hotel, Mrs Hillier was indisposed; 'understandably exhausted by our long journey', George said.

At first he seemed distracted, twitchy, and after only five minutes excused himself to go upstairs and check on his companion. Like a devoted pet, Cora thought. It was late summer and they sat outside in the hotel's private garden, watching Georgie chase pigeons. He told Cora he was astounded by how much his godson had grown, and when Georgie ran up to him and jumped on to his lap, Cora had had to look away, so shocking was the likeness. 'He's adorable,' George said minutes later, watching the child gallop across the parterre in front of them, 'quite adorable.'

They made polite, if somewhat stilted, conversation, mainly about his work and his recent exhibition in London. And from time to time one of them asked the other, 'And do you ever hear anything of . . .' But when, eventually, Cora picked up her purse and said, 'It's getting late and I must not keep you,' he reached over and grabbed hold of her hand. 'I hear things, you know, even in London. I hear you have a new lover . . . a *young* lover.'

Cora smiled. So, word *had* got back to him. Sylvia could always be relied on. 'And what if I do?' she asked, pulling her hand free.

He looked away and said nothing for a moment. But as she rose to her feet, he said, 'Don't go yet. Stay a little while longer.'

'A little while longer?' she repeated, staring at him. 'That's what you used to say to me . . . stay a little while longer Cora, and I did. But you did not stay a little while longer for me. I think you should go and check on Amy,' she added, pulling on her gloves. 'You haven't been up to look in on her for over an hour.'

And then she called out to her son and bid him adieu.

'What about your aunt's marriage to Prospero?' Sylvia was saying.

'Hmm?'

'What would you like to have recorded about that?'

'Oh, well, one must include that, and all the changes at that time. It was, I suppose, the beginning of the end . . . in Rome.'

The year after Antonin's death, and months after the death of James Staunton in Rome, Cora returned to France, to an apartment situated off the Rue du Faubourg Saint-Honoré, in Paris. It was an area she knew well. She had given the matter considerable thought and could think of no better place to live. Expatriate Rome, she had decided, was too small, too confined, and she had no wish to live permanently with her newly widowed aunt. In Paris she would be free, without any need to look over her shoulder. And where better to be a widow?

A trust set up by James Staunton ensured that her son's educational and personal expenses were more than adequately provided for, and with a small income from investments she was at last 'of independent means'. Georgie was to be despatched to boarding school in England, her aunt resided in another country, and she had no husband to curtail her activities. She also knew that George made regular trips to Paris.

At that time reminders of the city's recent struggle were visible everywhere, but for Cora nowhere was more poignant than the burnt-out ruin of the Tuileries Palace. The opulent, lavishly furnished rooms, built by Catherine de Medici and home to the sovereigns of France for hundreds of years, had perished, and all that remained was the charred façade. But Paris, like Cora, was about to go through a process of reinvigoration and reinvention. New wide streets and boulevards, pleasure gardens, squares and fountains would give the city an altogether bright and modern feel. Paris reawakened Cora to her love of city life, and the bustling cafés, thronged streets, constant movement of people and vehicles, the daily spectacle of the city's wealthy fashion-conscious residents, made her feel as though she was living at the very hub of the universe, the capital not just of France, but of the world.

For a number of years Cora's routine remained unchanged. She spent her mornings idly shopping, buying brocades, feathers and lace to add to hats and costumes, visiting her seamstress, or passing through the endless rooms of paintings and marbles in the Musée du Louvre galleries. Each afternoon she pulled on her riding habit and bowler, ordered her horse to be brought round, and set off side-saddle for the Bois de Boulogne. Evenings were filled with the opera, theatre, and endless dinners where she indulged in her love of conversation, updating herself on the political swirls and rumbles from Rome and London.

Cora's aunt was by now a formidable force in Rome, and, at the age of seventy-one, had remarried. A colonel in the Noble Guards of his Holiness the Pope, Prospero Cansacchi was a decade younger than Fanny Staunton, with an ancient lineage, a palazzo, and a title.

Fanny's marriage pleased Cora greatly, and she wasted no time in placing an announcement in the London *Times: Mrs Francesca Staunton, widow of the late James Staunton of Rome, aunt of the Countess de Chevalier de Saint Léger, was married to Count Prospero Cansacchi di Amelia, at Amelia, Italy, on Saturday last.*

The newly styled Contessa Cansacchi visited her niece in Paris, but whilst Cora relished the relentless merry-go-round of the French capital's colourful nightlife, her aunt still preferred the cosiness of expatriate Rome. The world of her stylish niece was exciting and glamorous, but it was much too fast and modern for the old contessa. But Rome, too, was changing, and the medieval town inside the ancient city walls had been all but swept away. The narrow streets and ramshackle buildings of Cora's early days had been replaced with grand civic buildings and fine hotels, and the construction of a vast monument to Victor Emmanuel had commenced on the ancient site at Capitoline hill, overshadowing the old Piazza d'Ara Coeli and dwarfing its tiny, crumbling fountain.

Many of the English expatriates, rattled by the changes and upheaval, had returned home, knowing that an era had ended. But each winter continued to deliver a few familiar if tired faces, as well as a steady stream of seemingly deliriously happy new ones, enjoying their first Grand Tour. Hungry for souvenirs, artefacts and paintings, the new visitors were different to the old ones: they were rich. And though Cora's aunt and others considered their seasonal guests to be rather insensitive, vulgar and brash, Cora had no issue with new money. Privately, she preferred many of the jolly new arrivals to the somewhat pessimistic and impoverished expatriates. She was enthralled by their bravado as much as their wealth, for where the expatriate set were able to exude a collective artistic sensibility and an appreciation for the antiquated beauty in their midst, their bejewelled visitors were able to purchase it.

Invitations to the elderly Contessa Cansacchi's soirees were highly sought after by visitors to Rome. Her apartment, though a little overcrowded with ornamentation, seemed to them to bear all the hallmarks of old money, with a distinctly continental style. And her soirees were invariably a mix of the old and new crowd, as well as Italian and French nobility. New arrivals, who had visited Paris en route to Rome, were told, 'Ah, so you were in Paris . . . you may have met my niece, the Countess de Chevalier de Saint Léger?' It was heady stuff for many of them, and partly what they had come to Europe for: to be educated, purchase art and make interesting connections. And when the Countess de Chevalier de Saint Léger was in residence, staying with her aunt, she only added to the array of foreign titles on offer. She was altogether different to anyone back in England.

As knowledgeable as she was fashionable, her gowns – all from Paris – were of exquisite taste, something money alone could not buy. Yet it was also noted that the younger countess had an easy ability to relate to the common man. Her manner was as of much interest and note as the size of her bustle or the height of her hair, the way in which she used her hands or held her glass or fork; the subjects she chose to speak about and those she preferred to remain silent on. She appeared to encapsulate all that was glamorous in a modern cosmopolitan society, and yet – and without offending anyone – she also broke any number of rules. She held opinions and challenged men quite openly, displaying a confidence that was rare and exciting and frightening at the same time. Her once golden hair had a silver hue, and was worn in a fashionable up-knot, usually adorned with an encrusted comb or exotic plume. Her face, everyone noted, had an uncommon youthfulness about it, and her usual expression of aloof detachment was softened by the teasing suggestion of a smile about her mouth, which men – and in particular the man who would be her next husband – found quite beguiling.

Chapter Sixteen

'*If you touch her again I'll kill you,*' *she says, in a new voice, and holding the knife out in front of them.*
'*Whores,*' *he says, and spits on the floor.* '*Bloody whores, both of you.*'
And then he turns and leaves the room.

'Paris! That was my zenith,' Cora said to Sylvia.

But they had already *done* Paris. Sylvia knew all about Paris. She knew full well that the *happiest days* of her life had been spent there, where he was – where George was – so often, so easily. It had been their place of rendezvous, and for so many years. Wasn't that why she had moved there, to be able to see him? Oh, Cora always claimed she had lived there because she loved the place, particularly at that time. But Sylvia knew better.

'I rather think we've covered Paris,' Sylvia said.

'It was his favourite city, you know?' Cora went on. 'The one place we could meet and . . . just *be*. The one place people didn't bother him, make demands on him, his time. Where he was able to be himself, able to relax.'

232

Sylvia nodded. 'But didn't Mrs Hillier keep a house there?'

Cora jerked. 'What has that to do with anything? I hope you're not including *her* in the book. I want no mention of her. None at all. Yes, she kept a house in Paris, as you well know, but she was in very poor health by then, bedridden, and quite unable to leave England. And anyway, she and George's friendship had long since ended.'

Sylvia chose not to mention Evie Dipple, George's muse and sitter at that time, reputed to keep house for him in London. Cora had turned a blind eye to it, so she would too.

'And I want absolutely no mention of that awful Evie Dipple woman either,' Cora suddenly said, as though reading Sylvia's thoughts. 'Or any of the others.'

'Of course not.'

After a few minutes, Sylvia – who had been silently practising, building up to it – said, 'Shall we make a few notes about your early life?'

'Fine,' Cora said, looking away, across the garden.

But as soon as Cora mentioned Standen Hall, Sylvia shook her head and put down her pencil. 'You need to be truthful, Cora. You're not being truthful *enough*.' She closed her notebook. 'But we can ponder on it, return to it tomorrow. It will allow you a little time to think things through.'

'Think things through,' Cora repeated vaguely.

Yes, she needed to think things through, she thought; unravel fact from fiction. The truth, the glimpses she had had of it of late, was hazy and blurred, and dreamlike. Had she dreamt her life? she wondered. If only her aunt were still alive, she would tell her what to do. For hadn't she always told her what to do, how to be, *who* to be?

But Sylvia's words – suspended about the ether *and* in print – had confused her further. Stories based on her life, inspired by *her version* of her life, had been recorded, over and over, with

233

differing permutations and endings, and always without any beginning. She glanced about the garden, back to her friend and away again.

Then, out of the blue, Sylvia said, 'Actually, if we aren't going to work on the memoirs, do you mind if we *do* talk about Paris again? Harriett is back there, you see, she has returned to Armand and I need to immerse myself – set the scene.'

'I thought they were at Lucca?'

Sylvia laughed. 'Really, dear, that was chapter fifteen; this is chapter twenty-four! Possibly the penultimate chapter.'

'Possibly? Dependent upon what?'

'Well, whether Armand takes her back, of course.'

'Of course? But haven't you decided? One would have thought as their creator you have *some* say in their fate.'

Sylvia raised her eyes, pensive for a moment, then said, 'Yes, to a certain extent I do. But I never decide my endings until I arrive there. And I chose Paris because you've always told me that it is the most romantic city, a city for lovers.'

Cora's head throbbed. The heat was stifling. A storm was forecast. Sylvia had read it out to her. And the whalebone, holding her in, holding everything in, made it almost impossible for her to breathe. Sylvia meant well, she knew that, but her constant fussing and need to please had become irksome, and almost as intolerable as the heat. She felt no sense of peace, or space, and that feeling of claustrophobia only added to her discomfiture. And the questions: always asking, wanting to know something about something – a date, person, place, who was who, who had said what to whom. She hadn't meant to snap, and had no wish to be discourteous or unkind, but really, surely Sylvia could see it was too much. And after all, it was her wretched story.

When she said, 'I may as well write the blessed thing myself,' she had meant it. But Sylvia had looked crestfallen, quite tearful, and so she had apologised, again. Then she said, 'I must take a walk. I need to think about things.'

'My dear, you need to settle yourself.'

'No . . . no. I have to sort . . . my head, my heart.'

Sylvia rose to her feet, laid the back of her hand across Cora's brow. 'Oh, but you feel feverish again, dear. Perhaps I should send for Dr Parsons.'

'I do not need a doctor.'

'Then stay where you are and allow me to read to you.'

'He's here, Sylvia. He's with us.'

'Who is here, dear? Who do you think is here?'

'He is. I've seen him, more than once, here in the garden, and in the house. He wishes to speak to me, I think, he wishes to tell me.'

'Tell you?'

'Yes. There must be a reason why he's come to me, here, now. You see, I think he knows . . . knows what is happening.' She looked at Sylvia. 'Oh, I know, I know what you're thinking, you're thinking I'm going mad with the heat, that I'm suffering delusions. But I'm not. I saw him as clearly as I see you now. He's here, Sylvia, he's waiting for me,' she added, and smiled. 'He still loves me.'

'Well, of course. Of course he's here with you, and of course he still loves you. He always did, always.'

Sylvia had seen Cora mouthing words to herself in the garden days before. She had followed her outside and, from behind the pergola, had watched her as she sat muttering and mumbling – presumably to George. She saw and made out enough to know that Cora believed she was speaking directly to him. It was beyond sad. For there was no one there – how could there be? He had been gone two decades. And yet, watching her, straining to hear her, Sylvia found herself turning time and again towards the sundial, looking for him, almost longing to see him.

Many of Cora's words had been silent, others mere sounds, melting into the air. But Sylvia distinctly heard her say George's name, and mention 'our grandson'. A few minutes after that, when Cora had yelled out, 'No', and appeared to look towards the pergola, Sylvia had swiftly moved off up a pathway through the woodland, towards the driveway back to the house.

It was late in the evening when the storm arrived, rattling windows and doors and glass panes, whistling down every chimney. It had been anticipated for days, but came with a force so great that rather than quell any delusions it took them a stage further.

Cora had been at sea. Somewhere between Southampton and Le Havre, or Marseilles and Civitavecchia. She had woken to pitch-blackness, a small cabin rocking, the great roar of a swell outside. She felt hot and sick, feverish once again. She had clung to her bed, wondering what year it was, to which port she was headed, and whether or not she was married, and to whom. Everything was muddled, tossed about by the roll and sway and hidden in the darkness. And thus she drifted in and out of slumber, and in and out of that first journey to Rome, glancing through carriage windows and tiny portholes, across a sea vast and deep and dark. Sailing away from England, away from them . . . and away from *him*, the man she had called 'Uncle John'.

When she heard the footsteps, felt someone climb upon the bed, arms reach around her, she could not be sure if it was not part of another dream. But when she heard herself speak, say his name, it seemed to her to be real . . .

'George?'

'I'm here.'

'I'm frightened.'

'There's nothing to be afraid of, my love.'

'But we might drown . . .'

'No, we shan't drown.'

'Don't leave me.'

'I shan't leave you.'

'I don't know what to do. What shall I do?'

He did not reply. And so she asked him again, without words, in silence: *what shall I do?*

You must do nothing.

You knew, didn't you?

Yes, I knew.

But how did you know? Who told you?

Someone. Someone told me . . .

I wasn't allowed to say anything, wasn't allowed to speak about any of it. Fanny said I must never speak about it, no one could ever know.

Hush now, you must sleep, must rest.

Then she felt his hand upon her hair, heard herself breathing, in and out, in and out.

Chapter Seventeen

If it happened again she would kill him. She had heard her say it. And if she didn't kill him then someone else would have to. Someone else would have to do it. If only her mother would come back and take her away from this place. Come back and gather them all up.

Summer wilted. Frogs and minnows shrivelled and dried and died in the sun-baked mud of ditches and ponds and streams. Lawns long yellow turned brown, and birds stopped singing. No sigh of nature could be heard, no breath of wind moved the trees and no petal stirred. But the out-of-towners and motor enthusiasts continued to flee to the country, honking horns on silent lanes, searching for a picture-postcard church, an open tea shop, and cooler air.

At Temple Hill, Cora waited for Cecily.

When she heard Sylvia mutter, 'That girl can't seem to stay away,' she said, 'Jack invited her, and *I* happen to like her calling in.'

Sylvia said, 'Are you aware she's planning to write a book about you?'

Cora laughed. 'Well, it's not the first, is it?'

'So long as you know what she's up to. It's none of my business, of course, my only concern is protecting you.'

'I hardly think I need protecting from Cecily.'

Sylvia's antipathy towards Cecily Chadwick was, Cora thought, like some queer jealousy. Every time her name cropped up, Sylvia's back straightened, face crumpled. She was suspicious of Cecily, Cora understood that, but it was surely unfounded. The previous day Sylvia had gone so far as to say she thought Cecily might be a gold-digger. She told Cora that she had seen Cecily more than once examining her possessions, looking beneath bits of china, scrutinising artwork for a signature, 'just as though she were placing a monetary value on them'.

But Sylvia had always suffered from jealousy. Not of Cora, but of anyone close to Cora. She had been jealous of George from the start. Had wasted no time in telling Cora of rumours, many of which Cora later discovered to have been incubated and hatched by Sylvia herself. And she had been the first, the very first to explain George's relationship with Mrs Hillier, and then later, for years, agree with Cora that he would never in a month of Sundays give up the older woman, that it was hopeless, that he simply did not love Cora *enough*.

'They visited the Academy yesterday,' Sylvia said. 'Have you told Jack? Does he know?'

She stared at Sylvia. 'Know what?'

'Well . . . that you are there, dear.'

Cora flinched, shook her head. 'No. And I don't intend to.'

John Clifford's sculpture 'Tinted Venus' was now at the Academy. She was there, on display and naked for all to see. It was easy enough to pass off the painting in the hallway; 'It was a gift,' she liked to say, 'from a dear old friend.' It had been Mr

Fox who had used the word 'erotic'. She had been shocked by his choice of adjective and had laughed at the time, saying, 'Gracious, I shall have to have it burned, else the people of Bramley will burn me!' He had laughed, but hadn't he given her a queer look?

Sometime later Jack had asked, 'It's not you, is it, in that painting in the hallway? It's just that it rather looks like you, or how I imagine you once looked.'

She had laughed again. 'I *am* flattered! I have no idea who the sitter was but I can assure you that it was not me, my dear.'

And Sylvia, too, did not know. Oh, she knew about Clifford's 'Venus', and about George's 'Madonna', but she did not know what had happened at Lucca. Though she liked to think she did. She did not know that George had painted her there, and years later presented her with the painting. Cora had given Sylvia a synopsis, an edited synopsis of those weeks at Lucca, and she, Sylvia, had added to it, as she always did. And yet it amused Cora. For so many clues were there, hanging in the hallway of her home. But even Edward had failed to realise that it was in fact herself as Aphrodite.

It had been some years after her marriage to Edward, during that first summer's visit to England, when George arrived by cab carrying a large canvas covered in brown paper. It was, he insisted, a gift, and he looked at Cora as he said, 'Consider it my belated wedding present to you both. I should have given it to you when you were married but I could not bring myself to part with it.' And she had been embarrassed, as much by his attachment to the canvas as the image upon it.

Edward had later commented to her that it was not, in his opinion, 'entirely suitable' as a wedding gift. But had he not realised then that it was her? For he had stared at it for some time, perplexed, before having it removed to the attic of his home.

Now she wished she were able to tell Cecily about the painting, the story that went with it, the child conceived during its execution. Cecily, she thought, understood art and would not be shocked. But no, it was too complicated, would mean explaining so much, which would only lead on to more. 'And then she would judge me . . . she would not understand,' she concluded.

And yet Cora could not help but smile whenever she thought of Cecily, because she inevitably thought of her grandson as well. She had watched them together, seen Jack's fumbling attempts to be indifferent, seen that look in his eyes, even when he glanced at Cecily for a second or two. And it had catapulted her back. So familiar was his look, his aura. Oh yes, he was smitten, in love. But they were both so young, and he was ambitious, had already told her that he had no wish to settle down until he was at least thirty. And Cecily? Cecily had informed her that she wanted to travel, see the world, and not be encumbered by family, and expectations and obligations. She was a modern woman in a modern world. It was all so very different now.

Sylvia was saying, 'I wonder what they'd make of it if they knew about you being there, in the Academy.'

'I'd rather not think about it, if you don't mind.'

There were no two ways about it: Sylvia would have to go, and soon. She was becoming a liability and knew far too much, Cora decided. She had not properly considered, had not properly thought through the implications of having Sylvia there, with Jack.

'John Clifford,' Sylvia said, wistfully. 'He was such a kind, dear little man.'

'Yes, he was,' Cora replied. She could still picture the elderly sculptor, standing in his dusty smock, surrounded by his tinted marble goddesses and nymphs. And hadn't he been the one to first warn her? Hadn't he been the one to tell her that 'dear

George' was not the marrying sort; that he was married to his art, his vocation? But she had dismissed Clifford's words, had continued her fantasy, for so many years – a lifetime.

When Sylvia announced that she was going out for a walk, Cora said, 'But you'll miss Cecily.'

'She has no wish to see me . . . and I'm quite sure you'd prefer me not to be here,' she added – newly cryptic, Cora thought.

When Cecily arrived she brought apples and raspberries, and some eggs. And, for a while, Jack loitered about in the doorway, looking nonchalant, or trying to, and saying things like, 'I'm just popping out to the courtyard', or, 'I need to have a quick word with Mr Cordery . . .' and then disappeared for five minutes and came back, twitchy, nervous, hands in pockets. But Cora was keen to catch up with Cecily alone. And so, eventually, she asked Jack if he'd be so kind as to run an errand for her, delivering a remittance to the shop in the village.

Cora did not particularly wish to hear about the Academy. It had once been George's domain, the world he had presided over without her. But she had to ask. It would have been impolite not to.

'And so, what did you see at the Academy, dear?'

'Golly, we saw so much, I hardly know where to begin.'

And then she did, she began a roll call of familiar names and old friends, and Cora stared at her, impassive, occasionally raising an eyebrow in recognition or nodding.

'Oh, and we saw quite a few of Lord Lawson's paintings as well.'

Cora smiled. And as Cecily reeled off famous titles, each one – still vivid – flashed through Cora's mind's eye. 'And Sylvia happened to mention that you were once his sitter,' Cecily added.

Cora closed her eyes. 'Dear Sylvia, she does get a little

confused about certain things, and this is one of them!' she said
and tried to laugh.

'But you knew him?'

Cora glanced away. 'Yes, yes, I knew him. I met him in Rome,
when I was very young – when we were all very young.'

'He was President of the Academy,' Cecily said, as though
Cora needed to be reminded.

'That is correct, he was. And a supremely gifted and talented
painter.'

Happily, the conversation moved on.

'. . . and then we took an omnibus and sat up on the top,
and went the whole way round Hyde Park, and Jack pointed
out where he lived with his mother . . . You never lived in
London?' she asked.

Cora shook her head. 'No, though I know it well, and have
stayed there often enough.'

'I'd like to live in London one day, I'd like to experience life
in a city.'

'Paris is the best city to experience life when one is young.'

'Do you ever wish you were still there?'

'Oh, sometimes, but only if I could be young again also,'
Cora said, smiling.

'Hmm. I can imagine you there, in Paris. It suits you more
than Bramley!'

It suits you more . . .

The words threw her back: they were the very words Edward
had used in Paris, when George brought them together again,
after so many years.

'It suits you more, more than Rome or London. Yes, Paris suits
you!' Edward had exclaimed, and all three of them laughed.

They were dining at the Café Anglais on the Boulevard des

Italiens. She and George had recently travelled together from Rome via the Riviera to Paris. And back in the French capital, they had attended the opera and theatre, and dined out together each evening. At that time George made frequent visits to the city and they had seen more of each other. To many in Paris they were a fixture, a couple like any other. So much so, that many there – none the wiser – simply assumed them to be *Monsieur et Madame*. And Cora, now styled the Countess de Chevalier de Saint Léger, had begun to think this was the way it would be. And she could live with it, she thought. She could live with George coming back to her once a month, perhaps, telling her there was no one but her, that he loved her, adored her. Such passion, she told herself, would only be diluted by a contract, a contract of marriage.

But that evening at the Café Anglais, Edward had overshadowed George. For his presence was commanding, his seniority unquestionable. And he had been charming, effusive; telling Cora he simply could not believe how little she had aged, or that the young English girl he remembered so well from Rome was now such a renowned society figure, a feted hostess. Like a fine wine, he said, she had only improved with age. But Edward's broad smiles and attentiveness had had a debilitating effect upon George's spirit, he had grown quieter and more sullen as the evening progressed. He sent back his steak, complained about the service, and made such a fuss about a draught from the door that they moved tables, twice.

Only years later did Cora learn of George's anguish that night. That after escorting her home and returning to his hotel with Edward, he had been unable to sleep and had come to her.

At two o'clock in the morning he had walked out from his hotel on the Rue de Rivoli into a seedy mix of nocturnal human debris littering the street corners and alleyways of the French capital. He told her that his body seemed decided upon a route without any consultation with his mind. Eventually, he had found himself in front of the stone steps leading up to the doorway of her apartment building. And through the closed shutters he thought he could make out a light within her room. He had stood there for some time, wondering what he should do. With his hands thrust deep into the pockets of his overcoat, he had shuffled and paced, up and down and up and down in front of the building, berating himself out loud and muttering expletives in any number of languages. At one point, he ran up the steps and held his hand over the cord of the bell, only to pull it away and run back down the steps. Then a light had gone on inside the ground-floor apartment. A window opened. 'Who is there? What do you want?' a female voice called out. And George quickly marched off back up the street, into the night.

Now Cora thought, if only he had pulled on that damned cord. Why hadn't he? What stopped him? She felt the dull ache of regret and longing, and years gone by. And she thought of her marriage, her final marriage, there in Paris the very next year. But it was not revenge. It had never been about revenge. Or had it?

There had always been gossip about George's affairs, and there had been so many by then. He had grown more handsome with age, his silvering hair and beard lending him a distinguished look which seemed only to emphasise his success. And what had once been his 'perfect vision' had aged, aged beautifully, as he repeatedly told her, but aged nonetheless. The waist had thickened, the pert chin had softened, and the hair, like his, had silvered and lost its sheen. Oh, Cora still had her admirers, George included, but she could not compete with youth. She was by then the mother of a young man, and had, everyone knew, been widowed twice, and the map of her life showed on her face.

The final agony came only a few months after that fateful

dinner at the Café Anglais, when Cora received a letter from Sylvia informing her that George had recently returned to London from Paris – with Evie Dipple. Had Cora seen them together? Did she know? Sylvia asked. She went on to say that she had heard he was 'smitten, quite besotted by the girl, and she – young enough to be his daughter! But I imagine you saw them, crossed paths, or perhaps heard that they were in town? I'm longing to know if you met them, and what you made of it all & of her. I understand she is an actress as well as an artist's model, & from somewhere in the East End, I believe. Quite something when one bears in mind what a snob George once was. Such hypocrisy!'

That George had elected to bring his young lover to Paris cut as deep as any goodbye. They could so easily have crossed paths and yet she had been kept in the dark; he had not even had the decency to warn her. The irony of her name, her title, and the fact his new love hailed from the East End of London was not lost on her either. And if we had met, if we had bumped into each other, she thought at the time, what would I have done? How should I have been? Am I nothing more to him than a former and occasional lover, an old friend? 'I am the mother of his children . . . the mother of his son.'

'Does it still feel strange to be here, back in England?' Cecily was asking, leaning forward, elbows on her knees, chin cupped in her hands.

'Sometimes. Sometimes I think I might wake up and discover that I have dreamed this . . . this particular part of my life, my dotage. Wishful thinking, perhaps,' she added, raising her eyebrows. 'You know, when I was young, when I was your age and first in Rome, everything felt *too* real . . . too vivid and alive.'

'Maybe it was that place.'

'Mm, that place, that time. It was all new to me, still foreign, exotic,' she smiled, 'and I, like a newborn baby, opening up my eyes for the very first time, dazzled by the splendour, the magnificence, the mystery of it all. Life is so intoxicating when one is young.'

It was Clifford who had said to her, 'We all lose our senses here, for a while at least. It's an inevitable though heady infatuation. We're made to fall in love – by history, the romance of the place. The possibilities seem limitless, and for a time we think we are immortal, like the ancient ruins surrounding us. You're simply infatuated, my dear. No more or less. It will pass.'

But it never passed.

Later that afternoon Jack came to Cora and asked if he could speak with her. And she guessed what was coming, had been anticipating it for weeks, but she was still unprepared. Now, he too sat with a notebook and pencil, saying he wished to record it, 'get it all down'.

'There's really no need, Sylvia is recording my memories.'

He told her he wished to know more about Jack, his name-sake; his grandfather, he called him.

'Oh well, he was a good man, a very good man, kind, discerning . . . gentle. Very like his father.'

'And I look like him, or so Sylvia said.'

'Mm, somewhat.'

They spoke about her aunt, and Cora described the palazzo apartment where they had lived with James Staunton and his son, Jack; pointing to various paintings and items of furniture that had once been there. Oh, how she wished he could have seen it, and seen Rome, as it used to be. They had been so happy there, a close family, she said. Herself, Aunt Fanny, James Staunton and Jack: a family of four. And she and Jack like brother and sister.

He frowned. 'But then you married him . . . Jack.'

She smiled, nodded.

'But was it not odd for one's uncle to become one's father-in-law? One's brother one's husband?' he asked. 'Must be queer to marry within one's family.'

Her heart shivered. 'Well, we were, for a time, like brother and sister.'

'And then?'

'And then we fell in love and were married,' she said, looking down, smoothing out the skirt of her gown. She glanced up, caught his eye. 'Not all marriages are born of passion, and I'm not sure it's a necessary foundation for an *enduring* marriage,' she said.

'And were you happy together?' he asked, staring directly at her.

She glanced away. 'Well, yes,' she replied, 'as happy as it was possible to be then . . . as happy as I knew how to be then.'

'You never speak about him.'

She shrugged. 'It was a long time ago, we were married for a very short time.'

'And his death, it was an accident?'

She nodded. 'Yes,' she said, 'an accident. He slipped and fell.'

It had been early autumn, she told him, barely a month before the birth of his father, Georgie. An English banker – a friend of the family – had arrived at the apartment in a state of great distress, followed by two men, carrying Jack. He was already unconscious, covered in blood from a gaping wound to his head. There was nothing Dr Small could do. He died hours later. 'I thought at the time I was dreaming, having a nightmare, that I would wake up and discover . . . something else. It's all a blur now, that time. I was nearing the end of my confinement and I think I slept all through those final weeks.' She shook her head. 'Hard to recall . . . hard to recall.'

For a few minutes his questions stopped. He sat pondering,

cogitating, jutting out his jaw, hand to his chin in that way he did – like George, like Georgie. Then he said, 'I always feel as though there's something you're not telling me. Please, don't take this the wrong way. I just have this . . . this feeling that . . .'

'Yes?' she said, looking up at him, her heart trembling.

'Oh, I don't know. I imagine it's all because, well, because I've not known anything about you, not properly, not up until now. You know, for a while you were almost a myth to me. I hardly believed you existed!'

She laughed.

'Mother always said you were . . . a little difficult, impossibly grand and rather . . . too beautiful. She said that she'd always suspected you had a few dark secrets. I think she thought you held things back, weren't completely honest with Father.' He paused, looked away. 'I think she almost resented you for the love you had for him.'

'Well, of course I loved him – I loved him very much. He was my baby, and the most loving and affectionate son. He always seemed to sense how I was feeling, whether I was sad or happy, or lonely. And he never had Ge— ack in his life. He was born in the midst of tragedy. Rather like you.'

He lowered his head. 'Yes, it would seem we were both jinxed.'

'Don't say that. You had a father who, had he been here now, would have loved you, oh so much. And a grandfather who would have adored you.'

He looked up at her. 'And what about *your* father?'

'I'm afraid I never really knew him,' she replied.

'But what was his name?'

'His name was Samuel . . . Samuel Stopher.'

'So you were born Cora Stopher?'

It was the first time anyone had put those two names together, but she simply smiled and nodded.

'And what did he do? Did he have an occupation?'

'He was a gentleman . . . a rentier.'

'A rentier?'

'He owned land . . . property.'

'In Suffolk?'

She nodded. 'Woodbridge, or thereabouts.'

'We should go and visit, you and I. I'd be interested to see it, where you grew up, where you hail from.' Then he laughed. 'I can't very easily visit South America, but Suffolk is within reach.'

After a little while, he put the notebook to one side, sat back in his chair and said, 'So, tell me about the great Antonin.'

And she was relieved, for she could speak about Antonin, her time at Chazelles, without any sense of trepidation. She could tell him how a dashing French officer had wooed her in Rome, married her and taken her to live in his castle. She could speak about a distinguished military career, a noble death and medals and honours. She could tell him of that short-lived but fortuitous union, and just as it had moved her on, so it moved them on.

Eventually, he said, 'And you never wished to marry again?'

She shook her head, glanced away. 'No, twice was enough. Quite enough.'

Chapter Eighteen

What she needs is a weapon, something weighty, something to knock him out with. He would be slow, would be drunk; was always drunk at night. And her aunt was frightened; she could see that, had seen and heard enough to know that husbands are not always tender and loving.

Yes, a weapon.

For three days Cora barely uttered a word to Sylvia. She was angry, angry at Sylvia's snooping, and at her ridiculous claims and insinuations. The only person she could rely on was Cecily, who had reported everything back to her, confirming her suspicions once and for all that Sylvia could not be trusted. The final straw – though there had by that time been enough to line a stable floor, she thought – had been her discovery of Sylvia's visit to Meadow Farm. And it had been Mr Fox who had reported that particular excursion back to Cora, having passed by on his bicycle.

She had hoped that Sylvia would take the hint, would

voluntarily depart and return to London. She had hoped that she would not have to ask her to leave. The former would perhaps allow them to salvage some scrap of friendship, in time; the latter would most definitely end it forever.

When she finally summoned Sylvia to the drawing room and said, 'I wish to speak to you, Sylvia, please sit down,' Sylvia had not smiled, and Cora suspected she knew what was coming. She produced her own notebook and quietly read out from it. Then she looked up at Sylvia and said, 'Well, do you have anything to say?'

Sylvia said, 'A litany of charges, it would seem, and no doubt all Cecily Chadwick's doing. But I have to tell you that I think you're being foolish, very foolish to listen to and trust that girl. In fact, I've been holding back my suspicions about her and her mother for some time.' She paused. 'I fear your blackmailers are closer to home than you realise.'

Cora laughed. 'The Chadwicks! Oh, Cecily and Madeline are not my blackmailers, Sylvia. I know exactly who—'

'You've always been naive,' Sylvia interrupted, 'always trusted the wrong people. It's why you're in the situation you're in today. Had you thought more, been more discerning in your judgement,' she continued, her voice now trembling, 'your life might have been different . . . and perhaps you would not have lost *him!*'

'How dare you. How dare you say that to me, after *everything*. You know nothing, nothing at all about real life. You've spent half a century lost in your own imaginings, making up stories that have no bearing whatsoever on real life, real love. You don't know what real love is.'

'I know what it's not – it's not what you did to him. That was unforgivable, and it will make you go mad – mad like her before you. It was revenge, pure and simple, and you know it.'

Cora stared at her. 'I think you've said enough, more than

enough. I've already sent for Cotton, he'll be here any minute. There will be a train back to London sometime soon, I'm sure,' she added, pulling on the bell by her side.

Sylvia rose to her feet. 'You can banish me and you can hide away here, but you can't escape, not now. Jack wants to know the truth, he wants to know who he is, and he's going to find out, he's going to discover *everything* about you . . . and about that awful aunt of yours,' she said. And then she turned and left the room.

The overcast sky and silent drizzle seemed appropriate weather for a departure. She sat down in the wagonette and glanced back at the house. No one had anticipated her arrival and no one had come out to wave her off. The door was already closed.

Goodbye.

It was her lack of status, lack of husband, she thought, that allowed people to treat her thus. And it had always been so. Had she been married, been a widow, the world would have viewed her differently. She would have been elevated to *belonging*, worthy of respect, protected by the love and esteem of a man, living or deceased. Without it, without that status, the world had been dismissive – of her, of her feelings. At best, it smiled at her politely. At worst, it simply ignored her. And, perhaps born from that invisibility, and from her immersion in fiction and a focus on other people, she too had often forgotten her own existence, had had to remind herself.

Mr Cotton slammed his door. 'All aboard!' he shouted and laughed. The vehicle turned, headed up the driveway, and Sylvia did not look back. As the motor bumped down the track, past the Chadwicks' privet hedge and white gate, through the trickling ford and up the hill on the other side, she kept her eyes fixed ahead. Passing through the village she saw Mrs Gamben standing in the doorway of the post office, a shawl wrapped about her head; the butcher – all waxed moustache and boater – standing next to his bang-tailed cob; and coming up by the village green she saw Jack and Cecily on the road ahead, his jacket spread over their heads. They stopped and stood aside as the motor passed by. Sylvia looked straight ahead.

She would not cry, could not cry. She would be back in London soon, home, to her meagre life, her tiny flat, and her safe habits for one. No one would say 'how dare you', no one would say 'that will be all'. She would catch a taxicab from Waterloo, and stop at the shop on the corner for milk and bread, and something for supper. They'd say, 'You've been away a while, Miss Dorland. Been anywhere special . . . had a nice time?' And she would smile, and tell them, yes, wonderful.

She would climb the five flights to her landing, pull out the key and open the coffee-brown door to her own small world. And everything would be just as she had left it. She would carry her bag to the bedroom, place it down upon a neatly made single bed, and then – only then – would she allow herself to cry.

A fire had been lit. They were drenched through, and Jack's jacket in a sorry state. But when Mrs Davey brought in the tea tray, she said she would see to it and took it away.

Jack said, 'We saw Sylvia, with Cotton . . .'

Cora smiled. 'Yes, she's had to get back to London . . . had a telegram earlier. Something to do with her publishers, I believe.'

'Has she gone for long?' he asked.

'I'm not entirely sure,' Cora replied. 'But I don't expect her back this summer.'

He glanced over to Cecily, raising his eyebrows. He said,

'Well, that is a shame . . . she never got to have a look at your story.'

'I shall take a look . . . if you'd like me to. I have an eye for a good story,' said Cora.

Cecily looked from Cora to Jack and then back to Cora. 'Yes, thank you, perhaps when it's finished,' she said, and Cora smiled and nodded.

It was not until later, when Jack walked Cecily home, that Cora had a chance to ponder the contretemps of earlier, Sylvia's parting words. She had managed, she thought, to mask any shock in front of her grandson and Cecily at tea, but she was still aghast, had hardly thought her friend capable. And really, none of it made sense. For what was there for Sylvia to be angry about? After all, she had been the one in the wrong, the one snooping and spying, tiptoeing about the place, *investigating*, determined to have her answers, desperate for a story.

. . . *that awful aunt of yours* . . .

Cora winced, shook her head. It was all her own fault, she thought. She had been naive, had trusted Sylvia and told her far too much too early on. And what had been said could never be unsaid, that was the problem. If she had never in the first place mentioned that wretched man, John Abel, all those years ago in Rome, Sylvia's appetite would never have been whetted.

She closed her eyes, shook her head. 'Such a foolish thing to do, and all for added drama, as if there wasn't enough!'

But one thing was patently clear: Sylvia had been jealous, and jealous for a lifetime. But jealous of whom, what, and why? Jealous of the drama, perhaps, envious of the action. Then another thought came to her: was it George? Had Sylvia, too, been in love with George? Had she, for all these years – and as she watched and read and listened to Cora – been in love with the very same man? But no, it was more complex than this, Cora mused. For there seemed to be another dynamic at play, lingering on the outermost periphery, confounding her, confusing her, whispering too quietly for her to hear.

And that parting diatribe, she thought, moving away from a vague suggestion, spewed out like a bile-filled held-back torrent . . .

. . . had you thought more, been more discerning in your judgement, your life might have been different . . . and you would not have lost him.

She closed her eyes. Love . . . *I know what it's not . . . it's not what you did to him . . .* But what did I *do* to him? Cora thought. My only crime was to love him. Sylvia was right, she conceded, she had lost George, and more than once . . . and for a long while after her marriage to Edward. And yet that was also what had brought him back to her.

How could she have said no to Edward? He had asked her to marry him any number of times, and he would not give up, had pursued her with letters and visits and such declarations. She frowned now at the remembrance of that time, his courtship of her. He had said he would take care of her, and of her son; he would make sure she had property of her own, and an income, too. She would be secure for the rest of her days.

It had been the news that George had been in Paris with Evie Dipple that made her realise she had waited long enough, that George Lawson was never going to marry her, or anyone else.

When she wrote to Edward to accept his offer of marriage she stipulated a number of preconditions: she would not be able live in England, she would not be able to run his house; she would prefer not to use his name, but retain her French name and title; and they would not be able to spend Christmases together. 'However, we shall be able to enjoy one another's company here on the continent, as and when your work permits . . . Regarding your very kind offer of a property, I have a hankering for somewhere quiet, a secluded place, the sort of place where one might never be found, and with enough space for my son and any family he might have in the future.'

Days later, she received a reply from Edward: he agreed to every condition. 'You have made me the happiest man in all of England,' he wrote. 'As to your house, I believe I have found the perfect location!'

In the end the marriage had been an arrangement that suited them both. Edward had continued to live and work in England whilst she continued with her life between Paris and Rome. She had returned to this country, to England, once or twice in the summer months, and Edward had visited her on the continent each winter. They had travelled together, touring France and Germany, Switzerland and Austria, and Italy as well.

And he had been true to his word. Shortly before they were married he purchased some one hundred acres of heathland, on the very edge of a quiet village, where he would build Cora her home. And though she did not see the place until a year after its completion, she had instructed him on some of the detail: the need for 'a south-facing canopied veranda, high ceilings and tall windows, well-stocked pleasure gardens, and pine trees'.

He was a good husband, and she had made him happy, very happy, for he had told her so, often. They had been married for almost six years by the time he passed away in his sleep at his home in London. She returned for the funeral, and for the reading of his will.

'They've quite clearly had some sort of bust-up,' Jack was saying. 'I don't believe for one moment Sylvia had a telegram from her publisher, do you?'

'Well,' Cecily began, relishing the feel of her hand in his, 'it's not entirely outside the realms of possibility. She is a writer, she does have a publisher . . .'

'Ah yes, I can just see it . . . Miss Dorland needed urgently, stop, *the end* not acceptable, stop, more words needed, stop, forthwith, stop . . .'

'Who knows, maybe she has to attend some sort of meeting, something important.'

'Rot! She and Cora have had a fall-out. You saw Sylvia in the car, she wouldn't look at us, didn't wave. And it's been building up for weeks, since Sylvia first arrived. I told you about the last time, when Sylvia came running out of the bushes and flagged me down on the drive like an escaped lunatic. And that wasn't their first upset either. It's quite obviously something to do with the stupid memoirs, and you know what? I knew it would happen. I warned Sylvia, told her the day she arrived that she had one almighty task on her hands.'

'I feel sorry for them both, but perhaps more for Cora than Sylvia,' Cecily said.

'Why's that?'

'Perhaps because she's a kinder person than Sylvia.'

They had reached the bottom of the hill and they stopped. They were yards from the garden gate but it was shaded here, private. He moved closer to her. 'Do you really think that?' he asked. She could tell from his eyes that he wasn't remotely interested in her answer. But she smiled and nodded as he moved his mouth to hers.

Chapter Nineteen

he knows the broken brick is there, under her bed, because she put it there. It had been left lying by the wall of the tanner's yard, and she knew as soon as she saw it that it was meant for her, meant as her weapon. She had carried it all the way back through the lanes and up the stairs to their rooms in her apron; and then placed it under the tiny bedframe. Next time he came, she would use it. She would. She would hit him over the head with it.

Within a week the temperature had fallen, the brightness faded. Clouds returned to their usual place. Autumn was in the air. Everyone said so, and everyone shared in the relief. It was over, at last. Things could return to normal now, they said.

At Temple Hill, windows and doors were firmly shut, fires were lit and blankets returned to beds. And Jack's trunk, brought down from the attic, now lay open in his room.

Cora dreaded his departure. She had no wish to be alone again. She had grown used to his company, used to him and Cecily about the place, coming and going, noisily, giggling and laughing, as though all of life was amusing. And sometimes it was, for they made it so.

There had been trips to Linford to order books and purchase stationery; and a trip to London, to Gamages, and to a tailor where Jack was measured for a new suit. He had protested, telling Cora that he did not need another suit, but she had insisted, saying it was important, the sign of a gentleman, to be well-dressed. Cecily went with them and they dined at Simpsons in the Strand before returning home. On the train, Cora had quietly watched them: the glances and smiles and not-meant-to-be-noticed gestures. Jack was in love, and in love for the very first time. Nothing, no other love, would be quite the same, she knew. But he was so young; they were both so young. They had their whole lives ahead of them. And she told him this, later that evening.

'I know, that you're very fond of her, as am I, but you can't allow yourself to be *too* attached . . . and you must not allow her to have too many hopes,' she said. 'It would be cruel.'

He adopted that demeanour she had become accustomed to: he looked away, shrugged and said, 'I know. I do know this.'

'I imagine I'll see a good deal less of her once you have gone . . .'

But Cecily had no intention of abandoning Cora. She remained enthralled by her faded beauty and dusty treasures, by her stories and her life. She was, to Cecily, cultured and worldly, and possessed with an attitude quite different to others of her generation or to anyone else in Bramley. And yet so much of her life remained an enigma, even to Jack. But perhaps it was this, Cecily thought, perhaps it was the not knowing which allowed others, including herself, to imagine and fill in the gaps. Oh, Cora had confided to an extent, she had told Cecily a few of her secrets, but without any context or chronology these things meant little. In fact, they only added to the intrigue.

One day shortly after Sylvia left, when Cecily arrived at the house and Jack had been out on his motorcycle, Cora invited her to join her in a stroll about the gardens. She seemed agitated, distracted, and as they walked across the lawn, she said, 'One thing you will unfortunately learn in time, my dear, is that not everyone wishes for your happiness . . . or good fortune.'

It was another one of her cryptic comments and meant nothing to Cecily at the time, because once again it was random, without context. Cecily said nothing, and they walked on in silence towards the arbour.

'There's to be a military display on the green tomorrow – soldiers from Aldershot. The Wiltshire regiment, and a band,' Cecily said, trying to lighten the atmosphere.

Cora shuddered. 'Why people want to watch soldiers perform acrobatics with guns and ugly machinery I don't for the life of me know.'

'I suppose it's rather exciting to some,' Cecily offered.

'Exciting? One would have thought life was exciting enough without any reenactments of war.'

'Not everyone's life has been like yours, Cora.'

'Hmm,' she murmured, resting her cane to one side, and drawing in her skirts for Cecily to sit down. 'The problem with the British is that they have not seen war at close quarters, not here, not on their own soil, not for generations.' She turned to Cecily, 'No one is alive to remind them of the futility – the carnage, the waste. No, the British go off and fight in other countries. It's very different when it's happening around you. I pray that I never see another war, that your generation – you and Jack – never see any war.'

For a few minutes they sat in silence. The garden was quiet, sleepy in the morning sun, the air cool.

'You must forgive me, Cecily. I'm a little out of sorts today,' she said, placing a bejewelled hand upon Cecily's. She wore a number of rings on her wedding finger and Cecily wanted to ask her which was from whom: which ring went with which man. 'In old age one's thoughts crowd in on one day after day,' Cora went on. 'It's an exhausting business,' and she turned to Cecily with a nervous smile.

She seemed troubled. Her eyes were tearful. And Cecily said, 'Is it Sylvia? Are you missing her?'

She looked away, shook her head. 'No, it is not Sylvia, and no, I am not missing her, as it happens. But I am not relishing the months ahead. I am not looking forward to . . .' She stopped, her lip trembled and for a moment she took on the countenance of a little girl, lost and frightened. 'I have spent so much of my life alone, one would have thought I'd be used to it by now. I've lived in foreign cities, foreign countries, on my own, and yet this country, England, is more foreign to me than any other place.'

'That's because you've been away for so long. It's understandable.'

She nodded. 'But enough of me, I want to talk to you about Jack.'

'Oh . . .'

'It's not easy, for you or for me, to see him go. I understand this,' she began. 'You are . . . attached, fond of each other, I know. But sometimes one has to relinquish attachments, we have to be selfless and brave.' She turned to look at Cecily. 'Am I making sense?'

Cecily nodded.

'I don't want you – either of you – to be hurt, you see,' she said and paused, looking downwards, breathing in deeply. 'People come into our lives without warning, and for a while they make us forget who we are. Only when they leave us are we reminded; only when they leave us do we have to return to who we were before. And that can be painful because we've been changed, and what fitted before, what seemed at least comfortable, is no longer so.' She raised her head, staring into the distance. 'We think nothing can ever be whole again,' she added in a whisper. Then she turned to Cecily. 'I spent a long time waiting for someone, waiting for someone to come back to me. I don't want you to make that mistake.'

On their last day together, like so many days before, Cecily and Jack went out on his motorcycle. She had told her mother, had had to tell her – after roaring past Mrs Moody in Linford – that yes, she sometimes rode pillion on Jack's bike, 'sort of side-saddle and on a cushion,' she added, as though it would make a difference. But Madeline was aghast, furious that Cecily had lied to her, astonished that all the times she had presumed her daughter to be up at Temple Hill, perhaps taking tea in the garden, she had in fact been 'speeding about the lanes with a young man. It's not only dangerous, it's improper!'

'There's nothing improper about it, women are buying them as well.'

Madeline shuddered. 'Next, you'll be telling me you're off to London to fight for votes!'

'Yes, I very well might.'

'Really, Cecily, I don't know what's come over you this summer. You've always been such a . . .'

'Good girl?'

'Yes,' said her mother, looking at her, mystified. 'And of course everyone will assume that you're courting now, you and he,' she went on, 'and I'm not entirely sure what I'm supposed to do.'

'I don't care what everyone assumes but I do care what you think, Mother.'

'What I think . . . what I think is that you're both too young.'

'But you were little older than me when you married Father.'

Madeline shook her head. 'That was different. Jack is about

to leave for university, Cecily, he's not going to stay here. He has a future mapped out for him, and I can't help but feel . . .'

'Yes?'

'That he'll leave you behind, dear.'

Perhaps he would leave her behind. The notion was one Cecily had certainly pondered, particularly after Cora's words to her in the garden. And she had drawn conclusions: he would leave her behind; he had no choice. He had said to her himself, 'it's a tremendous opportunity'. And it was. A university education could not be passed over, no matter what. It would set him up for life. Oh, that she could have the same path and spend three whole years studying, reading, surrounded by erudite people – people she could learn from, people who spoke about poetry and literature and art, people who had travelled and seen places and been places; people who led interesting lives. Oh, that she could be *someone*.

But there was a chink of light, a hope, flickering at the back of her mind – or the front, depending on her mood. He would return, during holidays and when he was able, and then, at the end, he'd be free. Three years, she concluded. I shall have to wait three years.

Nothing had been said. No words about their future had passed between them, though they had spoken often enough about foreign places, places they had read about, heard about, would like to see. She imagined them strolling along the banks of the Seine, the Danube, the Tiber, arm in arm, a handsome couple. And sometimes she imagined them together at Temple Hill . . .

Three years. I shall wait three years, she told herself. Cora's warning to her had, she thought, been about wasting an entire lifetime waiting, and she would certainly not be doing that. Three years was not a lifetime.

But as his departure date loomed, she became aware of the

clock, of the minutes and hours, the slipping away of time and the inevitable goodbye, when he would leave Bramley and move on. And the flicker of hope died.

Jack's life, she imagined, would be as glamorous as his grand-mother's. Faster, modern, and not yet abroad, but on a path to somewhere: somewhere far more sophisticated than Bramley. He would, perhaps, remember her – the village girl, that inno-cent country girl, the one he had been quite fond of at the time. The one he had taken up to London, and rode about with through the lanes. The one he had kissed on a hot day at the top of some hill he couldn't quite remember. In years to come he would return there, to Bramley, at first to visit his grandmother, Cora, and then, after her death, to stay at the place himself from time to time, for he would surely inherit it. And Cecily, too, might be there, might be invited up to Temple Hill for tea. He would take her hand in his and say hello, politely, then step aside to introduce his wife . . .

Oh, the agony!

It would not happen, it could not happen. She could never allow it to.

But the thought, the image, kept coming back to her. She saw herself – rounded, matronly, a brood of noisy, ruddy-faced children and a quiet husband by her side. And him, Jack, lean and dapper, smiling on benignly, sympathetically. But sometimes there were no children or quiet husband, just her: thin and bespectacled and monosyllabic, a spinster of the parish, a school-mistress, speaking about the weather, the last sermon, and Miss Combe's new electricity.

He would say, 'Cecily Chadwick, well I never. I hardly recog-nised you . . . still in Bramley, eh?' For she had never gone anywhere, other than that day excursion to the coast each summer. There had been no travelling, no countries visited or cities explored; there had been no great adventure, and no other loves. And she would smile, grateful for the acknowledgement, the remembrance, and then laugh – and make a joke of her lack of a life. 'Oh, but I could never leave Bramley,' she would say. 'After all, I'm settled here, and it is so wonderful to live in a place where everyone knows who you are.'

He would introduce her to his children, all lined up and quite as beautiful as he, and with exotic names and precocious but enchanting demeanours: Nathanial, Atalanta, Theodopholis and Hermione. And they would look at her with pity in their eyes, but not for her but for their father, that he could ever have loved someone so plain and parochial, that their successful and debonair father could have been so short-sighted. And they would not know what to say, or how to be, and so he would intervene and make small talk, until it was time for her to leave. Then they would all heave a sigh of relief, and tease him that he had once had a thing for poor Miss Chadwick.

When he released her hand he said, 'You never know, I might get back at Christmas . . . come and say boo!'

She smiled.

'Otherwise it'll be Easter.'

'Yes, Easter,' she repeated.

'It's not that long.'

'No.'

'We've our whole lives ahead of us, you know.'

'Of course, I know that.'

'Don't be sad . . . please, don't be sad.'

They stood in the fading twilight by the gate and all she could think was that by morning he would be gone. And all she could hear were the whispers of the coming days and weeks: *the poor thing went about with him all summer . . . bound to happen . . . he was hardly going to settle down here – with her.* And she would have to brave it, have to smile through it all as thought it had been nothing, a brief flirtation, a passing fancy.

'But we've had a fine old time to ourselves,' he said.

'Yes, we have.'

He looked away. 'I can't promise you anything . . . I can't—'

'It's perfectly fine, Jack. You don't need to say any more. I understand.'

She smiled and turned away. She heard the latch on the gate drop, clickety-click, his feet upon the track, and a door quietly close.

Chapter Twenty

*T*he movement of cold air stirs her. The cover has been pulled back. She can hear the rasping sound in the blackness, smell him as he moves closer. 'Come here my little lovely, come to Uncle John now . . .' She tries to wriggle free, but he has hold of her, is pulling at her nightgown, and as she struggles, as she struggles to reach down beneath the bed, the soft cotton tears, releasing her like a baby from the womb and her hand to the floorboards, the brick . . .

Cora could smell the mustiness of an English winter. It was a smell she vaguely remembered: a mingling of damp plaster, rotting wood and vegetation, the smoke of coal fires, and coldness. Coldness. The house felt newly strange and suddenly much too large for one person. She had no need for so much space. Though she might have had, once, when the place was first built, when she still had a son, anticipated a daughter-in-law, envisaged grandchildren. When Georgie told her that he planned on having a large family, 'to make up for the deficit'.

'Deficit indeed!' Fanny had repeated, laughing.

'That's what he said. I suppose it's because he's grown up alone.'

'Well, he'll have to find himself a wife first, and she'll need to be a robust girl, my goodness yes,' Fanny went on, smiling. 'But at least you have the place, the space for this enormous family he's planning.'

Cora moved to the window, gazing out at the excavations for the new monument in honour of the King. Her aunt had told her that it would take over two decades to build and be so vast it would dominate the city's skyline.

'No one knows who anyone is any more,' Fanny was saying, 'it's all changed, anyone of quality seems to have gone, and instead, we have a constant stream of loud Americans to plague us. Tourists they call themselves. They come for a week and fly about the place with lists and maps and itineraries – such frenzied haste.'

'It's the same in Paris,' Cora replied. 'The Americans are *everywhere*.'

Cora had travelled by train from Paris to Rome, as she did each and every Christmas. Edward remained in England, spending Christmas with his family, as he had done each year since their marriage. It was, as her aunt liked to remind her, an unusual domestic arrangement. Twice a year Edward visited her, and she had returned to England the previous summer, staying for two weeks under the roof of his fine stucco-fronted house in Kensington, only ten minutes' walk from George's London home.

As Cora turned away from the window, Fanny returned to the subject of Georgie. 'And how is your darling boy?' she asked.

'Georgie,' Cora repeated, and immediately felt the warmth of maternal blood run through her veins. Georgie, she thought, and could not help but smile. 'He's hardly a boy, he's a grown man now,' she said. 'He is well, very well, and I believe he's charming everyone in London.' She moved about the room, picking up ornaments, examining them, as if to check that they were the same ones that inhabited a place in her memory; running her fingers along polished marble and mahogany; the velvet pile of a sofa, a chair.

'And does he see much of . . . of his godfather?' Fanny asked.

'Oh yes, he sees him from time to time. But of course George is very busy at the Academy, and still travels a good deal.'

'And you? Do you still see him?'

'I saw him in Paris last . . .' she saw her aunt wince and stopped. 'But why do you ask if you do not wish to hear? Why does it pain you to hear me speak about him?'

'Because it's not right for you to see him, not now you're married. He had his chance – so many chances – and you waited for him . . . waited for him for so long. You simply can't allow him to walk in and out of your life, not now.'

'I have to see him; you know that. It's impossible for me to banish him now.'

'But don't see him alone, Cora, please. There's enough gossip already about you and your marriage . . . and him.'

Cora shook her head. 'I no longer care what the old expatriate wives of Rome are saying about me. And there'll always be gossip about George. There always has been.' She turned away from Fanny. 'But, seeing as you've mentioned it, tell me, what is the gossip?'

Fanny did not immediately reply. Cora turned to her. 'Well?'

'That you and George continue to see each other in Paris, alone, that his breakdown was in no small part due to your marriage and . . .'

'And?'

'Georgie.'

Cora sighed. 'George and I see each other when he is in Paris, of course – we're friends, we'll always be dear friends.'

'Friends? And does your husband know just how friendly you are with . . . the President of the Academy?'

'As for his breakdown,' Cora went on, 'he was simply exhausted. Everyone at the wedding could see that. Everyone knew how hard he'd been working . . .'

Fanny shook her head. 'No, it was a blow and it hit him hard. I saw. I was there, remember?'

Cora said nothing.

'But he leads such a queer life,' Fanny said, changing tone, shifting in her chair.

'Why do you say that?'

'No wife, or family, an older married lady his constant companion. It's not normal. But he was always a little peculiar, I thought. Charming but a little peculiar.'

'George was ambitious, single-minded in his vocation, his art. He's a very private person and requires solitude in which to work. He could not cope with a family, family life. And Mrs Hillier is not his *constant companion*, not any more. She no longer travels and has, I believe, been in poor health for some time.'

'It always seemed to me . . .' Fanny began, then hesitated, choosing her words carefully. 'It always seemed to me as though he was fearful . . . hiding something.'

'Hiding something? Oh, perhaps his emotions. But now I understand that genius, real artistic genius, can take every ounce of passion from a man, so that . . . he's left with little to give, to share with another,' Cora replied, staring at a framed mini-ature of her son.

'Hmm. Jack knew, didn't he?'

Cora kept her gaze fixed on her son's face. 'Knew?'

'About you and George . . . later, he knew about you and George.'

'I'm not sure what you mean, or what Jack thought . . . about

271

anything. But do not, please, rewrite *that* particular chapter. Jack's death had nothing whatsoever to do with me, or George, as you well know, and if he was concerned he never said. And I married him, didn't I? I did as I was told.' She moved over to her aunt, sat down opposite her. 'You know . . . you know that I loved George. I still do. I can't change that. I can't change what my heart feels.'

'No, you can't say that, not now. You have a good husband, one who cares about you, who loves you.'

'Oh, I know that, of course I do, and I'm immensely fond of him, too. But let me ask you this: did you cease to love your husband, James, when he died?'

'No, of course not.'

'But you love another now?'

'Yes, but that's quite different, he's a different person and this is another stage of my life.'

'Exactly.'

'But James is dead, Cora; George lives and Edward—'

'Edward is my husband,' she interrupted, rising to her feet. 'He understands that George and I were . . . are close, that we remain firm friends.' She walked over to the window. 'And yes, George lives, but so perhaps does another man . . . so perhaps does John Abel.'

And that was it. The name – the unmentionable name – had been uttered, silently shattering three decades of carefully arranged words, and everything between them.

She turned to her aunt. 'I'm sorry, but I'm afraid it's a little late in the day for you to lecture me on the morality and virtues of a faithful marriage.'

Fanny did not look at her, but Cora could hear her breathing as the name ricocheted about the room: impossible to grab hold of and take back. And what she had said was true enough: John Abel might yet be alive. And if so, where did that leave her aunt? There could be no moral high ground. Not then, not ever. They were both guilty.

When Cora asked Mrs Davey to close up various rooms, the housekeeper reminded her that they had never in fact been opened up; that the morning room and a few of the bedrooms were still stacked with crates, yet to be unpacked. Something to do over the winter, Cora thought: unpack and go through it all, sorting. Mr Cordery would have to bring the crates down to the drawing room; she would open them up there, where it would be warm. She would be able to review it *all*, her life. Unravel the knot.

She had not heard from Sylvia and did not expect to. But she would write to her in time, eventually. She would send her a Christmas card, perhaps. And she could rest easy about the people at the farm. Cecily had been to call on them and they had told her that they had never heard of any other John Abel. The name was a coincidence, nothing more. They were perhaps related in some convoluted way to *him*, Cora thought, but it was a common enough name, or had been, once. And the letters had stopped, for now at least.

Yes, she would be able to address things now, without bother-ation and interruptions. She would have time and peace; space to think. She would be able to work through everything, put it in order; write it all down. Or perhaps Cecily could . . . After all, she was young, part of the modern world. What was once shocking and scandalous was . . . not so unusual now. People were more forgiving, more understanding, surely. And all fam-ilies had secrets, hidden away somewhere.

She would unravel the knot and work backwards. Go all the way back to the beginning, to that time before, before they had moved on, before new countries and new names, before the inventing and reinventing began. She would go back to where *she* first started. Because she needed to make sense of the start in order to make sense of this end. And there was an end, looming, she knew. It was why she needed to set things in order, why she needed to put things straight. There should be no mess for Jack to have to deal with. Death, she often thought, should be peaceful, any ripples for those left behind soothing. But at other times she was filled with panic, terrified of the dark void ahead, and of meeting those she had – in life – escaped.

I must not think of death, she told herself; otherwise it will surely hear me and come knocking . . .

So she tried to look forward to bleak winter, to the drawing in of days and long dark nights. She tried to settle herself in autumn, watching clouds and drizzle, and a pale English sun. And she waited for Cecily to call.

She had, she realised, been testing Cecily over the course of the summer, slipping in details here and there, but still not entirely the truth. She had been sounding her out, watching her reactions. And the girl had not once appeared shocked, had not flinched. She had been sympathetic, understanding. She had passed the test.

I shall tell Cecily the truth, she decided; ask her to write it all down. But there remained one problem: which version and for whom? Well, for Jack of course. There was only him. But would he want to know? Perhaps it would be better for her to omit certain details, to leave it to fate and the future to unravel. Yes, perhaps. She had no wish to cause him any unnecessary pain or distress, or to burden him further. No. Her desire was simply to put the record straight – for herself, in her own mind; to release her burden and be in possession of that state generally known as a clear conscience. She would ask Cecily, take her advice. After all, she cared about Jack, and who knew what might happen between them in the future.

Thankfully, Cecily was not going anywhere. They would no doubt spend some of the long winter evenings ahead together, for Cecily had already said, 'Don't worry, Cora, I'm still here.' Yes, so long as she had dear Cecily calling on her, with that sweet open mind and sunny disposition, she would not succumb to loneliness, not give way to *the others*. And she must stay warm, speak to Mrs Davey about the fires; make sure there was enough coal and logs. Oh yes, she must stay warm.

The mere thought of an English winter made Cora shiver. That harsh chill which permeated one's clothing and flesh and bones. She had told people that it would be her first in six decades, but this was not strictly true, because she had come back once, briefly, in the depths of winter.

Standing by an open grave, her face too cold to move, her heart numb, Cora had watched her son's coffin as it was lowered into the frozen earth. But even then, as he was delivered into that cold hard ground, he had become a memory, nothing more than a memory. He was a name, another name, soon to be added to a churchyard of chiselled names. And the realisation that his presence – his face, his voice, all of him – was already dimming and being forgotten, struck her . . .

Those who had known him would remember his laugh, his smile, his humour, and his bravery. They would speak of him for a while, clinging on to those remnants, but slowly, with time, they would forget. In years to come his name might crop up in conversation, someone might say, 'Ah yes, George Staunton, I vaguely remember him. Whatever happened to him?' But the name would fade, the tombstone fall, and, eventually, inevitably, disappear into the undergrowth of that quiet corner of the churchyard.

Perhaps one day someone would notice that leaning tombstone covered in lichen and ivy. They might bend down, pull away the weeds, and then – moving their hands over the stone – say the name out loud once more. And for a moment, just a moment, they might wonder who he had been, George Staunton; whose child, whose husband, whose father. They might try to imagine what someone of that name looked like, how he spoke, what made him laugh or cry. But they would never be able imagine the baby born in Rome, nor the circumstances surrounding his birth. They would never be able to picture the boy who had grown up in France, or envisage the young man who had returned – so dazzlingly handsome and suntanned – from two years in India. His lifetime, the thirty-three years he had walked upon the earth, had ended, abruptly, one Saturday morning in January.

In the years that followed, after her son's death and before her final return to England, visits to old friends – and to acquaintances she had made on her incessant journeys – kept Cora busy. There was little else for her to do at that time, and she was in fact of no fixed abode. Her circle of friends had slowly diminished. Many of them had passed away, others had returned home, to England or America. In Rome, there was a new crowd, a younger crowd, a mix of English, American and European artists, travellers, and new business people, as well as the usual fugitives and misfits.

But Rome was not the same place. The city had changed shape. The antiquated ruins and monuments remained, weathered further by the passing of years, crumbling through ignorance and neglect, and now like gargantuan tombstones strewn haphazardly about the place, randomly interrupting the new order and tidiness of modern Rome. But the small medieval city, the Rome of Cora's youth, had been all but swept away.

On her last visit to the city, she sat each morning outside the Café Santa Maria in the Piazza d'Ara Coeli, and from under the shade of her parasol watched the exotic human traffic pass by like contestants in a fancy dress parade: young Romans strutting like peacocks, elderly peasants cocooned in grubby cloth, and wealthy English tourists in their distinctive upper-class garb for hotter climes. The English tourists, known for their good manners, always smiled and nodded, *'Buon giorno.'* They assumed her to be Italian, Roman, and she never let on. Never said, 'But I am also English.' Instead, she surreptitiously studied them as they studied their maps and guidebooks and discussed their itinerary for that day.

The invisibility of old age allowed her to observe and listen. It enabled her to bestow these unknown friends with detailed identities, so that by the time they moved on she knew them all the better for *not* having spoken with them. Later, as she walked through the shadowed streets off the Corso she often fancied she could hear the revelry of a party from an upstairs window. And sometimes she would stop, stand and listen to sounds that were there but not there: the French military band playing on in the Piazza Colonna, the cheers and thunderous echo of a carnival. But there were times when her loneliness was acute, the sense of singularity suffocating, the absence of familiar voices deafening.

Each afternoon she visited the Protestant Cemetery, arranging flowers or tidying the potted plants within the box-hedged graves. And here, sitting on the old iron bench under the shade of cypresses, silent conversations flowed.

Rome reinvigorated her, body and soul. Paris was simply exhausting. And London, on those rare occasions she had flitted in and out, was jarring and judgemental, too big and brash. And the lack of light, that interminable smog, rendering its streets dank and inhospitable, depressed her spirits. In the cacophony of the English capital she had always felt like an alien, an outsider, for it was the place from which she had fled, and then returned too late in life to be fashionable.

Travelling from city to city, country to country, had for so long been the ebb and flow of her life. And though no one was waiting for her in Rome or Paris, or anywhere now, continuing this movement allowed her to luxuriate in the sensation of busyness. She was able to talk of train times, schedules and itineraries, departure and arrival dates, arrangements and contingencies, as though they mattered; as though her time was valuable, as though others depended upon her punctuality and *were* waiting.

She knew her way to the Eternal City the way anyone knows the path that leads them home. From a train carriage window she checked off the sequence of familiar vistas, counting down landmarks, towns and cities. And later, travelling back over that same landscape, they were checked off again, in reverse order.

On her final journey, returning to England for good, she had been unusually reticent, had no interest in making any new friends. Standing upon the deck of a steamer, taking in England's ragged hemline – quiet, contemplative, inconspicuous, she hoped – she offered little conversation and made no mention of any connections. On that last journey she simply played the part of an elderly lady returning from an indefinite period abroad. And when those standing alongside her turned to her and said, 'Ah, so good to be home,' she simply smiled. 'Yes indeed, so good to be home.'

'. . . We'll live like gypsies . . . divide our time between Rome and Florence, head to Paris in the spring . . . and the south of France perhaps in autumn.'

'But not England?'

'No, not England. Who needs England?'

'And you'll stay with me?'

'Of course, I shall . . . I'll never leave you.'

'Not even if I had done something . . . wicked?'

'Hmm, something wicked . . . If you had done something wicked, well, I rather think I'd love you all the more for it.'

And so she gives in, moves her mouth to his, and seals her fate.

Book Two

England 1923

Chapter Twenty-One

ylvia had said it out loud, and silently, too: *Cora is gone
. . . Cora is gone . . .* She had to; had to remind herself. It
would take time, she told herself, to grow used to the idea. And
it was why she had sought out the photograph, why she sat with
it in her hands. But it was still queer to think of *her* dead, a
person no more. Difficult to accept that she had been mortal,
just like everyone else; impossible and too painful to think of
her beneath the sandy soil of an English churchyard.

Perhaps it would be easier if she had seen the grave, witnessed
the burial and been a part of that ceremonial goodbye. She
would, she thought, have been able to say adieu. She would have
been able to let her know.

For years Sylvia had pondered a hello and not a goodbye. She
had anticipated a reunion, reconciliation, imagined them
embracing, forgiving, smiling at one another, herself saying, 'I
shall hear none of it; it is all in the past now.' She had imagined
returning once more down that sweeping driveway in Mr
Cotton's wagonette, and Cora, standing there upon the doorstep
– waiting for her, just as she had that sultry summer's day twelve

years ago. How pleased Cora had been to see her . . . She had said, 'Here at last!' and then playfully chastised Sylvia for her tardiness, telling her that she had been waiting patiently all morning. And Jack had been there too: eager to finally meet his grandmother's oldest friend. He had said, 'I've been longing to meet you . . . have heard so much about you.' That was how it had been, hadn't it?

Yes, it had been a perfect day. One etched on her memory.

But there could be no reunion, not now, not ever. That indomitable spirit, that indefatigable soul had departed this life and moved on – as she always had.

Sylvia stared at the photograph. She ran a finger over the tear: a scar on her memory, and on her heart. But it was too late, too late to offer Cora her happy ending, too late to assuage her loss or make amends: too late to tell her. And there was an added torment bound up in those few hushed words to a painter, so long ago in Rome.

'But had I known . . . had I known . . .' she whispered, shaking her head.

And then she closed her eyes once more as she relived that bittersweet moment, when Cora had clung to her weeping, saying, 'He says we have no future, no future together . . . he says it cannot be . . . that he cannot marry me . . . will never marry me . . .'

But how wonderful it had felt to hold her, to have Cora in her arms, so weak and fragile, and lost. 'You have me,' she had said. 'You have me, and I shall never ever walk away from you.' And yet she had. For hadn't she walked away that summer, twelve years before? Hadn't she left Cora then, weak and fragile and lost once again, afraid, alone and old?

'I let her down! I walked away . . . just as he did . . . I was no different.'

Sylvia had not been able to attend the funeral, though Cecily had been kind enough to telephone a second time to inform her of the arrangements. The first call, the one to tell her Cora had died, had come out of the blue. And Cecily had been quite cold, Sylvia thought: perfunctory in her approach. But Sylvia was not used to receiving telephone calls. The only telephone at the Windsor was in the arched alcove of the lobby, where, on the rare occasion it was in use, people liked to loiter about, listening. It had a sign above it which read, FOR RESIDENTS' USE & EMERGENCIES ONLY, in red letters upon white. It was a queer, perplexing contraption and Sylvia had no use for it. And that day, when Mrs Halliday came into the dining room and said, 'Do excuse me, Miss Dorland, but you're wanted on the telephone,' Sylvia had been mystified. For who would call her? She had no kin.

Mrs Halliday had handed her the parts, whispering instructions, 'To the ear, dear . . . that's it . . . now say hello . . .' Sylvia thought she heard a voice: 'Sylvia . . . Miss Dorland, is that you?' But the line had been bad and, not sure what the call was about or to whom the voice belonged, Sylvia had been circumspect, reticent.

'Yes,' she had said, elongating those three letters, phrasing the word as a question.

'It's Cecily.'

'Cecily . . .'

'I hope you remember me . . .'

Cecily Chadwick. 'Yes, yes. I remember you. Of course I remember you. How lovely to hear from you.'

'I'm calling with some . . .'

But Sylvia did not catch the words and had to ask her to speak up.

'*Sad* news,' Cecily said, louder, and with emphasis. 'It's Cora, I'm afraid she passed away on Friday. I thought I should call . . . call and let you know.'

And that was it. Cecily may have said more, Sylvia could not remember. She had been too stunned, too upset to take in anything else. She had said goodbye and then stood for some time clutching the receiver, unsure what to do with it *or* the news. When Mrs Halliday reappeared, she asked, 'Bad news, dear?' She took the receiver from Sylvia's hand, hung it up, and led her back towards the dining room. But Sylvia had said no, she could not face anyone, could not eat now. 'My friend, my dearest friend has passed away.'

She did not cry, not that day. She simply returned upstairs to her room and sat quietly until it was time for bed.

Perhaps Cecily said something about the funeral during that first call. Perhaps she had told Sylvia she would call again to let her know the arrangements. Either way, Cecily had called again a few days later, and that was when she had also said that she had something for Sylvia from Cora.

'Actually, I've had it in my possession for quite some time,' she said. 'She asked me to make sure that it was passed on to you in the event of her death.'

Cora: ever the planner.

But there was no way Cecily could get up to London, not at that time. Not with the funeral and everything else she had to deal with, she said, but perhaps in a few weeks, when things were calmer.

An obituary in one of the London newspapers was simply titled, 'Death of the Countess de Chevalier de Saint Léger Lawson', and read:

We deeply regret to record the death which occurred at her home in Bramley on Friday of last week of the Countess de Chevalier de Saint Léger Lawson, who had been in failing health for some time past . . . The Countess was in her eightieth year and had a very wide circle of friends both here and on the Continent, to whom her passing is a matter of sincere regret. The Countess was thrice married and by her first union, to Mr John Staunton, there was a son, Captain George Staunton RHA, who met with his death in a hunting accident many years ago. Her second marriage was to the Count de Chevalier de Saint Léger who was killed in the Franco-German War; while she was wedded on a third occasion to Mr Edward Lawson, late President of the Royal Institute of British Architects, and father of Lord George Lawson, late President of the Academy.

The Countess was born at Standen Hall in Norfolk, and was the niece of the late Contessa Cansacchi di Amelia who passed away some time ago in Rome. A renowned and fashionable figure within Continental society, the Countess resided a great deal abroad, in particular in Rome and Paris, and was noted for her cosmopolitan tastes and for her fine collection of art and antiques . . . The funeral took place at St Luke's Churchyard, Bramley, on Wednesday afternoon, where the remains of the deceased lady were laid to rest . . .

The piece went on to list the chief mourners, and to say that 'the grave had been prettily lined with moss and bunches of violets by Mr Cordery, the head gardener at Temple Hill'. It then listed the floral tributes, and Sylvia was pleased to see her own name.

Of course there were mistakes, inaccuracies. How could there not be? Cora had spent a lifetime confusing and confounding everyone with her story. And she had always lied about her age, was ten years older than the age they quoted. But she would have been satisfied, Sylvia thought, to be a decade younger – even in death. And the obituary recorded most of the official version: almost all of the important names were there. And yet, Sylvia could not help but wonder where the information had come from, for someone had tidied it all up. That someone had to be Cecily.

Sylvia cut out the obituary and pasted it into the scrapbook, the one she kept that charted Cora's life, and now death. It included every announcement – the birth of each of her sons, their deaths, and the deaths of each of her husbands; her marriages; court circulars, drawing-room appearances, and clippings about George. But there had been so many about George, particularly after his death, that she gave up cutting and pasting *him*. Also in the scrapbook were two pencil sketches of Cora by John Clifford, and another by George (all three from Rome, when Cora had been no more than twenty); a ribbon Cora had given her at around that same time, and various notes confirming appointments and rendezvous. Sylvia liked to look at those notes, the handwriting, the young signature long before the loops and swirls of the double C flourish that became her customary abbreviation. There was a lock of pale golden hair, various pressed flowers, and postcards and telegrams, and a small swatch of blue silk Cora had sent her shortly before her marriage to Edward. The photograph, the one taken in the garden that day at Temple Hill, would go in there also, Sylvia decided: at the very end. It was the only one she had of them together.

Some weeks after the obituary, the same newspaper announced a sale at the house:

The trustees of the estate of the late Countess de Chevalier de Saint Léger Lawson announce a sale to be held at her home, Temple Hill, including the whole of the antique and modern appointments: Louis XIV and Empire escritoires, secretaires, commodes and tables. Two fine old English mahogany and oak long-case clocks. Beautiful Chinese silk embroidery and antique Italian tapestry. Rare old French trousseau chests, French, Italian and English oil paintings and water colours, Italian carved cabinets, settees and chairs in old English, 890 volumes of books, plate, needlework, tapestries, French linen, clocks, bronzes, Italian marble sculpture, ornamental china and porcelain, Venetian air twist and other glass and crystal, English oak dining furniture, together with the usual indoor and outdoor effects . . .

So, Cecily was selling it all. Cora's precious cargo, gathered over a lifetime and brought back to England, was to be sold off, flung back across the counties of England, the countries of Europe. And that announcement, the announcement of the sale at the house, inspired more tears than any obituary. Because all of those things, every item of furniture and glass and linen, each book and painting and each piece of china, were all that was left of her, all that Cora had left to the world of herself. And Sylvia could picture it all, picture it all so vividly, the dismantling of that life.

Chapter Twenty-Two

When Cecily arrived she was not at all as Sylvia remembered her. A glamorous woman, festooned in fur, had replaced the gauche and awkward girl of Sylvia's memory. And she was taller, much taller than Sylvia remembered. She moved across the room with an alarming confidence, leaned forward in a haze of perfume and pressed her lips to Sylvia's cheek. Sylvia released a short, sharp gasp. She could not recall the last time anyone had done such a thing. She watched Cecily place a brown paper parcel on the low table and dispense with her fur, draping it along the back of the armchair. 'Golly,' she said, as she sat down, 'what a day.'

It was stormy outside. Sylvia had noticed. She had watched the weather at the window for most of that day: the constant drizzle interrupted by intermittent downpours, the petrified limbs of the trees in the park opposite against the low sky. Later, she had heard the wind, coming in angry gusts, and then the bells: an ambulance or fire engine, perhaps. And she could only wonder at the drama unfolding somewhere.

'Yes, what a day,' Sylvia said, eyeing Cecily as she opened up

290

her handbag and took out a familiar cigarette case. 'I hope it hasn't been too much trouble for you, coming up to town,' she said.

'No trouble, no trouble at all,' Cecily replied. She flicked a lighter, tilted her head and released a plume of smoke into the dimly lit room; then she placed the handbag on the table in front of them, next to the brown paper parcel. 'Actually, we're up for a few days.'

'Ah, I see,' Sylvia said and nodded.

It made sense. Yes, it made sense. *This* Cecily did not look like a schoolmistress from the country, not at all. This Cecily was undoubtedly used to trips up to town, to hailing and dashing about in taxicabs, in a flurry, in a rush. This Cecily was different to the one before. She wore the new shorter length skirt, her hair was cut fashionably short, too, and, Sylvia noted, she left an imprint of her painted lips at the end of her cigarette.

Sylvia leaned forward, pushing the glass ashtray across the polished wood, and said, 'Oh, I must show you something.' She reached down to the shelf beneath the table and handed Cecily the photograph. 'I'm afraid it got torn . . . caught in an album or some such thing, I can't quite recall now.'

Cecily stared at the image. Yes, she too could remember that day. 'Feels like a lifetime ago,' she said. 'So much has happened since then.'

And it had for her, and for the world, but less so for Sylvia.

Right up until her move to the Windsor Hotel, four years ago, Sylvia had followed a daily routine unchanged and unaltered for over half a century. The move had been disruptive but inevitable. And the Windsor had undoubtedly been the right choice. It was situated round the corner from her former flat, and almost all of the residents were elderly ladies, like herself. Most were widows, who had had a husband, or two, and children, or not. Many of them were colonials who had returned from India and the Far East after the war had ended. It was one of the things Sylvia liked about the Windsor, the class of person. And it made the conversation all the more interesting to hear about places like Bangalore, Kashmir and Calcutta, and verandas and bungalow lifestyles. She had even toyed with the idea of writing a novel set in India, loosely based on her new friend Mrs Evesleigh's life. Oh yes, the Windsor had been the right choice. These women understood expatriate life, and Sylvia had been able to talk about her time in Rome, and about her dear friend, the Countess de Chevalier de Saint Léger Lawson. A few claimed to know or recognise the name, thought they had heard it – or part of it – before, and then usually asked, 'Any relation to *Lord* Lawson?'

'Stepmother,' Sylvia replied, 'and dear friend, as was I.'

Inevitably, there then ensued some discussion about George Lawson: his life and work, his affairs – and rumoured illegitimate children.

'Well, I really wouldn't know about *that*,' Sylvia responded, running free, but enjoying the debate and that tingle of attention.

Sylvia had had special cards printed to announce her move to the Windsor, and though she had only managed to send out a dozen or so of the fifty, later cutting up the unused ones to use as bookmarks, she *had* sent one to Cora, with a note on the reverse, saying, 'My dear, I do hope that you are well, and that we might be able to catch up one day in the not too distant future. As ever, Sylvia.' She had hoped for a reply, a note to say 'Good luck' or something along the lines of 'Wishing you well in your new home', but nothing came.

The war, Sylvia agreed with the other ladies, had changed everything and everyone. No, nothing would ever be the same. But they had their memories, memories of how things had once been, memories of lost places, lost faces. Even now, four years later, The War consumed a great deal of their time, and energy.

But Sylvia had had no children or grandchildren to lose, and though she had lived through and witnessed the seemingly never-ending horror, and had imagined – or had tried to imagine – circumstances not her own, she had for the most part been buried in the execution of the book she and Cora had begun years before, the book they had worked on during the summer of 1911. It would not be Cora's memoirs, could not be Cora's memoirs, but it could be the story of her life, Sylvia had decided. The story of her life as it could have been. And it was to be Sylvia's peace offering. For she had planned to write to Cora, enclosing the first draft, once it was finished. She would not and could not, she had decided, do anything with it without her friend's blessing.

But time had run out and now the manuscript lay in a drawer, and Sylvia was unsure what to do with it. Unsure, that is, until Cecily's second telephone call. And as soon as Sylvia heard Cecily say the word 'manuscript', her heart leapt. Cora knew, had obviously remembered, and it seemed as though from beyond the grave she was giving it her blessing, sanctioning it.

And it was understandable, commendable, Sylvia reasoned, that Cora wished Cecily to see it first, particularly in view of the circumstances. But she must not be *too* eager. There was an etiquette to be observed, a way of handling these things, just as there was with everything else. She would wait, wait until later, once they had crossed bridges, so to speak. Then she would offer Cecily a sherry and produce the manuscript. She had imagined Cecily's face – though it had been different, younger, and altogether more open – the look of astonishment, surprise, then the tears and smiles; and she had heard her say, 'Oh Sylvia, she would have been so happy, so grateful . . .' And Sylvia would say, 'It's the book I have been writing for over fifty years, my final work.' And they would raise their glasses to—

'. . . Sylvia?'

Cecily was still holding the photograph in her hand and Sylvia thought she had perhaps missed a question. 'Mr Fox died . . . passed away last year,' she said, presumably for a second time, and quite as though Sylvia and he had been close.

'Oh dear, how sad.'

She went on, and Sylvia realised that she was working her way through those in the photograph, and beyond it, to a village, bustling and busy, going about its business. That summer's day – that moment, that second – when they had all smiled at the camera and Mr Trigg had hit a switch, they had been frozen in time, together, forever.

Sonia Brownlow married Jack's friend, Noel, Cecily was saying now. But he had been killed in action only weeks after their wedding. She had married again, another army man, and was living out in India, Cecily thought. 'And did you see Marjorie, Sonia's sister, in the newspapers?' she asked.

Sylvia shook her head. 'No, was she married?'

Cecily laughed. 'No! She was arrested, at a suffragette parade. But I believe she's been released.'

'Arrested,' Sylvia repeated, Gracious.'

It baffled Sylvia why these women did such things, why they wanted to vote. Some things were better left to men, she thought: politics, fighting, voting; making decisions.

'Whatever happened to Miss Combe?' Sylvia asked. 'I rather liked her.'

'Poor Miss Combe,' Cecily said. 'You know, she never got her electricity. She passed away quite suddenly, unexpectedly, during the very first days of the war.'

'And your friend, the one from the shop, the post office, where is she now?'

The farmer – or farm worker, as it turned out – that Annie had been waiting for finally arrived and married her the year before war broke out. They produced three children before he was killed in action in 1917. And though Annie remained a widow, there was someone in her life, Cecily said.

'And your mother . . . your sister?'

Cecily's sister, Ethne, was married to the new rector, a Mr Meredith Ballantyne, and Madeline continued to live at the same house, the one her husband had built. Rosetta had moved in, Cecily said, after Ethne moved out. But Bramley had changed, people had gone, businesses had disappeared. 'It is all different,' she said, 'not at all as you'll remember . . .'

They spoke about various other people in the village. Cecily mentioned a few names Sylvia could not recall, and, bizarrely, Sylvia mentioned names Cecily could not recall.

'I imagine you saw the details of the sale?' Cecily said.

'Yes, I did. But it strikes me as a great shame,' Sylvia replied, noting the 'CC' ring on Cecily's finger. 'I'm not sure she would have wanted it *all* going under the hammer.'

'But we can't keep it,' she shrugged her shoulders, 'we just can't. We don't have the space.'

'But surely if you lived there, at Temple Hill . . .'

Cecily smiled, shook her head. 'No, it has to be sold, I'm afraid. You see, there was little to no money, and we certainly can't afford to run a big house like that, not on the money I earn. I don't think Cora had any idea quite how impoverished she was . . . and probably just as well.'

'She was never very good with money,' said Sylvia.

'It's so sad that the two of you never saw each other again after that . . . that little upset you had.'

'*Upset?* Oh, but we never fell out, not really. I loved her, loved her dearly, and I think, I hope, she knew that . . . but yes, I wish I had seen her again. Just once, once more.'

Cecily looked away. She said, 'I'm afraid she was very confused at the end, had absolutely no idea who anyone was. It was a blessing, really.'

'When did it start, the confusion?'

Cecily shook her head. 'Oh, years ago, during the war. She simply couldn't accept what happened, what was happening around her. It was very hard for her.'

'Yes, of course.'

'But she had become forgetful, a little confused, even before that time.'

'Yes,' Sylvia said, remembering.

'She thought she was back in Rome, thought she was young again . . .' Cecily leaned forward, stubbed out her cigarette. 'It was sad,' she added, closing her eyes for a moment, shaking her head again. 'Because she was so . . . so vulnerable, so . . .' she glanced up at the ceiling and then laughed. 'You know, she began to wear her hair down,' she said, looking directly at Sylvia and wiping away a tear.

'Down?' Sylvia repeated.

'Yes, *down*. And sometimes with a moth-eaten plume or an ancient paste clip in it, but she looked so pretty, quite beautiful with that long white-white hair,' she went on dreamily. 'Yes, very pretty.'

'It's how she wore it when she was young.'

'And right up until the end she was always dressed, always in one of her costumes, as though about to go somewhere, or receive someone.'

'It's how it used to be . . .'

'She was sweet, childlike . . . and very talkative, too. Do you remember her queer accent?'

Sylvia smiled, nodded. How could she forget?

'You know, when I first met her, when she first came to Bramley,' Cecily continued, 'it seemed to me as though she was

296

always . . . delivering a speech, harking back to Rome, to what once had been. I was really quite awestruck – I rather think we all were, then,' she said wistfully. 'She was so intriguing, so enigmatic, and oh, how we all hung on to her every word!'

Yes, Sylvia thought, *how I hung on* . . .

'And she always seemed so . . . so extraordinarily wise . . .'

How people had fawned and courted her, Sylvia thought – even then.

'And forgiving. She was forgiving, wasn't she?'

Sylvia smiled, nodded. Yes, she was forgiving. She forgave *him*; despite everything, she forgave George. And now Sylvia was pleased she had given them that time, those final few months together.

'I was so sorry . . . when I heard, heard about Jack. It must have been hard, very hard for you,' Sylvia said, and not without empathy. 'And you know, I did write. I wrote to Cora at the time,' she added.

Cecily nodded. 'It was hard for us all,' she said and sighed. 'But by then everything had changed. The village had thinned out, altered its shape and character. And so too had she. You see, it was then, during that time, that she dispensed with her title, decided she wanted to be known simply as "Mrs Lawson". She didn't go anywhere, hardly ventured outside. And people began to say that she was mad, quite mad. They said that the place was haunted, that she lived amongst ghosts and spoke more with the dead than with the living. And perhaps it was true. But then she lingered on there for so long, for so many years, too long, surrounded by all her statues and bronzes . . . lost in her memories.'

Yes, Sylvia thought, picturing Cora's dust-shrouded para-phernaila, how dark the house must have been: dark and dusty, and filled with things no one would ever dream of having indoors nowadays. How could she *not* have gone back, stuck there, surrounded by it all? But she had the name, the only name she ever wanted, in the end: Mrs Lawson.

Cecily continued. She had called on Cora regularly, she said, but the place – the house and Cora herself – appeared sadder and shabbier on each occasion. Like Dickens' Miss Havisham, it seemed to her as though Cora was trapped in time, 'in a moment – a day, a month, a season, a year – she simply couldn't let go of or release. She became a relic, a relic of a bygone era.' But even before this, Cecily said, she had witnessed Mr Fox and a few others alter tempo. The tide turned, and just as though they – the very same people who had once been mesmerised – had been jilted at the altar, as though they had been wooed and courted and then somehow let down, they turned on her. They began to say that she was and always had been deluded, that she had simply made things up, and that she was nobody special.

By the time the war ended, she had gone, Cecily said, closing her eyes for a moment. 'She was lost . . . and I suppose we were all browbeaten, disenchanted, uninterested in titles and former lifestyles, or any tales that did not involve a Military Cross.' No one associated old Mrs Lawson with any famous names; no one was interested, she said. One decade had altered everyone's perspective, and Cora, the Countess de Chevalier de Saint Léger, her connections and memories of Paris and Rome, had been forgotten. 'No one knew she was there.'

'In these past few years,' Cecily continued, 'since the war, she just seemed to . . . shrivel up, literally shrink. Mrs Davey stayed on with her, of course, and Mr Cordery, too. But she had few if any visitors, apart from yours truly. And she had no idea who anyone was anyhow, no idea what time she was in.'

Cecily told Sylvia that Cora's bed had been moved downstairs, into what had been her drawing room, and a live-in nurse employed to take care of her. The canvas of her life, which had once been epic – in miles and scale and vista – grew smaller and smaller, until it became nothing more than the view from that bed.

'But I'd like to talk to you,' Cecily said, turning to Sylvia, altering her tone, 'about something she told me . . . something she told me on one of the last occasions I visited her.'

It had been shortly before that final, rapid decline, said Cecily. Cora had sat in her usual chair, overdressed, tiny and hunched. She had asked Cecily about her journey, whether she had had a good crossing. And Cecily had smiled and nodded. What else could she do? Cora had asked her the very same question on her previous visit. She was confused, thought she was back in Rome, and there seemed little point in attempting to dislodge her from her dream. She told Cecily that she was glad not to be in England, 'so cold at this time of year', and then she leaned forward in her chair and said, 'I shan't ever go back there, you know. Not now.'

'Well, you can be wherever you wish to be,' Cecily replied.

'He wants to visit Cyprus in the spring . . .' she said, absently.

'That would be nice.'

'We might go to Egypt, see the Nile, the pyramids.'

'How lovely.'

'But I'll never go back there. I can't ever go back there.'

'No.'

'You understand, don't you?'

Cecily nodded.

'And he shan't go back either,' she continued. 'He prefers it here, you see. Oh yes, he always did . . . he never wanted to leave me, but he had to. It wasn't because of Freddie. He didn't know . . . had no idea,' she added, lifting her hand to the locket round her neck.

None of it had made any sense to Cecily. And she was herself distracted, keeping an eye upon the time, glancing to the clock on the mantelpiece. And the muddled ramblings of a deluded old lady had not been compelling enough to unravel. Not then. The same names came up again and again: Freddie and George, or Georgie, and Jack and Fanny. All jumbled in with 'he' and 'she' and 'him' and 'her', and 'they'. How could it make sense? A lifetime spewed out without any chronology; the names of people long since gone, and – bar one – never known to Cecily. It was sad, pathetic, and the events of the preceding decade had washed away any romantic ideas Cecily might have had about the elderly woman sitting in front of her. Reality had arrived in 1914, futility in 1917.

'Did you see him?' Cora had asked, moving in her chair, tilting her head to peer at Cecily.

Her spine had curved with age, pushing her head forward so that it hung down and appeared too large for her small frame. Mrs Davey said she barely touched food, and though she had long given up smoking, Mrs Davey told Cecily that she still enjoyed the occasional glass of wine.

'See whom, dear?'

'Well, Jack, of course. They're outside . . . they'll be back at any minute. I said to them not to go far, said you were coming . . .'

And thus it went on, this movement back and forth in time, and names, and words, and words and words. Then silence. From time to time the flicker of amusement crossed her face, and she almost laughed; and then she would frown, appear perplexed or bewildered, move about in her chair, scanning the room with her eyes, searching for . . . sense? Order?

She said, 'He was a shoemaker.'

'Who, dear?' Cecily asked. 'Who was a shoemaker?'

'He was . . . Uncle John . . .'

'Uncle John?'

'Do you remember him?'

Cecily shook her head. 'No, I never knew him. Was it a long time ago?'

'Best forgotten,' she said, then added, 'You mustn't tell her, don't tell Fanny we've spoken of him.'

'Of course I shan't tell her . . . but what happened to him?'

She didn't answer. She disappeared back to that place Cecily couldn't reach. But the pain – on her face, in her eyes – was easy enough to see.

'What happened to Uncle John, Cora?'

She winced, closed her eyes and shook her head. 'Mustn't tell.'

'Mustn't tell what?'

She opened her eyes, and without looking at Cecily, staring down into her lap, she whispered, 'I killed him.'

For a moment Cecily said nothing. She was unsure what to say. 'I'm quite sure you did not kill anyone,' she said at last, in an unusually condescending tone.

Cora looked up at her. 'Oh, but I did. I hit him over the head with it!'

'With what? What did you hit him over the head with?'

'It had to be done . . . had to be done. He was a brute, a monster . . . and I didn't understand. We went to Jersey,' she went on, her eyes half closed, lowering her head. 'Yes, Jersey . . . to the Lebruns . . .' She raised her head again. 'Do you recall them, Philip and Mary?'

'No. I never knew them.'

'We couldn't go back, you see. No, not ever, she said. But Mr Staunton was a good man, such a *good* man.'

'Mr Staunton? Jack's grandfather?'

None of it made any sense.

'Did Mr Staunton know any of this . . . about Uncle John?'

But she didn't answer, didn't seem to hear. 'Fanny warned me. But I never thought they'd find me.' She glanced up at

Cecily. 'It was my brother, you know, my eldest brother, Samuel . . . he ended up there, in Jersey . . . working for the Lebruns. I suppose Mary thought she was bringing us back together. But he wanted money, nothing more. He said he'd write to the newspapers, tell them.' She shook her head. 'My aunt had only just married again . . . become a contessa. I suppose he thought I was rich . . .'

'You mean to say you were blackmailed . . . by your *brother*?'

'He said he'd tell *him* . . . tell him where we were, how to find us. But how could he tell him if he was dead? And I *had* killed him . . . Fanny told me. Yes, it wasn't bigamy, she said, because he was gone . . . it was only bigamy if I had not killed him, you see.'

No, Cecily did not see. Could not see. It was all coming too quickly. Bigamy, blackmail, murder, it was bizarre, too preposterous to contemplate, almost impossible to comprehend.

'She was his housekeeper, you know,' Cora was saying, 'and he was such a good man . . . Mr Staunton.'

'Mr Staunton?'

'Yes, Mr Staunton . . .' She lifted her head and looked at Cecily. 'Have you had your hair done, dear?' she asked.

When Cecily stood up to say goodbye, moved over to her and took her hand, she said, 'But you don't have to go upstairs yet. Fanny will be with the little ones, will have put them to bed by now.'

In the hallway, Mrs Davey appeared.

'She's very confused,' Cecily said.

Mrs Davey nodded. 'They're all here with her. She can't escape them, or the past. But she's happy enough . . . happy to be amongst them.'

'I'm not so sure,' Cecily replied, putting on her gloves. 'She has some uninvited guests, I think.'

'Do you think any of it is true?' Cecily asked Sylvia now.

Sylvia took a moment, then she smiled and said, 'Well, of course it's not true! Oh, there may have been an Uncle John, once, somewhere in her family, and he may have been something of a brute, but I'm afraid everything else is complete nonsense. She was clearly deluded, as you say – very confused.'

'But where on earth did it all come from?'

'From her imagination . . . she was always one for a story. You should know that. Don't you remember all her tales about Rome and Paris?'

'Yes, of course I do, but they *were* true, weren't they?'

'Hmm. Not all of them, no. Cora liked to add her own twist, embellish, add a little detail here and there. She adored drama, and the truth of the matter is, she could not recall her childhood even twelve years ago. But it's sad, makes me very sad, that she was so lost at the end . . . so estranged from reality.'

'Yes, yes. You're right. Of course, you're right.' Cecily glanced to her wristwatch. 'Gracious, I should be going soon.' She reached for the paper bag on the table: 'I've brought you the letter, and my manuscript,' she said. And Sylvia, thinking she had misheard her, almost laughed. '*Your* manuscript?'

'Yes, I mentioned it to you on the telephone, remember?'

And just as the sun slowly rises, the horrendous reality of the situation began to glimmer and break in Sylvia's mind, the word 'manuscript' echoing once more down a crackling telephone line. She said nothing, and Cecily handed her an envelope with the words 'Miss S. Dorland' written on the front in Cora's hand, and underlined twice. Cecily said, 'I've had this letter for so long, seems rather strange to be finally handing it over to you.'

Sylvia tried to smile. 'I shall look at it later,' she said, putting it to one side, watching Cecily as she pulled out a small pile of paper held together by a red elastic band. 'And here is the manuscript,' she said, rather triumphantly, Sylvia thought. And she pushed the bundle across the table towards Sylvia. The capitalised title on the frontispiece read, *A Desperate Heart*.

'It's a novel then?' said Sylvia.

'Yes, as I said on the telephone, it's loosely based on Cora's life and, I hasten to add, not quite finished. But I'd value your opinion . . . She had such a remarkable life, inspiring, I think.'

'Yes, it was certainly that,' Sylvia conceded.

'I'd appreciate your opinion . . . thought you might take a look, point out any obvious mistakes . . . and I wondered if you might be prepared to elucidate on a few other matters . . . and not necessarily for the book.'

'Oh?'

'The truth is, I'm still rather confused about Cora's marriage to Edward. Why she kept it a secret for so long, and why she married a man so very much older than she was. He was an old man and she still quite young, not that much older than me when she married him. I know it can't have been a . . . a proper marriage, a physical relationship, nor even for the company, the companionship of a husband, because they never lived together. I presumed it was for some sort of security, but then . . .' she paused.

'Then?'

'Then, more recently, I've been pondering her relationship with George. You see, I'm aware that she knew him long before she married Edward, and though she was always rather guarded about their friendship, later, when she was . . . confused, she spoke of him so much. It was always George this, George that. She very rarely mentioned Edward, or Jack, or Antonin.' She paused again, scrutinising Sylvia. 'I realise now that they were closer than I had at first thought, that she may . . . well, may perhaps have been in love with George – and not his father?'

She said this as a question, but Sylvia offered no reply. And she quickly went on. 'Of course, I may be wrong, but even so, it must have been queer to George for his friend, one of his contemporaries, suddenly at that late stage to become his stepmother.'

Sylvia smiled. 'Oh, I don't suppose George ever viewed Cora as a mother, even a stepmother. But you are correct, they were close, very close friends, and for many years.'

'You were there, at the wedding? You knew them both, George *and* Edward?'

Sylvia nodded. 'Yes, I was there. I knew them both.'

'And you never detected anything . . . between Cora and George?'

Chapter Twenty-Three

*I*n the taxicab, en route to the Café Royal, Cecily wondered if she had misinterpreted Sylvia's reaction to her novel, which had been odd to say the least. She had forgotten about Sylvia's obsessive nature, that all-consuming love she had for Cora – anything and everything to do with Cora. She had appeared surprised when Cecily mentioned and then produced the manuscript, despite the fact that they had spoken about it on the telephone, for hadn't Sylvia said then, *Oh how lovely, I'm so pleased?*

But Sylvia seemed to think she had some divine right over Cora's life, as though she owned the copyright to it, all of it. As though only she knew the truth. And oh, how she guarded it! When she said, 'I'll try and take a look at it, but I am actually rather busy,' Cecily could have laughed, and almost had. For what was there for Sylvia to be busy with, there at the Windsor? What was there for her to do?

She lit a cigarette. The traffic on Oxford Street had ground to a halt and she stared at the murky shapes waiting in queues to be transported home. But she saw none of them. The photograph, reminiscences, and the memory of that summer had stirred her, taken her back. Back to a time when everything shone, back to a time when even the prospect of war had not been enough to dampen hopes and dreams . . .

She had been home for a day when Rosetta mentioned his name, told her that Jack Staunton was in Bramley, at Temple Hill. 'Don't suppose her ladyship's too happy about him going off up in them aeroplanes neither.'

'Aeroplanes?'

'Well, yes, he's learning to fly. Been having lessons over at Farnborough. You ask your mother if you don't believe me.'

So she had asked her mother. 'Is it true that Jack Staunton's back and that he's learning to fly?'

'Yes, it's true. Though for the life of me I can't understand why he's got himself caught up in that nonsense.'

'I can,' Cecily said, watching her mother, bent over the sewing machine. 'Do you know how long he's home for?'

Her mother didn't look up. 'He's been to call a few times, enquired after you, asked where you were,' she said, fiddling with the fabric under the needle as she spoke.

Cecily sat down in the chair opposite her mother. 'But how long is he here for?'

Madeline glanced over her spectacles at her daughter. 'I'm not sure, he didn't say. But I told him you'd been in Paris for almost a year. He couldn't believe it. Yes, I said, she's never going to settle in Bramley, not now. But I told him that due to the situation you'd come home and were living in London. Very wise, he said, very wise. And Walter, too, is keen to see you. You know he adores you, would marry you in a heartbeat, and yet you keep him hanging on . . .' she looked away, shook her head. 'It's cruel, I think. Really, I do.'

Cecily rose from her chair, walked to the window. Daylight was fading, the tops of the trees golden in the twilight. 'I can't marry Walter. I've told you before, I don't love him in that way.'

'In *that way*?' her mother repeated and then laughed. 'My dearest girl, do you really think all of life is about being in love? It's about making the best of what we have, and being gracious – and thankful – in our acceptance of that.'

Cecily closed her eyes, didn't answer for a moment, and knew full well that she should not answer. She knew that she should leave it at that. But she couldn't. She turned to her mother. 'No. You're wrong. It's not about acceptance, Mother. It's about creating the life you wish for . . . dream of. Creating a better world, a better place in which to live. Otherwise, what is our life about? What is our legacy?'

'My legacy is you,' Madeline replied quickly. 'You and Ethne.'

Cecily sighed. 'The world is changing, Mother, and even if there is a war, it will continue to change, for better or worse. We can't stand still, we can't stop progress.'

'Progress? Your generation are too preoccupied with progress. Is it not enough to have a life and someone to love?'

Cecily didn't answer. Yes, she thought, of course it is. It's the most important thing, surely, to have someone to love, to be loved.

'I'm surprised he hasn't called today,' her mother went on. 'Jack Staunton, I mean. I told him you'd be home Saturday. In fact, I was surprised he wasn't at church this morning. Of course, she never goes . . .'

Jack Staunton. Each mention of the name caused a flutter.

'Oh well,' Cecily said, 'we probably have nothing in common now. He was always . . . rather arrogant, I think.'

'Jack? No, he's not arrogant, dear, quite the opposite. And, considering everything . . .' Madeline paused, looked across the room to the empty hearth, 'considering everything, it's really very encouraging.'

She had wondered what her mother meant by 'encouraging', but chose not to ask. 'Poor Walter,' her mother began again, 'seems to work all the hours God sends.'

'I can imagine,' said Cecily, turning away, staring out through the open window in the direction of Temple Hill. 'I wrote to him, you know. When Mr Gamben died, I wrote separate letters to each of them . . . How is Annie?'

'As happy as the day is long.'

Cecily smiled. 'All she ever wanted was to get married and have a family.'

'Well, it's enough for some of us. And Luke's a good husband to her. He loves her and he loves that baby.'

'I'm happy for her.'

She was looking forward to seeing Annie again, but they had lost the place with each other during the course of the past two years. And Walter, dear Walter, he had almost proposed to her the night before she left for Paris – would have done so had she not stopped him. And was it not in fact Jack Staunton's words she had borrowed to deter Walter, when she told him that she had no wish to be tied down, no desire to be married for at least another five years?

Jack. Almost three years had passed since she had stood and kissed him at the top of that hill. Almost three years since she had felt her heart split in two and thought she'd never, ever recover. Almost three years . . .

After he left she had wondered if he would write, had longed for him to, just to see her name in his hand. And she had waited. But nothing came, not even a postcard. Then, early the following year, having managed to persuade her mother to allow her some of the money her father had left to her, she had gone travelling with Aunt Kitty and cousin Erica. They had been away for six months, had visited Paris, the Riviera, Rome, Naples, Florence, Geneva, the Rhineland, and almost every place with a church or cathedral in between. By the time she returned home, Jack had been and gone. He had stayed at Temple Hill for only a few weeks that summer, due to his own somewhat hectic itinerary. Then another Christmas came and went without any sign of him. He was ski-ing, Cora had said. And that Easter, 'away with friends . . . on the Riviera.' Their paths, it seemed, were destined not to cross, and Cecily – by then determined that they should not cross – enrolled on a secretarial course in London (with French as an extra). By winter she had returned to Paris, sharing what she described to her mother as a shoebox off the Champs-Elysées with a girl from her course.

'Almost three years,' she said out loud in the taxi.

'Almost three years,' she murmured, standing by the window in her mother's workroom.

'Mm? What's that, dear?'

'Oh nothing. I think I'll take some air, have a walk in the garden.'

As she moved towards the doorway, she said, 'Oh, and how is Cora?'

'I'm not entirely sure. No one ever sees her but Mrs Fox seems to think she's gone a little doolally.'

Cecily stopped. 'Doolally?'

'Mm. Communing with the dead, she said.'

'And how does she know?'

'Edith Davey – the housekeeper up at Temple Hill, is very friendly with the cook at the rectory. They speak.'

'You mean they *gossip*,' Cecily said and moved on.

Outside, the air was soft, fragrant with the scent of honey-suckle and jasmine. It felt good to be back there, home, out upon that hillside once more. And yet so much of the place reminded her of him. But how could that be? How could the place she had lived for so long be infused with the presence of someone who had only been there, in her life, for a matter of weeks? How could he do that to a place and to her?

It made her angry and perplexed her. I have done it, she thought, sitting down upon the warm stone of the steps to the lily pond; I have hung on, dragging a romantic notion forward, from here to Europe and back again, and then to Paris and London. I have done it to myself. So, he called and enquired after me, she mused. It means nothing . . . nothing. He has nothing better to do with his time here . . . is most likely awful now . . . like those graduates in London who say, 'Bramley? Is that a new college?' and then laugh. Well, if he comes, if he were to appear now, I shall be indifferent, she thought. Yes, I *am* indifferent . . .

She had been sitting on the steps for no more than five minutes when she heard the voice. 'Hello stranger, your mother said you were out here.'

'Reckon we'd be better cutting down Piccadilly,' the cab driver said, interrupting.

'I'm in no rush,' Cecily replied.

She was only thirty minutes late, only nine years behind, and she wasn't ready to step back into *now*. Not yet. She wanted to remember, needed to savour those weeks, those few weeks, not quite amounting to months, that they had had together before the war, before he said, 'I'll be back soon.'

They had picked up where they left off. Resuming what was unconcluded with a new sense of urgency and without any questions. Resuming a courtship begun three years before. Those who did not know might have used the word 'whirlwind'. Because within weeks Jack had asked her to marry him, at the top of the hill – the place they had first kissed. And within a heartbeat she had said yes.

But he was like that, she thought now. He knew what he wanted and went after it, as though aware of the limitation on time. As though he knew.

They married four days after the declaration of war, at St

311

Luke's in Bramley, and afterwards Cora hosted a small reception in the garden at Temple Hill. The week after their return from honeymoon – five days in Brighton – Jack signed up. Like most others he enlisted for a 'temporary commission for the period of the war'. He was assigned to the Rifle Brigade. But of course it was not where he wanted to be. Jack wanted to be in the air. And he was one of a few who had already taken a turn up in the sky.

Jack got his wish early the following year. After attending a military school in Birmingham and gaining his flying certificate, he was attached to the Royal Flying Corps' Number One Squadron, and almost immediately deployed to the war zone, piloting biplanes over the fields of France and Flanders on recon-naissance missions. He was happy to be doing his duty and thrilled to be flying.

Cecily lived in fear and dread. She never knew for sure when her husband was flying, or where he was, would only find out about his movements after the event, in the form of a letter, a telegram or, occasionally, a phone call. Shortly after their marriage she had had a telephone installed at their cottage. 'For emergencies only,' she had said, only to regret it later. Because the very last thing she wished for was any emergency call. She wanted to hear from him, Jack; wanted to hear his voice and know only that he was safe, alive.

Whenever he managed to secure leave, he came home to Cecily at their rented cottage on the north-west fringe of Bramley – exhausted. He was understandably sombre, less ebul-lient. But by then everything and everyone was changing. Young, fit and able-bodied men had disappeared from the village, and it was left to the women to do the jobs the men had previously done. Cora's servants had been halved in number, and then halved again, as her kitchen and parlour maids joined the war effort, and left for farm or factory work. Her precious garden had been dug up, turned over to produce vegetables and accommodate livestock. She was left with Mrs Davey, and a daily, and her gardener, Mr Cordery, who was too old to enlist.

Cecily followed events in the newspaper; she read of the losses to the British Fleet and to the army, and then, with even greater horror, of the losses to the Royal Flying Corps. She became used to the distant sound of air raids and bombs dropped by German zeppelins along the coast. And Cora told her it was different to any of the wars she had known before. It was a modern war, she said, voracious in its appetite for young souls, relentless in its cruelty.

On Jack's last leave, Cecily savoured each second of each minute, barely sleeping so that she could watch him while he slept, take all of him in. And that was all he did, sleep, for three whole days. But on his final day they had gone back to Brighton, with Cora.

The place had been crowded with army personnel and couples unashamedly walking hand in hand; young women in their Sunday best clinging on to their sweethearts; parents walking proudly alongside their uniformed sons – all of them enjoying those precious hours before the inevitable 'Adieu' and that grim journey back across the Channel. Under the strange and intense winter sun that day, the young men in uniform appeared to Cecily almost iridescent. They were there and alive, but not really there; destined for glory, destined for death, they were already going, already gone, already ghosts.

And there were the others, too, the walking wounded and injured, in mud-caked tattered uniforms, staggering on crutches, sitting along the promenade in bath chairs; some missing limbs, others disfigured or badly burned. Jack had made a point of stopping to speak to them, shaking hands, slapping backs, making jokes. They all did that, Cecily noticed. As though they had been at some macabre, nightmare party and could laugh about it now, momentarily, before re-entering that doorway, and the cacophony of the theatre.

Cora had seen injured soldiers many times before, she said, after the Crimea, as first deserters and then disorientated soldiers slowly made their way home to England; and on the streets of Rome, after Garibaldi marched on the city. She told Cecily that she thought her sensibilities had long ago been anaesthetised to life's tragedies and war's casualties, but even she struggled with the sights that day.

They had sat hand in hand opposite Cora on the train journey back to Linford. And from time to time Jack lifted her hand to his lips and held it there, eyes closed, as Cora chattered on. But there had been signs, even then, of Cora's confusion and muddled memory; early signs, which went unnoticed.

'Did we have luncheon today?' she had asked.

And they both laughed, thought she was ragging them. Jack said, 'Yes, and you said it was daylight robbery. Three shillings, remember?'

She shook her head.

'Whitstable oysters, consommé, turbot Marguery, fillet of beef and peach cardinal. A feast!' Jack said.

She smiled. 'Ah yes, of course.'

Later, alone in the bedroom of their cottage, they had lain on the bed staring at each other. He said, 'Don't cry, please. I'll be back soon, a few weeks . . .'

'Promise me, promise me hand on heart you'll come back . . . promise me you shan't let yourself get killed?'

He held his hand to his heart. 'I promise.'

'And you'll never ever forget that promise, will you?'

'Never.'

Against the odds, Jack had survived almost two years in the Royal Flying Corps, and had been promoted from Flying Officer to Lieutenant. But he had been in Number One Squadron, deployed on reconnaissance duties and not fighting. When he telephoned Cecily two days after returning to duty to tell her that he was to be promoted to Captain and that the squadron was to become a dedicated fighter squadron, she said nothing. She closed her eyes and knew: knew immediately that aerial combat would be infinitely more dangerous than reconnaissance. But he seemed oblivious to any peril, and spoke only of his new aeroplane, a Nieuport 17, and its powerful engine and large wings.

The telegram to say Jack was 'missing' arrived the day after Cecily found out – had it confirmed – that she was expecting the first of their 'unruly horde'. She had already posted a letter to her husband, saying:

My darling man, I have news! Are you sitting down? I imagine that you are. I imagine you are lying on your horrid uncomfortable bunk as you read this. But even so, brace yourself, darling . . . you are to be a father! Yes, that's right, YOU ARE TO BE A FATHER! This means that you really do have to stay safe and come back to me . . .

Cecily did not cry, she did not shout. She sat down. And she stayed very still and very silent for some time, holding on to that telegram, pondering that word: missing. Missing was not dead, she reasoned; missing was inconclusive. And Jack had promised. It took her a while to realise that the strange whimpering sound, the sound of an injured animal, was coming from within her and not from outside.

Hours later, she walked out from her cottage towards the village, towards Temple Hill and Cora. It was early autumn, the sky was clear and cloudless, the hedgerows still green, and purple with blackberries. But she saw none of the day. She walked in a daze along the gritted road, past the whitewashed cottages and tile-hung shops of the village, across the stepping stones of the ford, and up the rabbit-hole tunnel towards the house. *Not dead, not dead . . . missing, not dead . . .* From time to time she placed her hand upon her stomach and thought of the life within her. And in her head she heard his voice: *I promise . . . never.*

She kept her gaze steady as she passed her former home, determined not to look at the gate, lest something of him – and her – was still there, an impression caught in the ether and only visible once lost. But at the very top of the track, as she emerged from the shadows, the sound of a motorcycle's acceleration on the other side of the valley made her stop and look up. She followed its sound along the winding lane towards the village, turned and stared back down the track, willing him to appear, anticipating the sight of him coming up the hillside towards her, to explain. She thought she could hear the machine, spluttering, stumbling through the ford and out the other side. But no one and nothing appeared at the bottom of the track, and as the sound of the engine slowly faded she too, moved on.

Cora was in her usual place, usual chair, leaning forward and peering through her old lorgnette at the newspaper laid out on the card table in front of her.

'Aha!' she said, glancing up as Cecily entered the room. But her smile quickly fell as she took in Cecily's expression. And before Cecily could speak, she whispered the name as a question. 'Jack?'

Cecily nodded. 'Missing.'

Cora closed her eyes.

If there was a specific time, a moment Cecily could identify as the start of Cora's mental collapse, when she had finally given in, given up, surrendered her mind, her sanity, that was it. The prospect of his loss – more loss – was simply too much.

As though shutting out reality, trying to deny that moment,

Cora kept her eyes closed. But even through sealed eyelids tears escaped. And Cecily, unsure and impotent, powerless to alter facts and details, unable to offer hope, simply stood and watched. Then, with her eyes still closed and seemingly unable to speak, Cora nodded. As though it were news she had been waiting for. When she finally opened her eyes, she said, 'We shan't give up hope. We must wait for him. He'll find his way back to us. He'll find his way home.'

The newspapers were quick to include Jack's name in the Roll of Honour. Captain J. G. Staunton, RFC was listed under 'Missing', above the column titled 'Previously Reported Missing, Now Reported Killed', and another, 'Previously Reported Missing, Now Reported Prisoners of War'. And the *London Gazette* kindly included him in their 'List of Dead'.

Jack had been missing for seven months by the time the letter arrived from the War Office. It enclosed a copy of the Geneva Red Cross 'List of Dead', and read: 'Staunton J.G., RFC, seen to fall in an air fight near Bixschoote . . . In view of the lapse of time, this report will be accepted for official purposes as evidence of death.' Ten days later, Cecily gave birth to their son.

As the taxicab turned on to Piccadilly, Cecily glanced at her wristwatch and thought of her boy. He was staying for a few days with her mother and Rosetta, whom he adored, and who idolised him. Rosetta had looked after him as a baby so that Cecily could continue to teach at the school. And her new charge had given her a new lease of life. Each day and in all weathers a bonneted Rosetta had pushed the perambulator proudly through the village, disappearing into the lanes, singing songs to little Jack. One of his first words had been 'Etta', which Rosetta had now officially adopted as her name.

Even then, during those very first days and months of her son's life, Cecily had spoken to him about his father, telling him how brave and fearless he was. And as her son grew bigger, she would hold him on her hip, pointing to the man in the framed wedding photograph on the mantelshelf and repeating the word 'Daddy', until one day he finally said it as well: 'Dada!' And Cecily wept.

She had taken her son to visit his great-grandmother, but by that time Cora had been distracted at best, and entirely absent at worst. There were glimmers, the odd moment when she seemed to know, appeared to realise that the baby in front of her was in fact Jack's son, her great-grandson. But there had also been occasions when she had stared at the baby in Cecily's arms, frowning, and asked Cecily to whom the child belonged. Once, possibly prompted by confusion over the name Jack, and after Cecily had once again tried to explain that Little Jack was Jack's son, she had asked her, 'Is it *my* baby?'

It was sad and bizarre and comical. And Cecily had had to remind herself how Cora might think such a thing. Lost in time, she had grasped the name, the name of a former husband with whom she had had her babies.

'No, dear, he's not your baby. He's my baby,' she replied, looking at the old lady through tear-filled eyes.

How Walter had laughed when she told him of that. He said, 'How can a woman of eighty odd think she has a baby?'

'Because she doesn't and can't let herself see the here and now. Inside her mind she's still young, forever young. She's gone back in time.'

Walter Gamben had been returned from the killing fields of France invalided, minus a leg, in the spring of 1918. Cecily had visited him at the military hospital at Winchester. Months later, after he had been discharged and returned home to Bramley, he had asked her to marry him. It was Armistice Day, the whole village half-deaf and dizzy from the sound of the church bells, everyone riding on a wave of euphoria, drunk on the idea of peace and the future. How many marriage proposals must there have been that day, Cecily later thought.

She had told Walter that she could not marry him, that she was still in love with her husband, still in love with Jack. She had tried to explain to him that some small part of her refused to believe that Jack was not coming back. For he had promised her and she could not give up on that promise. Not yet. Walter said he understood, and that he'd wait. 'Even if I have to wait ten years,' he said, smiling at her with such optimism, such hope. Then he said, 'You know, I sometimes feel guilty . . . guilty that my happiness has been brought about by another's misfortune. For had Jack been here you wouldn't be with me now.' Cecily told him he was wrong, told him she would still have been there for him; 'the what ifs could go on and on – what if I'd never met Jack, what if there had never been a war – but we're all part of each other's lives, each other's story, and always will be.'

But it was the unwritten story, the one about herself and Jack, that she most often returned to, and dreamed of: the *what if he is alive, what if he comes back to me*. She had already spent what seemed like a lifetime imagining that story. A story bound up in missing faces and places, and journeys yet to be taken. It was the fantasy of youth and idle optimism, pulled forward in time and springing back like elastic. Nothing could change the past; it had happened, it had gone, but what if . . . what if . . . what if . . .

But the war had ended and Jack had not returned. He had not come back to her. He had not been able to keep his promise. And as life took on a new normality, hope faded and loneliness set in. Each evening, alone in her bed, Cecily returned to her musings, to Jack, and their unspent future . . .

They would have been happy together, surely, blissfully happy and in love. They would have gone on to have more children, that 'unruly horde' they had spoken of. And they would have lived in Bramley, possibly at Temple Hill. After all, it was the perfect house for a large family. There would have been a swing in the garden, a slide, bicycles lying about the place; and noise, oh, so much noise. She would glance up from the manuscript in front of her, look out through the window and see them, see him – her husband, the father of her children. And he would sense her gaze, turn to her and smile.

How it could have been, how it should have been, if only . . .

It had been impossible for Cecily to let go of that dream, and of him, Jack. It sustained her, kept her warm, offered her sanctuary and became her escape. It was the luxury in her life, that imagining, that what if. And she realised she could write it any way she wished, change and alter it at whim; introduce new situations, new characters, test Jack's love for her and test her own for him. And thus, night after night, she rewrote history. There was no declaration of war and Jack never fell from the sky. No one aged or died, and time simply moved back and forth, like waves upon a shore. Days were repeated, rerun with amendments and with added colour and detail. And she returned again and again to that moment when the world had spun on its axis and everything around them – and beyond them – had seemed possible and within reach.

Cora had once said to her, 'We all have a plan . . . a plan of how our lives will be, but it is never what happens because we're all mortal, all fallible. And because human beings make mistakes – follow others' mistakes. We are easily led from our path. But we can find our way back, eventually, if we are able to remember what it is we first wished for.'

On Armistice Day, after she had returned home from the celebrations, after Walter's proposal, Cecily sat up until dawn reading through her old journals. Thinking of her son, his future, she deliberated on destroying the blue cloth-covered books. So much had been promised, so much had been hoped, and she had no wish for him to one day read and feel that loss. Then she picked up her pen and wrote:

It is that morning of once before now, that morning I first saw you . . . and I feel the heat. I see lambent ferns and waist-high nettles . . . a demoiselle butterfly skimming the pond. I see dragon-flies, minnows and jam jars, yellow gorse and purple heather, and poppies, scarlet and black. I see fox-coloured tiles and tall chimneys, and lines of silver on blue. And you say, we have our whole lives ahead of us. Our whole lives, you say, looking back at me.

Now it is early evening. The sun has slipped beneath the trees. I move through the last remnants of slanting sun upon grass, golden, parched and dry, and I hear you whispering: when this whole rotten business is over . . . when this whole rotten business is over, you say. And my heart burns but I am still. I can wait. I can wait.

The sun slips further, I hear the first owl, and I feel the edge of summer.

The baby in my arms laughs as I swing him through that fading twilight, round and round, and round again. And when I stop and look up I see you standing by the hedge once more in your cricket whites, smiling back at me, at us.

Yes, it was a stunning thought, my darling. You were my stunning thought, burning and poignant and blurring my mind.

Cecily glanced up at the lights of Piccadilly. That dark time had gone. It was over. The only thing that mattered now was the man waiting for her in the bar of the Café Royal. And their future together.

'Anywhere here is fine,' she said to the cab driver, pulling her wallet from her bag.

Chapter Twenty-Four

The letter lay unopened on the shelf of the mantelpiece. Sylvia sat with Cecily's manuscript scattered about her.

She had looked through it, read a number of chapters. But it was appalling – and quite insensitive – she thought, for Cecily to have brought it to her. Then again, the girl had always been presumptuous. Had overstepped the mark years ago. And Cora was naive and silly to have trusted her so. As for the manuscript, it was, as far as Sylvia could make out, simply the work of a rather vivid imagination, and not an accurate account of Cora's life at all. *Loosely based*, Cecily had said. Well, it was certainly founded on delusions, presumably Cora's. What on earth had she told Cecily? And what could she, Sylvia, say to Cecily about it?

It was curious to Sylvia that Cecily had been unable to remember the people at the farm. When Sylvia said, 'And what about that nice young family at Meadow Farm?' Cecily had stared back at her blankly. 'The Abels, I think they were called,' Sylvia had added. No, Cecily shook her head. 'They can't have been there for very long,' she said. 'It's been with the Stephenson family since before the war.'

Of course Sylvia was testing Cecily to see what she knew. When Cecily went on to talk of Cora's confused ramblings, and the mention of 'someone called Uncle John', it was obvious to Sylvia that she had never been told the name, the full name. Thus, she had never made any connection with the people at the farm. Uncle John was simply Uncle John: a monster, deprived of identity, and now confined to fiction. Sylvia had made sure of that. And she had done so out of loyalty and love, nothing more.

In truth, Cora had never *consciously* told Sylvia the full name either; certainly not then, not that summer. But Sylvia had a long memory, there had been little to cloud it. And even during Cora's fever, at the height of her delirium, when she repeated the name out loud, Sylvia already knew it. She knew John Abel and the Uncle John mentioned in Rome all those years ago to be one and the same.

When Sylvia visited the farm, she had done so in order to establish whether one John Abel was related to the other John Abel. It seemed almost too much to hope that this would be the case, that a young farmer would be able to furnish her with those missing pieces of a story which had fascinated her for the best part of fifty years. And yet, there were too many coincidences for there not be a link, for she had heard the rector inform Cora that the family came from Suffolk.

Sylvia had duly told the young man that she heard he hailed from Suffolk, and then lied, telling him that her parents, too, came from that county, the Woodbridge area, and that they had spoken of a John Abel, one who had married a woman by the name of Frances . . . a Frances who had gone to live overseas? The young farmer clearly knew something of the story, for he had nodded and, glancing at his wife – smiling knowingly, Sylvia thought – he said yes, that would be his Great-Uncle John. Then he turned to Sylvia. 'You're not from the Mother's Union, are you?'

Sylvia shook her head.

'Parish council?'

'No. I'm simply staying in the village for a while and I . . . I heard the rector mention—'

'Ah! That old busybody, I might have known.'

'John!'

'We came here to get away from nosy parkers,' he said, staring at Sylvia.

'John!' his wife said again.

'I do beg your pardon,' said Sylvia, turning away, about to head back to the village.

Then he began, 'I never knew him, but I know enough about him . . .'

He had been a shoemaker, he said, like his father before him. 'It was the family trade, see, then.' And yes, she was correct, his namesake had married a woman named Frances, or Fanny, as she was known, the daughter of a local tin man. They had moved away from Woodbridge to the East End of London. But things had gone wrong there, for his great-uncle's wife had 'up-ed and off-ed', left her husband and disappeared without trace. 'It were the great mystery in the family, that.'

'And your uncle – great-uncle – whatever happened to him?'

The young farmer looked at his wife and then back at Sylvia. 'He's long since been gone.'

Sylvia smiled, nodded. 'Of course, I realise he must have passed away by now but do you know *where* he passed away? Did he . . . live for long after his wife departed?'

'Lived till he were nearly ninety. Never married again, couldn't, you see.'

'Yes, I see,' Sylvia said, thinking aloud. 'But something must have made her – your great-uncle's wife – flee like that, in the depths of the night, and taking the poor child with her?'

'Who said anything about night? Or any *poor child*?' he asked, narrowing his gaze.

'Oh, forgive me. I'm a writer. I somehow imagined that it was at night . . . and I thought I heard tell that there was a child involved.'

The three of them – Sylvia, the young John Abel and his wife – stood under the shade of a stone archway leading to the farmyard, where a pile of manure lay steaming in the sunshine. John Abel leaned on his rake as he explained to Sylvia that it was his grandmother who had first told him the story of how her brother's wife had vanished.

'She knew her, of course, knew Fanny Abel. Didn't like her.' He shook his head. 'Said she had had highfalutin' ideas. Woodbridge not good enough for her . . . London not good enough for her! No pleasing some folk, eh?'

'No, indeed.'

'And you're right, as it happens, there were a child, a girl, but not theirs, some relation of hers, of Fanny Abel's. My grandmother reckoned she and the girl must have went overseas, changed their names, because he looked for them for years, did Uncle John, placed advertisements in the newspapers, done all of that.'

'And he never discovered what became of them?' Sylvia asked.

'Didn't your mother say she ended up a duchess or something?' the woman broke in, addressing her husband.

'That's right!' He laughed; then, scratching his head, he said, 'No, no, it weren't Fanny Abel, 'twas the girl, the girl what ended up a duchess.'

Now Sylvia laughed too. 'A duchess! Gracious me. But however did your mother hear that?'

'Woodbridge is a small place, missus . . .'

'Miss.'

'Aye, Woodbridge is a small place, and she knew the family, see, some of the family at any rate. One of them had went off to work at . . .' he looked towards his wife.

His wife stared back at him blankly for a moment, then she said, 'Wasn't it Jersey?'

'Jersey, that's it. He went off to be gardener to some folk at Jersey, but they must've had connections in Woodbridge, I reckon – imagine it's how he got the job. Anyhow, they knew, must've known, because they were the ones it came from, the ones what told him. Imagine, eh? Imagine finding out that your own sister was aristocracy!'

'Ah, so he was the girl's brother, this gardener in Jersey?'

He scratched his head again, looked back at his wife. 'I think that were it, weren't it? You remember better than me.'

'Yes, that's it,' his wife replied.

'Aye, well, they'll all long since be dead so we'll never know now, but I fancy the notion that I'm related to the nobility,' he said, smiling and winking at Sylvia.

'Fascinating. And your great-uncle, he died eventually at . . . at Woodbridge?'

'He was locked up,' the woman replied quickly.

'Locked up?'

'Mm. Put away. Best thing for him,' she said, glancing from her husband to Sylvia. 'He was a . . . a—'

'Nothing were proven,' the farmer interrupted, suddenly raising his voice. 'It weren't proven and shouldn't be repeated. Some silly young girl's word against his.' He turned to Sylvia. 'Best let sleeping dogs lie, eh?' he said. Then he raised his cap to Sylvia, 'Good day to you, missus.'

Walking back from the farm that day, Sylvia knew what she had to do. But, trying to look forward and not back, she struggled to contain her emotions, struggled with the knowledge that she had been the one to lie. The confirmation that Uncle

John had not only existed but that he had lived to the age of ninety meant she owed Cora an entirely different story, one that absolved her and gave her back the life she could and should have had.

But could she? Sylvia thought now; could Cora ever have had that life, the life she so wanted – with him, George? Sylvia reordered her thoughts. She did not want to think of her own intervention. She *had* made amends. She had given Cora that life, given it to her in a book begun as a memoir now rewritten as a work of fiction. Yes, she had given her back her life, something Cecily could never do. That was why she came to me, Sylvia thought, to sanction Cora's memories, to fill in the gaps. *You were there*, Cecily had said. Yes, she had been there.

When Cora married Edward Lawson at the town hall of the eighth arrondissement in Paris, three days after her fortieth birthday, she became stepmother to her son's father, wife to his grandfather. But only Sylvia and Cora's aunt knew this. Edward remained almost as oblivious as his son. And he, like others, was intoxicated by her – that aura of experience, that enigmatic smile. For Cora had lived, she had seen life, and felt it, too. And now she seemed to guard its secret. If one could only keep hold of her, pin her down. In the meantime, one could watch. Watch *her*. The way she spoke – to a waiter, a dignitary or a dear old friend – was something to behold. The way she tilted her head and blinked as she listened to those same people as they spoke to her; the way she drifted effortlessly from one language to another. And the places she knew and the people she quoted, and her knowledge, and empathy, that ability to relate to each and every person, no matter how extraordinary, no matter how mundane, as though she was completely captivated, immersed in their experience.

And all the while George saw this. She belonged to him, and yet he had never owned her. He loved her, but he had thought he needed something more. Something he would see and know, something he would recognise when it presented itself to him. It had been her; it had been her but not her. How could it be her? He had walked away. How could it be her if he had walked away? And his father, pandering and fawning like a lovestruck adolescent – it was despicable, sickening. It had made him feel physically sick. Cora was almost young enough to be his granddaughter!

And that day, that fateful day in Paris, when Cora married Edward, how bittersweet it had been. Even at the time, the marriage had had the scent of scandal about it. In ignorance, people's main concern had been the fact that Edward, a long-time widower, respected member of the English establishment and father of England's greatest painter, had elected to wed a woman almost three decades his junior, *and* one residing on the continent, *and* one with a dubious past. For no one was quite sure of her credentials or where she hailed from. But it mattered not to Edward. He was in love, bewitched, mesmerised. No one in attendance at the nuptials could have been in any doubt about that.

Cora's son and her aunt were both present at her marriage, and a notable mix of artists, architects, English, French and Italian friends – including the Hilliers and George – attended a second ceremony at the British Embassy and a reception there afterwards. It was unbearably hot: the temperature in Paris that summer's day hit one hundred degrees Fahrenheit. And though each of the long windows of the embassy rooms remained wide open, the air was stifling, oppressive.

Circumnavigating the room, holding on to the arm of her new husband, Cora looked radiant and much too youthful, people commented, to be the mother of a young man. Edward smiled broadly, barely lifting his eyes from his new bride. And in his speech he thanked his son, George, for bringing himself and Cora together.

That was when Sylvia noticed George's expression, one she would later describe as 'bewildered detachment'. He shuffled, looked down at the floor and kept pulling out his pocket watch, as though he needed to check the time of his next appointment. Oh, how Sylvia had felt for him! Whatever he had done to Cora it seemed cruel beyond words that she was standing there in front of him as his father's bride – his stepmother.

Was Edward Lawson aware? Sylvia had wondered. Did he know what had taken place – what was, perhaps, still taking place – between his son and his new wife? But surely it was obvious. It was to Sylvia. For she had studied them for years, followed the strange and fragile dynamic of this denied, ongoing and furtive love affair.

When George shook his father's hand, he simply said, 'Congratulations, sir,' and then added, 'I wish you both a long and happy life together.'

'I only hope that one day, and in the not too distant future, you can find yourself a Cora,' Edward replied, red-faced, delirious with the occasion. 'But I don't suppose there is another Cora in the universe,' he added, gazing at his wife.

No, there was not another Cora in the universe. How could there be? Who, other than Cora, would have had the vision, imagination and skill to invent such a character? For Cora *had* invented herself, and then reinvented herself again and again, honing and perfecting her creation, each one of her selves better than the one before. But she had had no choice. Robbed of identity early on in life, she had had to become someone else.

And that day, all George could do was stand back and watch, like everyone else. Watch a woman who seemed only to improve with age.

Sylvia was not sure if she was the only one to notice the one person Cora did *not* kiss on that her wedding day. They came face to face, stood and smiled at each other, but nothing more. And later, as everyone was leaving, bidding each other a weary adieu, and kissing once again, Sylvia saw them standing together in a corner. Cora had her hand upon George's arm, and it seemed to Sylvia as though George was refusing to look at her. Then, at last, he raised his eyes to her and smiled: a sad, affected smile. As Cora turned and walked away, towards Edward, George watched her intently, but she never looked back at him. Not once. Though Sylvia had willed her to.

Later, Sylvia travelled back to the hotel with George, who seemed exhausted, monosyllabic. The hotel lobby had been busy and – 'Much too hot to retire' – George suggested they take a nightcab together in the lounge. He ordered iced tea for them both and they sat in silence for some time, watching others come and go: the rigmarole of travellers.

'It was an elegant reception,' Sylvia said at last.

'Mm, yes,' he replied, absently, gazing across the room.

'I'm sure she'll be happy . . . sure they'll both be very happy.'

He said nothing.

'She looked very fine,' Sylvia persevered. 'Everyone looked very fine.'

He moved forward in his chair, placed his glass down upon the table in front of him, and with his eyes fixed on it, he said, 'Why did you tell me those things, Sylvia? Why did you make up that story about Cora, all those years ago, and then tell me?'

'I'm not sure what you mean. Which particular story are you referring to?' she asked. 'There have been quite a few, you know.'

He lifted his head to look at her. 'The one where Cora was

330

wanted for murder. The one you told me in such extraordinary detail in the Piazza del Popolo that day. *That* story.'

Sylvia glanced at the letter. She was unsure about opening it, reading it. Unsure what it would say. It could say so much, she thought. Until opened, it could say so much . . .

And it was typical of Cora to have the final word. Even from beyond the grave she *would* have the final word. But there was a sense of unspent luxury to be derived from looking at the envelope, anticipating its contents, her words. It was bulky, clearly contained more than one sheet of paper, and the know-ledge that it had been written some years ago was intriguing. It came from one who had not only gone, departed this life, but from another time also. It had been sealed by Cora, passed on to Cecily and then kept, stored in an unknown place through seasons and years, until now, when it had finally arrived at its destination, its intended recipient. There was something impos-sibly romantic about all of this to Sylvia. And, in a peculiar way, it seemed a shame to break the seal, open up the pages, read the words.

Sylvia would wait; find the right moment. It deserved that. *She* deserved that.

Chapter Twenty-Five

The plane came down near Bixschoote, in Flanders. Others had seen him fall. That he had survived the crash was almost unimaginable, but not impossible. He was an accomplished pilot, without doubt one of the best. And he had already had a few 'star turns', earned his badge as a flying ace, shooting down more than a dozen enemy aeroplanes.

Those working in the fields stopped. They raised their heads to the blood-orange sky, to that halting, whirring sound. And as they watched its steady, smoking descent, they began to walk and then run across the flat earth. They saw it bounce and burst into flames, saw a figure emerge from the burning wreckage, stagger, and then fall. They took off tunics and shirts and jackets and smothered the flames. And then they carried the burned body back to the farmhouse of Monsieur and Madame Ricard.

For a number of weeks – no one would ever know how many – the rescued pilot lay unconscious in a cellar in Flanders. When he finally opened his melted eyelids, he was unable to see, unable to hear, unable to speak. Badly burned, with broken legs, broken ribs, a broken shoulder and fractured wrists, he drifted in and out of consciousness for more weeks, oblivious to his surroundings, unaware of what had happened. When he did, eventually, gain consciousness, complete consciousness, he was unable to tell anyone his name, unable to remember. His memory had gone. But he had spoken, had uttered a few words the evening he was rescued, before he passed out.

Monsieur and Madame Ricard's daughter, Susanne, told him that when he was rescued, as the plane burned, he had told her that his name was Jacques, and later, in his delirium, he had spoken of a Cee-cee, or something sounding like that. But all clues to his identity – his uniform, any papers or documents he had had on him – had perished.

Jacques' recovery was slow. It was months before he was able to climb from his bed and stand on his feet, months before he was strong enough to learn to walk again. But as his physical wounds slowly healed, his mind began to throw things back to him, offering him snatches of nameless people and places, glimpses of moments: a church steeple, a village green; an elderly woman with a shock of white hair and piercingly brilliant blue eyes; and a girl, a young woman, whose lips he so wants to kiss.

As time went on these things came back to him more, in dreams and, encouraged by him, in conscious moments, too. The elderly woman, the one with the white hair, speaks to him in French, and another woman – one he suspects is his mother, suspects has gone, died – sometimes appears at the foot of his bed. But the girl, the girl with the lips he longs to kiss, comes back to him more than anyone else. She smiles at him from shadows, in sunlight and moonlight, next to painted gates and sun-bleached canvas, sitting on a garden bench and lying back upon a bed. And she says his name: she says *Jacques*. He knows that this is the Cee, the Cee-cee. And in his dreams she stands very close to him, staring at him, smiling. She says, 'Promise me . . . promise me.' She says, 'Never ever forget.'

But how many months have passed? He has no idea. No idea. He belongs nowhere, has nowhere to go. And though they continue to hide him, he catches time: colours changing, fallen leaves, snow, and then the thawing, a gradual warmth. He hears them speak of ploughing, planting, and then harvesting. When Susanne returns from one of her meetings, she talks of a final push, and tells him, 'It will be over soon, the war.' A final push, he thinks. But he can't remember any war. Can't remember where he came from, or who he is. And he sees only the scarred face of a stranger looking back at him from the glass.

Susanne has nursed him, bathed his wounds and changed his dressings. She is the one who has fed him, brought him up from the cellar to look at the sky, the sunset. She is the one who helped him take those first steps through the pain. And she speaks to him in English. She says, 'The body chooses how and when it heals itself. It chooses its time, like the mind. When the time is right, your memories will return.'

But as summer slips to autumn, nothing comes: no parents, no siblings, no family. And Cee-cee continues to stare back at him, elusive, impossible for him to take hold of: 'Never ever forget.'

Lying in his bed, staring up at the cobwebbed beam, he hears the tail end of a conversation, one he has heard before, one that makes no sense. A woman says, 'She is afraid of being discovered, being found.' Another asks, 'Why?' The woman says something he can't quite hear, and then, 'My husband adored her.' But who are these people? And whom do they speak of? Later, when Susanne finds him sitting on the floor, weeping and surrounded by broken glass, she wraps her arms about his neck and holds him to her. She strokes his head, whispers in his ear, and she says his name: Jacques.

She has a familiar softness, a scent similar to something before. And there's a craving in him, a longing to languish in that

334

softness, to taste and know that scent. But something stops him and he pulls away.

'I'll be dead to them all by now,' he says. 'Forgotten . . . mourned and forgotten.'

She shakes her head. 'I think not, Jacques. I think there's someone waiting. Don't you?'

He wanted to say yes, because he hoped that there was, and part of him – that irrational, instinctive, illogical part of him – knew that there was. Yes, Cee-cee was waiting. Somewhere. She was waiting. And in his dreams he wanted to take hold of her, tell her that he was alive and coming back to her, if only he could remember. He wanted to reach out and touch her and know that she was real, and maybe then he would remember who he was, had been.

He was sitting on the bench outside the farmhouse when he heard the noise. He could see Monsieur Ricard nearing, coming up the cypress – lined lane on his bicycle, ringing his bell and calling out, 'Vive la France! Vive la France!'

Unsteadily, he rose to his feet.

'The war is over. *Finis!*' Monsieur Ricard shouted, dropping his bicycle to the ground. '*Finis!*' he said again, crossing his hands in front of himself. Then he grabbed Jacques by the shoulders, kissed him on both cheeks and rushed in to the house. '*C'est finis! C'est finis!*'

At the celebrations in the local village square, Jacques joined in with the others, drinking and singing and cheering 'Vive la France!' and falling into the fountain wrapped in a flag not his own. And later, as dawn broke, standing by the gate to the farmyard, Susanne wrapped her arms around his neck again and said, 'So, Jacques, do you want to kiss me?'

It was a clumsy, drunken kiss, and only made his head spin more. But the sensation of another's lips upon his own, of arms wrapped around him and a world spinning was too familiar. And as he pulled away, trying to steady himself, his mind, he saw two figures standing at the top of a purple-coloured hill under a vast blue sky, kissing.

'Cee-cee,' he murmured, 'Cee-cee . . .'

Susanne stepped back, listening, watching.

'Cee-cee-ly . . . Cee-cee-ly,' he said, and he fell against the gate and dropped down to his knees. His head bent, he stared at the ground and didn't speak. Then he raised his face, closed his eyes to the light and exhaled one word: 'Cecily.'

'Cecily? And who is Cecily?' Susanne asked, crouching down next to him.

'She's my girl,' he said, opening his eyes, looking into hers. 'She's my girl,' he repeated, shrugging his shoulders and trying to smile. He glanced away, tilting his head to one side, frowning, searching. 'No . . . no, she's my wife, I think.' He straightened himself, nodded his head. 'Yes . . . she is, she's my wife. I'm married. I'm married to Cecily . . . my Cecily.'

And he placed his head in his hands and began to weep.

Chapter Twenty-Six

*H*e was there, sitting up at the bar reading a newspaper, and she smiled as she moved towards him. Even now, four years after his return, four years after he had returned from the dead, Cecily's heart leapt at the sight of him, his presence made all the more precious by his long absence.

But he had kept his promise, as she knew he would: he had come back to her.

Cecily had refused to relinquish hope. Inspired and reassured by stories in the newspapers, tales of missing soldiers and prisoners of war returning home months after the cessation of fighting, she had clung on, waiting, expectant. And though she had never quite been able to envision how he would return, when he would return, or how she would react or how he would be, she knew in her heart that he was not dead. And if he were not dead, he would, eventually, find his way back to her.

When it happened, there was no forewarning, no trumpet call, nothing to herald his arrival.

It was early evening, a weekday – perhaps a Tuesday or Wednesday, she could never quite remember. The sky was overcast, the air damp and threatening rain. She had gone out to the garden to take in the washing hanging from the line he had put up for her, years before. She was already late to collect her son, had spent the previous hour reading and marking Class Three's homework. As she gathered up sheets that had hung out since dawn, a figure appeared on the periphery of her vision. She did not turn, not immediately. She heard her name, a familiar male voice. But it had happened before, and would happen again. The sound of Jack's voice, her name, carried in the wind, echoing back to her, inflected in sighs and sounds. But the blur at the edge of her vision did not move and began to take on a shape. And as she turned her head, turned to face him, she saw at first only a bearded stranger, a black eyepatch and a stick; a dishevelled man in shabby clothes. And when he stepped forward and began to move towards her, she stepped back, pulling the collected bedlinen in front of her as though it were a shield.

Later, she would replay this scene over and over, see it in slow motion: see herself, arms filled with linen, turn slowly, so slowly, and him, at the end of the pathway, standing watching her, perfectly still; see herself step back as he begins to move towards her, see her arms fall, white linen float down to the grass; and as the landscape moves, the sky comes down and the earth rolls out like an unfurling carpet, bringing him back to her.

'I was beginning to think you were taking your revenge,' he said, easing himself up on to his feet.

'Revenge?' she repeated, wrapping her arms round his waist.

'Keeping me waiting so long,' he whispered. 'I missed you.'

'And I missed you. But thirty minutes is *not* two years, Jack Staunton.'

He smiled, shook his head. 'It wasn't two years . . . was it?'

'Almost.'

She placed her bag on the marble counter, watched him as

he turned to the barman to order her a drink. Even now, she found it difficult not to stare. Older, injured, war damaged, he was perfect to her. The burns, flesh still charred when he had appeared to her that day, had healed as best they ever would. There were scars: scars from new skin and scars on old skin. The skin grafted to his face, his eyelids, cheeks and nose, as well as to his neck and hands, masked some of the damage to his young, once fit and able body. And the somewhat patchy beard he would not part with.

But the lack of early, proper medical attention to Jack's injuries, including his two shattered legs, meant they had not healed the way they should have, could have. One leg remained badly twisted, at the knee and at the ankle, and made walking difficult without the aid of a stick.

Watching him, she said his name, and he turned to her. 'What's that?'

'Oh nothing. Nothing at all.'

'So, tell me,' he began, sitting down and swivelling his chair round to face her. 'How was Cynthia? Did she like it, your story?'

'Her name is Sylvia, Jack, not Cynthia.'

'Of course, Syl-via.'

'Think . . . saliva?' she suggested. 'Though it's not her name.'

He smiled. 'How was dear Saliva?'

She shook her head: 'You really have no recollection of her at all, do you?'

'No, should I?'

'Perhaps. She was, I think, your grandmother's oldest friend. And that summer – the one when we first met, before the war – she was there, quiet, unmarried, rather touchy, slightly troublesome, and quite obsessed with Cora.'

'I'm sorry,' he said, 'but you are painting a pretty dismal image. Do I really need to remember Sylvia?'

She lifted her hand to his face. 'No, my dear, you don't. The only person you need to remember is right here. Anyway,' she went on, 'in answer to your question, I've left it with her, which was the plan.'

Sylvia had read some of her manuscript there and then: some of the first chapter. As Cecily sat drinking the tea a woman called Wendy had brought in to them, she had watched Sylvia's mouth twitch, watched her raise a hand to her spectacles, pushing them back up her nose, watched her turning pages. She had listened to her breathing, the occasional sigh. Eventually, Sylvia had looked up at her, smiled and said, 'hmm, yes . . . interesting.' And that was all.

Cecily had wanted more, had said again, 'I'd value your opinion . . . I'll leave it with you if I may.'

'How was she with you?' Jack asked.

Cecily shook her head. 'She's no different. No different at all to how I remember her,' she said, lighting a cigarette. And as her husband took a glass from the barman and placed it on the polished marble in front of her, she smiled at him.

'What is it?' he asked, taking hold of her hand. 'Tell me.'

'Oh, I was just thinking about everything, on the way here in the taxicab. I was remembering all those days and nights . . . all those days without you . . . and thinking about Cora, remembering all of it.'

He nodded. 'I knew it would be tough. But I did offer to come with you . . .'

She shook her head. 'No, it was best, I think, that I went on my own. Anyhow, you don't remember her.'

'And perhaps with good reason.' He pushed his folded newspaper across the marble. 'Take a look,' he said.

A headline read, 'Lawson's Lost "Aphrodite" Found.' Beneath it, a small back and white image of the painting, and Cora's young face staring out at her.

She said, 'You did the right thing.'

'You mean *you* did the right thing. She left it to you. Left everything to you.'

'She thought you were dead. We have done the right thing,' she added, placing her hand over his.

'It always strikes me, the irony – me having lost my memory, coming back to my only blood relation, who had no memory of me, could not remember me.'

'But she did! She did remember you. She spoke about you all the time, it's just that she didn't recognise you, didn't recognise the *you* that returned, and she had gone anyway, left us by then . . .'

He glanced down at her hand over his. 'It makes me sad to think she never knew, never realised that I'd survived and come back.'

'I've told you before, you need to try and take comfort from the fact that in her mind you were there, with her. Everyone she ever loved was with her.'

Cora had failed to recognise the battered, bearded man with eyepatch and stick as any relation. And certainly not as her grandson, not as the unblemished, handsome young man who had gone off to fight, to fly aeroplanes. He had been killed and, in an attempt to accept that, or perhaps in order to protect herself from that, she had simply slid further into a world inhabited by ghosts. She did not hear the war veteran in front of her claiming to be Jack or, if she did, chose not to. Too much time had elapsed, and those in front of her were not those she remembered.

On one occasion she had even spoken to Jack about Jack, telling him he must meet her grandson. 'He likes cricket,' she said, vaguely. 'He's a leg-spin bowler, you know.'

Cecily and Jack gave up trying to explain. They visited her, sat with her, listened to her nonsensical conversation and jumbled words and names. Sometimes she recognised Cecily, and once she asked her, 'Who is he, that man? Is he *your* husband?' As though he might perhaps be *hers*. 'Yes, he's mine,' Cecily replied, smiling at Jack, winking. 'He's mine and I love him.' Cora's face had erupted into a smile, a wonderful breathtaking smile Cecily would always remember. 'And does he love you?' she asked.

Cecily turned to Jack. 'Well?'

'With all my heart,' he said, looking from Cecily to his grandmother.

And for a moment, just a moment, Cecily thought she saw something in Cora's eyes, a fleeting recognition, as she stared back at him and said, 'Yes, of course you do.'

'What time do we need to be there?' Jack asked.

'Seven, I think. Mr Davidson, the curator, wants to meet us, meet you. He wants to introduce you to the biographer.'

'Whose biographer?'

'Lawson's, of course. Don't tell me you've forgotten, I told you this morning, remember? The retrospective is to coincide with the publication of the book, *The Life, Letters and Work of George Lawson*.'

'But why do they want to meet us? If it's to talk about the painting, I know nothing about it. Do you?'

Cecily shook her head. 'No, nothing really, other than it's by him, and of her.'

'Oh God, they're probably going to ask all sorts of questions, like when and where it was executed and so on and so forth.' He shook his head. 'You know I can't handle too many questions.'

She tightened her grip on his hand. 'Don't worry. I'll answer any questions they might have as best I can.'

He glanced to his watch. 'I suppose we should get a move on.'

She didn't reply. And when he turned to her, he asked, 'What are you smiling at now?'

She shook her head. 'Oh, nothing really,' she said. 'I was just thinking about how Sylvia will react to my novel. I just hope she's not shocked.'

'Why on earth would she be shocked?'

'Because . . . because it bears little comparison, I think, to the true story.'

'She's a novelist, it's fiction. And you said you gave them all a happy ending. Can't do better than that.'

Yes, she had given her heroine a happy ending, an ending no biography or memoirs could ever do. Whether it was the right ending, the one Cora would have wished for, she would never know but she suspected that perhaps it was. Because though Cora had never confessed to any great love affair with the painter, George Lawson, she had spoken of him in such a way that it had been plain to see she had once loved him. When she told Cecily of her marriage to his father, Edward, she had simply said that he was a good man, a good husband, but that it had been a mistake for her to marry again. And by the time she told Cecily about that marriage, Jack had gone, and Cora was already muddled about who was who and where she was. Quite often it had been difficult for Cecily to know whom she was speaking about, and she continually made mistakes with names and places and dates. But there had been clues: in the painting, and in the names themselves. She had, after all, named her son after George, and mentioned that he was godfather. Could he, Cecily wondered, have been the father of her son?

It had been a thrilling thought for a while, that Jack could be Lord Lawson's grandson, that her own son could be his great-grandson. But as Cora sank further into her dementia it became impossible to ascertain the truth, and impossible to pose those questions. Cecily had waited, hoped that Cora might say more, say something, and though she had, none of it made any sense.

Now, it no longer mattered whose son Jack's father had been. Jack had no memory of him, none at all, and very few of his mother. 'But do I need to remember?' he had asked her, whenever she tried to coax memories. 'Can't we just live for now, look forward?' The only thing that mattered to Jack was here and now and the future. And so that's what mattered to Cecily now, too.

'When are you going back,' Jack was asking, 'to pick it up?'

'I said I'd call in on Friday before we go down to collect the children.'

'It'll be interesting,' he said, smiling, lifting his glass, 'for you to hear what she makes of it all.'

'She won't like it,' Cecily said. 'I know that. But I'm going to ask her again about George Lawson and Cora.'

'You really want your story to be true, don't you?'

'No, not necessarily, but I would like to know the truth.'

'Did you tell her about the Uncle John character, the blackmail?'

She sighed. 'Yes, and she said the same as you. Said it was all nonsense.'

'I never said it was nonsense,' he replied, tenderness in his voice. 'I simply said that it didn't seem feasible. She may well have received some unpleasant letters, though you never found any, did you?'

'No. No, there were very few letters at all.'

They sat in silence for a moment, then she said, 'You know, you once told me – years ago, I think it was on your last leave – that you'd found out something about Cora.'

He laughed. 'You're not expecting me to remember what it was now, are you?'

'No, I suppose not,' she said, sighing. 'You said you couldn't tell me until you had spoken to her about it . . . whatever it was.'

'Well, whatever it was, we'll never know.'

Chapter Twenty-Seven

*S*ylvia had already moved the envelope about the room: from the mantelshelf to the window sill and back again. Now it lay on the table in front of her. She enjoyed looking at it. It made her happy to see it sitting there, waiting to be opened. She would find the right time. Until then, she could wallow in its potential, imagine its contents . . .

My own dearest Sylvia, Forgive me, forgive me, forgive me . . .

My dear Sylvia, Can you find it in your heart to forgive me?

Dearest Sylvia, Soon, I shall be gone, and I cannot bear that thought without first making amends with you . . . my only true friend . . .

Dear Sylvia, Mr Cordery is planting out the herbaceous border and I was wondering if there are any violet plants to be had in London at this time of year . . .

Sylvia, I am at a loss to know WHAT to say to you, even now. The fact that you took it upon yourself to speak to X and visit Y is beyond me, but . . .

Sylvia placed the envelope on the table in front of her. She poured herself a sherry. Then she sat down. She tried to ignore the cream paper in front of her. She looked about the room, sipping the warm

345

liquid in her glass. It was at moments like these she often wished that she had taken up smoking, or another hobby: something one could pick up and put down, something to distract oneself with. But now the envelope was shouting out at her, begging to be read. And that was what she had been waiting for: beseechment.

She picked it up, read her name out loud. Then, slowly, running her index finger under the flap, she severed the seal and lifted the paper to her face. It smelled of violets, the scent of Cora. And she sat with it, unsealed, in her hands for some time. It was the first step. She glanced at the clock: five to seven. She would wait five more minutes.

It was a difficult five minutes. Time seemed to slow down, minutes stretched out, self-consciously, as though knowing they were being watched. Finally, the clock chimed the hour and she pulled out the sheets. One, two, three, four, five, six, seven, eight: eight pages from Cora! Her heart soared.

The letter was dated 15 September 1917. Sylvia lingered for a while on that date, making calculations: seven years after they had last seen each other . . . six years ago . . . and wasn't that the time when Jack went missing? She read the first three words a few times over, out loud and slowly, knowing she could loiter there in safety: 'My dear Sylvia . . . my *dear* Sylvia . . . *my dear* Sylvia . . .' It was a good start, a nice opening. She cast her eyes down over the page. Certain words sprang out: Cecily's name, Jack's name, the word blackmail and a few capitalised words, which appeared to her rather angry. She took a deep breath and began.

My dear Sylvia,

    How very queer it feels to be penning a letter to you once more, and in the knowledge that by the time you read these words I shall be no more . . . for I am to ask Cecily to pass this on to you in the event of my death, which I fear cannot be too far away.

    Much has happened since we last saw each other & none of

346

us I am certain could ever have imagined or begun to comprehend
the obscene horror upon us now. I am unable to make any sense
of the carnage & see only the <u>WASTE</u>. Like everyone else, I have
prayed & pleaded with God, I begged him to keep Jack safe, to
end this fighting, but my darling boy is 'missing', & though I try
to keep Hope and Faith, to live within that state, God's voracious
appetite for young souls offers me no hope at all. I do not see my
grandson returning & experience tells me I will not be spared.

It is this sense of waste that has caused me to reflect upon my
own life, & I see now only the brevity of our time here, that it
lasts but a moment, & I begin to understand that the most important thing of all is to be <u>TRUE</u> to oneself . . . something I have
struggled with, due perhaps to the absence of anyone to remind
me & other things which I shall come on to. I realise also that
before I am able to forgive myself I must forgive others . . . and
so, dear Sylvia, I want you to know that <u>I forgive you</u>. Though I
cannot condone your underhand tactics, & consider blackmail
wholly immoral & beneath you or any decent human being, I am
quite sure by now you bitterly regret such an undertaking. However,
I know you were desperate, & I see also that I was much to blame.
Furthermore, I know that you were not alone, & that the coincidence of another at the same time as yourself was unforeseen &
not in your plan.

The withholding of information can be peculiarly frustrating,
not least for the withholder . . . What you failed to grasp was
that I had to protect dear Jack. He had a future ahead of him.
Indeed, he WAS the future, the very best of me, and all I had left
of George. It was this, & this alone, which caused me to question
the merit & potential ramifications of allowing the truth to be
told. No one else mattered a jot. They have all gone, and though
George & Edward's reputations would be held up to scrutiny, their
judgements perhaps questioned, I think the truth would only add
to intrigue & the myth of George in particular.

I am including some pages from your notebook, the ones I tore out — confiscated, though I rather think they read like a novel & if you were to do anything with them, I would prefer that you took out the extraneous detail & imagined dialogue . . .

As regards 'The Beginning', that part of my story you were so very desperate to hear about & for so long, and which I rather think you know a little about by now, I leave it for you to decide whether or not to include it in any book. Is it relevant? Of any interest? I am still unsure. Also, I must admit that my memory is not what it was, & thus some things continue to elude me. However, & most peculiarly, certain details of my early life, which have remained something of a blur for so long, have recently come back to me, & I am able to confirm a few Facts. So, to the beginning . . .

Heart pounding, Sylvia turned the page.

I was born & baptised Coral Lillian Stopher in the year eighteen thirty-three. My parents' names were <u>Coral & Samuel</u>. Both originated from Woodbridge in Suffolk, which is where I was born & where my father was employed as an under-gardener & outdoor servant at a place called <u>Standen Hall</u>. I lived at this place — with my parents, sister & two brothers — in rooms above the stables. The Lillian in my name came from my maternal grandmother, a woman I cannot recall and possibly never knew, and my parents used this name for me, its abbreviated version — Lily. Thus, I was once Lily Stopher.

When I was perhaps six or seven years of age we left Standen Hall, for reasons I know not, but I suspect that my father lost his job there for he had nothing to go to and we nowhere to live. It is my belief now that we were homeless for some time, for I have memories of walking many miles & of sleeping out in fields, under stars.

It was around this time that my mother disappeared, though I do not recall her actual departure or any 'Goodbye', she was simply there and then not there, & I always assumed she would be coming back, that she had not abandoned us, perhaps because I had been told by someone at some stage that she had simply 'gone for a while'. Not long after this my father too must have 'gone', for I have very few memories of him without her, my mother. As I say, my memory is not what it was & there are gaps and this time is one of them.

My siblings were eventually placed into the care of various scattered family members, & I into the care of my maternal aunt, who had married a shoemaker, a man by the name of JOHN ABEL. *Aunt Fanny and Uncle John at that time resided somewhere in the vicinity of* ~~Bethnal Green~~ *the Whitechapel area, in East London, and I recall little of it apart from the brutality of the man, my uncle. He fitted into that world & my aunt did not. But I do remember our rooms, how cramped and gloomy and very small they were, & how vast and sinister-looking the lunatic asylum on the old Roman road. That building haunted me before I understood why. I had no idea then that it was in fact the very place my mother had 'gone for a while'.*

My memory of our departure – the night we fled, & the events preceding it – is now muddled & vague . . . due perhaps to the fact that it is a memory for so many years unpractised, not exercised, but instead <u>exorcised</u>. I can have been no more than twelve years of age, certainly of an age when I should be able to recall more, but though I have tried I am unable to summon detail, or perhaps I have no wish to.

Here, there was a line crossed through, and crossed through so many times it was impossible to make out the words.

What I do know is that my aunt and I took off into the night knowing we had committed a crime, knowing the law would not protect us, knowing people were hanged for murder and tried for desertion, knowing my aunt could not afford to go through Parliament and obtain a divorce. We travelled first to Jersey, later to Paris, & thence onwards to Rome, where my aunt had secured a position as housekeeper for a Mr Staunton. It was the start of a new life, she told me, and a place where no one would ever find us. She was true in this, for in the doing I never again saw any member of my family.

It was many years later that I learned the truth of what happened to my mother, that when she left us she had in fact walked to London, whereupon she was found in a desperate & hysterical state on the streets, and later committed to the Bethnal Green Lunatic Asylum. She had been incarcerated there for over twelve years by the time the cholera epidemic swept through its doors and rescued her. As to my father, he passed away the year I was twenty-one, at the workhouse at Colchester, the very same place he had been headed when he left my siblings & myself in a derelict barn by a roadside. One imagines he had gone there looking for work and, unable to secure any employment, could not face returning to four hungry, motherless children.

My mother's fate has been an immovable stain on my mind, for I long ago realised poverty & insanity to be irrevocably linked — that one simply preceded the other, and my mother's madness to be the direct result of a bleak existence. My aunt once told me that three of her eight brothers had been committed to the Country Lunatic Asylum, the same three who had tried to move on in life, the same three who had had Removal Orders placed on them, returning them back to where they had started, back to the parish of their birth. I understood early on how madness could rescue a person & obliterate pain, that money afforded comfort & comfort afforded reason.

My life overseas enabled me to crawl out of that mire & become someone. Had my father not lost his job we would not have become homeless, & perhaps my mother would never have taken it upon herself to walk away one day down the old London Road. We would

*have remained together, & I would have had a family, my own family.
But I would never have met George, never have become who I am
— or once was. These are the things I ponder upon now, how my
life should have been or could have been. And it is a queer conun-
drum. One offers me an <u>identity</u>, a family, and perhaps a sense of
belonging . . . the other, <u>opportunity</u>. But which, I wonder, would I
have chosen, then, had I been able?*

*So that was the beginning, Sylvia. That part of my story you
so wished me to tell you. I was born poor, horrendously poor,
nothing more or less. Unlike you, I was not a banker's daughter,
I was a servant's daughter . . . and, even worse, an unemployed
under-servant's daughter. Poverty made my mother go mad,
ruptured my family, & drove my aunt to desperate measures.*

*When I told you in Rome all those years ago that I had killed a
man, I was not lying, for it was how it seemed to me at that time. I
yearned to tell the truth, to confide in someone, you, and for you to
understand that possibility & be able to make a choice, to be my
friend or not, & to see me as more than that which I had come from.
And you did . . . and yet you used my confession & my trust in you
to betray me, electing to repeat it, without context or furnishing of
background from me. However, it is a long time ago, & we are older
and wiser, and the world has changed.*

*Please do not be sad about this last chapter — ironically, the
start of my story — or about our 'upset' or by my passing. My life
has been rich and full, & friendships do not last forever. In many
ways you have achieved much more in your life than I. You leave a
legacy in your words, your books, & I leave nothing other than my
memories, which I am doubtful anyone will be interested in now,
but perhaps.*

Here the pen changed. And the hand, too, appeared altered.

I have spent a great deal of time cogitating & pondering this letter, and if I am to be honest, completely honest — and that is my intention — there is another matter to set straight, and this may come as something of a shock to you.

As regards my 'Comte de Chevalier de Saint Léger', he never existed.

Sylvia looked up. 'Never existed? But of course he did! I met him, I met him in Rome . . .'

There was no wedding at Le Havre or anywhere else, & there was no fine chateau in the Loire. There is and never was any Comte de Chevalier de Saint Léger. There was however an Antonin de Chevalier, my rather gallant French army officer & lover of three years. When I met Antonin, after Freddie passed away, I longed to escape from Rome, longed for change. I had been living on hope for so long, the hope that G would return there & to me, and, like any insubstantial diet, my near empty life had left me famished & weak. When I took little G off to France — to stay, or so I told everyone, with Antonin's family — it was not with the intention of staying away for two years, & of course I had had to tell my aunt that I was engaged to be married, otherwise she would never have allowed me to go. When I wrote to her, and to you too, about the place 'Chazelles', it was not altogether a lie, the house was indeed called Chazelles, but perhaps more dilapidated farmhouse than castle, & buried in obscurity in rural Nièvre.

It was in fact my aunt who decided that I was residing in a castle & that Antonin's family must have a title lurking somewhere, all good French families did, and she embraced this notion long before I. That is not to say it was forced upon me, but rather that I chose not to enlighten her on the truth of my circumstances. I chose not to disillusion her. She had been through so much & had such hopes and dreams for me. I think I realised then that

I could return to Rome as someone else, someone quite different, & so caught up with my new & improved self & the possibilities ahead that it was impossible for me to relinquish the idea of that new identity. Everyone who mattered in Rome had a title — genuine, defunct or bogus — so why should not I also?

After Antonin was killed I had no choice but to return to Rome — as his widow. My aunt believed I had married Antonin at Le Havre, and we had indeed been living as man & wife, I was long used to referring to myself as such & had been 'Madame de Chevalier' for over a year. I am not altogether sure now where the 'Saint Léger' came from, or why I added it to the name. I rather think I must have felt the name needed something more, and that it had a nice ring to it. The only time I can recall any problem was when I married Edward — with all the various paperwork, or lack of. But of course he saw to all of that.

One thing I wish to make clear is that there was no plan or premeditation on my part. It was an evolutionary process, a small detail, which began as a misunderstanding & developed into something more. In the end, of course, the name secured not George but his father, a man who would have done anything to stop G & me from marrying when we were young. I suppose one could say then that my revenge — if indeed it was revenge — was not simply on George but on his father, too. And yet, like my first marriage, that union was an arrangement that suited both parties. Edward offered me much needed security — a home (my first & only home) & an income. In return, I gave him the Countess de Chevalier de Saint Léger Lawson. Je pense, quid pro quo.

But enough. It is late & I am weary . . . and yet it is impossible for me to end this without mentioning George. I think you & you alone know that my life has been shaped and defined by him, his presence, that he was and remains my only one true love. That love began over seventy years ago in Rome, is with me now & shall go with me after death. If I am to be remembered for anything, I hope it will be for my love of him, & as the mother of his sons.

And so, I leave it with you, dear Sylvia, to decide how & what to record, if anything at all. I have always felt alone in this world, an exile even before I became one. But we are, I think, all in transit . . . hopefully, to something better.

The letter was signed: *Yours, Cora Lawson.*

Sylvia stared at the signature. Then, as though emerging from the depths, she gulped and swallowed, and began to weep.

By the time Sylvia first met her, Cora had already dropped the last letter of her given name and assumed the name Staunton, the name that would become hers through marriage. At that time, the focus of attention had been on Cora's aunt, the new Mrs James Staunton. There were rumours then that Mr Staunton had advertised for a new wife. And there was gossip and intrigue then about who she was or had been, and where she hailed from. Everyone knew there was a secret, but no one guessed that the secret was murder – attempted or otherwise, or desertion, or bigamy. No one had had the imagination for that: no one apart from Sylvia.

It had at first been all the little things, the tiny incidental details, which allowed Sylvia to build a picture. And then the mistakes: the mention of an 'Uncle John', and Cora's knowledge of things she should not have had knowledge about; and sometimes the fear, as well. Long before Aunt Fanny's tutelage paid off, before the reinvention was complete, Cora had been a mass of contradictions, both in character and in what she said. And Sylvia, the budding novelist, had not only been captivated and inspired, she had taken note. Cora was older than her years and Cora still cried for her mother; Cora was streetwise and savvy, and Cora was afraid of strangers; Cora was reticent and studied, and Cora was verbose and impetuous; Cora was from Suffolk, and Cora was from London; Cora had been an only child, and Cora had siblings – all dead. And so it went on.

It was easy enough to see that Cora lied, but what Sylvia wanted to know was *why* she lied; what inspired the lies and contradictions. When she had asked Cora, 'Did you run away?' Cora had not appeared shocked. They had been sitting on the bench by the fountain in the Piazza d'Ara Coeli, and Cora had simply stared at her and said once more, 'I am not allowed to tell anyone . . . but I'll tell you one day, I promise.' And then she lifted Sylvia's hand and kissed it. No one had kissed Sylvia's hand before, no one had ever promised her anything. No one was like Cora.

Then, George Lawson arrived in Rome. Cora fell in love and had no time for sitting by fountains with Sylvia. Cora changed. And stories were practised and put in order. Sylvia heard them, each one slightly more polished than the last, until there was a final, definitive version. And it was impressive; Sylvia could not have done better herself. But George Lawson was not the man for Cora. Sylvia knew this. He was self-centred and ambitious, determined to prove himself. He would not stay in Rome; he would not marry Cora. He was using her.

When Sylvia penned her note to George, telling him she had information she thought he ought to know, her only thought had been Cora: protecting her from an inevitable heartbreak. And when she met him that day and he said, 'If this is another rumour about Cora or her aunt, I rather think I've heard them all,' Sylvia knew he had not heard what she was about to tell him. No one had. Not even Cora.

She explained that this was *not* idle gossip but had come from Cora herself, and though she had been sworn to secrecy, she felt duty bound to tell him. Yes, he wanted to know what it was

Cora had told her. And so Sylvia told him the truth. Or what she thought might be the truth.

She had no idea then that her actions – motivated by nothing other than love, the desire to protect the person she loved – would carve the future path of Cora's life; or that as a result of those actions Cora would spend all of her days estranged from love, would make it her mission to prove something and become someone, or that that someone would be George Lawson's stepmother. Sylvia never imagined that.

And yet it was she, Sylvia, who had comforted Cora after George broke off with her and left Rome. It was she who had held Cora in her arms and smiled down at her when she said, 'You're the best friend anyone could ever have, Sylvia.'

Chapter Twenty-Eight

The doorman saw them into the taxicab. It wasn't far to walk, but it was easier for them, easier for Jack. Piccadilly was busy and progress was slow. Through the window Cecily watched the drifting crowds, those milling about the statue of Eros, amidst pigeons and fruit barrows, under the rain-laden sky; she could hear the echo of music drifting out from an arcade, and newspaper boys shouting about curses and Pharaohs, and 'Lord Carnarvon struck dead!' And there was perhaps some queer synchronicity at work that day, she thought, when the taxicab finally pulled up opposite the Academy, outside the *Egyptian Hall*.

They were on time. West End church bells were chiming seven o'clock as they walked through the entrance of the Academy. Mr Davidson was waiting. He stepped forward to introduce himself. 'Please, do come this way,' he said. He led them through the vast lobby, past vaguely familiar sculptures – Cecily knew she had seen before – then down a corridor and into a panelled room. There, another man stepped forward to shake their hands. 'Stephen Fowler, a pleasure to meet you both.'

Mr Davidson asked them to take a seat. They sat side by side upon a long leather chesterfield sofa. He laid out some paper-work on the table in front of them – which Cecily was expecting, which their solicitor had already looked over – for her to sign. After signing her name – Cecily Staunton – a few times over, Mr Davidson offered them a glass of sherry. Still on his feet, he made a toast: 'To "Aphrodite"!' And the three raised their glasses and repeated it. Then he sat down in the armchair opposite Mr Fowler, and said, 'As you know, Mr Fowler has spent these last few years researching Lord Lawson's life and work, and he has a few questions he'd very much like to ask you.'

Cecily reached over and took hold of Jack's hand. She said, 'I'm happy to answer anything I can. Unfortunately, my husband's memory is not what it was.'

The men nodded at Jack.

Mr Fowler began. 'The painting, "Aphrodite", was, I believe, executed at Lucca some sixty years ago. Would that be correct?'

Cecily heard Jack sigh. 'I'm really not sure when, exactly, it was executed,' she answered, 'Cor— my husband's grandmother had it hanging in her hallway for a number of years, certainly since nineteen eleven, but I'm afraid I have no idea where it was before that, or any dates.'

Mr Fowler smiled and waved a hand, as though it was of little importance. 'She was, we believe, his regular sitter during his time at Rome. And we are, I think it is safe to say,' he paused and turned to the other gentleman, 'almost certain that she was his "Madonna". The faces are identical, the treatment the same. Wouldn't you agree, Mr Davidson?'

'Oh, without doubt.'

Mr Fowler cleared his throat and went on. 'For my own part, there's . . . a niggling. Yes, a niggling. Call it a dilemma, if you will.' He paused, lowered his head and glanced over his spectacles at Jack. 'Your grandmama gave birth to a child some nine months after she had returned from her stay at Lucca with Lord Lawson and Mrs Hillier. That child – your father, sir,' he said, nodding to Jack, 'was given the name George, and George Lawson was duly conferred godfather.' He said this last word rather more loudly, and then paused, again, as though giving Cecily and Jack time to absorb these facts, an unfolding theory. 'Lord Lawson wrote often of this child – your father, his godson – George, or George, as he seemed to prefer to call him. And sums of money – considerable amounts and over many years – were sent to banks in Paris and Rome . . .'

It was obvious to Cecily where the conversation was headed, what was being implied, and so she continued to hold on to Jack's hand, gripping it tighter from time to time.

Mr Fowler sighed heavily. 'Unfortunately, almost all of Lord Lawson's personal correspondence was destroyed by his family after his death. He was secretive by nature, and his surviving journals and personal papers are . . . hard to decipher – written in code, perhaps. But there's one name, a name that appears time and again in his early journals, and then again in later ones. It's a name I have been unable to identify or locate. And so, what I would like to ask you is,' he paused, looked from Cecily to Jack and back to her, 'what was the countess's given name?'

'Cora, her name was Cora,' Cecily replied.

He looked away, shook his head.

'That's not the name?'

He closed his eyes and sighed. Then he looked at her. 'No. And it's a shame,' he said and laughed. 'I thought I had discovered the missing piece,' he said, wringing his hands. 'Yes, the missing piece,' he said again.

Mr Davidson turned to him. 'Hmm, not even remotely alike,' he said.

'There were . . . no other names? Middle names?' Mr Fowler asked, looking from one to other once again.

Cecily turned to Jack, shaking her head. 'Not that I'm aware of,' she said. And Jack shrugged his shoulders. She looked back at Mr Fowler: 'But what is the name you're looking for? Perhaps it will mean something if I hear it.'

'Lily. The name is Lily.'

Cecily managed not to say anything, or nod. But she did smile.

Chapter Twenty-Nine

Cecily said she could not stay long. 'Jack's waiting at the hotel, and we have to get back to collect the children from my mother's.'

'Ah yes, of course,' said Sylvia. 'How are they? I forgot to ask you last time.'

Cecily opened her bag, pulled out her wallet and took something from it. 'Here,' she said, extending her hand.

Sylvia stared at the photograph: a dark-haired boy in a sailor suit, holding another child, his sister, on his lap. 'Aha, so that's little Jack.'

'Actually we call him Jay. It was too confusing with two Jacks in the house . . . He'll be five in a few weeks' time. And that's my baby, that's Lily,' she said, moving over to Sylvia to look at the photograph with her. 'She's grown a lot since then – they both have. She'll be three in October.'

'Lily? And what made you choose that name?'

'It's what my father called me when I was young, before he passed away. He always called me Lily.'

'I see,' said Sylvia, staring at the photograph.

Unlike the little boy, whose hair was straight, and parted at the side, the baby in the picture had a mop of dark unruly curls. And whilst the boy looked back at the camera with a serious face, the baby looked elsewhere, laughing.

'So when was this taken?' Sylvia asked.

'Oh, only a few months ago, at Christmas,' Cecily replied, smiling at the image. 'But children grow so quickly.'

'Jack must be very proud.'

'He is . . . adores them both.'

Sylvia handed back the photograph and Cecily returned to her chair.

'It would've been nice to have seen Jack,' said Sylvia.

'I know, I'm sorry, but he's not always comfortable with strangers.'

'*Strangers?*'

'He doesn't remember people, Sylvia. He has very few memories of anyone really, from before the war.'

'I see. And the children, little Jack – I mean, Jay – how was it for him when his papa returned?'

'Daddy,' Cecily corrected her. 'It's been four years, Sylvia. Jay was little more than a baby when his daddy came back.' She shrugged, 'Jack's simply Daddy, like any other . . .'

Sylvia nodded. 'And Jack copes? Copes with the children?'

Cecily laughed. 'Oh yes, he copes very well. In fact, he rather prefers their company to anyone else's. They don't see his disability, his injuries, they see the man, their father. Jack as he is now is the only Jack they've known.'

'And you? It must be quite . . . quite hard for you, dear.'

She shook her head and laughed again. 'No, it's not hard for me, not hard for me at all. I feel immensely lucky – extraordinarily lucky. My husband came back, with four limbs and a face, scarred perhaps but recognisable – to me. God spared Jack, spared me. I have my husband, the father of my children. I have *everything*.'

They moved on. Cecily told Sylvia that she and Jack had attended the private view of the exhibition of George's work, adding, 'We've loaned them the painting, the one from the hallway at Temple Hill.'

Sylvia tried to remember.

'The one of Cora? Painted by George in Italy?'

No, she could not recall it. But it did not surprise her to hear that Cora had had such a painting, she said. 'I've no doubt she had quite a few by him.'

'No, that was the only one.'

'And so it's on loan to the Academy?'

'Yes, indefinitely. It's one of the few pieces we're not inclined to sell. Jack says it's our pension,' she added, smiling.

'And I imagine it'll provide a very generous pension, too.'

'We have everything we need,' Cecily went on, 'and anyhow, it would cost a fortune to insure and look quite out of place in our cottage.'

They sat in silence for a moment or two. Sylvia deliberated on what to say about the manuscript, lying on the table in front of them. But she was still distracted by Cora's letter, acutely conscious of its presence beneath her, under the cushion. It would be interesting to see if Cecily mentioned it, asked her about it, she thought.

'About your novel,' Sylvia began, 'it's a reasonable enough story though I'm not sure one could say it is Cora's story.'

'It's fiction, Sylvia,' Cecily said, a little defensively, Sylvia thought. 'I should perhaps have explained that . . . it's inspired by her life rather than based *on* her life.'

'But you said *loosely based*; you did use those words, Cecily.'

Cecily smiled, nodded. 'Yes, I did, and perhaps that was misleading,' she said. 'But I must ask you, did you like the ending?'

Sylvia glanced across the room, up to the cornicing. She could see a cobweb or two. She would have to speak to Mrs Halliday about it later, get her to send someone up. Then Cecily spoke again. 'Is the ending feasible?'

She turned to Cecily. 'Nothing is ever *entirely* unfeasible in fiction,' she said.

'And in Cora's life?'

'I'm afraid I can't say. You would have to ask Cora that question, I think.'

'But she's not here, and you are. Do you think it's possible that Cora and George could have married, had circumstances been different?'

Sylvia laughed. 'Had circumstances been different, my dear, anything might have been possible. And as I said before—'

'No, you didn't say before,' Cecily cut in, exasperated, irritated. 'Oh, and there's something else: why did Cora think George was buried in Rome when his grave is here in London?

'Because she needed to . . . and because I gave it to her.'

'You *gave* it to her?'

Sylvia nodded. 'I wrote it that way, in *A Roman Affair*.'

For seven days after George's death, his body lay in the Octagon Room at the Academy. Crowds of mourners queued to pay their respects, to file past the coffin festooned with flowers and wreaths, and draped in patriotic colours, like a war hero who had died for his country. The newspapers proclaimed his death a 'tragedy'; the nation was bereft.

Weeks earlier, George had been diagnosed with angina. His doctors had informed him that he needed to cut down on his workload, needed to take a rest. He had written to Cora in Rome, telling her that he planned to take a sabbatical, and that he would like to spend it in Italy, with her. And she had quickly replied, full of plans: they could take a house outside Rome, somewhere quiet, she suggested; and they could perhaps travel north, if he felt up to it, to Bagni di Lucca, where the waters and hot springs would surely do him a power of good. Yes, she would look into it, she told him.

When Cora learned of her son's accident, she immediately despatched a telegram to George informing him of the situation, telling him that she was about to set off for England. Two days later she sent another – to inform him of Georgie's death. Stunned by disbelief, by the sudden and abrupt end to her son's life, she failed to notice George's silence, his absence at their son's funeral. She had no idea that hours after George received her second telegram he had had a stroke; no idea, as she stood in a snow-covered churchyard with one George that the other had just taken his last breath.

Cora insisted on going to the Academy. She told Sylvia she could not return to Rome before paying her final respects. And so, stiffly upholstered in mourning, she held on to Sylvia's arm as they climbed the steps of the entrance to the Academy. She seemed able, Sylvia thought then, to divorce her shattered spirit from that swell of public hysteria. For no one in that murmuring line of sombre-faced strangers would ever have guessed. No one shuffling across that marble floor could know that she had just buried her son; or that the man whose coffin they queued to see was in fact the father and the man she had loved for almost half a century.

And yet, it seemed to Sylvia that, in death, George Lawson, late President of the Academy, England's greatest painter, unmarried, with no apparent heir, and owned by everyone, belonged only to one: the woman gripping her arm.

When a man, some sort of official in uniform, asked, 'Did you know him?' Sylvia quickly replied, 'Yes, we both knew him . . . long before he became famous.'

'Thought so. Saw you'd both dressed proper. Not everyone has the decency to do that these days,' he said, and moved on.

When it came to their turn, Sylvia stepped to one side and Cora walked forward alone. She placed her hand upon the coffin, closed her eyes for a moment, and Sylvia saw her mouth a few words. Then she turned to Sylvia and nodded. They walked back through rooms softly humming with desultory conversation, following the snaking line out into the lobby and past Clifford's 'Tinted Venus' without a second glance.

'Yes,' Sylvia said again, 'it was my gift to her, dedicated to her . . .' She paused and smiled. 'But I'm afraid you'll have to wait for my new book for your answers,' she added in a new bold voice.

'You've written a book about her, about Cora?'

'Well, they've all been about her, one way or another, I suppose. But this one is different. It's the story of her life,' Sylvia said, 'the *true* story.'

'Oh, and according to whom?'

'Well, according to me, of course. As you know, I was there for a great deal of it, and, as Cora's confidante, was for most of her life privy to her innermost thoughts and secrets. That is why she wished me to record her memories, but alas it was not to be.'

'How wonderful,' said Cecily, rising to her feet. 'Well, I shall look forward to reading it. What's it to be called? Have you a title yet?'

'*The Memory of Lost Senses.*'

'*The Memory of Lost Senses,*' Cecily repeated. 'Mm, I like it.' She pulled on her coat and picked up her manuscript.

Sylvia watched her and said, 'I thought you had something to tell me, something about Cora?'

'Did I? Oh no, I simply wondered about the letter – her letter to you, that was all. Was it . . . was it as you imagined . . . what you expected?' she asked, fastening buttons.

'It was indeed, and it will help me with the final part of my book,' Sylvia said, moving forward in her chair.

'Please, don't get up, I can see myself out.'

There was no kiss.

Wendy was quick to respond to the bell, and even quicker to return with the bucket of coal. 'Having a clearout, are we?' she said to Sylvia, crouching down by the hearth, eyeing the paper and envelopes, the tattered shoeboxes piled up on the table.

'Sorting through . . .'

'Don't forget, it's Mrs Evesleigh's birthday. There's tea and cake in the lounge at four.'

'Ah yes, of course,' Sylvia replied, watching the flickering.

'Do you want me to take any of this?' Wendy asked, nodding her head towards the table. 'I can dispose of it, you know. You don't want to be having a bonfire in your room, now do you?'

Sylvia feigned a little laugh. 'Thank you, Wendy, but I shan't be having any bonfire, at least, not today. Just burning a few old letters, that's all.'

There was plenty of time, Sylvia thought, hours until Mrs Evesleigh puffed out her cheeks to extinguish a few tiny pink candles. In the meantime, Sylvia could have her own burning ceremony. And it gave her something to do: a task for the afternoon. I am the only one who knows, she thought, placing the first envelope upon the fire, watching the cream-coloured paper slowly ignite and burn . . . *the only one who will ever know.*

Cecily stared out of the train carriage window to row upon row of soot-blackened houses, back-to-back gardens, washing lines and fences and paths, huddled and dismal under the lowering smog. She caught glimpses of crossings and platforms and faces, and high streets foreign to her; shops she would never enter, trams and buses she would never take. She forgot for a while that she was about to see her children; forgot Jack, sitting opposite her.

She had known about Lily for years, known since that stormy summer's afternoon when they sat waiting for a deluge that never came; when she told Cora that her father had called her Lily, not Cecily, and Cora had said, 'Mine too.' But what could be gained by revealing the name? What could be gained now? Everything was in place and where it ought to be; and she had left it so.

Jack had said, 'A coincidence, eh? The name being Lily.'

'Hmm, it's a common enough name, I suppose.'

They had been in another taxicab, heading back to their hotel, exhausted from standing about the crowded picture galleries of the Academy surveying George Lawson's life's work; and, at the same time, elated from seeing their painting hanging there. But Cecily's private joy had been the 'Madonna', Lawson's most famous work, the one which had catapulted him to success and, for years, had been enjoyed only by royal eyes. The painting was vast. It took up an entire wall of one room – easily the most crowded room. And there, right at the centre of the enormous canvas, a vaguely familiar face: eyes downcast, almost closed, and lips slightly parted as though in mid-sigh. And for Cecily it spoke of the pain of love, and of a life of loss.

'Do you think they were actually implying that my father was Lawson's lovechild? That he and Cora had had an affair?' Jack had asked, staring out at the wet lamplit street.

'It did sound like that, didn't it?'

'Scurrilous . . . Perhaps I should sue them,' he had added, turning to her, smiling.

She could not tell him. She had promised Cora. And that promise – like Jack's to her – had been kept.

But that morning, when she had called on Sylvia to collect her manuscript, and had teasingly said, 'Oh, I have something to tell you, something about Cora,' she had thought of telling Sylvia; or rather, of leading Sylvia to a place where she might tell *her* more. But it was clear to her that Sylvia was not going to divulge anything, whatever she knew. And she had been in an odd mood, odder than ever. There had been little point in asking about Cora's letter, though she had, simply for politeness' sake.

'She just seems so . . . so bitter,' Cecily said now, continuing to stare out of the carriage window, musing aloud.

She was rankled by Sylvia's attitude, and wondered why she had been so unkind, for she had said nothing at all constructive, offered Cecily no words of encouragement or praise. *A reasonable enough effort . . .*

Then Jack said, 'Perhaps it was unrequited love.'

Cecily turned to him. 'The only person she's ever loved is Cora.'

'That's what I meant. There's your answer,' he said, raising his eyebrows, smiling at her.

When they arrived back at Bramley, Jay was waiting at the bottom of the track, perched on the wall of the bridge where the ford had once been. He looked smaller than she remembered – even from a few days ago. And as she stepped down from Mr Cotton's motorcar, he was there, helping his father climb down at the other side, wrapping his arms around him as though he'd been gone for years and not days. He barely drew breath as he walked back with them, regaling them with what had happened in their absence: Lily had refused to eat Rosetta's dumplings, had thrown one across the kitchen floor; she had behaved atrociously at bathtime, 'screaming the whole place down, *and*,' he added, with emphasis and pausing for dramatic effect, before what Cecily knew to be the *pièce de résistance* – 'she took a wee in the garden, on Granny's lettuces.'

'Jack!' said Cecily, in an attempt to silence her husband's laughter.

Then, as though remembering something called manners, Jay looked at his mother and asked, 'Have you had a nice time, Mummy? What have you been doing?'

'Well, I went to call on an old lady, a friend of your great-grandmother's.'

'Golly,' he said, 'she must be *ancient*!'

'Yes, she is quite old. She's a writer, a novelist, like me.'

'What does she write about?' he asked, moving on up the track, clutching his father's hand.

'Mm, romantic things . . . men and women falling in love, that sort of thing,' she replied.

'Ugh!'

'But she's been writing a book about your great-grandma, a book about her life.'

'Why doesn't she write a book about Daddy?' he asked, releasing his father's hand, rummaging in his pocket and pulling out a piece of folded paper. 'That'd be far more interesting than a book about some old lady, specially a *dead* old lady.'

Cecily smiled. 'Jay, she wasn't just some old lady; she was Daddy's grandmother, your great-grandmother. And she wasn't always dead, or old. She was once a little girl and lived in a castle, and she lived in a castle in France as well. Imagine that?'

But they had reached the gate and her son had turned away from her, stretching out his hand to present his father with the paper aeroplane he had made for him earlier that afternoon. And Cecily, home again and feeling complete, paused for a moment to savour it, savour it *all*: the familiar scent of pine and woodsmoke, the soft twilight air; that sense of wholesomeness she knew money could not buy. Then, feeling the pull, she turned her eyes to the ever-narrowing track, beyond the silhouetted limbs of arching branches to the circle of light at the top.

And she watched her, Cora – Lily – turn and walk away, vanishing into the dusk, into her world, another place in time.

One day Cecily would tell her children of their great-grandmother, that she had been Lord Lawson's stepmother, been his Madonna and his Aphrodite, too. And that she had been quite a character.

But for now it was enough to be home, with Jack, with her children. And as she watched her husband walk up the pathway holding on to their son's hand, and saw Rosetta appear in the doorway, their daughter on her hip, she knew everything that mattered was there in front of her.

She heard the latch on the gate drop, clickety-click, her feet upon the path, and a door quietly close.

It is evening and the sun is still high, shining in through the wisteria tumbling across the small open window. The room is hot, the black paint on the window frame bubbling and peeling in soft curls. She sits barefoot on her aunt's lap and it feels good to be held, secured. She can hear her sister in the field outside, her cousins and little Johnny, too. 'Your mother has had to go away for a while, just for a while,' her aunt says, answering her questions, stroking her hair. 'She needs a little rest.'

'And Father?' she asks, swinging her legs up, glancing to her toes, her feet.

'Well now, your father is . . .' but she doesn't finish the sentence. She says, 'And you're to come and stay with me and Uncle John in London. Now isn't that nice?'

Samuel has already gone – to relations in Framlingham, someone said.

'And Jemima and Johnny, are they coming as well?' she asks.

'No, dear, they are to stay here with your Uncle Daniel,' her aunt says.

She nods. She knows she must be brave, must not cry. Then she turns

371

to her aunt, looks up at her and says, 'But when will she be back? Do you know? Did she say?'

'Oh, soon,' her aunt replies, kissing her forehead. 'Very soon.'

'And will she know where I am, will she know where to find me?'

'Well, of course she will, Lily. She knows you're with me . . . knows you're safe with me.'

FALLING

A LOVE STORY

Also by Jane Green

Bookends
Jemima J
Mr Maybe
Babyville
Straight Talk
Spellbound
The Other Woman
Life Swap
Second Chance
The Beach House
Girl Friday
The Love Verb
The Patchwork Marriage
The Accidental Husband
Tempting Fate
Saving Grace
Summer Secrets

FALLING

A LOVE STORY

Jane Green

MACMILLAN

First published 2016 by Macmillan
an imprint of Pan Macmillan
20 New Wharf Road, London N1 9RR
Associated companies throughout the world
www.panmacmillan.com

ISBN 978-1-4472-8851-0

1 3 5 7 9 8 6 4 2

A CIP catalogue record for this book is available from the British Library.

Typeset by Ellipsis Digital Limited, Glasgow
Printed and bound by CPI Group (UK) Ltd, Croydon, CR0 4YY

FALLING

A LOVE STORY

ACT ONE

Chapter 1

'It's lovely,' she lies, in her most gracious of voices, looking around at the tired wood panelling lining the walls of the living room, floor to ceiling. As she looks down, her gaze lands on well-worn salmon-pink shagpile carpeting and she quickly conceals her horror.

Emma wonders if this house might not be beyond even her capabilities to transform. Perhaps the landlord would let her paint it? Surely he would let her paint it – who wouldn't want to lighten up this room, so dark it feels more like a cave? She would paint it for free, *and* pull up that carpet. Maybe she would be lucky and find a hardwood floor underneath; even if it was merely concrete, surely it wouldn't cost too much to stick down some inexpensive sisal.

This room could be transformed, she determines. Lipstick on a pig is her speciality.

Her landlord, or potential landlord, smiles. 'Hey, I know it's not everyone's taste today,' he says. 'Why do people want everything to be grey and modern?'

Emma is surprised by his comment, surprised frankly

by his interest in making small talk. 'I hate that look,' Emma offers. It happens that she does agree, quite passionately, in fact. 'None of those decorated houses feel like real homes.'

'Exactly!' he says in delight. 'This is a home.'

Struck by his words, by the obvious sincerity with which they are spoken, she turns to look at her potential landlord for the first time. She can't help but feel struck by the sight of him. He is not too tall, only a few inches taller than her, with skin tanned by the sun and an easy smile that seems to put her at ease. It isn't so much that she finds him attractive, but rather that there is something familiar about him, a recognition, a sense of having somehow met him before.

Perhaps because she has remained silent, he goes on to add, 'At least, it was a home. My grandparents lived here for forty years.'

Yes, thinks Emma, *it looks like it. It smells like it, too.* The air is fusty. Of course old people had lived here. That explains the wood panelling and the floral wallpaper in the family room; it also explains the salmon-pink carpet and avocado-green bathroom suite with matching tiles.

'How would you feel about me putting . . .' Emma pauses, wondering how to say this diplomatically. She doesn't want to jump in and tell him she'd like to tear everything out and start again. He probably doesn't want to change any-thing; his voice had softened when he mentioned his grandparents. She has an odd reluctance to offend him, and senses she'll need to take this slowly if she wants this house. '. . . a woman's touch on the house?'

'A woman's touch!' The landlord smiles and nods approvingly. 'That's exactly what I've been saying this house needs for years. A woman's touch.'

She follows him into the kitchen at the back of the house and her heart sinks slightly. It hasn't been touched since the fifties, rough wood cabinets bumpy with layers of white paint, although pretty black iron hardware. Formica worktops with large cracks, and linoleum floors. A stove that is so ancient it's fashionable again, and, surprisingly, a large modern stainless-steel fridge.

Emma looks at the fridge and raises an eyebrow as she looks over at the landlord.

Damn, she thinks. What was his name again? Donald? Derek? Something like that.

'The old fridge gave up last year,' he explains. 'The tenants picked out this one. And I paid for it,' he adds quickly, as if to reassure her that he is a good landlord, on top of everything, ready to jump in and deal with problems.

'Great,' says Emma, wandering over to the back door and peering out through the glass onto a fenced-in garden, or what could be a garden if the weeds were cleared. 'Can I go outside?' she asks, already out the door.

He follows her out, apologizing for the weeds. They both stand there as Emma looks around, her imagination already firing. There are two filthy peeling rattan chairs stacked off to the side, surrounded by boxes and baskets: in other words, rubbish.

The landlord turns to look and immediately apologizes. 'I haven't been out here,' he explains. 'Obviously all of that will be gone. I can replace those chairs with new ones.'

Emma is again struck by him. His eagerness to please doesn't seem solely mercenary. He wants her to know that he cares about the house and yard. 'Do I get to choose what kinds of chairs the new ones are? Like the fridge?' Emma says.

'As long as they're not too expensive.'

'I am the expert at renovating on a shoestring.' She smiles.

'You're my kind of woman.' He laughs, as Emma flushes slightly and turns away. A flirtatious landlord is the last thing she wants right now. 'Sorry.' He apologizes immediately, realizing his mistake. 'I was kidding. But I'm happy for you to choose things as long as they're within the budget.'

Emma looks up at the sky, noting the sun, looking at the shadows to try to figure out which way the garden faces. 'South-west,' she guesses, and he turns to her with a smile.

'You're a sun worshipper?'

'With this pale English skin?' She laughs and shakes her head. 'I turn into one giant freckle in the sun. But I am a gardener. At least, a frustrated one. For years and years, I lived in flats in London dreaming of having a garden of my own. Then for the last five years I've been on the top of a high-rise in Battery Park.' Good lord. Why is she suddenly giving him her life story?

'Ah, so you're a city girl.'

'Not by choice.'

'You're ready to be out here?'

'Ready to be steps from the beach, in a gorgeous town where the pace of life is relaxed and the pressure is off? No. Definitely not.'

He laughs. 'I've lived here my whole life, and wouldn't move anywhere else. How did you find Westport?'

'I have a friend who lives here, who I used to work with. She moved out three years ago after she had a baby, and she loves it. I've been out to visit her quite a few times, and something about this place feels right. I never thought I'd be able to move out here permanently, but . . . I needed to make some big changes in my life. Moving somewhere like this, with a quieter pace of life, seemed like a good first step.'

'I saw on your application you're a banker. That's quite a commute.'

'Actually,' Emma says, 'I took a package. I'm now officially unemployed, albeit with a very nice severance. I hope that won't be a problem?'

'As long as you pay your rent, nothing's a problem. What are you going to do here in town?'

Emma is struck again by the sincerity of his interest. He is not just making small talk, she is sure of it. He's looking at her, making her feel like he cares about what she'll say next. She shakes her head. 'Thankfully, I have enough to have a little bit of breathing space. I don't really know. I've always had a dream about doing something with the home. Interior design, gardening, that sort of thing. I've been doing an online course to get the official qualification. Now all I need are clients.'

'And a house to do up.'

'And a garden to transform. Preferably one that faces south-west.' She grins as she looks around the garden.

He grins, too. 'Then you've found it. It seems that you and this house were meant to be. Although, you couldn't do anything major to it without consulting with me.'

'Of course.' Emma laughs politely. She couldn't move in *unless* she did something major with the house. As it is, it's completely awful, but stepping back to take it in, even with all its flaws, she thinks she could turn this into a charming beach cottage.

The landlord seems like a nice guy. He may be resistant to her changes at first, but she surmises that she could ask forgiveness rather than permission for most things. If he walked into this room and found the wood painted a lovely chalky white, the floors covered with sisal, the single light bulb replaced with a pretty glass pendant light, surely he would be thrilled. Who *wouldn't* be thrilled at someone transforming their house for nothing? He would undoubtedly get more money for it next time he decides to rent it out.

The truth is that Emma Montague isn't looking for somewhere permanent just yet. She's just looking for a place to call home for the next year or so. A year to try to recover from the last five years of working in finance in New York. A year to try to figure out what kind of life she wants to live. For five years she has lived a life that wasn't hers. Five years of utter exhaustion; five years of keeping her head down and working like the devil, putting away enough money to be able to afford to do what she is doing now, leaving the rat race and pursuing her dream. Her goal is to figure out what her dream is. Right now she only knows that the first step is to find a world and a life that feels likes her own; a life in which she finally feels she belongs.

It starts with a house. She is itching to buy, but it is more sensible to rent, making sure this is where she wants to live. Still, the rentals down by the beach, here in Westport, Connecticut, are mostly prohibitive for a single girl with a budget, even an ex-banker. The last thing she wants to do is blow all her savings on rent.

This house, this dated, fusty house, is entirely within her budget, precisely because it *is* so dated and fusty. It is the perfect size – two bedrooms with a living room, kitchen, and family room that would make a perfect office.

And best of all there is a garden, or rather more than enough space for one. She can finally plant vegetables. She can put a gravel path down the middle, can grow tomatoes, cucumbers, and lettuce, plant roses and clematis over the fence at the back. She imagines a long, rustic table, a small group of friends sitting around, bottles of rosé, and candles interspersed with galvanized steel pots of lavender running down the centre. Laughter. Happy faces. Everyone lit by the glow of summer and love.

Emma shakes her head to bring herself back to earth. She knows only one person – her friend Sophie Munster

– here in Westport. She has no other local friends she can invite to sit around the table, and since she's something of an introvert, it may take a little while to find them. But she will find them.

Although a bit of a loner, she is loyal, and fun, when she finds people with whom she is comfortable. She is thinking of taking up yoga, and maybe knitting. There are evening classes at the local yarn shop, Sophie says. They should both go. Sophie grew up here, although she went away to boarding school. She has friends from grade school, though, and seems to know almost everyone in town. Surely it's only a matter of time before Emma's fantasy of summer evenings comes true.

For as long as she can remember, Emma Montague has had a fascination with America. Growing up in her upper-crust family in Somerset, England, sent off to boarding school, then moving to London after university to enter the world of banking, she had the persistent belief that this was not supposed to be her life.

As a little girl, she had never quite felt she fitted in. She was loved and treasured, but her boisterous, overbearing mother and loving but somewhat beleaguered and introverted father didn't quite know how to connect with their quiet, studious child. The place she felt happiest, the place she found her solace and joy, was in the pages of books.

She read all the time. It was so much easier than dealing with the chaos of her playmates during breaktimes. She was close to one or two of her classmates, but she only liked seeing them one at a time. Otherwise, she was happier with her books. She was the child with the torch under the duvet late into every night. She would breeze through a book in a day and a half, then read it six more times.

She fell in love with America through the pages of these books. Her dull, patrician life in Somerset felt very staid compared to the lives of Jo and her sisters in *Little Women*, and Katy in the What Katy Did series. She devoured the stories of Laura Ingalls Wilder and dreamed of having a farm out in the middle of nowhere, growing all her own vegetables, raising her own animals.

Life then got in the way, sweeping her up into the cut-throat world of London finance, not because she had a passion for finance, but because it was what all the girls were doing at that time. First London, then New York. Finally, now that she has extricated herself, it looks like she has a shot at the kind of life she might actually want to live.

Westport, Connecticut, may not be Walton's Mountain, but there are enough trees for her to pretend, and the beauty of the beach on the doorstep is something she now realizes she has always wanted.

When she was living in Manhattan she would go running along the river every day before work. The sunlight glinting off the water brought a calm and peace to every morning. She hadn't known how much she wanted to be by the water until Sophie drove her to Compo Beach for a walk one weekend. That was the moment she knew this was where she wanted to be.

There had been a tremendous expectation for the life Emma was supposed to have led, at least from her parents. And she had tried to fit into the life they had designed for her. Namely, to work at a pretend job for a few years to enable her to meet the right kind of husband, before quickly getting pregnant, giving up work, and going on to raise three or four beautiful children in a lovely stone manse in Somerset. Preferably near her parents. Have a couple of dogs, Gordon setters or pointers, possibly golden retrievers; have lots of local women friends who come for coffee. Get involved in the village fair and perhaps, given her love of books, institute a reading mentoring programme in the less well-off town twenty minutes away.

Emma knew the path well, as it was the path so many of her childhood friends had taken. At thirty-seven, she is the only one still unmarried, apart from Imogen Cutliffe, who is one of the leading lights of British screen and stage and about to star as the lead in a film starring Bradley Cooper. Emma is the only one who continued to work and rise up the corporate ladder, putting all her focus on making money. It wasn't that she cared about money for the sake of money, rather it was the only path out: making enough money to retire from banking in her thirties, and the freedom to pursue her dream. If she could figure out what her dream was.

She hadn't known her life was going to turn out like this. For a long time she imagined she would indeed follow the path her parents expected of her. She dated Rufus Fairfax for years throughout her twenties, not because she loved him, but because her parents loved him and he seemed to tick all the right boxes. He was a banker in the firm where she worked, he was handsome (although he had not an ounce of sex appeal, as far as she was concerned), and he was of the right stock. Clever, but not very funny; in fact, he was achingly dull. But they looked so good together! They seemed to fit so perfectly together that everyone assumed they would get married from the moment they started going out. And Emma had presumed everyone was right, that everyone knew something she did not, and she was the one who must have been wrong.

She determined to make it work. She and Rufus spent their weekdays in London, both of them burning the candle at both ends, and their weekends in the country, usually staying with friends in crumbling old piles that were impossibly draughty, with terrible food and lots of drink to distract from the fact that everyone was freezing cold and permanently starving.

Rufus had a huge group of friends from boarding school that Emma always found rather awful. They were shockingly loud, and arrogant, fuelled by absurdly expensive bottles of wine that they ordered in restaurants to prove they could afford them. They shouted inside jokes from when they were all thirteen, their wives and girlfriends sitting with smiles plastered on their faces, pretending to be amused.

Emma started leaving these evenings early, claiming headaches and making her way up to bed during those country weekends, earplugs tucked into her overnight bag to help her sleep through the inevitable banging and shouting in the early hours of the morning when the party eventually broke up.

None of this fazed Rufus, who proposed to her four times. The first time, he did so after a romantic dinner at Hakkasan, having gazed at her over the course of the evening with a hopeful kind of love that Emma found slightly discomfiting. Each time, Emma said she just wasn't quite ready. Eventually, five years ago, Rufus issued an ultimatum: if she wouldn't marry him, he would find someone else who would, and with a great dramatic flounce, he packed up his things and left their Kensington flat. Emma knew he thought she would beg him to come back within a week or so, but from the minute he was gone, she felt nothing other than tremendous relief.

She had been playing the part of adoring girlfriend, probably – hopefully – soon-to-be wife, for so long that she had forgotten how liberating it was to simply be herself. She saw girlfriends from university she hadn't seen for ages because Rufus disapproved of their drinking ('Darling, there's nothing quite so ghastly as a woman publicly drunk'). She got into bed at seven thirty p.m. with hummus and chips for dinner, and spent hours watching terrible reality television that Rufus would never have condoned.

She was happy, and happier still when she was called in to her superior's office and asked if she would consider taking up a position with the bank in New York. They were starting a new private wealth management operation, specifically for English expatriates living on the East Coast of the United States, and they needed someone to head client relations.

They would put together a package, they said. All moving expenses would be paid. She would be set up in an apartment, and there would be a healthy relocation allowance. They offered all of this as if to sweeten the deal, as if Emma weren't using everything she had, sitting in her office in her oh-so-staid black Givenchy skirt and Manolo Blahnik d'Orsay heels (the perfect combination of elegant and sexy), not to break out in a scream of joy and twirl around the room, punching the air and whooping in a mad happy dance.

It was the fresh start she had been longing for, and better still, in New York! The place she had always imagined living! Well, perhaps not quite New York City. She preferred to see herself in rural Vermont, or Maine, but at least it was across the pond, and she would get a green card, and at some point surely, surely, she'd make it out of the city and into the farmhouse of her dreams.

This is not the farmhouse of her dreams. This isn't even the beach cottage of her dreams. But it could be. With just a little bit of work, if her oddly welcoming landlord acquiesced, she could transform this into something, if not quite magnificent, at least beachy, and airy, and filled with charm.

They walk back through the house, Emma trying to see through the wallpaper, the linoleum, the salmon-pink flat shagpile carpet, as the landlord shows her out.

'It was great to meet you, Emma,' he says, meeting her

gaze with a friendly smile and shaking her hand with a grip so firm she crumples slightly before flexing her fingers.

'Ouch!' she says, laughing.

'I'm so sorry!' he says, clearly mortified.

'It's fine.' She smiles. What a friendly man he is. 'It's just, I wasn't expecting that.'

'I'm Italian,' he says, by way of explanation, which makes no sense to Emma whatsoever. 'My family is known for its handshakes.'

'Really?' She peers at him.

'No. I'll work on it. Do you want to think about the house and let me know when you've made a decision?'

'That sounds great,' she says, wishing she could remember his name.

'Dominic,' he says, as if reading her mind.

'Dominic,' she says confidently, as if she had remembered all the time. 'Thank you so much. I'll be in touch.'

'I can't believe you didn't invite me!' Sophie walks back into the kitchen, having put her soon-to-be two-year-old down for a nap. 'I would have loved to see it. Which house is it again?'

'The grey one with the overgrown garden?' says Emma, scooping up a handful of Goldfish crackers from the bowl Sophie's son, Jackson, hadn't touched. 'On Compo. About four in. Maybe six. I don't know. Close to the end of the road.'

'But it was awful?'

'It wasn't *awful*. It's just that it wasn't great. But I've looked at everything online, and if I want something great it's going to cost me at least twice as much. It seems ridiculous to pay so much money on rent, especially since I don't know what I'm going to be doing or where I'm going to land. I'd much rather be frugal, or at least moderately frugal, and rent something I can turn into my own.' She sighs. 'If he doesn't let me change the inside I'll just do it and say I'm sorry afterwards. At least we've established that he's definitely fine with me putting a garden in. And I could put a gorgeous garden in.'

'That won't help you much in winter.'

'No, but it will give me something to look forward to. And can we not talk about winter yet? It's June, for heaven's sake. The last thing I want to think about is snow.'

Sophie shakes her head. 'I can't believe you're actually going to be moving out here!' She grins suddenly. 'This is the most exciting thing that's ever happened to me.'

'Apart from marrying Rob and having Jackson, you mean?'

'Well, yes. Apart from that. But it will be just like old times when we worked together. We can hang out every day. Imagine if we could get Hilary Trader to come and live here, too. God, we'd have fun. We're going to have fun anyway, even if it's just you and me. Do you need a second opinion about the house? Because I'm really happy to go see it if you need me to.'

'Oh, you're sweet,' says Emma, blanching in horror at the thought of her friend, in her immaculate, brand-new, pseudo-modern farmhouse, every wall horizontally planked

with perfect high-gloss white wood, her kitchen a panorama
of white marble and grey cabinets, every chandelier hanging from the ten-foot ceilings a perfect cluster of crystal
globes dripping from polished nickel fixtures, walking into
the grimy little cottage by the beach.

'You would hate it,' Emma says. 'You would think it the
most disgusting house you have ever seen.'

Sophie looks offended. 'Why would you say that? Just
because I live in a new house doesn't mean I can't appreciate older homes.'

'Darling, this house isn't just old, it's dead. I have huge
plans for it if I decide to take it, and I'm not even sure
about that. But I honestly don't think, even you, with your
glorious taste, would be able to see through the brown
flowery wallpaper and threadbare salmon carpet.'

Sophie wrinkles her pretty little nose. 'That sounds
gross.'

Emma laughs. 'It is. But all that can be changed. I'm going
to see a couple more rentals later this afternoon and, hopefully, by the end of the day, I will have made a decision.'

Chapter 2

Her phone rings just as Emma has put the last box down in the living room of her new home. She sighs looking at the screen, ready to divert it to voicemail. But she can't actually divert it, for her mother knows that if she gets voicemail after fewer than about seven rings, it is because Emma is choosing not to answer the phone. She silences the ringer instead.

The last person Emma wants to talk to is her mother. The last person Emma *ever* wants to talk to is her mother. But it's been a while, and better to get it out of the way, do her good deed for the day.

She thinks about Sophie, whose mother, Teddy (short for Theodora), lives in Westport and is as close to Sophie as a sister. Sophie always says she doesn't need a lot of friends, although she does in fact have tons of friends, most of whom she has known her entire life. She says this because her mother is her best friend, and Emma always smiles and says how lucky she is, not understanding how such a thing is possible.

The thought of *her* mother, Georgina Montague (born

Georgia but changed to Georgina shortly after realizing her newly embarked relationship with Simon Montague was serious), being her best friend is nothing short of hilarious.

Emma has never felt particularly comfortable around her mother. In fact, she finds herself shrinking into corners to allow her mother to take centre stage. She has always been aware that with her quieter personality and her occasional need for solitude, she is a source of both bewilderment and irritation to her mother. Her mother wants to be closer, too, she knows, wishing for the kind of daughter who goes shopping with her, accompanies her to fund-raisers, and provides her with the grandchildren she so desperately wants.

In many ways, moving across the Atlantic was the best thing for Emma and her mother. They don't have much in common, and their different personalities often result in Georgina unwittingly belittling Emma. Her barbs seem to be couched in tremendous good humour, or so it appears, unless you are paying the closest of attention.

Their relationship was better while Emma was with Rufus. Emma's parents adored Rufus, naturally, and still haven't quite got over the fact that Emma broke up the relationship. Rufus married the next little blond thing to come along, eight months after he and Emma broke up. Emma was stunned when her parents were invited to the wedding.

She presumed they wouldn't go, but they did, declaring it a high old time, with excellent grub and a darling bride who couldn't wait to start making babies with good old Rufus, who seemed over the moon.

Emma did what she always did when her parents unknowingly offended or upset her. She said goodbye as if nothing was wrong, then took a break from them. In the past, those breaks had sometimes lasted for six months or more. But they didn't notice. Her mother left numerous messages, not seeming to realize that anything was wrong, or perhaps hoping that if she pretended nothing was wrong it might entice her daughter back.

The hurt would heal – it always did – and Emma would eventually get back in touch, and there would be no mention of her going AWOL for six months, or however long it had taken to nurse her wounded feelings. Her mother cheerfully blundered through life, never noticing the bombs she threw around her (for Emma was not the only one to find her overbearing and insensitive), cheerfully carrying on as if life was peachy.

'Hi, Mum.'

'Hello, darling!' booms her mother's voice over the phone. 'Just checking in with you. Isn't the big moving day coming up? Daddy and I were wondering if you needed help. It's a bit busy over here with all the summer festivals coming up, and you know how Daddy likes to enter his vegetables in the village fete, but we could absolutely jump on a plane if you need us. It's very hard moving on your own, though I know you've done it before, darling. But you were in your twenties then, and I don't want you to put your back out. Plus I'm terribly good at organizing, as you know, and I'm worried that you have no one to help you.'

In the room filled with nothing but boxes, Emma shakes her head. Her mother will take any opportunity to point out her single status. It used to upset her, but she has learned to let the comments wash over her head.

'It's fine, Mum,' says Emma, knowing how much her mother hates being called Mum, infinitely preferring what she sees as the far more palatable 'Mummy'.

'I changed the date of the move, so I'm already in my new place, actually,' she says, looking around the room defeatedly at the number of boxes. It's not as if she were downsizing. She had lived relatively anonymously in her flat in Battery Park, a small one-bedroom that she had always thought of as pleasantly minimalist.

She'd had no idea that her books would take up so many boxes. Nor her artwork, now stacked in three piles against the wall. Where did all this stuff come from?

Dominic had had the dreadful salmon carpet professionally cleaned, and had regrouted the bathroom. The new bright-white grouting did little to help the avocado-green tiles, but at least Emma thought she could bear to step into the shower.

After looking at other far more lovely, but pricier options in neighbouring towns, her only choice if she wanted to stay both solvent and by the beach was this one. She had phoned Dominic the next day to confirm. He sounded delighted, that unusual sincerity in his voice again – but on the other hand, who wouldn't be delighted with one quiet tenant with lots of books and no dogs? Two weeks later, she was preparing to head out, having given up her sparkling New York City apartment for . . . this.

'Darling! You should have said! How is the new place? Is it gorgeous? Do you love it?'

Emma suppresses a snort. 'Not exactly. I think the best way to describe it is that it has a tremendous amount of potential.'

'That sounds like a perfect project for you,' says Georgina. 'What can we send you for a housewarming present? What about a lovely teapot? Or a set of bowls? Actually, I have those lovely green bowls from Grandmère' – when had Grandma become 'Grandmère', Emma thinks wryly – 'which would be perfect for a young, well . . . youngish girl on her own. Why don't I send those?'

Emma instantly pictures the bowls, a faded green milk glass, possibly pretty once, now scratched and stained after years of use.

'It's okay, Mum,' she says. 'I don't need a housewarming present. At least, not yet. Let me get settled, then I'll let you know what I need.'

Chapter 3

A dull thud on the front door makes Emma jump. She can't imagine who could possibly be visiting her. She puts down a stack of books, eyeing the door nervously. 'Hello?' she calls, as her hand hovers over the door handle.

'Hey,' she hears from outside. 'It's Dominic DiFranco. I wondered if you needed some help.'

Opening the door, Emma is simultaneously grateful and slightly nervous. Is it normal for the landlord to show up whenever he feels like it? She looks over his shoulder but there is no car in her driveway.

'Where do you live?' she asks. 'Did you walk over here?'

'It seemed silly to drive,' says Dominic, gesturing to a large red pickup truck in the driveway next door. 'Given that I live next door.'

'You do? Why didn't you say anything?'

'What if it had freaked you out?' he says.

'What if it's freaking me out now?'

'Is it?'

'A little.' Emma frowns. This is something he should

have mentioned. Surely this is relevant. She knows nothing about him, she realizes, thinking how unbalanced that is.

'Don't let it. I inherited both of these houses from my grandparents when they died. They lived in this one, and rented out the one I now live in. I do the opposite. I live next door with my kid, Jesse. It helps to supplement my meagre income as bartender-slash-carpenter.'

'You have a kid? Sweet. How old is he?'

'Six. He's the coolest. You'll meet him soon. I'm surprised he hasn't poked his nose in already to meet the new neighbour.'

'Thank you for the warning! I'll look out for him. So you're a bartender? That's cool. Where do you work?'

'The Fat Hen?' He looks at her, expecting a reaction.

She stares at him, not sure what she is supposed to say. 'Great.'

'You don't know it?'

Emma starts to laugh. 'How would I know it? I've been living in town for, oh' – she looks at her watch – 'approximately four hours and thirty-six minutes.'

'We've been on Guy Fieri's show.' His chest puffs up proudly. '*Diners, Drive-Ins and Dives?*'

His pride is endearing. Emma smiles as she watches him, certain now that whoever said all men are little boys at heart was right. 'Should I have seen it?'

He gasps. 'Yes! Yes, you should have seen it! It's the greatest show ever invented.'

He's sweet, she realizes. A big kid. 'I'm not a big television watcher,' Emma admits reluctantly.

'How about the games?'

'What games?'

'Weekend sports. Baseball. Basketball. Come on. You've got to watch football, at least?'

'Nope.' Emma shakes her head and laughs. 'I'm so sorry, but not even football.' She peers at him. 'When you say football, do you actually mean American football? Or *real* football?'

'You mean soccer? Soccer is soccer and football is football. What's American football?'

The teasing is fun. She hasn't had a sparky, teasing conversation for a very long time, she realizes. Her old colleagues took themselves too seriously to engage in conversations like this. 'American football? It's like rugby for wimps. With helmets and padding.'

'Oh, ha ha,' says Dominic, shaking his head. 'I think maybe we should take the topic of sports off the table. You should come down to the Fat Hen, though. I'm working tonight. I'll get you a good seat at the bar and make sure you're looked after.' He leans forward, lowering his voice conspiratorially. 'First shot's on me.'

'Shot!' Emma barks with laughter. 'Good lord! Do I look like a shot girl to you?'

'Everyone looks like a shot girl to me. What's the point of drinking if you don't start off with a shot? Tell you what. I'll help haul boxes for you if you promise to come and have a drink at the Hen tonight. It's the perfect introduction to town. The real Westport. Not the prettied-up, perfect version.'

Emma appraises him. Of course he doesn't like the prettied-up, perfect version of anything. How could he? Everything about this man is real. *Integrity*, she finds herself thinking. *He has integrity.* 'I suppose we'll find out tonight which I prefer,' she says, challenging him gently on his preconception of her. 'And thank you, I would love some help with the boxes. I've got far more books than I realized and I'm not sure where to put them.'

Dominic looks around the living room. 'You want me to build some shelves in here? I could make some beautiful built-in cabinets.'

'Actually, I wouldn't mind some in there.' She points to the family room. 'I was thinking of having that as a little library-cum-office. Would you be able to build some shelves in there? I was just about to order some of those stepladder bookshelves, but having built-ins would be even better.'

'Sure. All part of the service. No charge.' He smiles at her. 'I can run to Home Depot today and pick up the wood. I'll just have to take measurements.'

'You would really do it? I was kind of joking. I didn't actually think you'd say yes.'

Dominic frowns. 'Why would you joke about that?'

'Because it would be unthinkably rude to actually ask for something so huge. Are you completely serious? Because I'd totally understand if you aren't.' Part of her feels guilty. She barely knows him, and yet she trusts him. If he means it, she wants him to do it.

'I'm totally serious.'

'Thank you,' she says. 'Truly. This is amazing.' She is smiling widely, unable to quite believe his kindness. 'Can I just ask one tiny thing?'

'What?'

'If you're going to build bookshelves, wouldn't it be better to remove the carpet first? You don't want shelves sitting on the carpet. If I pull it up while you're gone, we can re-cut it to fit around the shelves. That will give a much more professional finish.'

Dominic looks at the carpet, thinking, before nodding. 'Okay. Sure. You pull the carpet up and we can refit it when the shelves are done.'

'Fantastic!' Emma's face is alight with pleasure that her plan to get rid of the hideous carpet has been put in motion so soon. 'Let's get these boxes stacked up against the wall so at least we can get the rest of the furniture in.'

Chapter 4

'You're right, this is . . . fine for a temporary place to live,' says Sophie, walking through the house and trying not to show how much she hates it. 'I mean, I really can't see what it's going to look like with all the boxes everywhere. And . . . that terrible wood.'

'I know. The wood. Isn't it awful? I'm dying to paint it all, but I need to move slowly. I've already got the landlord to agree to take the carpet up, which will then mysteriously disappear. "Oh bugger! Those bloody rubbish disposal men took it by mistake. I only propped it up against the wall outside because there was no room for it inside. Oh, I'm so sorry. How about I replace it with some lovely fresh, new, clean sisal? My treat. To make up for my mistake."'

Sophie laughs. 'Poor landlord. He won't know what's hit him. So what's the story with him? Is he cute?'

Emma starts to laugh. 'Absolutely not. First of all, have you not heard the expression about not doing your dirty business on your own doorstep?'

'Are you kidding? Where better? He could slip through

the sliding doors at night and have his wicked way with you. So, is he cute?'

'Sophie, no. First of all, he's not my type at all.'

'What's your type?'

'Not him.'

'Methinks the lady doth protest too much.'

'I promise you, Sophie. He's not for me. But he seems like a lovely guy and he did help me move all the boxes.' Emma sits up as she hears the sound of a car. 'In fact, here he is after his Home Depot run. So now you'll get to see for yourself.'

Sophie joins Emma to look out the window, giving a low wolf whistle as Dominic climbs out of his truck and goes to the back, hauling planks of wood off the flatbed.

'Are you kidding?' she says. 'He's ridiculously sexy.'

'Not going to happen,' says Emma. 'We couldn't be more different.'

'You don't have to marry him, but a summer fling would be an excellent idea. Whoa. Who is that?' A small boy, a miniature version of Dominic who looks to be about six years old but sports a Mohican, climbs out of the passenger seat and walks to the back of the truck to help.

'That,' says Emma, 'is his son. Jesse. Yet another reason not to get involved.'

'What's the story there?' Sophie is intrigued. 'Divorced?'

'I have no idea. Honestly, Sophie, I've just met him. I certainly don't want to start peppering the poor man with questions. He's my landlord, after all, and he lives next door. I don't want him to think I have any ulterior motives.

I just want us to . . . be friends.' She pauses. 'I did say I'd go and have a drink at the Fat Hen with him tonight, though.'

Sophie turns to her, open-mouthed. 'Oh my God! Are you kidding? You're having a date with him already?'

'It's not a date. He's the bartender there. He's just trying to make me feel at home. He's not trying to get into my knickers.'

'What?'

'It's an English expression. Never mind. Why don't you come with me?'

'And gate-crash your date? I don't think so! What are you wearing?'

'This!' Emma gestures down at her old clothes. 'Oh, go on. Come. It will be much more fun if you're there.'

'I guess Rob could put Jackson to bed. It will give me a chance to get the lowdown on Sexy Dominic and the small son.'

Emma gives her a long, hard gaze. 'I shouldn't have invited you, should I?'

'Too late now. How about I pick you up at seven?'

Chapter 5

The Fat Hen parking lot, just off Riverside Avenue, is filled with pickup trucks, motorcycles, and the odd Audi and Range Rover. As Sophie parks the car, she explains to Emma that it is indeed a Westport institution, home to bikers from all over the state, as well as a popular spot for the brave hedge-fund manager who likes to experience the rough-and-ready of the real world from time to time. It's known for having the best burgers for miles, as well as live music three times a week, and karaoke on Mondays.

Neon signs adorn the walls, throwing glowing light into the otherwise dark space. A long bar runs along one wall, packed three deep, with a small restaurant area at the back. It is loud and raucous, filled with a mix of regulars and people stopping in to experience the famous joint.

And it is probably the last place on earth Emma would ever choose to go. Her world, at least the world she has most recently left in New York City, is filled with genteel cocktail bars. In her world, she orders French martinis, Prosecco cocktails with St Germain, Negroni Royales. She perches on bar stools surrounded by handsome, clean-cut men in sharp suits who eye her as soon as she walks in, considering whether to talk to her. This scene is about as far away from that world as you can get, and even though she willingly left all that behind, she's a little intimidated by what greets her here.

Emma grins as she pushes through the throng of people at the bar, trying to catch Dominic's eye to let him know she's arrived. Her blond, naturally curly hair is scooped up in a clip at the back of her head, with a few tendrils hanging loose. She's wearing an oversized white shirt and dark jeans, with flat espadrilles on her feet, only because she figured flip-flops probably weren't right for a night out, even to the Fat Hen. The only jewellery she wears is a large gold cuff on her right wrist, the last gift she gave to herself when she left the bank, and the last time she would spend serious money on something so utterly frivolous. She hasn't taken it off since.

Sophie is with her, rather more done up. Sophie has known about the Fat Hen all her life, but she hasn't ever been to the bar before, although Rob has. He warned her she was a little too dressed up, but Sophie ignored him. She dressed for herself, she'd told her husband, not for the bar she was going to, and so she had, wearing towering platforms, white jeans, a flowing shirt. With dangling earrings and blow-dried hair, she gets admiring glances from the men at the bar as she walks in, as tall and slim as a model, and so very much more glamorous than most of the women here.

Dominic is chatting with a group at the other end of

the bar, and as he looks over, he notices Sophie first, then lights up as he sees Emma.

'Hey!' He comes over with a grin, clearly thrilled they are here, thrilled to show off his workplace. 'You made it!'

'I did.' Emma finds she has to shout. 'This is my friend Sophie.'

They shake hands as Dominic turns to a couple of guys sitting on stools. 'Hey! Get a move on, and let these ladies sit down.'

'No, no, it's fine,' Emma starts to say, but the men immediately stand up and offer their stools. Smiling a grateful thanks, she and Sophie sit down as Dominic pours them a couple of shots and slides them over.

'*Salut*,' he says, pouring himself one, too. The three of them down the shots in unison. 'Welcome to the neighbourhood.' He smiles, instantly refilling their glasses.

'Bugger,' says Emma, as she lifts the glass to her mouth. 'We're not going to be driving home after this, are we?'

'That, my darling,' says Sophie, downing the second drink, 'is what Uber is for.'

Dominic, overhearing, snorts as he shakes his head. 'You bankers,' he says. 'Uber!'

'I'm not a banker,' Sophie says defensively, although she's smiling. 'Any more. If I were, I wouldn't be here, would I?'

'Good point,' says Dominic. 'Another shot?'

'No!' Emma interjects. 'No more shots. Let's have proper drinks. I'll have a vodka martini, straight up, with olives. Sophie?'

'Vodka and grapefruit juice.'

'Coming right up, ladies.'

Sophie leans towards Emma as Dominic turns to pour the drinks. 'He is very cute,' she says. 'If I weren't married . . .'

'Thankfully you are, and thankfully, I am not you.'

Sophie looks up as Dominic approaches. 'So, Dominic. I saw your very cute son today. How old is he?'

Dominic's face breaks into a smile at the mention of his son. 'He just turned six, and thank you. He is very cute, I agree. Jesse. Light of my life.'

'Do you have a sitter?'

'I have a few. A friend's daughter often comes over when I'm working, then there's a high school student around the corner, and I have an old friend who fills in if I can't find anyone else. They're all great with him. He's the kind of kid who will go to anyone.'

'Where's his mom? Is she in town?'

Emma tries to catch Sophie's eye to give her a warning look – this feels far too intrusive to ask someone she doesn't know – but Dominic is unfazed.

'His mom took off just after he was born. She didn't want a kid, but by the time she found out she was pregnant it was too late. She had him, then left when he was about four months old.'

Sophie's mouth opens in shock. 'Are you serious? She's not in touch with you at all?'

Dominic shrugs. 'Nope. I tried. I used to email her pictures of Jesse and updates about what he was up to, but then the emails started bouncing back. We haven't heard from her in years.'

Emma is disarmed by his candour about something so personal. Sophie, meanwhile, can't hide her shock. 'So you're raising him all by yourself? Are your parents around? Do they help?'

'Nooo!' Dominic laughs. 'I mean, they're around, but we don't see them too much. They're in Trumbull, but they're kind of busy doing their own thing.'

'So you're, like, the perfect man?' Sophie, Emma realizes, is drunk. Not sloppy drunk, but uninhibited drunk, as she leans across the bar, smiling.

Dominic looks at Emma. 'I like your friend,' he says.

'This is what happens to her when she downs three drinks in as many minutes,' says Emma, wondering how it is that she is managing to hold her drink so much better than Sophie.

'Is she married?'

'Very much so. With a very large and strong husband. The jealous kind. You know the type.'

Dominic shakes his head and whistles. 'I shouldn't have poured you guys all those shots, should I? Is he going to show up and punch me?'

'Only if you're very unlucky.'

'Will you two stop talking about me as if I'm not here?' Sophie says. 'Anyway. I am married and very happily, but Emma isn't. Emma is very definitely single, and isn't she gorgeous, Dominic? Don't you think she's pretty?' Sophie raises her eyebrows a few times, gesturing towards Emma with her head. 'I just want you to know that if you were interested, you would have my blessing.'

'That's very kind of you,' says Dominic, laughing, as Emma turns a bright red and silently wishes the floor would miraculously open up and swallow her whole. 'But I don't think it would be a good idea. Landlord, tenant, that whole thing. It can get messy. Also, I'm . . . seeing someone.'

'Okay?' Emma rolls her eyes at her friend. 'Can you just stop now?'

Sophie throws her hands up in the air. 'Okay, okay! Forgive me for trying to do some good in the world. So. Who are you dating? Is she cute?'

Dominic just shakes his head and laughs, excusing himself as he goes to serve a group of women at the other end of the bar.

'He really is cute. And nice. Did you notice? He's really nice,' Sophie says, turning to look at Emma and seeing that she is mortified. 'I didn't mean to embarrass you. Sorry.'

'I think maybe after we've finished these drinks it's time to go home.'

'No way!' says Sophie. 'This is the most fun I've had in years.'

Emma makes it a habit not to get drunk, but this evening she's well on the way. At the very least, she has bypassed tipsy and moved firmly into that slightly more serious, happy stage of intoxication. She has a very large glass of water alongside her martini, which she is sipping regularly.

She doesn't like being drunk because she doesn't like being out of control. It has been such a long time since she's been in a situation like this that she's forgotten how much fun it is. She isn't plastered, not nearly as drunk as Sophie, but she is giggly and loose, and having fun with all the men in the bar – so many men! so friendly! – who are talking to them. She is having fun with the fact that Dominic is keeping an eye out for them and warning off any men he doesn't like the look of.

It's been a while since Emma had fun. It has definitely been a while since she has been anywhere where men have given her an appreciative glance.

For a while, when she first moved to New York, fresh out of her long-term relationship with Rufus, she dated non-stop. Everything was so exciting – the men! the bars! the way strangers would walk straight up to her in a restaurant and hand her their business card.

It didn't take long for her to realize how empty that was. Every man she dated inevitably ended up having a long list of other women he was taking out on the side. She had never heard of the word *exclusive* in terms of dating. Apparently, it was an American thing. Emma had always presumed that if, after around four or five dates, you liked each other and you ended up in bed together, you were 'going out'. Who would ever imagine that a person would be doing the same with someone else, or indeed, a number of someone elses? Well, everyone in New York, it seemed. Everyone but her.

It never felt like an even playing field. For every man Emma was interested in, there were at least three tall, skinny, leggy model-types who flung their Keratin'd hair around and smiled their perfect, white-toothed piranha smiles while elbowing Emma out of the way.

She couldn't compete with such high-maintenance gorgeousness, nor did she want to. At work, she put on her uniform – the designer uniform that all the female bankers were expected to wear: the Givenchy, the Dior, the Jimmy Choos, the Manolo Blahniks. She blow-dried her hair and expertly applied make-up every morning before leaving her apartment for work. But as soon as she got home she tore everything off and slipped into jeans and a T-shirt, scrubbing her face, pulling her hair back into a messy bun. On the weekends she let her curls burst free.

But every time she went out for dinner with one of the men she had met when she was done up for work, or at a client meeting, she knew she had to maintain the image or they would lose interest. After a while, she didn't want to pretend any more. After a while, it just seemed easier to *not* date. And even though all of her work colleagues thought she was crazy moving out to the suburbs as a single, childless woman – *Westport! But you're not married! You're never going to meet anyone in Westport! What are you going to do in Westport?* – she knew she stood a better chance of meeting a real person there, someone who wasn't obsessed with a perfect trophy girlfriend hanging off his arm. More than that, she realized that in the life she wanted to live, meeting a man just wasn't the most important thing.

There were other things that Emma wanted to accomplish, things other than a picture-perfect relationship that may have been hollow beneath all the flash and charm. A business of her own that fuelled her creativity. A peaceful life. She dreamed of sitting in her own garden surrounded by hydrangeas, sipping a glass of wine and breathing in the salty air; going for daily walks along the beach; renting a kayak and taking it out on the water. She wanted to be living her life, finding friends, and if someone happened to come along whom she found interesting, then great. She wasn't going to go looking for him.

She was perfectly happy building a new life by herself.

In fact, the last thing she needed was a man to complicate things. Although, with a couple of drinks under her belt, there was nothing wrong with the tiniest bit of flirting. Was there?

Later in the evening, a girl comes into the Hen and Emma sees every man in the bar appraise her as she sashays through the crowd with a very plain friend. She walks right through the crowd, stopping several stools down from where Emma and Sophie are sitting.

'Dom!' She leans over the bar, pulls Dominic in with a proprietorial hand around the back of his neck, and gives him a long kiss on the lips.

'Wow.' Sophie leans towards Emma with a frown. 'That's the girlfriend? How disappointing.'

She is pretty, Emma thinks, pretty beneath all the make-up. Her hair is very blond, and very hairsprayed. Her eyelashes are false, her T-shirt tight and low-cut. She's sexy as hell.

'Why? She's a bombshell,' says Emma.

'She looks like she just walked out of Ruby's Two.'

'What the hell is Ruby's Two?'

'It's where the girls are.'

Emma continues to look bemused.

'A strip club! It's where all our hedge-fund husbands go for their boys' nights out. And trust me, it's not exactly . . . not exactly sophisticated.'

'Are you calling his girlfriend cheap?'

'Yes!' slurs Sophie delightedly. 'That's exactly what I'm calling her. She's nothing compared to you. And without the make-up she's probably as rough as anything.'

'You're mean when you're drunk.' Emma sits back, looking at her friend in astonishment, narrowing her eyes to try to focus more clearly.

'I'm not mean. I'm just more honest. Seriously.'

Before Emma can respond, Dominic comes over with the blond girl. 'Ladies, I'd like you to meet Gina.'

Sophie puts on her most gracious smile. 'So nice to meet you,' she says, as Emma admires her capacity to switch gears so quickly. 'I'm Sophie.'

'How do you do?' Emma extends a hand to Gina. 'I'm Emma.'

Gina's smile is polite, if not warm. 'Which one of you is the tenant?'

'Me.' Emma raises a hand. 'I just moved in this morning.'

'I guess we'll be seeing a lot of each other,' she says eventually. 'I stay over a lot next door.'

'Great,' says Emma. 'You'll have to pop in for a cup of tea.'

'Right,' says Gina, who mumbles vaguely – something along the lines of how nice it is to have met her – then walks off to the other end of the bar.

'Not exactly warm and fuzzy.' Sophie pretends to whisper this, but she is within earshot of Dominic.

'I'm sorry.' He turns to face them. 'She's a nice girl underneath, but not much of a woman's woman. It's just insecurity.'

'Why is she insecure?' Emma is perplexed. 'She's gorgeous.'

Dominic shrugs. 'Isn't it a female thing?'

They all turn to see Gina, at the other end of the bar, who smiles at them before beckoning Dominic over. It's clear he has no choice.

'Gotta go,' he mutters.

'Wuss,' mutters Sophie, as Emma just shakes her head and laughs. 'You know why she just did that, right? Claimed her territory?' says Sophie, as Gina slides her arms around Dominic again, from the other side of the bar, and kisses him deeply. 'She's threatened by you.'

'Why on earth would she be threatened by me?'

'Because . . . I don't know. There's something. I think he might like you.'

'Don't be ridiculous,' says Emma. 'Never have there been two people less compatible than my landlord and myself. Just because neither of us is married doesn't mean we're going to jump into bed together.' She doesn't know why she feels the sudden need to defend herself, to insist that there is no possibility of anything happening, when she is beginning to notice she feels happy whenever he is around.

'It might be fun.'

'I'm not planning on finding out. Don't you think it's time we made a move to go home?'

Chapter 6

It takes a while for Emma to open her eyes. She isn't sure where she is at first. The room is brighter than she is used to, and it smells different. Her head is pounding. As she swims up to consciousness, she cracks open one eye to see the light flooding in through the French doors in the bedroom.

Ah. It comes back to her. She is in the rental house. There are boxes everywhere. The light is flooding in through the sheer white Ikea blinds on either side of the windows. She hadn't drawn them last night, not that it would have made a difference – they wouldn't keep out the brightness of this summer's day.

Last night. Oh God. The drinking. She makes her way to the bathroom, ripping open a box and digging through it until she finds a bottle of painkillers. Tipping two tablets into her hand, she leans over and puts her mouth to the tap, swallowing the pills with a mouthful of lukewarm water before walking back to bed and sinking into the covers with a moan.

Emma doesn't remember the last time she had a hangover. However bad she is feeling, though, Sophie must surely be feeling worse. Sophie didn't drink any water, and Sophie was hammered. Emma pats the bedcovers for her phone, and, squinting at the screen, she taps out a text.

You alive?

The dots appear, before one word. **No.**

Emma grins and puts the phone down, closing her eyes to wait for the painkillers to take effect, trying to remember what happened last night. Dominic had been sweet and solicitous, looking after them at the bar, pouring them drinks on the house far longer than he should have. His girlfriend, Gina. Bitchy. Probably not who she would see him with only because he seems so nice, and she seemed . . . insecure and rude.

Nothing terrible happened, she is sure. And it was fun, even though it's not something she wants to do on a regular basis. Someone asked for her number; she can't remember who. She only remembers giving it to him, with one digit off.

An hour later, having dozed off again, Emma wakes, this time feeling guilty. There is so much to do today, so many boxes to unpack, so much organizing. She pads into the kitchen to dig out a jar of instant coffee from one of the boxes. (She hates instant coffee but always has some on hand in case of emergencies.) As she hauls the boxes from the high pile in the corner, there is a knock on the door. She's not as alarmed as she was the first time this happened, but she still can't help but wonder who could be knocking on the door.

'Hello?' Emma calls from the kitchen.

'It's Dominic,' comes the voice. 'I've come to start working on the shelves.'

Emma catches sight of herself in the door of the microwave. She's in men's boxer shorts and an oversized T-shirt, with her hair a tangled, frizzy mess. Shit. She doesn't particularly want to be seen like this, but she is stuck. She runs to the bedroom, grabs an elastic band off the bedside table and scrapes her hair back into a bun, then goes to the door, opening it a crack and peeking her head through.

'I'm not even dressed,' she says. 'Can you give me five minutes? I had no idea you'd be here so early.'

'It's eleven o'clock,' says Dominic. 'Bit too much drinking last night?'

She blushes, but laughs. 'Thanks to you constantly refilling, yes.'

'Here.' He hands her a cup of coffee through the door. 'I thought you might need this.'

'Good God! Are you the greatest landlord ever?'

'I aim to please,' he says.

'Thank you. This is amazing. Can I just put some clothes on? Give me five minutes. Is that okay?'

'See you in five minutes.'

Emma runs to the bathroom and looks at her face in the mirror. Her eyes are puffy, her skin greyish. She washes her face and splashes it several times with icy cold water, pinching her cheeks to bring some colour back into them. Her make-up bag sits on the dresser; she looks at it, but no. It would be ridiculous to put make-up on. Maybe just the tiniest bit of concealer to hide the shadows under her eyes.

Her clothes are still packed, but she finds a clean T-shirt and denim shorts. A roll of deodorant – the shower will have to wait – a spritz of perfume, and a shake-out of her hair before gathering it back again, and she is, if not her best self, at least presentable.

Not that it should matter in the slightest, she tells herself. But she wants to redeem herself after last night.

She's soon back to open the door again. But when she does so, she's greeted by a surprise.

'Hello.'

There is a small person next to Dominic, holding a toolbox. Emma crouches down to look him in the eye. She isn't very used to small people. Most of the women she worked with in New York were single, and those who were married tended to keep their families and work lives separate. Emma hasn't spent very much time with children at all. She sees Sophie's son, Jackson, from time to time but he is so young, and her time with him sporadic.

It's not that she doesn't like children, it's that she never feels entirely comfortable around them. She wonders whether it's better to talk to them the way she hears other adults talk to them – in a singsong voice, like a child herself – or to talk to them as if they are adults themselves.

Because she is never sure who to be or how to act, she is convinced this awkwardness makes her someone whom children will dislike. She once read that it is good to crouch down to look children in the eye so they see you as being on their same level. Hence her crouching now.

'I'm Emma,' she says, holding out her hand to shake his. 'You must be Jesse.'

Jesse doesn't say anything, but he takes her hand, even though he doesn't look her in the eye. Emma wishes she had something fun to tempt him out of his shell. A dog! A cat! Any kind of small animal. But she has nothing other than herself to offer. 'I like your haircut,' she says lamely. 'Is it a Mohican?'

Jesse looks at her then. 'Mohawk. It's called a Mohawk,' he says gravely, as if he were the teacher and she the student.

Emma nods. 'In England, where I come from, I think we used to call them Mohicans, but Mohawk it is.' She's aware that she is babbling and worries that she's sounding stupid, so she stands up, gesturing them both inside. 'I guess you're going to help your dad?' she says eventually, as Jesse nods and marches past her, lugging the toolbox with him and setting it down in the little room that will be a library, before opening it and extracting a tape measure.

Emma leaves them to it. They are measuring, and sawing, and sanding. It all seems very professional. Every now and then she hears Dominic talking to his son, as if he were a colleague and not his child. He asks Jesse's opinion, and waits to hear what he has to say, appearing to seriously consider everything the child offers.

'Should I put this shelf here or here?' she hears.

'Put it higher so she can fit big picture books on it, too,' says Jesse.

'Great idea,' says Dominic. 'I bet she has a lot of picture books.'

Emma experiences a slight pang when she hears this. She doesn't actually have many picture books, but she does have an awful lot of hardback novels, and more than a few coffee-table books. She is tempted to go in and check on their progress but doesn't want to interfere. Perhaps she should make them some fresh lemonade.

Emma busies herself in the kitchen, squeezing lemons, adding sugar, then unpacking her pots and pans, the pantry items, putting everything away. Halfway through one of the boxes, she finds her wireless speaker and sets up her playlist on her phone to play the sounds of summer.

Seconds later the voice of Jack Johnson fills the air. Emma sings along, moving through the tiny galley kitchen. For the first time in a long time, she feels the burdens of work, of banking, the stresses and pressures of the career treadmill, beginning to lift. As she continues to unpack, she swells with the thought that this is her life now. That she has a future filled with all kinds of possibilities. A wave of excitement builds deep inside.

Dominic comes out of the library and stands in the door-way. It takes Emma a little while to sense that she is being watched; she flushes a bright shade of red when she sees him.

'You look happy,' he says.

'It must be this house. I think it's having a magical effect on me.'

'It's living by the beach. It has a magical effect on

everyone. It's why I would never leave. I think it's the light, but it feels different from anywhere else in town. Living down here reminds me of growing up. Kids are out on bikes, free-range. Like time has stood still.' He pauses. 'Want to come see the shelves? We're almost done.'

'Sure. I made you lemonade.' Emma puts down the dish-cloth, picks up a pitcher and glasses, and follows him into the library. She takes a deep breath before looking at what he has built. The shelves are ever so slightly sloping to the right. Not all of them, but at least two. There are giant seams at the top, and although they will clearly do the job of holding books, they are hardly a thing of beauty.

'Fantastic,' says Emma, mustering every dramatic skill she has ever possessed. 'I can't believe you've done this in just a few hours. Wow! These are brilliant.'

'I'm pretty good at making things,' says Dominic, proudly.

'My dad can build anything,' says Jesse, proudly.

'You are clearly a man of many talents,' says Emma, as her brain furiously ticks, figuring out how she's going to fix the sloping shelves and seams.

'Want me to start loading the books on them?' says Dominic, good-naturedly. 'I can put the carpet back, too, if you'd like.'

'No, no, it's fine,' says Emma quickly. 'I'm going to paint the shelves and I haven't decided what colour, so I'll put the carpet back after I've painted. Thank you so much for this. It's amazing.'

'No problem,' says Dominic. 'I'm going to run over to

the deli and grab something to eat for Jesse and me. Can I get you something?'

'I'm fine,' says Emma. Actually, she's starving but she doesn't want to ask anything more of Dominic. 'But thank you. For everything. Maybe you guys can come over for dinner one night this week so I can thank you properly.'

'That would be great,' says Dominic, although Jesse narrows his eyes slightly and says nothing, Emma notices, realizing that Jesse may like her as a neighbour, but he may not feel the same way about a friend who might get in the way of his time with his father. 'Speaking of dinner,' Dominic continues, 'I'm having some friends over on Wednesday for a barbecue. Good people. You should come. You can bring your friend Sophie if you'd like.' With that, Dominic and Jesse gather up their tools and say goodbye.

Two hours later, Emma returns from the hardware shop with mouldings, moulding pins, filler, sanding blocks, primer, and paint. The boxes left to unpack will have to wait. The shelves are only a few millimetres off, but Emma knows it will be all she focuses on every time she looks at them. She can nail pins into the back and lift the shelves to straighten them; put the moulding onto the fronts of the shelves to disguise everything else. She will fill the gaps with caulk, prime them, and paint them a glossy pale greige. All subtly done, so they are perfect and it won't look like she went back to 'fix' Dominic's hard work.

She will turn them into something beautiful. This is what she does. This is what she is good at. And there is nothing she loves more than a challenge.

Chapter 7

'I've made delicious cake,' says the extremely well-groomed and flawlessly made-up woman who ushers Dominic inside, where a perfect lemon almond cake sits atop a white china plate stand. Cans of fizzy drink are stacked on the worktop, next to a silver ice bucket filled with ice, glasses, and whimsical napkins with an illustration of a glass of wine and text: *It's 5 o'clock somewhere!*

'And I have cookies and fruit for the kids. Hi, Jesse!' Lynn says, as she leans down and gives Jesse a high five. 'Weldon's in the playroom, sweetie. You want a juice box or some cookies before you go?'

Jesse shakes his head before running up the stairs to the room above the garage that was once a spare room but has now been converted into a playroom, complete with a basketball hoop for a passion Weldon's dad very much hopes he will soon develop.

Dominic sits down on the stool at the worktop, looking around. 'This house is beautiful,' he says to Lynn, getting up quickly to examine the open shelving on one side of the kitchen. 'I love these shelves.'

'They aren't new!' Lynn says.

'I know, but I never noticed them. I just built shelves for a new tenant so I'm noticing shelves in a way I hadn't before.'

'I didn't know you were handy.'

'There are a lot of things you don't know about me,' says Dominic.

'Really?' Lynn raises an eyebrow. 'Want to tell me more?'

Dominic blushes. He had no intention of flirting with Lynn, the mother of Jesse's best friend since preschool. He knows Weldon's dad, even though he doesn't see him much, since Tom commutes into the city every day. Tom is more of a weekend dad, the kind who throws himself into coaching Little League and driving his kids everywhere at the weekend, because during the week he's lucky if he even gets to see them.

Dominic has lived in this town his entire life. He grew up going to school with the kids of policemen, garbage collectors, actors, and writers. He grew up in a time when everyone knew everyone else, when there were few class distinctions, when nobody cared how much money anyone had, or how big your house was. Very few families even lived in big houses back then. Now the McMansions in town have reached absurd proportions, much like the one he is sitting in now.

Dominic remembers the house that was here before. The Bennett house. He used to go to school with the Bennett kids. He got stoned, many times, in their unfinished basement, while the laundry tumbled around and around in the giant old machines on one side of the room.

That house is long gone. Lynn and Tom squeezed within the boundary lines a giant gabled manse that stretches out, almost meeting the edges of the plot. There is room for a small pool, with a high white fence to keep the neighbours out.

The floors of the giant house are a bleached driftwood grey, shiny chandeliers hanging wherever you look. Beautiful furniture has been tastefully arranged by a decorator, huge clamshells filled with tall white orchids, shelves dotted with the odd vase, a shagreen box, three artfully stacked coffee-table books. Everywhere there are vast gaps of empty space. Dominic has often wondered if there is a junk room somewhere, a small cosy space that houses all the *stuff*, a room that feels like part of a home. Because this isn't a home. This is a magazine spread. He often finds himself wondering how Lynn and Tom actually live in this space rather than tiptoeing around trying to keep everything perfect.

More and more frequently, Dominic finds himself around families like this. The husbands are gone most of the week, the wives rattling around in these giant, beautiful, soulless houses. He is aware that as one of the few fathers present, he is something of an . . . attraction? Distraction? He is aware – and it has taken him a very long time to fully realize this – that with his golden Italian-American complexion, his thick dark hair, his big brown eyes, and, okay, he'll go there, his butt (every girlfriend he has ever had has gone on and on about his butt), he's a welcome addition to the Mommy and Me groups.

If he hadn't gotten involved with the parents of other children, he would have gone out of his mind with boredom when Jesse was young. It wasn't that he didn't adore his son, but there were only so many days he could take him to the playground, or the bookshop, or the museum, or the maritime aquarium in Norwalk. The jellyfish were beautiful, but only for the first two hundred times. After that, even the seahorses got old.

Having a young, handsome, single man in regular attendance was the most exciting thing that had ever happened at the Mommy and Me groups. A couple of women were standoffish and rude, never looking at him, barely responding when he said hello. They were the worst kind of *new Westport*, he felt: horribly entitled snobs. Later, though, he discovered that both those women had huge crushes on him (not that they would ever have done anything about it) and couldn't bring themselves to even meet his eye lest they turn beetroot red.

Regardless, Dominic found he loved the groups. He loved how the women gossiped, how they knew everything about everyone in town and had no compunction about sharing what they knew 'within these four walls only'. The women would look at each other solemnly, crossing their hearts that they would never tell anyone. But Dominic knew they would spill the beans about everything they'd learned as soon as they left the driveway.

He loved that he got to see beyond their black Range

Rovers and gigantic, multi-carat diamond studs, to realize their insecurities and their fears. He also got to see their kindness, and their humour, and their willingness to help anyone in their community. He got to learn who they were before they became power mommies.

It was only a matter of time before Dominic fell for one of them. They all made such a fuss – flirting, welcoming him with open arms, teasing him, loving seeing him blush. They loved that he fixed things, that he was 'good with his hands'. He'd walk into their houses for playdates and notice broken light fixtures, or shelves that needed putting up, or doors that didn't close properly, and he'd grab his toolbox from the truck and get to work. No charge, naturally, while the women simpered and smiled, thrilled at having a man around who knew what to do.

Amy was different. She didn't flirt, and didn't tease, although she did talk. They started organizing their own playdates outside of the Mommy and Me group, and after a few weeks she confessed her unhappiness. She was trapped in the wrong life, she said. She was desperately lonely, she said. She and her husband had nothing in common, other than their daughter, Sara. She was convinced her husband was having an affair with a young colleague in his office who Amy had just discovered was accompanying him on all his business trips.

Dominic tried to be a good friend, to listen and advise without getting too involved. Amy could talk to Dominic, she said, because he was a man and understood her feelings in a way her girlfriends couldn't. Then they stopped talking about Amy's problems, and started talking about themselves. They found themselves smiling every time they saw each other. Amy would open her front door, beaming, and Dominic would find that he couldn't stop beaming in return.

They were both high on the other's company, on what neither of them acknowledged out loud was an unspoken attraction. Acting on it, Dominic knew, was a terrible idea. It wasn't that he hadn't had affairs with married women in the past – he hadn't always been the thoughtful, considerate man he was today – but it would only lead to heartache for everyone involved. It wasn't as if Amy was his soulmate.

There were times, though, late at night, when he couldn't stop thinking about her, wondering whether perhaps she *was* the woman he was supposed to be with. He would tell himself that he only felt that because she was unavailable. He had always been drawn to the unavailable because it wasn't real, it posed no real threat, it could only ever be an exciting fantasy.

And then something did end up happening. It couldn't *not* have happened. It was only a matter of time, no matter what Dominic may have tried telling himself. They had dropped the kids off at a gym class and were waiting together in her car. They had done this many times before, but that day, neither of them could look at the other, and all Dominic could think about was touching her. The conversation had halted, and without thinking about it, without planning it, they were kissing, and it was electric, and amazing, and passionate, and life-changing.

Or it could have been, had Amy's husband not announced, two days later, that he was being transferred to Chicago and they were all moving. It was for the best, said Dominic, who was simultaneously devastated and relieved.

He had learned his lesson. However much he might flirt, however much some of these mothers might flirt back, he wasn't going to get emotionally involved again.

'So who's the new tenant?' says Lynn, cutting him a generous slice of cake, but none for herself. 'I'm off the carbs,' she announces, sliding the plate over to him. 'You can clearly eat whatever you want, but it's Paleo all the way for me right now.'

'You look great,' says Dominic, because it's what he is supposed to say, although she does look great. Who wouldn't look great, he thinks, with daily workouts and hours of pampering?

'Really?' Lynn is delighted. 'Okay.' She leans forward conspiratorially. 'I'm only telling you this because I trust you and I know you'll be honest with me. I haven't told anyone else, not even my husband, so you have to swear not to say anything.'

This is why I love these playdates, thinks Dominic, delighting in being, once again, an honorary mom. 'Swear,' he says solemnly.

'Okay. I went to the dermatologist last week. I got the works.'

'What does that mean, the works? Botox?'

'Oh, honey, Botox was just the beginning. I had Botox, Restylane, Sculptra, and Thermage. I had my lips reshaped and my crow's feet removed. Look!' She pouts and turns her head slightly to one side. 'Cheekbones! I've never had cheekbones in my life!'

'You do look fantastic!' says Dominic, recognizing his place in these friendships – he's the handsome guy who makes these women feel good about themselves, brings a little bit of excitement into their lives without ever crossing the line. 'If you weren't married I would—'

'You would!' Lynn bursts into peals of delighted laughter before squeezing his arm in a completely nonsexual but appreciative way. At least, that's what he hopes. 'So tell me about the tenant. Is she young and hot?'

Dominic takes a bite of cake as he thinks about how to respond. The truth is, there is something about Emma that is enormously compelling, even though he would never think to describe her as young and hot. It's not that she isn't either of those things, but her qualities are under-stated. She is attractive, yes, in her mid-thirties, he guesses, and seemingly industrious and clever; a good person.

But finding someone attractive is not the same as being attracted to her. It was great that she came to the bar the other night, and she was cute and funny when she was slightly drunk, and that English accent of hers is adorable, but there's nothing more. He just likes her. She's someone he can see being the perfect tenant – reliable about paying the rent, pleasant to have around. But other than that, she's really not his type.

Gina, on the other hand? Gina is his type. Physically, at least. Italian American like him, she's fiery as hell, and smoking hot. She gives him shit all the time, but in a way that is completely familiar to him, and honestly, it might be the hottest sex he's ever had. Gina is up for it all the time, and there's nothing she won't say or do. She's definitely not the girl he's going to marry – she's never done anything beyond spending the night and is always gone before his son is awake – but for right now, he's having fun, making no promises. It seems to work for both of them.

'The tenant seems great,' he says, pushing Gina, or rather Gina's mouth, out of his head. 'I don't really know her. English. Quiet. Retired banker. I try not to get too close.'

'That sounds like the perfect approach,' says Lynn, who places her hand on his arm again and squeezes it just a second too long.

Chapter 8

Patience has never been a virtue of Emma's. She wants the house to look gorgeous, cosy, and welcoming, but immediately. She doesn't want to sit around waiting for primer to dry before she commits to more sanding, more coats of paint, and still more sanding after that. The prep never seems to end.

Finally, the shelves are done, and dry. There was so much paint left over that she carried on painting the orangey brown wood panelling on the walls. She is nervous about Dominic's reaction but can always strip it if he hates it. Would he hate it? How could he hate it? Look how much better it looks already! Look how this room has been transformed with just a coat of paint!

Her glass desk is perfect at the end, a small love seat in a slub linen pushed to one side, piled with printed cushions and a cashmere throw. White ceramic Chinese stools offer occasional seating, sitting atop the new sisal carpet that stretches to each corner. It is officially the cosiest, prettiest office ever, with an orchid sitting on the desk next to a bleached wooden lamp that cost next to nothing.

The rest of the cottage is still dark and dismal, but this room? This room! Emma pulled off the white slatted blinds, most of which were broken, and stapled a large piece of sheer canvas over the window. It is completely private and allows a soft light to filter through. And simple linen curtains hang on either side, hiding the staples and framing the window.

It is gorgeous, she thinks, every time she walks in. She sits on the sofa, looking around the room and admiring the transformation she has wrought in such a short space of time.

Even the vertical planking no longer bothers her. Now it is a glossy pale grey, and four large black-and-white prints of delicate flowers cover most of the wall.

She picks up her phone to check the time. Almost five. Dominic said his barbecue was kicking off at five – time for the quickest of showers and some clean clothes in order to meet his friends.

Reluctantly, she uncurls herself from the sofa and heads out of the one perfect room in the house, gingerly walking over the brown carpet in the hallway to make her way to the bathroom.

Emma has never enjoyed walking into parties alone where she doesn't know anyone. She has never been particularly good at small talk, although she manages to hold her own after years of working in the city and attending social events that would be good for business.

She had never liked those kinds of parties, or truthfully,

any parties at all. She was much better on a one-on-one basis, or with small groups of people she knew well and felt comfortable with.

Much the same thing used to happen at each party she attended in her years of living in New York. It was either in some fabulous apartment in New York – a loft in the East Village, a classic eight-room apartment on the Upper East Side – or at someone's weekend house, whether a shingle house in Southampton or a renovated farm in Millbrook. The women would all be beautifully dressed (white linen shifts in the Hamptons; jeans, heels, and gauzy tops in both the city and the country), and would all shriek with excitement upon seeing each other, gabbing furiously as the husbands converged around the drinks, usually served from a permanent bar tucked into a small nook somewhere in the apartment or house.

The men would drink single malts and straight vodkas, while the women invariably chose some cute, pretty signature cocktail for the night. As the evening progressed the women would keep to their side of the space, and the men would keep to the other.

Occasionally the twain would meet, particularly if a sit-down dinner was involved, but even then, the men would shout to each other across the table, leaving Emma bewildered at their lack of manners. There'd been more dinners than she could count where she'd sat next to a man she hadn't met, and peppered him with questions about himself, only so she didn't have to sit in an uncomfortable silence. She was never obtrusive, but polite and gracious, only to have him break off mid-conversation to shout something to a friend sitting across the table.

Either that, or Emma would eventually run out of questions, and then, instead of asking her anything about herself or initiating any other subject of any kind, her dinner partner would just carry on eating in silence, leaving Emma chewing her chicken, or short ribs, wondering how early she could leave without causing offence.

Emma's mother may have been a nightmare, but she was a stickler for manners, for being gracious, and always – almost always – immaculately behaved. What would she have done in these situations, Emma used to think, imagining her mother turning to her father and saying, with a sniff, 'NQOCD.' *Not quite our class, dear.* It was quite as awful an expression as 'not PLU,' which her mother used frequently – *not people like us* – but, of course, Emma's mother never realized that these expressions were only ever used tongue-in-cheek, never seriously.

Emma thought back to one party in particular, in East Hampton. She'd been dating a man named Evan, the only man she knew at a party filled with the usual mix of braying bankers and their trophy wives, who showed off their worth with crocodile clutches and heavy gold men's watches dragging down their tiny wrists.

The dinner was interminable. She sat next to an imperious know-it-all, and afterwards, when they all retired to the vast conservatory, she almost sank with relief at the prospect of a quick escape.

After the meal, the men disappeared, apparently to the

barn, which housed whatever it is men like to do late at night, leaving Emma in a room filled with women she didn't know, none of whom had spoken to her all night.

She excused herself politely, removed her heels, and slipped silently out the back door, walking back to the house they were staying in. She gratefully crawled into bed and was fast asleep by the time Evan joined her, hours later, so drunk that his snoring woke her and kept her awake for the rest of the night. She ended things as soon as they arrived back in New York.

As Emma approaches Dominic's cottage next door, she shakes her head to clear the memories. Parties are decidedly not her thing, but a barbecue in the garden at her landlord's house . . . at least there will be no pressure to perform. At least the crowd won't consist of self-absorbed bankers and intimidatingly gorgeous and perfect women.

At least there is that.

She pushes open the gate that separates the two gardens, hearing the buzz of happy chatter and children's squeals. A group of people are standing around a trestle table covered in a red-and-white checked tablecloth, with bottles of wine and soda, and a big aluminium bucket filled with ice and cans of beer wedged underneath.

The table is covered with platters of crisps and dips, giant bowls of pretzels, and M&Ms mixed with popcorn. Children grab handfuls of the snacks when their parents aren't looking and run back and forth between them and a great big inflatable pool and slide at the bottom of the garden, not wanting to miss a second of the fun.

'Daddy! Daddy!' Jesse's at the top of the slide, yelling for his father. 'We need more water! We need the hose!'

'Okay, buddy!' Emma sees Dominic put his beer down and grab the hose, pulling it back down to the slide. 'Coming right up.' He turns and sees Emma, and grins broadly.

'You made it! I'm so pleased. Help yourself to a drink – I'll just finish this off, then I'll come and introduce you to everyone. Hey, AJ?' A tall man at the other end of the garden looks up. 'This is Emma, who I was telling you about. My tenant.'

'Emma!' As AJ shouts her name, everyone turns to look at her, with smiles and waves. Emma walks over, shakes hands with people as she tries to remember everyone she's introduced to – AJ and Deb, Joey, Frank, Kevin, Tina, Johnny, Andrea and Victor – before someone hands her a cold beer and she takes a grateful swig.

'The English tenant,' AJ says, a great big bear of a man with a huge smile behind his thick beard. 'How's your landlord treating you?'

'So far, so good. But ask me again in another week.'

'Dominic says you were a big-time banker. How do you like our slow life out in the suburbs? He says you're retired.'

Emma laughs. 'That makes me feel like a pensioner. I'm not retired; I couldn't afford to retire. But – well, I've retired from banking, I suppose. So far I'm loving it. No stress, no pressure, no working all hours of the day and night. I'm in heaven, although I can't do this forever. I'm just taking a short break before I decide what to do next.'

'And how did you find Dominic?'

'Craigslist.'

'Really? Now that's a great story.'

'It is? There's no great story there. I just answered an ad for a rental house, and . . . voilà.'

AJ shrugs and winks knowingly. 'It's not a great story *yet*.'

'What do you mean?' Emma feels a faint blush coming on, as he unselfconsciously teases her. 'There's no romance. Anyway, he's dating someone.'

AJ laughs good-naturedly. 'Gina's not someone you *date*. She's someone you . . . do other stuff with. I'm sorry, I'm just teasing you. You're single, Dominic says, and you seem like a great girl. What's wrong with wanting my friend to be happy?'

Emma laughs. 'That's very sweet, but it's a terrible idea. What if it all went horribly wrong and I had to move out? What if we ended up hating each other and then had to continue living next door, with me having to ask him to fix the tap every time it broke? Terrible idea. The worst.'

'What if you ended up falling madly in love and discovered you were each other's soul mates?' AJ says, as a woman walks over and leans tenderly against his shoulder. Emma realizes she must be Deb, who was introduced to her along with AJ. Now Deb shakes her head with an exasperated smile at Emma.

'Is he teasing you? I'm sorry. It's what my husband does. It's like some bizarre initiation rite he has to go through with all the women Dominic's interested in.'

'Oh. That's okay. Dominic's not interested in me. It's not what you think. I'm just the tenant.'

'He's not? Are you sure?' Deb asked.

'Very sure.' Emma laughs, excusing herself to go into the kitchen. How bizarre of his friends to be so preoccupied with the idea of her dating him. She felt she had to get away from the scrutiny. Perhaps she can help with the food.

'Can you baste the ribs?' says a woman, struggling to pull a lasagne out of the oven. 'I'm Andrea. Andrea Leung. We met earlier?'

'Of course,' says Emma. 'Are you from around here?'

'We live in Massachusetts, actually, but we're here visiting friends. Penelope?' She turns suddenly, calling out to a sweet little girl sitting at the kitchen table. 'Run outside and check on Grace and Victoria.' She turns back to Emma. 'Sorry. Just needed to check they're not getting into trouble.'

'Of course. How do you know Dominic?' Emma asks, to be polite more than anything else.

'I don't. My husband, Victor, went to school with AJ, and we're staying with them, so he brought us. He seems lovely, though. You're lucky.' She smiles, turning on her heel to take the food outside before Emma can close her mouth, which had dropped open in surprise at the comment, or have a chance to correct her. But she has to wonder what is going on. Why does everyone assume she has some kind of romantic connection with Dominic?

She turns back to the ribs, basting them with the sauce, ready to put them in the oven as Jesse runs into the kitchen, feet soaking wet from the slide. With a yelp and a loud cry, he goes skidding into the kitchen table, banging his head, collapsing in a small heap on the floor.

'Jesse!' Emma races over and feels his head. 'Are you okay?'

Jesse is furiously trying to blink back tears as he nods. 'I'm okay,' he says in a small voice, trying very hard not to cry.

'Let me feel,' says Emma, hoping he doesn't cry, because she has absolutely no idea what to do with a crying child. She runs her hand over the side of Jesse's head, where she can already feel a bump forming. 'Oh dear,' she says. 'You've got a big one.'

'A big what?'

'A big, ginormous volcano erupting out of your head.'

'It hurts.' He blinks back more tears.

'Can I rub it for you? Sometimes that helps. And we can put some ice on it, too. How does that sound?'

'Okay,' he says, as Emma rubs his head just the way her mother used to rub hers. Leaving him for a second, she goes to the freezer and pulls out a bag of frozen corn that looks like it's been living in there for years. And just behind it, she spies a box of frozen Fudgsicle lollies.

'Okay.' She goes back and drops down onto the floor next to Jesse, the bag of corn in one hand, a Fudgsicle in the other. 'The corn's for your head, the Fudgsicle's for your mouth. You know chocolate is the very best thing for bumps and bruises, right?'

'No,' says Jesse. But he reaches for the Fudgsicle as

Emma holds the frozen corn to his head. Just then Dominic walks in, his face sinking when he sees his son's tear-stained face.

'Buddy! What happened?' he says, rushing over to pick Jesse up.

'I'm okay,' says Jesse, who is more interested in sucking the Fudgsicle than in discussing his wound. 'I skidded on the kitchen floor.'

'Wet feet,' explains Emma.

'Emma looked after me. I feel better now,' he says, as Dominic winces when he feels the bump, before putting him down on the floor.

'No running with wet feet,' says Dominic sternly. 'What did I tell you?'

'Sorry, Dad. Can I go back to the slide?'

'Only if you walk.'

''Kay,' says Jesse, Fudgsicle in his mouth, as he turns and runs out of the kitchen.

'No running!' shout Dominic and Emma together. Then they look at each other and laugh.

'Sorry,' says Emma, who finds herself holding the bag of corn again. 'I hope you weren't saving the corn for anything special. It's clearly vintage.' She turns the bag over to look for a sell-by date. 'Goodness, sell by the fourteenth of October, 2010. This could be worth some serious money. Have you considered contacting *Antiques Roadshow*?'

'It's frozen,' says Dominic, who is smiling through his embarrassment. 'The sell-by dates don't matter in the freezer.'

Emma wrinkles her nose with a laugh. 'I think five years is pushing it.'

'You thought I was going to *eat* it? Oh, you're funny. That corn is only there for bumps on the head. That's why I bought it.'

'Of course you did. What else is in there, I wonder, that is purely for medicinal purposes?'

'This,' says Dominic, pulling a bottle of vodka out of the freezer. 'Want some? Go on. It's after five. Live a little.'

'You're a horrible influence when it comes to alcohol,' says Emma, although she doesn't protest as Dominic reaches for a couple of glasses and pours them each some vodka on ice.

'It's summer. We're at a party. We're not getting drunk; we're just having a drink. Here. Cheers,' he says.

Emma realizes that she hasn't stopped smiling since Dominic walked into the room. 'Cheers,' she says back, then downs the vodka in one.

'We should totally get together for a girls' night out,' says Deb, AJ's wife, later in the evening as they are sitting around, messily gnawing on ribs and coleslaw, reaching for the large pile of wet wipes in the middle of the table. 'That would be so much fun. What do you think? I'm still on the kids' vacation time, so I'm making the most of it before school starts.'

'I'd love to,' says Emma, thinking how much she actually would, how every single one of Dominic's friends has been welcoming and warm, without an ounce of competitiveness.

Gina isn't here – she wonders why for a moment, and then dismisses the thought, happy simply to have spent time in such pleasant, relaxed company. These are the kinds of people Emma would never have met in her New York banking world, and she feels relieved again to be where she is now.

They are teachers, builders, personal trainers. The people, she thinks ironically, who work for the people she once worked with. They are real, fun to be with, and completely down-to-earth. A few weeks ago she wouldn't have fitted in, she thinks. Or they would not have accepted her, not in her short skirts and high heels. But sitting here today, wearing jeans and flip-flops, her hands sticky from the ribs, laughing as the afternoon turns to dusk, she is nothing other than the tenant, fitting right in.

AJ wanders over. 'Dominic said he built shelves for you. How did he do?'

'They're fantastic,' lies Emma. Although it is true, the shelves do look pretty fantastic now, after her ministrations.

'Really?' Both AJ and Deb look dubious. Deb lowers her voice. 'He's a great guy but a master carpenter he's not. He built us a bench for our foyer and it collapsed the first time AJ sat on it.'

'Hey.' Dominic comes over. 'I heard that. That's got nothing to do with the bench. That's AJ's beer gut.' He reaches over in an attempt to pat it, but AJ wrestles him away.

'All I can say is don't give up the night job,' says AJ with a guffaw.

'I built beautiful shelves for Emma, didn't I?' says Dominic, turning to Emma for confirmation.

'You did.' Emma nods.

'Even if they fall down if you put anything on them?' AJ laughs.

'You don't believe me? Come and see. You don't mind, Emma, right?'

Crap, thinks Emma. *He doesn't know I've thrown the carpet out. He doesn't know I've painted his beloved orange wood-panelled walls. He doesn't know I've chucked the broken white slatted blinds. Why did I open my mouth?*

'Sure,' says Emma, with some hesitation. 'But the house is a bit of a mess. I don't know that today's a good time . . .'

'I don't care about that. Come on, I need to prove to these guys that I can build a decent set of shelves.'

Emma closes her eyes for just a second. *Ask forgiveness,* she thinks. *Apologize once he's seen it, and hope to God he appreciates what it looks like now.*

Please do not let him be angry.

They walk across the garden, through the gate, Emma trying not to sink into a pool of guilt and misery. She thinks about whether to prepare him, about what she should say, but suddenly they are at the door, and then inside the house, and then, all of them, standing in the doorway of the office.

'Oh my God!' says Deb. 'This is *gorgeous.*'

'Wow!' says AJ. He stands there silently for a moment.

'I take it all back. Man, this room looks fantastic. Wow, Dominic. You did an awesome job.'

'Thanks,' says Dominic, his brow furrowing as he frowns at the room.

'I'm really sorry,' Emma says to Dominic, under her breath. 'I got a bit carried away with the paint. I was only going to do the shelves, but then I got some on the walls and I was only going to paint a section but it looked weird so I ended up doing the whole thing. I'm really sorry,' she says again. She arranges her features into an expression of apology as she looks at him, but he doesn't look back at her. He's too busy looking around the room.

'What happened to the carpet?' he says, after a pause.

'Ah. The carpet. I put it outside while I was painting because there were so many boxes on the floor that I kept tripping over it, and the bin men took it. I mean, I presume they took it by mistake, because when I went to bring it back in the next day, it had disappeared.'

'I love this rug!' says Deb. 'Is this sisal? This is so fantastic.'

'Where are the blinds?' asks Dominic.

Emma finally takes a stand. 'I threw them away,' she says firmly. 'Dominic, most of those slats were snapped in half. They had to be chucked.'

'They did,' says AJ, looking at his old friend. 'I came into this house before you rented it to Emma, and those blinds looked like crap. So did the carpet. In fact, the rest of the carpet *still* looks like crap. This room now looks like something out of a magazine. You should be paying her to do this. You'd probably get more rent if she did over the whole house.'

Emma smiles her relief and gratitude at him.

'He's right,' says Deb, turning to Emma. 'You know, I'd love some help with our house. Is that something you would do? Would you be able to come over and advise me?'

Emma, beaming, says, 'Sure, I'd love to,' then sneaks a look at Dominic.

'Oh, come on, Dominic,' she says. 'You have to admit the room looks better. I am really sorry about the carpet. And the blinds. And especially about painting the wall. But look how bright it is now. Don't you think it's lovely?'

'I just didn't expect this,' Dominic says eventually. 'This house has been the same since my grandparents lived here. I liked that it was the same, because it reminded me of them and when they lived here.'

'Dude.' AJ shakes his head. 'This house has looked like shit for years. I knew your grandparents, may they rest in peace, and back then this house looked fine. But now? I don't even know how you manage to rent this place, it's so dated. You should let Emma update the whole thing. She obviously has fantastic taste. She should do this professionally.' Turning to Emma, he asks, 'Have you considered it?'

'It's definitely something I'm thinking about,' says Emma. 'But it's early days. I need to get settled here first, but someday soon I might get serious about it.'

'As a contractor I could introduce you to at least two

people right now who need your help. You let me know if you want me to make the introductions, because you've really got talent.'

Emma swells with pride. She has always loved turning a house into a home, creating a warm, elegant, cosy space, but the dream of turning that into a business has never been anything more than that – a dream. Dominic's upset is forgotten at the prospect of AJ finding first clients for Emma, and as they all walk back to Dominic's house, Deb chattering about how they could redo the kitchen and redecorate the family room, Emma thinks she should just tell AJ she'll meet whoever he wants her to meet. What is she waiting for?

Dominic's been quiet as they've all trooped back. They are about to go through the garden gate when he takes a deep breath and turns to her.

'You've done a beautiful job,' he says. 'I'm sorry I was a bit weird about it. I didn't expect you to have changed the house so much.'

'Oh God, I'm sorry. It was really selfish of me. I didn't think you would be upset. I kept thinking you would be thrilled at how good it looked, but I never considered your emotional attachment to the house as it was, or the implications of all the changes I made. I didn't mean to do anything to upset you.'

'You didn't,' he says. 'I was a little shocked at first, but honestly, you've done a beautiful job. I can't believe you did all of that by yourself. It looks incredible.' Then he frowns. 'What the hell did you do to the shelves? I swear they didn't look like that when I left the other day.'

'Oh, just some mouldings I nailed on to make them look thicker. I think it's a more modern look.'

'Well, they're great. I can't take any of the credit.'

Emma smiles. 'A little bit of the credit. You can definitely take a little of the credit. We make a good team.'

He looks at her with a small smile, the tiniest hint of a raised eyebrow, not saying anything, just looking at her. Emma finds herself flushing pink, and looking away. That isn't what she meant, she thinks. She doesn't quite know what to say next. Saying anything else will only make it worse.

'Better get back,' says Dominic, pushing the gate open and stepping aside to let Emma through. As she passes, he guides her by placing a hand, very gently, on the small of her back. As she feels his hand there, the strangest feeling comes over her, from the tips of her toes to the top of her head.

Safe, she finds herself thinking. *I have come home.*

Chapter 9

Emma wakes up early the next morning, crawls out of bed to make some coffee, then brings it back with her, slipping between the sheets again, revelling in the luxury of a lazy morning.

All those years she dashed out of bed, went running, on a literal or proverbial treadmill from the minute her feet hit the floor to the minute her head hit the pillow later that night. How she is loving the lack of stress, the fact that she has nowhere to be, no one to report to, nothing to do other than lie between these sheets and sip coffee, watching the sunlight filtering in through the sheer curtains: another beautiful day in paradise.

The phone buzzes on the bedside table next to her, and Emma reaches over to see who's calling. Her mother.

'Hello, darling,' she hears through the phone. 'I hope I'm not disturbing you. I know it's early, but you're always so busy.'

'Not so much since moving out to the suburbs,' says Emma. 'It's fine. How are you?'

'Very excited, darling! Guess what?'

'You won the lottery?'

'Don't be silly, darling. No. But Cousin George is engaged.'

'Oh, that's great. I didn't know he was seeing anyone, though.' Emma barely remembers Cousin George. He's younger than she is by a good few years. She remembers him as a feminine and rather pretty boy. And almost certainly gay, she had thought, although, given her mother's news, clearly incorrectly. As a child she babysat and played with him on the rare occasions he and his parents visited them. He is a cousin of her father's, whose family is more aristocratic than her mother's. Hence her mother's involvement, for she distanced herself from her side of the family, embarrassed by their distinct middle-classness.

'He's been going out with the Honourable Henrietta Chapman,' says Emma's mother, as Emma mentally rolls her eyes. No one but her mother would bother putting in the *Honourable* bit, but of course she has to repeat every title she comes across, as if doing so will somehow elevate her in the eyes of the world.

'That's nice,' says Emma.

'It is nice,' her mother replies. 'It's wonderful, and I have offered to throw them the engagement party here at Brigham Hall.'

Brigham Hall didn't use to have a name. It didn't use to be called anything other than home. But years ago, Emma's mother decided that every smart family lived in an old stately home with a name, and therefore their own old, not terribly stately home must have one, too. Weeks were spent trying out possibilities. Should it be a Manor? A Farm? A House? The name Brigham appeared to have been pulled out of thin air, although Emma's mother claimed it was from her own mother's side of the family. Brigham House sounded like an orphanage, they all decided. Brigham Farm was nice, except it wasn't really a farm, they just had a few acres and a couple of sheds, which didn't really count. Brigham Manor was very nice, too, thought Emma's mother, but her husband thought it too grand, too pretentious. So Brigham Hall it became, complete with personalized stationery and an embosser for the envelopes.

'Put it in your diary, darling, because you're expected to be there.'

Emma resists a bark of indignant laughter. 'Expected to be there? What does that mean?'

'It means that all the family are coming, and you haven't been home in over a year. Everyone's asking for you. Especially George.'

Emma sputters with laughter. 'Why on earth would George be asking for me? I haven't seen him in years.'

'Exactly. That's the point. He very much wants you to meet the Honourable Henrietta. He still says you're his favourite cousin.'

'I'm sure that's not true. He barely knows me. And Mum, you really don't have to call her "the Honourable" every time you mention her. I'm not sure it's really the done thing.' *Ouch.* Emma's mother has never taken criticism well, but better, thinks Emma, for her mother to hear it from her than from anyone else.

'I didn't . . . I mean, I know you don't actually use that term. I'm only saying it for you.' Her mother stammers slightly, embarrassed at being caught out.

'Naturally,' says Emma. 'I don't know if I can make it, though. It's such a long way and it's not like George and I are close. What's the date?'

'September the fifth,' says her mother. 'Not too long. Write it down, and do your best. Darling, I know you have a busy life and I know it's far to come, but it would mean a lot to all of us. Especially me and your father. He misses you and he's not doing so well.'

Emma's heart skips a beat. 'What do you mean? Is he sick?'

'He has a touch of gout again, and you know what a bear he is when he's not feeling well. He'd love to see you, darling. Try to make it. I know you will.'

Emma sighs. 'I really don't know. Let's talk nearer the time. I'll do my best.' She knows she won't, however, knows already that she will come up with an excuse, any excuse to avoid a great big family reunion.

'Didn't you get the invitation? I sent it last week. I'm surprised you haven't received it by now.'

'I haven't been out to the mailbox in days,' says Emma, realizing as she speaks that it's true. 'It's probably in there. I'll go and check now.'

'All right, darling,' says her mother. 'Let me know when your flight gets in and we'll send someone to pick you up.'

Emma doesn't bother telling her mother that chances

are she won't be coming. She merely says goodbye, putting it out of her mind.

It really has been days since Emma has checked the mail. This business of not working is great, but it's also disastrous for any kind of routine. It would be so easy to just while away the days drinking coffee in bed, renovating the house, and binge-watching TV series on Netflix, as she has been doing evening after evening, alone in her little house.

But a promise to her mother cannot be broken, she thinks to herself with a small smile. She'll just retrieve the invitation and then jump into the shower. She pushes open the door and trots over the lawn, still damp from the morning dew, to the mailbox. As she does so, the front door next door opens and Dominic walks out.

Shit. Emma is in her sleeping shorts and a baggy T-shirt, which is far too sheer to be worn without a bra, as she is wearing it now. And her hair! Oh God. She hasn't touched it since she woke up. Despite not having had the misfortune of seeing herself in the mirror, she's pretty certain it will look the way it always looks when she wakes up, before she has had a chance to shake it out or scrape it back: flat on one side, sticking up at the back and on top, tight curls at the nape of her neck where the night sweats have got her.

And, oh no – oh God, please, no! Last night, at Dominic's party, the drinks kept flowing, and while she hadn't drunk enough to be hungover now (thank God, because it could be so very much worse), it was bad enough that last night she fell into bed without washing off her make-up, which means there is undoubtedly mascara smudged half-way down her cheeks.

She's not supposed to see anyone. It's 7:32 in the morning, for God's sake. She's supposed to run to the mailbox, grab the irritatingly large stack of catalogues and handful of bills, and get back behind the safety of her front door without being spotted. Now Dominic is waving hello with a big smile, and – oh God! No! He's walking over. Emma grabs the mail and clutches it to her chest to hide the fact that her T-shirt is nearly transparent just as she realizes that she hasn't shaved her legs for days.

She slides a hand through her hair, attempting to shake it out slightly as she smiles a hello, backing slowly towards the house, hoping she can get away with the smile and nothing more.

'Hey!'

Nope. Dominic is almost upon her, and no hole in the ground is opening up to swallow her, so she is just going to have to brazen it out. Maybe she will get lucky; maybe he wears contact lenses and will have forgotten to put them in. Maybe a miracle will happen.

Why, she thinks, for a fleeting second, does she even care?

She watches him curiously, half expecting him to recoil with horror at what she looks like, but his smile is as natural and open as it always is.

'You're up so early,' he says, as Emma takes a step back-wards, realizing – and how could this possibly be any worse than it already is – that she hasn't yet brushed her teeth. So not only did she not remove her make-up last night, she didn't brush her teeth either. Her breath is so stale she can taste it.

'Early riser,' she says, attempting to speak without letting any breath out of her mouth, so her words sound vaguely strangled.

'Wasn't that a fun party last night? My friends thought you were great.'

'Thank you.' Emma shoots a desperate look at her front door, so near, and yet so far. 'I thought they were great. You're up early, too.'

'Yeah. Jesse's sitter cancelled and I have a doctor's appointment at nine. I've been phoning around the sitters to find someone.'

'Did you?'

'Not yet.'

'I can look after him,' Emma finds herself saying, without meaning to. 'I mean, I'm right next door. It's totally fine. You can send him over whenever you want.'

Dominic's face lights up. 'Really? You wouldn't mind? That would be awesome.'

'It's no problem. What does he like to do?'

'Jesse's the easiest kid in the world. He'll do anything. You can stick him in front of the television and he'll be happy. Or on the computer – he'll gladly play Minecraft for days on end.'

'Can I take him out? I mean, if I have any errands or anything, would he come?'

'That would be great. Let me put the car seat in your car just in case. Wow. Thank you, Emma. This is saving my life.'

'It's nothing. The least I can do. Just bring him over whenever you're ready. I'm going to get dressed, okay?' she says, finally making it to the safety of her house.

Only once she has successfully escaped her front lawn does she remember that she's not exactly a natural when it comes to small children. She loves teenagers, with their strong opinions and sense of moral outrage, loves children when they are old enough to have an adult conversation. But a six-year-old? Why did she offer to babysit a little boy she barely knows, when she has no idea how to talk to children his age? What on earth could she possibly have been thinking, other than how to get away as quickly as possible?

But Dominic had brought his son over and left. Jesse, now that he is here, seems entirely comfortable. He walked in, went straight to the sofa, where he sat down with his iPad mini, and has barely said a word for the past hour.

Emma has made herself busy with what she is calling work, although it's hardly that compared to what she is used to. She has Pic Stitched together a photograph of her office/library, the before and after shots, and is posting them online. She has put them on a local Facebook page and the classified sections of local websites, along with copy that offers inexpensive interior design services.

She wishes she had more photographs, more rooms that

she had designed. While Jesse is busy playing online games, Emma examines the cabinets in the kitchen, standing in the doorway for a while, looking around. She has a moment of feeling guilty for not engaging with Jesse more, trying to talk to him or find something they could do together. But looking at his complete absorption in whatever is on the screen of his iPad, she decides he is fine, probably happier to be ignored by her. She turns back to the kitchen cabinets. She could easily spray-paint them white after taking the doors off, giving the room an open-shelf look. She could add the leftover moulding from the library onto these shelves to thicken them up, make them look more substantial.

It's a pity there are no splashbacks on the kitchen work-top. The Formica surfaces are among the ugliest things she has ever seen. She goes back into the library, stopping for a second to admire her work – such a pretty room! – before sitting at her computer to search for some kind of plastic worktop sheeting. There must be something. Some kind of sticky-back plastic or contact paper that will mask those worktops.

She finds something online, rolls of sticky plastic printed to look like marble – contact paper. It isn't expensive, and she buys two rolls, recognizing the nervous thrill she always gets from buying something online – it is likely to be either disastrous or the greatest thing she has ever seen. But it's cheap, so she'll find out which it is in about three days.

The blank wall facing the window needs something.

Open wooden shelves like the ones she re-pinned on Pinterest the other day. Maybe a small butcher block island underneath, but narrow, enough to provide another work surface and some storage but not crowd the room.

She pulls her tape measure out from a drawer and makes measurements, noting them down in her phone. She's so inspired, she hates having to sit still. She turns back towards the boy on the couch.

'Jesse?' She has to ask three times before he looks up, so absorbed is he in his iPad. 'Do you want to come to Home Depot with me?'

'Sure,' he says, jumping up, eyes still glued to the screen. 'That's my dad's favourite shop.'

'Great. We could go somewhere else, too. Maybe grab some ice cream?'

Jesse's eyes are big. 'Before lunch?'

'If you don't tell, I won't tell.'

'Deal!' he says, high-fiving her as they walk out the door.

Emma runs through a number of beginner conversations as she steers the car up Compo and onto the Post Road. She could ask Jesse about school, what grade he's in, what his favourite subjects are, but she instinctively knows how boring that would be. She remembers a friend who had a routine with little kids. He would ask them what job they had and whether they were married, whether they had any children, and they would invariably burst out laughing.

Emma thinks about what would happen if she asked

Jesse if he's married, cringing in horror at how ridiculous she would sound. She can already picture his sideways glance of disdain.

She turns on the radio instead, scrolling through until she finds 95.9 The Fox, grateful for Steely Dan, amazed that Jesse starts singing along right away. He knows all the words, more than her, even, and she starts to laugh.

'How do you know this?'

'This is what my dad and I listen to all the time.'

'Steely Dan?'

'All the old music. Neil Young. Lynyrd Skynyrd. The Allman Brothers.'

'You're a pretty cool little kid.' Emma laughs. She feels amazed at how relaxed and open he seems with her after their silent morning together. 'You know that, right?'

'Yup,' nods Jesse. 'I know. Hey, did you ever go to the Humane Society?'

'What's the Humane Society?'

'It's where you go to rescue animals.'

'I haven't. I don't have any animals. Which is a shame. I'd kind of love something to keep me company, but I'm not sure I could handle a dog.'

'I love animals,' Jesse says, staring at her with great seriousness and intensity. 'I wanted a cat for my birthday, but Dad is worried it will get run over. I don't know why. Our neighbours have three cats and they've lived here for ages and they're fine, and they live outside and inside, too.'

'So he won't allow you a cat?'

Jesse shakes his head with such a solemn look on his

face that a ridiculous idea blooms in Emma's head. Surprised, she shakes herself, trying to dispel it. Of course Emma shouldn't get a cat. For starters, she has no idea if animals are even allowed in her lease. Although, surely, given that she is babysitting Jesse today, her friendship with Dominic has reached a level where she could persuade him to say yes, even if the lease said no.

Now that she realizes she's talking herself into it, she stops to wonder why the prospect of a cat suddenly seems appealing. She'd never considered having an animal before. Is it for her, or is it to try to endear herself to Jesse? And why would she want to be doing that, anyway?

Because he's a kid, she thinks. *And he's my neighbour. Because he's sweet, and doesn't have a mother, and wants a cat. And if I got one, we could share it.*

She doesn't stop to be shocked by her own thoughts. Instead, she finds herself saying, 'Shall we go and have a look?' After a pregnant pause, she adds, 'Just to see.'

Jesse nods, grinning widely. By the look on his face, she can tell the two of them are now in this potentially naughty outing together.

When they arrive at the shelter, Emma is really planning to just look. She thinks they can get away with wandering the corridors gazing at the animals, maybe playing with one or two, but leaving empty-handed a few minutes later.

She didn't expect the shelter to have kittens, much less a tiny tabby female who is the last one left. She didn't expect the kitten to curl up in her hands, nudging Emma's chin over and over as her whole body shakes with purring.

Then Jesse sits cross-legged on the floor, the cat crawling all over him, up his shirt, as he heaves with giggles and nuzzles the tiny creature.

'If we got her,' Emma says, 'not that we're going to, but if we did, what would be a good name for a kitten like this?'

'I would call her Hobbes,' says Jesse.

'Hobbs like the clothing shop?' Emma thinks about her mainstay in London.

Jesse frowns. 'No. Like the comic *Calvin and Hobbes*. The tiger. She's kind of like a tiny brown tiger.'

She laughs. 'I like it.' And then, not quite believing the words that came out of her mouth – what has happened to the good girl, with all those years of banking in her past? – she says, 'Should we?' Even as she speaks, she realizes that it isn't really a 'we' question. This cat would be hers. But she can't help acknowledging she'd be willing and happy to share her with Jesse for as long as she lives next door to him.

'For real?' His eyes grow big.

'Do you think your dad would go nuts if I brought home a kitten?'

'No!' he breathes, his eyes still large. 'We had a lady live there two years ago who had two cats, and the last person had a big dog. He would be fine! For real, though? We can get this kitten?'

'Hobbes. Yes. We'll have to get a litter tray at Home Depot, and a cat flap.' Then she feels the moment fill her with a warm glow. 'I haven't had a cat since I was a child.

This is actually very exciting!' she says, as Hobbes crawls on top of her foot and looks up at her with a plaintive mew.

'Gosh, you are gorgeous, Hobbes,' she says, scooping the kitten up and burying her nose in her soft fur. Then she turns to Jesse. 'Let's do it!' she says. 'But let's leave her here while we go to the shop to get everything we need, and we'll pick her up on the way home.'

In the end, what shocks her most isn't her impetuous decision, but rather that she finds herself standing in the aisle of the shelter with a small child hugging her legs, his eyes closed and a huge smile on his face.

Before long, she and Jesse are in the car, post Home Depot, the back filled with shelves, brackets, long thin boxes of thin veneer tongue-and-groove wood planks for the kitchen floor, cat litter tray and litter, cat flap and kitten food, and one cardboard box punctured with lines of round holes, from which Hobbes squeaks all the way home.

Dominic's truck is in the driveway when they pull in next door.

'Uh-oh,' says Emma, with a wave of regret. She was trying to do something nice for Jesse, as well as for herself, but she really should have checked with him beforehand – he is her landlord, after all. All of this only seems to be striking her now.

'Do you really think it's okay?' she asks Jesse.

'I think he'll be fine,' Jesse says, in a worryingly mature

manner for a six-year-old. 'Anyway, once he sees Hobbes, he's going to fall in love. Like we did.'

'Let's hope so,' says Emma, as Dominic walks out the front door and comes over to the car with a big smile on his face.

'Hey, buddy!' He gives Jesse a high five as he looks at the packed car. 'You look like you need some help unpacking your vehicle, ma'am,' he says to Emma with mock formality. Then he frowns as Hobbes's unmistakable mewling comes from inside the box.

'I'm really sorry,' says Emma, and she immediately starts babbling. 'We're hoping you're going to be okay with this and I realize I should have checked with you first but—'

But Jesse stops her by bursting out with, 'We got a kitten!' Before Dominic can react, before he has a chance even to speak, Jesse pulls open the box and grabs the tiny Hobbes and places her in his father's hands.

Dominic's face instantly softens. He looks down, startled, before burying his nose in the kitten's fur, just as Emma had. The kitten starts to purr like an engine, clearly making her own bid for Dominic's compliance.

Emma catches Jesse's eye. *Bold move*, she mouths approvingly.

Jesse shrugs, as if he can always be relied on to know the right thing to do when it comes to his father.

'Whose kitten is this?' says Dominic. 'It's adorable, but I mean, I don't know . . . Jesse, we need to talk about this.'

'It's not mine. It's Emma's. But she said she'd share it with me. And it's not an it, it's a her. Her name is Hobbes and she's really Emma's, but mine, too. And we bought a cat flap and Emma says I can come over anytime and play with the kitten, and please, Dad, say it's okay? Please? It's the only thing I've ever really, really wanted.'

Dominic pauses. But not for as long as Emma might have expected. 'Okay,' he says, his eyes still lit up at the tiny kitten in his hands. 'She's adorable. Hobbes. Sorry. Hobbes is adorable.' He raises an eyebrow at Jesse, who nods in delight. 'Hobbes as in *Calvin and Hobbes*?'

Jesse nods, and Dominic glances at Emma. 'Figures,' he says to her. 'His favourite comic strip for years.' Now he meets her gaze squarely. 'I'm fine with you having a cat. I guess. I don't really have a choice, do I?'

Emma doesn't know what to say, but he doesn't look angry.

Then he surprises her by saying, 'Do you want me to put the cat flap in for you?'

'That would be fantastic.' She suddenly feels shy, touched by his easy acceptance of her impulsive cat-rescuing. 'Thank you.'

'You're welcome.' His tone now is quiet, and more serious, too. 'Thank you for looking after Jesse. Obviously the two of you had a good time.'

'It was the best,' says Jesse. 'And we stopped for ice cream on—' His face falls and he turns towards the houses. 'I mean, nothing. We didn't have ice cream. We drove by the ice cream place and said maybe we'd come back after lunch. Right?' He turns to Emma with a warning glance.

'Absolutely,' says Emma, who doesn't point out the

chocolate drips all the way down his red T-shirt, drips that his father is looking at right now with wry amusement.

'So you didn't have any ice cream, huh?' Dominic says.

'Nope.' Jesse shakes his head with great vigour. 'I know I'm not allowed to eat ice cream until after lunch.'

'So those brown stains on your T-shirt? Is that . . .' Dominic leans forward and examines them. 'Coffee? Have you been drinking coffee?'

'I just let him have a tiny sip,' says Emma. 'I'm so sorry. He spilled my coffee all down his T-shirt. Right, Jesse?'

'I'm really sorry, Dad. It was hot and I spilled.'

Dominic grins. 'It's okay, buddy. Come on. Let's get Hobbes inside and get this cat flap installed. And it seems there may be some new shelves that need putting up?'

The rest of the day is punctuated by the intermittent sounds of the drill as Dominic installs the cat flap in the back door, before putting the shelves up in the kitchen, Emma handing him each drill bit or bracket as he needs it. Jesse spends his time playing with the kitten, rolling up strips of aluminium foil into balls and shrieking with delight as Hobbes bats them into the corners of the room, sliding across the floor as she skids towards them.

'If I'd known a kitten would make him forget about the iPad,' Dominic says, whispering under his breath, 'I would have gotten him one years ago.'

Emma smiles as she unwraps hardware and hands it to him. 'It's not about what happened,' she says. 'It's what happens next.' She blushes slightly, realizing how this comment, one of her standard lines, could be misinterpreted.

'So what happens next in your life?' says Dominic, reaching up to position a shelf. His T-shirt rides up, exposing the tanned skin on his stomach and waist, and Emma, flushed with guilt for noticing, quickly looks away.

'What do you mean? Work? Well, I just posted some stuff today about helping people out with interior design. Hopefully that will lead to something.'

Dominic glances at her with a grin. 'I didn't mean work. How does a woman like you end up single? Who's the unlucky guy who let you get away?'

From anyone else, Emma would think it was a leading question, but from Dominic, who is so comfortable with who he is, it is entirely natural that he would say whatever is on his mind. 'Do you say that to all your tenants?' Emma laughs. 'Is that your way of flirting with me?'

'Only a little,' says Dominic. 'I can't help it. I'm Italian. It's my way of making friends. But seriously, you seem like you should be married with a couple of kids, baking chocolate chip cookies for the school bake sale.'

'You know, I really think you should have quit while you were ahead,' says Emma. 'You went straight from saying I was cute to comparing me to a suburban housewife from the last century.'

'Listen, some of these local housewives are hot. I'm telling you, I would never say anything derogatory about housewives.'

'So it was a compliment?'

'Absolutely. But you are single, right? I assumed you were, only because there are no comings and goings here.'

Emma sighs. 'One of the downsides of having your landlord live next door.'

'Maybe, but look at the upsides!' He gestures to the shelves.

'Granted. No, there are no men right now. There have been too many recent changes in my life for me to focus on relationships. I just need to settle into my new life before I'm ready for that stuff.'

'When you are ready, you just let me know. I'll tell you all the places to go to meet the single men, which nights, and what to avoid.'

'The Fat Hen?' She is joking, but she feels a slight pang. Suddenly she's not sure she wants Dominic to send her off to meet the single men.

'Nah. You don't want to meet men at the Hen. Not the kind of men you'd want to spend quality time with. I might be the bartender, but in all honesty I'd have to say that.'

Emma pauses, not sure she should be asking, but she wants to know; now seems like the perfect time. 'How about you? You're dating Gina?' She tries to make the question seem casual. Light. As if she doesn't much care.

'Dating.' He seems to muse over the word. 'I hadn't even really thought of it as dating. Gina isn't really someone you date. I guess you could just say we're hanging out together. We've known each other a long time. It's . . . fun.'

'Sometimes the relationships that grow out of long friendships are the very best of all,' says Emma.

Dominic laughs. 'This is definitely not a relationship. I'm not even sure that it's fun a lot of the time. Gina is one tough woman, but . . .' He shrugs. 'It is what it is.'

'What does that mean?'

'It means it's fine for right now. Neither of us wants anything more serious.'

'Men always say that. But I find invariably the women do want something more serious. A man always thinks that he's on the same page as the woman he's with, then wonders why she's so devastated when he says, "Let's both go back to being friends."'

Dominic is amused. 'You sound like you have bitter experience.'

'No,' she says. 'It's just that I think you're wrong about Gina. I think she's more interested in you than you think. She definitely seemed interested enough to be unfriendly to other women.'

'You?'

'And Sophie.'

'Don't take it personally. Gina doesn't like women. Especially if they're pretty. If you weighed four hundred pounds she would have loved you.'

Emma laughs as her phone buzzes, a text from Sophie, which she excuses herself to read, realizing that it isn't just her phone buzzing, but her whole body. Is she imagining it, or is there real chemistry between them? She hadn't expected it, wasn't looking for it, but now that it is here, it seems to be making her feel more alive; at any rate, it is making her smile.

Rob's on a last-minute trip and my mom's babysitting Jackson. Want to go out tonight?

Emma reads the text and thinks to herself, *Yes*. She does need a night out. There are only so many nights binge-watching shows on Netflix that a girl can take. She needs to go out with a friend and have a couple of drinks and have some fun.

'Dominic? You know how you just said you'd tell me the fun places to go in town? I don't think I'm quite ready to go hunting for a man, but I am ready for a girls' night out, and you clearly know all the right places. If we wanted to have some fun, where would we go?'

'That was quick!' he says, before insisting she get her phone back out and make a list of all the places they should go.

Chapter 10

It is a gorgeous, balmy summer night. Emma asked Jesse
to kitty-sit while she's out, and already she can hear him
crooning at Hobbes to try to entice her from behind the
sofa as Emma finishes getting ready.

She is wearing a white floaty dress that shows off her
tan. Her hair is down, tumbling around her shoulders in
beachy waves. Skinny gold hoops are in her ears, and a
long beaded necklace with a tiny seed pearl tassel falls to
her waist. She has sprayed a shimmery golden oil on her
shoulders, her chest, and down her arms, and is glowing
as she steps into the living room before leaving to pick up
Sophie.

'Wow,' says Dominic, seemingly stunned into silence as
he looks at her approvingly. She didn't expect Dominic to
be there. Jesse had wolfed down a grilled cheese sandwich
in her kitchen before crawling across the living room to
extract Hobbes from behind the sofa, never mentioning
that his dad might be dropping in. She knew Dominic
would come over after she left to watch Jesse but thought
he'd wait until she was gone. She was aware of a vague

disappointment that he wouldn't see her looking so pretty. She knows she looks pretty only because she feels pretty, prettier than she has felt in ages, and she registers a tiny thrill that he is seeing her looking her absolute best. Why she cares about what Dominic thinks is not something she is willing to think about just yet.

'I'm just bringing Jesse his juice box,' says Dominic, sitting on her sofa and looking away, gesturing to the small box on the table before looking back at her with a slight shake of his head. 'You look amazing.'

'Thank you!' If Emma wasn't glowing before, she lights up at the compliment. She grabs a small straw clutch and slips her feet into strappy wedges. 'Is this the right look for the place you recommended?'

'You're going to blow them away.'

Emma smiles her way out of the house, into the car, over to Sophie's house, and all the way to Southport, the smile, the buzz, the glow never leaving her.

'Why are you so gorgeous and smiley?' asks Sophie when she gets in the car.

'I don't know,' says Emma. 'I'm just happy.'

And she is.

'I don't get it,' Sophie keeps saying, glancing over at her friend as they drive over to the bar. 'Did you do something?'

'What do you mean, did I do something? Like what?'

'I don't know. Did you have a facial? Did you change . . . I don't know, something? You look ridiculously gorgeous tonight.'

Emma snuggles further down in her seat, unable to wipe the smile from her face. 'I think it's leading a stress-free life. Honestly. I feel like a different person since I moved out here and gave up my job. Sophie, I love living by the beach. There's something about the light there that is completely and utterly magical. I wake up every morning feeling happy and . . . I think that's it. It's just my new life.' She's not ready to admit, even to her closest friend, that she is starting to realize there is something about her landlord that she can't quite shake off. It isn't an obvious attraction, but the more she sees him, the more he seems to be growing on her. His kindness, his comfort in his skin, his ease in the world. All of it makes Emma feel safe.

Sophie peers at her with disbelief. 'Are you sure you're not in love or something? Is there anything you want to tell me?'

Emma frowns. 'There isn't,' she says, after a pause. 'But there is. I know that doesn't make sense, but I think I might be feeling something for Dominic. I'm just not quite sure what it is.'

Sophie's eyes widen. 'What does that mean? You're attracted to him? Not that I'm surprised, but I didn't think you were interested. God knows you've spent enough time telling me you're not.'

'I wasn't. I don't know what this is. I just feel . . . calm . . . when he's around. And I find myself smiling in anticipation at the thought of seeing him. I like seeing him. I'm starting to want to see him more and more. And I really don't know what any of this means.'

Sophie leans back. 'I knew it. The very fact that you kept saying he wasn't your type at all means he's your type. Of course he's your type. He's *everyone's* type. He's like, manliness personified.'

'What's the matter with you?' says Emma, laughing. '*Manliness personified?* Have you been taking drugs? He's not manliness personified!' She cracks up. 'He builds a terrible bookshelf, for your information. Although I do admit the kitchen shelves were slightly better, and the cat flap is really quite good.'

'Cat flap?'

'Ah, yes,' says Emma. 'I knew there was something else I hadn't told you. Jesse and I got a cat today.'

Sophie starts to laugh. 'Jesse and I? Okay. That's it. You're already part of the family.'

'I'm really not,' says Emma. 'I just babysat him today and we went to the Humane Society and ended up with a cat. I feel for this little kid. He's very grown-up for his age, you know – he's only six – and he clearly adores his father. I can't imagine what he's been through, being abandoned by his mother.' Her face is serious, almost tearful as she thinks about Jesse, his closeness to his father, the incredibly close relationship they have.

'Did you find out any more about what happened?'

'Not yet. But I'm sure I will. I'm sure it's good for him to have a woman around who does nice things for him.'

'Unlike that awful woman his dad's banging?'

'Sophie, don't be crass. But yes.' She smiles. 'Unlike that

awful woman his dad's banging. Apparently, however, that relationship is not serious.'

Sophie shoots her a sideways glance. 'He told you that? Well, of course he did. How could it be serious when he has a beautiful, talented, single woman living next door who makes that girl look like an old tramp? He's totally falling for you.'

'Okay, stop,' says Emma. 'Seriously. I love you but I'm not ready to predict the future. He's lovely, and I'm happy, and we need to sit back and just let this unfold the way it is supposed to.' She gives her friend a hard stare. '*If* it is supposed to. Meanwhile, let's go and have some fun. What are we drinking?'

Chapter 11

A large crowd of people fills the forecourt of the restaurant, beautiful people lounging on the rattan sofas dotted around the small square, the bar at one side five deep in men with dark tans, and women in floaty sundresses and high-heeled sandals. There is a buzz of laughter, excitement, and potential filling the air as Sophie and Emma thread their way through to get a drink.

This is awful, thinks Emma, catching the eye of an older man with an open shirt through which a copious amount of chest hair pokes out. He raises his glass in a toast, with what she can only interpret as a lascivious self-congratulatory smile. Everything about him seems sleazy. Emma looks away, rethinking the whole idea of a night out in what appears to be the worst kind of singles bar.

Emma has never done the singles scene. As someone who does not like crowds, and who is not actively looking for excitement, she cannot compete with the kind of women who now surround her. Emma is pretty, but she knows she is a *quiet* pretty; she is more girl-next-door than sex siren. As Sophie muscles her way to the bar, Emma steps back slightly and looks around. The laughter here is a little too loud, the men a little too tanned, the women a little too *done*. All cleavage, and legs, and teeth, and necks thrown back to expose golden clavicles. Blow-dried hair, glossy and long, curled at the ends to bounce on bare, brown shoulders; legs lean and muscled from hot yoga and Pilates, fingers heavy with cocktail rings glistening in the fading light.

Small globes twinkle overhead, strings of tiny fairy lights woven through white hydrangea trees in giant square planters. There is an air of possibility, as if anything could happen here. Indeed, as Emma backs away from the cluster at the bar, another man lays a hand on her arm as he moves past her. She looks up as he smiles and winks in a way that makes her want to run home, crawl under the covers, and never go out again.

'Isn't this fun?' says Sophie, eventually reappearing with two French martinis as they find the last available sofa and settle down. 'I never go out to places like this any more. God, being married is boring. You're so lucky.'

Emma looks at her as if she is entirely nuts. 'You actually think this meat market is more appealing than curling up in bed with the man you love? Oh my God, Sophie, have you lost your marbles? Do you not smell the air of utter desperation?'

'Nope,' Sophie says happily, looking around. 'I think this is fun. Two men told me I was beautiful while I was waiting at the bar, and a third asked for my number.

Honestly, I haven't had this much attention for years. I should come here more often.'

'Which men?' demands Emma.

'Just some guys.'

'Was one of them wearing an open-necked shirt with a mat of curly chest hair?'

Sophie pauses. 'Maybe.' She looks around with a frown. 'Isn't everyone here wearing an open-necked shirt with a mat of curly chest hair?'

Emma bursts out laughing. 'Come on, Soph, you have to admit this is pretty awful. You would have to be desperate to come here on a regular basis.'

'I think it's great. If I weren't married this is totally where I'd come.'

'You're only saying that because you *are* married, so it's fun. If you actually were single and this were about the only option available for you to meet some potential suitors, you'd kill yourself. The only decent men in this place have wedding rings on, and that's not good either. That guy over there' – she points to a tall, good-looking man in red trousers and a blue polo shirt – 'the one all over the skinny blonde with the big boobs? He's got a wedding ring, and I'll bet you my pension she's most definitely not his wife.'

'Don't be such a Debbie Downer. Come on, play the game. If you could have a date with anyone standing in this courtyard right now, who would you choose?' Sophie sips her drink as she challenges Emma, who looks around with a slight grimace.

'There really isn't anyone.'

'I know, I know, because the cute landlord isn't here . . .'
Emma shoots her a warning look. 'Okay! Sorry! Of the
available men in this courtyard right now, if you absolutely
had to pick someone to go on a date with, who would you
pick? And by the way, before you say chemistry isn't something you can predict and you don't go out with people
based on what they look like blah blah blah, I already know
all of that. But you have to pick someone. Just for the
record, if I had to pick someone, I would choose the guy
in the red pants and the blue shirt.'

'Ew!' Emma shakes her head. 'He is so full of himself.
That's not my type at all.'

'He's not full of himself. He's confident. He's probably
a trader who lives in a great big gabled new house in Greens
Farms with four small children and a wife who thinks he's
in a business meeting right now. I didn't say I'd marry him,
but he's my type. So who would you pick?'

'If I absolutely had to . . .' Emma looks around, her
eyes finally landing on a man deep in conversation with a
friend, short brown hair, slightly geeky glasses, no interest,
it seems, in the women around him. 'Him.'

'Really? Him?'

'Yes. He looks interesting. And normal. He looks like
an architect or a graphic designer.'

'He does. And he actually looks like a nice guy. No
wedding band, either. Just saying.' Sophie takes a big swig
of her martini, then stands up. 'I'm just going to the bathroom.'

Emma continues people-watching while Sophie is gone,

wanting to feel a little less uncomfortable than she does. She tries not to catch anyone's eye, for even though she is single, she doesn't want to look single, doesn't want anyone here to think she's the sort of woman who comes to a place like this in the hope of meeting someone.

Sophie is gone for a long time. Emma gets out her phone and busies herself scrolling through her Facebook news feed, when suddenly Sophie is back, clearing her throat, and introducing her to the guy with the glasses Emma had pointed out, and Doug, his friend.

'I just started chatting with these guys,' says Sophie, 'and this is Jeff. He's a real estate agent. I told him that you were renting but were probably going to start looking to buy something in a few months, so I thought I should introduce you.' Sophie makes big eyes at Emma as the men step forward and shake her hand.

'Here,' says Sophie, pulling a chair forward. 'Join us. Sit down.'

When Sophie finally sits, Emma leans towards her and says, under her breath, 'Girls' night?'

'Single friend needs sex?' says Sophie, equally quietly, as she smiles brightly, raising her voice to a normal level. 'Emma? Jeff is divorced and lives very close to you at Compo Beach.'

'Really?' says Emma, forcing a smile, for small talk was not something she had anticipated on her girls' night out. 'What street?'

'Appletree Trail?' says Jeff, as Emma shakes her head.

'I don't know it. I'm sorry. I've only lived here for about five minutes.'

'Where's your place?'

She explains as Jeff's face lights up. 'Dominic's house? I love that house. Now *those* are two properties that are going to be worth some real money. I can't believe he hasn't sold them yet and cashed in. Every real estate developer in town wants those houses.'

'Really? What's so special about them?' asks Emma.

'One's on a double lot. If you combine them, you can build a big house and a pool. That's pretty rare down by the beach, unless you're on one of the private roads. I've talked to Dominic about selling for years, but he won't do it.'

'How do you know Dominic?'

'We were at school together. I've known him forever.'

Emma is starting to feel more comfortable. The fact that he knows Dominic means he must be a good guy. 'Do you know his son, Jesse?'

Jeff nods. 'He and my nephew, Chad, are pretty friendly. They're in the same class at school.' He smiles. 'Big first-graders come September.'

And Emma risks asking the question she hasn't been able to ask anyone else, not even Dominic. 'Did you know Jesse's mother?'

Jeff laughs. 'Oh yes. Everyone knows Jesse's mother. I've known her and Dominic for most of my life. We all grew up together. Stacy is . . . huge fun, but a party girl.

Not the type who ever wanted to settle down. She's a holy handful.'

'What does that mean?' Emma couldn't help asking.

'Stacy's a wild one. I don't know, I kind of thought she was crazy, but Dominic's always liked a bit of crazy.'

Emma opens her eyes wide. 'That doesn't sound good.'

Jeff shrugs. 'He is such a great guy. He would do anything for anyone, and we all love him, but he's always been a disaster with women. His parents were totally nuts. I remember going to his house as a kid and his parents would literally be screaming at each other. One time when I was there, his mom cracked his dad over the head with a frying pan and there was blood everywhere. The police were always going over there. Dominic grew up in crazy drama, and for years he's dated the kind of women who like crazy drama, and then he wonders why he gets hurt. Stacy was never really interested in him. I mean, she liked that she had him wrapped around her little finger, but there was no way she was the type to settle down. She was a huge partier, and – Oh, I shouldn't say this. This is gossip.' He trails off.

'My lips are sealed,' encourages Emma.

'She wasn't exactly the faithful type. Stacy was never faithful to anyone, and then she got pregnant, and she didn't find out until it was too late. So she had the baby, and boom! Took off. Dominic woke up one day because the baby was crying and he discovered that Stacy had literally run away in the middle of the night. And that was it. I don't think he's ever heard from her again.'

'Oh my God. That's really awful. But she must come home at some point, to visit or something? She doesn't know Jesse? What about her family? She must be in touch with some people, surely?'

'There are a couple of girls in town who know where she is, but they're loyal to her and won't say. Apparently she doesn't want to be found. I heard she moved to Alaska, but who the hell knows. So Dominic is raising that kid by himself.'

'He's a great kid.'

'He is. So, what brings you to Westport? What's your story?'

'I don't really have a story. I was working in banking, gave it up, and just moved out here for a quieter life.'

'So you did what they all dream of doing and managed to get off the treadmill.'

'I did.'

'Boyfriend? Husband?'

'None of the above.'

Jeff nods thoughtfully. 'Hm. Interesting. So maybe you and I could go look at houses sometime? If you're actually interested in buying something.'

'I'd love to,' says Emma.

'And maybe we could grab dinner or something afterward?'

'Oh! That would be nice,' says Emma. He is nice-looking, and perfectly pleasant, but there does not seem to be an ounce of chemistry between them. She thinks of Dominic. She likes Jeff. She very much likes that he's not a banker type. But she doesn't like him as much as Dominic. She doesn't trust him the way she trusts Dominic. She pushes thoughts of Dominic aside, bringing her focus back to Jeff. She had no idea she was about to be asked on a date, given how little they have talked. Perhaps she's wrong, perhaps it's not a date. The only thing they have established they have in common is Dominic, and that doesn't really count.

'What are you guys talking about?' says Sophie, who has been engrossed in conversation with Doug.

'We're planning house hunting and maybe dinner,' says Jeff.

'Ooh, a date! So quickly! I like your style.'

'Thank you,' he says, before checking his watch. 'Damn. We have a dinner. We have to go, unfortunately. It was so nice meeting you. Here.' He roots around in his wallet, pulling out a business card. 'Call me and we'll set up that date.'

'Oh. Okay,' says Emma, eyeing the card suspiciously. This isn't how it is supposed to happen, surely? Granted, it has been a while since she dated, but isn't he supposed to take her number? Or her email, at the very least? Isn't he supposed to be the one who gets in touch with her rather than the other way around?

As Jeff and Doug walk away, she fingers the card and turns to Sophie with a frown. 'Call me old-fashioned, but isn't he supposed to take my number if it actually is a date? This feels like business. I think he only suggested dinner because he thinks he might get a house sale out of it.'

Sophie shakes her head. 'I don't know. I have no idea how dating works these days. Honestly, I think it's probably okay. You don't have to call him, though. I'd email him and leave the ball firmly in his court. You can just say it was nice to meet him. Was he nice? Are you interested?'

'I don't know,' says Emma. 'He was pretty forward, but all we talked about was Dominic. He knows him pretty well, and he filled me in on some of his history.'

'Oooh. Gossip! Let me get us more martinis. Then I want to hear all about it.'

The house is quiet. Jesse is on the sofa, fast asleep, a blanket over him, and Hobbes curled up in the crook of his neck. Emma pauses, smiling at the scene of domestic bliss, when she sees the glow of a candle in the garden.

Opening the sliding doors, she steps out to find Dominic, sitting in an Adirondack chair with a glass of what looks like it might be whiskey, earphones firmly in place, his eyes closed. He doesn't see her until she is right in front of him, and when he does, he opens his eyes and jumps.

'I'm so sorry!' Emma says, lowering herself into the chair next to him with a smile. 'I didn't know you were sleeping. I didn't mean to give you a fright.'

'I wasn't sleeping. I was listening to some music, and I didn't want to wake Jesse. Did you have fun?'

Emma frowns. 'I'm not sure I'd call it fun. It's a bit of a "scene". Sophie loved it.'

'You didn't?'

'I'm more of a quiet, glass-of-wine-in-a-corner kind of

girl. We met someone who knows you, though. A real estate agent. Jeff Mulligan?'

Dominic smiles. 'Yeah. Another townie. I've known him forever. Small world, huh?' He peers at Emma. 'I think I know everyone in town. So, did he ask you out?'

Emma feels herself blush. 'I'm not sure. He suggested dinner, but he didn't take my number.'

'Did he give you his business card?'

'Yes!' She laughs. 'So I don't quite know what he meant by dinner. I think he sees me as a prospective client.'

'Jeff sees everyone as a prospective client. Which doesn't mean he won't also see you as a prospective something else. Although I'll admit I wouldn't have thought he's your type.'

'No? What do you think my type is?' Emma leans forward to see him better. It's so dark, his features light up every now and then as the candle flickers in the breeze.

'I don't know,' Dominic says slowly. 'Why don't *you* tell me?' The candlelight glints in his eyes as he looks at her, as he leans towards her, never taking his eyes from her face. Emma's heart skips, then stops. They stare at each other, not speaking, the garden completely silent, as a cat yowls from the garden opposite, breaking the spell.

'I'd . . . better go inside,' she says softly.

Dominic sits back, the moment gone, both of them wondering what has just happened; what might have happened had the cat not stolen that moment away.

Emma can't stop smiling. She locks the front door feeling as if she is walking on air. What did it mean? What *does* it mean? None of this should make sense; this is not the kind of man she thought she would fall for. Even that sentence sounds ridiculous. What kind of man *did* she think she would fall for? A banker? A hedge-fund manager? One of the tanned men at the bar tonight, buoyed by alcohol and their own narcissistic sense of self-importance? Jeff? She shudders.

Has she fallen for Dominic? Has *he* fallen for *her?* That moment, in the garden, when they stopped speaking, when they just stared at each other as Emma's heart skipped a beat before racing wildly. Wasn't that the moment he was supposed to kiss her? She could feel it, could sense it in the air, the intimacy, the chemistry, the excitement, but then, the cat. He had pulled away.

There was something there. She felt it. She is old enough and experienced enough to recognize chemistry, even in the most unexpected of places. She does like him. Every time she sees him, she feels happy. Sometimes when she's in the house, and she hears his truck pull in the driveway, without even realizing she is doing it, she starts to smile. She doesn't know when this started. She thinks of him guiding her through the garden gate the other night, his hand on the small of her back, the feeling of safety that came over her. She feels safe with him. He is the kind of man who would look after her. He is the kind of man who *is* looking after her. *Look at how he takes care of Jesse.* She is still smiling as she thinks of him building her shelves, helping her out in the kitchen, and just now, in the garden, almost . . . almost . . . kissing her.

Could she see herself with a man like Dominic? A few months ago she would have said no. Not because he wasn't a city boy, but because they come from such different worlds. She thinks of the world she comes from, the world she moved across the Atlantic to escape. The formality and pretentiousness of her aspirational mother, the expectations everyone held for her, expectations that led her into banking in the first place. And during those New York years, all the parties, the one-upmanship, how relieved she is to have escaped to a quieter life.

'Stop!' she says out loud, realizing how ridiculous it is to project into the future, to think about what kind of a life she might have with Dominic. This isn't what she does, what she has ever done. She has never been the sort of woman to dream about getting married. On girls' nights out, in her twenties, even when she was with Rufus and knew the path down which she was supposed to be travelling, she was never comfortable having the conversations the girls sometimes had: where they would get married, what kind of flowers they would have, what – oh, how many times did she listen to this one – the dress would be like.

Emma was never interested. She shakes her head now to dislodge her thoughts. Why is she even thinking about whether she could see herself and Dominic together? It's not like she's looking for a relationship with anyone. The fact that he makes her feel good is irrelevant, surely. She has bigger things to focus on – living purposefully and on her own terms, perhaps for the first time ever in her life.

Twenty minutes later she is brushing her teeth when she hears a car pulling up outside the house. Padding into the library, toothbrush still in her mouth, she leaves the lights off to peer through the window, knowing she can't be seen. Who could it be, so late at night?

A Jeep is in Dominic's driveway. Emma stands to one side and watches as the lights go off and the car door opens. And out steps Gina, who pauses for a minute to shake her hair out. Emma's heart sinks.

Of course. That was why he left. Gina was coming over. Emma got it completely wrong. He wasn't about to kiss her. That was all in her imagination. Why would he have kissed her when he has Gina?

Feeling stupid, and disproportionately sad over something so silly, Emma goes back into the bathroom to rinse her mouth, then crawls into bed. She tries to distract her sorrows with a few pages of the book on her bedside table. But it doesn't work. Eventually, finally, she falls asleep.

Chapter 12

The Jeep is gone by the time Emma wakes up, earlier than she normally would, only because Hobbes pads along her pillow, purring, curling herself up in the crook of Emma's neck, and licking her chin with a rough, raspy tongue.

Emma nuzzles Hobbes for a while, going over everything that happened the night before with Dominic. The talking, the sharing, the intimacy.

This morning she finds herself embarrassed. He has a girlfriend; she needs to push him out of her head, at least in any capacity other than helpful landlord.

I will be friendly and polite, but a little cool, she thinks. *I will ensure that he does not think his tenant is interested, that if I was a little flirty last night, or a little too revealing, it was just because I was a little drunk, not because I have a crush on him, or anything ridiculous like that.*

As she thinks this, she pictures him in his jeans and T-shirts, pictures his dimples when he smiles, the way he pushes his hair back when it falls into his eyes as he's working, and she finds that she is smiling to herself. Horrified, she wipes the smile off her face as she hears a noise.

'Hello?' She jumps out of bed and runs into the living room, to find Jesse standing in the middle of the room, still bleary-eyed with sleep.

'Jesse? How did you get in?' She is careful to lock all the doors every night, city girl that she is. She frowns, clearly remembering having locked both the front door and the back last night, after Dominic left.

Jesse grins. 'Cat flap.'

Emma can't help but smile. 'Ah! The infamous cat flap!'

Jesse drops down to the floor and easily slips through the flap to the other side, popping up to wave at her through the glass of the window, before coming back through.

'Well, you're a boy of many talents, aren't you? Have you come to see Hobbes? You did a wonderful job of looking after her last night. She was so happy when I came home.'

'Can I feed her?' says Jesse, spying Hobbes in the corridor and running over to get her, which sends her darting under the bed in fear.

'Yes. And be gentle. Move slowly so she doesn't think you want to play a game of chase, and she'll come to you. Have you had breakfast?'

Jesse shakes his head.

'How about I make pancakes?'

Jesse's face lights up, and Emma walks into the kitchen, makes a fresh pot of coffee, checks for eggs, flour, and milk, and gets to work.

At some point while she is spooning homemade pancake

batter into the frying pan, Emma decides that she is not going to stress about making conversation with a six-year-old. In fact, she's not even going to try. She is going to let Jesse lead the way. If he doesn't speak, she will make herself busy doing something on the computer. Making conversation with a six-year-old, finding common ground, is altogether too anxiety-inducing for someone who doesn't consider herself good with children. With that decided, she slides a few of the finished pancakes onto a plate for Jesse, puts them on the table, and heads back into the kitchen to clean up.

'Where are yours?' says Jesse.

'I might eat some later,' calls Emma, sponge already in hand.

'Oh.' Jesse pauses. 'But then they'll be cold.'

'Good point,' says Emma. She puts down the sponge, puts two more pancakes on a plate for herself, and sets it down opposite Jesse and sits.

'Is it okay for us to eat together?' she asks.

Jesse nods happily as Emma suppresses a smile.

'These are good,' he says in surprise, taking a huge bite, talking as he chews.

'It's vanilla extract,' confesses Emma. 'It's the secret ingredient. Can you close your mouth when you chew because . . . *ew!* I can see all the food in there.' Much to her surprise, Jesse instantly closes his mouth. 'And I added a bit of sugar,' she continues. 'You're not supposed to, but frankly I think everything's better with a little sugar added to it. I'm a bit of a sugar addict, you know.'

'I love sugar, too,' says Jesse, his mouth again open and full. 'You know what my favourite sandwiches are?'

'No. Can I guess?'

Jesse nods.

'Pesto chicken, Fontina cheese, and tomato?'

He makes a face.

'Chicken, dill, and mustard sauce? Roast beef and horse-radish? Gravlax and dill?'

Jesse clearly has no idea what she is talking about, but Emma is having fun. She could go on all day, thinking up exotic sandwiches a six-year-old would never have heard of, let alone tasted.

'Sugar,' he interrupts her, with a whisper and a devilish grin.

'What?' Emma feigns horror.

'I do it when my dad's sleeping.'

'I know you expect me to be shocked,' says Emma, 'but that's what my mother had as a treat after the war. White bread, thick butter, and sugar.'

'Butter?' Jesse is intrigued.

'Oh yes. She says it's all about the butter.' Emma leans forward and drops her voice. 'I could make one now, one with butter, one without. We could both sample them so we can decide which kind is better. What do you think?'

Jesse nods vigorously, as Emma pushes her chair back to go to the kitchen, grateful she had the foresight to buy a fresh loaf of bread yesterday. It isn't the processed sliced white bread that her mother loves, but it will have to do. She cuts four thin slices, removes their crusts, and slathers thick slabs of cold butter, straight from the fridge, on two of the slices.

She pulls the silver sugar shaker out of the cupboard, smiling as she always does when she uses it. It is a ridiculous thing for a single girl to own, she knows, the kind of old-fashioned object no one has any more, and certainly not someone with no husband or children. But her mother gave it to her, and it was a remnant of her childhood, and it always makes her think of her childhood home when she uses it. She gives each piece of bread a liberal sprinkling of sugar, then another, and then presses each pair of slices together to make two sandwiches, and cuts each in half again for her and Jesse to sample.

He has pushed the plate of pancakes away in anticipation of this forbidden treat. They each pick up a butterless sandwich and take one bite, staring into each other's eyes, Emma forcing herself not to grimace at the overwhelming sweetness.

'It's good,' says Jesse, mouth filled with bread and sugar, as he grins.

'Next,' says Emma, handing him the sandwich smeared with butter. Jesse takes a bite, then closes his eyes, a slow smile spreading on his face as Emma takes her own bite. She has heard her mother wax lyrical about sugar sandwiches since she was a tiny girl but has never before tried one herself.

'Oh, wow,' Emma says, her tongue searching out the grains of sugar and thick creamy butter mixed in with the yeasty dough. 'That is delicious.'

'Mmmmmm!' says Jesse, wolfing down the rest of the sandwich. 'Butter!'

'I never thought I'd like it, but that was amazing. I'm guessing you don't want the rest of your pancakes?'

'I do!' Jesse pulls the plate back and carries on with his official breakfast. 'Do you think Hobbes would like sugar sandwiches?' he asks Emma.

'Only if they were coated in cat food,' she says.

'What is cat food made of?' asks Jesse.

'I have absolutely no idea. It says turkey in gravy and beef, but who knows what else.'

'Can I see if she likes pancakes?'

'Okay. But I don't think she will.'

Jesse pulls off a tiny piece and puts it on the floor in front of Hobbes's nose. Hobbes sniffs it, then, to Jesse's delight, bats it across the room, running after it, trying to pull it out from under the chair with her paw.

There is a knock on the back door, startling Emma, who looks up to see Dominic's face in the glass.

Oh God. Again. At least she doesn't have mascara smudged under her eyes. Still, why does this man have to keep seeing her at her worst? *Why should it matter?* she reminds herself. *Friendly but cool tenant*, she thinks, beckoning him in.

Friendly but cool.

'What's going on here?' says Dominic, as relaxed and easy in his skin as he always is.

What was I expecting? wonders Emma. *Some kind of weird morning-after-the-night-before? Nothing happened.*

Look! He isn't behaving any differently, which means I don't have to get weird. She takes a breath and tries to relax, even though it's hard to look at him, particularly given that smile, which causes a small flip in her stomach. She looks away.

'I'm just making breakfast for Jesse,' she says, making big eyes at her young breakfast companion, trying vainly to telegraph that he hide the last of the sugar sandwiches.

'Is there enough for me? I'm starving.' Dominic walks over and picks up Emma's sugar sandwich. 'What is this? Egg?' Before anyone can say anything he pops the whole thing in his mouth.

'Oh my God, this is good! What the hell is this? It tastes like sugar!'

Jesse grins.

'It's a sugar sandwich. With butter,' says Emma, reluctantly. 'I'm so sorry. It's all my fault. It's my mother's favourite treat and I had to introduce it to Jesse. But I'll hypnotize him and make him forget he ever tasted it, I swear.'

'Can you make me another one?' says Dominic, high-fiving Jesse, who whoops in delight, before reaching over and grabbing one of Jesse's pancakes. 'I've got bacon in the fridge if we also need bacon,' Dominic adds.

'Yes to the bacon.' Emma's face is serious. She's both relieved Dominic isn't angry, and pleased at the suggestion of the three of them sharing breakfast. 'Bacon is always needed. Go and get the bacon.'

And before long they are all three sitting down at the

table, to a feast of pancakes, more sugar sandwiches, and crispy bacon glazed with maple syrup (Dominic's idea). They sit, and laugh, and tell jokes, while Jesse gets Hobbes to try out everything to see what she likes (just the bacon).

Emma forgets that she saw Gina park her Jeep in Dominic's driveway late last night. She forgets that Dominic has a girlfriend, that she is supposed to be embarrassed to have given him any indication that she is interested in him. She forgets that she went to bed feeling lonely and sad. She is too busy having fun.

'You got something here,' says Dominic, gesturing to his own lips as he looks at Emma.

Emma flushes a bright red, her hand flying to her mouth. 'Did I get it?' she asks as she brushes her lips.

'No. Here.' He reaches forward and brushes his fingers over the side of her bottom lip, and her breath catches as he looks in her eyes. 'Got it,' he says quietly, his smile fading. A second passes. Then Emma jumps up.

'I'm going to clear up,' she says, and she can't look at him, knows that her face is bright red, that she is flushed from head to toe.

'I'm going to take Jesse to camp,' says Dominic. 'Come on, buddy. Let's go.'

'No!' says Jesse. 'I want to stay here and play with Hobbes.'

'You've got to go to camp,' Dominic says in his stern voice. He turns to Emma and adds, 'And Emma has work to do, right?'

'I do,' says Emma, the flush finally fading. 'But, Jesse,

I meant what I said. You can come over anytime. Hobbes will be right here waiting for you when you get home from camp.'

'Can I come over as soon as I get home?'

'Absolutely. The cat flap is now yours to use as you please.'

'Look, Dad!' Jesse drops to the floor and scoots through the cat flap, waving delightedly from the other side.

'Oh God,' groans Dominic. 'I'm really sorry, Emma. I didn't think he'd be in and out of your house with the damn cat flap. I can tell him not to. I don't want him bothering you.'

Emma finds herself slightly insulted by the suggestion that Jesse might be bothering her. 'He's not bothering me,' she says. 'He's sweet. We had a lovely time before you arrived.'

'Great. Thanks. How to make a guy feel wanted.'

Emma laughs. 'I didn't mean that! I just meant we were having fun – he's lovely.'

'As long as *I'm* not unwanted, we're all good.'

Don't blush, she thinks. *Don't blush, don't blush, don't blush.*

She knows he is watching her but she can't meet his eyes.

'We're all good,' she says, not taking the bait. Not looking at him, willing herself to keep her cool.

'Okay. Jesse, let's go. See you later, Emma.' And with a smile, he and Jesse are gone.

Chapter 13

Later that morning, when Emma's phone buzzes, she looks to see a number she doesn't recognize. She picks up to find a woman on the line who saw her ad on Craigslist offering interior design services.

They have recently moved to town, the woman says, and have purchased an older Colonial house on Marion Road. They don't have a big budget, and she has no idea how to decorate, no furniture, and really needs some help. She has been into a couple of local shops and spoken to the in-house decorators, but the furniture would be a fortune and she needs to keep the cost down.

She saw Emma's pictures on Craigslist and loved the style. She says it is exactly what she's looking for in their new house. Could Emma come and see it? Is there any chance she might be available that afternoon because she's itching to get started, and having an empty living room might be fun for the kids but she really, really wants to get some furniture in before Labor Day rolls around in early September, which isn't long, given that it's now mid-summer, and she's too scared to make those big decisions by herself.

Emma agrees to go over at two o'clock. Then she takes as many pictures as she can of her tiny galley kitchen, with its faux marble worktops and open wood shelving on rustic black brackets, before running out to the corner shop by the railway station to stock up on magazines. She hadn't expected to see a client so quickly and needs to cobble together some kind of portfolio, some indication of her style, and quickly.

She swings by Staples, picks up a ring-binder and plastic page covers, and spends a couple of hours clipping pages from magazines – *Coastal Living*, *Better Homes and Gardens*, *House & Garden*, *Elle Decor*. All are ruthlessly milled for examples of the style Emma loves. Before long, she loses herself completely in the task, letting go of her sense of time, of place, even of self, in a way that is almost magical. She certainly never felt this way working in the city.

This, she realizes, is what she does best. She can re-create any one of the rooms she sees on these pages for a fraction of the cost most designers would charge. She can walk into a shop like HomeGoods and bypass everything until she finds the one lamp, the one tray, the one mirror that is exactly, but *exactly* like the one in that gorgeous magazine spread, and the result will look just as good as a room created by a designer whose expertise costs a small fortune.

She can do this Fairfield County look – the white sofas, the turquoise accessories, the grey woods, the obligatory Buddhas everywhere you look – with her eyes closed. All she needs are the clients. If this woman – Lisa is her name – works out, who knows where it might lead.

Thank you, God. Emma offers a silent prayer, grabbing her new ring-binder and a notebook in which to record all that Lisa is looking for. Taking a quick glance in the mirror, she pauses, noticing how different she looks from her banking days. For this meeting, she has gone for understated chic – dark jeans, ballet flats, a good linen shirt, and her ubiquitous chunky gold cuff. On her shoulder, a designer handbag – the one designer handbag – left over from her old life. She may not be interested in the labels any more, but it is good for potential clients to see that she is a woman who shares their good taste. She looks chic and understated. A little make-up and hair pulled back in an elegant chignon complete the look. *If I didn't know better,* she thinks, looking in the mirror, *I would say I was a seasoned interior designer. If I didn't know better, I would say I look like a woman who knows what she is doing.*

With that, she closes the door and sets off.

Chapter 14

The house is probably from the 1940s, Emma guesses, as she pulls up. Someone has added a curved portico over the front door, which adds character and charm, and there are pretty panelled window boxes on the first-floor windows, which would be lovely spilling over with lobelia and ivy, but are empty and forlorn.

The landscaping is tired. Half-naked yews, old enough to be huge, but mostly bare, apart from the top, flank the front doorsteps. Creeping fir, a weeping maple, various untended plants line the front of the house, and there is cracked tarmac on the driveway.

The house is pretty, or at least could be pretty, with a little bit of TLC, thinks Emma. She instantly imagines the quick fixes that could transform the front. Gravel the driveway, for starters. Pull out all the landscaping – those terrible old, bare yews – and replace it with something simple and clean. Boxwood balls perhaps, or a holly hedge.

Paint the front door a glossy grey; fill the window boxes; install large square iron planters on either side of the steps.

Lisa answers the doorbell as Emma looks around,

making mental notes. She is Emma's age, with dark hair pulled back in a ponytail, a striped T-shirt and white jeans, bare feet, and a toddler on her hip.

'So nice to meet you!' She invites Emma in, handing the baby to a young au pair as they pass the living room, bare but for a brand-new huge sofa and dark wood coffee table, a couple of sad chairs pushed back against the wall. Beyond is the library, containing a glass desk and bookshelves, empty but for a few novels on one shelf.

'You do have some furniture,' Emma comments, walking through the kitchen and noting the table and chairs – Restoration Hardware, she's sure – and the slipcovered sofa in the sunroom.

'Yes. But none of it makes this place feel like home,' says Lisa. 'I have no idea how to make a room the kind of place you want to spend time in. I thought getting the sofa and coffee table would make it inviting, but it still looks cold.'

'At least you chose a great sofa and coffee table,' says Emma, encouragingly. 'There's so much we can do to dress it up. And the glass desk in the library is perfect – it's exactly what I would have chosen myself.'

Lisa's face lights up. 'Well, thank goodness I did something right. My husband's birthday is over Labor Day weekend, and I'm planning to throw him a party. It'll probably be outside in the yard, but I want everyone to see our house. We moved from the city a year ago and I'm totally embarrassed that the house still looks like this. I want it to be beautiful. And I have so little time to get it right before the party. Can we go see the rooms and I can tell you what I'm thinking?'

Emma follows Lisa into the living room and the library, then upstairs, hiding her nerves, hiding her fear that she will be found out as an amateur. Will Lisa be able to tell this is Emma's first job? But as she walks through the house, her confidence returns; she can see exactly what it needs to be transformed into a wonderful home: sisal rugs, sofas, a couple of chairs and side tables. Abstract paintings in coastal shades of blue and green, cushions, lamps, and trays. Window blinds. Emma could create gorgeous rooms here just by shopping for about three days, and there is no doubt in her mind that the result would be beautiful.

Lisa isn't asking Emma to spend hours in D & D Building gathering beautiful fabrics and wallpapers, putting them together on mood boards with sketches and photographs. She merely wants to give Emma a budget and send her off to local shops, where she will choose porcelain Buddhas, and crewel cushions, and mohair throws, and everything else she needs to create a finished, magazine-worthy house that Lisa can show off to her friends.

'You basically want me to shop for you,' says Emma at one point, as they flick through the ring-binder she had put together, Lisa exclaiming over every single page.

'Yes!' says Lisa. 'That's exactly what I want. I want you to send me pictures just to check that I like what you've chosen, although honestly, I don't even know what I like. That's the problem – I get so overwhelmed. I want to show you a picture of a living room and I want you to make mine look just like that, but within our budget.'

'And that,' says Emma delightedly, 'is exactly what I can do. I've brought a file of designs. Why don't we look through and see if there are any rooms in there that you love? Or even parts of rooms that you love. Light fixtures or window blinds.'

'Let's do it,' says Lisa, opening the file again and sighing with pleasure at nearly every picture Emma has included.

'I love this,' she says, over and over. 'Oh my God, look at that fireplace!'

'We could do that pretty easily with your fireplace if you wanted,' says Emma. 'I have a handyman who could stucco over the brick and make it look like sandstone to give you that very modern, clean look. It wouldn't cost a lot and would give your living room a lovely contemporary feel.'

'I love that idea!' Lisa turns to her. 'Emma, you are the perfect person. I love every single room you've picked out in here.'

Lisa's phone interrupts her with a buzz, and as she excuses herself to take the call, Emma stands up and wanders around, looking out the windows, thinking about where she might buy the furnishings she has in mind, if she is lucky enough to get the job.

Then Lisa comes back into the room. 'I'm so sorry. That was my husband. He has a late meeting tonight.' She rolls her eyes – clearly this is something that happens a lot. 'We were supposed to be going to a farm dinner in Redding, but he has to cancel. I've got two tickets now to get rid of.' She sighs. 'You wouldn't be interested, would you? I'm never going to find anyone who can get a babysitter organized in time. It would be a shame to let the tickets go to waste.'

'Really? Why don't you go with a friend?'

'To be honest, I'm kind of exhausted anyway,' Lisa says. 'I'd be much happier if I knew the tickets were being used.'

'What exactly is a farm dinner? It sounds fascinating.'

'Oh, it's a great concept. They do these a few times a year; each dinner features one of the hottest local chefs, and great wine, and they set up these long tables in the orchard. We went last year, not long after we moved here from the city, and it was amazing. The food was terrific, and we met some really nice people. I know we've only just met, but I'd love it if you took our place. Really. You should go.'

'Are you absolutely sure?'

'Yes! Go. Just give them our names when you get there.'

'Can I write you a cheque?'

'Don't worry about it. This is the beginning of what I hope will be a great working relationship. Send me a proposal with pricing so I can sit down with my husband and get back to you as soon as possible? Because seriously, I'm ready to get going on this, like, tomorrow.'

'Done,' Emma says with a laugh. 'And thank you so much for the farm dinner tickets. I'll let you know how it goes.'

Floating on air, Emma says goodbye and makes her way home.

*

'I can't come,' says Sophie. 'We're going out for dinner with a couple from my Mommy and Me group and we've already cancelled three times. I'd much rather go to a farm dinner with you, believe me, but I can't cancel on them again. I've spent the whole day praying she'll phone and say she's not feeling well or her husband's stuck in the office, but she just texted to say she can't wait to see us, and they've booked a table at the Whelk.' Sophie sets down her mug of coffee and stretches out her legs as Jackson plays between her feet.

'Why are you going out for dinner with people you don't like?'

'I don't exactly not like them. I just don't think they're really our type. They've been pursuing us for months. Every time I see her, she says we have to get together with our husbands and go out for dinner, and I always smile and say, "Yes! We must!" but I never follow up in the hope she'll just forget about it. Eventually I just had to bite the bullet and issue an invitation. Then I kept cancelling, thinking our plans would just fade away and she would forget about it, but she kept texting. Eventually I ran out of excuses, so we're just going to get it out of the way.'

'So what am I going to do with these tickets? I'll have to give them to someone. Can *you* give them to someone? I don't even know anyone in this town other than you.'

'How about sexy landlord?'

'Give Dominic the tickets?'

'No, silly. Ask him to go with you.' Sophie rolls her

eyes. 'You know you want to. He'll be the perfect dinner companion. Go and knock on his door and ask him.'

Emma groans. 'I can't.'

'Why not?'

'I just . . . it's overstepping.'

'What on earth are you talking about? He invited you to his barbecue, and it sounds like the two of you are hanging out a ton. This is your way of paying him back. Why don't you just text him? Here. Give me your phone.'

Without waiting for Emma to say yes, Sophie grabs it from the coffee table and scrolls through her screen of contacts until she finds Dominic.

'Hey, Dom,' she types, looking up at Emma, who shakes her head vigorously in horror.

'He's not Dom,' she says. 'Dominic.'

'Okay. Sorry. "Hey, Dominic. Someone just gave me two tickets to a farm dinner in Redding tonight. Want to come?"'

'Don't say that,' says Emma. 'Say, "Is there any chance you want to come?"'

'Why? So you can be all English and reserved and pretend you don't really want him to come? Too late. I pressed Send.'

Emma groans. 'It's too forward. Now I'm embarrassed.'

'Oh . . . oh . . .'

'What?'

'The dots!' Sophie shouts. 'He's responding already!'

'What does he say?'

'He says . . .' She pauses dramatically. '"Yes! Sounds

great!!!"' she reads from the screen. 'Note the exclamation points,' she adds with a wink. 'Then he finishes with, "I'll pick you up. What time?"'

'Pick me up? That's funny, since he lives next door. Tell him five.'

'Done. Now I have to help you figure out what to wear for your date.'

'It's not a date,' grumbles Emma.

'Just because you extended the invitation doesn't mean it's not a date. And not only is it a date, it's your first date, technically.'

Emma shakes her head. 'Every time you call it a date it makes me freak out with nerves, and it sets the expectations so high I'm bound to have a horrible time. It's not really a date, is it? Isn't it just two new friends going out?'

Sophie stares at her friend. 'I'm sorry, Emma. I didn't mean to freak you out, but I do think this is a date. I know you're nervous, but don't be. We've already established he's lovely. Now you just have to relax and be yourself. Oh, and look gorgeous.' She grins. 'Can I help you pick out what to wear for dinner on the farm? I'm thinking floral dress, with a fabulous straw cowboy hat.'

Emma shakes her head with a laugh. 'You're incorrigible. Okay. I will do my best to relax and be myself. As for the floral dress, that I have. But where am I going to get a fabulous straw cowboy hat?'

'My wardrobe. I'll drop it off in about an hour. You're going to look beautiful. Let's blow Dominic away!'

*

The dress is indeed floral, and floaty, with a vintage feel that Emma loves. She feels feminine and beautiful in this dress, which she fell in love with years ago in a tiny shop on Westbourne Grove, but has barely worn, because it has never felt quite her style.

Her hair is clipped back into a bun, tendrils hanging loose, with thin gold hoops in her ears and flat leather sandals on her feet. The tiniest bit of make-up, a woven raffia clutch, and the cowboy hat. She'd thought at first that the hat would be ridiculous, but even she has to admit it's perfect when she catches sight of herself in the mirror.

The doorbell rings. Dominic doesn't have to say anything for Emma to see that he approves. His eyes widen with a smile when he sees her, and he nods almost involuntarily.

'You look beautiful.' He says this as he places a hand on the small of her back, again, to guide her out the door, and again, just like the last time he did it, Emma feels her nerves disappear. A feeling of absolute safety washes over her as she lets him guide her to the truck.

'This is definitely the right truck for a farm dinner,' she says, as they pull out of the driveway. 'You're going to feel right at home.'

'I love a farm,' says Dominic. 'I worked on farms when I was a teenager. That was back when there were a ton of farms and farm stands around here. You wouldn't even have recognized this town back then. It really was a small New England town when I was growing up. Everyone on Main Street knew you, people kept tabs on you everywhere, even at the grocery store. If you misbehaved, the shop-keepers would call home and tell your mom.'

'I wish it were like that now,' says Emma. 'I grew up in the country in England and it was much the same. I loved it, although of course back then I couldn't wait to leave and move to London.'

'I would never want to live in the city,' says Dominic. 'Even though I don't always like how the town has changed, it's my home.' He shrugs. 'There isn't anywhere else I could imagine living. My parents moved up to a retirement community outside of Trumbull, but I have to say, I can't imagine ever leaving Westport, even though I never go to Main Street any more.'

'What? No Brooks Brothers board shorts for you?' jokes Emma.

'Right. Because I look like a Brooks Brothers board shorts shorts kind of guy.'

'You look very dapper tonight.' She looks at him, in a button-down white shirt and jeans.

'I made an effort for you.' He looks over at her and grins, and Emma smiles back, as her heart skips the tiniest of beats.

They turn up a dirt road and follow the hand-painted signs to *Dinner on the Farm Parking* through an open wooden gate, into a meadow filled with parked cars. They park and climb out, following another couple along a mown grass pathway through a wildflower meadow. A few minutes later they reach a large open field filled with people standing around sipping elderflower cocktails, helping themselves to hors d'oeuvres off trays borne by young, smiling women in linen aprons and chunky boots.

Dominic grabs two glasses off a tray, and they toast each other and take a sip.

'I had no idea this was a thing,' says Dominic, looking around with a smile. 'I like it, though. It makes me feel comfortable, at home. Just like we were talking about on the way here. Reminds me of what the town was like when I was growing up.'

'Where do you think the actual dinner will be held?' Emma looks around but can't see any tables.

'Through there, maybe? See the sign to the orchard?' A passing waitress overhears and stops with a smile.

'The dinner? It is in the orchard but we don't let anyone over there until it's time. There's a whole theatre involved in getting the tables ready, and we wait to bring everyone in all at once.'

'This is really nice,' says Dominic happily, helping himself to a small spoon of shrimp with dill pesto and quinoa. 'And delicious,' he adds. His mouth is full as he speaks, and Emma laughs as she takes a spoon and tries the food herself.

It's not long before everyone is invited into the orchard. The scene they find there is beautiful. Four long trestle tables stretch between the apple trees, globe lights strung between the branches, votives in mason jars winding down the centre of each hessian-covered table, bamboo chairs lining each side.

The lights twinkle in the fading sunlight as waiters stand

to one side, greeting the guests with smiles. Everyone first glimpses the magical setting, then looks for seats. Emma glances around, trying to spot people she hopes, prays, may be nice, chatty, fun for the night.

Before she can think too long, Emma and Dominic sit with two couples their age, who introduce themselves as soon as they sit down. Emma already has them pegged – she worked with people just like them in New York. The men, good-looking and clean cut, wear huge expensive watches on their wrists. She knows even without looking that they will each sport a Panerai, or a Rolex Daytona, and she flicks her eyes down to check, seeing that indeed one is a Panerai, the other an IWC. *Nailed it*, she thinks. *Bankers.*

The women are well groomed and friendly, but clearly not very interested in Emma. Out of politeness, she attempts to make small talk, asking them about their lives, their babies, where they worked before they had babies. Both of them are former bankers, undecided as to whether they will return to work. Emma knows in both cases they will not; she has worked with too many women like them, and she feels like she knows exactly how their lives will be laid out ahead of them. They have children and leave banking, thinking they will go back, but they will love being stay-at-home moms, even though a lot of the time they are bored. They will employ a nanny or au pair to take care of the boring parts – the endless trips to the children's museum, the aquarium, the soft play zone – and will spend their time getting back into shape and looking good enough to keep their husbands' interest. The children will grow, will start kindergarten, and the wives will get involved with charities, will tell people they used to be bankers, conferring on themselves a status they gave up to be full-time mothers, because they still want to be defined as something more than merely a wife.

When their children reach high school their friends will slowly start working again, and they will realize it is no longer a status symbol to be a stay-at-home mother. They will look for something not too taxing to fill their time. Good God, they will realize. Whatever did they do with all that time? They will work in local shops, or start businesses, or help out at the school library. Many will become real estate agents, although most will struggle to find clients in a town overrun by middle-aged women going into the real estate business once their children have started high school.

Oh yes. Emma knows these women well, thanks to Sophie and her vocal feelings about them. She can see their whole lives laid out in front of them in a way they will not be able to for years. As the women answer her questions, she wonders whether they will ask her anything about herself, but she is entirely unsurprised when they don't. Once she stops asking them about themselves, they grow quiet.

'I saw what just happened,' Dominic says, dropping his voice so they can't hear. 'They were as interested in you as their husbands were in me.'

'Their husbands weren't interested in you?'

'Nah. I don't work at a hedge fund or bank. I told them I was a bartender and their eyes glazed over.'

'But everyone loves the Fat Hen! Why didn't you tell them you worked there? You know they would have wanted you to be their new best friend if you'd told them.'

'That's exactly why I didn't tell them,' murmurs Dominic. 'The Fat Hen has enough of those types. I definitely don't want to encourage any more.'

'I'm sorry,' whispers Emma. 'I think we got stuck with the duds.'

'We have each other,' says Dominic. 'And I couldn't be happier with the company I'm keeping tonight.'

She flushes with pleasure, just as the feta and watermelon is set on the table, and she can distract herself with the food. They chat about this and that, until the plates are removed, when Dominic turns to her and asks, 'How is it you don't have a boyfriend? I asked you before but you didn't give me a straight answer.'

This time, she manages not to blush and commands herself to hear the question as one from a friend and not a flirtation. 'I'm pretty self-sufficient,' Emma answers. 'Honestly, I'm not sure I'm a good girlfriend. I had a very long relationship when I was younger and everyone expected us to get married, but I think I'm a bit of a lone wolf. It's a terrible thing to admit, and not the thing you're supposed to say, but I'm perfectly happy being on my own. Why are you smiling?'

'Lone wolf,' he says. 'When I was a kid I used to be in

a rock band and we called it the Lone Wolves because that's what everyone called me. The Lone Wolf.'

'So you're independent, too?'

'It's different for a man. We're expected to be. But I don't know how easy it would be for me to share my life with anyone, either.'

'Really? You seem so open. You seem exactly the kind of man who would, should, have a partner.'

'Yeah. I know that's how it seems, but my model for marriage wasn't a great one.'

Emma remembers what that real estate agent Jeff had said about Dominic's parents: the fighting, the drama, the violence.

'Your parents? Were they not happy?' She already knows the answer but wants to hear it first-hand from Dominic.

He laughs. 'That might be the understatement of the century. They hate each other, but they're still married. I think my mom planned a huge bunch of kids, but after me she had a ton of miscarriages, and I think the whole thing was a huge disappointment to her. They're very Italian, which means there's always a lot of shouting, but in my family's case that comes with a lot of anger and a lot of . . .' He shakes his head. 'This is boring.'

'No. It's really not. I imagine that growing up in a family like that must have scarred you in some way, must have made you reluctant to get involved with anyone.'

'I didn't think so when I was younger, but I realize now how often I was attracted to women who brought drama to a relationship. Everything I thought I wanted to avoid

from my own childhood: the shouting, the anger, the turmoil? I always seemed to pick women who brought exactly
that into my life.'

'But not now?'

Dominic pauses. 'I had a girlfriend once. I was about
seventeen, and we would fight all the time. There was this
one night when we were yelling at each other, and I was
so angry, I swear to God it's the only time in my life I
actually have come close to laying a hand on someone.
I didn't. But I was scared that I was going to. And I realized then that if I didn't make a conscious choice to live
differently, I was going to follow my parents' path. And
I didn't want that. That night changed me completely. I
learned that it's all a choice, and that choice is up to us.
And then of course Jesse came along, and it's always different once you're a father. I'm different. Not only do I
always have to put Jesse first, I've had to learn what it is
to have a relationship. I know it's my kid, but it's the first
real long-term relationship I've had as an adult. I've had
to learn to be selfless. To put someone else before me. And
I've had to try to teach Jesse that we're the only ones in
control of our happiness. It's been a great lesson.'

'So now you're ready for the woman of your dreams?'
says Emma.

'Maybe.' He looks at her. There is a long pause.

'Gina?'

'That's over,' he says simply.

Emma fights the delighted grin that is itching to get out.
'Didn't I see her come over late last night?'

'She did. And I ended it.'

'I'm so sorry.'

Dominic stares at her. '*Are* you?'

She is quiet for a minute. 'I don't know. Are you?'

'No. It was pointless. It wasn't going anywhere. It wasn't fair, either to her or to me.' Dominic reaches for the basket of cornbread, takes two pieces, hands one to Emma. Without looking at her, he reaches for the butter and keeps his eyes down as he slathers some on his bread. 'I found myself thinking about other . . . things,' he finally says.

Emma's heart jumps. 'Other things?'

Dominic looks up and gives her a slow smile. 'Yes.'

They make it through the lamb-and-date meatballs, the braised short ribs with succotash and roasted beetroot, through the burnt caramel ice cream with toffee apple slices. They make it through talking, and drinking, and laughing, and looking at no one but each other.

They make it through coffee, and fine, delicate ginger-and-lemon cookies, and mint tea with tiny chocolate biscotti.

They make it halfway up the mown pathway on the way back to the car park after dinner, couples behind them, couples in front.

'Look,' says Dominic, pausing along the path and pointing out something glistening beyond the trees. 'A pond. Shall we check it out?'

Emma nods, and as they step off the path and through the long grass, Dominic reaches out and takes her hand, and a warmth settles over her entire body as she feels his hand wrap hers.

They walk down to the pond, and stop when they reach the water, turning to each other at the same time. Emma is hardly able to breathe.

Dominic reaches out and places a hand on her cheek. And then she is in his arms, his mouth is on hers, her mouth opening as his arms wrap around her body and she sinks into something that feels so familiar, so right, that when they finally disengage, when they open their eyes and look at each other, her cheeks are wet with tears.

'Why are you crying?' Dominic asks, looking at her with wonder.

'I have no idea,' she says, which is absolutely true.

They kiss at every red traffic light on the way home. They do not talk about what will happen once they get there until they pull into the driveway. Then Dominic asks if she will wait in the car while he pays the babysitter and sends her home.

Emma sits in the car, astonished by what has happened. She watches Dominic, standing in the doorway paying the babysitter, feeling a jolt of lust in her loins, something she hasn't felt in a very long time. She's not even sure she has ever felt exactly this before.

She looks at him from inside the darkened car, tasting him still on her tongue, remembering from earlier in the evening what he feels like, the shape of his head, the texture of his hair, and a shudder runs through her body.

She wants to drink him in, eat him up. She wants to fold herself into him so tightly that the two of them become one. She wants to consume and be consumed, in a way so unlike the Emma she has always been, that when the baby-sitter leaves and she finally gets out of the car and joins him in the house, her legs are shaking.

'Sssshhh.' Dominic puts his finger to his lips, indicating that Jesse is fast asleep, before pulling her back into his arms. They stand at the foot of the stairs, kissing, and when he takes her hand and motions her upstairs, she nods, and follows him up into the master bedroom, where he inches her back, until she falls backwards on the bed, laughing softly.

He dips his head down, kisses her neck, pushes the strap of her dress down, and the laughing stops, replaced with a sharp, ravenous intake of breath as she pulls his head back up, needing his mouth to be on hers.

Dominic kisses his way down her body, pulling her dress down, fumbling around her back to undo her bra and throw it across the room. He lingers on her breasts, slips a hand down inside her underwear, as she lets out a small, pleasurable moan. She reaches down to undo his jeans, unbuttons his shirt to feel his skin against hers.

She marvels at the intimacy of these acts, and how she feels so comfortable performing them. It should feel so strange, she thinks, guiding him into her, feeling him inside her as he props himself on his hands and gazes at her. But everything feels so right. So very different from before. From ever before.

*

The last time Emma had sex was through Tinder. She is not a Tinder girl, but everyone she knew was doing it, everyone said she had to do it. She thought, after a while, that she *should* try it. Though people used the app mostly for sex, surely there were some who found relationships unexpectedly, and if they did, why not her?

She was swiped by a handsome artist who lived downtown. Naturally. He was in his late twenties, and confessed to always being drawn to older women, which threw Emma slightly, for she didn't consider someone in her mid-thirties an older woman. They went to the bar of a basement restaurant in the West Village, where he was greeted by the hostess, the bartender, and even the manager, who came out from the back to give him a bro hug.

They sat at the bar and had dirty martinis, two for her, three for him. They talked about nothing very important, but he was good-looking, and young, and his interest in her made her feel desirable and beautiful. It had been a while since she had felt desirable and beautiful. Attention from the lecherous men with whom she worked didn't count – that was all part of the game.

She couldn't see herself with this Tinder man in any meaningful way, but the attention was flattering, and easy. Towards the end of her second martini, she began to feel like Mrs Robinson. How old must Mrs Robinson have been? Much older than thirty-five. In her late forties, at least, thought Emma, picturing Anne Bancroft in the film, her age indeterminate, a young and gorgeous Katharine Ross as Elaine. *She was much older than me,* thought Emma, looking at the bloom of smooth skin on the artist's cheek, *but I think I now know how she felt.*

'Want to come back to my place for a . . . coffee?' murmured the artist, after he had kissed her, at the bar, in full view of everyone, his tongue snaking into her mouth in a way that was both embarrassing and exciting.

She knew that coffee was not on the agenda, and she nodded. Why not? It would be something new for her.

Emma was not the sort of girl to have a one-night stand, had never, in fact, *had* a one-night stand. Emma was a good girl, a rule-follower. The only rule she had ever broken was not marrying Rufus. It was high time she did something unexpected.

So, yes, she would go back with him; yes, she knew coffee would be forgotten once they walked into his loft; no, they didn't have enormous chemistry. His kissing, in fact, was very . . . enthusiastic. *Too* enthusiastic. And wet. There was no build-up, no excitement, no anticipation; one minute his face was in front of hers, the next his tongue was plunging around her mouth. *That's okay*, she thought; that didn't mean the sex itself would be awful. Maybe it would be wonderful, despite the bad kissing. Why not have wonderful sex with someone young and handsome, and fun?

She should have listened to her feelings about the kiss. For she soon learned, a bad kisser was not a good start. A rough, wet, overenthusiastic kisser meant a rough, wet, overenthusiastic everything.

Emma did go back to his apartment, where he threw her

on the bed in a way that he perhaps thought was dominant and sexy but was in fact the opposite. His tongue was too big, his touch too impersonal. There was no chemistry, and it was too late. Emma felt too guilty to get up and leave.

It was, thankfully, quick. She spent the few minutes it lasted thinking about a pair of shoes she had passed on the way to meet him, wondering whether they would go with a white dress she had hanging in her wardrobe. As soon as it was over he grabbed his iPhone from the bedside table and started reading texts. She watched as he hovered over the Tinder app, and she started laughing.

'You're actually going to swipe *now?* Seconds after you've finished having sex with someone?'

At least he had the grace to look embarrassed. She left, vowing not to have regrets. She had tried Tinder, and clearly it was not for her. The sex was definitely not for her.

Not long after, when she found herself out with a group of women, all talking about Tinder and their sexual escapades, she was gratified to discover she wasn't alone. Most of them were disappointed, complained that sex was a commodity, felt disposable. There was no intimacy, they agreed, and worse, no pretence or effort to give them pleasure.

And yet these women kept doing it, addicted to the swiping, to being swiped, to the possibility that one of the swipes might, just might, turn into something more. Not necessarily a relationship, but at the very least, great sex.

Not Emma, though. She deleted the app from her phone.

No sex at all was better than selfish sex. She threw her energy into her work (and bought a small, discreet vibrator online).

Until now. Until Dominic, who has made her heart smile these past few weeks. She hasn't thought about him much, hasn't allowed herself to think about him, because the two of them seemed so mismatched, from such different cultures and classes, but there is no question she has a warm glow of happiness whenever he is around.

They have become friends, with an ease and openness that Emma isn't quite sure she has experienced before. With that friendship, she has found herself looking at him, with something she refuses to recognize as lust.

But it is lust. Oh God. It is definitely lust.

He doesn't stop looking at her as he moves inside her, Emma's legs wrapped around his back, her hands moving over his arms, his shoulders, his chest. He dips his head to kiss her, over and over, smiling, watching her face as she feels an orgasm beginning to build, tipping her head back and moaning as the feelings overtake her body, as he allows himself to be overtaken with her.

Afterwards, as she lies in his arms, Dominic talks. He tells her stories about his family, his friends, his hopes and dreams.

'I must go soon,' she whispers, and he nods, and keeps on talking. He is still talking when she falls asleep.

ACT TWO

Chapter 15

It takes Emma a while to orient herself. Her eyes are closed as she fights her way upwards, out of the deepest of sleeps, with the vague awareness that something is different.

Everything is different.

The smell of the room is unfamiliar. She is pressed against something warm. Something breathing. Last night comes back to her in a flood, flashes of memories like Polaroids, flitting through her mind. The dinner. The kiss. The drive home. The strap of her dress being slipped off her shoulder. The hand moving . . . *oh!* There is a flicker deep down as she gasps ever so slightly and opens her eyes.

She didn't mean to fall asleep in Dominic's arms. She didn't mean to spend the night in Dominic's bed. She is pressed against him, or is he pressed against her? The two of them are in the middle of the bed, squeezed together. She can smell his cologne, the musky scent of his skin. She didn't think she liked cologne, but Dominic always smells delicious, even when he is building shelves, and she sniffs deeply now, drinking him in.

She wants to kiss him, to reach out and stroke him, but

what if last night was a one-night stand? What if he wants nothing to do with her now? What if it is awkward, and awful, and they are not able to look at each other?

Damn, she thinks. *Why did I allow this to happen? Where am I going to live if it all goes horribly wrong?*

She turns her head and squeals in fright. Standing right by the side of the bed, up close, staring at her with narrowed eyes, is Jesse.

Oh *shit*.

She has no idea what to say. She wouldn't have wanted Jesse to know they were more than friends. She wouldn't have wanted him to know anything until she was sure there was anything to know.

'Hey,' she whispers, pulling the covers up under her chin, attempting a natural smile as if it is completely normal to find the next-door neighbour in your father's bed. 'How did you sleep?'

Oh God. Why did Jesse have to be standing here?

'Are you okay?' she whispers, when he doesn't answer. 'We had a sleepover with your dad last night,' she says lamely. 'We didn't plan it but, obviously, I ended up staying over.'

Jesse just stares at her.

'Why don't you have any clothes on?' he says eventually.

'It was so hot,' she says. 'I think maybe the air conditioning was broken. Was it hot in your room? No? It must just be in here, then. I do not want your father to see me with no clothes on, though. Would you mind passing me that dress on the floor over there so I can put something on before he wakes up?'

Jesse squints at Emma, deciding whether to believe her, knowing, she suspects, that her story doesn't quite add up, but eventually he gets the dress and throws it at her, quite unpleasantly she thinks, although she's in no position to say anything.

'What about Hobbes?' says Jesse. 'Who's looking after Hobbes?'

'Why don't you go through the cat flap and check on her?' says Emma brightly. 'I'll get dressed and maybe I'll make us some breakfast. How does that sound?'

Jesse shrugs but leaves the room. Emma hears the back door slam as he goes out into the garden on his way next door. She slips the covers back to get dressed, before an arm lays across her chest to stop her. She turns to see Dominic's eyes open, and for a second she is nervous about what he will say, until a slow smile spreads on his face.

'Morning,' he says, pulling her gently towards him and kissing her. For all her concerns – about him, about Jesse – she can't help but giggle.

'Get off me!' She attempts to push him away, which only makes him squeeze her more tightly.

'This is great,' he says. 'This is like having my own teddy bear.' And she finally relaxes in his arms, snuggling down in the bed, rolling over until she is looking into his eyes.

'Jesse came in,' she says. 'I'm so sorry. I honestly wasn't planning on staying the night, but I fell asleep, and when

I woke up it was to see him standing next to the bed.' She frowns a little. 'I don't think he's happy.'

'Why isn't he happy?' Dominic takes a strand of her hair between his fingers and twirls it around and around. 'I love your hair, by the way,' he says. 'Curly hair turns me on.'

Emma starts to laugh. 'You're just saying that. Curly hair turns you on? I don't believe you.'

'Okay. Let me revise. *Your* curly hair turns me on.' He smiles. 'Or maybe it's you that turns me on.'

'I do?' Emma smiles back at him.

'You do. Everything about you. Your curly hair. Your English accent. Your hands . . .'

'My . . . hands?' Emma grins.

'You have the most delicate hands.' He takes her hand in his, entwining her fingers with his own. 'I noticed them right when you moved in. They're beautiful. You move them when you talk, in this really graceful way. It's like watching ballerina hands.'

'You're weird,' sputters Emma, although she is unspeakably flattered.

'Also, your body turns me on' – he raises an eyebrow – 'big-time.' He kisses her, and she relaxes into the kiss, so relieved this is still lovely, so relieved he isn't changing his mind, hasn't woken up to what he believes is a terrible mistake.

But she's still concerned about Jesse. She pushes Dominic away reluctantly. 'Not now. Jesse's going to be back any second and I said I'd make breakfast. Is that okay?'

'It's more than okay. You're turning into quite the breakfast-maker, it seems. Lucky us. Lucky me.'

After one more lingering kiss, Emma pulls on her dress. She watches Dominic watching her every move, with a lazy smile on his face. She smiles back before going downstairs.

Once there, she moves around the kitchen, finding bowls, plates, opening the fridge for the eggs and milk. She cuts slices from a loaf of sourdough bread, puts them into the toaster; beats the eggs and seasons them; melts butter in an old cast-iron skillet she finds at the back of a cupboard – as good as new after a very good wash.

This feels nice, she thinks. Cooking breakfast for Dominic and Jesse. Jesse clearly wasn't happy with her being in his father's bed, but why would he be? He's had his father to himself for his entire life; of course he doesn't want to share him. Not that Emma is looking to share him. Good *God*! She laughs out loud at the very thought. Still, it must have been disconcerting for him, and she understands that. Luckily, it won't last, thinks Emma. Look how she and Jesse bonded over Hobbes; look how much fun they had been having together before this morning. This is a tiny blip in what is clearly a friendship. She knows Jesse likes her, she can tell. He likes the fact that she talks to him like an adult; he doesn't have to know it's only because she doesn't know how to talk to children.

Breakfast will go a long way towards healing his shock at finding her there this morning. He's a little kid, after all. A little kid who has no mother, who will surely blossom with a spot of love and nurture. Of course his father adores him, Emma has no doubt of that, but Jesse needs a woman in his life to look after him, and right now, even if it's only temporary – God, why is she even thinking like this? – she can give him some of that maternal warmth. She will start by making him the most delicious eggs he has ever tasted.

Emma sets the table properly. She goes into the front garden and snips off five blue hydrangeas, setting them in water in a mason jar that she puts in the centre of the table. She lays the knives and forks at each place setting, with glasses of juice, the coffeepot in the middle on a coaster.

She places the toast on a napkin-covered plate, standing the slices up, as if they are in a hotel dining room. She finds grape jam in the fridge, and scoops some into a small ramekin, placing it on a small plate with a teaspoon.

She has no idea why she feels the need to create a scene of domestic bliss, only that she wants them both to sit down to something that is both delicious and beautiful. She wants this to feel special.

'Breakfast!' she calls, and hears Dominic clump down the stairs. Her stomach lurches as he walks in wearing boxer shorts and a navy T-shirt that rides up as he stretches. *You are gorgeous*, she thinks, gazing at him for a moment, savouring a feeling she now knows for certain she has never felt in quite this way before.

'I know what I want for breakfast.' Dominic comes up behind her, murmurs into her neck, sliding his hands around her waist. Then the back door opens, forcing them to jump apart as if shocked.

'Breakfast!' Emma says to Jesse with false brightness. 'Come and sit down!'

'I don't like these eggs.' Jesse sits, sinking his head in his hand as he stabs at the eggs with his fork, a scowl on his face.

'These are scrambled eggs, English style,' says Emma. 'They're creamy and delicious. I promise you'll like them.'

'They're really good,' says Dominic, scooping some into his mouth, then turning to Emma. 'Wow. These actually *are* really good. What did you do?'

'The secret is lots of butter, and very slow stirring over low heat so they cook slowly. It makes the eggs creamy rather than rubbery.'

'Jesse, you'll really like them,' says Dominic. 'Come on. Try some.'

Jesse reluctantly lifts a forkful to his mouth, grimacing as he chews, before jumping up and spitting them in the sink.

'Jesse!' says Dominic, with a laugh. 'That's not very nice.'

'They're gross!' says Jesse. 'Slimy and disgusting.'

'Come on, buddy. Sit down. You don't have to eat them, then. Have some toast.'

Emma feels herself almost on the brink of tears but remains silent and tries to mentally talk herself out of it. *Don't be silly*, she tells herself. *He's only a child and he's punishing you for being here. Don't take it personally.*

She looks at Dominic, who is gazing at his son with unconditional love. *How can he not say something?* she thinks. *How can he laugh? Surely this is a learning oppor-tunity.*

You may not like the food, she thinks, although she doesn't even believe that, for who would not like these creamy, buttery scrambled eggs? *But even if you don't, you don't jump up from the table and make a big song and dance about spitting it out.*

You put the fork down and say, 'No, thank you. I'm not hungry.'

Dominic is encouraging this bad behaviour. Instead of showing Jesse another way to cope with his distress, he is smiling at him indulgently, which will surely give him the wrong message, make him think his behaviour is accept-able.

It's a teaching opportunity, she thinks. And she will not let it pass.

'Jesse,' she says gently, as Jesse crosses his arms in a sulk and refuses to look at her. 'It's very rude to spit food out. I just went to a lot of trouble to cook you breakfast. You didn't have to eat it, but it would have been more polite to just say you didn't want it.' He refuses to look at her. 'Jesse, my feelings are very hurt.'

He mutters something under his breath.

'What? I can't hear you.'

'I don't care!' The words burst out of his mouth. 'I don't care about you. I don't even want you here. Why are you here? Go back home! Go back to your house. We don't want you here!'

'Jesse,' Dominic finally interjects. 'That's not very nice. Say you're sorry.'

'No,' says Jesse, kicking the table leg, pushing the chair back, and running out of the room. As he heads upstairs his sobbing can be heard loud and jagged through the thin ceiling of the small house.

'I'd better go talk to him,' says Dominic. 'He'll be fine. He's never good with the idea of me having girlfriends. Wait here. I shouldn't be too long.'

But Emma doesn't want to wait. Poor Jesse, she thinks. She understands why he would not be happy about the prospect of his father having girlfriends.

Is that what she is? she wonders. A girlfriend? It is far too early to use that term. A friend who is a girl, she thinks. That's what he meant. A friend who is a girl, a friend with, obviously, benefits. *Girlfriend*, in the loosest possible sense of the word.

She washes up quickly and quietly before letting herself out the back door and returning to the safety of her own home.

Chapter 16

Later that morning, Lisa phones, her voice high with excitement. Her husband has given her the go-ahead to get the house decorated on the budget they discussed, so she'd like Emma to get started right away. Should she accompany Emma to the shops? she asks. Emma senses she is nervous about giving up control, even though she doesn't want to do the hard part.

'You can,' says Emma dubiously. 'But it can be very hard to picture how things are going to work in the room until you see them all together. But don't worry, I won't buy anything that can't be returned if you don't like it, and I can always text you photos if you'd like. You have the big pieces already, all I really need to do is accessorize.'

'Okay,' says Lisa. 'Don't worry about texting photos. I trust you. Do you think you'll be able to get it done by the end of next week?'

'It's tight, but I should be able to do it,' says Emma. 'Why don't I come over on Friday morning at nine to get the rooms set up. Does that sound okay?'

'Is there any chance you could come by on Thursday morning, instead?'

Emma realizes that she's going to need to get started right this minute. 'Sure,' she says to Lisa. 'I'll see you then.'

She starts with Pier 1, where she finds bamboo side tables that look far more expensive than they actually are. She adds three big faux orchids, knowing she will have to break the baskets they are glued into and find something else to put them in.

At the charity shop she finds two mid-century modern chairs, and a pair of white Foo dog lamps that have been sitting there for months. They are whimsical and fun, and she gets them for less than sticker price.

Just as she's leaving she finds a set of three huge black-and-white photographs, close-ups of flowers, grainy and gorgeous. The three would be perfect hung together, on the library wall.

On to HomeGoods for more lamps — she's always felt that pools of warm light do more than anything else to cosy up a space — a large sisal rug for the living room, and a grey-and-white geometric one for the library.

She picks up porcelain Buddhas and turquoise shagreen boxes. At West Elm, she buys both wooden and lacquered trays and chocolate-brown geometric poufs. At Pottery Barn, she finds more cushions, and throws, silver-rimmed candle holders, with huge three-wicked barrel candles to sit inside.

Her car is filled. She phones Lisa on the way home and asks if she can drop things off in her garage as she has no room in her house at the moment to store anything. She makes Lisa promise not to look at anything she has bought. Not yet.

But Lisa greets her as she pulls up, can't resist sneaking a peek into the bags as she helps Emma carry them inside. 'Buddhas!' she says in delight. 'I love the Buddhas. Oh, and look at those cushions! They're gorgeous.'

'I'm on the right track, then?'

'Oh please, please, can we set some of it up now? I'll help. Please?'

Emma can't say no. She's dying to see it herself. But once Lisa has helped move the furniture to put the rug down, she banishes her upstairs, making her promise not to come down until it's all done.

She works quickly. The bags are put in the hallway as she drapes the throws over the back of the sofa, and piles the cushions on top. The trays are placed on the coffee table with the shagreen boxes. She needs a few stools, she thinks to herself. Maybe in porcelain. She can order them online tomorrow.

The tables look great, and the mid-century chairs, too. They could be re-covered, Emma thinks, in a thick linen, but for now, with cushions, they are fine. She switches on the lamps, takes some books that are already shelved and stacks them horizontally, looking at them with a discerning eye. She needs more, she realizes. So much more. Now she can see the gaps. Artwork for the wall. More objects. She can hang the artwork and the curtains on Thursday. Emma casts an expert eye around the room, making notes on a pad to remind her what else to buy. Lucite chairs for the office, she thinks, writing it down. An upholstered bench in front of the fire. Tables for either side of the fireplace. She'd seen two nice demilune tables at the charity shop but hadn't thought she had a place for them. Now she realizes she does.

'I can't wait any longer.' Lisa has crept back into the room 'Emma!' she cries delightedly. 'It's *beautiful*. It looks like something out of a magazine!' She can't seem to wipe the smile off her face as she tiptoes around her own house, running her fingers along the sides of the trays, picking up the little sculptures on the bookshelves, admiring the vases. 'I can't believe how different you've made it look!'

'Just you wait,' says Emma. 'I have more plans for these rooms.'

'What do you think about more bookshelves?' Lisa pauses. 'Not just for books, but I was thinking about maybe building some shelves in this corner to display stuff. Like one of the pictures in your file – do you remember? They were dark grey and glossy and absolutely beautiful. Do you think that would work?'

Lisa is talking about the bookshelves in her own house. 'That would be stunning,' Emma says. 'I could draw something up for you to give to your carpenter.'

Lisa's face falls. 'I don't have a carpenter. Do you know anyone?'

Emma pauses. The bookshelves in her own house look beautiful, but only if you don't look too closely. Pull off her carefully nailed-on moulding and everything slants to the right. Could Dominic do a better job if she helped him? Would he do a better job with a spirit level and an assistant? She could be there to catch the mistakes. Surely this would be good for him, a job doing what he really loves to do.

'I do, actually,' says Emma. 'I can see if he's free right now to come and take a look.'

'That would be fantastic,' says Lisa. 'I am so glad I found you, Emma. This is going to be great!'

Emma stands back as Dominic measures the wall, asking Lisa a series of very professional questions. Emma is quiet. It's probably not a great idea for Lisa to know she and Dominic have anything other than a professional relationship.

'Emma? Can you just show Dominic the picture in your file? I want shelves just like that.'

'Absolutely.' She turns to Dominic. 'I can get those to you as soon as I get home,' she says, and the twinkle in his eye brings a flashback of him moving inside her, smiling down at her, and for a second she loses her words. When she shakes her head to dislodge the thought, he is hiding a grin.

'Are you okay?' he says.

'I'm so sorry. I just got lost in thought for a second.'

'Creative types!' laughs Lisa, seemingly oblivious to the sexual energy raging between them. 'If Emma gets you the picture today, do you think you could start immediately? How long would it take?'

'I could get you something by next Friday.'

'Can you make it next Thursday?'

'That's tight. I don't know.'

Lisa lowers her eyes, looks up at him through her eyelashes. 'Pretty please?' she asks in a little-girl voice, and Emma suppresses a laugh.

Dominic sighs. 'Seeing as you asked so nicely. Let me give you a price when I get home and figure out the cost of the materials and labour, and if it's good with you, I'll get going immediately. I should be able to have the shelves done in time. Like I said, it's tight, but I think I can do it.'

'Thank you so much.' Lisa's voice is almost back to normal. 'Let me show you out.'

As soon as the door closes behind Dominic, Lisa whirls back into the room with her hand on her heart. 'Oh my God!' Lisa exclaims. 'He's completely gorgeous. You didn't tell me your carpenter was so hot. He was so handsome I could hardly look at him.'

'Really?' Emma wrinkles her nose. 'I guess I don't really see it. You think he's handsome?'

'And tall. And sweet. *God!* It's a good thing I'm happily married or I'd be extremely tempted right about now.' She peers at Emma. 'Do you really not think he's *adorable*?'

Emma sighs. 'Okay. Yes. I do think he's very handsome. But I can't let that get in the way of us working together.'

'How do you know him?'

Emma thinks for a second, her mind trying to come up with a plausible explanation, but it doesn't feel right to lie to a client. She can tell the truth, just not, perhaps, the whole truth.

'I rent one of his cottages,' she says. 'He actually built those shelves in the picture you're talking about.'

'Why didn't you say anything?'

'I didn't want you to think I was recommending a friend. If you want him to build them, I'm sure he has the time, and I can oversee them to make sure they're perfect.'

'I'll oversee him anytime you want,' says Lisa, and they both laugh. 'Are you married?' she then asks, out of the blue. Emma blushes and shakes her head.

'Is he?'

'I know where you're going with this,' warns Emma with a laugh.

'Seriously? Why not! If I were single and he was my landlord he could *fix my shelves* anytime he wanted.'

'I don't know that we're terribly well matched,' says Emma, aware suddenly of her well-spoken British accent. 'And I'm not looking for anything at the moment.' Which had been true, up until the moment Dominic kissed her. But certainly her first client wasn't the person she should be making any confessions to.

'The best things in life always find us when we're not looking for them,' says Lisa, now serious. 'Okay, I'll stop. But the two of you look good together. I could see it. And *I* would.' She smiles. 'If I were you.'

Chapter 17

By late that afternoon, she's back home. Everything she needs is at her fingertips. Emma sits at the computer, Hobbes on her lap, losing herself completely as she trawls websites, changes search terms, and zeroes in on all the accessories she needs to complete Lisa's house.

Just past six she hears the cat flap open, and seconds later Jesse is in her doorway. By the smile on his face, it looks as if he's got over his morning tantrum.

'Hey, Jesse.' She pretends the last thing she heard him say about her was not that he wanted nothing to do with her.

'Hi,' he says. 'Have you seen Hobbes?'

'She's right here.' Emma slides her chair back, gesturing to her lap. Jesse comes over and pets the cat. 'Want to take her? Maybe the two of you can cuddle up on the sofa. I can put a movie on if you like.'

'Sure,' Jesse says. She notices now that he's carefully keeping his gaze on the kitten, and doing his best not to look at her at all.

She hands him Hobbes, gets up, and puts a movie on,

grabbing a packet of M&Ms from the kitchen and pouring them into a bowl.

'Ssssh,' she says, putting the bowl on the table in front of the sofa. 'Don't tell your dad.' She turns to go back into her office when Jesse speaks.

'I'm really sorry, Emma,' he says. 'For what I said. I didn't mean it.'

Relieved, and moved, she turns carefully and sits next to him on the sofa. 'That's okay, sweetie. I'm sorry I upset you.'

They look at each other and Jesse nods, then giggles as Hobbes inches her way up his chest and starts to suck on his earlobe. Emma stands up, makes her way into the bath-room to wipe away her tears. It seems like everything is going to be all right.

A knock on her door brings her out of the bathroom, and she opens it, unsurprised to see Dominic standing on the doorstep.

'Hi, you.' He leans forward to kiss her, but Emma turns it into a quick peck, whispering that Jesse is there. She doesn't want to upset the apple cart again.

'I wondered where he'd gotten to,' says Dominic. 'He can't see us. Give me a proper kiss. I deserve one after you were all weird with me this afternoon.'

'I wasn't weird. I was being professional. I didn't want Lisa to suspect my reasons for recommending you.' Dom-inic pulls her close as she loops her arms around his neck. 'She thinks we look good together,' says Emma when she pulls away.

'I knew I liked her.' He lets her go and walks across the threshold, entering the cottage and heading over to where Jesse is lying on the sofa.

'Hey, buddy. I'm going to run out and get burgers and corn for dinner.' He turns to Emma. 'Want to join us? I'm just throwing stuff on the grill.'

'Really?' says Emma, who hadn't much thought about dinner. She wasn't terribly hungry but presumed she would do what she had been doing almost every night and just throw together a salad from whatever she had in her fridge.

'Sure. If I buy salad stuff can you make it? Is it okay if I leave Jesse with you while I run up to the grocery store?'

'Salad stuff I have. And yes, of course Jesse is fine to stay here.'

Dominic drops his voice. 'Is he, though?'

'After this morning?' She drops her voice, checking that Jesse is glued to the TV. 'He apologized.'

'Good.' He rolls his eyes. 'Children.' And off he goes.

When he gets back, they all gather at Dominic's house. Emma is careful not to touch Dominic all evening in front of Jesse. Every now and then Dominic will take her hand, or reach over for a kiss, but she doesn't want to upset Jesse, doesn't want to do anything that might disturb the détente they seem to have reached. She's still not sure she understands it, neither why Jesse got quite so upset nor why Dominic seems completely unaware that this might be an issue.

Dominic grills outside while Emma shucks the corn and gets a big pot of water to boil. She sets the table, getting a reluctant Jesse to help, while Dominic brings in a platter of food.

They crack open beers, even though Emma would normally drink wine. This year, in this house, in this town, with this man, an ice-cold bottle of beer has become summer personified. Everything about the evening is perfect.

Jesse is quiet but sweet. Towards the end of the evening, fireflies glimmer on and off in the darkening yard. When Jesse starts yawning, Dominic says it's time for bed.

Jesse starts whining that he wants to stay up, that he never goes to bed this early.

'You know what?' Emma says, when twenty minutes have passed and Dominic has clearly forgotten that he was supposed to be sending Jesse to bed, even though Jesse can barely keep his eyes open. 'How about Hobbes has a sleepover with you tonight?'

Jesse's face lights up. 'In my room?'

'Sure. If your dad says yes.' She looks at Dominic, who laughs, raising his hands, knowing he now doesn't have a hope in hell of saying anything *other* than yes.

'Why doesn't your dad take you up to bed while I go and get Hobbes. I can bring him in as soon as you've brushed your teeth.'

'Do I have to brush my teeth?' Jesse says – but not to his dad, to Emma.

'Absolutely you do. Unless you want them all to fall out. Go on, go up now, and by the time you're done, Hobbes will be curled up on your pillow.'

Dominic shoots her a grateful smile as he heads upstairs with his son. Emma watches them before heading next door to get Hobbes. *They need a woman*, she thinks. *The pair of them need someone like me.*

When Dominic comes back downstairs, he stands behind Emma at the sink and slips his arms around her waist. It is weird, she realizes, that it is *not* weird. There is no dancing around each other, trying to figure out what the other is thinking or feeling; there is no awkwardness, no trying to take it slow, no slight discomfort that exists at the beginning of a new relationship. How weird it is that they moved past that so quickly and completely.

Dominic seems quite unlike any man she has ever met, perhaps because he is not playing games. He seems completely open about how he feels about Emma, and doesn't particularly want to hide it from anyone. Even his own son. Emma has spent a large part of the evening attempting to fob off his amorous advances – because of Jesse, not because she wasn't ready and willing to receive them.

'Poor little guy,' Dominic says as he nuzzles into her neck. 'He's exhausted. No idea why. All that running around at camp, probably. Thank you for bringing the kitten. I honestly don't know how I would have got him into bed otherwise.'

'It's a pleasure.'

'You even got him to brush his teeth. I should be giving you a medal.'

'I'm just relieved he's feeling better. That whole tantrum earlier really upset me.'

'I know. I'm sorry. And I'm sorry we haven't had a chance to talk about it properly. If it makes you feel better, this time he's prepared.'

Emma frowns. 'What do you mean?'

'I told him you might sleep over again, that adults are allowed to have sleepovers, too, and that you are a special friend. I told him I really like you, and I want him to really like you, too. I also said that he and I would always be a team, and that no one would ever get in the way of that.'

'And you think he's okay with that?' Emma can't wipe the smile off her face. He wants her to sleep over again! All of it said so easily, so simply. She doesn't know what to do with the feeling that gives her.

Other than enjoy it.

'I don't ever want you to think this relationship is only about sex,' says Dominic, sliding his hands around to cup her breasts. 'But the sex was so damn good last night, do you think it would be terrible if I picked you up and carried you upstairs to bed so we could do it again?'

'Yes!' Emma is horrified. 'You can't pick me up! I'm way heavier than you thi—' She can't get any more out before Dominic has swept her up, not in a romance-novel kind of way, but hoisted over his shoulder. She yelps with laughter before remembering that they are both trying to get Jesse to fall asleep, so instead she thumps his back all the way up the stairs.

Is it possible, she thinks, lying in the dark, just able to see the outline of Dominic's body as he gently snores, *is it possible for something to get so very much better in twenty-four hours?*

And is it possible, she thinks, reaching out and stroking his arm over the sheet, feeling its contours, *to feel so strongly about someone I barely know? Someone I would never choose for myself? Someone I never would have thought would fit into my life or my world, at least not the life that's always been expected of me.*

There is something about Dominic. About all of this, that feels . . . right. From the moment he first put his hand on the small of her back, entirely innocently, a gentlemanly gesture to guide her through the garden gate, she felt she had come home.

What was it Lisa had said earlier today? That the best things in life always find us when we're not looking for them?

Now, more than ever, she knows that to be true. She barely even knows Dominic, but feels, for the first time, that she has found everything she has been looking for; this is where she fits in; this is where she belongs.

Chapter 18

Dominic suggests the diner for breakfast the next morning, and Emma is relieved. She realizes she's been vaguely worried about confronting another scene with Jesse like the one at breakfast the day before. Although it is only a blip in a catalogue of lovely times together, she doesn't want to upset him again, and perhaps sitting together in a restaurant will make that less likely.

She gets dressed and goes to wash her face in the bathroom, where she finds Hobbes curled up fast asleep on the bath mat. Picking her up, she tiptoes downstairs and goes back home to brush her teeth and jump in the shower before meeting Dominic and Jesse outside by the truck.

It all feels so curious, she thinks, bouncing in the passenger seat of the truck as Dominic and Jesse loudly sing along to Neil Young, that this should feel so much like a family. Perhaps this is how every woman feels, dating a man with children. Perhaps this is how every woman feels when she has found what she didn't even know she was looking for. Emma should recognize family, for she was loved by her parents, but she didn't feel like she belonged, didn't feel she had the right family, even though they were clearly hers.

As for dating, they are not *dating*. Not exactly. They have only been on one date, to the farm dinner, and that wasn't really official. Nor has he mentioned taking her out. She is not sure what this is, other than fantastic sex, much laughter, and sweetness.

It may not have a label, but right now it feels lovely, and that is enough.

At the diner, Jesse is greeted by everyone, all of them commenting on how big he is, how grown-up. They tuck into a booth where Emma tries to order a fruit platter and rye toast, only to find Jesse insisting she needs to have pancakes instead, because the pancakes here are the best, and if she hasn't had them she is missing out.

Emma pauses. Pancakes drowning in syrup are the very last thing she wants right now, but she also wants to please Jesse, wants him to like her. If she has to eat a few pancakes to help that happen, she will sacrifice the fruit and toast.

Dominic tells stories throughout breakfast about Jesse, all of them funny, all of them delighting Jesse, though he has clearly heard them many times before.

'Tell Emma the one about my head splitting open like a watermelon!' He bounces excitedly on the banquette seat. 'And the time you forgot me in the restaurant! Go on! Tell her!'

'I'm not sure I should, buddy,' says Dominic. 'I don't think those stories are good for my brand.'

'Dad.' Jesse raises an eyebrow at his father, who bursts

out laughing and proceeds to fill the rest of breakfast with more stories of Jesse's childhood.

'Remember when you took the scissors out of the kitchen drawer and you decided to give yourself a haircut?' As Dominic recounts the tale, Jesse rocks back and forth with glee. He knows every word of this story but can't tear his eyes off his father, delighted at hearing his childhood over and over again.

'Oh man.' Dominic shakes his head, laughing. 'He cut huge chunks out of sections of his hair. It was terrible. He came in to show me with a big smile, thinking he'd given himself this great haircut, and he looked like he'd just stepped out of the circus ring. I had to shave it all off.'

'But you left me a Mohawk!' Jesse shouts.

'Not that time. There wasn't enough hair.'

Whatever Jesse was going through yesterday seems to be over, for the most part. He is as sweet with Emma as he was before he found her in his father's bed. When Dominic reaches for her hand as they walk out of the diner, Emma is glad to see that the flash of discomfort in Jesse's eyes passes quickly.

They drop Jesse at camp, then drive to Torno Lumber to buy materials for Lisa's shelves, before Emma goes off to buy more accessories for the house. She stops at Gold's for sandwiches for lunch, bringing them home to watch Dominic first construct the basic shelves in their backyard, leaping up from time to time to give him advice.

'I'm not sure that's completely level. It may be me, it probably is me, but can we just check it?'

They stop and check; stop and check; even when Emma is wrong, and she is wrong only once, they stop and check.

She brings her laptop outside, sitting under the shade of the apple tree while he saws, sands, and hammers. They stop, although only briefly, for a short but sweet lovemaking session after lunch.

One night, with a start, Emma realizes she has spent every night for the past week with Dominic. They haven't discussed it, but as each evening rolls on, they just both assume she will stay. And she has. She needs her own bed tonight, though. She has a lot to do tomorrow; they both have a lot to do, finishing up Lisa's house. And to be honest, she has to confess to herself that it will be good for her to have some space. Everything has happened so quickly, she feels a need to catch her breath, just to be sure it's all real.

After so many days away, Emma's house is a peaceful and welcome respite. But a lonely one. She pours herself a glass of wine and sits in the garden, where she immediately realizes she can hear Jesse laughing and Dominic calling him over to help with the grill, and her self-imposed exile seems ridiculous.

And yet she should have a night to herself. It can't be right to have this instant relationship in so short a time. Emma goes back inside, pours another glass of rosé, curls up on the sofa with Hobbes, and attempts to lose herself in a novel.

It doesn't work. She puts the book down every few

paragraphs and picks up her phone, checking for emails, texts, any kind of distraction.

At ten o'clock, just as she is trawling through Netflix looking for a series she hasn't yet watched, Dominic texts her.

I miss you.

I miss you, too, she types, the smile wide on her face.

I'm going to bed now, he types. **I wanted to say good night.**

Good night, she types. **Sleep well.**

He sends an emoji kiss, and nothing else.

There is a part of her that had hoped he would suggest her coming over. She would have gone, even though she knows she needs the night alone. The relationships that burn brightest and fastest burn out the quickest, she reminds herself. She has learned this the hard way, with exciting friendships that failed.

A couple of years ago, at a party on the Upper West Side of Manhattan, Emma had watched as a very tall, rather stunning girl stalked in. She looked like a model, angular and chic, but it turned out she was actually a chef in a wonderful restaurant Emma had recently visited. The two of them spent the whole night chatting.

It felt immediately like they had known each other for years. It was one of those mutual girl crushes that women so often experience. They couldn't believe how much they had in common, how much they thought alike, how they were both interested in the same things, namely, interiors, food, design.

'We have to get together,' said Anna, the girl, and they arranged to meet for lunch the next day. There were many lunches, coffees, dinners, and outings over the next few months. When they met one another's mutual friends they joked that they were each other's New Best Friends. But it was true: Emma hadn't found anyone in years who seemed to connect with her in quite the way Anna did.

The two of them went on adventures together, climbing into Anna's old VW Beetle convertible and driving out to fantastic farmers' markets in upstate New York, staying with friends of hers in Millbrook. Anna almost immediately became the best friend Emma had always wanted.

If she had been honest, she would have had to admit she didn't love Anna's friends. She found them pretentious and rather full of themselves. One of them, Albert, was the king of the malaprop. Emma would listen to him denigrate a fellow artist, using incorrect words in incorrect ways, and she would smile to herself as she sat there saying nothing.

She and Anna spent almost every weekend together, would text each other throughout the week and talk several times each night on the phone. Until, one day, Emma's text wasn't returned for a few hours. Anna eventually responded with an emoji unhappy face. She was sorry, she'd said; she'd been really busy.

Emma suggested coffee a few days later. Anna wrote back saying she had to work. She included a kissing emoji this time, as if that would make Emma feel loved.

Emma quickly discovered she felt like she was in a

romantic relationship and the other person was backing off. She had no idea what she had done. They had become instant best friends, until the day they weren't.

She decided not to pursue Anna, certain that the friendship would get back on track as soon as her friend wasn't so busy. It was simply work-related, she told herself. This probably happened to Anna sometimes, and she just hadn't known her long enough to experience it before. So she waited, patiently . . .

Anna never contacted her again.

They ran into each other a few months later in a restaurant. She saw Anna, head close together with a girl Emma didn't recognize, two good-looking men sitting opposite them. And that was when she knew she had been replaced with another instant best friend.

It hurt tremendously. Emma wasn't used to being dumped. But she also had to admit the warning signs had been there, she had just failed to recognize them. Anna had regularly dismissed women she knew as being too high-maintenance, too bitchy, too needy. They had been friends, Anna had said about one or another woman she knew, until she realized they were awful. Emma lost count of the number of times she heard this. She thought that would never happen to her; she thought their friendship had been different.

She crafted texts many, many times. *If I did anything to upset you,* she wrote to Anna, *I would love to know; I'm so sorry if I said anything to offend you; I would never knowingly have done anything to jeopardize our friendship.* But she never sent them. She deleted the number, which she had never known by heart, then blocked it. One night a few months after the previous encounter, she saw Anna again, this time sitting with another new friend at a different restaurant. This time, she went over, despite the pounding of her heart, and with a big smile, tapped Anna on the shoulder. She was friendly but slightly disinterested, cool but polite.

'Anna.' She bent down to kiss her. 'What a nice surprise to see you here. I saw the review in the *Times* the other week. Congratulations.' She turned then and nodded to the other people around the table, now watching her curiously. Turning back to Anna, she said, 'You look wonderful. So good to see you. Have a great evening,' and with a wave she turned on her heel and walked out. She had known Anna would never realize how upset Emma had been when she disappeared, nor how discombobulating it was to see her now. But most of all, she had realized that Anna would never know how un-Emma it was for her to behave in the way she had just behaved, affecting an air of gracious disinterest. Because as close as she had thought she and Anna had been, she now knew they had really not known each other at all.

Emma was, at least, able to let go after that. She no longer worried about what she might have done to push Anna away. She had no idea whether Anna had tried to call after that chance meeting, thanks to blocking her number, but sometimes she liked to think she would have tried.

It had been just like a romance. The intensity, the delight at finding someone with so many shared interests, the way the mutual attraction had fizzled out. Emma hadn't been needy, or high-maintenance, or bitchy, but Anna was someone who moved through people, who gathered them easily because of her beauty and charisma, and discarded them just as easily and quickly. Perhaps it was from boredom, perhaps it was just because she was careless of any feelings but her own. All Emma was certain of was that she wouldn't jump into any friendships, or relationships, that quickly again.

However, here she is sleeping over every night with Dominic, for all intents and purposes, rushing things in a way that is bound to end badly. Yet there isn't the buzz of nervous excitement she has had before at the beginning of relationships. There is, instead, huge passion. But the relationship doesn't feel dangerous. She doesn't feel that she and Dominic are anxious about having found each other. If anything, their connection to each other feels calm, and safe, and – she doesn't even really want to think this it's so unlikely – *right*.

Nevertheless, she believes she needs this night off. She is glad she is in her crisp, cool sheets, glad that she can stretch a leg out to the other side of the bed when her own side gets too hot. She is glad that when she finds herself awake at two a.m., she can turn the light on and get back to sleep by reading, without worrying about waking anyone else up.

And at that early hour, before she has a chance to become

absorbed in the book, she can lie in bed and think about all that has changed over the last week; the loveliness of not being alone, the fun it has been to get to know Jesse, to find herself cooking dinner for someone other than herself, to feel part of a family that is, this time, the right family for her.

Emma is awakened by the telephone. Sure it is Dominic, she is surprised to see *Unknown* on the screen. It's either withheld or overseas.

'Hello, darling,' peals her mother's voice. 'We haven't spoken for a while so I thought I'd check that you were still alive.'

'I'm very much alive,' says Emma, getting out of bed and padding to the kitchen to get some coffee on. 'Alive and busy.'

'Busy? Did you get another job? Oh, I'm so pleased, darling. Daddy and I have been worried about you, out in the country all by yourself with no one you know.'

'I told you, it isn't the country. It's the *suburbs*, which is a different thing entirely. I'm surrounded by people, and I got my first decorating job last week.' Of course, Emma knows her mother will refuse to acknowledge the word *suburb*, having spent her entire life attempting to erase her roots. She ignores Emma's mention of the word.

'Darling, that's wonderful!' she says. 'Who is the job for?'

Emma smiles at her mother's question. What difference does it make who the job is for? It's not like her mother would know anyone in Westport. 'It's for a woman my age who doesn't know how to decorate her house. I'm just doing two rooms, for now, but it's a start. She's thrilled.'

'I'm so pleased for you. But I also called because I do want to make sure you've booked your flight for Cousin George's engagement. Remember? I'm throwing the party here at home?'

Oh, God. How had this so completely slipped her mind? 'I'm so sorry, Mum, completely forgot. Give me the dates again and I'll see if I can work it out. It may be difficult, though,' she lies. 'I have a few more clients I'm meeting with, so it really depends on the work situation.'

Her mother gives her the dates, as Emma's heart sinks, picturing a party at which she will know no one other than family members she hasn't seen in years. She realizes she will probably have nothing in common with any of them any more, if indeed she ever did. And with that thought, she can't help thinking about how comfortable she has felt with Dominic and Jesse.

'Mummy?' She resorts to 'Mummy' only when she wants something, but a thought has just occurred to her. 'Would it be okay if I maybe brought someone with me?'

Her mother is instantly suspicious. 'What sort of someone?'

'My landlord, actually. He's terribly nice, and he's never been to England, but I'm sure he'd love to go. I have no idea whether he would come. It probably wouldn't work, but if he could, would that be okay?'

'Your landlord?' Her mother is shocked. 'Darling, why

on earth would you offer to bring your landlord to a family party in England? I know you're trying to prove you're a good tenant, but isn't this a bit *too too*?'

'We're sort of seeing each other,' says Emma, reluctantly, for she really doesn't want her mother knowing anything about her life.

'Emma!' booms her mother in surprise. 'Why didn't you say that in the beginning? Now I understand! But, darling, I'm not sure that a family party is the best place for him to meet everyone. And you haven't been living there very long. Isn't it a bit early to be thinking about bringing him to England to meet your family? I don't know, Emma. I'm not sure this would be the right time.'

Emma says nothing. If Dominic can't go, she won't go either. If anything, it makes the decision easier.

Later that day, on the way to Lisa's, Emma mentions to Dominic that her mother has phoned. Emma's thinking about going to England, she tells him. Has he ever been?

'I've never left the country,' he says. 'I don't even have a passport.'

'How can you not have a passport?' Emma, who has had a passport as far back as she can remember, is aghast.

'Why would I need a passport when I've never left the United States? My driver's licence is my ID.'

'But what if you suddenly decided to hop over to, I don't know, Mexico, or the Caribbean for the weekend?'

Dominic turns and looks at her, shaking his head with a laugh. 'Do you know me? Do I look like someone who would decide to hop over to the Caribbean for the weekend? Rhode Island? Yes. New Jersey? Yes. I've even been to Maine for the weekend, which I won't be doing again in a hurry because it was so far away. But the Caribbean? Never.'

'I'm so sorry,' says Emma. When she was growing up on the relatively tiny island of Britain, everyone she had ever met had a passport. It was so cheap and easy to hop on a ferry or a plane and go on holiday. The English lived for their holidays. Who wouldn't have a passport over there?

Of course someone like Dominic has never left the United States. Why would he need to? she thinks. America is so vast, you could spend your life picking different places to visit on holiday every year and you'd still never get to see the whole country.

'I'm an idiot,' she says. 'I'm sounding like a snob. It's just that in England almost everyone has a passport. Maybe you should get one? Maybe' – she takes a breath, hardly believing she's saying this – 'we could all go away some-where for a holiday sometime?'

'You're right. I should definitely have a passport,' says Dominic. 'Now that I have myself an English girlfriend. She's positively spiffing,' he continues, in a really bad Eng-lish accent as Emma groans.

'Please don't do that,' she says. 'That's the most horrible English accent I've ever heard.'

'Toodles. Pip pip!' he says, as Emma shakes her head.

'No one in England ever says that,' she says. 'Seriously.

Please stop. It's very difficult for me to continue being attracted to a man who sounds worse than Dick Van Dyke in *Mary Poppins*.'

Dominic's face falls. 'Really? I'm that bad?'

'Oh, Dominic,' she says with a sweet smile. 'You are so very much worse.'

The shelves go up at Lisa's, and they are beautiful. More than beautiful; they are perfect. Dominic has done a great job.

Emma is slightly surprised, but relieved and delighted. She works right alongside him, priming, applying the first coat of paint. Tomorrow he will come back by himself to sand, and apply the second coat. Saturday will see the third coat, so Emma will be able to finish the room on Wednesday, by which time most, if not all, of the furniture she has ordered will have arrived.

'We make a good team,' says Dominic, looking over at where she is painting. 'I like this. You and I.'

Emma smiles. She is liking it, too.

Chapter 19

The weeks sail by, filled with ease, and fun, and a peace that Emma has never known before. One Saturday afternoon, after Dominic and Emma have spent the morning finally creating the garden Emma has long dreamed about, Dominic announces that AJ and Deb are coming for dinner that night. Does Emma have anyone she wants to ask? It might be fun to turn it into a small party.

She will invite Sophie and Rob, not knowing anyone else to ask. She worries, for a brief moment, that her friends might not have anything in common with Dominic's, but she pushes the thought away. This week has been so busy, finishing the decorating for Lisa, that she hasn't even had a chance to speak to Sophie. It will be nice for them to meet Dominic properly.

He is insisting on grilling his usual burgers, but Emma persuades him to try something a little different. 'Not steak,' she groans, after his first suggestion. 'How about tuna?'

Dominic grimaces. 'Do we have to have fish?'

'Who doesn't like fish? Okay, I can see that you don't particularly like fish, but I do. Most people do. I'll do a simple pasta with pesto to go along with it. I promise that everyone will love it. Maybe I'll do a shrimp ceviche to serve beforehand . . .'

'Why are you getting so fancy?' He peers at her. 'Are your friends fancy?'

Emma laughs. 'No, my friends are not fancy, but I want to do something nice. Let's do burgers with sourdough rolls, tuna and pesto, ceviche, and a tomato, mozzarella, and prosciutto salad. How's that? Unfancy enough for you?'

'I like the pro-zhiutt,' says Dominic.

Emma stares at him. 'Pros*ciutto*?' she says.

'That's not how you pronounce it,' says Dominic earnestly. 'In Italy, they never pronounce the *O*. It's pronounced *proZHOOT*, *mohʒaRELL*, *riCOTT*.'

'I'm sure that's not right,' says Emma, who has been to Italy many times and has never heard anyone there ask her if she wanted some *proZHOOT* or *mohʒaRELL*. 'Maybe it's an American thing?' she says, finally, to appease him.

'Nah,' says Dominic happily. 'It's Italian. I can get the best *proZHOOT* ever. Want me to do the shopping? I can pick it up now if you want.'

'That would be great,' says Emma, giving up on pronunciation. 'Do we have enough to drink? Shall I stop at the liquor shop?'

'Sounds good to me. Can you drop Jesse off at the School of Rock for his guitar lesson?'

'Sure,' she says, but a slight feeling of dread settles on her. Despite the admittedly nice moments they've shared, she and Jesse have not yet quite found their groove again. At first, after that awful morning, she'd thought he'd settled down. But in the past week or so, he has not been the sweet little boy he was before he realized that she and his father were more than just friends. Emma has noticed him becoming increasingly suspicious, and cool. She tries to convince herself that with time she can win him over for good, but she can't help feeling a little apprehensive. He loved her before, of course he will love her again, right? Still, the prospect of spending time with him on her own makes her nervous. What if he doesn't talk to her?

In the car on the way to his guitar lesson, her fears are realized. Jesse is silent, speaking only when necessary, and then in monosyllables.

'What songs are you learning at the School of Rock?' Emma turns her head to glance at him in the backseat, in a bid to engage him.

Jesse shrugs. 'Don't know.'

'Is it rock? Stuff I would know?'

'No.' He refuses to look at her. After a while she gives up, reaching forward to turn on the radio, softly singing along until they reach their destination. As soon as they do, Jesse jumps out of the car without saying goodbye, leaving Emma both upset and angry.

How is a six-year-old allowed to behave like this? she wonders. Then she berates herself for not following him and forcing him to say goodbye. But she wouldn't have done that, she thinks. Couldn't have done that, lest it bring on another meltdown.

It's not good for a small child to have this much power, she thinks, aware that her mood has been brought down, that she is now obsessing about making Jesse happy.

She wishes she knew how.

That evening, setting up for the dinner she and Dominic have planned, Emma tries to settle the butterflies in her stomach. Will her friends like him? Will he like them? Why does she care so much?

'You look amazing,' Sophie whispers in her ear as they hug on the doorstep, having merely texted for days. 'Oh my God, are you totally in love?'

'Stop,' says Emma, kissing Rob hello, then squealing in delight as she sees Sophie's mother, Teddy, emerging from the car with Jackson.

'Teddy, I haven't seen you in ages!'

'Is it okay to bring her?' says Sophie. 'I knew we should have asked, but I totally forgot to text you and I know you love my mom.'

'I'm thrilled,' says Emma, giving Teddy a big hug. 'How are you?'

'All the better for seeing you,' says Teddy, as Jackson pulls on her long white braid. 'Ouch. Jackson, sweetie. Be gentle with your old grandma.'

'You're hardly old,' says Emma. 'You're the youngest fifty-something I know.'

Teddy breaks into a big grin and leans forward to plant a kiss on Emma's cheek. 'Fifty-something! I knew there was a reason I loved you.'

'Come and meet the others,' says Emma. 'Let me get you all drinks.'

'This looks fantastic.' Sophie bypasses Emma's ceviche to lift the aluminium foil off a catering pan revealing a huge chicken parm, smothered in tomato sauce and dripping with cheese.

'Oh my God,' swoons Sophie, picking a piece of cheese off the side. 'Did you make this? This tastes incredible.'

'I did not,' says Emma. 'I made all the other stuff, which Dominic said was far too healthy for his friends, so he insisted on making chicken parm. Please tell me you'll eat my ceviche?'

'He made this? All by himself?'

'He's an amazing chef, especially when it comes to Italian food, and all of it is insanely fattening, which means I'm going to weigh three hundred pounds by the end of the summer.' She casts a look at the pan. 'It may be worth it, though.'

'I'll say it is.' Sophie is almost drooling. 'He cooks, too? Is he the perfect man?'

Teddy joins them, putting Jackson down and peering out the kitchen window. 'Where is this perfect man of yours? Is he the rather macho bearded one by the grill?'

'No, that's his friend AJ.'

'Of course it is. He's the handsome one by the table, then.'

'Yes. That's Dominic. I'm not sure he's *my man* yet, though. Not really.' Emma attempts a laugh.

Sophie shoots her a sceptical look. 'You're completely

starry-eyed and you've been sleeping at his house every night. I'd say that pretty much makes it official.'

'Sophie!' Emma blushes. 'I just – ' She lowers her voice. 'His son doesn't seem completely happy about us being together, so I'm trying to be discreet about it. I don't want to rock the boat. I figure if we take it slowly, he'll have time to get used to it.'

'I thought Jesse adored you?'

'Well, he's gone back and forth. We got along great at first, but not any more. Now he sometimes looks at me strangely. I'm afraid he thinks I'm the devil sent to steal his father away from him. I'm trying to prove that I have no intention of getting between the two of them.'

'It'll be fine,' Sophie says, shrugging off Emma's concern. 'You're a wonderful person, and Jesse will realize you're a great addition to his family. He's incredibly lucky to have you. He should know that.'

'He's six years old. I'm not sure he's capable of recognizing any of that. But he did like me before, so hopefully he'll get over this and we'll go back to being friends.'

'You're the loveliest woman in the world. He'll get over it.' Sophie gives her a hug, and asks, 'Can I take anything outside?'

'Grab the crisps. Come and meet AJ and Deb. And, of course, Jesse.'

When they get outside, they find that Jesse is busy with Dylan, a friend who has come over for a playdate. They are grabbing handfuls of popcorn from the table before cramming them in their mouths as they race around the garden.

Emma watches, wanting to tell them to slow down, not to fill up on popcorn, to leave room for the chicken parm and for the hot dogs Dominic is grilling. But she says nothing, reminding herself she is not Jesse's mother. She's noticed more and more that he sees her efforts to guide him as telling him off, and Jesse clearly doesn't believe she has the right to do that. Emma knows she doesn't have the right to do that, either.

Perhaps, in time, she will be able to exert more influence. She can see that Dominic is an amazing father, brimming with love, attention, and appreciation for his child. But he doesn't set boundaries the way she would, rarely setting Jesse straight if he is rude or behaving badly, which is not how Emma would parent.

Even though Emma is not a parent.

Teddy sits next to her on the Adirondack chair, toasting her with a frozen margarita in a plastic cup. They sit in companionable silence for a while, watching Dominic, AJ, and Rob chatting by the grill, and Sophie and Deb animatedly discussing their shared obsession with Etsy.

'This is nice,' says Teddy, after a while. 'He is nice.' She nods her head in Dominic's direction. 'This is good for you. He's good for you.'

Emma finds herself smiling as she nods. 'Things are going well. It's early days but it feels good.'

'Early days are irrelevant,' Teddy says. 'When it's right, it's right. Do you know, when I met my husband – Sophie's father – I came home that night and told my mother I had met the man I was going to marry. He went home and said the same thing to his father. We had barely spoken, just seen each other across the room and shared one dance before the night was over, but both of us knew. Dominic may not be who you would have chosen for yourself, but here you are. It's quite clear the two of you have found something special in each other.'

Emma looks at her curiously. 'You can see that he isn't what I would have chosen for myself?'

'He's from a very different world than yours. Even I can see that. But he's a very good man. I see that, too. And he loves you.' She looks steadily at Emma. 'It would seem you love him, too.'

Emma shakes her head. 'I don't know that we're talking love yet. It's far too early.'

'It may be too early for either of you to admit it, but it's there. I am something of a witch, Emma, and I can tell you that this is the man for you. You're going to live happily ever after.' She smiles. 'The son will come around.'

'That's the challenging part,' says Emma. 'But I'm working on it.'

Teddy goes off to talk to the others, and Emma notices Jesse is still tearing around the garden with Dylan, approaching their table for his third canned soda. Really, Emma's not surprised that he's acting like a crazy person, given that he's just consumed his weight in sugar. She watches him finish the drink and reach for another.

'Hey, Jesse, if you're thirsty, maybe you should have some water?'

Jesse barely pauses as he reaches for a fresh can from the galvanized bucket on the ground, and he doesn't even look at her as he swigs the beverage. He looks quite defiant, thinks Emma, who doesn't say another word.

'A Valium?' mutters Sophie, who has come up beside her and witnessed the whole exchange.

'You know what you need, Jesse?' Emma now calls out, loudly enough for Jesse to hear. 'You need a trampoline.' Jesse stops in his tracks and stares at her, his eyes widening as his mouth opens.

'I do.' He starts nodding. 'I do. I do need a trampoline.'

'I think it would be a great thing for you to get rid of some of this energy.'

'That and chucking the soda,' mutters Sophie under her breath, although Emma hears her loud and clear.

'I think we should buy you one,' says Emma. 'A late birthday gift, seeing as I didn't know you when it actually was your birthday.'

'Really?' Jesse is now hopping up and down. 'Did you ask Dad? Did Dad say yes?'

Emma looks over at Dominic, who heard her raised voice when she made the suggestion and has been watching the exchange attentively ever since. 'What do you think? Can I buy Jesse a trampoline?'

'I think that would be a great idea,' Dominic says with a smile. 'Jesse? What do you say?'

'Thank you!' shouts Jesse, running over and flinging his arms around Emma as her eyes, completely unexpectedly, fill with tears. Relieved, even thrilled, she hugs him back. It's not precisely how she would have chosen to pave the way back into his heart, even temporarily. But for now, it will do.

As the hours tick by, Emma realizes it is obvious to all that she and Dominic are a couple. Yet she also can't help but notice that Dominic has been careful not to kiss her or touch her all evening.

Perhaps he doesn't want his friends to know, she thinks, although Deb had sidled up to her earlier in the evening and whispered how thrilled she and AJ were that Emma and Dominic seemed to have such great chemistry. It is more likely, she knows, that he is being reserved for Jesse's sake. While at first he seemed oblivious to Jesse's resentment of her, they have discussed it enough since that first morning that Dominic is more sensitive to it now. Still, Emma tries not to let her imagination run riot with fantasies that his standoffishness is about something else.

Finally, towards the end of the evening, Dominic slips his arms around her waist from behind as she is talking to Sophie and Deb, and kisses her neck. She savours the feeling of his arms around her, even as she suspects this display is fuelled by alcohol.

'Now that's a bold move,' says Deb, looking from one to the other. 'We can definitely all see you've progressed from the landlord/tenant relationship now.'

'No.' Dominic shakes his head. 'I do this with all my tenants.'

'It's true,' says Emma, leaning back into his body, marvelling at how solid and safe he feels. 'It was in my lease.'

They all laugh.

'Seriously, though,' says Deb with delight. 'The two of you are a couple?'

'We're a beginning,' says Emma, and at the same time Dominic says, 'Yes, we're a couple.'

Emma pulls away and turns to look at him. 'Are we? Are we a couple?'

'Aren't we?'

'We haven't even been on a date!' she says. 'Well, except for that farm dinner – but that wasn't official because I invited you.'

'That counts!' says Dominic. 'Anyway, we've found plenty of other things to keep us busy . . .' He grins.

Sophie claps her hands over her ears. 'Too much information,' she says, before removing her hands. And then she glares at them in mock outrage. 'What do you mean, you haven't been on an official date? A real, formal "man asks a woman out" date? What have you been doing?' Then she laughs. 'No, don't answer that! You must go on a date! It's terrible that it hasn't happened.'

'It's all been a bit more organic than that,' explains Emma. 'We've just sort of fallen into a relationship. We've kind of gone beyond dating.'

'Bullshit.' Sophie turns to Dominic. 'You need to take

her out for dinner. You can drop Jesse off with us and I'll babysit him. He can even sleep over.' She winks. 'Go somewhere nice. Wednesday night?'

'Sophie!' Emma starts to laugh. 'I don't even know if I'm free on Wednesday night.'

'Trust me,' she says. 'You're free.' Then she looks at Dominic. 'You don't work at the Hen until Thursday, right?'

'Right.' Dominic grins.

'So now you both can go on your first official date. Take her somewhere you love. Don't go to a place that's trendy or cheap. You're welcome.' She turns away with a smile. 'Honey?' she calls out to Rob. 'Can you bring me another glass of wine?'

'I don't even know anywhere trendy,' Dominic says to Sophie. 'What does that even mean?'

'It means somewhere that opened up in the last year that's filled with very glamorous people who are overdressed and filled with their own fabulousness. They tend to be very loud. Don't take her anywhere like that.'

'I don't know anywhere like that.' Dominic feigns horror. 'The restaurants I go to – when I go to restaurants at all – have been here forever. They're small. And cosy.'

'Perfect. Take her somewhere like that.'

Chapter 20

Love. Does he love me? Is this the real thing? Emma moves around the kitchen, cleaning up her house before she gets ready for her date, pausing with shock and surprise.

I love him, she thinks, her breath catching in her throat before a slow smile of wonder settles on her face. *I love him.*

She couldn't tell him. Wouldn't tell him. It would be too risky, would make her too vulnerable – what if he is frightened away?

She is certain, though, as she puts the dishcloth down and moves to the bathroom, that she does love him. For a long time now, Emma realizes, she has been worried about her capacity to love. She didn't love Rufus, the only other man she was supposed to have loved. She liked him very much, to be sure, but not in the way she needed in order to marry him. And her relationships in the years since have never blossomed into anything even close to what she's experiencing now.

Emma has never quite believed that love would happen for her. It certainly happened to others, perhaps just a few lucky people, but she had thought, had always known, she wouldn't be one of them. That kind of love wasn't going to happen to her, and she had accepted it.

And yet here she is. And it does seem to have happened. It is passionate, and sweeping, and dramatic, but in the most comfortable of ways.

I know you, she thinks, from the very beginning, when she first came to see the house. *I recognize you. Here you are.*

Their relationship is ease and safety. It is quiet recognition. It is going on their first date together, after weeks of sleeping together. It is so easily starting to spend all their time together, virtually living together, so easily finding herself no longer worrying about what she looks like first thing in the morning. She makes the effort to feel beautiful now, secure in the knowledge that she doesn't need to, that he likes her whatever she looks like, even with terrible bedhead and pillow marks on her cheek.

She remembers having read something once about a psychologist who had spent years studying married couples, and who was able to predict very quickly whether newly-weds would stay together and be happy or see their unions end in divorce. His predictions were unerringly accurate.

He'd discovered that successful marriages boiled down to kindness. Not necessarily the obvious kindness, like bringing someone a cup of coffee in bed, although that was a lovely sort of gesture, and important. But what he pointed to was the kindness of attention. When one partner asked a question of the other, or asked for an opinion, or wanted to talk about a problem, in a successful relationship the other partner always stopped to offer their full attention. By doing so, they met their partner's most fundamental emotional needs.

The article had stuck with Emma. And in the weeks since she's moved in, she hasn't been able to stop thinking about it. The couples in disastrous unions, this psychologist said, were constantly in fight-or-flight mode. They were verbally or sometimes physically combative, always preparing to attack or be attacked.

Looking back, her relationship with Rufus had indeed been combative. They would verbally spar, jousting with words and sarcasm.

The relationship with Dominic is different, not just because he is from such a different world. There is true kindness in their interactions. She thinks about how even when she met him that first day, looking at the house, he had listened to everything she said, really considered her words and responded. Dominic makes time for her, listens to her, is calm, and steady, and so grounded that he makes her feel calm, and steady, and grounded, too.

So this is love, she now thinks. *I was right*. It isn't a roller coaster of emotion, but rather a feeling of a kind of calm, a peacefulness.

And there is no doubt in her mind that she has come home.

Emma blow-dries her hair, then uses a curling iron to twist it into the loose curls that Dominic loves, the loose curls that make her feel feminine and beautiful.

She left his house this morning, telling him he couldn't come over until he was ready to pick her up for their date. She wants this to be a real date. She wants to feel excited, feel the thrill of anticipation, and she wants Dominic to feel it, too.

She has no idea where they are going, but Dominic said casual. Not too casual, though, she thinks. It is August already, almost the end of summer, and the evenings are warm. Warm enough for her to wear what she has chosen to wear all summer, one of the pretty linen shifts and loose printed tea dresses that make her feel feminine and pretty.

She chooses a strappy white linen dress tonight, to show off the deep, golden tan that has developed over the summer. Suede espadrilles with a small heel, a gold shark's-tooth necklace, and a sheer grey chiffon wrap.

The lightest touch of bronzer, highlighter on her cheek-bones, gloss on her lips. They may have been together just a short while, but Dominic has seen her first thing in the morning. He knows what she looks like without all the accoutrements. She doesn't need to dress up for him, but it is nice to dress up for herself. *He loves me with or without make-up.* And then, mid-thought, she stops.

I love him, she thinks again, getting up to leave.

The bar at Tarantino's is packed. Dominic greets a dark-haired man with a bro hug, and then they are led through the bar and into the restaurant.

'I reserved the quietest table we have,' the man says, taking them to one in the window, and laughing because nowhere in the restaurant is it truly quiet. 'What can I get you to drink? Dominic, you want your Tito's martini?'

'Always,' Dominic says with a grin. 'Emma?'

'Could I have a glass of Prosecco?'

'Coming right up.'

Emma sits back and looks around at the bustling Italian restaurant. 'I love it.'

'I've been coming here forever,' says Dominic. 'Sophie told me to bring you to my favourite joint, and this is it.'

'Do you know everyone in here?' Emma laughs as people look over to catch Dominic's eye and wave.

'Pretty much. The combination of being both Italian *and* a townie. My family lived right here, in Saugatuck, for years. I went to school with pretty much all the local business owners down here. It's a tight-knit community.'

'What's Saugatuck?'

'A neighbourhood. The best neighbourhood.' He winks.

'Have you ever wanted to live anywhere else?'

'Never. This is home. I like that wherever I go, I know people. The whole town is filled with memories for me. I remember tearing around on my bike with a pack of neighbourhood kids when I was young; I like that I grew up here when there was Bill's Smoke Store, and the Remarkable Book Store, and Sally's. I don't have any wanderlust in me. I guess we're very different that way.'

'No,' says Emma. 'Obviously I left England for the United States, but honestly, I had never really felt at home there. Oh, don't get me wrong. My parents loved me. I'm much more like my dad than my mum – she doesn't understand me at all, and of course my dad was always at work while I was growing up, so I was left feeling like I must have been a changeling. Living in London wasn't much better, so I was happy for the transfer to New York. I lived in Manhattan for years, but I always knew it wasn't where I wanted to spend the rest of my life. I think I've found my place now. I'm really not sure I would ever want to go anywhere else.'

'I think we find our place when we make a decision to do what's right for us rather than always keeping everyone else happy. From everything you've told me, it sounds like you spent your whole life following someone else's plan. This sounds like the first time you've respected yourself enough to do what is right for you. And you're right, that's when we find our place.' He smiles.

Emma's heart lurches. *I love you*, she thinks, clamping her mouth shut in a tight smile to make sure the words don't escape. 'Cheers.' She raises her glass, instead, and takes a sip of her Prosecco.

'By the way,' she says, 'I forgot to tell you. I ordered the trampoline on Monday and it should be here in a couple of days. Do you think we can put it up together?'

'I wouldn't have you do it yourself. Not when we make such a great team. Listen, thank you for buying that for him. I know he's struggled with you and me a bit, but hopefully it will all get better. I hope you haven't bought the trampoline to try to make him feel better about you, because I wouldn't want that.'

'I've thought about that,' says Emma. 'I've worried

myself about whether I'm subliminally trying to bribe him, but I don't know that I am. Honestly, he's just crazy about trampolines and every time we pass those kids in the house on the corner jumping up and down, he stares with such longing, it just breaks my heart. I really want to try to do something nice for him.'

Dominic smiles. 'You're right. He has been talking about a trampoline forever, and he does stare at those kids every time we drive past. I can't believe you noticed that.'

'I can't believe you didn't buy him a trampoline earlier,' she jokes.

'I was waiting for someone else to pay for it,' he says. 'Seriously, though, thank you. This is incredibly meaning-ful to me. And Jesse. That you would notice and then do something so nice.'

'It's my pleasure,' says Emma, as Dominic reaches over and strokes her hand. 'I think he's such a great kid. This really isn't a bribe, but a part of me does hope that eventually he'll see I'm not a bad person.'

'I don't think he thinks you're a bad person at all,' says Dominic. 'You have to remember it has only ever been him and me. I've been very careful to keep any relation-ships I've had away from him. Gina never spent the night, for example. He's really had no experience of seeing me with anyone on an ongoing basis.'

'So why have you let him see *us*?' says Emma, in a tone of voice so light it doesn't give away what she is really thinking, hoping, wanting to hear.

'You know why,' says Dominic.

'I do?' Her heart skips a beat.

'Is it too early to say it?'

'Say what?' says Emma, whose voice catches in her throat.

'That . . . this. Us. Feels . . . right. It does to you, too, doesn't it? Feel right?'

'Yes.' Emma laughs to dispel her nervousness and her slight smudge of disappointment that he didn't say what she so wanted to hear. She pushes it aside.

Dominic's face is now serious. 'I mean it, Emma. I don't know what it is about you . . .'

'Is it my English accent? My excellent teeth?' She bares them. 'Is it my curls?'

Dominic laughs. 'Why, yes. It is in fact all of those things, but more than that, it just feels . . . I don't know. Different. I feel safe with you. I love . . . being with you. It's the easiest, most comfortable relationship I've ever had.'

'Is it a relationship, then?' Emma says.

'Isn't it?'

'Yes?'

'Yes!' He wipes an imaginary bead of sweat off his forehead. 'I was getting worried.'

The waiter approaches the table. 'May I tell you about today's specials?'

'Thank God!' Emma looks at him. 'Saved by the linguine.'

The waiter frowns. 'We don't have linguine today.'

Emma shakes her head with a laugh. 'Never mind. My mistake. Tell us what you do have.'

The food has been eaten, the wine has been drunk, and Emma and Dominic have not stopped talking all night. She has heard his stories. And she has shared her own.

'Did you know you liked me as soon as you met me?' she teases, late in the meal.

'Almost as soon as I met you. I didn't walk away thinking, *Wow, that tenant is super hot.*' He laughs as Emma makes a comically disappointed face, growing serious before taking her hand. 'It was more than that, Emma. I liked being with you, from that very first time. Even when you came to look at the house, I kept thinking about you. I was so worried you wouldn't take it! And after you signed the lease, I found I really looked forward to seeing you. When I'd leave my house and come out to the driveway, I would dawdle a little, hoping you'd come out and see me.'

Emma is moved by his words, surprised that his feelings mirrored her own so exactly. The feelings that well up inside her are almost more than she can deal with, an explosion of happiness deep inside her belly. She has to lighten the mood, so she laughs again and says, 'Oh God! I was doing the same thing. I'd hear your truck pull in and suddenly remember that I had to go to the mailbox.'

'Remember when you went to get the mail early one morning and I came over to talk to you? Oh my God. Your face!'

'I was devastated. It was the one time I didn't want you to see me. I'd just rolled out of bed and I looked terrible.'

'You looked adorable.' Dominic's eyes twinkle at the memory. 'I think that was the moment I really started to fall for you.'

'Have you fallen for me, then?' *I love you*, she thinks.

He smiles. 'Let's just say I like you.'

'I like you, too,' says Emma. 'I really like you. I really, really like you a lot.'

The smile leaves Dominic's face as he looks at her. 'I love you,' he says, serious now.

'Oh, thank God!' Emma bursts out, almost weeping with relief, before laughing at herself. 'I'm sorry, Dominic. I'm so relieved to hear you say it. I love *you*. I love you, too.'

Dominic leans forward and kisses her, pulling back for just a second to look at her, smiling into her eyes before kissing her again.

'I wasn't expecting this,' says Dominic. 'You. Us. All of it. I was happy to grow old with Jesse.'

'I wasn't expecting it either.' Emma laughs again, turning as they hear a burst of noise from the sidewalk outside.

They both watch a woman throw her head back with laughter as she's about to get into a large white Suburban. She looks over to the restaurant just as she gets in the car, and when Emma turns back to Dominic, the colour has drained from his face.

'Are you okay?' Emma rests her hand on Dominic's. 'What's wrong?'

'That woman.' He turns to her with an unfamiliar look in his eye, frowning. 'That was . . . Stacy.'

'Stacy?'

He's silent for a moment, looking dazed. 'Jesse's mother.'

'Oh my God.' Emma's hands fly to her mouth. 'She's in town?'

'It would seem so,' says Dominic, now distant. Cold.

'I can't believe she's here and she hasn't been in touch. How can she not want to see Jesse?'

Dominic's face hardens as he calls the waiter over. 'Can we have the cheque, please? We have to go.'

Dominic doesn't talk all the way home. His jaw is clenched and twitching with anxiety. Emma sits staring down at the dashboard, unable to look at him, wanting this journey to be over as quickly as possible.

What just happened? she thinks. He just told her he loves her. How could seeing his ex-girlfriend derail him so? He had said Stacy hadn't meant much to him, other than giving him the greatest gift in the world in Jesse. If that is true, why is he so tense, so distracted, so clearly upset?

Emma stares out the window as they drive over the bridge, not even noticing the reflection of the lights in the water. Up until ten minutes ago, her life was perfect. What the hell just happened?

Can it have changed so quickly? In seconds? Was this all a terrible mistake? She turns her head from time to time to look at Dominic. She is sure he knows she is looking at him, but instead of turning to look back, or reaching over to give her hand a reassuring squeeze, he stares stonily ahead, not saying a word.

'Is there something I can do to help?' Emma tries, halfway down Compo Road South. She wants to ask him why he's reacting so strongly, what his behaviour means, but she's frightened of the look on his face.

'I'm fine,' says Dominic, who clearly isn't fine. Emma looks at his hands on the steering wheel, wondering if she should reach over and touch him, stroke his arm, squeeze his hand. But he has an impenetrable wall around him.

'Thank you for a lovely evening,' says Emma, getting out of the truck in the driveway and hesitating. For a while now she has been going automatically to Dominic's house, brushing her teeth and washing her face in his bathroom at the top of the stairs, climbing into his bed, and falling asleep curled up in his arms.

'You're welcome,' says Dominic, distractedly.

'I think maybe I should sleep at mine tonight,' Emma says, which isn't what she wants at all. She wants him to snap out of whatever it is he's going through and put his arms around her. She wants him to apologize, tell her again that he loves her, that the words they'd said to each other at dinner and the happiness they'd found together were more important than anything Stacy might have meant to him or done to him.

But instead he says, 'Sure. That's probably a good idea.' Dominic gives her a perfunctory peck on the lips and turns to walk into his house. Clearly his mind is still elsewhere. She doubts he even realizes he is walking away from her.

Emma stands as still as a stone, feeling like her entire world has collapsed.

She makes it inside, closes the door, and locks it before she realizes there are tears staining her cheeks. She tries to steady herself. *Just give him a few minutes*, she admonishes herself. Obviously it's a big deal for him to see her; he'd told her before that he had no idea where she was living or anything. *Just give him some time*. The poor man must be traumatized. If he would let her, she would try to comfort him, reassure him.

Dominic is sure to knock on the door eventually and apologize. How is it possible that one second he is telling her he loves her, and seconds later, when he glimpses his ex, he's changed his mind? It's not possible. It must be that he is upset, and if that's the case, he will come over. He would not deliberately leave her without an explanation for this long.

Her mind starts spinning again to darker thoughts, which grow darker as the night progresses and there is no word from Dominic. No reassuring text, no quick hug to let her know that he is okay, that what they have is still real.

In the early hours she sits straight up. What if he has realized he's still in love with Jesse's mother? What other explanation could there be for his behaviour?

Emma pictures the woman she saw so briefly from inside the restaurant. It had been hard to really see what she looked like. A redhead, slim, leather trousers and some kind of brightly coloured top. Was she pretty? Hard to tell. Probably. Was she the kind of woman Emma could see Dominic with? Well, yes. She looked like all the women who hang around the bar at the Fat Hen and try to chat Dominic up. She looked like the kind of woman Emma would have imagined Dominic to be with, before she fell in love with him herself.

She is up all night, intermittently crying and feeling numb, exhaustion wreaking havoc with her emotions. She starts off concerned about Dominic, knowing he will come to talk to her, for isn't she his partner? His lover? Isn't she the woman he just tonight claimed to love?

But he doesn't come.

At four in the morning, exhausted and bewildered, she gives up trying to go to sleep and makes herself tea.

A few weeks ago, I was the most self-sufficient, independent woman in the world, she thinks. *I had everything going for me. I had left the city and found a great little house and I didn't need anyone. I had finally accepted that I was better off on my own, that I didn't really fit in with other people, and that was fine. Good, even. This is exactly the kind of heartache and misery that comes with trusting someone else, looking to someone else to make you happy. I'm a loner. I've always been a loner, and I should never have tried to be someone else. This was my mistake in thinking I could have a relationship, that a connection, love, would make me happy. See how it ended up? I should have known better than to have given this much power to another person, allowed myself to get hurt in this way.*

She replays the end of the evening over and over, as if watching the movie in her mind will somehow shed more light on the matter, offer some clarity, help her understand. The only conclusion she can draw is that Dominic has to still be in love with his ex. And she has come back. Which means Emma's relationship with Dominic is over. Which means that everything in her life has to change.

She can't stay here, in this house. She can't deal with the pain of living next door to him and seeing him every day.

At five in the morning she sits down at her desk and goes online to look at rental properties in the area. At five fifteen she stops, unable to believe she has to move again, unable to believe this is happening to her.

This is why I don't have proper relationships, she thinks. *This is why I have avoided falling for anyone all these years. This pain of ending is almost unbearable. How am I supposed to deal with it? How do I move through this and get back to being the whole person I was before I gave my heart away?*

At six, she picks up her phone and calls the very last person in the world she would normally think to call. But there is no one on this side of the Atlantic who would be awake.

Her mother picks up after two rings.

'Darling, what a lovely surprise. I was just about to leave for a tasting for the engagement. I've found the most wonderful caterer. She's doing these little crab choux pastries after I told her about the ones we had at the Connaught the other week, and the most divine mini roast beef and Yorkshire puds. I haven't got long, darling. Everything okay?'

'I'm fine,' says Emma, as her voice cracks and a sob escapes.

'Darling! Are you crying? What's happened?'

There are a few seconds of muffled silence as Emma tries to stifle her sobs. 'I'm sorry, Mummy. Just a bad day.'

'Bugger the caterers,' says her mother. 'I've got all the time in the world. Why don't you tell me what's going on?'

'I'm just having a bad day,' repeats Emma, who has never told her mother much about her personal life for fear of her mother's judgement. 'I'm really fine. It's just a mild case of the blues.'

'You know what you need?' says her mother.

'What?'

'A nice sweet cup of tea for starters,' she says. Emma manages a smile. She had forgotten how her mother believes, like most Brits, that a nice sweet cup of tea is the cure-all for anything and everything. 'And,' her mother continues, 'you need to come home and let Mummy and Daddy look after you. I know you said you probably weren't going to come to the engagement, but darling, there's nothing like being looked after at home when you're feeling down. I won't even ask you to come to the party if you don't feel like it. You can sleep in your own bedroom cuddling up with Ritalin.'

'What's Ritalin?'

'Not what. Who. It's our new cat. She's completely bonkers. We called her Mittens originally, but we quickly changed it to Ritalin. She's mad all day long, and has driven the dogs potty, but at night she's very sweet and she loves to cuddle. I'll make you lots of cups of tea and Daddy's very good at pouring generous single malts. I'll make you shepherd's pie and trifle. You'll feel better in no time. Will you come, Emma? I don't know what's going on, darling, but I do know that being at home is the very best place to be when life isn't going the way you want it to.'

'I'll think about it,' says Emma with a sniff, grateful for her mother choosing to be loving and sweet. Emma had forgotten her mother could be loving and sweet. For the first time in perhaps forever, returning to her childhood home is starting to sound appealing.

'That's what you've been saying ever since I told you about the party. Why don't you just say yes? I can also update the numbers for the caterer.'

'You're sure I don't have to be at the party if I don't feel like it?' says Emma dubiously, knowing that the last thing she will feel like doing is being paraded around in front of a group of family members she hasn't seen in years, and strangers she has no interest in meeting.

'Quite sure,' says her mother.

'Okay,' says Emma with a deep breath. 'I'll come.'

Her decision to visit England leaves her with a feeling of such relief that she decides the only way to get through the rest of the day is to get out of town. Showering quickly and dressing, she drives to the train station, averting her eyes from Tarantino's as she goes by, a swell of tears threatening to fall as she thinks about their evening last night, still unable to understand how something can change so drastically so quickly.

With a coffee-to-go cup in hand, she walks up the stairs to the platform and waits for the Metro-North into the city, no idea where she will go when she is there, knowing only that she wants to spend the entire day away from Dominic, away from Westport, away from memories that have become so painful overnight.

She puts earphones in on the train, and listens to podcasts from BBC Radio 4, all of them sweeping her back to a land she had been so determined to leave behind for the bigger, brighter lights of America, a land that now feels like the only place where she will find solace and refuge.

Even the voices are comforting. The English accents on the BBC are lulling her into a sea of daydreams. Was this a terrible mistake, moving to America? What if she packed up everything and went home? What would she do back there? Where would she live? Who would she see?

Emma has largely grown away from the friends she had when she was younger. They are Facebook friends now, which are not the same as real friendships at all. She scrolls through her news feed on a daily basis, curious to know what people are up to, what they look like, but with no desire to sit down with any of them in person.

Would she go back to London, perhaps? Brave her way through the crowds, the unfamiliar people? The last time she was there, for work, she found herself in restaurant after restaurant, café after café in the West End, surrounded by people who looked familiar, people she thought she ought to know, but didn't. It made her feel strangely displaced. In her old neighbourhood in New York City, she ran into at least three people she knew every time she left her apartment. She realized then that London wasn't home. Not any longer.

Where else in the UK might you go as a thirty-something single woman? If not London, where? Brighton? These days, it seems to have become spectacularly trendy. She doesn't know Brighton, only remembers visiting the pier with her grandparents when she was very young.

If she were to go back to England, her parents would want her back in Somerset. But could she live in the English countryside? Wouldn't she die of loneliness?

She wouldn't belong any more, she thinks. She has been away too long. Maybe, for now, as comforting as England seems, she just needs to focus on getting through the day. Maybe she shouldn't worry about the future. Maybe she should just focus on what she could do today to distract herself from thinking about last night.

At Grand Central Station, she walks around the main concourse like a tourist, head tipped back, looking – really looking – at the ceiling for the first time. She wanders through the passageway leading out to Lexington Avenue, stopping at all the stands, trying on jewellery, examining small artworks, buying a pair of delicate crystal earrings. All around her, people are rushing back and forth; she thinks how this used to be her, always rushing. She had always wanted to stop at these stands and look more closely at what they were selling, she just never had the time.

Her thoughts are all over the place . . . remembering when she used to work and had no time . . . wondering what she will do without Dominic . . . trying on earrings and thinking they would look lovely with the blue sundress, the blue sundress she wore last week when she and Dominic went to the farmers' market . . . oh, how she misses him . . . should she go to a museum? . . . Dominic . . . she's going to be a tourist for the day . . . please God let it not be over.

Tears spring in her eyes each time Dominic's name enters her head, but she refuses to give in to the deep sadness she feels, made worse by sheer exhaustion. Distraction has always been the best way Emma has known to avoid fear and sorrow, so she walks out of Grand Central and strides through the streets in no particular direction, until she finds herself outside the Guggenheim.

She enters the museum and spirals down from the top, stopping to take in the Calder mobile, the Klee paintings, the Kandinsky gallery. The art isn't soothing in the way she had hoped. Every time she stops to look at a picture, she finds her mind wandering back to the evening before.

On to Central Park – perhaps a walk will stop the thoughts crowding her mind. But the hordes of nannies and their charges only make her think of Jesse. She has grown so attached to him, despite the ups and downs of their connection. Seeing all these babies and small children only fills her with sorrow at not being able to continue to be part of his life.

She walks up Madison Avenue, window shopping. Expensive designer labels have never really been her thing. She indulged in them when she was working for the bank, only because she had to look the part, had to have the labels everyone else had. She would have been quite happy dressed head to toe from Zara, but everyone at work compared labels all the time, and the label you wore meant something.

She remembers the day just after she first moved to New York, when a female colleague complimented her on her shoes.

'Thank you,' she had said, delighted. 'They were only thirty dollars from Nine West.' She thought she was sharing her bargain of the month with a friend who would be impressed with the deal, but instead she saw a look of disdain pass over her colleague's eyes.

'Oh,' the other woman had said. 'I thought they were Lanvin.'

Emma went out the next day and bought the Lanvin pumps, an eerily close approximation of what she already owned. She bought the Hermès belts and scarves that everyone else wore, the Dior suits and dresses. She dressed in a way that was well beyond her years.

Her biggest clothing splurge was a Chanel jacket. She was accompanying a colleague to Chanel, intimidated at the quiet luxury of the shop, and at what she perceived to be the condescension of the sales assistants. Although afterwards she realized how nice they had been, that it was her own feelings of inadequacy that had made her so quick to judge them.

Her friend tried on a suit, and while Emma was waiting, she had slipped on a jacket. It was black and white, classic bouclé, with an intricate trim of beads and ruffles. It was quite beautiful, if unlike anything she would ever wear.

Two sales assistants gasped and said it was the most perfect fit they had ever seen. Emma's colleague came out and said Emma absolutely had to have it.

'I don't think I'd ever wear it,' Emma had protested.

'That's the kind of jacket you can wear to a gala, or throw over a T-shirt and jeans. Trust me. You'll live in it.'

'Okay. Sold!' Emma had laughed, until she handed over her credit card, and picked up the receipt. The jacket had cost thousands and *thousands* of dollars. She blanched as she picked up the pen to sign the receipt with a shaking hand. It had never occurred to her to ask the price of the jacket. A few hundred dollars, she had presumed, because it was Chanel. A stretch, perhaps, but one could manage it. But a few thousand? She was too embarrassed to back out.

She did wear it, once, after which it sat in her wardrobe for the next year. Eventually she sold it through a high-end charity shop, making back a fraction of what it had cost her.

The thought of wearing it now is enough to make her laugh. Thank God she is out of that world, she thinks. Thank God she doesn't have to 'label up' in order to fit in, or mask her insecurity about being perceived as *good enough*.

She walks up Madison past all of the shops she used to know so well: Chanel, Hermès, Stella McCartney, Dior. Their windows are filled with gorgeous chiffons and silks, thick cashmere sweaters for autumn, exquisite leather handbags as soft as butter. Emma couldn't care less. During these past few months in Westport she has loved pulling on a simple cotton dress, slipping on shorts and a T-shirt, living in flip-flops or sandals.

Everything about living there had been perfect, until she risked the life she was finally building for herself by getting involved with someone.

She stops at a small café, goes inside, sits down on the banquette against the wall to order an iced coffee. It is after lunch now, but she has no appetite. She hasn't eaten anything all day, but the thought of food makes her feel queasy.

She doesn't want to go home, but she needs to sleep. She supposes she could stay in a hotel for the night. She's not quite ready to hear what Dominic has to say; not quite ready for it to be over. She recognizes that part of her wanting to stay away is a hope that he will be shocked by her absence. If he thinks she has disappeared, will he reconsider whatever decision he might have made?

She feels childish thinking that way, but still, reflexively, she glances at her phone, even though she's switched it off. It would be too painful for her to check it every fifteen minutes, hoping for a call, a text.

The silence has been the most difficult thing of all.

Dominic didn't come over and apologize after their awkward goodbye. He didn't wake up in the night, missing her, sending her a text. He left her on her own, all night long.

The phone starts whispering, begging her to turn it on. She stares at the black screen, her fingers moving, darting back and forth to the on button, sheer force of willpower eventually leading her to slip it back into her bag.

'They're terrible things, those mobile phones, aren't they?' says a voice next to her. It is a voice that is instantly recognizable, a voice that belongs to a typically patrician Upper East Side Lady Who Lunches, the kind who thrived in a bygone era. Emma turns to see an elderly woman, with silver hair extravagantly coiffed and waved in a way it doubtless has been since the sixties. Her arthritic curled fingers are weighed down by heavily jewelled chunky rings that Emma feels certain are real, or at the very least copies of real ones that are stored in a safety-deposit box.

There is a small dachshund on the seat next to her, wearing a smart quilted vest. The woman is wearing a Hermès scarf around her neck, a cream suit with large gold buttons, and neon-green Nike trainers.

Emma doesn't respond to her comment about mobile phones, merely smiles and nods in a way that she hopes will convey the message that she isn't in the mood for talking. She offers a tight smile before rooting around in her handbag, wishing for a magazine or book to show she is too busy immersed in other things to talk. But there is nothing there. No book or magazine has miraculously materialized in her bag in the last three minutes.

Emma sighs, taking a sip of her coffee, resolving to drink it quickly and leave, knowing that she is about to be pulled into a conversation with a stranger when the very last thing she wants to do is talk to anyone at all.

'I can't decide which one to use,' says the woman, not taking the hint. 'My iPhone, my iPad, or my BlackBerry.'

Emma turns to look at the woman with an unwitting smile on her face. She has to be in her eighties. Emma's own mother, in her sixties, has very little idea how to use any of the new technology. In fact, her mother has only just made the transition from a flip phone because Emma's father has been complaining about how long it takes her to send a text, her fingers hovering over each number as she tries to figure it out. Emma smiles to herself now, remembering hearing from her dad that someone had downloaded Candy Crush on her mother's phone. Apparently now she's addicted, and plays it for hours every night in bed.

Her companion in the café has opened her handbag and draws out her three different devices. *Okay*, Emma thinks to herself, *I give up. I can drink an iced coffee in peace some other time.*

'That looks terribly complicated,' she says. 'Are you sure you need all of those things?'

'Not really,' the woman replies. 'The iPad is easiest for me to watch things on. I use the iPhone as my phone and calendar. But the BlackBerry is the easiest one for me to type on, and I do a lot of typing for my blog.'

Emma's smile is now genuine. 'You have a blog? That's wonderful. What do you blog about?'

'It's Confessions of an Old WASP. Or C.O.W.' She chuckles a little. 'I have quite a following, you know. Eight thousand unique hits a week.'

'That's amazing. What do you write about?'

'My life. Often I reminisce about how it was in the old days, compared to now. I write about what happens each day, the things that make me stop and think, the people I talk to.'

'Like me? Should I be worried?'

She leans forward. 'It depends on whether you reveal anything interesting or not.'

'How am I doing so far?'

'Very dull.' She smiles. 'But we've only just started. Clearly, you're not from here. I've always loved English accents. How long have you been in New York and would you ever go back home?'

'I've been here for almost five years, and I love it. I have loved it. I was here in Manhattan for most of that time but I've just moved out to the suburbs.'

'Which suburbs? Westchester?'

'No. Connecticut. Westport.'

'Why, that's lovely! I had great friends many years ago who had a wonderful house on, oh, what was it called . . . on the water. Grand mansions.'

'Beachside Avenue?'

'Yes, that was it. Delightful people. They used to have dreamy parties in the summer on their grand lawn. It was extraordinarily Great Gatsby-ish, and terribly glamorous. Goodness. I haven't thought about them for years. I think, my dear, you may have just given me my next column. Who throws parties like that any more? People should!'

'I think people probably do throw parties still, they just aren't as elegant as they used to be,' says Emma. 'I'm the wrong person to ask, though. I've only recently moved there and I hardly know anyone. The only parties I've been to are barbecues at my boyfr—' She stops. She doesn't know whether he is her boyfriend. 'My landlord's house. And they're not very glamorous.'

The woman peers at Emma. 'I'm Cece,' she says.

'Emma. It's lovely to meet you.'

'Emma. What a classic English name. Lovely. So . . . parties. Are the parties at your landlord's or your boyfriend's? I presume you started to say *boyfriend*. Or are they indeed one and the same thing?'

Emma swallows the lump that unexpectedly rises in her throat.

'Oh, my dear.' Cece sits back. 'I am so sorry. I didn't mean to say anything to upset you.'

'It's fine,' says Emma, although it clearly isn't. She blinks the tears away. 'It really is. My landlord *was* my boyfriend. At least, I thought he was, but something happened last night and it seems to be over.' She blinks again. 'I'm so sorry.' She laughs tremulously, wiping her eyes with a paper napkin. 'I didn't mean to get emotional on you.'

'Forgive me if I'm intruding with this question,' says Cece. 'But sometimes it is far easier to talk to a stranger than a friend. What happened last night? It may help to talk about it.'

So Emma does. She tells this lovely older woman about the evening, and about Dominic: how they are from such different worlds but have found something lovely and special together, something that neither one of them expected, something that has made her feel safe and happy for the first time in her life.

She tells her about wanting to say *I love you*, how Dominic finally said it last night. She describes the both of them unexpectedly seeing his ex, the mother of his child, how he reacted, how he didn't talk to her for the rest of the evening.

She tells her how she spent the night alone, expecting to hear from him, expecting him to come to her side, apologize. She is only in the city today because she can't bear to hear that their relationship is over. She knew from the way the colour drained from his face last night, from his silence afterwards, that he is still in love with Stacy. That he has always been in love with Stacy. And while she has no idea whether Stacy is back temporarily or whether she is back for good, Emma cannot settle for being second best.

When she is finished, Cece pats her hand. 'My dear,' she says. 'What a story, and what a difficult night you have had. I suspect you are exhausted. When we are tired, everything seems so very much worse. May I tell you what I think, because I do have some thoughts?'

Emma nods.

'I think the greatest gifts we can give each other in a relationship are the gifts of kindness and communication. It seems that Dominic was unkind last night not to share with you what he was thinking, but he is a man, and most men are, as we know, somewhat limited. It may be that what you saw as unkindness was merely thoughtlessness. He was clearly discombobulated at seeing the mother of his child after so many years, but it may not be, as you have assumed, that he is still in love with her. It could be any number of things that upset him, and until you ask him, you won't know.

'In my experience, it is always better to confront these things. If you were to go home and ask him to explain, I'm quite sure he would give you clarification. I don't mean to offend you, Emma. I hardly know you, but it seems to me that you have created a drama in your head that may have nothing to do with reality.'

'You don't think it's over, then?' It is the first time all day that Emma has allowed herself even a glimmer of hope.

'I don't know. But neither do you. And you won't know until you've spoken to him.'

Emma is quiet for a long time. She stares at the woman, and notices for the first time, beneath her designer labels and big jewellery, what she hadn't noticed before: a kindness in her eyes. And, more than that, she notices that the woman meets her gaze directly, that she is paying attention, seeing Emma, and listening. Emma takes a deep breath.

Perhaps she should have guessed that this woman would surprise her when she noticed the trainers on her feet. 'You're right,' says Emma. 'Thank you.' Then she hesitates. 'You're not going to write about this, are you?'

'I probably will,' says Cece. 'But not in a way in which anything about you would be recognizable. What if I were to describe you as a delightful South African lady I met downtown who had recently moved to Rye? Would that be all right with you?'

'It would be fine,' says Emma, smiling.

She leaves with Cece's business card and promises to read her blog and get in touch. Next time Emma's in the city, says Cece, she will take her out for lunch.

The simple human connection she's made with someone older and wiser has lifted her spirits. When Emma finally settles herself on the train heading back to Connecticut, she pulls out her phone and turns it back on with her heart pounding, praying for something from Dominic.

And there she finds what she's praying for.

Text after text after text. Asking where she is. Apologizing. Telling her he wants to explain. Asking her to call him as soon as she can.

Chapter 21

Dominic has not experienced serious anxiety for a very long time. The last time he found himself tensing up on a regular basis was when he was dating Stacy. She was pregnant, still drinking, not looking after herself, doing things he was convinced would hurt the baby.

He wanted to marry her back then. She was so exciting, so vibrant. They made a great-looking couple; they were such an *obvious* couple: the childhood classmates who would live happily ever after. It was hard for him to see any other outcome, any other path to walk along for the rest of his life.

And yet there was so much that wasn't working in their relationship. Her drinking, for starters. Could he really picture himself with a woman who was so careless about alcohol? If she were sober, if she could *get* sober, he knew they could make it work. If she calmed down, learned to control her explosive temper, didn't pick fights while under the influence, they could make it work.

There were at least two Stacys, he'd learned. Sober Stacy was sweet, funny, huge fun. Drunk Stacy was mean and angry and belittled him in front of anyone who would listen.

On the nights they didn't go out, she would curl into him on the sofa as they watched movies; she was playful, affectionate, and he would wrap his arms around her, imagining the family they would have. They had great conversations back then. Where would they live? Saugatuck? The beach? In their fantasy world, on Beachside Avenue. They discussed how many children they would have. (Two. A boy and a girl: Jesse and Sophia.) And what pets they would have. (A German shepherd for their son, and a cat for their daughter.) It all seemed so perfect. Too perfect to be real.

Every time Dominic relaxed, hoping this was the end of the madness, praying she wouldn't drink again, just as she had promised during those loving, sober moments, he would be disappointed.

Over time, the more frequently she drank, the nastier she became. She told him he was pointless, clumsy, and stupid. She didn't love him; he was a loser who was never going to do anything with his life. She said she hated him, she deserved better, she was only with him because she pitied him.

Dominic knew she didn't mean it, but the words hurt. The longer they were together, the more damage they did. And in time, he started to believe he was as worthless as she told him he was. All the lessons he had learned during his first bad relationship – the one in which he came close to physical violence – his decision to live mindfully, to make the right choices, went out the window.

Then Stacy got pregnant. It was an accident; she was using a sponge as contraception, and neither of them knew why or how it had failed. But it had happened, and at first it seemed to be a wake-up call for Stacy and he was convinced things would change. She cut down on her drinking, which gave him hope. But she didn't stop entirely, and before long he realized his belief that things would get better was just wishful thinking. Before too long, if anything, she became even more abusive. He had trapped her, she would insist; he was manipulative; he had somehow orchestrated the pregnancy in order to control her.

His anxiety grew throughout her pregnancy; he was so worried her behaviour was going to damage the baby. She stopped coming home entirely towards the end of it. She would tell him she was staying at Tanya's, or Lisa's, and he would call, or drop by with her pregnancy vitamins, and be told that she had just run out to get something from the gas station, or that she was staying there but hadn't arrived, or that she had decided to stay with another friend in Fairfield.

Dominic grew tired, exhausted not just by Stacy's antics but by his fears about the baby. That was all he could think about. As long as the baby was okay, nothing else mattered.

When Jesse emerged, he was perfect. His Apgar score was a perfect ten. Dominic couldn't believe not only his relief but the pure joy he felt when he first held his son in his arms.

He also assumed that having the baby would force Stacy to grow up. But she didn't care. She barely looked at Jesse when he was born. Once they got home, she went through the motions of mothering an infant, but it was obvious to everyone that she didn't bond with her baby. When Jesse woke crying in the night, it was Dominic who went to him. Always. Stacy didn't breast-feed. Dominic was the one who sterilized the bottles, warmed the formula, changed the baby, rocked him to sleep, worried when he cried.

One night, Stacy disappeared. She took everything that was hers and sneaked out in the middle of the night. No note. No explanation. Dominic didn't know whether to be devastated or relieved.

In some ways, it was easier. Having a relationship with Stacy was like having two children to take care of. He was constantly worried, angry, or scared. More than anything, he was terrified of what she might do to the baby. She had hit him only once, when drunk, but he knew it wouldn't be the last time. The thought of her raising a drunken hand to their son kept him awake at night, and he knew then he had to protect Jesse, could never leave him alone with her if she had been drinking.

When she finally left, he was relieved, although the thought of raising Jesse to adulthood as a single parent, of being the only adult in the house, was equally terrifying.

He knew then he would never live on anyone else's terms. That he would never again tolerate behaviour that was fuelled by rage, or alcohol; that he would never put his son, or himself, in that position again.

He had too much respect for himself. And he was able to make a choice. He would never make the wrong one again.

Relieved as he was that Stacy had gone, as he settled into daily life with his infant he kept thinking that she would get in touch. Jesse was her child. He could understand her walking away from *him*, but her own flesh and blood? He knew that she would have to eventually return.

But as time went on, and she didn't reappear, and he didn't hear a word from her, he began to wonder. He tried to find her, for Jesse's sake, always aware that Jesse was equal parts of both of them. That was when he discovered how completely she had vanished. Her parents didn't know where she was. Even her best friends claimed not to. He started searching on the Internet and couldn't find a trace of her anywhere. At one point, he considered hiring a private investigator to find her. But he really didn't have the money. And then he started to be honest with himself, and admit that while he felt obliged to look for her, he didn't really want to find her.

By the time Jesse was three, he started to ask about his mother. By then, he had noticed that most other kids had moms and he was the only one with a daddy and no mommy. Dominic explained that she'd had to leave, but it didn't mean she didn't love him, that one day she would be back to see the gorgeous son they had created.

As the years went by, he occasionally heard rumours that she had returned for a visit. Someone would say she had been spotted in town, or that a friend of a friend had talked to her. But he never believed that she could come back to town and not want to see her son. So it was easy for him to dismiss the rumours. The Fat Hen had been her hangout. Mario's. The Black Duck. If she was in town, surely he would have run into her somewhere.

And after all these years, finally seeing her felt as if someone had taken a knife to his heart and twisted it. How could she be back in town and have made no attempt to reconnect with her son?

And what about Emma? He knew his reaction had rattled her, knew he needed to reassure her. He also knew that if he opened his mouth to speak, all that would come out would be a howl of pain. His perfect, wondrous little boy. How could Stacy not want to see him, to know him? She doesn't know he has her crooked smile and long fingers. How could she have abandoned her son the way she has?

This morning he couldn't wait to get to Sophie's to pick Jesse up from his sleepover. He lifted him up and held him close, squeezing him hard, kissing him all over.

'Dad!' Jesse wriggled out of his clasp, insisted on being put down, immediately running off towards the car, giggling. 'Get off me.'

Dominic couldn't stop looking at him as they drove home. His beautiful boy. With a mother who didn't want anything to do with him. How could she be here and not want to see who her son had grown up to be?

And so he has spent the afternoon on the phone. He has asked everyone he can think of where Stacy is. He has settled Jesse in with a sitter and driven to the Commuter Coffee Shop, Dunville's, AJ's hardware shop, the Fat Hen to ask if anyone has seen her. He has been to the Black Duck, and finally, he goes home. He may not be able to find Stacy, but he does know where to find Emma. If nothing else, she will make him feel better. She always does. Emma, who is so good for him. So good for Jesse. So good.

He had texted her that morning, eager to explain why he'd been so preoccupied and upset, longing to make things right. He'd had a terrible night's sleep. Last night he'd gone through the box that was stored at the back of the wardrobe, the box that contained all the old photos of him and Stacy. They were both different people back then, he'd realized, as he stared at the images. Different people living a different life.

He thought he had said goodbye to Stacy long ago, but seeing her brought back memories he'd buried, and pain he hadn't felt in years. And the only person who might be able to make him feel better wasn't around. Where *was* Emma? He had gone over there this morning, but the house was empty. It was only then that he realized how his behaviour the night before must have seemed to Emma, especially right after the conversation they had just had in the restaurant before they saw Stacy out the window.

He texted her multiple times but got no response. Had he screwed things up? She couldn't have done a runner – her things were still everywhere – but why else would she have disappeared? Why else would she have ignored his texts and messages all day?

And his anxiety, the kind he hadn't felt for so many years, came roaring back. That terrible, heart-jumping, unsettled feeling, when you know that something in your life is terribly wrong, or about to go terribly wrong, and you don't know how you're going to fix it.

He loves Emma. He doesn't want to screw this up. He should have spoken to her last night; he realizes that now. But he'd been too blown away by seeing Stacy standing there in the middle of town, laughing like she hadn't a care in the world. He'd been too upset, his mind racing with everything Stacy's return could mean, his thoughts a jumble, his emotions so in turmoil he doesn't even remember the drive home from the restaurant now. He doesn't even remember the last thing he said to Emma.

But he does know Emma is the person he is supposed to be with. Not Stacy. Never Stacy. Or indeed any of the dramatic, volatile, unpredictable women he had dated before Emma.

She has brought a peace and calm to his life he hadn't known was possible. She makes him feel good. More than good, *loved*. It has taken him forty years to understand what it is to be loved. Now that he has found it, he can't lose it.

But now he can't find her.

Where *is* she? He checks his phone once again to see if she has responded to his texts, and when there is nothing there, his chest tightens; the pain only gets worse as the day goes on. He feels like he is barely able to breathe by the time he hears a car pull up next door. He jumps up and dashes out the door, certain Emma has finally returned; she would never just leave like that, never just walk out like Stacy . . . With a jolt he realizes it is not Emma's car he sees, but a white Suburban. The same white Suburban he saw last night. Outside the restaurant. His heart stops.

Stacy gets out of the car and stands beside it, looking at him with an unreadable expression on her face. Dominic just stares, not knowing what to say. He may have spent the day looking for her, but he never expected her to come looking for him.

'Hey,' she says softly, slowly approaching. 'Remember me?'

Dominic doesn't take his eyes off her until she is standing in front of him.

'You look good,' she says, with the crooked smile that is so familiar to him it is almost heartbreaking. 'It's been a while.'

'Over six years,' he says, after a pause.

'But who's counting.' Stacy seems awkward.

Dominic just looks at her.

'Can we talk?' she says.

'Sure.' He is staring at her intently now, trying to see if she will meet his gaze. 'What do you have to say?'

'Can we maybe go inside?'

Jesse is still inside with the babysitter. It's the last place Dominic wants to go.

'We can go for a walk,' he says. Stacy nods, and the two of them turn to set off towards the beach.

'I'm sorry,' Stacy begins. 'I should have said it years ago, but I didn't know how. I didn't know anything. I am sorry I abandoned both of you in the way that I did.'

Dominic spent years imagining these very words coming from her mouth, but now that he is actually hearing them, he is stunned. He doesn't feel the relief he sometimes thought he would feel; he feels . . . confused. Angry. Conflicted.

'I know it doesn't help or make it better. I was not in a good place, and it has taken me a very long time to get to a good place. I really wish I could turn back the clock, and do things differently, but . . .' She trails off. 'Dominic, I can't do anything other than apologize and try to show you that I've changed.'

Show me? he thinks. *How is she going to show me? And what makes her think I even care? Saying she's sorry doesn't change anything.* He's too pissed off to respond to her. They walk in silence until Stacy speaks again.

'What's Jesse like?' she says.

Dominic stops walking and turns to her with a spark of anger in his eyes. 'I don't know what you want me to say. You've been gone for six goddamn years and now you come back and want to know what your son is like? If you'd stuck around, you would know. If you'd made any attempt to get in touch with him in the past half dozen years, you would know.'

'I know, Dominic. That's what I'm trying to tell you. I

know you're right, and I'm sorry. I don't have an excuse. I was overwhelmed, and unprepared for motherhood. I was destroying myself with my drinking. I never intended to hurt you. I had to learn how to take care of myself.'

Dominic can't control his fury. 'You didn't hurt me,' he spits. 'I don't care any more that you left; my life is fine now. But you did hurt Jesse. And I do care about that. How could you leave your son? What kind of mother disappears and never ever gets in touch? Never even calls to see how her kid is doing? Never writes a letter, never sends a text, nothing? How dare you just show up and ask what he's like? How *dare* you?' He is shaking as he speaks, and he half expects Stacy – the Stacy he used to know – to spit her own fury right back at him, to come up with excuses, and accusations of her own. But to his shock, her face crumples as she starts to cry.

'You're right. You're right. There is nothing I can say in my defence. I didn't want to be a mother. I thought I could pretend I wasn't. I thought if I left and started a new life somewhere else, I could just forget about everything and everyone I'd left behind, including Jesse. But of course it doesn't work like that. There hasn't been a day that's gone by that I haven't thought about him. Dominic, I was drinking. I am an alcoholic. I know that now. But I am sober today, and I have been for two years. Long enough that I thought my life was getting better, that I could go on and try again. I knew you must have been disgusted with me, and wouldn't want to see me. But I had managed to find someone, and I was in a relationship that I thought was serious. I got pregnant, and at first I was so happy. I thought it was my second chance. I miscarried six months ago. Ever since then I haven't been able to stop thinking about the child I already have. I was finally able to realize what I had left behind, and I knew it was time for me to come back and get to know him.'

'So you thought you'd just come back and pick up where you left off?'

'No. I get that I abandoned him. I know I don't have any right to walk back into his life and be his mother. That's not what I'm asking. But I would like a chance to get to know him. I would like to be . . . if not a mother, then someone like, I don't know, a favourite aunt.'

Dominic has no idea what to say. This, of all things, is the last thing he expected Stacy to ever say to him. He had never imagined something like this happening and he has no idea how he feels about it. He closes his eyes for a few seconds to regroup. 'Are you staying in Westport? Are you back for good?'

'I don't really know what I'm going to do in the long run. The relationship I was in . . . wasn't as serious as I had thought.' She shrugs. 'I'm a real estate agent now, in Florida. Fort Lauderdale. I have a good life there, but I needed to come back and see if I could meet Jesse.'

'How long are you planning to be here?'

'Ten days.'

Dominic nods. 'Okay. Let me think about it. This is a lot to take in, and I have to think about Jesse. I don't know how he's going to react, and he's my priority.'

'Of course. I know you're an amazing dad. You were always an amazing dad.'

'Well, I didn't have much of a choice,' says Dominic, surprising himself with the bitterness in his voice before he checks himself with a sigh. 'I'm sorry. I shouldn't have said that. I'm glad you got your life straightened out. I need to figure this out with Jesse, and Emma.'

'Emma?'

'My girlfriend.'

'Serious?' Her eyes flash.

'Very. What happened with your boyfriend?'

Stacy looks away. 'I sank into a depression after the miscarriage, and it turns out he wasn't such a great guy after all. He couldn't deal with it, so he dumped me for someone else. So.' She turns back to him. 'I'm single again, which means I'm also able to devote however much time I need to Jesse. Obviously I'm not here for long this time, but I can come back. I plan on coming back.'

'I'll bear it in mind,' says Dominic. 'Listen, I had better get back. Here's my number. If you give me yours, I'll get in touch after I've thought about this. I need a little bit of time.'

'Of course,' she says sadly. 'I understand. I know you want to protect Jesse, and I don't want to mess him up more than I have. I just want to be in his life. I'd love to see him before I go back to Florida, if you think that will be okay.'

Dominic nods, and the both of them turn around at the same time to make their way back to the house. He can't quite figure out what he's feeling, now that she is actually here and offering to be a part of their son's life. It seems to be some kind of mixture of sadness, regret, and relief. And the tiniest bit of fear.

'Thanks, Dommo,' she says as they reach the house. They both stand awkwardly by her car as she reaches up and kisses his cheek. He stands stock-still, saying nothing, not even moving, as she gets in the car and drives away with a small wave.

No one has called him Dommo since Stacy. It sweeps him back to years ago, to the memory of what it felt like to be crazy in love, to think that the high of that crazy love was going to last forever. He doesn't feel anything for Stacy any more . . . but even so, that one word sets him off on an impromptu trip down memory lane, bringing back feelings he thought he had buried long ago.

He has no real emotional connection to these memories: Stacy as a young girl, sliding her hands into the rear pockets of his jeans; the two of them with part-time jobs delivering Chinese food for the Little Kitchen; Stacy drinking and shouting.

He shakes his head. He doesn't want to think about Stacy any more. Where is Emma?

He is still standing there when he spots Emma's car rounding the curve of the road and pulling into the driveway. He walks towards her to greet her, put his arms around her, apologize, but when she gets out of the car, she doesn't look him in the eye. Instead, she takes a step backwards, clearly uncomfortable.

'Hi,' she says, meeting his eyes only briefly.

'Hey,' he says awkwardly, not sure how to act in the face of her reserve. 'How are you?'

'I'm okay,' she says. And then she takes a deep breath and meets his eyes. 'I think maybe we need to talk.'

Dominic's heart plummets when he hears those words. They never mean anything good. Did she see Stacy? Did she see her reach up and kiss him on the cheek? *We need to talk* usually means *This is over*. It means *I have changed my mind*. It means *I may have told you last night that I loved you, but it was because of the wine, and I didn't mean it, and even if I did in the moment, I woke up this morning and knew all this – us – has been a terrible mistake.*

Dominic follows Emma into her house and stands before her in the living room, feeling slightly sick, as she puts her bag down, takes a deep breath, and turns towards him.

'I needed some time away to think today,' she says. 'I realize that you and I have probably rushed into things here. I wasn't looking for a relationship, and this . . . this thing . . . just crept up on me, on both of us. We probably took it much too quickly.'

Dominic's face falls. He can't believe his worst fears are coming true.

'It's been lovely,' Emma says, willing herself not to cry, 'but I saw your face last night when you saw your ex.' She can't seem to say the name *Stacy* out loud. 'I know you probably aren't even aware of it, but I think you're not over her. There are things you need to resolve with her before you're ready for a relationship with someone else.'

She pauses, remembering the old lady in New York, and the advice she'd offered. 'Is that what's going on for you?'

'Wait,' Dominic says. 'I don't understand. What's going on for *you*? What are you saying?'

'I'm saying we should maybe have some space while we figure this out. If your ex is back in town and you're still in love with her, you need to spend some time with her. I think you're amazing, Dominic, but I can't be second best in your life, and I want you to be happy. If she's the one who's going to make you happy, then you need to be with her.'

Emma blinks away her tears. She crosses her arms, the way women do when they're trying to protect themselves from pain.

Dominic steps towards her, smiling.

'What?' Emma looks confused. 'Why are you smiling?'

'I'm sorry,' he says, as he takes another step towards her. As he continues to move, Emma steps backwards until her back is literally against the wall of the living room. 'This is because you think I'm still in love with Stacy?'

'I watched your face last night when you saw her get into her car,' says Emma. 'I saw it in your eyes. You didn't say a word all the way home. You never bothered to say good night or come and see if I was okay.' This time tears do spring into her eyes.

He finally stops smiling when he sees her tears. 'That was shitty of me, Emma, and I am sorry. I was thrown by seeing Stacy last night, you're right. But not for the reasons you think. I was upset. I didn't sleep all night, but not because of my feelings about Stacy. This is about Jesse, not me. To know that she's back in Westport? To see her after all these years when she walked out on our son without even a backward glance?' This time it is Dominic's eyes that fill with tears. 'That's what I couldn't deal with.'

'So . . .' Emma looks up at him. 'You're not in love with her?'

'Are you kidding? Stacy is a nightmare. I'll admit, I was shocked last night when I saw her and realized she was actually back. For real. It was like a horror movie.' Dominic smiles. 'She's not the one I love. I'm in love with *you*. Completely.' He puts his arms around Emma as she leans into his embrace. 'Wholeheartedly. With everything I have. I love you, Emma. There is no one in the world I want to be with more than you. You make me happy, and calm, and just . . . better. You make me a better person.'

Emma allows herself to be held, and all the discomfort and anxiety of the day slips away as if it had never existed. *Thank God*, she thinks. The pain of the last twenty-four hours was almost unbearable. If that's what relationships are like, she is better off without them. Except here she is, in Dominic's arms.

'I did see Stacy today, though,' Dominic says, and he feels her body instantly stiffen.

'What?' She attempts to pull back, but he refuses to loosen his embrace.

'She came here because she wants to get to know Jesse.' This time he does loosen his grip on Emma. 'She says she's sober now. She wants to get to know her son.'

Emma stands back to face him, forcing herself to be calm, not to let her panic show. 'Isn't this what you wanted?'

Dominic shakes his head with a sigh. 'I don't know any more. All these years I was furious with her for walking out on him, but now that she says she wants to get to know him, I don't know what to do. What if she lets him down? She doesn't plan to move back here. She just wants to meet him. What if she's nothing but a huge disappointment?'

Emma takes a deep breath. 'I don't know that you can stop it. If she's a huge disappointment, she's a huge disappointment. I think it's better that you let Jesse find out for himself. Maybe she really has changed and she can be a mother to him.' As she speaks, Emma is stunned to find she almost chokes on the word. Jesse has a *mother*. All this time, she has harboured this secret hope that *she* will be his mother, that *she* will be the one to step into the void his real mother left. She never anticipated that Jesse's real mother would come back.

Dominic looks at her, his face serious. 'This doesn't change anything,' he says. 'Well, obviously it changes things for Jesse, but not for us.' He pauses. 'I want to be sure you're hearing me, Emma.'

She looks up into his eyes and nods. She just hopes he knows his own mind as well as he says he does.

'I love you, Emma,' he says, leaning down and kissing her.

And this time, she lets herself believe him.

*

Later that evening, in the kitchen, Dominic's phone buzzes. He reaches over to grab it off the worktop where it's plugged in, charging, but not before Emma notices it's a text from Stacy.

He sighs. 'She wants to know if I've thought about it and if she can meet up with Jesse this weekend.' He looks up at her. 'What do I do?'

'You should say yes,' Emma replies. 'She's only here for a few days. You should maybe let her take him to the playground or something.'

'Really? You think that's a good idea?'

'You have to try,' says Emma. 'You'd never forgive yourself for cheating Jesse of this chance to meet his mother. And he deserves to know who she is, for good or ill. Maybe she will let him down again. But there's also the very real possibility here that Jesse could have a mother. That's what you've always wanted, isn't it?'

'Okay.' He nods. 'Okay. You're right. Playground. That's a great idea. I'll set it up.'

'That sounds perfect,' says Emma, but she feels slightly sick, knowing that Dominic should go, too. It would be insane to let Jesse go off with Stacy by himself, before he gets to know her. Still, she wishes she knew how to get rid of the creeping insecurity she has had since last night.

She knows she has nothing to worry about; she thinks, *hopes*, she has nothing to worry about.

Her disquieting sense of distrust now has nothing to do with Dominic. This is about Stacy, a woman who may or may not have ulterior motives, a woman who may or may not still yield a power over Dominic. She is, after all, the mother of his child. If Dominic felt he ever had to choose, what choice would he make?

Emma shakes her head in an effort to physically dislodge her thoughts. *This is madness,* she tells herself. *Dominic hasn't given you any reason to doubt his love.* If anything, he's been refreshingly clear about his feelings. All she needs to do is follow Cece's advice and listen, pay attention to what he's saying, what he's doing. All she needs to do is stay present, and everything will be fine.

'Are you okay?' Dominic looks over at her as she nods and forces a smile. 'This is hard for you, isn't it?'

'Not hard,' she says. 'But weird. I just didn't expect Jesse's mother to come back. It isn't something I was prepared for.'

Dominic nods. 'You and me both. I'm upset, too. All these years I wanted her to want to have a relationship with him, but now that she's here, I just feel anxious. It's going to be okay, though,' he says, more to soothe himself than Emma, it seems. 'Whatever happens, we'll figure it out. Maybe next week, after she's gone, you and I can go away for a night? Somewhere romantic?'

Emma is startled, remembering the phone call with her mother at the beginning of this endless day. How could she have so completely forgotten? And how can she now tell Dominic what she has done? 'Dominic, I can't. I'm so sorry about what I've done. But, well . . . Do you remember I told you about my cousin getting engaged, and my mother throwing him a party in England, how I probably wasn't going to go?'

Dominic nods.

'Well, the last time I spoke to my mother, she was still upset by my decision. I spoke to her again early this morning, when I was so upset, and she was worried about me, and told me she wanted me to go home. At the time, I thought she was right. So I changed my mind. I'm so sorry I forgot to tell you. I've already booked the flight.'

'Oh. Wow. Okay,' Dominic is surprised. 'So when are you going?'

'Next week.'

'For how long?'

'Just a few days.'

Dominic pauses. 'Why don't I come with you?'

Emma's eyes open in amazement. 'Are you serious? You would really come to England?' She frowns. 'But you don't have a passport.'

'I do now.'

'What?'

'Well, I got myself one after you seemed so horrified when I was building those shelves for Lisa. I thought maybe one day we could go away on vacation, so I got an expedited one as a surprise.'

Emma starts to laugh. 'You want to come and meet my whole family? You think you're ready for the craziness of my childhood home?' She imagines Dominic and her parents, and her laughter gets louder. 'Actually, my childhood home isn't all that crazy, and my father's really quite normal, but my mother? Are you sure you're ready for my mother? I'm not sure *I'm* ready for this.' It is impossible for Emma to hide her excitement. 'Really? You really want to come?'

'She'll love me.' Dominic grins. 'Mothers always love me. I flirt a little, charm a little, and they fall head over heels in love.' He laughs, then adds, 'I do want to see where you grew up. And' – he narrows his eyes at her – 'I want to see what you'll look like when you're old.'

'Do not tell my mother you think she's old. She'll never let you in the house.' As Emma laughs, she wonders what her mother will make of Dominic. She may well think he's charming. She will certainly think he is exotic, with his American accent, dark skin, big brown eyes, and strong arms.

'I very much want to meet your parents.' Dominic steps back and leads Emma to the sofa, where they both sit, curled into each other. 'I'm really serious about this, Emma. I'm serious about you. I know this is quick, and I know we've only had one proper date, but . . . I don't even know that I should say this . . .'

'Say it,' encourages Emma softly.

'I feel like this is *it*.' He looks at her, and she nods, a lump in her throat. 'I can't believe how freaked out I got when I realized you were gone today. It really made me realize that I feel like I'm where I'm supposed to be with you, and I'm who I'm supposed to be. This all feels fated somehow, you moving in, us getting together. It feels *right*.

I know you just said you thought we were rushing things, but I also know you understand what I'm talking about. So maybe we shouldn't jump ahead and use . . . the M-word, or anything like that, but I see us together for a long time.'

Emma nods, unable to speak.

'I mean, a really long time. A really, *really* long time. Maybe forever.' He frowns. 'I don't want to scare you off. Am I scaring you off?'

'You most definitely are not scaring me off,' says Emma, leaning in to kiss him. 'I've been terrified of saying it out loud. I feel exactly the same way. It feels preordained, even if you and I come from different worlds. I do feel I was meant to meet you, rent your house, for a reason. I do see us together for' – she laughs – 'a really, really long time. And I would be thrilled if you came to England. As long as you prepare yourself for my mother.'

'If she's anything like you, I'll adore her.'

Emma lets out a bark of laughter. 'She's *nothing* like me.'

'Then I'll just pretend.' He leans his head to kiss her properly, when they both jump apart at the sound of the cat flap.

'Where's Hobbes?' Jesse, just dropped off from a late playdate, let himself into the backyard to crawl through and head straight for the kitten in the corner. 'Dad? Can we go to a movie tomorrow? Can we? Please? Pretty please?'

'Hmm. Let me think. I have a lot to do. I just took on a new job to make some cabinets for a nice lady across town.' He watches his face fall. 'But hey, buddy, don't worry, we're heading into the weekend. We can definitely go see something. What do you think, Emma? Want to come with us?'

Emma looks at Jesse, expecting him to make a face, or scowl at her, or shake his head at his father. But instead, much to her surprise, he nods delightedly before running over and grabbing her hand.

'Come on, it'll be fun!'

'Okay,' she says. 'I'm in.' And then, to Dominic, 'Can I steal you for one second?' Jesse is already on the floor, playing with Hobbes, as Dominic allows himself to be led into the other room where Emma whispers quietly, 'What about Stacy? Weren't you going to the playground with Stacy?'

'Doesn't this sound like a whole lot more fun? I'll text her and maybe Jesse and I will meet her for ice cream in the afternoon. How's that?'

'That sounds perfect,' says Emma, wondering if Dominic believes her, if she is as convincing as she hopes.

Chapter 22

Emma stayed over again. It was as if the blip, if indeed a blip it was, had never happened. In the morning, they had a big breakfast together, then on Saturday they went to the movie Jesse selected. It was a wonderful day. A healing day.

After the movie, Jesse couldn't wait to show Emma the burger bar they always went to after a film. He told Emma which burger she needed to order, and how she needed to eat it – with no tomato, no cucumber, and extra mayo, which Dominic explained was kind of a rule in the family. All in all, for the first time since Jesse walked in and found her in his father's bed, Emma started to feel that they had turned a corner.

Every time she felt a worrying thought about Stacy creep in, she pushed it away. She knows Dominic texted her back, knows they are going to Sweet Frog for frozen yogurt later in the day, but she refuses to worry. The whole situation had exhausted her, emotionally and physically. The thought of Stacy re-entering their lives had seemed so terrifying, but now, after more consideration, Emma can see what a good thing this could be for Jesse. She could almost believe everything she had said to Dominic.

And after Jesse's seesawing emotions since he realized they were together, he seems to have finally accepted her. The three of them seem – she is almost too scared to say this, to even think it, but she can't deny it any longer – the three of them feel like a family.

After lunch they stop at the Athletic Shoe Factory to get Jesse some new trainers. Dominic wanders off into the shop next door as Emma supervises the fitting. The salesman unboxes the pair they'd picked out, and when Jesse tries them on, he tells him to stand up and 'walk over to your mom'.

Emma fully expects Jesse to correct him with a snap, to insist she isn't his mother, but Jesse says nothing, merely walks over to Emma, who finds her eyes stinging with happy, relieved tears.

They drive home, Emma enveloped in a warm glow of happiness. Now she is filling Hobbes's bowl with cat food. Dominic is upstairs talking to Jesse, no longer able to put off telling him about the London trip, which requires that they leave him behind so he doesn't miss school. It's not for long, Emma knows, but she's apprehensive about his reaction just the same.

The house is quiet. Emma enjoys the peace for a few minutes before she has to run next door and grab some eggs from her fridge. Just as she turns to go, she hears Jesse raise his voice. She pauses, listening, sorry, though unsurprised, that Jesse is upset. She hears Dominic murmuring in a low voice, although she can't make out what he is saying.

And then she hears Jesse's voice rise again. 'I hate her,' he says.

Emma knows it isn't true, yet it feels as if a knife is twisting in her heart.

'I hate her,' he says again. 'If she wasn't here, you wouldn't be going to England and I wish she wasn't here.'

'Come on, buddy.' Dominic's voice is soft, placating. 'You know you don't hate Emma. I'm only going for a few days and you're going to have fun with Nonna and Papa.'

'I'm not. You've never been away before and I don't even know Nonna and Papa. I don't want you to go. Emma can go by herself! Send her away! I don't want her here any more. Make her go.'

'You don't mean that,' says Dominic in what Emma has come to recognize as his *soothing* voice. 'You love Emma. I know you do. And you love her being around.'

'I do *not*!' screams Jesse, sobbing now. 'I *hate* her. You and me are the team. She's not on our team and we don't need her and I don't want her. You keep bringing her on our team and I don't want her any more. Send *her* to England and you stay here with me.'

'Buddy, I'm sorry you feel that way,' Emma hears Dominic say. 'I promise I won't be away for long, but I've already bought my ticket. I know you don't want Nonna and Papa to stay, but remember what happened last time they were here?'

'They've never stayed here.'

'Yes, they have,' says Dominic. 'You were about four. They stayed for two nights when I went to a wedding in Rhode Island, and you had chocolate ice cream and cannoli for dinner every night.'

There is a pause. A lowered voice. 'I did?'

'Yes. You did,' says Dominic. 'And they took you to the toy shop and bought you whatever you wanted. That giant bear over there? That was what you wanted. Remember?'

Another pause. 'Maybe.'

'I bet they'll do that again. What's your favourite food in the world?'

'French fries.' Jesse is reluctantly being pulled out of his hysteria.

'What else?'

'Chocolate ice cream.'

'What else?'

'Chocolate chip cookies.'

'I can pretty much guarantee that Nonna will give you French fries, chocolate ice cream, and chocolate chip cookies for breakfast, lunch, and dinner. You know what else?'

'What?'

'You know how you think your dad is the best cook in the world? Guess who taught him everything he knows? That's right. Nonna. You think my chicken parm is good, wait till you try Nonna's lasagne. Oh my God, Jesse, you will think you have died and gone to heaven.'

There is a brief silence. 'What does that mean? Is that bad?'

'No! It means it's good! It's amazing! It's the best thing you'll ever eat in your life. I'm jealous you're getting to eat all that amazing food and not me.' He pauses, then frowns. 'I don't know about the toy shop, though.'

'What do you mean, you don't know?'

'Maybe I should tell them not to take you. All those things you don't want. Those *Star Wars* things. That Lego. The stuff you never talk about when you watch TV and see those ads.'

Emma can practically hear Jesse smiling as his father teases him. 'What I really want is a hoverboard.'

'Then you better let Nonna and Papa stay here, because I'm not planning any trips to the toy shop soon, but I guarantee they *are*. Although . . . I think you may be a little young for a hoverboard.'

'Okay,' grumbles Jesse, whose heart is no longer in the protest. 'Do you think they'll take me to Skyzone, too?'

'Most definitely. Why don't you and I make a list of all the fun stuff you're going to do when I'm away? And listen, buddy? There's something else I need to talk to you about, too.'

'What is it?'

'Come sit down with me, buddy. I need to talk to you about your mother. You know how you sometimes ask me questions about her, and want to know what she's like?' There is a pause and Emma imagines Jesse's nod. 'You know she hasn't lived here for a long time, but I just found out that she's back in town for a visit.' He pauses again and Emma pictures Jesse's eyes widening in surprise. 'I know this is a lot for you, and it's totally fine if you don't want to see her. But she has asked me if she can meet you. She knows all about what a fantastic kid you are, and she wants to get to know you. But if you don't want to, that's absolutely fine. This is all up to you.'

Jesse seems to be processing all this big information.

'If you want to, I thought maybe we could meet her for ice cream later today. What do you think?'

Emma holds her breath.

'Ice cream?' says Jesse. 'Where?'

Chapter 23

Waiting for Dominic and Jesse to return from getting ice cream with Stacy is the longest hour and a half Emma can remember. She spends it outside in what she has finally transformed into a sweet little vegetable garden. Dominic had bought wood and made raised beds, filling them with soil dropped off by one of his landscaper friends.

It was too late to plant seeds, so Emma had run to the garden centre and bought the last of the straggly pumpkin plants and squashes, a few aubergine plants, and two tomato plants, just enough to give her some of the pleasure of picking her own vegetables.

She had put a large flowerpot in the middle of the garden, filling it with pink geraniums that spilled over the sides and made her think of the south of France, and there's a small stone bench that she perches on now, taking a break from pulling weeds.

Weeding is like a meditation for her. When she is bending over, digging around for the green invaders, pulling them up by the roots and forming small piles that she lifts into garbage bags, she is thinking of nothing, her brain entirely focused on clearing the beds. When she has weeded as much as she can, she gets the clippers from the garage and clips the boxwoods she had planted around the edges of the small garden into a small, perfect hedge.

She has barely thought about the fact that Dominic and Jesse are with Stacy. And they have been gone for quite a while.

As she sits on the bench, hot and sweaty, she hears a screen door slam. She looks up to see Dominic striding towards her.

'Hey,' he says, bending down to give her a kiss. 'I see you've been busy.'

'I can't believe how many weeds there were after such a short period of time. I have to make a point of getting out here and weeding more often.'

'Summer's over,' says Dominic. 'You won't have to worry about it for almost a year.' He sits next to her on the bench before sighing.

'Everything okay?' says Emma. 'How did it go?'

Dominic frowns and shakes his head. 'I can't tell. Jesse was kind of quiet with her. She asked him a lot of questions about school, and what he likes to do, and he answered everything, but it wasn't like there was this big bonding moment.'

'Surely you didn't expect that?' Emma looks at him in surprise. 'Jesse must have been overwhelmed.'

'He didn't seem overwhelmed. He seemed, if anything, bored.'

'He's six years old. He probably had no idea how to

express anything. Don't they say that little kids never react to big things in the way we expect? I'm sure there's a ton of stuff going on in that little mind of his, and you'll probably get to hear about it when you least expect it.'

'Yeah, you're right. I do know that. I just thought he'd talk to me when we left. I asked him if he had any questions or wanted to ask me anything, and all he wanted to know was when the new *Star Wars* movie is coming out.' Dominic starts to laugh. 'That is not what I expected him to say.'

Emma laughs, too. 'He'll probably ask you about his mum on the way to school, or when you're giving him a bath or something.'

'I hope so. I mean, I hope he talks about it sometime. The only thing he asked me was what to call her.'

'What did you say?'

'I said to call her Stacy. I didn't know how else to answer the question. If after this quick trip she really stays in touch with him, and they form a relationship, then maybe he'll call her Mom someday, but I think that has to be his choice. She can't ask that of him, and I would feel weird telling him to call her that. What do you think? Do you think that's okay?'

'I think you did great,' smiles Emma. 'I would have said exactly the same thing.'

'Thanks. She wants to pick him up on Monday and take him to the toy shop.'

'Did you say yes?'

Dominic frowns. 'I said I'd think about it. I'm worried

that it's all happening too fast. She won't be here for long and I don't want to get him too attached too soon.'

'He won't. It's only a couple of days. And it's the toy shop. Let her spoil him if she wants to, and let him get to know her. Nothing huge is going to happen in such a brief period of time. She's not going to be able to hurt him in a few days.'

She takes Dominic's hand. 'If you don't take the risk of allowing him to be loved by her, you're also keeping him from something momentous, something you said you've always wanted.'

Dominic closes his eyes. 'I know, I know. But wanting it when she wasn't around, when it was only an abstract concept, is very different from wanting it now that she's here and could hurt him again.'

'It's like falling in love,' says Emma. 'You have to give it everything you have or you'll miss out on all of it, the highs and the lows. You have to close your eyes and jump, hoping that you'll be caught, that you'll emerge better for the experience.' For a moment, Emma pauses, wondering when she had come to feel this way about love. She never believed any of this before. It was all new. It was Dominic. 'You have to allow this to happen between Jesse and Stacy, however scared you are. You have to step back and allow him the experience of getting to know his mother.'

'You're right. I know you're right. So I let her pick him up?'

'Yes. If you still feel weird about it, you can always go with them.'

'I think I still feel weird about it.'

'So accompany them. You'll feel better.'

'You know what makes me feel better?' He smiles at her. 'You. You always know exactly what to say. How did you get to be so smart?'

Emma smiles. 'And you thought I was just a pretty face.'

They spend Sunday working in the garden and watching Jesse have the time of his life on the trampoline. Not surprisingly, he falls asleep right after dinner, which is a great thing both because the next day is finally the first day of school and because it gives Emma and Dominic the kind of quiet night at home they treasure. A healing night.

The next day, after Jesse goes to school, Emma spends the morning working, posting new photos of her work online, while Dominic goes out on a carpentry job. Just after lunch, Emma takes a break to text Sophie.

I miss you! Want to have tea later today? How about Neat at four?

I miss you, sister! comes back, seconds later. **But, ugh, I've got a gym class with the boy this afternoon. How about tomorrow morning?**

Client meeting ☹ **Lunch?**

Can't. Ugh. Shall we text tomorrow and see if we can squeeze in something quick?

Sure! Emma fills a line with the kissing face emoji, then loads her car with returns she has to drop off, and mail she has to send, and sets off to do her errands, singing out loud to Jason Mraz as she makes her way up the Post Road.

She is driving across the bridge on the way to Whole Foods when she sees them, and her breath catches in her throat as she sits in traffic, unable to tear her eyes away.

Dominic is holding Jesse's left hand, Stacy his right. They are doing the one-two-three-swing with him, something Emma and Dominic have never thought to do with him themselves. Jesse seems too old for that, too big, far too mature to enjoy it, but there he is, being swung, and all three of them are laughing, looking like the most perfect, perfectly happy family you could ever wish to see.

Emma finishes her errands in a haze. She admonishes herself not to jump to conclusions; she resolves to listen, and pay attention, and thereby gets through the afternoon. She is cooking dinner when they get home. She is on her second glass of wine, with loud music on in the kitchen to try to distract her from her fears.

She hears the front door open and sees Jesse, a blur running upstairs to his room. Dominic looks happy, happier, she is sure, than she has seen him look in ages. Maybe ever.

She feels sick.

'How's my girl?' He bends to kiss her and she kisses him back, forcing a smile, trying to pretend that everything is fine. All she can think of is the image of the three of them, Jesse swinging between his two parents, delight on each of their faces.

'I'm fine. How did it go?'

'It was fine.' Dominic shrugs. 'Nothing dramatic. We

had a good time. Jesse had a good time, and so far he hasn't asked me anything.'

'I saw you, you know,' she says, instantly reprimanding herself for mentioning it. She hadn't wanted to say anything, but the words, the feelings, wouldn't stay in.

'You did? Where?' There is nothing but innocent delight on his face.

'On the bridge. Swinging Jesse.'

Dominic shakes his head. 'Oh man. I told him he was too big and too grown-up, but it was Stacy's idea. And she was right. He loved it.'

'I saw.' Emma turns away.

'Emma? Honey? What's the matter?'

Emma shrugs miserably before turning back to face him. 'I'm sorry. I hate myself for feeling this way. I saw the three of you together, and you looked like the perfect family.' Her voice wobbles. 'I'm the one who feels like the intruder now. I'm thrilled that Jesse has the chance to get to know his mum, but I'm scared, and I grew more scared after I saw you today. You looked . . . happy.'

'I *was* happy,' he says quietly, taking her hands. 'I was happy because Jesse knowing his mother is something I've always wanted. This has nothing to do with me. I love you, Emma. You are the only woman I want to be with, ever. Even if there was something between me and Stacy, which there isn't, at all, but even if she thought, I don't know, that she'd come back to try to make it work with me, it wouldn't matter.' He sighs. 'How can I say it so you can hear me?'

Emma looks at him. 'I don't know. I think it's just this stupid thing I'm going through. I feel better, though, hearing you say that.' She gives him an embarrassed smile, allowing herself to be gathered in his arms. 'And the wine helps.'

'Okay, I'm glad you feel better. Because there's one more thing.' He holds her tight. 'Stacy has asked if Jesse can stay with her while we're away.'

Emma steps back, furrowing her brow. 'What? I thought she was leaving.'

'She was. But she said she can change her flight to spend more time with Jesse.'

'Do you feel safe enough leaving Jesse with her? He doesn't really know her.'

Dominic nods. 'I know. But he doesn't really know my parents, either. I don't know what to do. She asked him if he wanted to come stay with her and he seemed to think it was the best idea ever.'

Emma is horrified. 'She asked him? Without checking with you?'

'Jesse had volunteered that Nonna and Papa were going to stay with him when we were away and she offered.'

'So what did you say?'

'I said we'd already made plans with my parents.'

'And?'

'And she said plans could be changed.'

'I don't like this,' says Emma. 'I think it's too much, too soon, and you can't be around to monitor what happens.'

'I know. That's how I feel, too, but Jesse was so eager

to be with her, and I keep thinking about what you said, about how sometimes you have to close your eyes and jump in.'

'Not when it's unsafe. I didn't mean let him stay with her all that time on his own.'

'She's sober now, Emma. I think she really is. And I've talked to other friends who know her, and they think she is, too. It's probably better than having him stay with my parents and their shouting. I think this might be a good thing, and I don't know how I can say no.'

Emma sighs. 'I can't tell you what to do, Dominic. If you think it's a good idea, then do it. I think it's a huge risk. She may be sober, but she hasn't shown herself to be responsible. Don't you want to give this some time, ease into this relationship slowly? Isn't that better for Jesse?'

'In an ideal world, of course that would be better for Jesse. But it's not ideal. I honestly don't know which is the lesser of two evils, Stacy or my parents. And I think Jesse will have a better time with Stacy. But it's more than that. I saw them together today. They seemed to be making a real connection. It made me feel like our trip was a good thing, I mean to give them a chance to spend a few days alone together. Maybe that's what they need to establish a real relationship. And ultimately isn't that what I want for him?'

'Okay,' says Emma, resigned. 'There's your answer. I hope she's good with him.'

'If today was anything to go by, she's going to be great. I agree with everything you're feeling, but I can see she's changed, Emma. And it's not like she's a stranger. This is someone I've known practically my whole life. I'll be honest and say I haven't trusted her in the past, but I really do think it's going to be okay.'

'Okay,' says Emma, going back to chopping peppers, knowing she has no say, she has to keep quiet. 'Okay.'

The days pass in a flurry. Jesse is distant with Emma again, excited at the prospect of staying with Stacy. She is not surprised. She understands that he is simultaneously excited at the prospect of staying with the woman who is his mother, and angry at Emma for taking his father away. Emma understands. On some level, and certainly from a six-year-old's perspective, she *is* taking his father away. Not emotionally, and certainly not for very long, but this is the first time, other than a night in Rhode Island two years ago, that Dominic has left Jesse overnight.

She understands that this is a big deal, and not just for Jesse.

Dominic's whole life has revolved around his son. His guilt at being a single parent, at not being able to give Jesse the proper family life he deserves, has meant that Jesse is indulged. He is a child used to having his father at his beck and call always.

Dominic has not had a life because he has given it to Jesse. He's kept his relationships from Jesse, working hard to ensure that they neither impact nor infringe upon his life with his son in any way whatsoever.

Jesse has no idea that Dominic has even dated. Until

now. And the woman his father is dating is taking him away.

The wicked stepmother, thinks Emma. *Isn't that the way these things work?* But wicked stepmothers rarely start out that way. A woman, a loving, kind, caring person, falls in love with a man who has children. She decides to work hard to earn the love of his children; surely they will respond to her overtures of kindness, affection, and warmth. She is a good person; all these children need in order to love her is a happy family, a stable and loving life.

She marries the man, ignoring the fact that the children are distressed, or angry, or in pain. They take the children shopping, redecorate their bedrooms, buy them toys, and accompany them to their favourite sports events in a bid to seduce them, but the children can tell they are being seduced, can smell the disingenuousness, and no amount of gadgets will give them their father's undivided attention again. Their dislike and distrust of the stepmother grows.

The children get more sullen and resentful. The stepmother grows more sullen and resentful. She has tried so hard! She has done everything for these ungrateful children! She has had enough of being nice. And thus, the wicked stepmother is born.

Emma knows how these things happen. She has read enough fairy tales, been friends with enough women who have stepmothers. She will not be one of those women. She will never try to get between Jesse and his father, will never try to take Dominic away from his son. And she will have patience with Jesse's feelings about her.

She's a good person, and kind. All Jesse needs is a stable, loving family. If Emma can give it to him, they will all, surely, live happily ever after.

Dominic comes downstairs, his hair wet from the shower, muttering in anger as he casts a dark look at his phone.

'What's the matter?'

'I knew it.' He shakes his head. 'I fucking knew it.'

'Knew what?'

'Stacy. Just called to say she couldn't change her flight without it costing her hundreds of dollars that she doesn't have. So she's going back, and now I have to tell Jesse that once again she's let him down.'

'When's she leaving?'

'Tomorrow.'

'I'm sorry,' says Emma. 'That sucks.'

'It really does. I really thought she had changed, but turns out she's as irresponsible as ever. I shouldn't have said yes. I should never have let her back in our lives.'

Chapter 24

'Whoa.' Dominic lets out a low whistle in the Virgin Atlantic upper-class lounge. 'This is *awesome*!'

Emma still has thousands of air miles from when she travelled with the bank. She would never have paid for these tickets, but she decided to upgrade, knowing that for Dominic, a man who has never even left the country, business class will be an experience he will never forget.

She finds a spare sofa in the lounge and curls up with a book, while Dominic goes off to explore. He has a head massage in the spa, and two dirty martinis in the bar, and orders a plate piled high with antipasti, which he brings back to the table for them to share.

'Is this really all free?' he leans forward and whispers.

'It's all included in the astronomical price of the ticket,' Emma whispers back, amused and touched by his wide-eyed wonder at something she has taken for granted for so many years.

'Emma?'

She looks up to see Caroline, a girl she used to work

with at the bank, a girl she hasn't seen since she left two years ago when she got pregnant.

'Caroline!' Emma stands up and gives the girl the obligatory air kiss on both cheeks before crouching down to admire a beautifully dressed toddler in what has to be the most top-of-the-range buggy she has ever seen. 'Is this the baby? Oh my goodness!' Emma says. 'He got so big!'

'That's Burke,' says Caroline. 'My husband is over there. Hunter. Did you ever meet him?'

'Not really,' says Emma, who remembers being briefly introduced at their engagement party. He was a big tall golden preppy man, filled with the kind of confidence that comes from being raised in a family that has always had the best of everything. 'Although I did meet him before you two got married. This is Dominic,' she says, as Caroline casts a curious glance over him and extends her hand.

'Nice to meet you,' she says.

'Hey.' He smiles. 'How are you doing?'

'Great. Thank you.' She smiles politely before turning back to Emma. 'So how is everything at work? I wish I could tell you I miss it, but I'm thrilled to be a stay-at-home mom.' Caroline lets out a peal of laughter, as Emma remembers how she never really liked Caroline. She seemed pleasant enough, until you realized how competitive she was.

Whatever anyone had done, Caroline had done better. If someone came in with a new bag, Caroline showed up the next week with the more expensive version; when

someone bought a house, Caroline would make sure everyone knew hers was bigger. Or more expensive. Or in a
more prestigious town.

When she and Hunter got engaged, Emma suddenly
remembers, Caroline showed up with a ring so big, she
joked that she had pulled a muscle in her finger trying to
hold it up.

She claimed it was Hunter's great-great-grandmother's
diamond, which they had had reset. No one quite believed
her. It could have been bought wholesale the day before
on Forty-Seventh Street, but that didn't make for such a
good story.

'I left the bank,' says Emma. 'A few months ago.
Burnout!'

'Good for you,' says Caroline. 'So you're a lady of
leisure, like me. Isn't it fun?'

Emma nods. 'It is fun, although I'm starting my own
interior design business.'

'I had no idea interior design was your thing,' says
Caroline. 'I ought to get you over to look at our house. I
wanted to do it myself, but frankly ten thousand feet is a
little overwhelming. Every time I start thinking about it, I
get the cold sweats, so of course we're living in it with no
wallpaper and not a single window blind anywhere. Can
you imagine?'

'Deathly.' Emma shakes her head, without a trace of
irony. *Now I remember*, she thinks. *You are awful.*

'I'm the carpenter,' Dominic offers. 'If Emma helps you

out, I come along as part of the deal and build a great bookcase.'

Caroline closes her eyes for a second before shaking her head with an embarrassed laugh. 'Oh God! I'm mortified. For a moment there I thought you were Emma's boyfriend. I'm so sorry. I couldn't quite make sense of the two of you together.' She lets out another peal of laughter, oblivious to the looks on Emma's and Dominic's faces. 'I'll definitely give you a call. Emma, do you have a card?'

You bitch, thinks Emma, fishing for a card, her heart pounding. *You fucking bitch*. She glances at Dominic, who also looks a little stunned, and knows she has to say something.

'Dominic *is* my boyfriend,' she says eventually, her voice shaking. *Fuck it*. She's not going to give her the card. 'And we work together.'

'We sleep together, too,' says Dominic, seeing Caroline's face fall. 'Apparently I'm a fantastic fuck.'

Caroline's mouth opens in a small O.

'So nice to see you,' says Emma, gathering her things and standing up. 'Enjoy your ten-thousand-foot monstrosity and the sunlight streaming through your curtainless windows.' Summoning as much hauteur as she can manage, hauteur that may, in fact, put Caroline to shame, she glides off, with Dominic at her side.

'What a bitch,' says Dominic. 'Who the hell is she?'

'Someone I used to work with. I'd love to tell you she is unique in her cattiness, but sadly that kind of attitude is one of the reasons I had to leave banking. There were some wonderful people, but too many like that. I just can't play that stupid game of "I have more money than you, therefore I'm better than you."'

'I really wanted to say that I was also overwhelmed in my *twelve-thousand-foot* house, but I thought she might have knocked me out.'

'She's far too polite to have knocked you out. She may have turned you to stone with a withering look, though.'

'Eurgh.' Dominic shudders. 'Please tell me that if she ever manages to track you down, you won't work for her? Life is too damn short to be around people like that. Too much negative energy.'

'I couldn't agree more. Shall we go to the gate and wait there? At least outside this first-class lounge with the masses, we won't have to see her again.'

As they walk towards the gate, Dominic turns to her. 'Your mother isn't anything like that, is she?' he says.

'Like Caroline? Why would you ask that?'

'I don't know. You said she was a roaring snob. If she's like that woman, this isn't going to go so well.'

'Are you nervous?'

'Yes. What if they hate me? What if I hate them? What will happen to *us*?'

Emma stops walking and turns to face Dominic. 'Well, my mother may be a roaring snob, but not remotely in the same way as Caroline. She's funny more than anything else. Once you understand that she's not to the manor born, her assumed superiority is hilarious. And she's not mean. Truly. My mother doesn't have a mean bone in her body.'

'Do you think she'll like me?'

'I think it's impossible for anyone not to like you.'

'That doesn't answer my question.'

'Dominic, I can't speak for my mother. I am sure she will love you, but even if she doesn't, it doesn't matter. I love both of my parents, but I moved across the Atlantic to get away from them. That should tell you everything you need to know about how much it matters to me whether they like you or not.'

'But it matters to me.'

'It shouldn't. *I* like you. I *love* you. Jesse loves you.' She smiles. 'That's all that matters.'

'Okay, you're right.' He nods. 'You're right. I have no idea where this anxiety came from.'

'It's all going to be fine,' Emma says. Hoping very much that's true.

They call Jesse just before they get on the plane. Dominic describes everything to him in detail. The lounge! The massage! The free food! He promises to try to find a TARDIS for him from England.

'How is he?' Emma looks over at Dominic, who is frowning slightly, staring at his phone.

'He's okay. Quiet. I think he was really looking forward to staying with Stacy. Jesus.' He shakes his head in disgust. 'Poor little guy. And now he's stuck with my parents, and I don't know if this is a good idea.'

'Which bit?'

'Getting my parents to stay with him. He doesn't really know them.'

'Don't you always say you think they'd be better grand-parents than parents?'

Dominic's laugh is bitter. 'They are, but that doesn't mean they're any good.'

'It's just a few days,' Emma tries to reassure him. 'I'm sure he'll be okay for just a few days. What specifically are you worried about?'

'I just haven't left him this long before. He said Nonna and Papa were having a fight. That's the thing I was worried about. That they'd get violent in front of him.'

'Violent? What kind of violent?' For everything Dominic has told her about his parents, he hasn't explicitly described any violence. Then, with a start, she remembers the man she met at the start of the summer, when she was out with Sophie. Jeff. The real estate agent. The one who had known Dominic when he was little, when his parents were still living in town. Hadn't he said something about Dominic's mom cracking his dad over the head with a frying pan? Something like that. She hadn't paid much attention because it was . . . well, it was *before*.

It's only a few days, she reassures Dominic. It will be fine. However badly his parents had got on when they were young, they're still together, aren't they? Not to mention they're in their seventies, and would have undoubtedly calmed down.

Jesse is going to be fine.

Chapter 25

'Muffin?' Georgina Montague shouts down the hallway to where her husband is trying to have a peaceful hour, tucked in the old battered wing chair in the library, with the paper and a small nip of scotch.

He sighs as he sets the newspaper down. They have been married forty years. For forty years he has pleaded with her not to roar through the house when she wants someone, and been duly ignored. If anything, he is convinced she now roars more loudly, just to spite him.

'In here.' He raises his voice just a little bit, knowing she probably won't hear. He can't bring himself to shout, nor is he willing to get up and go to her. This chair is perfectly comfortable, Petey's nose is resting on his good foot, and the foot that is still recovering from gout is resting on the ottoman.

'Where are you, Muffin?' shouts Georgina, drawing closer, for he knows she knows exactly where he is, where he *always* is on a hot day. Or a cold day. Or a rainy day. The library, which is the only room in the house he considers 'his'. It's too warm for a fire today, more's the pity.

He glances out the window at the unseasonable Indian summer and sighs. He never quite got the hang of gardening, and summer is only enjoyable for about four weeks. By mid-July he's always longing for jumpers, and thick socks, and hikes with their chocolate lab, Petey, pushing the leaves out of the way with his walking stick.

He is an autumn/winter person, he had decided long ago. Georgina, or Muffin, as he calls her – as they, in fact, have called each other for the best part of forty years – adores the summer.

He looks out of the library's French doors, sighing as he sees the large white marquee sitting on the lawn, tables and chairs stacked up on one side. When Georgina asked him if they could throw an engagement party for his nephew George, he thought she meant a bit of wine and a few nibbles in the living room. It's why he said yes. He thought it would be a relatively quiet affair.

There have been men shouting in his garden all day as they hoisted up the marquee, and lorries filled with equipment that they have put in the barn, turning it into what is apparently called a caterer's kitchen.

Simon Montague loves his wife. He doesn't love crowds. He can only tolerate the kind of parties at his house where, at a certain point, he is able to quietly disappear. He enjoys people very much, but only for limited periods of time, and only if he can escape by himself to recharge his batteries.

This library has always been his refuge, but it's not much of a refuge today, with all the activity right outside the door, the men shouting back and forth, the bursts of raucous laughter.

Why can't people be more respectful? he thinks sadly, waiting for Georgina to come pounding into the room.

'Thought I'd find you in here,' she pants, resting in the doorway.

'Why were you shouting for me, then?'

'Habit,' she says brightly, ignoring his irritation.

'Muffin,' he says sadly, as another burst of laughter comes from outside. 'Is it really too much to ask for people in our house to be quiet?'

'They're not in our house, darling. They're outside.'

'But it's so disturbing! Every few seconds there's a burst of shouting or laughter. Why can't they do their job quietly?'

'They're almost finished,' she says. 'Don't be an old grouch, Muffin. I know you hate lots of people, but George and Henry are thrilled.'

'You're calling her Henry now?'

'Apparently everyone calls her Henry. They'll be here in time for supper tonight. I know he can't wait to see you. And I've made a lovely beef Wellington for you.' She smiles, seeing the look of pleasure on her husband's face. 'With apple crumble for pudding. See? I'm trying to look after you amidst the madness.'

'Party's tomorrow evening?'

'It is. Will you be sociable? Just for one night?'

'Just for one night,' grumbles Simon. 'But you mustn't do this again, Muffin. Truly. You know I only agreed to host an engagement party because I thought it would be small.'

'Darling.' Georgina leans over to give her husband a kiss on the cheek. 'How long have we been married? When it comes to parties, when have I ever done anything by halves?' She smiles at him indulgently. 'Are you able to run to the cellar and get that lovely wine? I'm putting out a plate of cheese and biscuits for when Emma arrives with her man. They should be here soon.'

Simon takes his foot off the ottoman with great reluctance and heaves himself out of the comfort of his chair. 'Know anything about this man?' he asks his wife as he slowly makes his way out of the room. 'Is it serious?'

'I imagine it must be if she's bringing him home to meet us. I trust you'll be on your best behaviour with him?'

'Me?' He turns to look at his wife, aghast. 'I have never been the one in this partnership that anyone has had to worry about.' He lets out a bark of laughter. 'Let's just hope he's looking after her. That's my only concern.'

'Ssssh,' says Georgina suddenly, her head cocked. 'Oh my goodness! I think I just heard a car door. I think they must be here.'

It has been ages since Emma has been to her parents' house. She has barely given England a second thought during her five years in the States. She has made a few sporadic trips back, but not to Somerset, only to London, for work, where she has stayed at the Four Seasons, dined at the best restaurants, had her parents come up from the country to see her, and taken them out somewhere fabulous for dinner.

She hadn't been back to Brigham Hall since she left. She told people she was from a beautiful part of the world, but her heart didn't ache for her house, the fields, the narrow country lanes overgrown with lush hedges.

At least, it didn't ache until today, driving along those winding roads with Dominic, seeing everything through his eyes, passing charming thatched cottages and village streets lined with pretty stone buildings older than anything Dominic had ever seen in his life.

She drives the hire car expertly, even though it has been years since she drove on this side of the road. As they draw closer to Yeovil she remembers it all, and she laughs in pleasure as she points out pubs she used to frequent as a teenager, fields in which she snogged teenage boys, buses she used to take, sitting on the top deck in the seat at the front, puffing on cigarettes and blowing smoke out the side of her mouth in a way she thought at the time was ineffably cool.

'*Snogged?*' Dominic starts to laugh. 'I've never heard anyone but Austin Powers use that word. I didn't think it was even real.'

'It most certainly is real,' says Emma. 'You know what it means, right?'

'Sure. Having sex.'

'No!' She laughs. 'It most certainly does not mean having sex. Oh my God, you think I was having sex with teenage boys in fields? What kind of girl do you think I am?'

'My kind of girl?' he says.

'Well, I wasn't. Having sex in fields. *Snogging* is kissing. Proper kissing. French kissing.'

'Do you mean with tongues?'

'Yes. With tongues.'

'So . . . making out?'

'Yes, exactly. Making out.'

'Hmmm. *Snogging.* I like that word. I'm going to call it snogging from now on. Do you want to go snogging with me?'

Emma cracks up. 'I can't actually believe we're having this conversation. Anyway, that's not how you'd say it. You'd say, "Fancy a snog?"'

'No way.' Dominic starts laughing. 'Is that really what you'd say? "Fancy a snog?"'

'Yes, but it's not *snahg*.' She starts to laugh. 'It's *snog*. Short *o*.'

'Snog. "Fancy a snog?"'

'Are you asking?' Emma is still laughing.

'I'm asking.'

'I'm dancing.'

'What?' He stares at her.

'Never mind.' Emma shakes her head, giggling. 'It's an old joke. The boy who walks up to the girl and says, "Are you dancing?" "Are you asking?" "I'm asking." "I'm dancing."'

'I don't get it.'

'No. It's an old saying. Must be an English thing.'

'Shall we pull over into a field and *snog*? I'm feeling competitive with all those old boyfriends of yours. I'm not going to feel like I've had the full English experience until I've snogged someone in a field.'

'When you say "someone", do you mean anyone at all? Like, say, her?' Emma gestures to a sour-faced older woman on the pavement.

'No thanks. When I say someone, I mean you.'

'I'll think about it,' says Emma. Once they have passed through the village, she veers to the left and parks. 'Come on.' She gets out of the car and pulls Dominic out, too, pulling him behind a bush where she snakes her arms around his neck and passionately kisses him.

'Mmmm.' Dominic starts to unbutton her jeans. 'I could get used to this.'

'Not now.' She giggles. 'I don't want nettle rash. Later. I promise you,' she says. She gives him another kiss, before dragging him back to the car.

A mile, another mile and a half, a left, a right, and the car slows as Emma drives through the wooden gates and up a winding driveway, rounding a small copse of trees to reveal Brigham Hall, nestled in a gravel driveway, fields stretching all around it, the setting sun turning the pretty stone a glowing pinkish gold.

'Whoa.' Dominic whistles, gazing at the house. Emma realizes with a start that it does look rather stately and grand, particularly to an American newcomer. She'd never thought of it that way when she lived here.

'You never told me you live in Downton Abbey.'

'Hardly,' Emma says. 'This is nothing. It just looks grand from here. Wait until you get inside. It's all falling apart.' She steps out of the car, pausing to really look at the stone Georgian house she has always taken for granted. Seeing it through Dominic's eyes, she recognizes how beautiful it is, how lucky she was to have grown up here.

As she stands by the car and Dominic busies himself with their bags, a chocolate lab suddenly emerges through the front door, his tail wagging furiously in delight. Emma flings her arms around him, covering him with kisses. As much as she has made America her home, this is home, too, she realizes. And for the first time since moving to New York all those years ago, she is happy to be here.

Chapter 26

'Hello?' Emma walks through the front door, Petey stuck to her heels, followed closely by Dominic, who puts their bags down in the hallway, next to the Wellington boots lined up under the coat rack.

The limestone floor is old and worn, dotted with aged Persian rugs, and a couple of riding hats sit on a console table. Dominic walks over and picks one up. 'Who rides?'

'No one any more. I used to, but obviously I'm not here. That's my old hat, I think.' She walks over and picks it up, smiling at the memory. 'I kept a horse at a stable down the road. Pennyflake was his name. I adored him.'

'Why are the hats out?'

Emma lowers her voice. 'Same reason the wellies are lined up by the front door. It's what you do when you're a *yah* living in the country.'

'A what?'

'A yah. Someone upper class, don't you know.' She exaggerates the accent as Dominic shakes his head with a laugh.

'I thought we spoke the same language, but I guess not.'

'That's exactly what I thought before I moved to America,' says Emma, putting down the riding hat. 'I kept asking where the shopping trolleys were kept, and was there a petrol station nearby. I couldn't understand why no one knew what I was talking about.'

Dominic stares at her. 'I'm not even going to ask,' he says finally, as Emma laughs and walks over to give him a kiss.

'I love you.' She looks into his eyes, seeing them crinkle as he smiles.

'I love you, too,' he replies, and then both of them jump apart as Emma's mother walks into the hallway.

'There you are!' she booms, coming over with a smile, kissing Emma on each cheek before embracing her in a quick, tight hug. 'I thought I heard a noise. Well, hello!' She releases her daughter and stands back to look Dominic up and down, before extending her hand. 'You must be Emma's friend. I'm her mother. Georgina Montague. How do you do?'

'Good, thank you,' says Dominic. 'How are you?' He shakes her hand enthusiastically.

'Well, let's get you upstairs,' she bustles. 'Daddy's just in the cellar, but put your things away, then come down and we'll all have a little glass of something. Muffin?' She turns and bellows down the hallway. 'Did you find the wine?'

'Your mother is terrifying,' says Dominic, as soon as they are safely behind closed doors in Emma's old bedroom. He looks around, taking in the evidence of Emma's life, long before he came into it. 'Why are there posters of boy bands on your wall still?'

'Because I basically haven't been back since I went to university. This is like stepping back in time.'

'Who are they, anyway?'

'Take That.'

Dominic looks blank.

'Huge band in Britain. That's Jason. He was my favourite.'

'Cute,' says Dominic, walking around the room and examining the gymkhana ribbons. 'Your mom must treat this room like a shrine.'

Emma bursts out laughing. 'Are you joking? The only reason this room still looks exactly like it did when I left for university is that my mother has probably never set foot in it since. My parents' bedroom is in the other wing. She never comes up here. It was brilliant for parties. I could sneak tons of people up here and my mother never knew.' She pauses. 'Can I just say something about her being terrifying? You didn't mean that, did you? She really isn't terrifying at all, once you get to know her. She's just quite strong and imposing. You can handle her.'

'Okay,' says Dominic, although he sounds doubtful. 'But if *she's* like that, what the hell is your father like?'

'He's a softie. My mother's the one who wears the trousers.'

'You mean pants.' He raises an eyebrow at her.

'When in England,' she says, as he grabs her and pulls her onto the bed.

*

'Really good to meet you, sir,' says Dominic, more respectful than Emma has ever seen him. He looks more
sophisticated than she has ever seen him, and more uncomfortable. And terribly American, she thinks, in his chinos,
blue button-down shirt, and trainers.

She looks at the trainers, then at her father's battered
old brogues. Her mother will have noticed them immediately, disapprovingly. Trainers, she would say, are only for
the gym. Thankfully, though, her mother is not casting
disapproving glances at Dominic, but is instead busy
bringing in the cheese platter, twittering on about someone's homemade peach chutney she had bought at one of
the country fairs over the summer.

'Come and sit down,' says her father. 'The girls are
drinking wine, but I'm on the scotch. Fancy a glass? I have
an excellent single malt, too.'

'Actually,' Dominic says, 'I'm more of a beer drinker.
It's not that I don't like a glass of Jack every now and
then, but this early in the evening I drink beer, sir.'

'Hmm,' says Emma's father, visibly pleased at being
called *sir*. 'I think we may have a couple of beers in the
outside fridge.' He stands up.

'Please, let me. If you tell me where they are, I can get
them.'

'That's very kind of you. Go through the kitchen into
the gallery, then to the garage. There's a small fridge in
there. I'm not sure what kind we have, but they should be
on the top shelf.'

'Is there anything I can get for you?'

'No, no. I'm quite all right with my nip here.' He toasts him with a smile. When Dominic is safely out of the room, he turns to Emma.

'Very nice young man, your American,' he says.

'He is nice, isn't he?' says Emma. 'I'm glad you like him.'

'I like the way he called me *sir*,' says her father. 'It reminds me of army days. Quite unusual to find a young person these days who has that sort of respect for the older generation. I approve, Emma.'

'You hardly know him.' Emma laughs. 'Which is not to say I'm not delighted you approve. He's a lovely person. I know we're not here for long, but hopefully you'll get to know him a little.'

'He's quite good-looking,' booms her mother from the sofa. 'Very glamorous and exotic with that suntan and that black hair. Where is his family from?'

'I believe Connecticut,' says Emma, being deliberately obtuse. 'Westport, originally, but now Trumbull.'

Georgina's face is blank. 'I mean, where is his family *from*? What country?'

'His grandparents were Italian,' she says.

'Aha!' beams Georgina. 'I thought I detected some Italian in there. We were just in Puglia, weren't we, Muffin? The most divine place. Where in Italy are they from? Has he spent a lot of time visiting his ancestral home?'

'I don't know. You'll have to ask him yourself about what region his family comes from. But this is the first time he's left America.' As soon as the words are out of her mouth she regrets them, for her mother opens her mouth in dismay. Luckily, before she can say anything disparaging, they are interrupted by the sound of the doorbell.

'George and Henry are here,' exclaims Georgina in delight, walking out of the room to get the door as Emma looks at her father in consternation.

'I thought it was just us,' she says. 'I thought the four of us were going to have dinner so you could get to know Dominic. I didn't know George and his fiancée were coming, too?'

Her father shrugs helplessly, placing a hand on her shoulder. 'You know your mother, darling. She can't help it. She has this compulsion to invite everyone. What's that she always says? *The more the merrier?* I'm sorry. You know I would have preferred it to be just us. Not that I don't like my nephew very much, but it would have been so . . . George!' Her father composes a welcoming smile on his face as a young, handsome man walks into the living room, striding over to shake his hand effusively.

'Thank you again for doing this, Uncle Simon,' George says. 'It's so kind of you and Aunt G. I don't know how we'll ever thank you.'

A large woman with a big smile and short blond hair bounds into the room, flinging her arms around Emma's father, who pales slightly as he pats her on the back, trying to extricate himself from her embrace. 'Uncle Simon!' she says into his shoulder, pulling back but not releasing him. 'As soon as we move into our new house we're having you both up to stay! That's how we'll thank you! Honestly, this is just so, so lovely of you.'

She finally releases him, as both she and George turn to see Emma, standing behind them.

'Good God!' says George, peering at her. 'Emma? Is that you? My favourite cousin?'

'It's me,' says Emma, astonished to see George hasn't changed in the slightest since he was a child. He is still spectacularly pretty, with delicate aquiline features. He's also beautifully dressed in a pale green cashmere pullover tied around his shoulders, green-and-pink argyle socks, mouse-suede Oxfords. He looks like something out of another era, as if Brideshead had revisited Brigham Hall by way of *Chariots of Fire*. He has floppy blond hair that he brushes out of his eyes, and perfect white teeth that sparkle as he comes over to give Emma a hug that she really doesn't feel entitled to receive.

He steps back to look at Emma, still clasping her arms. 'You look positively glowing,' he says. 'Aunt G says you're in love and we get to meet the lucky fellow. In the meantime' – he lets her go and steps back – 'I'd like you to meet my beautiful fiancée, Henrietta.'

'How do you do?' Emma holds out a hand only to find herself enveloped in a fierce hug. Henrietta is rather large. And, there's no other way to put it, rather manly. She has a huge smile, twinkling green eyes, and dimples. In a white shirt and beige trousers, with ballet flats on her feet, she is friendly and warm, and if Emma didn't know better, she might think Henrietta was perhaps a somewhat feminine bloke, with a penchant for ballet flats.

It is all very confusing, she thinks, as the door opens

and Dominic steps back into the room, with an open can of beer in his hand.

'Well, hello,' says George slowly, and, if Emma didn't know better, she would swear seductively. 'You must be Emma's lucky man. I'm George. The little cousin.'

'Hello,' says Dominic, shaking his hand. 'Hey.' He waves to Henrietta. 'I'm Dominic.'

'Hello!' The wave wasn't enough for her, though. She bounds over and gives him a cheerful hug. 'I'm Henry.'

Dominic looks confused.

'Henry is short for Henrietta,' explains Emma, while stifling a case of the giggles. 'The engagement party is for George and Henrietta.'

'Henry,' corrects Henry.

'It's quite confusing,' says Emma.

'I know. Everyone thinks George is marrying a man!' With that Henry throws her head back and lets out a belly laugh. Emma, Dominic, and Emma's father Simon all smile rather uncomfortably just as Georgina comes back in the room.

'Ah, here you are,' she says merrily to the happy couple. She claps her hands and puts an arm around Henry's shoulders. 'And you've met the wonderful Henry! Isn't she the most perfect addition to the family? Don't you adore her?' Henry turns as she and Georgina gaze affectionately at one another.

'Dominic?' Emma says loudly. 'You wanted to borrow the computer? Let me just show you where it is. Back in a sec.' She takes Dominic by the hand and leads him out.

Once they are safely in the library, both of them collapse in nervous giggles.

'What's going on?' says Dominic. 'I'm very confused. It must be an English thing, but is Henry a man or a woman? I think George is a man, although I'm not totally sure. And Henry is marrying George? Have I got that straight? Meanwhile, I think Henry's got the hots for your mother.'

'Oh God.' Emma snorts with laughter. 'Don't. That's the most horrible thing I've ever heard.'

'It's true. You know it's true. That's why you're laughing.'

'Yes. Henry was looking at my mother rather adoringly.' She winces. 'You don't actually think she's got the hots for her, do you? Because that would be ever so slightly wrong.'

'I don't know. Maybe it's an English thing but George seems gay, not that there's anything wrong with that, and Henry seems to be, well . . . a man. Which is maybe why George wants to marry her. Him.'

'We're being awful,' says Emma with another giggle. 'We must stop. Although, I did always think George was gay,' says Emma. 'Which might explain his attraction to Henry.'

'And me.'

'Oh God! Yes! When you walked in, George looked like he had died and gone to heaven to find the hunky American of his dreams standing at the gates.'

'I want to tell you that's the craziest thing I've ever heard, but yeah. That's pretty much what he looked like.

You told me a little bit about your family, I know, but apparently you've kept the best part a secret!'

'I didn't know!' Emma laughs. 'I haven't seen George properly since he was a little boy. When I heard he'd got engaged, I was a bit surprised. I guess for all these years I'd assumed wrong.'

'Guess so.'

'Guess so,' echoes Emma. 'Henry seems nice, though. In a very jolly hockey sticks kind of way.'

'What does that mean?'

'English public schoolgirl. Super excited and enthusiastic about everything.'

'When you say school*girl*, you actually mean . . .'

'At least she's nice. Look, we'd better get back. If my mother becomes too impossible, we'd better have a plan of action. It won't do to dissolve in hysterics in front of everyone.'

'We need a code word,' says Dominic. 'How about *birdcage*?'

'Oh, you're funny. Fine. *Birdcage* it is.'

'If I say *birdcage*, that means you have to get me out of there, fast. Got it?'

'Got it,' says Emma. Then she ruefully shakes her head at Dominic. 'I really thought we were going to have a quiet evening when my parents could get to know you. I'm sorry.'

'Don't be. It isn't what I expected either, but it's probably more fun.'

*

'This cold pea soup is really good,' says Dominic, as they sit around the dining room table.

'It's not meant to be cold,' mutters Emma under her breath. 'It's my mother's cooking.'

'What?' says her mother, from the other end of the table.

'Dominic said the soup is cool,' says George, winking at Dominic. 'I think that's American slang for *delicious*.'

'Oh, I'm so glad,' says Georgina. 'I was worried it wasn't quite hot enough. I do love to cook, but I'm not always so good with timing.'

'She's right,' says her husband jovially from the other end of the table. 'Delicious food, always cold.'

'Or overcooked,' booms Georgina with a laugh. 'I'm lucky you love my overcooked broccoli.'

'Sounds delicious,' says Dominic quietly, going back to his soup.

'So, Dominic.' George lays down his spoon. 'You look like you're in shockingly good shape. Is that from working out or is it something in the water over there?'

'I don't work out,' says Dominic with a smile. 'Not any more, anyway. I was a gym rat in my twenties, but now I mostly stay in shape with a lot of physical labour.'

'Like what?'

'Dominic's a carpenter,' says Emma. 'He made the most beautiful bookshelves for my house.'

'That's right,' says George. 'Now I remember. Your mother told me he's your landlord. That's handy. A hunky landlord who makes things.' He shoots Emma an approving glance. 'You certainly hit the jackpot.'

'I don't just make things,' Dominic says. 'I work as a bartender, too.'

'A what?' Georgina says, turning to Henry and saying under her breath, but loudly enough for everyone to hear, 'I can't understand anything he says. It must be the accent. What did he say?'

'He said he works as a bartender,' says Henry loudly.

'A bartender?' says Georgina, composing her features into the politest expression she can muster. 'How . . . fun.'

'*Fun* is not the word I'd use,' Dominic says with a laugh. 'That's where the muscles are from. I haul boxes of wine and liquor up and down from the cellar all day long.'

'Nice,' coos George, as Henry bursts out laughing.

'Stop teasing him,' she tells George.

Emma and Dominic exchange confused glances.

Birdcage? mouths Dominic as Emma shakes her head and laughs.

'What about your family?' says Georgina. 'What line of business are they in?'

'My dad worked in the restaurant business,' says Dominic. 'He was a cook.'

'A chef!' Georgina perks up. There's something she can work with. 'How nice! Maybe he can give me some tips on timing.'

'That's not really—' Dominic starts to speak but Henry interrupts, much to Emma's relief. Emma doesn't care what kind of job Dominic's father had. She doesn't care if he was unemployed his entire life. But her mother would. And the less Georgina knows about Dominic's family, the better.

At least until she gets to know him, and fully accepts him into the family.

So Henry's interjection saves the day. 'Emma!' she says brightly. 'George says you love living in America! We were thinking about going over to the States for our honeymoon. I've always wanted to see New England. What do you think? Would you help us work out where to go?'

'Of course,' says Emma, 'I'd be happy to. I'm dying to hear all about the two of you. Where did you meet?'

'You tell it,' says George, looking at Henry. 'You always tell it so much better than me.'

'It's terribly unromantic.' Henry giggles. 'It was in Tesco Metro. I had a group of friends coming for dinner, but I'd burnt the stew – complete accident, I didn't realize the burner was misaligned – so I was desperately trying to cobble together something passable at the last minute.'

'One of her dinner guests was a chef,' says George. 'So she had to impress.'

'Did your hands meet over the potatoes?' asks Emma.

'Almost!' Henry says. 'I had paused by the cauliflower, trying to decide whether I ought to buy it, when George started talking to me.'

'She was actually wearing a sweatshirt saying *Oxford University*.'

'I didn't go to Oxford, though,' says Henry. 'Far too stupid!' And she starts laughing. 'I did a cordon bleu course instead.'

'Which means she is a far better cook than I will ever be, but we started talking about Oxford . . .' says George.

'And all my best friends went there, and George knew all of them, including two of the people coming for dinner.'

'So I gave her my recipe for tandoori cauliflower, not knowing she was already an amazing cook . . .'

'And I invited him for dinner.'

'And the rest,' says George, reaching for Henry's hand, 'is history.'

'He never left.' Henry rolls her eyes as George looks at her adoringly.

Emma shoots a look at Dominic as they give each other the tiniest of shrugs. Clearly they both got it very wrong.

'And now the two of you are about to embark on the journey of a lifetime, starting tomorrow night!' says Georgina, from the end of the table. 'I'm utterly thrilled to be the one hosting your engagement party. The two of you are going to be gloriously happy forever.'

'Thank you,' says George. Then he shoots a fond look at Emma and Dominic. 'Maybe there will be another announcement soon . . .'

'Oh, I don't know about *that*,' Emma's mother says clearly, her hearing suddenly fine.

'I'll clear.' Emma, bright red, jumps up, gathering plates and whisking them into the kitchen. She loads the plates into the dishwasher, aware her heart is pounding, embarrassed for Dominic, who surely must have heard her mother's remark, embarrassed for herself. Dominic probably didn't understand. He may have assumed her mother was simply implying that it's too early in their relationship to be considering marriage. But Emma knows better. She knows her mother too well. It was a clear statement that Emma should not be marrying someone like that. That Dominic is beneath her.

A wave of dismay washes over her. This is why she left to take a job in New York. She didn't want to deal with her mother's bullshit any more, her passive-aggressive digs, her ridiculous snobbery.

I shouldn't have come back, she thinks. *It's so much easier when I see them on my turf, when they fly to New York for a week and I can take them to dinner, to a show, perhaps a lunch or tea and send them off sightseeing. But this? Being in my childhood home, having to deal with my mother's snobbery and not being able to escape, is awful.*

Emma places her hands on the kitchen worktop and steps back, looking at the floor, taking a few deep breaths. The sound of footsteps behind her startles her, and she looks up to see Dominic coming through the kitchen doorway, juggling a stack of plates.

'Are you okay?' he asks, concern in his eyes.

'I'm fine.' She forces a smile. 'It's just always a challenge, being home.'

'Was it what your mom said? Not knowing about an announcement?'

Emma shrugs. 'Kind of. It just seemed so unnecessary. I know we haven't been together long, but she didn't need to point it out.'

Dominic smiles. 'That wasn't what she was pointing out and you know it.'

Emma swallows hard. 'What do you mean?'

'Someone like you? Someone who grew up with *this*?'
He gestures around the kitchen. 'Someone like *you* does
not end up with someone like *me*. Even I see that.'

Emma stares at him as Dominic sighs.

'Look, I knew as soon as I met you that we are from
very different worlds. I feel like I've stepped into the queen's
palace here. Your parents can definitely see I don't belong.
I'm okay with that, but yeah, the thought of you and me
getting formally engaged and having a party here like the
one your parents are throwing tomorrow is crazy. If my
parents came, they would be so intimidated, they would
get drunk and end up throwing up on one of the antique
rugs.'

Emma's face falls. 'Are you saying you and I are pointless? That it can't go anywhere? That maybe we shouldn't
be together?'

'What? No!' He steps towards her and places his hands
on her arms. 'God, no. I know that what you and I have
is rare, and really special. I also know that we come from
very different backgrounds, and not everybody's going to
understand that. I get that your mom doesn't understand
it. I get that most of the people who are going to show up
tomorrow for the party aren't going to understand it, either.
They're going to wonder what you're doing with a guy
like me. But that's okay. I know what we're doing together,
and you know what we're doing together. That's all that
matters. You know that, right?'

Emma's eyes are filled with tears as she nods. 'I do know
that. I needed to hear it from you. Thank you.' She sniffles

again. 'I'm sorry about my mother,' she adds. 'I was hoping she would behave better.'

'Honey, I'm a bartender at the Fat Hen, remember? This is nothing. She says anything else, though, and I'll take her down. Boom!'

Emma starts to laugh as she allows herself to be pulled in for a hug, the anger, embarrassment, and angst all gone.

'What's going on in here?'

Emma smiles as her mother bustles in. 'Nothing. We're just clearing up. We'll go and get the rest of the plates.'

She takes Dominic's hand and leads him back to the dining room. She may have forgiven her mother for the time being, but the last thing she needs is to give her the opportunity to say anything else.

Chapter 27

'I could get used to this,' says Dominic, settling back on the bench, nursing his pint of Guinness as a ploughman's lunch is set in front of him. 'Beer, bread, and cheese. Does life get any better?'

'Cheers.' Emma lifts her vodka and tonic in a toast to Dominic and her father, relieved that the three of them have managed to get away.

The caterers showed up late that morning, with teams of men to finish off the marquee. A lorry had trundled down the driveway even earlier, just after seven, dropping off vases filled with sweet peas and peonies, banging, clattering, shouting. The noise they'd made seemed entirely unreasonable, Emma felt, so early in the morning.

And Georgina bustled in and out of the house directing everyone, pretending to be stressed, although Emma knew she was loving every second.

Emma had grabbed some toast, made tea for herself and Dominic, and sneaked quietly back upstairs to bed, thinking it was the only peaceful place in the house. It quickly became apparent that there was no peaceful place in the house; the noise and banging could be heard everywhere. In the end Dominic and Emma got dressed and went for a walk.

It was noon by the time they approached the pub. Neither of them could face going back to the house, so they headed inside the eighteenth-century building. There, tucked into a corner with a stack of newspapers and a pint, was Emma's father.

'Dad? What are you doing here?'

He had put his paper down and groaned. 'It's the noise. I can't bear it. Your mother's gone into overdrive and I had to get out. I've got enough here to read to keep me busy for hours.'

'May we join you?'

His face lit up. 'Of course.'

The three of them toast each other and sip their drinks as Emma's father closes his eyes in pleasure. 'I love your mother,' he says, his eyes still closed, 'but she does drive me up the wall.'

'My father's an introvert,' Emma says unnecessarily to Dominic, reaching over for a piece of his cheese. 'And my mother, as you have probably realized, is an extrovert. It makes for an interesting partnership, don't you think, Dad?'

'Interesting is the polite way of putting it.' He smiles.

'And I' – Emma gestures to herself – 'just in case you haven't already guessed, take after my dad.' For years, Emma realizes, as she speaks, she had thought she ought to be different. More like her mother, more outgoing, more

ambitious, but suddenly she knows she is perfectly content
to be like her dad; to be herself.

'It's funny,' Dominic says. 'You seem really outgoing.
You're not shy at all.'

'That's not really what introversion is about,' says Emma.
'Although everyone seems to think otherwise. Being an
introvert really means you recharge your batteries by being
alone. You can be sociable and outgoing and enjoy people,
but only for limited amounts of time. Large groups and
lots of stimulation exhaust an introvert. Literally, for every
hour spent at a party, an introvert will need two hours on
their own.'

'I'm the opposite, clearly,' Dominic says.

'Indeed you are,' says Emma, smiling. 'Definitely an
extrovert. You're okay on your own, but when you're
feeling drained or tired, you make yourself feel better by
inviting a ton of people over, or going to work at the Fat
Hen.'

'It's true.' Dominic nods as he sips his pint. 'Does that
mean an extrovert and an introvert shouldn't be together?'

Emma's father laughs. 'You might think that from
looking at Emma's mother and me, but no. I think it's
rather good for you to marry the opposite. It brings balance
to your life. If my wife didn't force me out from time to
time, I'd never leave the house.' He pauses thoughtfully.
'I would actually be quite happy never leaving the house.
But I also know that in order to live a full life, I have to
have other experiences. It's good for me. And I wouldn't
have it any other way. Except when she says she's throwing

an engagement party and it turns out to be the equivalent of a wedding.' He shakes his head in dismay.

'Speaking of, where are George and Henry today?' Emma asks.

'George has found some spa in Yeovil and has booked a massage.' Simon says this without expression, leaving it to Emma to raise her eyebrows. 'And Henry is accompanying him to get her hair and make-up done.'

'Henry wears make-up?' asks Dominic.

'Not that I've seen,' admits Emma's father. 'But there it is. I'm also slightly unclear as to what exactly could be done with her hair. It's terribly short.'

'Have you planned your escape route for tonight?' Emma teases her father.

'I was thinking about booking a room at the Summer House. Just in case the party's too noisy. Although we do have the box room at the front of the house,' he adds. 'I'm sure the bed in there is shockingly uncomfortable, but if I have to escape to a quiet spot, I think that's probably going to be the quietest I can find.'

'What on earth is a box room?' says Dominic with a frown.

'It's a junk room,' explains Emma. 'It's the tiniest bedroom where you put everything that doesn't fit anywhere else.' She turns to her father. 'Can we join you?'

'That *will* be cosy.' Her father laughs as they lean towards each other.

Dominic watches the two of them and sees, suddenly, how much they look alike, how similar they are.

Years ago, his mother had told him that when he met the girl he was going to marry, he should look at her mother to see how she would turn out. For some reason, that piece of advice stuck with him.

He remembers it now, thinking of Georgina Montague with a slight shudder. She was undeniably a handsome woman when young – Dominic has seen the old black-and-white photographs in silver frames that dot every surface – but she is a bit of a battle-axe now. Clearly she was never tiny in the way Emma is; her stoutness and imposing bosom add to her commanding air. Seeing Emma here, next to her father, Dominic breathes a sigh of relief. He is clearly the parent she takes after in every way.

Dominic's phone buzzes and he lights up when he sees it's Jesse calling. He excuses himself to take the call outside.

'I like him,' says Simon Montague, when Dominic has left the room. 'He seems like a lovely chap, and he quite clearly adores you.'

Emma feels the warmth of happiness spread through her body. 'Thank you, Dad. That means a lot to me.' She pauses, knowing she shouldn't pose the question she's about to ask, but she can't keep the words in. 'Does Mum like him?'

'She really doesn't know him,' says her father diplomatically. 'And you know your mother. She still thinks you're going to find yourself a nice English fellow and settle down in Somerset. Preferably a peer.' He raises his eyebrows, then continues, 'Your having found yourself a serious American boyfriend means there's a very real possibility that you'll never come back for good. And although you and your mother have had your . . . issues over the years, she loves you very much, and that's a bitter pill for her to swallow.'

Emma sits back, surprised. She hadn't looked at it like that, hadn't ever considered the possibility that her mother wouldn't like Dominic because she fears he will take Emma away from her forever. Has she been too harsh on her mother? She is surprised to feel a wave of compassion.

Dominic walks back in, distracted.

'Is everything okay?'

He shrugs. 'Jesse's okay. He's not loving his grandparents being there. I mean, he's thrilled they've taken him out and bought him toys, but he tells me they're screaming at each other all the time. He's stressed and upset.' Dominic shakes his head. 'I shouldn't have done it. I thought they might have calmed down, but it doesn't sound like a great situation.'

Emma sinks down on her seat, filled with guilt and remorse. 'I'm so sorry,' she says. 'It's only another couple of days. Do you think he'll be okay until then?'

'I guess,' Dominic says. 'I just feel guilty, and a little foolish to think they might have been different with him. I hope he is going to be okay.'

'Listen,' Emma reminds him. 'You survived an entire childhood with them, and you turned out fine. However bad they are with each other, they're still loving with him, aren't they? And kids are resilient. He'll be okay.'

'I won't do it again, though,' Dominic says. 'I can't have

my parents look after him regularly. I mean, that's why they never have, and he doesn't really know them. I was always scared this would happen. I don't want him around that kind of shouting.' He looks at Emma then. 'At least with us he sees what a good relationship is.'

'He does,' says Emma, taking his hand. 'He will forget this visit with his grandparents, but he won't forget the example we're setting for him. That's what counts.'

It is Emma's turn to excuse herself. She goes to the bathroom and stares at herself in the mirror, smiling. Everything Dominic says, that they are setting an example for Jesse what a relationship can be, that he knows this is it, makes Emma happy. She knows this is different, knows this is for real. The only fly in the ointment is the childish need she still has for her parents' blessing.

She already has her father's – of that she is sure. But if she doesn't have her mother's approval, she can learn to live without it.

Chapter 28

'Oh God!' Georgina Montague throws her hands up in the air as she walks into the kitchen from the garden.

'What's going on?' Emma is doing up the ankle straps on her Manolo Blahniks, wishing she had brought evening flats rather than high suede Mary Janes. Now she will have to spend the entire evening tiptoeing around so that her heels won't sink into the lawn.

She is wearing a black silk dress she has had for years, her go-to cocktail dress for parties in New York, although it probably isn't what's worn for an English engagement party under a marquee in a garden. She owns a million floral tea dresses, any of which would have been perfect. Oh well. Emma sighs, seeing the first guests stride down the driveway in their pretty sundresses. They'll just have to presume that she has become completely New-York-ized over the past few years.

'What's the matter?' She looks at her mother as Dominic walks into the kitchen, breathtakingly handsome in a navy blazer and pale blue shirt.

'The barman's throwing up in the back loo,' Georgina

says. 'Food poisoning, he says. He's been retching for the past hour and tells me he can't work at the party. I don't know what we're going to do!' She throws her hands up in the air again for dramatic impact. Then she pauses, and swivels neatly to settle her gaze on Dominic.

'Wait a moment,' Georgina says. 'Dominic. Didn't you say *you* were a barman?'

'Mum, come on. We're guests,' says Emma. 'It's not fair to ask him. Phone the caterer and ask them to send a replacement. And if they can't, people can just serve themselves.'

'I *have* phoned the caterer,' snaps her mother. 'They don't have anyone else. Apparently it's one of the busiest Saturdays of the year. As for your suggestion we have people serve themselves?' She snorts with derision. 'I don't think so. This isn't that kind of party, and our friends certainly aren't those kinds of people. We *must* have a barman.' She stares at Dominic. The seconds tick by.

'It's fine.' Dominic gives an easy shrug as he breaks Georgina's stare and looks at Emma. 'Honestly. It's no problem. It's what I do. Do you have any signature drinks I need to know about?'

'I knew there would be something I'd forget. No! We don't have any signature drinks. Oh lord.'

'Don't worry. Let me go out and see what you have. Maybe I can come up with something.' Everything about his manner is reassuring. Emma watches her mother's shoulders visibly relax as she smiles at him graciously.

'Oh,' she says, just before she turns to leave the kitchen.

'You can borrow a white shirt from my husband. The trousers are fine.' She casts an eye over his khaki trousers. 'I would have preferred black but never mind.'

Emma is suddenly furious. How dare her mother be so patronizing. How dare she treat Dominic like a member of the staff, especially when he's doing such a huge favour for her. But Dominic places a hand on her arm and holds her back until her mother disappears through the doors into the garden.

'It's okay, Emma,' he says gently. 'She's hugely stressed, obviously, and at a party this size, having a bartender get sick is a big deal. I'm happy to help. She's just trying to make sure the evening's perfect.'

'Because she's so bloody insecure she thinks that a barman in the wrong trousers will make her look like a failure. Heaven forbid. My God. It's pathetic.'

'Yes. It is. Which is why you need to feel sorry for her, not get angry. She can't help it. It's okay.'

'Are you absolutely sure about this? Because honestly, at this point I would be quite happy to pack up our stuff and go to a hotel. I just don't know that we should stay.'

'They're your parents,' says Dominic. 'And they're getting older, and they're not going to be here forever. You hardly ever see them. Let's just accept your mom's insecurities and forgive her. She can't help it. Remember, she's just doing the best she can with the knowledge that she has.'

'When did you get so forgiving and generous? And wise?'

'I'm not sure I am. If it were my parents, I'd fucking kill them. But they're yours, so I'm able to be forgiving and see their good side.'

'There's a good side?'

Dominic pauses as if he's thinking. 'Well, your dad's awesome,' he says finally, and Emma laughs.

'Come here.' He takes her in his arms. 'It's all going to be okay.'

'Dominic?' They hear her mother calling from the gallery. 'Are you coming? I have the shirt here for you.'

'I promise to make you a very stiff drink,' he says with a smile, kissing Emma before walking off to join Georgina and take care of the bar.

The marquee, or, as Dominic kept referring to it, much to her mother's chagrin, *tent*, is packed to bursting with the guests. George and Henry are moving through the crowds, greeting friends, being introduced to ancient family members Henry has never met.

Henry, it has to be said, looks not unlike a man in drag. She is wearing red lipstick, which is entirely the wrong colour for her, and heavy eye make-up that no beautician worth her salt would ever have chosen for her. Her hair has been curled, and now has a pink streak in it that Henry described with a hoot of laughter as 'great fun!' She is wearing a belted green dress with a knee-length skirt that does absolutely nothing for her, and she has large sparkly multicoloured hoops in her ears.

Emma has greeted her relatives, family friends of her

parents she hasn't seen for years, and people from the village she has known her entire life. She has had the same
conversations over and over again: yes, America is exciting;
no, she isn't married yet; the barman is her boyfriend, and
he is helping out because the original barman has a stomach
bug; yes, I think he's terribly handsome, too; no, I'm no
longer with the bank.

She goes to the bar frequently, for constant refills and
reassuring kisses, but Dominic is busy. She can't expect
him to look after her as well as the other guests. So she
moves to the other side of the marquee, wishing he weren't
helping out, wishing he were by her side so she wouldn't
be quite so bored.

'Em-ma,' says a familiar singsong voice, and she turns,
catching her breath, utterly stunned to see a tall, lanky man
standing there, the top buttons of his shirt open to reveal
the beginnings of a suntanned chest. A chest she used to
know very well. A body she used to know almost as well
as her own.

'Rufus.' She forcibly replaces the surprise with a smile
and gives him an air kiss on either cheek. 'What a lovely
surprise. No one told me you'd be here.'

'I didn't know I'd be here myself.' Rufus laughs. 'I'm
up staying with Kat and Jonti for the weekend. I had no
idea they were attending an engagement party, much less
one at the Montagues'. Of course, I insisted on gate-
crashing.'

'Oh. I hope my mother doesn't see you,' says Emma,

knowing how appalled her mother gets when people show up without an invitation.

'I'm not really gate-crashing,' says Rufus. 'I phoned her first. I told her I was up for the weekend and she invited me immediately.'

Emma frowns. 'When was this?'

'Yesterday morning. Clearly she didn't pass on the information.' He laughs.

Emma finds herself looking at him, unable to believe she spent so many years with him. This was the man she woke up with every morning. She knows all his habits: the way he soaps himself in the shower, the way he shaves while grimacing into a tiny magnifying mirror stuck to the wall. He likes to sit on the loo for hours, reading the papers, sometimes with a glass of scotch on the window ledge next to him. He loves soft, creamy scrambled eggs for breakfast, with burnt wholegrain toast. He finds cruel humour hilarious. She knows the expression on his face when he orgasms. And what it takes to get him there.

She blinks. It has all come flooding back to her. She knows him so well, and here they are, making small talk, like strangers.

'I heard you got married and have children now,' says Emma, awkwardly, not knowing what else to say. 'Congratulations. How old are they?'

'I have Charlie, who's four, and Daisy, who's just turned two. They are adorable, naturally, as all small children are.'

'And your wife? Is she here, too?'

Rufus grimaces. 'Little bit of a problem at the moment.'

Emma stares at him. 'What do you mean?'

'We're on a little bit of a break. Having a few issues with . . . with our marriage.'

Emma can't hide her look of surprise. 'You're having issues? Aren't marriage and kids what you always wanted?'

'Well, yes. Absolutely. But my wife seemed to think I'd be home all the time once we had kids. She doesn't seem to understand that I can't change my schedule – all the after-work meetings I have to attend – just because I have children now.'

Emma tilts her head. 'Do you mean long drunken dinners with the boys four nights a week?'

Rufus gives her a sheepish smile. 'You know me so well.' He shrugs. 'You always understood.'

'I did, but I didn't like it. I never had a problem with you going out with the boys, it was just that the boys were so ghastly I never wanted to go.'

'That's what my wife thinks, too. She would never dream of going, but she doesn't want me to go either, which is where the problem started.'

'You're really allowing nights out with the boys to get in the way of your marriage when you have two tiny children?'

'Well, it's not just that,' says Rufus. 'You said I always wanted marriage and kids, which I did, but . . .' He pauses and looks away.

'What?' prompts Emma.

'I always wanted that with you,' he says simply, without a trace of his signature sarcasm.

Emma doesn't respond. She has no idea what to say.

'Clearly we've both moved on.' He shakes his head. 'I think I may have made a terrible mistake. I married the first girl I met after we split up. I didn't really give us a chance to get to know each other, to find out if we were compatible. I just met her, we fell into this thing very quickly, and I proposed without really thinking it through.'

'Oh God, Rufus. I'm sorry.'

'Nothing to be sorry about. I just don't think we have very much in common.'

'Other than your two children,' Emma points out.

'Well, yes. Obviously it's not ideal circumstances, to have had the children. I did rather think I might have been making a terrible mistake when I showed up in church on our wedding day. I was quite drunk, you know. But I didn't know how not to go through with it. And she announced she was pregnant before I had a chance to confess my un-happiness, and how could I say anything after that?'

Emma reaches out and rubs his arm sympathetically. 'I don't know what you do in a situation like that,' she says. 'It sounds impossible.'

'It just got worse from there,' he says, seemingly relieved to be able to talk about it. 'We weren't friends. We weren't partners. We were two people who happened to have chil-dren, but we had nothing else in common. I didn't feel love when I looked at her. I felt resentment. And she felt the same way about me. Anyway, I'm sorry. I didn't mean to talk your ear off. I certainly didn't mean to complain. I moved into a flat in Notting Hill a couple of months ago and I'm making the best of things. How's your life? You look wonderful.'

Emma smiles. 'Thank you.'

'No, I mean it,' says Rufus. 'You're absolutely glowing. America clearly suits you.' He pauses. 'I should never have let you go.'

Emma laughs. 'You didn't let me go, Rufus. I left. Or at least, it was my decision for us to split up.'

'But I should have worked harder for you. I shouldn't have let you just walk away without fighting to try and get you back.' He steps closer to her, looking meaningfully into her eyes, and Emma shrinks back. If she didn't know better she would be certain he was about to kiss her. Rufus pauses, Emma freezes, with no idea what to do, and the moment hangs in the air until they both hear his name being called.

'Rufus!'

Emma turns around to see her mother bearing down on them, delight in her eyes as she gives Rufus enthusiastic kisses on both cheeks. 'What a gorgeous surprise!'

Emma turns to her. 'You knew he was coming,' she says, trying to keep the belligerence out of her voice.

'I completely forgot!' her mother replies, still smiling. 'Gosh, you look handsome. Doesn't he look handsome, Emma?'

Emma nods uncomfortably.

'And is it true that you're a single man again? Oh, Rufus! I am so sorry.' But she can scarcely hide her glee. 'Emma, did you hear that? Rufus is single again!'

'I know,' Emma says flatly. 'We were just discussing it.'

'Were you? Oh, it's lovely to see you, Rufus. And even lovelier to see the two of you together. I know, I know, I'm just an annoying old woman, but the two of you do still make the most beautiful couple.'

Emma shakes her head with scorn as her mother innocently throws her hands in the air. 'What? Don't glare at me just for pointing out the obvious. Emma's gone all *American* on us,' she says, turning to Rufus. 'She brought her American *boyfriend* here.'

'Boyfriend?' Rufus raises an eyebrow. 'I had no idea you had a boyfriend. Where is he?'

'Behind the bar,' says her mother. 'He's a barman.'

'Oh,' says Rufus, with an amused smile. 'A *barman?* That's . . . nice.'

'It's certainly helpful,' trills her mother. 'Especially tonight, when the original barman we booked got ill.'

Rufus turns and studies Dominic as Emma cringes. 'He looks very American,' he says finally. 'All good looks, big muscles, and white teeth.'

'Thanks,' Emma says guardedly, unsure if this is a compliment.

'Not at all who I would have imagined you with,' Rufus continues, turning back to face her.

'Couldn't agree more,' says her mother.

Emma closes her eyes just for a second, reminding herself to breathe deeply. 'You need to stop, Mother,' she says, her voice shaking with fury. 'I've already had enough of your digs at Dominic. If I hear you say one more thing about him, if I hear you dismiss or refer to him disdainfully one more time, we will both leave. I swear to you this is not an empty threat. It will take me five minutes to pack my suitcase, and we will go to a hotel for the remainder of this trip. Dominic is the best man I have ever known, and if you can't see that, if you are only capable of judging him by where he's from, or how much money he does or doesn't have, you will lose both of us.'

Emma's voice is low, quiet, and resolved. Rufus has already backed away, leaving this to the two of them. Her mother stares at her before opening her mouth.

'First of all,' says her mother, flustered but doing her best to save face, 'I do not like the way you are talking to me. Secondly, this is not about Dominic, this is about you. I know you think he's the man you're going to end up with, but let me tell you, marriage is no piece of cake. It's one of the hardest things you will ever do, and it's hard enough when you marry someone from your own back-ground, let alone someone from another world. I don't care that Dominic is American. I don't care about that. He may be a nice man, but he's from a completely different class. He's a barman, for heaven's sake. He doesn't under-stand your world, and you can't possibly understand his. I am delighted that you are having fun, Emma, but I do not think this is the man for you. He is not the man you are going to marry.' She recovers her composure and steps back. 'And frankly, darling,' she adds, in a louder voice, 'he's not exactly PLU, is he?'

Emma's heart is pounding as she stares at her mother.

PLU. People like us. The most ridiculous epithet ever invented. It was the absolute worst thing her mother could have said.

'*You* weren't *PLU*,' says Emma, with a bitter laugh. 'But you seem to have conveniently forgotten your roots. I've had enough. The guests will have to help themselves to their own drinks.'

Turning on her heel, she strides to the bar, takes Dominic by the hand, and leads him upstairs to pack.

Emma never thought it would come to this. She never thought she would have to make a choice between her family and her man, but her mother has given her no option. Even if Georgina were to knock on the bedroom door and apologize, Emma isn't sure it would make enough of a difference.

Life is so easy when you are young, she thinks. You can say and do almost anything, safe in the knowledge that an apology will make everything better. The older you get, the more impact those harmful words and deeds have. Once said, those words cannot be unspoken.

Her mother is not the type to apologize. She has fallen out with friends over the years, and once crossed, she writes people off forever. Those few who have managed to stay in her inner circle have long joked that her parties are the most fun because they are always filled with new people, that you are unlikely to see the same faces three years in a row.

Emma is fighting tears as they both fill their suitcases.

She still hopes her mother will come up, say something, apologize, ask forgiveness, at least try to stop the two of them leaving. But she knows such a gesture would be out of character.

No one is in the house as they carry their luggage down the stairs.

'Are you sure about this?' Dominic pauses in the entrance hall to look at her. 'You're sure you want to just leave without saying goodbye? You're sure you want to fly all the way home without resolving this?'

'I'm sure,' she says, on the brink of tears.

'Emma.' He steps forward and reaches out for her arms, holding her steady. 'Your parents aren't young. And they're set in their ways. Think about this. Anything might happen to them and you would never forgive yourself if you left now, like this. I understand why you're so upset, but you're going to feel better if you can find a way to forgive her.'

Emma closes her eyes and shakes her head. 'I can't right now. Maybe I'll feel differently in the morning, but right now I can't even look at her.'

'Okay.' He nods after a long pause. 'I get it. Is there a place nearby for us to stay?'

'I already called the Summer House. They have a room.'

'Let's go, then.' He picks up both suitcases and walks through the door. With one last look behind her, pained by the very real possibility that she and her mother will never resolve things, that this may be the last time she comes here, Emma walks down the steps.

They are getting into their car when they hear a shout.

George approaches, running from the side of the house, concern on his face.

'Where are you two off to?' he says. 'Aren't you staying here? Isn't it too early to leave?'

Dominic puts the bags down and starts to walk back to the house. 'Hi, George. Emma will explain. I left my phone upstairs.' He disappears inside.

'I'm so sorry.' Emma turns to George. 'My mother and I had words, and . . . it just doesn't feel right to stay here any more.'

'Did she tell you she thought *Dominic isn't PLU*?' He does a shockingly good imitation of her mother.

'Please tell me she hasn't been saying that to everyone? Please don't make this worse than it already is.'

'She hasn't.' George lays a reassuring hand on her arm. 'I just know Aunt G. It's her favourite phrase. She doesn't realize that one's only supposed to use it ironically. She treated Dominic like a servant. I'm so sorry, Emma. I saw it happening, but I didn't know how to stop it. For what it's worth, I am thrilled you both came. I think Dominic is wonderful in every way, and I think the two of you are perfect for each other. And I don't think you should give a stuff what anyone thinks, least of all your mother. I love her, don't get me wrong, and I couldn't be more grateful to her for taking Henry and me under her wing in the way she has, but I think she is completely wrong about this.'

Emma's eyes fill with tears. 'Oh, George,' she says. 'Thank you. You have no idea how much better you've made me feel.'

'Trust me, I've had to deal with all kinds of crap now that I'm engaged to Henry. Everyone always thought I was gay, and all my friends think Henry's a secret lesbian.'

Emma composes her features in a way that she hopes conveys surprise.

'No one understands what we're doing together, but honestly, Henry's the most amazing girl I've ever met. She makes me laugh every day, and she's kind, and sweet, and huge fun. We are going to have an amazing life together, and I really have fallen completely in love for the first time in my life. I know everyone thinks this is a disaster waiting to happen, but I don't care what they think. Henry and I will prove them wrong, just as you and Dominic will prove your mother wrong. Besides, your mother's the greatest snob in the world, so really, you should automatically discount everything she says.'

Emma throws her arms around him in a tight hug.

'You should come and see us in America,' she says. 'Seriously. Any time. Thank you for saying everything you've said. And I didn't think you were gay,' she adds.

George pulls back and shakes his head with a smile. 'Darling, everyone did. I don't believe you for a second, but I forgive you. We would love to come and see you and the very hunky Dominic in America. I'll email you when you get home.'

'What was that about?' Dominic has found his phone and come back to the car. He looks questioningly at Emma, who is sitting in the passenger seat waiting for him, frowning.

'George was amazing,' she says, recounting what he said to her.

'Very amazing, you're right,' says Dominic. 'He's not who I thought he was.'

'I'll tell you one thing I'm sure of: he's genuinely in love with Henry. When he talked about her, he went all mushy. It was sweet.'

'I love that he said no one approves of their match. What the hell does anyone know? The only people who matter are George and Henry.' He pauses. 'And Dominic and Emma.'

'Yes.' Emma nods as her mother's words once again echo in her head. 'You're right. Let's go. I need to get out of here.'

Chapter 29

The view from the hotel dining room stretches across the fields. Emma gazes out the window. She never misses England when she is in America, does not give it a second thought. It is only when she is here, driving through pretty country lanes overhung with a canopy of green, winding through villages of old stone houses and thatched roofs, gazing out of windows onto rolling fields and meadows, that she misses it.

Their table is quiet; there's only one other couple here, on the other side of the room. Dominic is tucking into a ful English fry-up, and Emma is sipping coffee to chase down the painkiller she had taken earlier. The tears she shed last night after leaving the house in the wake of her fury left her with a pounding head, and she is only just starting to feel human again.

'Isn't that your father?' Dominic says through a mouthful of pork sausage.

Emma turns, as Simon sees her and gives her a cautious wave. She waits for him to come and join them, but instead he walks in the other direction. She excuses herself from the table to find him sitting on a bench outside. When she sits next to him, he takes her hand and squeezes it, and she lays her head on his shoulder, saying nothing, as the tears threaten to spill yet again.

'How did you know I was here?' she says eventually.

'I have friends in high places,' he says with a small smile. 'I took you tea in bed this morning, only to find you'd disappeared. Your mother then told me what had happened, and I knew there were only a couple of places you could have gone. Come home, Emma. You still have three days before you're supposed to leave, and we both want you to come home.'

Emma shakes her head. 'I'm sorry, Dad. We're leaving today. I changed the flight. We're being picked up after breakfast.'

Her father's face falls, suddenly looking old, older than Emma has ever seen him.

'You're leaving? Already? Oh, Emma.' He shakes his head. 'We can't end your trip like this.'

'Daddy, I'm sorry. I am. But Mum said terrible things last night. I couldn't stay. I just can't do it.'

'She didn't say any of those things to hurt you.' Her father sighs. 'She thought she was helping.'

'Helping?' Emma snorts. 'I don't need helping. I brought Dominic to England with me to meet you because we have something really special. When was the last time you met someone I was dating?' Her father says nothing. 'Exactly. The last boyfriend of mine you met was Rufus, because nothing since then has been serious enough to warrant my introducing you. But this is. I know he isn't what she expects, I know he doesn't meet her ridiculously high, snobby standards, but her values are completely messed up. She'd rather I marry some pompous, entitled banker who installs me in a mansion with a live-in housekeeper and a subscription to the yoga club to keep me busy while he spends his weekdays in the city sleeping with whoever he wants.'

'That doesn't sound like a bad deal, actually,' her father says, after a pause.

Emma can't help but laugh. 'Right. Because that's really what every mother wants for her daughter. Daddy, the things that are important to her are not important to me. I've made money, I've lived in that world, and I don't care about any of it. I've found a really good man in Dominic, and you know he's a really good man. He's solid, and calm, and he has huge integrity. He does everything he says he's going to do, when he says he's going to do it. Daddy, I lived in New York City for years and pretty much all the men I met were players.'

Her father raises a questioning eyebrow.

'They played around,' she explains as he gives her an understanding nod. 'They would say they would call and wouldn't, or would show up late, or would cancel at the last minute, or things would seem to be going fantastically well until I discovered they were dating three other women at the same time as me. Dominic doesn't have a dishonest bone in his body, and he makes me happy. He loves me, and I love him.'

Her father sits for a while, nodding. 'Do you have good conversations?' he asks eventually. 'Is he intellectually stimulating? Does he find you intellectually stimulating?'

'We talk about everything,' she says. 'Does he have a degree? No. Is he sophisticated and well travelled? No. But he cares about people and is devoted to his son. If I need intellectual stimulation, I can get that anywhere. I can join a book group, or go to lectures. One person can't be expected to fulfil all your needs; that's just unreasonable.'

'True,' says her father, now turning to face her. 'My darling girl, I want you to be happy. All I have ever wanted was for you to be happy. I am sorry that what your mother said was so insensitive and wounding. But' – he takes a deep breath – 'I can't say that I entirely disagree with her.'

The colour drains from Emma's face.

Simon puts his hand on her arm. 'I think he is a wonderful man,' he says. 'And I can see that he makes you happy. I am just asking you to consider that you are from two very different worlds. Your mother is, as you know, inclined to believe that class is the single most important issue, but I take a different viewpoint. You were raised here in Somerset. You've lived in London. You're an English girl through and through. I have supported your time in New York because I believe adventures are good for the soul, and the time to have adventures, to explore new territories, is when you are young. But once you decide to settle down, you have to come home.'

Emma stares at her father. 'Daddy, I never planned to come home. I'm happy in America. Westport is my home now. I know you don't want to hear it, but I feel more at home there than I have ever felt here.'

'But you and Dominic do come from very different worlds,' her father says eventually, struggling to find the right words that will make her understand. 'It seems you're compatible now, but in the long run that can be very difficult. It isn't as easy as you think.'

'We are compatible,' says Emma, relieved that her father can see that. 'And yes, we do come from different worlds, but we can create our own world for the two of us. We already have.'

'I just want you to be sure,' says her father.

'I am sure,' she says. '*We* are sure.'

'You have to find a way to make up with your mother.' Simon sighs. 'I'll talk to her, of course, but you know how difficult she can be. I'm not sure you should fly back to the States without having spoken to her.'

'I have nothing to say to her.' Emma is resolute. 'I'm sure I'll feel differently over time, but not today. She treated Dominic like a servant, because she believes he *is* below her . . . I'm not speaking to her today. Not yet.'

Her father gives a small smile. 'I know where you get your stubbornness from.'

Emma looks at her watch. 'Daddy, they'll be here to pick us up any second. I have to go.' And with that, she stands up to give him a hug goodbye.

Chapter 30

Emma looks out the window as they leave the airport on their way back home. She looks at the weeds growing through the cracks in the sidewalk, the back-to-back traffic, the looming grey buildings lining each side of the high-way, and a warmth spreads through her body. *Almost home*, she thinks, instantly comforted by the familiar sights and sounds. Home.

Dominic is quiet next to her, humming something, tap-ping his fingers on the steering wheel, a smile on his face. Emma shoots him frequent glances, knowing how excited he will be to see Jesse, days earlier than planned.

They pull off the highway, wind their way along Bridge Street, down Compo, pulling up in front of their side-by-side cottages. In the driveway is an unfamiliar old station wagon, at least twenty years old, the type of long, bulky car that few people drive these days.

'You ready to meet *my* parents now?' Dominic hesitates on the front path after unloading the suitcases from the trunk of the car.

Emma is about to answer when the front door is flung

open, and Jesse tears across the yard. 'Daddy!' he yells, flinging himself into his father's arms.

Emma stands back, watching them both, hoping Jesse might say hello to her, might have missed her, but he is far too busy chattering away to his father. He crawls all over him, kissing him, reassuring himself that his father is back, that he's not going away again.

'Say hi to Emma,' Dominic says eventually.

Jesse turns and gives her a dutiful smile then a wide grin. 'Hi!' He waves, and Emma laughs in relief, turning to walk next door to her own little house. But as she does so, she sees Dominic's mother emerge.

She is wearing a floral apron over beige trousers and a brightly coloured shirt. A short woman, she is well padded underneath the apron, and weighed down with copious amounts of chunky gold jewellery. Four large necklaces of varying lengths fall between her substantial bosoms; she wears large clip-on earrings and oversized rings. It is her hair that is the most extraordinary thing, standing high above her head, sprayed into a rock-solid beehive, accessorized by a large sparkly ladybird hair slide.

'Dominic!' She walks over and gathers Dominic in her arms, covering his face with kisses, leaving lipstick imprints all over his cheeks.

'Hey, Mom.' Dominic squirms ever so slightly but allows himself to be kissed before pulling away. 'I'd like you to meet Emma.'

She turns, surveying Emma up and down. Approvingly, Emma hopes.

'Okay,' she says, looking at Dominic with a nod. 'Okay.' Turning back to Emma she says, 'Call me Nonna. Everyone else does. Come in. I just made fresh cannoli for your father and Jesse, but there's more than enough for you. This kid.' She gestures to Dominic while looking at Emma. 'There's nothing this kid loves more than Nonna's homemade cannoli. How 'bout you, Jesse? What do you think of Nonna's cooking?'

'Good!' says Jesse, who is too distracted with the delight of having his father home to focus. They all laugh and enter the house.

'Hey, Pops,' says Dominic. 'This is Emma.'

At the table, Dominic's father is reading the paper and nursing a cup of coffee. Instead of looking up, he merely grunts, and reaches over for a cannoli from the plate that sits in the middle of the table.

No one speaks.

'Sit down,' says Dominic's mother, pulling out a chair for Emma. 'You want some coffee?'

'Emma only drinks coffee in the mornings,' says Dominic. Emma reddens, not wanting to put anyone out, not wanting to appear different in any way. 'She drinks tea in the afternoons.'

'I'm fine,' Emma says quickly.

'Tea?' says his mother. 'Very fancy. We only got coffee in our house. Are you sure you don't want some? Just a small cup? Go on.' She sets a cup of coffee in front of her.

Emma doesn't mention that there is tea in this house; she knows because she bought it herself.

'You know who came to see us?' Dominic's mother says. 'Stacy! I didn't know she was back in town. She came over and took Jesse out the first day we were here. She looks great. And she's doing really well, making a ton of money in real estate. It was good to see her.'

Dominic shakes his head. 'You didn't check with me before letting her take Jesse out?'

His mother shrugs. 'What's to check? She's the boy's mother. And she was leaving, so she wanted to get some time with him. I think she's really turned a corner. She says she's coming back to town.'

'Oh man,' Dominic mutters under his breath as Emma reaches over and takes his hand, giving him a supportive squeeze. *Don't say anything else*, she thinks.

'It will be like the old times,' his mother says. 'Good to have her around again. Sweetie, take a cannoli,' she says to Emma, who is staring at her, aghast at her insensitivity. 'No cannoli? I also got Italian cookies. Here.' She gets up from the table and pulls out a large round tin from the pantry, opening it to reveal chunky cookies stuffed with jam and dusted with icing sugar. 'Try one.'

Emma shakes her head. She feels sure that the comments about Stacy were deliberate, intended to let Emma know she will never be relevant in their eyes, that Stacy is the true heir to the throne.

'I'm fine,' says Emma.

'Just one,' says Dominic's mother. 'A small one.'

'Leave her alone,' roars Dominic's father, the first words

she has heard him speak. 'For Christ's sake, she says she doesn't want anything to eat.'

Emma watches Dominic's mother's face fall. 'Maybe just a small one,' Emma says, reaching for the tin.

'Thank you for staying with Jesse,' Dominic says, changing the subject. 'I know he's had a fantastic time, right, Jesse?'

Jesse makes a face, then quickly plasters on a smile and nods when he sees his grandmother look at him.

'I fattened him up,' she says proudly, reaching over and pinching his cheek. 'He was all skin and bone when I got here. You like Nonna's cooking, don't you, sweetie?'

Jesse nods, squirming away from her hand.

'Will you shut up about food?' says Dominic's father, shaking his head. 'All you talk about, all the goddamn time, is food. What you're gonna be cooking, what we're gonna be eating, what we haven't eaten. Jesus Christ. It's enough to drive a man crazy.'

'Why don't you shut up?' says Nonna, her own voice rising. 'Why you always got to ruin everything? I feed my family because I love them; that's what you do for the people you love. What do *you* do? Sit at the table in your undershirt, sweating, talking shit, putting down everyone around you.'

Dominic's father sits back, pushing the newspapers away. 'Putting down everyone around me? Dominic, do you see me putting down everyone around me?' He doesn't wait for an answer. 'No, I ain't putting down everyone around me. Just you, because you drive me fucking crazy.'

'Language!' says Nonna.

'Ah, shut up,' he says, going back to his paper. 'Everything you say gets on my last nerve.'

'You should try living with you,' spits Nonna. 'It's enough to drive a woman to suicide.'

'Is that a promise?' says Dominic's father.

Emma gulps her coffee down in one and pushes her chair back. 'I'm so sorry,' she says, 'but I have to get going. It was so nice to meet you.'

'I'll help you with the suitcase,' says Dominic, also standing up. They are outside quickly, and Emma turns to Dominic. 'Good God,' she says when they are safely out of earshot, when they can no longer hear Dominic's parents bickering. 'That was fun.'

'Yeah. Welcome to my childhood. At least it didn't get physical.'

'That was *awful*. Why are they even married? They hate each other!'

'Old-school Catholics. Divorce isn't allowed. But yeah, I think they've hated each other for years. I also think they couldn't survive without each other. It's a terrible, angry, screwed-up marriage, but they completely depend on each other. If my mother died, my father would go to pieces, I swear.'

'Please tell me we'll never treat each other like that.' Emma is now serious, putting down her suitcase outside the front door as she turns to him.

'We will never treat each other like that,' he says. 'Since

Jesse was born, I have lived my whole life determined to be nothing like them.' He leans in to kiss her.

'And what was all that about Stacy? Was that some passive-aggressive dig to make sure I know they prefer her?'

Dominic laughs. 'They hated Stacy! That's the least of your worries. It's just my parents being my parents. Ignore them.'

With that, Jesse bursts through them, pushing them apart, running into the house with Hobbes.

It is a relief for Emma to be on her own for a bit. Dominic has asked her to come back for dinner once his parents are safely out of the way. His fridge and freezer are now, apparently, filled with food. Emma knows that after dinner she will stay over, as she has done so many times before, but she needs this quiet time to think.

She doesn't like the comments Dominic's mother made about Stacy. She doesn't like that Stacy is back, either, although she's trying to like it, to welcome it, knowing it's good for Jesse.

She doesn't like that suddenly nothing is as straight-forward as it was before.

Her mother's words reverberate around her brain, as do her father's, even though she tries to push them aside. Their words are now tangled up with the ones spoken by Dominic's parents: who they are, what they said, how they treated each other. It was unsettling to see them, especially given her parents' concerns.

She had thought her parents wrong about her and Dominic. She hadn't thought their different worlds mattered. Emma corrects herself: she *doesn't* think it matters. And yet . . . meeting Dominic's parents . . . She cannot help but wonder if her mother and father are right.

Emma has no frame of reference for any of this. Dominic's mother and father are unlike anyone she has ever known. She has no idea how to talk to them, or what she would ever find in common with them other than Dominic himself. She tries to imagine what would happen if she and Dominic got married – if, say, her parents threw them an engagement party along the lines of the party they have just thrown for George and Henry.

She imagines Dominic's parents with her parents, with their friends, in their house. She imagines her mother's face listening to Dominic's father shouting that his wife drove him 'fucking crazy'.

It would not be pretty. She shakes her head to clear it. She has to stop thinking along these lines. She has no idea who Dominic's parents really *are*. Or how to behave around them. She thought she and Dominic could create a world of their own, a world in which it didn't matter where they both came from, or how different their backgrounds were. But what if she was wrong?

What if they did get married? she wonders. She is beginning to imagine it, the tiniest of thoughts, floating at the very edge of her brain. There is no rush, but isn't there only one real outcome for a relationship such as theirs, a relationship that is so easy, so filled with kindness and love?

They could get married here, she thinks. Perhaps on a country farm, lanterns hanging from branches, someone playing guitar, friends sitting on hay bales scattered through an orchard. That farm in Redding where they went the night Dominic kissed her; that would be perfect.

Or something small. Unassuming. Maybe they wouldn't invite their parents at all. Maybe they would just take the train into New York on the spur of the moment and get married at city hall, with no one present except Jesse.

There would be little point in trying to combine their two families, but perhaps, if they did throw a proper wedding, and the parents were there, they could figure out a way to manage it all.

It's only one day, she thinks. Anyone can put up with anything for one day.

But there is another nagging thought that she can't quite get rid of. What if she is wrong? What if George is wrong? What if their worlds *are* too different for them to find a way through?

She cuddles Hobbes, hoping for some comfort. A couple of days ago it felt like she didn't have a care in the world; now her head is spinning, her thoughts tumbling around. Is she making a terrible mistake? Should she end it now, before they are too entrenched?

But . . . but . . . they are so happy here. With their little side-by-side houses in Westport, by the beach, with Jesse. They are so happy in their own little world. And that world includes other people who like them both. Sophie and Rob like Dominic. They don't think he's *beneath* them because he doesn't work in finance, isn't hugely wealthy, isn't ambitious in the same way they are. All his friends seem to like her, to accept her. It doesn't bother them that she's English; they don't think she's a snob.

She considers this for a long time, telling herself how silly she is for thinking this is going to be anything other than great. She hopes that any nagging doubts will soon disappear.

Not long after, Dominic knocks on the door. The coast is clear, he tells Emma. His parents have gone home, and dinner is ready.

She has no appetite, but she follows him next door and sits at the kitchen table, pushing her food around her plate, uncharacteristically quiet.

'Are you okay?' Dominic asks after Jesse has finished and gone upstairs to put his PJs on. Emma is quiet as he pours her a glass of red wine, as she wonders how to voice the jumble of concerns in her head.

'I'm fine,' Emma says, in the way all women say they are fine when it is quite clear to everyone they are not.

'Something's the matter.' There is a look of concern on his face. 'What is it?'

Emma pauses. Should she share her concerns with him, or is that unfair? How can she tell him that meeting his parents has brought her own parents' words, their worries, flooding back? She can't help but wonder if they are right.

Is it too much to expect them to find the middle ground for the rest of their lives?

Jesse appears suddenly in the doorway, now in his pyjamas. 'Emma?'

'Yes, sweetie?' She is grateful for the interruption.

'Will you put me to bed?'

Tears well up in her eyes. She turns to hide her reaction, but Dominic can see how affected she is by the power of those six words: *Will you put me to bed?*

'Of course.' She blinks hard and gets up from the table, heading to the kitchen sink so she can pretend to get busy washing up. 'Just give me a couple of minutes, okay?'

Jesse heads back upstairs as Dominic slides an arm around Emma's waist.

'Wow,' he says. 'I told you he'd come around eventually.'

'You did.' Emma nods. For now, her other concerns have retreated into the background.

This is more important.

'What do you want me to read tonight?' Emma walks over to the bookshelf as Jesse climbs into bed.

'The book you bought me,' he says. 'The one about the anteater who eats the aunt.'

Emma is surprised. When she bought him Roald Dahl's *Revolting Rhymes* earlier that summer, he had expressed no interest in it whatsoever. She told him this was her favourite writer when she was a child, and offered to read him a couple of the stories, but Jesse had said no, throwing the book on a chair and going straight back to his Minecraft game on Dominic's computer.

As far as she was aware, he hadn't even looked at the book, but now it seems she was wrong. She opens it to 'The Ant Eater', and starts reading, complete with exaggerated accents, both English and American, much to Jesse's delight.

As she reaches the middle of the story, she feels a small hand slip into hers, and she stops, just for a second, to enjoy the spontaneous affection.

Dominic walks past the bedroom door and hesitates, leaning against the door frame for a few seconds to watch them, his eyes alight with love. Emma pauses, thinking that Jesse will ask his dad to take over, but he doesn't. He lets her continue.

As she finishes the story, Jesse wriggles down, into the curve of her body, the perfect fit. He rolls onto his side, as she spoons him, tucking his small frame into her own. He takes her arm and pulls it over him, never letting go of her hand.

They lie there for a few minutes, before Emma gently pulls her hand away.

'Good night, Jesse,' she whispers. She stays where she is for a few seconds more, listening to him breathe.

'I love you,' she whispers, because that is what his father says to him every night, the last thing Jesse hears before he goes to sleep.

But he doesn't say anything back. Jesse is already fast asleep.

Not an hour later, Emma crawls into Dominic's bed, snuggling into his outstretched arm as Jesse had snuggled into hers.

This is what it's all about, she thinks.

Love. Commitment. Family. The superficial stuff is irrelevant. Stacy is irrelevant. His family background is irrelevant. Cuddling with Jesse tonight was transcendent. *I am going to make this work*, she thinks. *No matter what.*

Chapter 31

Emma walks around Terrain, wanting to buy something, unsure exactly what that something might be, or indeed, if there is anything here that she really needs. The retail space is gorgeous; she could move a bed into a corner of the shop and live here happily for the rest of her life. She wanders around slowly, trying to decide whether to purchase a marble cloche, a gorgeous cheeseboard, the distressed wood tray.

There are plants everywhere. Emma has never been good with indoor plants, invariably killing them within a month. She sees dozens of terrariums on display, but she's pretty sure she would kill whatever plants are kept inside those, too.

She is meeting Sophie and Teddy for tea in the café, but Sophie just texted her to say that she's still waiting for her mother, who is stuck behind a school bus, hence Emma's impromptu shopping interlude.

She pauses by a row of cool Wellington boots, tries on a French quilted jacket that she probably wouldn't ever wear. She fingers scarves, moves slowly along the glass jewellery cabinet, walks to the front of the shop and picks up every candle, smelling it, until she hears her name.

'Emma!' Sophie is bustling through the shop's displays, her hair loosely pulled back in a messy bun, immaculate in tight jeans, a white T-shirt, ballet flats. She is wearing no make-up but looks stunning. Behind her is her mother, Teddy, elegant in similar clothes, a cashmere cardigan, the same huge smile as Sophie.

'You both look so gorgeous,' says Emma, hugging them.

'I'm so sorry we're late,' says Sophie, as the three of them walk to the café counter to order tea.

'My fault, I'm afraid,' says Teddy. 'We timed it horribly. I always forget about the school buses. I don't know why they don't pull over. They used to, when I first moved here. When Sophie was in school, the drivers always let you pass.'

'The driver on *my* route always lets me pass,' says Sophie.

'It must be because you're young and beautiful. I sat behind him almost the entire way to your house to pick you up, with a huge line of cars behind me. I only minded because I knew I was going to be late, but there was nothing I could do. I turned on NPR and listened to a fascinating interview with Terry Gross. The woman behind me was not happy, though. She honked a number of times.'

Sophie rolls her eyes. 'That's probably why he didn't let any of you pass. Frankly, if I were a bus driver and had a woman behind me, honking, in a Range Rover, I'm pretty sure I wouldn't let her pass, either.'

Startled, Teddy looks at her daughter. 'How did you know it was a Range Rover?'

Sophie just shakes her head and laughs, turning to Emma. 'Have *you* noticed the daily uniform in town?'

'Lululemon clothes, straightened hair, and a Range Rover? That uniform?'

'That would be the one.'

'No,' says Emma, shaking her head. 'I can't say I've noticed.' And all three laugh.

They take their teas to a table and sit down, shrugging off jackets and slipping them onto the backs of their chairs.

'It's so chilly now,' says Teddy, rubbing her arms and warming her hands around her mug of tea. 'I'm always surprised when the temperatures start falling again every September.'

'We're practically in October,' says Sophie. 'I saw Christmas decorations in a shop the other day, which made me feel ill. Much too early.'

'I completely agree.' Teddy rolls her eyes. 'They put them out earlier every year. Soon we'll be looking at garlands and tinsel in July.' She turns to Emma. 'Sophie mentioned you just got back from England with Dominic. How did that go?'

'It was . . .' Emma pauses. She can't lie. She can't say it was wonderful. She can't not say that they cut their trip short because of the way her mother treated Dominic, because of the things her mother said. She sighs. 'It was interesting,' she says eventually. 'And kind of awful, if I'm honest.'

'What happened?' asks Sophie in alarm.

Emma tells them the whole story. She tells them about England, about her parents, about her decision to ignore them and her belief that they didn't know what they were talking about until she met Dominic's parents. She tells them how she's realized that he *does* come from a very different world, and that while she knows what she has found with Dominic and Jesse is very special and worth fighting for, she cannot get rid of the sinking feeling that her parents may be right.

It is a relief to talk about this. It has been pent up inside her for days, and it has started to put a wedge between her and Dominic.

When Jesse asked her to read to him, requested that she perform the nightly routine that by rights used to belong to his father, she thought she could push her fears aside about there being too many differences between them for it to work.

Her doubts are not so easily dismissed.

It isn't that she wants a big life, or more money, or – heaven forbid – the trappings of the life she left behind in New York; it's that she was raised with museums, and art galleries, and theatre; she was raised with horseback riding, and ballet, and hunts. It isn't that she wants any of that today, but that she has spent her life thinking that she was supposed to want those things, supposed to end up in much the same life as the one in which she was raised.

'What do you think?' she asks finally, her worried eyes

moving from Sophie to Teddy, and back again. 'What do you think I should do?'

'*Do?*' Teddy frowns. 'What do you mean?'

'Should we carry on, or should I leave now before anyone gets too hurt? It worries me that we're so different. I don't care that he's a bartender and a carpenter. I've never cared about that stuff, but' – she pauses, embarrassed to admit this, but seeking advice from people she trusts – 'is it okay that he doesn't have any ambition? It's not like he's dreaming of one day opening his own bar, or becoming a master carpenter and founding the number-one cabinetry installation company in Fairfield County, with a team of fabulously talented men working for him. Is that okay? He's really happy exactly where he is, and although part of me loves that about him, I don't quite understand it.' She sighs and buries her head in her hands. 'God! I can't even believe I'm saying this. I never thought any of this would matter. One of the things I love about him is that he's not competitive with anyone. He's more comfortable in his skin than any man I have ever met.'

'Why do you think that is?' asks Teddy.

Emma pauses to think. 'He says he wasn't always like this. I think it's because he made a deliberate choice not to be like his parents. I think part of making any choice as deliberate as that must give you a sense of peace.'

Teddy peers at her, mystified. 'And isn't that the same as the deliberate choice you have made to leave your old life behind and follow your heart? I don't see what the problem is.'

'That's all true.' Emma nods. 'I have made a deliberate choice and in so many ways I am happier than I ever thought I could be, or would be. But what if all that isn't enough?' She muses out loud. 'Even though he is making a deliberate choice to be something other than his destiny now, don't we all turn into our parents over time? How can we avoid following that pattern as we age? We make choices about how we want to be seen in the world, but as we grow older don't we all forget to hold those constructs up, don't we all start falling into the patterns of our youth? Doesn't our essence always win out? And if so, what's Dominic's essence?' She pauses for breath, unaware of the tinge of hysteria in her voice. 'And that's not the only thing. We're so different. He likes sports, and beer, and bars. I like books, and theatre, and good wine.'

'No, you don't,' says Sophie, laughing.

Emma stares at her. 'What do you mean? Of course I do.'

'You don't. I mean, who am I to tell you what you like and don't like, but I've known you for quite a long time, and I've only seen you drink pinot noir and Whispering Angel, which is good but not that good, and vodka. Secondly, when was the last time you went to the theatre?'

Emma sits back. 'I am *desperate* to see *Hamilton*.'

'But when was the last time you went?'

'A while ago,' says Emma sheepishly.

'A year? Two years? More?'

'Maybe a couple of years.' Emma attempts to brush over

it. 'The point is, I want to see *Hamilton* and I can't bring Dominic with me because he hates the theatre.'

'First of all, isn't *Hamilton* mostly rap?' says Sophie. 'It's not exactly Arthur Miller. I'm pretty sure he'll love it. Everybody loves it. Secondly, if you really think he'd hate it, take someone else. Take me! Take my mom!' Teddy nods her head enthusiastically. 'So what if he doesn't like theatre?'

'I really like theatre,' says Teddy. 'I'd love to see *Hamilton*.'

'You're missing the point,' says Emma, as Teddy beams a benevolent smile upon her.

'I don't think so, my dear,' she says gently. 'I think we very much get the point. The point is that you're terrified that Dominic is not who he appears to be, even though all the evidence suggests he is *exactly* as he appears. And, you want him to be just like you, to want the same things you want, to like doing the same things you like doing, to fulfil all your wants and needs.'

Emma looks at her. 'When you put it like that, it sounds completely crazy.'

Teddy nods. 'It does, doesn't it?'

'But it isn't unreasonable to want to have the same aspirations. The same likes and dislikes. Isn't that what good relationships are based on?'

'In my experience,' says Teddy, 'good relationships are based on kindness. On putting the person you love before yourself. On thinking of what you can do to make that person happy. Good relationships require kindness, commitment, and appreciation. I think you have all of those, do you not? Despite what you just said about being frightened of him becoming like his parents, you're not really worried about that, are you?'

Emma hesitates, thinking. 'Maybe not,' she says eventually. 'But if your lifestyle choices are different?'

'They aren't so different, though, are they?' says Sophie. 'You both love your homes, the beach, leading a pretty quiet life. It's not like one of you wants to be out at fancy restaurants every night while the other is a hermit. You care about your friends, and Jesse. Isn't that the stuff that matters?'

'You don't think the other things get in the way? You don't think my parents are right? That we are from such different worlds, that relationships are hard enough, that throwing two people together who come from such different places means their union is destined for disaster?'

'I don't think that.' Sophie looks at her mother. 'Do you?'

Teddy shakes her head. 'That's what friends are for,' she says. 'You don't have to watch football games with Dominic. I'm sure he's got lots of friends who can hang out with him for that. Just as you have people who can go to the theatre with you.'

'Not that you actually go to the theatre,' mutters Sophie, shrugging as Emma shoots her a look.

'He is a wonderful man.' Sophie leans forward. 'You cannot throw this away because of some ridiculous, superficial reason. You're more worried about being judged by other people; that somehow they will think Dominic isn't good enough for you, which means that you're worried you're not good enough.'

Teddy looks at her daughter approvingly.

'She's right,' she says to Emma. 'Even though it may be difficult to hear. The Emma who is worrying about what people think, or how you might be judged, isn't the Emma I've come to know this summer. I've known you a while, and the Emma you have become, the Emma I have gotten to know since you met Dominic, is my favourite Emma of all.'

'*She's* right,' says Sophie. 'The two of you are great together. And think about Jesse. He's attached now. There is more at stake than just the two of you.'

Emma nods. There is a long pause before she asks, 'You really don't think we're going to turn into his parents?'

Teddy lets out a bark of laughter. 'I hardly think so, Emma. It is true that we often re-create our childhoods. However dysfunctional they may have been, we experience those feelings as "home", and re-create them in some form in our adult lives. But it is also true that we have a choice, and if we are lucky, and aware, we seek out the very opposite, which is exactly what Dominic has done, and what you are doing now.'

As Emma listens, she feels the weight of anxiety lift for the first time since she and Dominic left England. 'I do love him,' she says, and she smiles her first genuine smile in days.

'I know,' says Sophie. 'This is all about your parents.

You moved across the Atlantic to get away from them. You moved because you didn't have anything in common with them. You didn't want the life they had, and you didn't want the life they wanted for you. That you are only now paying attention to what they think is craziness. From what you've always told me, your mother doesn't want what's best for you, she wants what's best for *her*, right? Doesn't she want whatever will somehow elevate her status in the world?'

'Thank you for the reminder. You are absolutely right.'

'I know. So can we just forget about your parents and move on?'

'Okay,' Emma says carefully. Then, 'Yes!' Her friends have told her it's okay to trust her instincts; they've confirmed for her that her choices are good.

'Shall we ask if they have champagne?' Sophie laughs. 'I think it would be entirely appropriate at this point to celebrate the first day of the rest of your life.'

That night, Jesse has a sleepover at a friend's and Dominic is out meeting a potential client before heading to work at the Fat Hen, leaving Emma alone. It's so rare these days, it feels luxurious. She cleans the kitchen and is about to go upstairs and jump in the shower when she checks the time.

It is too early to turn in for the night. She could run to the bar and have a quick drink with Dominic, surprise him. Excited at the prospect of his face when he sees her unexpectedly, she checks her hair in the mirror, shakes it out, adds some lip gloss, then picks up her handbag and slips out the front door.

The parking lot is jammed with cars. She circles a couple of times before two people walk out of the bar, making their way slowly to their Honda at the back. She waits patiently, waving a thanks when they pull out, manoeuvring her way into the spot.

The place is heaving. She weaves her way through, excited to reach the bar, to see Dominic in his element, so much louder, more outgoing, gruffer than he is when he is not working a crowd. He has described it as acting, talked about having a 'bar persona', much like a stage persona, explained that as soon as he walks through the doors of the Fat Hen, he turns into Dom rather than Dominic. Dom, who flirts with the ladies, who winds up the men, who is quick with his hands, and with the queue, to ensure he gets the biggest tips of any of the bartenders there.

There are two girls leaning on the bar, with their heads tilted and waterfalls of hair falling over their shoulders. Even from a distance Emma can see them flirting with Dominic. They are what she would have once presumed were exactly his type. He is laughing with one of them, a blonde, and when she turns her head Emma recognizes her at once. The woman he was seeing when Emma first moved in. *Gina*.

She stands stock-still, heart pounding. She rarely thinks about what happens at night when Dominic is not with her, about what he is doing when he is at work. Of course he flirts, she knows he flirts, but it's always felt a bit abstract to her. She's never considered the possibility that it would be with former girlfriends.

Emma is not the sort of woman who is inclined to surreptitiously pick up a boyfriend's phone when he is in the shower to scroll through texts, checking to see what he is up to. She is very well aware that if you snoop, you are unlikely to be happy with what you find. And you won't be able to do much about it without revealing the snooping, anyway.

She remembers a man she used to work with who would regularly scroll through his boyfriend's phone. One morning he came to work almost in tears, having discovered an email confirming a brand-new subscription to Grindr.

There was no other evidence of cheating, no other indication that his boyfriend had done anything but sign up for the sake of curiosity. All the women at work had gathered around to offer their opinions. Most of them believed the boyfriend had probably signed up just for fun, to see who else in the area might be on it. After all, there were at least three men in the office who were married but rumoured to prefer playing on their own team.

He didn't know whether to confront his boyfriend or not. The consensus among the women at work was a resounding no. Far better to say nothing – because opening that particular door was bound to be a disaster. It would be different, they all said, if he had found evidence of a date, or an intimate text – something concrete. But subscribing to Grindr alone was definitely not grounds to reveal your despicable nature as a snoop.

Emma trusts Dominic. She certainly met her fair share of untrustworthy men while living in New York. It has never crossed her mind that Dominic was anything like them. In fact, the whole point is that he's not. She doesn't think for a minute that he would do anything to betray her.

From where she is standing, she can't hear what is being said, but she can clearly see Gina leaning across the bar, showing off her spectacular cleavage and laughing as she says something, her right foot, encased in the highest of heels, sexily rubbing up the back of her left calf.

Dominic moves closer to her to hear what she is saying, then stands back with a smile, a shrug, and a shake of his head. At that moment, he looks up and sees Emma. His eyes light up as he waves her over. Gina turns to see what has caught his attention, and irritation washes over her face as she recognizes Emma.

'The tenant, right?' says Gina, as Dominic leans over the bar and gives Emma a long kiss on the lips, pulling away, then coming back for one more.

Emma can't help turning to Gina with a happy smile when Dominic finally steps back. It's not something she does very often, but right now it feels oh so extraordinarily good to be here, with Dominic, who is so clearly in love with her.

'The tenant.' She smiles. 'Right.'

ACT THREE

Chapter 32

Autumn is upon them for good before they have noticed it's time for the seasons to change. One day the trees are green and lush, the next they are multiple shades of red, orange, and gold, the leaves drifting into the streets and covering up the last vestiges of summer.

With the changing seasons comes a routine that makes Emma feel settled and secure. And happy. She and Dominic have not talked about officially moving in together, and yet they seem to have moved in together. Most of her clothes are now at his house, and it has been months since she spent the night in her own, next door.

She still has her office there, though. The redecorating she did for Lisa has led to more clients, more work, and she has now redone the living room in her cottage as part showroom, part conference room.

She put up a Nobilis wallpaper that looks like bleached-out horizontal planks of wood. An L-shaped cream sofa is piled with tan and orange cushions and a large orange mohair throw. The coffee table is simple, a low square orange shagreen table with a Perspex box resting on top, and the latest interior magazines in neat piles for inspiration.

She painted the window frames a glossy chocolate brown, and had cream linen blinds made. Dominic boxed around the ancient, ugly fireplace with MDF, which Emma then faux-painted to look like limestone. Above the fireplace hangs a round, polished wood mirror, and hanging on the walls are abstract paintings in shades of orange, red, and brown.

Dominic wasn't at all sure of the colour scheme. 'Beach houses should only be blue,' he had said.

Emma hadn't wanted to point out that the colour scheme of the house when she moved in was everything *but* blue. Brown, salmon, and a grungy floral had been the order of the day when she first walked in. Now that it is finished, Dominic tells anyone who will listen that it is the most beautiful room he has ever seen, and Emma the most talented woman he has ever known.

'We should move in *here*,' he says one evening, walking through the front door to say goodbye before he leaves for work. He no longer needs a regular sitter; every night Emma is next door at his house, at the house that is really now their house, where she puts Jesse to bed.

Jesse can still be difficult. When he is tired, or feeling overwhelmed, he sometimes reverts to blaming Emma for everything that is wrong in his life. Sometimes she hears him shouting at his father, 'We don't need her! I hate her! Emma has ruined everything!' She is still wounded by those

words, even though she knows he is just a child, he doesn't
mean it. And it passes. It always passes.

It is clear he doesn't mean it when he snuggles into her
in bed. It is clear he doesn't mean it when he tucks in beside
her and pulls her arm over his small body.

Emma hasn't whispered 'I love you' again, although there
have been many times when she has wanted to. And she
believes he may be on the verge of loving her, too.

Stacy seems to have dropped off the face of the earth.
She sent Dominic a couple of texts when she first got back
to Florida, and said she would come back towards the end
of October. But October is almost gone, and there has
been no word from her. Emma is starting to relax into the
routine they had before.

'Well, we *could* live here, I suppose,' she says to Dominic. 'But you don't really want to live here. It's much
smaller than your house. We'd all be on top of each other.
You just want to live somewhere stylish.'

'Who'd'a thunk it?' Dominic laughs, shaking his head.
'Me, wanting to live somewhere stylish.'

'I could redo your house, you know,' says Emma. 'All
you have to do is say the word and I will gladly take on
the project.' She smiles. 'No charge, of course.'

'You're hired!' Dominic says with a laugh. 'I want you
to, of course, but I also kind of like it the way it is. Maybe
in the spring, when you move in officially, we can do it.'

Emma stares at him. 'What?'

'We can do it in the spring.'

'Hang on. Did you say when I move in?'

'I did.'

'I'm moving in? Since when? Am I part of this decision?'

'I'm telling you now.' He moves over to the sofa and sits. 'Unless you don't want to?'

'I just hadn't thought of making it official. I thought things were pretty good as they are.'

'Things are great. But you're sleeping at my house every night anyway. And you're already using this house as your office. Why not move in for real? When we get married, you're going to be living there anyway.'

Emma can't breathe. 'What did you say?'

Dominic speaks very slowly, as if he were talking to a small child. 'I said, when we get married, we're going to be living together anyway, so we may as well live together now. Or in the spring. Whatever.'

A slow grin spreads itself on Emma's face. 'Are you proposing?'

'No!' Dominic frowns. 'When I propose it won't be like this. I'm going to have champagne, flowers, a ring . . . the whole damn thing.' He watches her face, nervous now. 'That is the plan, though, isn't it? We are doing this, aren't we?'

'Doing what?'

'This. The whole thing. Living. Together. Marriage. All of it. This is it for me, Emma. Do you feel the same?'

Emma never wanted to marry Rufus. She hadn't thought

she wanted to get married at all. But in the past few months, she has been happier than she has ever been.

'Yes,' she says now, twining her arms around his neck as she kisses him. 'I feel the same.'

Chapter 33

'Snow!' Jesse bursts into their room, waking them up.

Dominic groans, turning over in bed. 'Jesse, it's six thirty-nine in the morning. Go back to sleep.'

'But it's snow, Dad! It's really snowing outside.'

Emma rolls over with a stretch. 'They did say snow was coming.'

'But not a lot, right? Just a couple of inches?'

'There's tons of snow!' says Jesse, running to the window and opening the blinds. 'Look!'

Outside is a blizzard of white. Emma puts her feet on the floor and shivers, wrapping her arms around herself. It's late November, too early, surely, for a serious snowfall.

Jesse grabs her hand and drags her to the window. As she stands there, a huge smile creases her face, and she's filled with childlike joy at the sight of the fat, fluffy flakes swirling outside. She squints at the pots in the garden. There's probably at least eight inches already.

'This is serious snow, Dominic,' she says, turning to him.

'Three inches?'

'At least eight. Maybe more. And it's coming down fast.'

'Aw, shit,' he groans, covering his face with the pillow. 'That means serious work.'

'Work?'

'Who do you think is going to be shovelling and clearing the snow? We had a huge snowstorm a few years ago and the roof collapsed. I'll have to clear it off the roof if I don't want a repeat of that experience. Maybe I'll call my buddy Glenn. He has a snowplough on his truck, and he can do the driveway. So much for a lazy day.'

'Dad? Dad?' Jesse dances up to his side of the bed. 'Can we build a snow fort? Please? You said you would build a snow fort with me the next time it snows.'

'I never said that,' says Dominic. 'When did I say that?'

'You did. You always say that. Will you? Can you get up now? Can we build a snow fort now?'

'We can't build a snow fort until it stops snowing,' says Dominic as Jesse's face falls.

'Can I go and play in the snow, though?' he says finally. 'Until it stops snowing?'

'Sure,' says Dominic.

'Do you have snow boots?' asks Emma. 'And snow clothes?'

'I have boots!' says Jesse. 'And jeans.'

As Jesse runs out of the room, Dominic pulls Emma in for a cuddle. 'He'll be fine,' he says. 'He'll come in when he's wet and cold.'

'You're tough.' Emma snuggles against him. 'I really

think he should have a hat and gloves, though. And snow trousers. I don't want him to freeze.'

'I know. We have the hat and gloves, but we don't have snow pants that fit him. We'll get a pair this weekend, okay? Look, don't worry. I guarantee he'll be back inside asking for hot cocoa in about five minutes.' Dominic groans. 'Oh God, I hate the snow.'

Emma is shocked. 'How can you hate the snow? I love the snow! It's the best thing about living here. Look at those gorgeous fat flakes. It's magical!'

'Yeah, the first snowfall is cool, I'll give you that, but then there's the work, and the weeks of filthy snow and gravel and sand piled up on every sidewalk. Ugh. Give me summer any time.'

'I can help you,' says Emma. 'With the shovelling.'

'Nah. You can make the cocoa, though.' Dominic smiles, pulling her in for a kiss. 'Do we have time for . . .'

Emma laughs softly as she moves a hand up his thigh, behind him to cup his buttock and pull him in. 'We always have time for that.'

'Where's Dad?'

Jesse played in the snow for almost exactly five minutes, just as Dominic predicted. He has had his cocoa, made popcorn, helped build a fire, and is now watching a movie. He's itching to go out and build a snow fort, but the snow has not yet stopped.

'Dad's shovelling snow,' Emma says. *Like he's been doing the past three hours*, she thinks to herself. She has to admit that she had no idea how much work this involved. They don't have snow in England, not proper snow, like here. She remembers the occasional light dusting when she was young, and going sledging – sledding, they say over here, she reminds herself – on flattened empty road-salt bags, feeling every bump as they careered down the hill, shrieking with excitement.

'Want me to get him?' she says, pouring the leftover cocoa in a travel mug to take out to him.

'Yeah,' says Jesse, already re-immersed in his movie. 'Tell him to come help me build a snow fort.'

'It's still snowing.' Emma laughs. 'He did say not until the snow stops falling. But I'll tell him.'

Emma puts her coat and boots on, and finds a hat lurking in the back of the hall wardrobe. The only gloves she can find are Dominic's yellow deerskin work gloves, so she puts them on and steps out the front door, pausing to take in the sight.

The blanket of quiet takes her breath away. The snow is still falling – smaller flakes now, not as wet and heavy – but they're swirling in the wind, and there is absolute silence. The roads have been ploughed, but the tracks have long since been covered over, and every tree branch has a thick duvet of white.

Dominic has shovelled the path to the driveway. He has been meticulous, leaving straight lines on either side. Emma walks up the path, stepping over the short picket fence dividing their two houses, following footsteps in the snow around to the back.

Through the garden gate, she pauses for a minute, her eyes trying to adjust to what she sees. Everything is white, apart from a black shape on the ground, covered in a thin dusting.

She moves closer, her brain not computing what that shape is, the only thing that shape can be. It is only when she reaches it that her heart stops, and she sinks to her knees next to Dominic, lying still, in the soft, soft snow.

Chapter 34

It's going to be fine. It's going to be fine. It's going to be fine.
How could it be anything other than fine?

Emma rocks back and forth in the snow, waiting for the ambulance to arrive, holding Dominic's hand, an unnatural calm coming over her; this is not how she would ever have expected to react in the face of something so potentially terrible, but she is almost numb.

She had phoned Sophie, her voice shaking with fear, to ask her to come and take Jesse. She told her briefly what had happened. Dominic must have been shovelling snow from the roof; he must have slipped and fallen. No, there was no blood. Yes, she was sure he was just unconscious; he was breathing. The ambulance was on its way. Jesse shouldn't know anything, not until they knew what was going on.

Emma keeps rocking, keeps murmuring.
Please be okay. Please be okay. Please be okay.

She senses a movement, and her heart leaps as Dominic stirs, then opens his eyes. Emma sinks with relief before bursting into tears.

'Ah, damn it,' he says, struggling to sit up. 'That'll show me, climbing on the roof in this weather. I slipped. Thank Christ it's snowing. It cushioned me.'

They both pause at the sound of sirens. 'I called an ambulance.' Emma is almost giddy with relief. 'I didn't know what to do.'

'We can tell them to leave.' Dominic stands. 'I just have a headache. I'm fine.'

The ambulance medics arrive and check his vitals. He seems fine. They declare him possibly the luckiest man in the world. He has what they describe as an 'epic' bump, and just to be on the safe side they're going to take him in to the ER. Just in case.

'I don't need to go to the ER,' says Dominic.

But Emma insists. He must go, she says. He should let the experts check him out, check to make sure everything is fine. Reluctantly, he allows her to lead him to the ambulance.

Sophie pulls up just as they are about to close the ambulance doors. She can hear Dominic arguing with the paramedics inside. She leans her head through the doors.

'Aren't you supposed to be dead?' Sophie asks him.

Dominic extends his arms. 'It's the second coming.'

'That's funny. But not really. Are you okay?'

'I'm fine. But your friend here' – he looks at Emma with a tender, if exasperated smile –'is making me go to the ER, just to be sure.'

'So I'll take Jesse?' Sophie looks at Emma for confirmation, and Emma nods from inside the ambulance as they close the doors.

Despite the snow, they get there in no time. The roads were empty, and the ambulance had four-wheel drive. There is no wait today. Dominic is brought straight into an examining room, where he's looked over and declared to be extraordinarily lucky.

'I do want you to have a CAT scan,' says the doctor, a young man, too young, thinks Emma, to be a doctor. 'Just to be on the safe side. We want to be certain we're not missing anything. I'm sure everything in there is absolutely fine, but let's not leave any doubt.'

'I'm sorry to have to tell you that nothing in there is fine,' says Dominic, 'according to my girlfriend.'

The doctor laughs.

'I really do feel okay, though,' says Dominic. 'Can't I just leave? I can come back to the hospital if the headache gets worse.'

'We need to make sure the headache isn't a sign of anything more serious,' says the doctor. 'With any luck, after the CAT scan you'll be good to go.'

Emma sits in the waiting room as Dominic is taken upstairs, scrolling through her phone, exhausted suddenly from the surge of fear, adrenaline, and relief that has swamped her system.

There is a knock on the door. It is the young doctor.

'Mrs DiFranco?'

Emma is about to explain they are not married, that her last name is Montague, but it is irrelevant. His face is serious, far more serious than it was earlier. She nods, more terrified than she had been before.

'Your husband is out of the CAT scan, but now he's being seen by the neurosurgeon. During the scan we found a small tear in one of his arteries, and some bleeding around the outside of the brain.'

Emma stares at him. 'What does that mean? You can stop the bleeding, can't you? He's going to be fine. Isn't he?'

The doctor's face is grave. 'He's going to need surgery, and the neurosurgeon is on his way down to come and see you. He'll explain the procedure in more detail, but essentially it involves drilling a hole in the skull to try to evacuate the haematoma and relieve the pressure.'

Emma nods, numb. 'Can I see him?'

'He's being prepped for surgery. But he's not conscious.' He takes a deep breath, as if he doesn't want to convey more bad news. 'I'm afraid he lost consciousness during the scan.'

The surgeon speaks to Emma briefly, but as soon as he walks away, she realizes she hasn't heard anything he said. Words flutter around her brain like confetti. *Haematoma. Herniation. Burr hole.*

But then a fragment of their conversation comes back to her. He mentioned – she is sure of it – that *the prognosis was better given that Dominic had had a lucid period.* Hadn't he? Had she imagined that?

She is shivering, so she puts Dominic's coat on to keep her warm, and in his pocket she finds his phone. She scrolls through his contacts, looking for his parents' number. Dominic may not be close to them, may only see them sporadically, but they need to know what's happened.

They arrive an hour later, moving slowly down the corridor, fear in their eyes. They seemed so intimidating the one time she had met them, but here, under these fluorescent lights, walking so tentatively down the corridor, they look frail and frightened.

'Mr and Mrs DiFranco.' Emma gets up from her chair in the waiting room. They turn to look at her blankly, with clearly no idea who she is.

'I'm Emma. I'm the one who phoned you. We met a few – ' She stops. It's not important. 'Dominic is about to come out of surgery.' She explains what the doctors are doing, removing the haematoma, drilling a hole in his skull to relieve the pressure, while his parents stare at her like rabbits caught in headlights.

She doesn't tell them that she has spent the past hour looking up epidural haematomas on her phone. She doesn't tell them that she is terrified. She keeps thinking of one phrase that loops over and over in her head: *Without prompt medical attention, an epidural haematoma carries a high risk of death.* What does *prompt* mean? she has asked herself over and over again. The ambulance came as quickly as it could, given the snow. Was it prompt enough? *Please, God, let it have been prompt enough.*

She has no idea how long Dominic had lain there in the snow before she found him. Had it been five minutes? Had it been longer?

She won't think about it. She can't.

'Is he going to be okay?' says his father.

'They haven't said. They did tell me it was good that he was conscious after his fall. But I'm sure he is going to be okay,' says Emma, as tears spring into her eyes. 'He's so strong.'

His mother nods, just as the surgeon strides down the corridor. 'Are you the parents?' He walks over and shakes their hands, then gestures to all of them to follow him into a tiny private curtained space off the main waiting room.

'The operation went well,' he says, as Emma closes her eyes in relief. 'We drilled a hole in his skull and seem to have successfully removed the haematoma and brought down the swelling. Mr DiFranco has been taken up to the ICU and we will be giving him medications called hyper-osmotic agents, which will further reduce any residual swelling.'

'Can you tell yet whether there will be any brain damage? Any seizures, or paralysis?' Thanks to her iPhone, Emma knows enough to ask this.

'It is too early to say,' he says. 'The next twenty-four hours are crucial.'

He offers a few more details to Dominic's parents – what a haematoma is, how it happened – as Emma sinks back onto the hard seat, drawing her knees into her chest and hugging them. She rests her head on her knees, and turns away from Dominic's parents and the doctor, as silent tears trickle slowly down her cheeks.

*

The ICU is quiet. There is a different doctor on duty now. Emma wanders around the hospital corridors, eventually circling back to the waiting room. Dominic's parents sit there numbly, nursing cardboard cups of lukewarm coffee, which they aren't drinking.

In the early hours of the morning, a nurse pushes the door of the waiting room open.

'He's awake,' she says. 'Would you like to see him?'

Emma jumps up, then hesitates. His parents should go first. She'll accompany them if they invite her.

But they don't invite her.

Emma sinks back into her chair, stung. *They don't know me,* she tries to reassure herself. *They only met me once, and so briefly. They have no idea what I mean to Dominic, what we mean to each other.*

She stops the nurse by placing a hand on her arm as she is about to head out of the waiting room. 'May I go in afterwards?' she asks, so quietly that Dominic's parents won't hear.

The nurse nods with an understanding smile. 'Of course.'

Ten minutes later, Emma is sitting next to Dominic's bed, holding his hand, as tears of relief course down her face.

'I thought you were dead,' she says, attempting to smile through her tears. 'For the second time in twenty-four hours.'

'I'm just tired,' he says. 'You don't need to cry about it,' and he squeezes her hand.

'How does your head feel? Are you in pain?'

'It's not so bad,' he says, closing his eyes for a second. 'I can't believe this happened.'

'I know. The random nature of life. But you're going to be fine.'

'Thank God you found me.'

'You have no idea how many times I've thought that since we got here. Promise me you will never get up on a roof ever again.'

'That's really not something I have to promise. I'm not even going to stand on a chair after this. How's Jesse?'

'He's fine. Sophie's been texting me. I'll tell her to let him know you're fine. He's sleeping over at her house.'

'And what about you? What are you doing?'

'I'm sleeping here. I'm not going to leave you, Dominic.'

'You should go home. You need a good night's sleep. I'm more worried about Jesse. I bet the little guy's scared.'

'Want me to bring him to see you tomorrow?'

'Not yet. I don't want him freaked out by all the hospital stuff. Maybe in a couple of days, when I feel a bit stronger.'

'Okay.' Emma can see he's getting tired, his eyes drifting closed every few seconds. 'I love you,' she says, and she leans forward and kisses him, sitting next to the bed for a few minutes until he is asleep.

Emma is so exhausted that she has to blink furiously all the way home just to stay awake. She doesn't even re-member the last time she was out driving at four thirty in the morning. The streets are deserted and silent, and the streetlights cast warm pools of light on the snow. *This is so spectacularly beautiful*, thinks Emma, driving slowly and carefully. Her first proper New England snowstorm. If only she were able to enjoy it.

She'd spoken briefly with Dominic's parents before leaving the hospital. They seemed as numb as she was, didn't seem to hear when she said she would take care of Jesse; too fragile and overwhelmed. As was she, but she had too many responsibilities, with Jesse, to give in to those feelings.

As Emma walks in the door of her cottage, Hobbes immediately curls around her ankles, looking up at her and mewing pitifully. She feeds her, makes her way slowly up the stairs, and pulls her clothes off before collapsing into bed.

Chapter 35

There are no texts from Dominic when Emma wakes up. She feels a surge of worry before remembering the signs at the hospital saying no cell phones allowed.

Poor Dominic. His mobile phone – the one she'd found in the pocket of his coat and used to call his parents, the one she'd so carefully returned to him when that kind nurse took her in to see him – is probably in a plastic bag in a cupboard somewhere, uncharged. She makes a note to herself to take his charger with her when she goes back to the hospital.

She checks her email, scrolls mindlessly through Facebook and Instagram before realizing with shock that it is almost nine in the morning. She had no idea it was so late, although she was up half the night, didn't get to bed until nearly dawn. She shakes her head to clear it. Things will get back to normal eventually.

She phones the hospital to see how Dominic is, but they won't give out information by phone to anyone other than family. *I am family*, she thinks, but she can't prove it, is too tired to have this discussion. She will go to the hospital as soon as she can.

Texting Sophie that she is coming to get Jesse, Emma jumps in the shower, swigging water straight from the tap to swallow a couple of ibuprofen, hoping they'll stop the pounding headache that comes with no sleep.

The streets are busier today, the roads no longer blanketed in white, but ploughed and already dirty. The Post Road is filled with traffic. Business as usual.

At Sophie's house, she gets out of the car and hops up the path. It may not in fact *be* the path, for there are a couple of feet of snow covering Sophie's entire front yard. She feels guilty leaving tunnels of footprints in the perfect white blanket, and she pauses in front of the house, looking up at Sophie's roof, where more thick snow sits, undisturbed, as perfect as a picture postcard.

Why did Dominic need to shovel snow from the roof? What was so important about our crappy roof on our crappy house?

She has to spend the day with Jesse, even though the only place she wants to be is with Dominic. It's not fair to leave Jesse, who must be so worried, even though he isn't showing it, with Sophie for the whole day. He needs to be with someone he trusts, someone with whom he feels safe.

With any luck, by the time she gets to the hospital, hopefully mid-afternoon, his parents will have left. If they were vaguely attentive to her yesterday, it was only because she knew more than they did when they arrived. But she is no one to them. At best, a temporary girlfriend to their son. A tenant. No one permanent.

Thank God the nurse let her in to sit with Dominic last night. Otherwise, Emma never would have seen him.

Wasn't it only in movies that they refused to let you see the patient if you weren't family? she thought last night. Clearly, given that they refused to tell her anything when she phoned, it happens in real life, too.

She told the nurses outside the ICU that she was his fiancée, surreptitiously slipping the Russian wedding ring – a gift from her parents on her twenty-first birthday, which she always wore on her right hand – onto the third finger of her left. It was almost true. They both knew they were going to get married. Not having formalized it yet didn't make their commitment any less meaningful.

Those nurses let her in to sit with him last night. Whoever answered the phone today wasn't having any of it.

Sophie's porch door is always open. Emma walks in and slides off her boots, and as Sophie comes from the kitchen to greet her, Emma starts to cry.

'I'm sorry,' Emma wails, as her face crumples.

'Are you kidding?' Sophie takes her friend in her arms and holds her tight. 'Let it out, honey. It's going to be okay. Jesse's upstairs watching TV. He won't hear a thing.'

When Emma's sniffles start to subside, she pulls away as Sophie reaches over to grab a box of tissues.

'I'm so sorry,' Emma says again. 'I'm just so tired.'

'Have you slept at all?'

'A little, yes. But I feel like I've been hit by a lorry. I think it's an emotional hangover.'

'I can't believe what happened. It's horrific. What do they say? How long will it take for Dominic to be released from the hospital?'

Emma tells her that when she left last night, or earlier this morning, things had been looking better. She doesn't know precisely what his recovery will entail, but the surgery had gone well.

'There's something I have to tell you,' Sophie says with a grimace. 'I was so worried about Dominic, about what would happen to him, that I phoned your parents.'

'My parents? Good grief, Sophie, why would you do that?'

'Because I thought things were looking really bad. I thought you might need them.'

'What did they say?'

Sophie's shoulders slump as she looks up at her friend. 'They booked a flight right away. They're on their way here.'

Emma shrugs. She's too tired, too worried to continue to harbour a grudge against her mother. She'll sort it all out later. 'Well,' she says, 'it wasn't necessary, but I can see you thought you were doing the right thing. It's fine,' she adds, as she sees Sophie's distraught expression. 'Honestly. Don't worry about it.' She peers at her friend. 'When you say on the way here . . . when, exactly?'

'Rob's gone to pick them up from the airport. They

should be here any sec—' They both turn at the sound of a car.

Sophie looks miserable. 'I'm sorry, Emma. I know you haven't spoken to them since your trip, and I would never have done this if I'd known Dominic was going to be fine.'

They both go outside, and Emma says nothing. She watches the car pull up, then park, watches Rob get out and pull suitcases out of the boot, watches the back door open. First her father, and then her mother get out of the car, blinking at the searing light outside.

'Darling!' Georgina drops her coat and rushes over, putting her arms around her daughter as Emma starts to cry.

Jesse bounces along in the backseat, a tall furry black hat on his head, his face almost entirely hidden by the strap in front of his nose. He is not strapped into his car seat because Emma hadn't taken it out of Dominic's car, and he is excited to be going to the Bluebird Inn for Texas French toast and chocolate chip pancakes, excited to be with new people who not only have shown up unexpectedly but have brought him a toy London bus, a black cab, and the Beefeater hat, which he may never take off.

Emma has promised him he can have whatever he wants, in a bid to keep him happy and distracted. Her parents are doing an excellent job on very short notice. Georgina, in the backseat next to Jesse, is telling him stories about their farm, which seem to entrance him. She even has photographs from home stored on her phone, and she and Jesse are swiping through them, as she patiently explains who all of the people are and what they do on the farm.

She is talking to Jesse in much the way she talks to everyone else, as if he is a friend she has bumped into in the village shop and is filling him in on local gossip. Emma keeps shooting glances at Jesse in the rearview mirror, convinced he must be bored, but he is smiling beatifically at her mother and happily looking at the photos.

They park in the old filling station next door to the restaurant and make their way inside, taking a table by the window. Jesse proceeds immediately to snap off the heads of two of the geraniums in the window boxes before her mother tells him to stop. Emma watches nervously, waiting for him to throw a tantrum, but he seems transfixed by Georgina and immediately does what she says.

'We'll talk later,' her mother had said earlier, when Emma had finished crying and stepped out of her mother's embrace. 'I want to hear about Dominic. Daddy has a very old friend who's a top surgeon at Yale, and he's already left him a message. We're going to get him the best help possible.'

'Thank you,' Emma says gratefully. 'I think he's in good hands, but it will be nice to get a second opinion.'

'That little one is wonderful,' says her mother now, watching as Emma's father takes Jesse's hand in the parking lot and leads him carefully around the idling cars to keep him busy while they wait for their food to arrive. 'I understand so much better now. I'm sorry, Emma, for what I said.'

'You don't need to apologize,' says Emma, realizing it's

true. There are far more important things at stake than what happened in England; she forgave her parents as soon as she saw them get out of Rob's car.

The food arrives soon after. Jesse delightedly digs into his chocolate chip pancakes, demanding that Emma's mother try some. Emma watches them with a tremulous smile, the first smile she has been able to muster since she found Dominic lying outside on the ground in the snow. It is quite clear that Jesse adores her mother. It is the very last thing she would have expected, that her difficult, judgemental, occasionally imperious mother would be an object of adoration in the eyes of a small boy. But there is no doubt that Jesse is smitten, and her mother, seeing herself reflected so beautifully in Jesse's adoring eyes, is smitten in return.

Emma would never have thought to phone her parents for comfort. But they are here, and she is comforted. The small mountain of carbohydrates on the table, drowned, as they are, in maple syrup, is comforting, too. Sitting at this table feels like a slice of normality in a world that has otherwise turned upside down.

'What's your name?' Jesse says, mid-chew, looking at Emma's mother.

'Georgina,' she says, pausing thoughtfully. 'How about you call me Gigi?'

Jesse nods, then glances at Emma's father. 'What about him?'

Emma's mother furrows her brow in thought.

Jesse spears another piece of pancake. 'Can I call you

Banpy?' he asks Emma's dad. 'My friend Dylan calls his grandpa Banpy, and I think you'd be a good Banpy.'

Emma's father beams. 'I don't see why not,' he says to Jesse. Then he turns to his wife with a happy shrug. 'Well,' he says, 'I didn't expect this!'

'Instant grandchild!' Emma's mother is beaming just as brightly. 'What an unexpected delight. And entirely worth the wait, if I may say.' Georgina gives Jesse an impromptu hug. Clearly he didn't follow their exchange, but he hugs her right back.

'Do you know when my daddy is coming home?' Jesse asks as they wait for the bill.

Emma takes a sip of coffee to stall for time, casting an anxious glance at her parents. But they can't answer this question for her. Taking a deep breath, she says, 'I don't know. He's had a big fall and they have to make sure he's completely fine before they let him come home. It may be a little while, but I can hopefully take you to see him in a couple of days when he's feeling a bit better.'

'Can't I go and see him today?' says Jesse.

'Not today,' Emma says. 'Today he's just sleeping, resting to get better.'

Jesse stops wriggling and looks Emma straight in the eye. 'What if he dies? Will I get to go and live with my mom?'

Emma is struck mute. She can't think of a thing to say.

'Jesse, don't say that, darling,' says Emma's mother calmly. 'I don't think he's going to die. It was a serious bump on the head, but the doctors think your father is going to be fine.'

Jesse shrugs an okay, but the rest of them can hardly breathe. Emma gives her mother a grateful glance.

She is not equipped for this. She has no idea how to talk to a small child about serious stuff. What if something terrible did happen? How would she explain it? What would she say, after she has already told him his father will be fine? She forces the thoughts away and turns to the waitress to take the bill.

Once they are in the car and Emma is driving them all back home, she thinks again how glad she is that her parents are here, that they can babysit, allowing Jesse to sleep in his own bed tonight instead of at Sophie's. She is almost starting to breathe normally when Jesse mumbles something behind her.

'What, darling? I can't hear you.' She turns the radio down.

'I want my daddy.' Jesse's face crumples as he starts to cry. Emma's mother immediately puts a large arm around him and holds him close, kissing him on the head.

'I want Daddy to come home,' he says, his whole body heaving. 'I want to see him.'

'I think we can go and see him tomorrow,' Emma says, although she's sure that tomorrow will be too early. 'I'll ask the doctors later. Why don't we all go home now, and you can introduce Gigi and Banpy to Hobbes, and maybe Banpy will even help you build a snowman.' She looks at her father helplessly, and receives a nod in return.

'Gigi can make hot chocolate and cookies, and I'll be back home before you go to bed tonight. How's that?'

Jesse is still crying, more softly now.

Emma reaches back and squeezes Jesse's hand. 'What about . . . if you sleep in our bed tonight? With me? On Daddy's side?'

Jesse looks up and nods. When Emma starts to pull her hand back, he clamps his on top and holds on for dear life, and that's how they drive, all the way home.

Back at the house, they decide that Emma's parents will stay at Emma's, while she stays with Jesse at Dominic's. Not surprisingly, exhausted by the events of the last few hours, Jesse cuddles up with Hobbes on the sofa and falls asleep. Emma finds she can no longer keep her eyes open, either, and her mother sends her upstairs to bed. Her legs are so heavy that she barely makes it up the stairs.

She crawls into bed, asleep almost as soon as her head hits the pillow. When she wakes up, staggering out of the deepest of slumbers, she's deeply disoriented. What time is it? she wonders. What day? The bed smells of Dominic.

Something is wrong; it takes her a few seconds to remember what it is. With the realization comes the worry, weighing on her chest. She lies there for a while, before remembering that Jesse is home and must be downstairs with her parents.

How long has she slept? Is Jesse still napping? She has to get up. She starts to stir, then sinks back into the pillows with relief as she hears Jesse clambering up the stairs. He appears in the doorway clutching Hobbes in his arms, before climbing onto the bed and depositing Hobbes on her chest.

'What have you been up to?' she asks.

'Banpy and I started to build a snow fort but it got too cold so he says we can't carry on today, but maybe tomorrow. And we watched *Harry Potter* one and two,' he says.

Emma sits up. 'Have I been asleep that long? Oh God.' She looks at her phone. It is a lot later in the day than she realized. She is desperate to get to the hospital to see Dominic.

She puts Hobbes aside, but before she even fully rises from the bed, Jesse turns to her and says, 'Nonna called. She said she's going to come and pick me up so I can stay with them. But why can't I stay here?'

Emma stills. Why would Dominic have made a decision like that without telling her? Jesse doesn't want to go; of course he doesn't want to go. But Emma can't do anything about it until she's talked to him. She supposes it's understandable for his parents to want Jesse to stay with them while Dominic recovers. They certainly don't want their grandson to stay with a woman they barely know, a woman they have shown no interest in getting to know.

But she can't do anything until she's talked to Dominic.

'Sleepovers can be fun,' she tells Jesse. 'Nonna will probably make something delicious for you. I'll talk to your dad today, and I'll probably pick you up tomorrow.'

'But I want to stay here with Gigi and Banpy.'

Emma smiles. 'They'll still be here tomorrow. You'll

have lots and lots of time with them. Lucky you, that everyone wants a sleepover with you.'

Jesse shrugs miserably, downcast. 'I said I wanted to stay home but they said I can't. I have to pick my five favourite toys to take with me, and anything I don't have, they'll buy me.'

'That sounds like fun,' Emma lies as Jesse scuffs the carpet with his foot.

'I really don't want to go.' His voice is threatening to break.

'I know,' she says, reaching out an arm as he snuggles up next to her, laying his head on her chest.

'I want to stay with Hobbes, too,' he says.

'It won't be for long,' says Emma. 'I promise I'll look after Hobbes for you. And while you're with your grandparents, your dad can get strong and healthy.'

Jesse thinks about it for a while before nodding reluctantly.

'I love you.' Emma kisses the top of his head, squeezing him tight.

'I love you, too,' says Jesse, not seeing the single tear drip down her cheek, which she quickly wipes away.

Emma jumps in the shower, but before she's finished, Jesse bursts in. She yelps, and grabs the curtain to make sure she's covered.

'Bye!' he waves from the doorway. 'They're here!'

'Wait. Don't they want to speak to me?'

Jesse shrugs, but before Emma has a chance to say

anything else, he has disappeared from the doorway. By the time she's thrown on a robe, they have gone.

'Did you talk to them?' she asks her mother, who is cleaning up the kitchen.

'I tried, but they weren't very interested. They barely said hello.'

'I'm sorry. They're not my favourite people.'

'No,' says her mother. 'I thought they were terribly rude. And now Jesse's gone. I was so enjoying him.' Her face is so downcast that Emma puts an arm around her shoulders to comfort her, in much the way she had been comforting Jesse earlier.

'Probably it's just for one night,' Emma says. 'I'll talk to Dominic about him coming back tomorrow.'

'I do hope so,' says her mother sadly. 'I have to say, I'm rather enamoured with him.'

'He clearly feels the same way about you,' Emma says with a smile.

But already the house seems oddly quiet. Things feel strange, and wrong. She tries to convince herself that there is a silver lining to Jesse's absence. She can focus on going to stay with Dominic at the hospital, and get a really good night's sleep.

Besides, she thinks wryly, surely it will motivate him to make a speedier recovery.

Showering has made her feel more human. She throws in a load of laundry, pulls on tracksuit bottoms, and fills a tote bag with toiletries, clean clothes, and a cushion. Now that she doesn't have to get home for Jesse, she can stay at the hospital all night. They may not find a bed for her, but she doesn't care. She *will* stay all night. She will stay as long as she is able, until Dominic is better.

Kissing her mother and father goodbye, she walks outside, grateful for the bracing cold air that instantly wakes her up.

When she arrives, she finds the hospital quiet downstairs, but the ICU oddly busy for early evening. She is buzzed in and puts her tote bag down in the waiting room before heading over to the nurses' station, stepping out of the way to avoid medical personnel walking quickly down the corridors, barely noticing they are about to run her over.

'Dominic DiFranco? Is it okay to see him now?' she asks.

The nurse looks at her blankly, as if she hasn't spoken.

'I'm here to see Dominic DiFranco,' she says again. 'I know it's not visiting hours but I've been home all day looking after' – she pauses – 'our son. Can I go and see him? I can see you're all very busy here, but I've been waiting a long time and I'm worried.'

The nurse falters. 'Take a seat in the waiting room,' she says eventually. 'We'll be right with you.'

Emma considers pushing through the doors and going straight to Dominic, nurses be damned. But she has never been a rule-breaker, and finds herself meekly following orders.

How odd, she thinks, that a hospital waiting room should feel familiar to her, should feel almost . . . homey. *Better get used to it*, she thinks with an ironic laugh. *You may be here for a very long time.*

She gets out her book and her cushion, crosses her legs on the chair, pulls her phone from her bag, prepared to fill the next few minutes with mindless activity. She hasn't checked her email for ages.

The door is pushed open just as her phone lights up. It is the neurosurgeon from yesterday, his face grave as he comes to sit down next to her. She smiles at him, relieved he is here; no one understands better than him what Dominic is dealing with.

He doesn't smile back. 'I am so sorry,' he says softly, as the smile slides off Emma's face and she stares at him in confusion.

He is so sorry for *what?*

He looks at her cushion, her book, her tote bag, closes his eyes for a second before looking back at her. 'Has no one called you?' His voice is soft.

'About what?'

He takes a deep breath. 'We don't know why this happened, but in the early hours of this morning Dominic had another catastrophic bleed. This one, unfortunately, caused a herniation of the brain stem.'

Emma looks at him blankly.

'The brain stem controls heart rate and bleeding. When it is compromised, the damage is irreversible. This second bleed was fatal.'

'I don't understand. What are you saying?' The fog is

rolling in, but it hasn't reached her brain, not yet. 'I'm so sorry,' she says. 'I don't understand.'

He reaches over and places a hand over hers. 'We did everything we could. Dominic passed away this afternoon. I am so sorry for your loss.'

Chapter 36

Emma doesn't remember getting home. She doesn't remember being asked who should drive her home, doesn't remember suggesting that her mother was the person to call. She has no idea that a nurse sat with her until both her parents showed up at the hospital. She has no idea that her mother cried all the way there, and all the way back, silent tears streaming down her face as she drove her daughter home.

Emma has no idea that when they got home, her mother wrapped her in the cashmere throw which had been draped over Dominic's sofa to hide the years of stains from Jesse's TV dinners, and had poured all three of them big tumblers of scotch, which they downed in one.

Emma has no idea that she couldn't stop shaking, couldn't speak; that the only sounds coming out of her mouth were very quiet whimpers.

She didn't cry. Not then. Her parents managed to get her up to her bedroom, where she lay down between Teddy and Sophie, who gathered her in their arms and held her until she fell asleep.

*

She wakes up sobbing, but she can't remember why. Once she has started, she can't stop. Her mother bursts into her room, and takes her in her arms as she wails, her whole body shaking.

Two days later, she leaves her bed and comes downstairs. Her mother watches her anxiously, settles her on the sofa like a small child and makes her milky, sweet tea, just like the tea everyone drinks in England when they are cold, tired, or sad. Emma doesn't speak for a while, merely sips the tea, staring at the floor.

'Mummy?' Emma looks up at her. 'What am I going to do?'

Her parents cancel their flight home. They tell Emma they will stay as long as necessary.

Despite their presence, the house feels empty and sad. She can't bear not having Jesse there, can't bear the lone-liness. She has written to Dominic's parents, begging, pleading to see Jesse, but there has been no response.

Emma hears from AJ that Stacy has returned to take custody of Jesse, that she is now planning to stay for good. She is Jesse's mother. Surely she is the best person for Jesse to be with now that his father is gone. Given that no one seems to be allowing Emma to be with him.

Emma's life isn't a life she recognizes, and isn't a life she wants. She doesn't shower, doesn't eat, wanders around the house aimlessly, picking up things. Almost everything she touches, even the tiniest of objects she has never noticed before, contains memories of Dominic. She can't believe she is never going to see him again.

It doesn't make sense. She sits at the kitchen table for hours, gazing out the window at nothing, vaguely aware of her mother's attempts at conversation. But Emma can't engage in conversation. Not yet. How can he have been here, how can her life, *their* life, have been fine? And now gone? How can he no longer be here?

Six months ago her life was full, and busy, and happy. She had moved out to Westport to start afresh; how can it be that in a few short months everything about her life had changed so utterly, become so much more than she ever thought it could be, and now it's gone? It's so much worse than if she had simply stayed in New York, unhappy. Now she has even less than she had before, when she didn't know what it was she was missing.

As the funeral approaches, she has to pull herself together. AJ has kept in touch, made sure she knows when it is, where to go. She hasn't been consulted about any of the arrangements. She probably wouldn't have been any use, even if she had been asked. His parents have made all the decisions.

On the morning of the service, Emma stands under the shower for forty minutes, letting the hot water wash over her, willing it to wash the grief away. But nothing helps. Looking at his bottle of shampoo, she finds herself sobbing. Anything can, and does, set her off.

As she sits in the bathroom, looking at her wet hair in the mirror, her face is almost unrecognizable, her skin so pale it is almost grey. She has dark circles under her eyes, and however much she tries, she can't see any life in them.

She dries her hair and brushes it back into a chignon, slips on a black dress from her city days, wondering why it is so big.

In one of the drawers downstairs is a huge pair of black sunglasses, left by someone once upon a time, long ago. Emma puts them on to hide her eyes, and stuffs her bag full of tissues from the boxes that Teddy has left on every surface.

She feels completely cried out, but she isn't. Every time she thinks the tears have run dry, they come again, in great racking sobs. While she is opening a can of cat food for Hobbes, or locking the front door, or in the shower, looking at a bottle of shampoo.

She keeps hoping this nightmare will be over. It's only the beginning, she knows, but if she thinks that, if she looks into the future and sees her life stretching out ahead of her, without Dominic, she may not have the strength to carry on.

Chapter 37

The funeral is packed with people Emma has never seen before. Here and there she sees a few familiar faces, but she keeps her eyes down, too frightened to speak, too frightened that if anyone approaches her, all that will emerge will be a howl of pain. Her parents leave her as they find seats, and she looks around, blinking, like a newborn child emerging into the world for the first time.

There is a cloud of grief in the room. Emma has been to funerals before, of course. Her grandparents, several aged aunts, a business colleague who had been battling cancer for years. But their deaths had been expected. People were prepared; they gathered to celebrate lives well lived. Those funerals were filled with moments of solemnity and sorrow, but also lovely stories, sometimes levity, a recognition of the impermanence of life.

But this? This is something completely different. She sees Dominic's childhood friends, and his friends' parents, his former teachers, many regulars from the Fat Hen, and all the bartenders in town. She sees Gina, AJ, and Joey, and in the front row, as if she has always belonged there,

Stacy. There are so many faces, so many people, so much sadness.

At the entrance there is a huge poster of Dominic, smiling his killer smile, a familiar twinkle in his eye. It looks to be a couple of years old, taken on a boat. Emma smiles when she sees his face, ten times bigger than life, immediately feeling the tears.

Another easel holds a poem. During the eulogy, Dominic's father tell the mourners it had been Dominic's favourite when he was a child.

Emma hadn't known that.

There was so much she hadn't known. She had always thought of them creating their own world, in their own bubble. And they had done exactly that. They had had six months in which to build that world, and it had been special, glorious. It didn't matter that so few of these people knew who she was and what she'd meant to him. It mattered only to the people they loved.

She sits next to her parents, and they hold her hands. The tissues in her handbag go untouched.

AJ gets up to speak. He tells a story about meeting Dominic in kindergarten, on the playground slide. He pushed him off, and then Dominic returned the favour, and they've been best friends ever since. He recounts the trouble they got into when they were young. He shares stories about their drinking games, and how they played on the railway tracks when they were still too young to know better, and how Dominic always got away with everything because everybody just loved him so damn much.

'Dominic was . . . oh boy.' AJ shakes his head, blinking away his tears before going back to the notes he's brought with him to read from. 'I can't even believe he's not here,' he says softly. 'Dominic was one of the greats. He was a really loyal friend, and he was an amazing dad, right, buddy?' He looks over to Jesse, sitting in the front row between Dominic's parents and Stacy, heartbreakingly unlike himself in a tiny suit and tie; his little face devoid of all expression as he fidgets and squirms, staying still only when he hears his name.

Jesse looks at AJ with a big nod and a sudden, unexpected grin. AJ gives him a double thumbs-up, and Jesse gives him one in return.

'He loved that kid with all his heart. And he loved Emma.' AJ looks over to where Emma is sitting. 'Emma was the great love of his life. Every time I saw him during these past few months, he said he finally had the family he always wanted.'

AJ doesn't take his eyes off Emma's while he is speaking. He's saying this for her, and he's saying this to her. She can't tear her eyes away from AJ's, can't see that everyone is leaning forward to see who she is.

'Dominic loved bartending at the Fat Hen. He loved building shit even though he wasn't very good at it.' There is a low murmur of laughter. 'Oh, come on. Everyone knew he wasn't very good.' AJ smiles at the memory, shaking his head as the crowd laughs. 'He may no longer be with us, but these past six months were the happiest of his life.

He left us too early, but he left us happy. I know he was happy.'

Emma's body shudders as she bites her lip, her whole body heaving in a bid to keep the sobs in. She didn't expect this to happen, doesn't want to embarrass herself in front of all these people she doesn't know.

The tears stream down her cheeks as she meets AJ's eyes and nods her acknowledgement, understanding, and thanks.

It is irrelevant that Dominic's parents never thought to contact her on the day he died. That they showed up to whisk Jesse away, not giving a thought to her. It is irrelevant that Jesse is sitting between his grandparents and Stacy, three people he barely knows, three people who don't know him nearly as well as she does, who haven't tucked up behind him in bed and read him Roald Dahl. It is irrelevant that most of the people in this room have no idea who she is, or indeed that she ever existed.

But they know who she is now, thanks to AJ. And they know that Dominic loved her. She just doesn't know what's going to happen to her now.

After the service, Emma waits at the edge of the room while everyone lines up to pay their respects to Dominic's parents. As the crowd shuffles and sways, she can just about see the top of their heads. She has to queue up and do the same herself. Her parents are waiting for her in the car. She has assured them she will be fine.

She can see that Dominic's parents are heartbroken. Broken. Their faces pulled down with grief. Although they smile and thank people, Dominic's mother looks as if she is about to keel over. Whatever residual anger Emma has been carrying about the way she's been treated dissolves.

When the crowd shuffles forward, Emma sees Jesse, standing between Dominic's parents, scuffing his foot along the floor as he always does when he's unhappy, or uncomfortable. Emma's heart feels like it has a vice around it. She stares at him, and he looks up, straight into her eyes, and freezes.

'Emma!' He races towards her, a six-year-old bullet, and jumps into her arms as he clutches her tight, sobbing into her neck, his arms and legs wrapped around her like a limpet.

Emma carries him to a chair at the side of the room and sits him on her lap, his arms still tightly around her neck, as she rubs his back and kisses him all over.

'I want to go home,' Jesse says, between the hiccups and sobs. 'Take me home, Emma. I want to come home with you.'

'I want you to come home, too,' Emma says. She didn't even realize, until this moment, just how much she has missed him. It seems he hadn't realized, either. 'Maybe for a sleepover? Maybe for the weekend?'

'No!' Jesse shouts, pulling back. 'I want to come *home*. Forever.'

'I want that, too, Jesse, but I don't know what's going to happen. I may not be living there any more. I don't know what's going to happen, but I'll try to find out, okay? I'll try to figure this out for you. I'm sorry this is so hard, sweetie. Are you with your mom?'

Jesse nods, and she can see the confusion in his eyes. Stacy may be his mother, but he doesn't know her. She may be his mother, but there's nothing familiar about her. She may be his mother, but that's just a word to him. She isn't a place to call *home*.

'I'm with Stacy a lot of the time, but I'm also with Nonna and Papa a lot, because Stacy isn't used to having a kid and they're helping her out until she gets used to it.' Jesse looks utterly miserable.

'Let's just sit here for a while,' Emma says. 'I'll talk to them.'

She waits until almost everyone has gone before approaching Dominic's parents.

'I am so sorry for your loss,' she says, as they stand there. Silence. 'I'm Emma,' she reminds them . . .

'Thank you,' says Dominic's father eventually, turning to speak to someone else.

Emma waits for Dominic's mother to say something, to open the door to . . . something. Anything. But she doesn't speak. She just nods and looks to the next person, to anyone else who will rescue her.

'I want to talk to you about Jesse,' Emma says. 'I know he's living with Stacy now, but I thought you could talk to her. Maybe he can come and have a sleepover with me? I'd love to see him. It doesn't have to be overnight. Maybe just a day. I could give her a break. And I think he needs to see his home. Where he used to live, with his dad. I don't think it's good for a child that young to be torn away from everything he—'

Dominic's mother raises her hand. 'Not now,' she whispers. 'I can't do this now.'

'She's threatened,' Sophie says, having materialized at Emma's side and pulled her away. 'She can't stand anyone else having had her son's love.'

'But they weren't close. Why should she care? He's dead, for God's sake. Is she really so awful that she wouldn't care about her grandson?'

'Maybe jealous? Insecure? Possessive? And grief-stricken after losing her son. However she's behaving now, we have to forgive her.'

'I promised Jesse I'd talk to her about having him for a sleepover.'

'Give her a few days to deal with this. That poor woman. Imagine losing your son.' Sophie shudders. 'I can't. As a parent, it's unimaginable.'

But what about Jesse? Emma thinks. *What about being six years old and losing everything you love in one fell swoop? Isn't that unimaginable, too?*

'Emma,' Sophie says, 'why don't you just ask his mom directly? Isn't he supposed to be living with her?'

'Yes, but I heard he's spending a lot of time with the grandparents.'

Sophie turns her head. 'Irrelevant. That's Stacy, isn't it? Go and talk to her.'

Emma looks stricken. 'Here? Now?'

'There's never going to be a good time. Do it now.'

*

'You're Dommo's girlfriend?' Stacy says, as Emma introduces herself.

Emma nods. *Dommo?* She had never heard him called anything other than Dominic or Dom.

'I wanted to ask about Jesse. We'd grown very close. I know he's living with you now, and I'd love to spend some time with him. Maybe have him for a sleepover on the weekends? I thought maybe it would give you a break . . .'

'Jesse talks about you a lot,' Stacy says gently. 'I can tell that he loves you. I think, in time, it's a great idea, but right now I'm trying to get to know him myself, and I don't want to confuse him, and I don't want him to feel torn.'

'I don't think he'd feel torn,' says Emma. 'You're his mother. No one can ever replace you, I know that, but it might be healing for him to have something from his old life, something that he associates with his dad . . .'

'No,' says Stacy. 'Not right now. I'm happy to talk again in time, but right now I need to strengthen my connection with him, and I'm not willing to do anything that might jeopardize that. If you want to give me your number, I'll get in touch when things are a little more settled with me.'

Emma feels a lump in her throat, and swallows hard as she nods. She has no power any more, no say. At least Stacy has expressed a willingness to allow it in the future. She takes Stacy's phone and taps her number into it, and the two women nod at each other as Stacy turns to go, leaving Emma feeling lonelier than ever.

Emma is almost out the door, aware that people are

staring at her, wondering about her, when she feels a hand on her arm. She turns to see someone who looks vaguely familiar, a man about her age, attractive, with glasses. She can't quite grasp who he is, until he introduces himself.

'The real estate agent,' she says. 'Of course. Jeff. I do remember you. We met that night at Artisan.'

'I never did call you, I know. I heard you and Dominic . . . well. That's irrelevant. I'm so sorry for your loss, Emma. He was truly one of the greats.'

'Thank you.'

'I just wanted to say, if you ever want to talk, or need a shoulder to cry on, I'm around.'

Emma tries to smile, is about to move away. But there's something else he clearly wants to say. He lays a hand on her arm. 'I heard you talk to Stacy. Maybe this is none of my business, but I heard her say she doesn't want you to see Jesse right now. Stacy has no idea what being a mother is like. She's doing what she thinks she has to do to try to establish a bond with the kid, but you'll be seeing him soon. I guarantee it.'

Emma blinks away a tear. 'How can you be so sure?'

'Because Stacy isn't cut out to be someone's parent. She never has been. You need to wait for Jesse to come back. He will. It's just a matter of time.'

Emma stares at him. She hopes he's wrong. She also hopes he's right.

Chapter 38

Her mother has told Emma that she will be happy again. Her mother has told her that although she may never stop missing Dominic, her grief will become a part of her, and his memory will lodge into her heart for the rest of her life. The pain won't go away, but it will become more bearable in time.

All Emma knows is that life will never be the same again.

Over the past couple of months, she has finally been allowed to see Jesse, who is shuttling back and forth between Dominic's parents and Stacy. Stacy hasn't yet found a job here, and she can't afford to leave Florida until she has secured something in Westport, so she shuttles back and forth. Jesse stays with his grandparents, albeit reluctantly, when she is not here.

Emma took him to the children's museum, and Shake Shack for a burger; he shook and clung to her when she tried to drop him off, begged her to let him come home. She tried to explain, as gently as she could, that it wasn't up to her, but she would try to see him as often as she could.

She is working again, no longer sleeping the days away in a fog of loss and pain, exhausted by grief. She is putting one step in front of the other, pretending to live a life, going through the motions, getting through each day as best she can.

One morning – it's a Tuesday, she thinks, but how can she be sure when the days and nights all blend into one another, each interchangeable – the phone starts to ring.

Emma does not often pick up the phone these days. There is nothing left to say. But on this particular Tuesday when the phone rings, Emma answers.

'It's Stacy. Jesse's . . . mom. I want to talk to you about Jesse. Are you able to meet me at the Sherwood diner in an hour?'

Chapter 39

It's late morning, and the diner is quiet, the early rush of businessmen and housewives in for breakfast having passed.

As soon as she walks in, Emma sees Stacy in a booth by the window. She slides in opposite, across the table, ordering tea from the waitress, wondering why she's been summoned. Maybe she's found a place to live in Westport, Emma thinks. Maybe she's coming back for good.

She stares at Stacy, looking for a glimpse into Dominic's life before she knew him. It is the first time she has seen her properly, close up. She is pretty, but weathered. *She has lived a hard life,* thinks Emma.

'How's Jesse?' Emma asks.

Stacy nods. 'He's good.'

There is a long pause. Emma decides to broach the subject head-on. 'Have you moved back here for good?' She struggles to keep her voice from trembling.

Stacy tilts her head. 'I've been splitting my time. I had planned to move back, initially, after Dominic died . . . but I've got a lot of commitments in Fort Lauderdale. It's kind of hard to extricate myself.'

'What about Jesse? Are you taking him to Florida with
you?'

Stacy shakes her head. 'Dominic's parents have him a
lot. They've been pretty good, although they're not so
young and I know it's been a strain.'

She takes a breath. 'You know, I came back to Westport
because I wanted to do the right thing by Jesse. I thought
it would be straightforward, that I could just rebuild a life
here. But I'm discovering it doesn't work like that. This is
hard for people to understand, but I have a life in Florida,
a good life, and a business, and it's hard to start all over
again in a town I left because I didn't want to be here any
more.'

'But you're willing to sacrifice that for Jesse? I think
that's wonderful,' lies Emma.

'I thought I was willing to sacrifice that for Jesse,' corrects Stacy. 'But I haven't changed, and my feelings about
this place haven't changed.'

Emma's heart sinks. 'You're taking Jesse to Florida.'

There is a pause. Stacy shakes her head.

Emma frowns. 'I don't understand.'

Stacy's eyes fill with tears, which she blinks away by
looking at the ceiling. 'I can't. I'm not cut out for this. I
want to be in his life, I do – he's a terrific little boy – but
. . . I never wanted to be his full-time mother. I've tried
so hard to do it, to be the replacement parent, but I can't.'

'These things take time.' Emma attempts to soothe what
she presumes is a case of frazzled nerves, panic at what this
means for Jesse; the weight of ensuring he is stable and

happy, suddenly crushing. She isn't sure what Stacy is saying, but it can't be good for this child; he can't be abandoned again. 'It's a huge adjustment for everyone. You're going to be fine, I'm sure of it.'

Stacy shakes her head. 'No. I haven't come by this decision lightly, Emma. It has been five months since Dominic died, and I have given it my best shot. Jesse is a great kid, and he deserves to have a mother. A full-time mother. I may have given birth to him, but I'm not his mother. And I may be good at the fun stuff, but not the everyday grind.'

Emma just stares at her.

'I know you think I'm a terrible person. Everyone will think I'm a terrible person, but I'm not. I'm just not mother material. I'm like the favourite cool aunt. You, on the other hand, *are* mother material. You're the one Jesse wants. He talks about you all the time, asks when he can move back in with you. You're the one he wants to be with.'

Tears spring into Emma's eyes. She had no idea Jesse felt the pang of loss as intensely as she does.

Stacy takes a deep breath. 'I want you to have legal custody of Jesse. If you want him.' A shadow of doubt crosses her eyes. 'I may have given birth to him, Emma, but I'm not his mother. You are.'

Epilogue

Emma sprinkles chocolate chips on top of the egg-soaked bread before carefully sliding it into the pan. She fries the French toast, flips it, then lifts it onto a plate. Two pieces for Jesse, two pieces for her.

'Birthday breakfast!' she calls, as Jesse, who has been up for hours, runs into the kitchen.

'Can we eat it in front of a movie? Please, please, please?' he begs. 'For a birthday treat?'

Emma never allows Jesse to eat in front of the television unless they are having a designated 'TV dinner'. She narrows her eyes. 'What movie?'

'*Star Wars?*' he says hopefully.

She slumps in disappointment. 'Again?'

'*Harry Potter?*'

'Okay,' she says, as he whoops, grabbing the plate to take into the living room. 'Be very careful,' she shouts, following him in to drizzle maple syrup over his toast and squeeze up next to him on the sofa pretending to be engrossed in a movie whose dialogue she can recite line by line in her sleep.

She watches him from the corner of her eye. He is completely relaxed, engrossed in the film for the nth time despite the numerous times he has seen it.

Lately, strangers have been telling them they look alike. It's not remotely true, of course. They look nothing alike, Jesse with his dark, birdlike features, and Emma, who is all peaches and cream, fair complexion, and wide-set eyes.

'You look like your mom,' people say. The checkout lady at Fresh Market, the sales assistant in the Gap, the woman who helps them in the children's section of Barnes and Noble. Emma always holds her breath, wondering if Jesse will pipe up that she isn't his mom, but he says nothing, just looks at Emma, who merely smiles, relieved she doesn't have to explain.

She may not be his mom, but she is beginning to feel like she is. Everything in her life has changed, and all of it now revolves around Jesse. She makes him breakfast in the morning, walks outside with him and waits on the little bench for the school bus to come and pick him up. She goes grocery shopping for his favourite foods to pack for lunch, and slides them into his lunch box with a silly drawing on a Post-it, every day.

Before, and she only ever thinks of it as *before*, Emma had spent her days trying to find design clients. Now she has joined a shop in town as their resident designer. She has a steady flow of regular clients recommended by the shop.

She makes sure she is always done with her work by the time the bus comes home, and always at the bus stop to greet Jesse when he hops off. She brings him inside, sits with him at the kitchen table, makes him his snack and listens as he tells her about his day.

She hadn't particularly wanted to be a mother, but now that she is Jesse's legal guardian, she has embraced her role as fully as anyone can. She structures her day around his wants and needs, things that need to be done at school. She used to judge the kinds of women who gave up full-time careers to have children, move out to the suburbs, and throw their lives into micromanaging their children's lives. But here she is, doing the same. And loving every minute of it.

Everything stops for a class party, a book reading, a Poetry Café in the school library. Her heart expands when Jesse stands up in front of everyone and reads aloud a poem he has written about summer, his eyes scanning the crowd of eager parents, his body unclenching as he spots her face, shooting her a quick grin and an almost imperceptible wave. She will be talking to some of the other mothers afterwards, and will feel something against her legs, a small arm winding around her body, and there he will be, not always looking at her, not always talking to her, but always, always claiming her as his.

Jesse bounces on the sofa and puts his plate on the table in front of them.

'When are my grandparents coming over?' he asks, as Emma looks at her watch. Dominic's parents, *Nonna and Papa*, see him occasionally, but they cannot seem to forgive her for raising their grandchild, even though it was what both Jesse and Stacy wanted, even though they confessed they were too old to raise him themselves.

Emma has tried to include them. She invited them for tea just after Jesse moved in with her, wanted to make them know she wouldn't get in the way of their relationship. She had made a proper English tea, hoping they would be seduced into liking her, or at the very least, accepting her.

She served petits fours, cucumber sandwiches with the crusts cut off, and smoked salmon on tiny rolls. She made buttermilk scones and served them with blackberry jam and proper English clotted cream that had her shriek with delight when she stumbled upon it in the refrigerator at Balducci's.

She had tried to express her love for their son, and then their grandson, with food, in much the same way she knew they had done with Dominic. But it had been a disaster.

Dominic's parents had sat uncomfortably at her table. They had answered her questions, but seemed to want to be anywhere other than there, in her kitchen, in a house that would always be their son's.

During the forty-five minutes they were there, they said almost nothing, both of them looking at their watches, clearly wanting to leave. When they did finally leave, Jesse asked what was the matter with them. Emma had no answers; she didn't know what to say.

She had tried and tried, sending emails, extending invitations, but there was no response. Dominic hadn't wanted a relationship with them; now she understood why. Their own discomfort in themselves, in their lives, in their skins, made everyone around them uncomfortable, too. That was why Dominic barely saw them, she realized. That was what made it all so difficult now.

Stacy has gone back to her life in Florida. She sends the occasional text, sometimes a photograph of herself. Just yesterday, Jesse received a big box of birthday presents. He thinks of her as a distant but loving aunt, just as she wanted.

The grandparents Jesse is asking about are *her* parents. Her sometimes difficult, self-absorbed mother and her diffident, quiet father have embraced Jesse, and embraced grandparenthood, with a joy and enthusiasm she could never have anticipated. From the moment they became Gigi and Banpy, they had forged an unbreakable bond with him.

The last time her parents came to stay, at lunch one day her father nibbled his sandwich, leaving the crusts in a neat pile on one side of the plate. Jesse did exactly the same. Emma implored him to eat his crusts, but he pointed to her father's plate. 'See? Banpy does the same. That's where I get it from. It's not my fault.'

'Are you telling me it's a genetic trait?' Emma burst out laughing.

'Yes,' said Jesse, even though they all knew he had no idea what she meant.

Emma looks over at Jesse, now glued to the television screen, occasionally reaching over to take a bite of his French toast.

'Gigi and Banpy should be here in about half an hour,' she says. 'They just went into town to get some stuff for this afternoon. And Sophie, Rob, and Jackson are coming, too. They wanted to see you before the party. I think they may have a small something for you.'

Jesse turns to her, his eyes wide. 'Do you think Gigi and Banpy have gone to get me a birthday present? Do you think it's a go-kart?'

'I very much doubt it,' she says, although knowing her parents, they will have indulged him and bought him exactly what he asked for. 'Although who knows. They do spoil you. Maybe, if you're *very* lucky, they got you *Star Wars* Lego.'

Jesse squirms excitedly. 'I hope it's the *Millennium Falcon*, Mom,' he says. This is not the first time Jesse has called her *Mom*. The first time it happened, she thought she had misheard. The second time it happened, she thought it was a mistake. This is the sixth time he has now said it.

She has ignored it up until now, but she can't ignore it today. She puts her plate down and moves closer to Jesse on the sofa, thinking about how to choose her words, what best to say.

'Jesse, can we talk about you calling me Mom?'

Jesse says nothing. She sees him swallow as he stares pointedly at the television screen. She picks up the remote control and mutes the volume.

'Sweetie, look at me.' He does so, reluctantly, as if he is embarrassed, as if he were trying on the word, was hoping to just slip into the habit with both of them pretending they hadn't noticed.

'I just want you to know, that if you do want to call me Mom, it's completely fine with me. You know how much I love you. And even though I haven't known you for your whole life, I know I'm going to be with you for the rest of our lives.' She pauses. Is she saying the wrong things? She feels stupid for not knowing what to say, for not knowing how to say it.

'The thing is, I didn't give birth to you, which you know.'

'Stacy's my *tummy mummy*!' He grins at the babyish term Emma had come up with.

'Right. Officially I'm your legal guardian, but as far as I'm concerned, you're my son. And I'm your mom. For-ever. If you want to call me Mom, I would be honoured.' She watches Jesse, who keeps staring at the television, then looks briefly down at his empty plate.

'Okay,' he says, grabbing the remote control and turning the volume back up. 'Mom? Can I have another piece of French toast?'

Emma takes his plate and heads into the kitchen. This is not what she ever expected her family to look like. She would give anything to have Dominic back by her side. But Jesse is her family now. There is no doubt about that. And she is his mother. No doubt about that, either.

As she makes her way back to Jesse on the sofa, the Rolling Stones drums in her head, 'You Can't Always Get What You Want'. She gives Jesse the plate, kisses him on the top of his head, and curls up next to him. There is no doubt that Jesse is what she needs.

Acknowledgements

As always, there are tremendous numbers of people to thank:

First, my brilliant team at Pan Macmillan. A huge thank you to Geoff Duffield, Jeremy Trevathan, Katie James, Catherine Richards, Charlotte Williams, James Annal, Anthony Forbes-Watson, and everyone else on the team – I consider myself the luckiest author imaginable to have such a creative and clever publisher.

Thanks always to my wickedly wonderful agent, mentor and friend Anthony Goff. To Leslie Gelbman, Louise Moore, and Dan Mallory for their sage advice and excellent taste.

For their help and guidance: Stacy Bass, Valerie Fischel, Wendy Walker, Glenn Ferrari, Randy Zuckerman.

To dear friends and my early readers: Patti Callahan Henry, Elin Hildebrand, Dani Shapiro, Lisa Lampanelli, Sharon Gitelle, Nicole Straight, Jerri Graham, Russ Hardin.

To brilliant Gus Walker, titles whiz.

And always, always, to my ever patient, beloved family, Ian, Max, Harry, Tabitha, Nate, and Jasper. And to my husband Ian, who showed me what it was to fall in love.